The
MX Book
of
New
Sherlock Holmes Stories

Part XXIX
More Christmas Adventures
(1889-1896)

The MX Book of New Sherlock Holmes Stories

Part XXIX
More Christmas Adventures
(1889-1896)

Edited by David Marcum

Traditional Holmes Adventures Compiled for the Benefit of the Restoration of Undershaw

First edition published in 2021
© Copyright 2021

The right of the individuals listed on the Copyright Information page to be identified as the authors of this work has been asserted by them in accordance with the Copyright, Designs, and Patents Act 1998.

All rights reserved. No reproduction, copy, or transmission of this publication may be made without express prior written permission. No paragraph of this publication may be reproduced, copied, or transmitted except with express prior written permission or in accordance with the provisions of the Copyright Act 1956 (as amended). Any person who commits any unauthorised act in relation to this publication may be liable to criminal prosecution and civil claims for damage.

All characters appearing in this work are fictitious or used fictitiously. Except for certain historical personages, any resemblance to real persons, living or dead, is purely coincidental. The opinions expressed herein are those of the authors and not of MX Publishing.

ISBN Hardback 978-1-78705-930-6
ISBN Paperback 978-1-78705-931-3
AUK ePub ISBN 978-1-78705-932-0
AUK PDF ISBN 978-1-78705-933-7

Published in the UK by
MX Publishing
335 Princess Park Manor, Royal Drive,
London, N11 3GX
www.mxpublishing.co.uk

David Marcum can be reached at:
thepapersofsherlockholmes@gmail.com

Cover design by Brian Belanger
www.belangerbooks.com and *www.redbubble.com/people/zhahadun*

Internal Illustrations by Sidney Paget

CONTENTS

Forewords

Editor's Foreword: Never Enough Holmes Adventures – Even at Christmas! by David Marcum	1
Foreword by Nancy Holder	16
"It is the Season of Forgiveness" by Roger Johnson	18
An Ongoing Legacy for Sherlock Holmes by Steve Emecz	20
Undershaw: Eliminating the Impossible by Emma West	23
Baker Street in Snow (1890) (*A Poem*) by Christopher James	33

Adventures

The Sword in the Spruce by Ian Ableson	35
The Adventure of the Serpentine Body by Wayne Anderson	50
The Father Christmas Brigade by David Marcum	79

(Continued on the next page . . . .)

The Adventure of the Fugitive Irregular by Gordon Linzner	98
The Incident of the Stolen Christmas Present by Barry Clay	112
The Man of Miracles by Derrick Belanger	134
Absent Friends by Wayne Anderson	156
The Incident in Regent Street by Harry DeMaio	175
The Baffling Adventure of the Baby Jesus by Craig Stephen Copland	195
The Adventure of the Second Sister by Matthew White	228
The Twelve Days by I.A. Watson	252
The Dilemma of Mr. Henry Baker by Paul D. Gilbert	285
The Adventure of the Injured Man by Arthur Hall	297
The Krampus Who Came to Call by Marcia Wilson	311

(Continued on the next page . . . .)

The Adventure of the Christmas Wish 332
    by Margaret Walsh

The Adventure of the Viking Ghost 345
    by Frank Schildiner

The Adventure of the Secret Manuscript 364
    by Dan Rowley

The Adventure of the Christmas Suitors 378
    by Tracy J. Revels

About the Contributors 395

These additional adventures are contained in
Part XXVIII: More Christmas Adventures
(1869-1888)

A Sherlockian Christmas (A Poem) – Joseph W. Svec III
No Malice Intended – Deanna Baran
The Yuletide Heist – Mark Mower
A Yuletide Tragedy – Thomas A. Turley
The Adventure of the Christmas Lesson – Will Murray
The Christmas Card Case – Brenda Seabrooke
The Chatterton-Smythe Affair – Tim Gambrell
Christmas at the Red Lion – Thomas A. Burns, Jr.
A Study in Murder – Amy Thomas
The Christmas Ghost of Crailloch Taigh – David Marcum
The Six-Fingered Scoundrel – Jeffrey A. Lockwood
The Case of the Duplicitous Suitor – John Lawrence
The Sebastopol Clasp – Martin Daley
The Silent Brotherhood – Dick Gillman
The Case of the Christmas Pudding – Liz Hedgecock
The St. Stephen's Day Mystery – Paul Hiscock
A Fine Kettle of Fish – Mike Hogan
The Case of the Left Foot – Stephen Herczeg
The Case of the Golden Grail – Roger Riccard

Part XXX: More Christmas Adventures
(1897-1928)

Baker Street in Snow (1890) (A Poem) – Christopher James
The Purloined Present – DJ Tyrer
The Case of the Cursory Curse – Andrew Bryant
The St. Giles Child Murders – Tim Gambrell
A Featureless Crime – Geri Schear
The Case of the Earnest Young Man – Paula Hammond
The Adventure of the Dextrous Doctor – Jayantika Ganguly
The Mystery of Maple Tree Lodge – Susan Knight

(Continued on the next page . . . .)

The Adventure of the Maligned Mineralogist – Arthur Hall
Christmas Magic – Kevin Thornton
The Adventure of the Christmas Threat – Arthur Hall
The Adventure of the Stolen Christmas Gift – Michael Mallory
The Colourful Skein of Life – Julie McKuras
The Adventure of the Chained Phantom – J.S. Rowlinson
Santa's Little Elves – Kevin Thornton
The Case of the Holly-Sprig Pudding – Naching T. Kassa
The Canterbury Manifesto – David Marcum
The Case of the Disappearing Beaune – J. Lawrence Matthews
A Price Above Rubies – Jane Rubino
The Intrigue of the Red Christmas – Shane Simmons
The Bitter Gravestones – Chris Chan
The Midnight Mass Murder – Paul Hiscock

These additional Sherlock Holmes adventures
can be found in the previous volumes of
The MX Book of New Sherlock Holmes Stories

PART I: 1881-1889
Foreword – Leslie S. Klinger
Foreword – Roger Johnson
Foreword – David Marcum
Sherlock Holmes of London (A Verse in Four Fits) – Michael Kurland
The Adventure of the Slipshod Charlady – John Hall
The Case of the Lichfield Murder – Hugh Ashton
The Kingdom of the Blind – Adrian Middleton
The Adventure of the Pawnbroker's Daughter – David Marcum
The Adventure of the Defenestrated Princess – Jayantika Ganguly
The Adventure of the Inn on the Marsh – Denis O. Smith
The Adventure of the Traveling Orchestra – Amy Thomas
The Haunting of Sherlock Holmes – Kevin David Barratt
Sherlock Holmes and the Allegro Mystery – Luke Benjamen Kuhns
The Deadly Soldier – Summer Perkins
The Case of the Vanishing Stars – Deanna Baran
The Song of the Mudlark – Shane Simmons
The Tale of the Forty Thieves – C.H. Dye
The Strange Missive of Germaine Wilkes – Mark Mower
The Case of the Vanished Killer – Derrick Belanger
The Adventure of the Aspen Papers – Daniel D. Victor
The Ululation of Wolves – Steve Mountain
The Case of the Vanishing Inn – Stephen Wade
The King of Diamonds – John Heywood
The Adventure of Urquhart Manse – Will Thomas
The Adventure of the Seventh Stain – Daniel McGachey
The Two Umbrellas – Martin Rosenstock
The Adventure of the Fateful Malady – Craig Janacek

PART II: 1890-1895
Foreword – Catherine Cooke
Foreword – Roger Johnson
Foreword – David Marcum
The Bachelor of Baker Street Muses on Irene Adler (A Poem) – Carole Nelson Douglas
The Affair of Miss Finney – Ann Margaret Lewis
The Adventure of the Bookshop Owner – Vincent W. Wright
The Case of the Unrepentant Husband – William Patrick Maynard
The Verse of Death – Matthew Booth
Lord Garnett's Skulls – J.R. Campbell
Larceny in the Sky with Diamonds – Robert V. Stapleton
The Glennon Falls – Sam Wiebe
The Adventure of *The Sleeping Cardinal* – Jeremy Branton Holstein

(Continued on the next page . . . .)

The Case of the Anarchist's Bomb – Bill Crider
The Riddle of the Rideau Rifles – Peter Calamai
The Adventure of the Willow Basket – Lyndsay Faye
The Onion Vendor's Secret – Marcia Wilson
The Adventure of the Murderous Numismatist – Jack Grochot
The Saviour of Cripplegate Square – Bert Coules
A Study in Abstruse Detail – Wendy C. Fries
The Adventure of the St. Nicholas the Elephant – Christopher Redmond
The Lady on the Bridge – Mike Hogan
The Adventure of the Poison Tea Epidemic – Carl L. Heifetz
The Man on Westminster Bridge – Dick Gillman

PART III: 1896-1929
Foreword – David Stuart Davies
Foreword – Roger Johnson
Foreword – David Marcum
Two Sonnets (Poems) – Bonnie MacBird
Harbinger of Death – Geri Schear
The Adventure of the Regular Passenger – Paul D. Gilbert
The Perfect Spy – Stuart Douglas
A Mistress – Missing – Lyn McConchie
Two Plus Two – Phil Growick
The Adventure of the Coptic Patriarch – Séamus Duffy
The Royal Arsenal Affair – Leslie F.E. Coombs
The Adventure of the Sunken Parsley – Mark Alberstat
The Strange Case of the Violin Savant – GC Rosenquist
The Hopkins Brothers Affair – Iain McLaughlin and Claire Bartlett
The Disembodied Assassin – Andrew Lane
The Adventure of the Dark Tower – Peter K. Andersson
The Adventure of the Reluctant Corpse – Matthew J. Elliott
The Inspector of Graves – Jim French
The Adventure of the Parson's Son – Bob Byrne
The Adventure of the Botanist's Glove – James Lovegrove
A Most Diabolical Plot – Tim Symonds
The Opera Thief – Larry Millett
Blood Brothers – Kim Krisco
The Adventure of *The White Bird* – C. Edward Davis
The Adventure of the Avaricious Bookkeeper – Joel and Carolyn Senter

PART IV – 2016 Annual
Foreword – Steven Rothman
Foreword – Richard Doyle
Foreword – Roger Johnson
Foreword – Melissa Farnham
Foreword – Steve Emecz
Foreword – David Marcum
Toast to Mrs. Hudson (A Poem) – Arlene Mantin Levy
The Tale of the First Adventure – Derrick Belanger

(Continued on the next page . . . .)

The Adventure of the Turkish Cipher – Deanna Baran
The Adventure of the Missing Necklace – Daniel D. Victor
The Case of the Rondel Dagger – Mark Mower
The Adventure of the Double-Edged Hoard – Craig Janacek
The Adventure of the Impossible Murders – Jayantika Ganguly
The Watcher in the Woods – Denis O. Smith
The Wargrave Resurrection – Matthew Booth
Relating To One of My Old Cases – J.R. Campbell
The Adventure at the Beau Soleil – Bonnie MacBird
The Adventure of the Phantom Coachman – Arthur Hall
The Adventure of the Arsenic Dumplings – Bob Byrne
The Disappearing Anarchist Trick – Andrew Lane
The Adventure of the Grace Chalice – Roger Johnson
The Adventure of John Vincent Harden – Hugh Ashton
Murder at Tragere House – David Stuart Davies
The Adventure of *The Green Lady* – Vincent W. Wright
The Adventure of the Fellow Traveller – Daniel McGachey
The Adventure of the Highgate Financier – Nicholas Utechin
A Game of Illusion – Jeremy Holstein
The London Wheel – David Marcum
The Adventure of the Half-Melted Wolf – Marcia Wilson

PART V – Christmas Adventures
Foreword – Jonathan Kellerman
Foreword – Roger Johnson
Foreword – David Marcum
The Ballad of the Carbuncle (A Poem) – Ashley D. Polasek
The Case of the Ruby Necklace – Bob Byrne
The Jet Brooch – Denis O. Smith
The Adventure of the Missing Irregular – Amy Thomas
The Adventure of the Knighted Watchmaker – Derrick Belanger
The Stolen Relic – David Marcum
A Christmas Goose – C.H. Dye
The Adventure of the Long-Lost Enemy – Marcia Wilson
The Queen's Writing Table – Julie McKuras
The Blue Carbuncle – Sir Arthur Conan Doyle (Dramatised by Bert Coules)
The Case of the Christmas Cracker – John Hall
The Man Who Believed in Nothing – Jim French
The Case of the Christmas Star – S.F. Bennett
The Christmas Card Mystery – Narrelle M. Harris
The Question of the Death Bed Conversion – William Patrick Maynard
The Adventure of the Christmas Surprise – Vincent W. Wright
A Bauble in Scandinavia – James Lovegrove
The Adventure of Marcus Davery – Arthur Hall
The Adventure of the Purple Poet – Nicholas Utechin

(Continued on the next page . . . .)

The Adventure of the Vanishing Man – Mike Chinn
The Adventure of the Empty Manger – Tracy J. Revels
A Perpetrator in a Pear Tree – Roger Riccard
The Case of the Christmas Trifle – Wendy C. Fries
The Adventure of the Christmas Stocking – Paul D. Gilbert
The Adventure of the Golden Hunter – Jan Edwards
The Curious Case of the Well-Connected Criminal – Molly Carr
The Case of the Reformed Sinner – S. Subramanian
The Adventure of the Improbable Intruder – Peter K. Andersson
The Adventure of the Handsome Ogre – Matthew J. Elliott
The Adventure of the Deceased Doctor – Hugh Ashton
The Mile End Mynah Bird – Mark Mower

PART VI – 2017 Annual
Foreword – Colin Jeavons
Foreword – Nicholas Utechin
Foreword – Roger Johnson
Foreword – David Marcum
Sweet Violin (A Poem) – Bonnie MacBird
The Adventure of the Murdered Spinster – Bob Byrne
The Irregular – Julie McKuras
The Coffee Trader's Dilemma – Derrick Belanger
The Two Patricks – Robert Perret
The Adventure at St. Catherine's – Deanna Baran
The Adventure of a Thousand Stings – GC Rosenquist
The Adventure of the Returned Captain – Hugh Ashton
The Adventure of the Wonderful Toy – David Timson
The Adventure of the Cat's Claws – Shane Simmons
The Grave Message – Stephen Wade
The Radicant Munificent Society – Mark Mower
The Adventure of the Apologetic Assassin – David Friend
The Adventure of the Traveling Corpse – Nick Cardillo
The Adventure of the Apothecary's Prescription – Roger Riccard
The Case of the Bereaved Author – S. Subramanian
The Tetanus Epidemic – Carl L. Heifetz
The Bubble Reputation – Geri Schear
The Case of the Vanishing Venus – S.F. Bennett
The Adventure of the Vanishing Apprentice – Jennifer Copping
The Adventure of the Apothecary Shop – Jim French
The Case of the Plummeting Painter – Carla Coupe
The Case of the Temperamental Terrier – Narrelle M. Harris
The Adventure of the Frightened Architect – Arthur Hall
The Adventure of the Sunken Indiaman – Craig Janacek
The Exorcism of the Haunted Stick – Marcia Wilson
The Adventure of the Queen's Teardrop – Tracy Revels
The Curious Case of the Charwoman's Brooch – Molly Carr

(Continued on the next page . . . .)

The Unwelcome Client – Keith Hann
The Tempest of Lyme – David Ruffle
The Problem of the Holy Oil – David Marcum
A Scandal in Serbia – Thomas A. Turley
The Curious Case of Mr. Marconi – Jan Edwards
Mr. Holmes and Dr. Watson Learn to Fly – C. Edward Davis
Die Weisse Frau – Tim Symonds
A Case of Mistaken Identity – Daniel D. Victor

PART VII – Eliminate the Impossible: 1880-1891
Foreword – Lee Child
Foreword – Rand B. Lee
Foreword – Michael Cox
Foreword – Roger Johnson
Foreword – Melissa Farnham
Foreword – David Marcum
No Ghosts Need Apply (A Poem) – Jacquelynn Morris
The Melancholy Methodist – Mark Mower
The Curious Case of the Sweated Horse – Jan Edwards
The Adventure of the Second William Wilson – Daniel D. Victor
The Adventure of the Marchindale Stiletto – James Lovegrove
The Case of the Cursed Clock – Gayle Lange Puhl
The Tranquility of the Morning – Mike Hogan
A Ghost from Christmas Past – Thomas A. Turley
The Blank Photograph – James Moffett
The Adventure of A Rat. – Adrian Middleton
The Adventure of Vanaprastha – Hugh Ashton
The Ghost of Lincoln – Geri Schear
The Manor House Ghost – S. Subramanian
The Case of the Unquiet Grave – John Hall
The Adventure of the Mortal Combat – Jayantika Ganguly
The Last Encore of Quentin Carol – S.F. Bennett
The Case of the Petty Curses – Steven Philip Jones
The Tuttman Gallery – Jim French
The Second Life of Jabez Salt – John Linwood Grant
The Mystery of the Scarab Earrings – Thomas Fortenberry
The Adventure of the Haunted Room – Mike Chinn
The Pharaoh's Curse – Robert V. Stapleton
The Vampire of the Lyceum – Charles Veley and Anna Elliott
The Adventure of the Mind's Eye – Shane Simmons

PART VIII – Eliminate the Impossible: 1892-1905
Foreword – Lee Child
Foreword – Rand B. Lee
Foreword – Michael Cox
Foreword – Roger Johnson
Foreword – Melissa Farnham

(Continued on the next page . . . .)

Foreword – David Marcum
Sherlock Holmes in the Lavender field (A Poem) – Christopher James
The Adventure of the Lama's Dream – Deanna Baran
The Ghost of Dorset House – Tim Symonds
The Peculiar Persecution of John Vincent Harden – Sandor Jay Sonnen
The Case of the Biblical Colours – Ben Cardall
The Inexplicable Death of Matthew Arnatt – Andrew Lane
The Adventure of the Highgate Spectre – Michael Mallory
The Case of the Corpse Flower – Wendy C. Fries
The Problem of the Five Razors – Aaron Smith
The Adventure of the Moonlit Shadow – Arthur Hall
The Ghost of Otis Maunder – David Friend
The Adventure of the Pharaoh's Tablet – Robert Perret
The Haunting of Hamilton Gardens – Nick Cardillo
The Adventure of the Risen Corpse – Paul D. Gilbert
The Mysterious Mourner – Cindy Dye
The Adventure of the Hungry Ghost – Tracy Revels
In the Realm of the Wretched King – Derrick Belanger
The Case of the Little Washerwoman – William Meikle
The Catacomb Saint Affair – Marcia Wilson
The Curious Case of Charlotte Musgrave – Roger Riccard
The Adventure of the Awakened Spirit – Craig Janacek
The Adventure of the Theatre Ghost – Jeremy Branton Holstein
The Adventure of the Glassy Ghost – Will Murray
The Affair of the Grange Haunting – David Ruffle
The Adventure of the Pallid Mask – Daniel McGachey
The Two Different Women – David Marcum

Part IX – 2018 Annual (1879-1895)
Foreword – Nicholas Meyer
Foreword – Roger Johnson
Foreword – Melissa Farnham
Foreword – Steve Emecz
Foreword – David Marcum
Violet Smith (A Poem) – Amy Thomas
The Adventure of the Temperance Society – Deanna Baran
The Adventure of the Fool and His Money – Roger Riccard
The Helverton Inheritance – David Marcum
The Adventure of the Faithful Servant – Tracy Revels
The Adventure of the Parisian Butcher – Nick Cardillo
The Missing Empress – Robert Stapleton
The Resplendent Plane Tree – Kevin P. Thornton
The Strange Adventure of the Doomed Sextette – Leslie Charteris and Denis Green
The Adventure of the Old Boys' Club – Shane Simmons
The Case of the Golden Trail – James Moffett
The Detective Who Cried Wolf – C.H. Dye

(Continued on the next page . . . .)

The Lambeth Poisoner Case – Stephen Gaspar
The Confession of Anna Jarrow – S. F. Bennett
The Adventure of the Disappearing Dictionary – Sonia Fetherston
The Fairy Hills Horror – Geri Schear
A Loathsome and Remarkable Adventure – Marcia Wilson
The Adventure of the Multiple Moriartys – David Friend
The Influence Machine – Mark Mower

Part X – 2018 Annual (1896-1916)
Foreword – Nicholas Meyer
Foreword – Roger Johnson
Foreword – Melissa Farnham
Foreword – Steve Emecz
Foreword – David Marcum
A Man of Twice Exceptions (A Poem) – Derrick Belanger
The Horned God – Kelvin Jones
The Coughing Man – Jim French
The Adventure of Canal Reach – Arthur Hall
A Simple Case of Abduction – Mike Hogan
A Case of Embezzlement – Steven Ehrman
The Adventure of the Vanishing Diplomat – Greg Hatcher
The Adventure of the Perfidious Partner – Jayantika Ganguly
A Brush With Death – Dick Gillman
A Revenge Served Cold – Maurice Barkley
The Case of the Anonymous Client – Paul A. Freeman
Capitol Murder – Daniel D. Victor
The Case of the Dead Detective – Martin Rosenstock
The Musician Who Spoke From the Grave – Peter Coe Verbica
The Adventure of the Future Funeral – Hugh Ashton
The Problem of the Bruised Tongues – Will Murray
The Mystery of the Change of Art – Robert Perret
The Parsimonious Peacekeeper – Thaddeus Tuffentsamer
The Case of the Dirty Hand – G.L. Schulze
The Mystery of the Missing Artefacts – Tim Symonds

Part XI: Some Untold Cases (1880-1891)
Foreword – Lyndsay Faye
Foreword – Roger Johnson
Foreword – Melissa Grigsby
Foreword – Steve Emecz
Foreword – David Marcum
Unrecorded Holmes Cases (*A Sonnet*) – Arlene Mantin Levy and Mark Levy
The Most Repellant Man – Jayantika Ganguly
The Singular Adventure of the Extinguished Wicks – Will Murray
Mrs. Forrester's Complication – Roger Riccard
The Adventure of Vittoria, the Circus Belle – Tracy Revels

(Continued on the next page . . . .)

The Adventure of the Silver Skull – Hugh Ashton
The Pimlico Poisoner – Matthew Simmonds
The Grosvenor Square Furniture Van – David Ruffle
The Adventure of the Paradol Chamber – Paul W. Nash
The Bishopgate Jewel Case – Mike Hogan
The Singular Tragedy of the Atkinson Brothers of Trincomalee – Craig Stephen Copland
Colonel Warburton's Madness – Gayle Lange Puhl
The Adventure at Bellingbeck Park – Deanna Baran
The Giant Rat of Sumatra – Leslie Charteris and Denis Green
    Introduction by Ian Dickerson
The Vatican Cameos – Kevin P. Thornton
The Case of the Gila Monster – Stephen Herczeg
The Bogus Laundry Affair – Robert Perret
Inspector Lestrade and the Molesey Mystery – M.A. Wilson and Richard Dean Starr

Part XII: Some Untold Cases (1894-1902)
Foreword – Lyndsay Faye
Foreword – Roger Johnson
Foreword – Melissa Grigsby
Foreword – Steve Emecz
Foreword – David Marcum
It's Always Time (*A Poem*) – "Anon."
The Shanghaied Surgeon – C.H. Dye
The Trusted Advisor – David Marcum
A Shame Harder Than Death – Thomas Fortenberry
The Adventure of the Smith-Mortimer Succession – Daniel D. Victor
A Repulsive Story and a Terrible Death – Nik Morton
The Adventure of the Dishonourable Discharge – Craig Janacek
The Adventure of the Admirable Patriot – S. Subramanian
The Abernetty Transactions – Jim French
Dr. Agar and the Dinosaur – Robert Stapleton
The Giant Rat of Sumatra – Nick Cardillo
The Adventure of the Black Plague – Paul D. Gilbert
Vigor, the Hammersmith Wonder – Mike Hogan
A Correspondence Concerning Mr. James Phillimore – Derrick Belanger
The Curious Case of the Two Coptic Patriarchs – John Linwood Grant
The Conk-Singleton Forgery Case – Mark Mower
Another Case of Identity – Jane Rubino
The Adventure of the Exalted Victim – Arthur Hall

PART XIII: 2019 Annual (1881-1890)
Foreword – Will Thomas
Foreword – Roger Johnson
Foreword – Melissa Grigsby
Foreword – Steve Emecz
Foreword – David Marcum
Inscrutable (*A Poem*) – Jacquelynn Morris

(Continued on the next page . . . .)

The Folly of Age – Derrick Belanger
The Fashionably-Dressed Girl – Mark Mower
The Odour of Neroli – Brenda Seabrooke
The Coffee House Girl – David Marcum
The Mystery of the Green Room – Robert Stapleton
The Case of the Enthusiastic Amateur – S.F. Bennett
The Adventure of the Missing Cousin – Edwin A. Enstrom
The Roses of Highclough House – MJH Simmonds
The Shackled Man – Andrew Bryant
The Yellow Star of Cairo – Tim Gambrell
The Adventure of the Winterhall Monster – Tracy Revels
The Grosvenor Square Furniture Van – Hugh Ashton
The Voyage of *Albion's Thistle* – Sean M. Wright
Bootless in Chippenham – Marino C. Alvarez
The Clerkenwell Shadow – Paul Hiscock
The Adventure of the Worried Banker – Arthur Hall
The Recovery of the Ashes – Kevin P. Thornton
The Mystery of the Patient Fisherman – Jim French
Sherlock Holmes in Bedlam – David Friend
The Adventure of the Ambulatory Cadaver – Shane Simmons
The Dutch Impostors – Peter Coe Verbica
The Missing Adam Tiler – Mark Wardecker

PART XIV: 2019 Annual (1891-1897)
Foreword – Will Thomas
Foreword – Roger Johnson
Foreword – Melissa Grigsby
Foreword – Steve Emecz
Foreword – David Marcum
Skein of Tales (*A Poem*) – Jacquelynn Morris
The Adventure of the Royal Albert Hall – Charles Veley and Anna Elliott
The Tower of Fear – Mark Sohn
The Carroun Document – David Marcum
The Threadneedle Street Murder – S. Subramanian
The Collegiate Leprechaun – Roger Riccard
A Malversation of Mummies – Marcia Wilson
The Adventure of the Silent Witness – Tracy J. Revels
The Second Whitechapel Murderer – Arthur Hall
The Adventure of the Jeweled Falcon – GC Rosenquist
The Adventure of the Crossbow – Edwin A. Enstrom
The Adventure of the Delusional Wife – Jayantika Ganguly
Child's Play – C.H. Dye
The Lancelot Connection – Matthew Booth
The Adventure of the Modern Guy Fawkes – Stephen Herczeg
Mr. Clever, Baker Street – Geri Schear
The Adventure of the Scarlet Rosebud – Liz Hedgecock

(Continued on the next page . . . .)

The Poisoned Regiment – Carl Heifetz
The Case of the Persecuted Poacher – Gayle Lange Puhl
It's Time – Harry DeMaio
The Case of the Fourpenny Coffin – I.A. Watson
The Horror in King Street – Thomas A. Burns, Jr.

PART XV: 2019 Annual (1898-1917)
Foreword – Will Thomas
Foreword – Roger Johnson
Foreword – Melissa Grigsby
Foreword – Steve Emecz
Foreword – David Marcum
Two Poems – Christopher James
The Whitechapel Butcher – Mark Mower
The Incomparable Miss Incognita – Thomas Fortenberry
The Adventure of the Twofold Purpose – Robert Perret
The Adventure of the Green Gifts – Tracy J. Revels
The Turk's Head – Robert Stapleton
A Ghost in the Mirror – Peter Coe Verbica
The Mysterious Mr. Rim – Maurice Barkley
The Adventure of the Fatal Jewel-Box – Edwin A. Enstrom
Mass Murder – William Todd
The Notable Musician – Roger Riccard
The Devil's Painting – Kelvin I. Jones
The Adventure of the Silent Sister – Arthur Hall
A Skeleton's Sorry Story – Jack Grochot
An Actor and a Rare One – David Marcum
The Silver Bullet – Dick Gillman
The Adventure at Throne of Gilt – Will Murray
"The Boy Who Would Be King – Dick Gillman
The Case of the Seventeenth Monk – Tim Symonds
Alas, Poor Will – Mike Hogan
The Case of the Haunted Chateau – Leslie Charteris and Denis Green
    Introduction by Ian Dickerson
The Adventure of the Weeping Stone – Nick Cardillo
The Adventure of the Three Telegrams – Darryl Webber

Part XVI – Whatever Remains . . . Must Be the Truth (1881-1890)
Foreword – Kareem Abdul-Jabbar
Foreword – Roger Johnson
Foreword – Steve Emecz
Foreword – David Marcum
The Hound of the Baskervilles (Retold) (*A Poem*) – Josh Pachter
The Wylington Lake Monster – Derrick Belanger
The *Juju* Men of Richmond – Mark Sohn

(Continued on the next page . . . .)

The Adventure of the Headless Lady – Tracy J. Revels
Angelus Domini Nuntiavit – Kevin P. Thornton
The Blue Lady of Dunraven – Andrew Bryant
The Adventure of the Ghoulish Grenadier – Josh Anderson and David Friend
The Curse of Barcombe Keep – Brenda Seabrooke
The Affair of the Regressive Man – David Marcum
The Adventure of the Giant's Wife – I.A. Watson
The Adventure of Miss Anna Truegrace – Arthur Hall
The Haunting of Bottomly's Grandmother – Tim Gambrell
The Adventure of the Intrusive Spirit – Shane Simmons
The Paddington Poltergeist – Bob Bishop
The Spectral Pterosaur – Mark Mower
The Weird of Caxton – Kelvin Jones
The Adventure of the Obsessive Ghost – Jayantika Ganguly

Part XVII – Whatever Remains . . . Must Be the Truth (1891-1898)
Foreword – Kareem Abdul-Jabbar
Foreword – Roger Johnson
Foreword – Steve Emecz
Foreword – David Marcum
The Violin Thief (*A Poem*) – Christopher James
The Spectre of Scarborough Castle – Charles Veley and Anna Elliott
The Case for Which the World is Not Yet Prepared – Steven Philip Jones
The Adventure of the Returning Spirit – Arthur Hall
The Adventure of the Bewitched Tenant – Michael Mallory
The Misadventures of the Bonnie Boy – Will Murray
The Adventure of the *Danse Macabre* – Paul D. Gilbert
The Strange Persecution of John Vincent Harden – S. Subramanian
The Dead Quiet Library – Roger Riccard
The Adventure of the Sugar Merchant – Stephen Herczeg
The Adventure of the Undertaker's Fetch – Tracy J. Revels
The Holloway Ghosts – Hugh Ashton
The Diogenes Club Poltergeist – Chris Chan
The Madness of Colonel Warburton – Bert Coules
The Return of the Noble Bachelor – Jane Rubino
The Reappearance of Mr. James Phillimore – David Marcum
The Miracle Worker – Geri Schear
The Hand of Mesmer – Dick Gillman

Part XVIII – Whatever Remains . . . Must Be the Truth (1899-1925)
Foreword – Kareem Abdul-Jabbar
Foreword – Roger Johnson
Foreword – Steve Emecz
Foreword – David Marcum
The Adventure of the Lighthouse on the Moor (*A Poem*) – Christopher James
The Witch of Ellenby – Thomas A. Burns, Jr.

(Continued on the next page . . . .)

The Tollington Ghost – Roger Silverwood
You Only Live Thrice – Robert Stapleton
The Adventure of the Fair Lad – Craig Janacek
The Adventure of the Voodoo Curse – Gareth Tilley
The Cassandra of Providence Place – Paul Hiscock
The Adventure of the House Abandoned – Arthur Hall
The Winterbourne Phantom – M.J. Elliott
The Murderous Mercedes – Harry DeMaio
The Solitary Violinist – Tom Turley
The Cunning Man – Kelvin I. Jones
The Adventure of Khamaat's Curse – Tracy J. Revels
The Adventure of the Weeping Mary – Matthew White
The Unnerved Estate Agent – David Marcum
Death in The House of the Black Madonna – Nick Cardillo
The Case of the Ivy-Covered Tomb – S.F. Bennett

Part XIX: 2020 Annual (1892-1890)
Foreword – John Lescroart
Foreword – Roger Johnson
Foreword – Lizzy Butler
Foreword – Steve Emecz
Foreword – David Marcum
Holmes's Prayer (*A Poem*) – Christopher James
A Case of Paternity – Matthew White
The Raspberry Tart – Roger Riccard
The Mystery of the Elusive Bard – Kevin P. Thornton
The Man in the Maroon Suit – Chris Chan
The Scholar of Silchester Court – Nick Cardillo
The Adventure of the Changed Man – MJH. Simmonds
The Adventure of the Tea-Stained Diamonds – Craig Stephen Copland
The Indigo Impossibility – Will Murray
The Case of the Emerald Knife-Throwers – Ian Ableson
A Game of Skittles – Thomas A. Turley
The Gordon Square Discovery – David Marcum
The Tattooed Rose – Dick Gillman
The Problem at Pentonville Prison – David Friend
The Nautch Night Case – Brenda Seabrooke
The Disappearing Prisoner – Arthur Hall
The Case of the Missing Pipe – James Moffett
The Whitehaven Ransom – Robert Stapleton
The Enlightenment of Newton – Dick Gillman
The Impaled Man – Andrew Bryant
The Mystery of the Elusive Li Shen – Will Murray
The Mahmudabad Result – Andrew Bryant

(Continued on the next page . . . .)

The Adventure of the Matched Set – Peter Coe Verbica
When the Prince First Dined at the Diogenes Club – Sean M. Wright
The Sweetenbury Safe Affair – Tim Gambrell

Part XX: 2020 Annual (1891-1897)
Foreword – John Lescroart
Foreword – Roger Johnson
Foreword – Lizzy Butler
Foreword – Steve Emecz
Foreword – David Marcum
The Sibling (*A Poem*) – Jacquelynn Morris
Blood and Gunpowder – Thomas A. Burns, Jr.
The Atelier of Death – Harry DeMaio
The Adventure of the Beauty Trap – Tracy Revels
A Case of Unfinished Business – Steven Philip Jones
The Case of the S.S. Bokhara – Mark Mower
The Adventure of the American Opera Singer – Deanna Baran
The Keadby Cross – David Marcum
The Adventure at Dead Man's Hole – Stephen Herczeg
The Elusive Mr. Chester – Arthur Hall
The Adventure of Old Black Duffel – Will Murray
The Blood-Spattered Bridge – Gayle Lange Puhl
The Tomorrow Man – S.F. Bennett
The Sweet Science of Bruising – Kevin P. Thornton
The Mystery of Sherlock Holmes – Christopher Todd
The Elusive Mr. Phillimore – Matthew J. Elliott
The Murders in the Maharajah's Railway Carriage – Charles Veley and Anna Elliott
The Ransomed Miracle – I.A. Watson
The Adventure of the Unkind Turn – Robert Perret
The Perplexing X'ing – Sonia Fetherston
The Case of the Short-Sighted Clown – Susan Knight

Part XXI: 2020 Annual (1898-1923)
Foreword – John Lescroart
Foreword – Roger Johnson
Foreword – Lizzy Butler
Foreword – Steve Emecz
Foreword – David Marcum
The Case of the Missing Rhyme (*A Poem*) – Joseph W. Svec III
The Problem of the St. Francis Parish Robbery – R.K. Radek
The Adventure of the Grand Vizier – Arthur Hall
The Mummy's Curse – DJ Tyrer
The Fractured Freemason of Fitzrovia – David L. Leal
The Bleeding Heart – Paula Hammond
The Secret Admirer – Jayantika Ganguly

(Continued on the next page . . . .)

The Deceased Priest – Peter Coe Verbica
The Case of the Rewrapped Presents – Bob Byrne
The Invisible Assassin – Geri Shear
The Adventure of the Chocolate Pot – Hugh Ashton
The Adventure of the Incessant Workers – Arthur Hall
When Best Served Cold – Stephen Mason
The Cat's Meat Lady of Cavendish Square – David Marcum
The Unveiled Lodger – Mark Mower
The League of Unhappy Orphans – Leslie Charteris and Denis Green
    Introduction by Ian Dickerson
The Adventure of the Three Fables – Jane Rubino
The Cobbler's Treasure – Dick Gillman
The Adventure of the Wells Beach Ruffians – Derrick Belanger
The Adventure of the Doctor's Hand – Michael Mallory
The Case of the Purloined Talisman – John Lawrence

Part XXII: Some More Untold Cases (1877-1887)
Foreword – Otto Penzler
Foreword – Roger Johnson
Foreword – Steve Emecz
Foreword – Jacqueline Silver
Foreword – David Marcum
The Philosophy of Holmes (*A Poem*) – Christopher James
The Terror of the Tankerville – S.F. Bennett
The Singular Affair of the Aluminium Crutch – William Todd
The Trifling Matter of Mortimer Maberley – Geri Schear
Abracadaver – Susan Knight
The Secret in Lowndes Court – David Marcum
Vittoria, the Circus Bell – Bob Bishop
The Adventure of the Vanished Husband – Tracy J. Revels
Merridew of Abominable Memory – Chris Chan
The Substitute Thief – Richard Paolinelli
The Whole Story Concerning the Politician, the Lighthouse, and the Trained Cormorant –
    Derrick Belanger
A Child's Reward – Stephen Mason
The Case of the Elusive Umbrella – Leslie Charteris and Denis Green
    Introduction by Ian Dickerson
The Strange Death of an Art Dealer – Tim Symonds
Watch Him Fall – Liese Sherwood-Fabre
The Adventure of the Transatlantic Gila – Ian Ableson
Intruders at Baker Street – Chris Chan
The Paradol Chamber – Mark Mower
Wolf Island – Robert Stapleton
The Etherage Escapade – Roger Riccard

(Continued on the next page . . . .)

The Dundas Separation Case – Kevin P. Thornton
The Broken Glass – Denis O. Smith

Part XXIII: Some More Untold Cases (1888-1894)
Foreword – Otto Penzler
Foreword – Roger Johnson
Foreword – Steve Emecz
Foreword – Jacqueline Silver
Foreword – David Marcum
The Housekeeper (*A Poem*) – John Linwood Grant
The Uncanny Adventure of the Hammersmith Wonder – Will Murray
Mrs. Forrester's Domestic Complication– Tim Gambrell
The Adventure of the Abducted Bard – I.A. Watson
The Adventure of the Loring Riddle – Craig Janacek
To the Manor Bound – Jane Rubino
The Crimes of John Clay – Paul Hiscock
The Adventure of the Nonpareil Club – Hugh Ashton
The Adventure of the Singular Worm – Mike Chinn
The Adventure of the Forgotten Brolly – Shane Simmons
The Adventure of the Tired Captain – Dacre Stoker and Leverett Butts
The Rhayader Legacy – David Marcum
The Adventure of the Tired Captain – Matthew J. Elliott
The Secret of Colonel Warburton's Insanity – Paul D. Gilbert
The Adventure of Merridew of Abominable Memory – Tracy J. Revels
The Affair of the Hellingstone Rubies – Margaret Walsh
The Adventure of the Drewhampton Poisoner – Arthur Hall
The Incident of the Dual Intrusions – Barry Clay
The Case of the Un-Paralleled Adventures – Steven Philip Jones
The Affair of the Friesland – Jan van Koningsveld
The Forgetful Detective – Marcia Wilson
The Smith-Mortimer Succession – Tim Gambrell
The Repulsive Matter of the Bloodless Banker – Will Murray

Part XXIV: Some More Untold Cases (1895-1903)
Foreword – Otto Penzler
Foreword – Roger Johnson
Foreword – Steve Emecz
Foreword – Jacqueline Silver
Foreword – David Marcum
Sherlock Holmes and the Return of the Missing Rhyme (*A Poem*) – Joseph W. Svec III
The Comet Wine's Funeral – Marcia Wilson
The Case of the Accused Cook – Brenda Seabrooke
The Case of Vanderbilt and the Yeggman – Stephen Herczeg

(Continued on the next page . . . .)

The Tragedy of Woodman's Lee – Tracy J. Revels
The Murdered Millionaire – Kevin P. Thornton
Another Case of Identity – Thomas A. Burns, Jr.
The Case of Indelible Evidence – Dick Gillman
The Adventure of Parsley and Butter – Jayantika Ganguly
The Adventure of the Nile Traveler – John Davis
The Curious Case of the Crusader's Cross – DJ Tyrer
An Act of Faith – Harry DeMaio
The Adventure of the Conk-Singleton Forgery – Arthur Hall
A Simple Matter – Susan Knight
The Hammerford Will Business – David Marcum
The Adventure of Mr. Fairdale Hobbs – Arthur Hall
The Adventure of the Abergavenny Murder – Craig Stephen Copland
The Chinese Puzzle Box – Gayle Lange Puhl
The Adventure of the Refused Knighthood – Craig Stephen Copland
The Case of the Consulting Physician – John Lawrence
The Man from Deptford – John Linwood Grant
The Case of the Impossible Assassin – Paula Hammond

Part XXV: 2021 Annual (1881-1888)

Foreword – Peter Lovsey
Foreword – Roger Johnson
Foreword – Steve Emecz
Foreword – Jacqueline Silver
Foreword – David Marcum
Baskerville Hall (*A Poem*) – Kelvin I. Jones
The Persian Slipper – Brenda Seabrooke
The Adventure of the Doll Maker's Daughter – Matthew White
The Flinders Case – Kevin McCann
The Sunderland Tragedies – David Marcum
The Tin Soldiers – Paul Hiscock
The Shattered Man – MJH Simmonds
The Hungarian Doctor – Denis O. Smith
The Black Hole of Berlin – Robert Stapleton
The Thirteenth Step – Keith Hann
The Missing Murderer – Marcia Wilson
Dial Square – Martin Daley
The Adventure of the Deadly Tradition – Matthew J. Elliott
The Adventure of the Fabricated Vision – Craig Janacek
The Adventure of the Murdered Maharajah – Hugh Ashton
The God of War – Hal Glatzer
The Atkinson Brothers of Trincomalee – Stephen Gaspar

(Continued on the next page . . . .)

The Switched String – Chris Chan
The Case of the Secret Samaritan – Jane Rubino
The Bishopsgate Jewel Case – Stephen Gaspar

Part XXVI: 2021 Annual (1889-1897)
Foreword – Peter Lovesey
Foreword – Roger Johnson
Foreword – Steve Emecz
Foreword – Jacqueline Silver
Foreword – David Marcum
221b Baker Street (*A Poem*) – Kevin Patrick McCann
The Burglary Season – Marcia Wilson
The Lamplighter at Rosebery Avenue – James Moffett
The Disfigured Hand – Peter Coe Verbica
The Adventure of the Bloody Duck – Margaret Walsh
The Tragedy at Longpool – James Gelter
The Case of the Viscount's Daughter – Naching T. Kassa
The Key in the Snuffbox – DJ Tyrer
The Race for the Gleghorn Estate – Ian Ableson
The Isa Bird Befuddlement – Kevin P. Thornton
The Cliddesden Questions – David Marcum
Death in Verbier – Adrian Middleton
The King's Cross Road Somnambulist – Dick Gillman
The Magic Bullet – Peter Coe Verbica
The Petulant Patient – Geri Schear
The Mystery of the Groaning Stone – Mark Mower
The Strange Case of the Pale Boy – Susan Knight
The Adventure of the Zande Dagger – Frank Schildiner
The Adventure of the Vengeful Daughter – Arthur Hall
Do the Needful – Harry DeMaio
The Count, the Banker, the Thief, and the Seven Half-sovereigns – Mike Hogan
The Adventure of the Unsprung Mousetrap – Anthony Gurney
The Confectioner's Captives – I.A. Watson

Part XXVII: 2021 Annual (1898-1928)
Foreword – Peter Lovesey
Foreword – Roger Johnson
Foreword – Steve Emecz
Foreword – Jacqueline Silver
Foreword – David Marcum
Sherlock Holmes Returns: The Missing Rhyme (*A Poem*) – Joseph W. Svec, III
The Adventure of the Hero's Heir – Tracy J. Revels
The Curious Case of the Soldier's Letter – John Davis
The Case of the Norwegian Daredevil – John Lawrence
The Case of the Borneo Tribesman – Stephen Herczeg
The Adventure of the White Roses – Tracy J. Revels

(Continued on the next page . . . .)

Mrs. Crichton's Ledger – Tim Gambrell
The Adventure of the Not-Very-Merry Widows – Craig Stephen Copland
The Son of God – Jeremy Branton Holstein
The Adventure of the Disgraced Captain – Thomas A. Turley
The Woman Who Returned From the Dead – Arthur Hall
The Farraway Street Lodger – David Marcum
The Mystery of Foxglove Lodge – S.C. Toft
The Strange Adventure of Murder by Remote Control – Leslie Charteris and Denis Green
    Introduction by Ian Dickerson
The Case of The Blue Parrot – Roger Riccard
The Adventure of the Expelled Master – Will Murray
The Case of the Suicidal Suffragist – John Lawrence
The Welbeck Abbey Shooting Party – Thomas A. Turley
Case No. 358 – Marcia Wilson

The following contributions appear in this volume:
**The MX Book of New Sherlock Holmes Stories
Part XXIX – More Christmas Adventures (1889-1896)**

"The Sword in the Spruce" ©2021 by Ian Ableson. All Rights Reserved. First publication, original to this collection. Printed by permission of the author.

"The Adventure of the Serpentine Body" *and* "Absent Friends" ©2021 by Wayne Anderson. All Rights Reserved. First publication, original to this collection. Printed by permission of the author.

"The Man of Miracles" ©2021 by Derrick Belanger. All Rights Reserved. First publication, original to this collection. Printed by permission of the author.

"The Incident of the Stolen Christmas Present" ©2021 by Barry Clay. All Rights Reserved. First publication, original to this collection. Printed by permission of the author.

"The Baffling Adventure of the Baby Jesus" ©2021 by Craig Stephen Copland. All Rights Reserved. First publication, original to this collection. Printed by permission of the author.

"The Incident in Regent Street" ©2021 by Harry DeMaio. All Rights Reserved. First publication, original to this collection. Printed by permission of the author.

"An Ongoing Legacy for Sherlock Holmes" ©2021 by Steve Emecz. All Rights Reserved. First publication, original to this collection. Printed by permission of the author.

"The Dilemma of Mr. Henry Baker" ©2021 by Paul D. Gilbert. All Rights Reserved. First publication, original to this collection. Printed by permission of the author.

"The Adventure of the Injured Man" ©2021 by Arthur Hall. All Rights Reserved. First publication, original to this collection. Printed by permission of the author.

"Foreword" ©2021 by Nancy Holder. All Rights Reserved. First publication, original to this collection. Printed by permission of the author.

"Baker Street in Snow (1890)" ©2021 by Christopher James. All Rights Reserved. First publication, original to this collection. Printed by permission of the author.

"It is the Season of Forgiveness" ©2021 by Roger Johnson. All Rights Reserved. First publication, original to this collection. Printed by permission of the author.

"The Adventure of the Fugitive Irregular" ©2021 by Gordon Linzner. All Rights Reserved. First publication, original to this collection. Printed by permission of the author.

"Editor's Foreword: Never Enough Holmes Adventures – Even at Christmas!" *and* "The Father Christmas Brigade" ©2021 by David Marcum. All Rights Reserved. First publication, original to this collection. Printed by permission of the author.

"The Adventure of the Christmas Suitors" ©2021 by Tracy Revels. All Rights Reserved. First publication, original to this collection. Printed by permission of the author.

"The Adventure of the Secret Manuscript" ©2021 by Dan Rowley. All Rights Reserved. First publication, original to this collection. Printed by permission of the author.

"The Adventure of the Viking Ghost" ©2021 by Frank Schildiner. All Rights Reserved. First publication, original to this collection. Printed by permission of the author.

"The Adventure of the Christmas Wish" ©2021 by Margaret Walsh. All Rights Reserved. First publication, original to this collection. Printed by permission of the author.

"The Twelve Days" ©2021 by I.A. Watson. All Rights Reserved. First publication, original to this collection. Printed by permission of the author.

"Undershaw: Eliminating the Impossible" ©2021 by Emma West. All Rights Reserved. First publication, original to this collection. Printed by permission of the author.

"The Adventure of the Second Sister" ©2021 Matthew White. All Rights Reserved. First publication, original to this collection. Printed by permission of the author.

"The Krampus Who Came to Call" ©2021 Marcia Wilson. All Rights Reserved. First publication, original to this collection. Printed by permission of the author.

The following contributions appear in the companion volumes:
Part XXVIII – More Christmas Adventures (1869-1888)
Part XXX – More Christmas Adventures (1897-1928)

"No Malice Intended" ©2021 by Deanna Baran. All Rights Reserved. First publication, original to this collection. Printed by permission of the author.

"The Case of the Cursory Curse" ©2021 by Andrew Bryant. All Rights Reserved. First publication, original to this collection. Printed by permission of the author.

"Christmas at the Red Lion" ©2021 by Thomas A. Burns, Jr. All Rights Reserved. First publication, original to this collection. Printed by permission of the author.

"The Bitter Gravestones" ©2021 by Chris Chan. All Rights Reserved. First publication, original to this collection. Printed by permission of the author.

"The Sebastopol Clasp" ©2021 by Martin Daley. All Rights Reserved. First publication, original to this collection. Printed by permission of the author.

"The Chatterton-Smythe Affair" *and* "The St. Giles Child Murders" ©2021 by Tim Gambrell. All Rights Reserved. First publication, original to this collection. Printed by permission of the author.

"The Adventure of the Dextrous Doctor" ©2021 by Jayantika Ganguly. All Rights Reserved. First publication, original to this collection. Printed by permission of the author.

"The Silent Brotherhood" ©2021 by Dick Gillman. All Rights Reserved. First publication, original to this collection. Printed by permission of the author.

"The Adventure of the Maligned Mineralogist" *and* "The Adventure of the Christmas Threat" ©2021 by Arthur Hall. All Rights Reserved. First publication, original to this collection. Printed by permission of the author.

"The Case of the Earnest Young Man" ©2021 by Paula Hammond. All Rights Reserved. First publication, original to this collection. Printed by permission of the author.

"The Case of the Christmas Pudding" ©2021 by Liz Hedgecock. All Rights Reserved. First publication, original to this collection. Printed by permission of the author.

"The Case of the Left Foot" ©2021 by Stephen Herczeg. All Rights Reserved. First publication, original to this collection. Printed by permission of the author.

"The St. Stephen's Day Mystery" *and* "The Midnight Mass Murder" ©2021 by Paul Hiscock. All Rights Reserved. First publication, original to this collection. Printed by permission of the author.

"A Fine Kettle of Fish" ©2021 by Mike Hogan. All Rights Reserved. First publication, original to this collection. Printed by permission of the author.

"Baker Street in Snow (1890)" (A Poem) ©2021 by Christopher James. All Rights Reserved. First publication, original to this collection. Printed by permission of the author.

"The Case of the Holly-Sprig Pudding" ©2021 by Naching T. Kassa. All Rights Reserved. First publication, original to this collection. Printed by permission of the author.

"The Mystery of Maple Tree Lodge" ©2021 by Susan Knight. All Rights Reserved. First publication, original to this collection. Printed by permission of the author.

"The Case of the Duplicitous Suitor" ©2021 by John Lawrence. All Rights Reserved. First publication, original to this collection. Printed by permission of the author.

"The Six-Fingered Scoundrel" ©2021 by Jeffrey A. Lockwood. All Rights Reserved. First publication, original to this collection. Printed by permission of the author.

"The Adventure of the Stolen Christmas Gift" ©2021 by Michael Mallory. All Rights Reserved. First publication, original to this collection. Printed by permission of the author.

"The Christmas Ghost of Crailloch Taigh" *and* "The Canterbury Manifesto" ©2021 by David Marcum. All Rights Reserved. First publication, original to this collection. Printed by permission of the author.

"The Case of the Disappearing Beaune" ©2021 by J. Lawrence Matthews. All Rights Reserved. First publication, original to this collection. Printed by permission of the author.

"The Colourful Skein of Life" ©2021 by Julie McKuras. All Rights Reserved. First publication, original to this collection. Printed by permission of the author.

"The Yuletide Heist" ©2021 by Mark Mower. All Rights Reserved. First publication, original to this collection. Printed by permission of the author.

"The Adventure of the Christmas Lesson" ©2021 by Will Murray. All Rights Reserved. First publication, original to this collection. Printed by permission of the author.

"The Case of the Golden Grail" ©2021 by Roger Riccard. All Rights Reserved. First publication, original to this collection. Printed by permission of the author.

"The Adventure of the Chained Phantom" and accompanying illustrations ©2021 by J.S. Rowlinson. All Rights Reserved. First publication, original to this collection. Printed by permission of the author.

"A Price Above Rubies" ©2021 by Jane Rubino. All Rights Reserved. First publication, original to this collection. Printed by permission of the author.

"A Featureless Crime" ©2021 by Geri Schear. All Rights Reserved. First publication, original to this collection. Printed by permission of the author.

"The Christmas Card Case" ©2021 by Brenda Seabrooke. All Rights Reserved. First publication, original to this collection. Printed by permission of the author.

"The Intrigue of the Red Christmas" ©2021 by Shane Simmons. All Rights Reserved. First publication, original to this collection. Printed by permission of the author.

"A Sherlockian Christmas" (A Poem) ©2021 by Joseph W. Svec, III. All Rights Reserved. First publication, original to this collection. Printed by permission of the author.

"A Study in Murder" ©2021 by Amy Thomas. All Rights Reserved. First publication, original to this collection. Printed by permission of the author.

"Christmas Magic" *and* "Santa's Little Elves" ©2021 by Kevin P. Thornton. All Rights Reserved. First publication, original to this collection. Printed by permission of the author.

"A Yuletide Tragedy" ©2021 by Thomas A. Turley. All Rights Reserved. First publication, original to this collection. Printed by permission of the author.

"The Purloined Present" ©2021 by DJ Tyrer. All Rights Reserved. First publication, original to this collection. Printed by permission of the author.

𝈂 𝈊 𝈈 𝈊 𝈈 𝈋 𝈈 𝈉 𝈈 𝈊 𝈈 𝈂

Editor's Foreword:
Never Enough Holmes Adventures – Even at Christmas!
by David Marcum

"It arrived upon Christmas morning...."
Sherlock Holmes – "The Blue Carbuncle"

Dr. John H. Watson met Sherlock Holmes on January 1st, 1881, in a laboratory at St. Bartholomew's Hospital, where Holmes, not-quite twenty-seven years old, was taking advantage of the empty facilities to conduct medico-legal experiments related to blood identification. Watson, himself only twenty-eight, had been grievously wounded at the Battle of Maiwand just a little over five months before, and during his subsequent recovery, he'd nearly died from enteric fever, also known as typhoid. By the time he made the month-long journey back to England on the troopship *Orontes*, he was still just barely recovered, and his mood was certainly grim as he faced an uncertain future.

Watson wrote that he had *"neither kith nor kin in England"*, and though it isn't recorded, one can only imagine how bleak was the Christmas of 1880 for this poor veteran, living on his meagre wound pension, and getting through every long dull day in an unfriendly city while residing in a small unfriendly hotel off the Strand. Unexpectedly running into an old friend, Stamford, in the bar of the Criterion on New Year's Day, and then subsequently being swept along to a meeting at Barts with a potential future flatmate, must have been the most excitement that had intruded into Watson's life since his return.

Based on their initial discussion at Barts, Holmes and Watson met the next morning to look at rooms in Baker Street. Watson moved in later that day, and Holmes the day after. The argument could be made that this arrangement saved Watson's life. He went from the desolate daily existence he'd had for weeks, slowly living beyond his means and with no set promise for a better future, to good rooms, a motherly landlady who helped him regain his health, and the mental distraction of a most unusual new flatmate. Within just a few months, Watson would learn that Holmes was a *Consulting Detective* – the first – and Watson began participating in various investigations as his health allowed. This certainly contributed more to his recovery than simply sitting around a bleak hotel room would have ever done.

Holmes lived in Baker Street from 1881 until autumn 1903 – around nineteen years, not counting the three-year period from April 1891 to April 1894 when he was absent and presumed dead following his battle with Professor Moriarty atop the Reichenbach Falls. Watson knew him that entire time – again, with the exception of The Great Hiatus, and that period of time in the mid-1880's when Watson spent some time in the United States – though he actually shared the Baker Street rooms with Holmes for quite a bit less than that – cumulatively around fifteen. His time there was broken up by those occasions when he married and lived elsewhere, with residences and medical practices in Paddington, Kensington, and Queen Anne Street.

Throughout all of these years, both of Holmes and Watson were involved in a great many investigations of varying levels of importance. There are those who think that Holmes's entire career consisted only of those cases related in the pitifully few sixty stories of The Canon, along with the one-hundred-forty or so "Untold Cases" such as the Giant Rat or the Red Leech – and unbelievably some people don't even want to acknowledge the legitimacy of the entire Canonical Sixty. However, over the course of a career that lasted decades, Holmes certainly carried out many thousands of investigations. (In "The Final Problem", Holmes states that *"In over a thousand cases I am not aware that I have ever used my powers upon the wrong side"* – and that estimate from the spring of 1891 must have been drastically low. Those who want – who *need* – to picture Holmes sitting around in his dressing gown for day after day and week after week in the Baker Street sitting room doing nothing, filthy and depressed and drugged and broken, and only able to function through Watson's caretaking while waiting desperately for a rare client to engage him for just a sliver of his vastly empty time are mistaken. That is not The Great Detective.

In fact, Holmes and Watson's lives were crowded with adventures. These overlapped and twisted and twined through one another, and the excitement never let up. Could anyone like Sherlock Holmes have lived a life of any other sort? Certainly not. And Watson, the recovered soldier and man of action, needed such a life just as much. Their days and years were full – and this would have been true in late December during the Christmas season just as much as any other time of year.

1881, that first year the two shared rooms in Baker Street, was when they became friends, and as Watson's health returned and he joined Holmes's investigations more and more, his assistance would prove to be initially useful, and then indispensable. By Christmas of that year, Holmes's practice would have been well established in the Baker Street rooms (following his move a year earlier from Montague Street), and

Watson would have had a good understanding of both Holmes's methods and personality. When Christmas rolled around, they would have already been working well together as a team for a number of months, so Christmas-themed investigations would pose no more difficulties than what had already occurred through the previous year.

For those who simply wish to read Holmes's adventures as they find them, each of the stories in this collection will be very satisfying. But for those who delve a bit deeper, there will be some who notice that there is a bit of overlap. Several cases, for instance, occur around Christmases in the same year, and those paying closer attention might see that they even occur on the same day. Don't let that worry you – it can all be rationalized. This is not a contradiction or an error, meaning that one story has to be chosen as the other as the "legitimate" account of what really happened on that day, and the other is a mere fiction. As someone who has kept a massive and detailed Chronology of both Canon and traditional pastiche for decades, I can assure you that it all fits together quite neatly.

Holmes and Watson's adventures often overlapped, with a piece of one case possibly consisting of just a short conversation lasting a few minutes before the day's events shifted to a piece of another case, and then back again. When Watson wrote the stories, he carefully selected the relevant threads for each separate case from this tangled skein of many concurrent cases, *The Great Holmes Tapestry* as I call it, to construct a self-contained and straight-ahead narrative of just one adventure. He didn't necessarily include what else was happening at the same time in another cases to avoid confusion. Thus, when written from beginning to end, a story will tell just that single investigation without pulling in threads from some other side-by-side case which would spiral the story beyond its scope. Think how twisted and intertwined the events are in your normal everyday life. How much more convoluted, then, were the lives of Our Heroes? As a deep-dive Holmes Chronologicist for forty-five-plus years, I assure you that all of the pieces of the puzzle fit. I'm thankful that Watson has taken the time to separate these events into digestible and self-contained pieces.

That's how the fifty-seven Christmas stories in this new collection can fit within the more limited years of Holmes and Watson's experiences and fixed number of Christmases. Some of these cases occur in the days leading up to Christmas, some on the day, and some afterwards. Some of the stories are inextricably plotted with the trappings of Christmas. Others are set during late December, and even though they could have occurred at any time of the year, they are certainly influenced by the season that surrounds them. In some tales there is festivity, and in others tragedy.

Watson might be having a bad year in this one, and Holmes in that one – the same as each of us have both high and low Yuletide seasons.

Sometimes more than one case takes place on a certain Christmas day, but they are cleverly written so that when reading them, it seems as if they stand alone. *"It arrived upon Christmas morning . . ."* said Holmes to Watson in "The Blue Carbuncle". He was describing a goose – a most remarkable bird – that held a bonny and bright little blue jewel. But he might have been describing any of the many stories that came his and Watson's way on and around the various December Twenty-fifths . . . .

And it isn't just the brilliant fifty-seven Christmas adventures in these three volumes that have to be taken into account – for there are quite a few other narratives beyond the extent of this set of books that also tell what Holmes and Watson were also doing at Christmas. Below is a list of *still more* Holmes and Watson Christmas Adventures. I highly recommend that the true student of The Entire Lives of Our Heroes seek them out as well. Read them and enjoy them – and study them too. Make notes as you go, and you'll start to understand just how the entire *Great Holmes Tapestry* of both Canon and pastiche fits together so brilliantly . . . .

Short Stories

The MX Book of New Sherlock Holmes Stories – Part V: Christmas Adventures (2016 – 30 stories)
- "The Case of the Ruby Necklace" – Bob Byrne
- "The Jet Brooch" – Denis O. Smith
- "The Adventure of the Missing Irregular" – Amy Thomas
- "The Adventure of the Knighted Watchmaker" – Derrick Belanger
- "The Stolen Relic" – David Marcum
- "A Christmas Goose" – C. H. Dye
- "The Adventure of the Long-Lost Enemy" – Marcia Wilson
- "The Case of the Christmas Cracker" – John Hall
- "The Queen's Writing Table" – Julie McKuras
- "The Blue Carbuncle" – Sir Arthur Conan Doyle *(Dramatised for Radio by Bert Coules)*
- "The Man Who Believed in Nothing" – Jim French
- "The Case of the Christmas Star" – S.F. Bennett
- "The Christmas Card Mystery" – Narrelle M. Harris
- "The Question of the Death Bed Conversion" – William Patrick Maynard

- "The Adventure of the Christmas Surprise" – Vincent W. Wright
- "A Bauble in Scandinavia" – James Lovegrove
- "The Adventure of Marcus Davery" – Arthur Hall
- "The Adventure of the Purple Poet" – Nicholas Utechin
- "The Adventure of the Empty Manger" – Tracy J. Revels
- "The Adventure of the Vanishing Man" – Mike Chinn
- "A Perpetrator in a Pear Tree" – Roger Riccard
- "The Case of the Christmas Trifle" – Wendy C. Fries
- "The Adventure of the Christmas Stocking" – Paul D. Gilbert
- "The Case of the Reformed Sinner" – S. Subramanian
- "The Adventure of the Golden Hunter" – Jan Edwards
- "The Curious Case of the Well-Connected Criminal" – Molly Carr
- "The Adventure of the Handsome Ogre" – Matthew J. Elliott
- "The Adventure of the Improbable Intruder" – Peter K. Andersson
- "The Adventure of the Deceased Doctor" – Hugh Ashton
- "The Mile End Mynah Bird" – Mark Mower

Holmes for the Holidays (1996)
- The Watch Night Bell – Anne Perry
- The Sleuth of Christmas Past – Barbara Paul
- A Scandal In Winter – Gillian Linscott
- The Adventure in Border Country – Gwen Moffat
- The Three Ghosts – Loren D. Estleman
- The Canine Ventriloquist – Jon L. Breen
- The Man Who Never Laughed – J.N. Williamson
- The Yuletide Affair – John Stoessel
- The Christmas Tree – William L. DeAndrea

- The Christmas Ghosts – Bill Crider
- The Thief of Twelfth Night – Carole Nelson Douglas
- The Italian Sherlock Holmes – Reginald Hill
- The Christmas Client – Edward D. Hoch
- The Angel's Trumpet – Carol Wheat

More Holmes for the Holidays (1999)
- The Christmas Gift – Anne Perry
- The Four Wise Men – Peter Lovesey
- Eleemosynary, My Dear Watson – Barbara Paul
- The Greatest Gift – Loren D. Estleman

- The Rajah's Emerald – Carolyn Wheat
- The Christmas Conspiracy – Edward D. Hoch
- The Music of Christmas – L.B. Greenwood
- The Christmas Bear – Bill Crider
- The Naturalist's Stock Pin – Jon L. Breen
- The Second Violet – Daniel Stashower
- The Human Mystery – Tanith Lee

Sherlock Holmes: Adventures for the Twelve Days of Christmas – Roger Riccard (2015)
- The Seventh Swan
- The Eighth Milkmaid
- The Ninth Ladyship at the Dance
- The Tenth Lord Leaping
- The Eleven Pipe Problem
- The Twelfth Drumming

Sherlock Holmes: Further Adventures for the Twelve Days of Christmas – Roger Riccard (2016)
- The Partridge in a Pearl Tree
- The Two Turtledoves
- The Three French Henchmen
- The Four Calling Birds
- The Five Gold Rings
- Six Geese at a Gander

Sherlock Holmes: Adventures Beyond the Canon – Volume I (2018)
- "A Gentleman's Disagreement" – Narrelle Harris *(A sequel to "The Blue Carbuncle")*

The Confidential Casebook of Sherlock Holmes (1997)
- "A Ballad of the White Plague" – P.C. Hodgel

Curious Incidents 2 (2002)
- "Green and Red trappings" – Valerie J. Patterson

The Sherlock Holmes Stories of Edward D. Hoch (2008)
- "The Christmas Client"
- "The Christmas Conspiracy"

The Misadventures of Sherlock Holmes (1944)
- "Christmas Eve" – S.C. Roberts

The Chronicles of Sherlock Holmes – Volume Two – Denis O. Smith (1998)
- "The Christmas Visitor" (Originally published in 1985)

Sherlock Holmes and the Watson Pastiche – Karl Showler (2005)
- "Fulworth Christmas"

Sherlock Holmes: A Case at Christmas – N.M. Scott (2016)
- "A Case at Christmas"

Sherlock Holmes: To a Country House Darkly – N.M. Scott (2017)
- "Christmas on Dartmoor"

The Secret Files of Sherlock Holmes – Frank Thomas (2002)
- "Sherlock's Christmas Gift"

The Secret Adventures of Sherlock Holmes – Paul E. Heusinger (2006)
- "The Christmas Truce"

Watson's Sampler: The Lost Casebook of Sherlock Holmes – William F. Watson (2007)
- "The Matter of the Christmas Gift"

Tales from the Stranger's Room (2011)
- "The Adventure of the Christmas Smoke" – David Rowbotham

A Christmas Carol at 221b – Thomas Mann (2018 – Novella)

A Julian Symons Duet – Julian Symons (2000)
- "The Vanishing Diamonds"

The Chemical Adventures of Sherlock Holmes – Thomas G. Waddell and Thomas R. Rybolt (2009)
- "A Christmas Story"

The Singular Exploits of Sherlock Holmes – Alan Stockwell (2012)
- "A Christmas Interlude"

Magazine Adventures

- "The Christmas Poisonings" – Barrie Roberts, *The Strand Magazine* (Issue No. 7)
- "The Affair of the Christmas Jewel" – Barrie Roberts, *The Strand Magazine* (Issue No. 9)
- "The Ghost of Christmas Past" – David Stuart Davies, *The Strand Magazine* (Issue No. 23)
- "The Christmas Bauble" – John Hall, *Sherlock Holmes: The Detective Magazine* (Issue No. 28)
- "Watson's Christmas Trick" – Bob Byrne, *Sherlock Holmes: The Detective Magazine* (Issue No. 46)

Novels

- *Sherlock Holmes and the Yule-Tide Mystery* – Val Andrews (1996)
- *Justice Hall* – Laurie R. King (2002)
- *Sherlock Holmes's Christmas* – David Upton (2005)
- *A Christmas to Forget at 221b* – Hugh A. Mulligan (2002)
- *Sherlock Holmes: Have Yourself a Chaotic Little Christmas* – Gwendolyn Frame (2012)
- *Sherlock Holmes & The Christmas Demon* – James Lovegrove (2019)
- *Young Sherlock Holmes* – Film Novelization by Alan Arnold (1985)

Film, Television, and Radio Adventures

- *Young Sherlock Holmes* – Film screenplay by Chris Columbus (1985)
- "The Adventure of the Christmas Pudding" *Sherlock Holmes* – Screenplay by George Fass and Gertrude Fass (April 4th, 1955 – Television Series)
- "The Night Before Christmas" *The New Adventures of Sherlock Holmes* – Script by Denis Green and Anthony Boucher (December 24th, 1945 Radio Broadcast)
- "The Adventure of the Christmas Bride" – Script by Edith Meiser (December 21st, 1947 Radio Broadcast)

- "The Man Who Believed in Nothing" – Script by Jim French (December 23rd, 2001 Radio Broadcast – Also published in *The MX Book of New Sherlock Holmes Stories – Part V: Christmas Adventures*)
- "The Christmas Ogre" – Script by M.J. Elliott (December 20th, 2015 Radio Broadcast. Text version published as "The Handsome Ogre" in *The MX Book of New Sherlock Holmes Stories – Part V: Christmas Adventures*)

And what has appeared in print doesn't even begin to match the level of excellent writing about Holmes and Christmas that one can find at fan-fiction sites on the web. In fact, for the last several years there has been a writing activity at *fanfiction.net* in which a group of authors compose and post something for the entire month of December, either a complete story, ranging from very short to full-length, to something serialized across the whole month. I've archived them in multiple binders and chronologicized them too, and it's amazing how it all fits together.

For more about the various Sherlockian Christmas stories, please see my essay "Compliments of the Season", an entry from my irregular blog, *A Seventeen Step Program*, at:

https://17stepprogram.blogspot.com/2018/12/the-compliments-of-season-sherlock.html

In the 2015 Foreword to the MX anthology volume *Part V: Christmas Adventures*, I wrote, ". . . *if there are already so many of them out there, why another book of Holmes Christmas adventures?*" As I explained then, for someone like me – and hopefully you too! – there can *never* be enough traditional tales about Holmes and Watson, two of the best and wisest men whom I have ever known. (And after reading and collecting literally thousands of stories about them for over forty-six years, I do feel like I know them.)

The other reason relates to the ever-increasing popularity of these MX Anthologies, and how it was time for *More Christmas Adventures*.

When I first had the idea for a new Holmes anthology in early 2015, the plan was to communicate with possibly a dozen or so "editors" of Watson's notes and see if they were interested in contributing. I had modest hopes that there might be enough new stories – maybe a dozen? – that could justify a new anthology. But the idea grew and grew until the first collection was three massive volumes of over sixty new adventures – really one big book spread out under three covers – and containing more new Holmes tales than had ever been assembled before in one place – at one time. (We've since surpassed that.)

A big part of what made the project so special was that the authors donated their royalties to the Stepping Stones School for special needs students, which was planning at that time to move into one of Sir Arthur Conan Doyle's former homes, Undershaw. By the time the first three books were released in October 2015, renovations were well under way at the school's future home, and it also quickly became apparent that the need for future volumes of *The MX Book of New Sherlock Holmes Stories* was very strong – many contributors reached out to me, wanting to contribute again, as did authors new to the party. The process for producing more anthology volumes was in place, a desire for more traditional Holmes stories is always there, and the school can always use more funding as provided by the sale of the books, so it was decided that what had initially been a one-time three-volume set would become an ongoing series.

Therefore, it was announced that there would be another anthology – but there was so much interest that it was quickly determined that *two* sets per year would be necessary, a general *Annual* in the spring, and another with themed stories in the fall. It turned out that the contributions for these spring and fall editions were so numerous that multiple volumes were required for each set. (Fortunately MX Publishing recognizes the value of these large collections, and doesn't try to limit their size as would some publishers – thus depriving the world of more great Holmes adventures. Rather, we add more and bigger books.)

With this set, we're now at 30 volumes, with more in preparation for Spring 2022, and I'm thinking ahead to a theme for Fall 2022. Right now we're nearing 700 stories from 200 contributors from around the world. We've raised over $85,000 for the school, with the very real possibility that it will go over $100,000 in early 2022.

At the time of publication, and as you will see mentioned in Acting Headteacher Emma West's foreword, it's been announced that the Stepping Stones School *at Undershaw* is changing its name *to Undershaw*, with the motto *"Eliminating the Impossible"*. With this action, the school further reaffirms its connection with the Sherlockian world, and I'm personally thrilled that these books can continue to assist in the great and important work that they do – while also bringing more and more traditional Canonical adventures about the True Mr. Sherlock Holmes to light, and into the hands of a world that is starving for them.

* * * * *

"Of course, I could only stammer out my thanks."
– The unhappy John Hector McFarlane, "The Norwood Builder"

As always when one of these sets is finished, I want to first thank with all my heart my incredible, patient, brilliant, kind, and beautiful wife of over thirty-three years, Rebecca, and our amazing, funny, brilliant, creative, and wonderful son, and my friend, Dan. I love you both, and you are everything to me!

During the editing of these particular volumes, I've been in the second half of my first year at my dream job – which has required a massive amount of figuring out new things in a hurry. (I've been dreaming about it every night, and – according to my wife – talking in my sleep for the first time in thirty-three years.) When the agency where I was a federal investigator closed in the 1990's, and I was figuring out what I wanted to do with my life, we lived near a beautiful park, and as I would walk there nearly every day with my son, seeing the trails and springs and streams and culverts big enough that kids were exploring them, and I realized that I was interested in infrastructure – and particularly working for that particular city. That led to my return to school to be a civil engineer. After a number of years working at various engineering companies, and getting my license along the way, and still wanting to work at the city, I was finally able to. Now I'm in an office just a few hundred feet from that same park. That has kept me extremely busy for the last few months, which kept me from replying to emails as fast as I would have wished, not to mention reading and editing stories as quickly as I did just a year ago, so I'm very grateful to everyone who patiently waited to hear back from me about their stories.

I can never express enough gratitude for all of the contributors who have donated their time and royalties to this ongoing project. I'm constantly amazed at the incredible stories that you send, and I'm so glad to have gotten to know so many of you through this process. It's an undeniable fact that Sherlock Holmes authors are the *best* people!

As mentioned, the contributors of these stories have donated their royalties for this project to support Undershaw, a school for special needs children located at one of Sir Arthur Conan Doyle's former homes. As of this writing, and as mentioned above, these MX anthologies have raised over $85,000 for the school, with no end in sight, and of even more importance, they have helped raise awareness about the school all over the world – which I'm told by the school is actually more important than the funds. These books are making a real difference to the school, and the participation of both contributors and purchasers is most appreciated.

Next is that group that exchanges emails with me when we have the time – and time is a valuable commodity for all of us these days! As mentioned, I don't get to write back and forth with these fine people as often as I'd like, but I really enjoy catching up when we do get the chance: Derrick Belanger, Brian Belanger, Mark Mower, Denis Smith, Tom Turley, Dan Victor, and Marcia Wilson.

There is a group of special people who have stepped up and supported this and a number of other projects over and over again with a lot of contributions. They are the best and I can't express how valued they are: Hugh Ashton, Derrick Belanger, Deanna Baran, Craig Stephen Copland, Matthew Elliott, Tim Gambrell, Jayantika Ganguly, Paul Gilbert, Dick Gillman, Arthur Hall, Steve Herczeg, Paul Hiscock, Craig Janacek, Mark Mower, Will Murray, Tracy Revels, Roger Riccard, Geri Schear, Brenda Seabrooke, Shane Simmons, Robert Stapleton, Kevin Thornton, I.A. Watson, and Marcy Wilson.

Next, I wish to send several huge *Thank You's* to the following:

- *Nancy Holder* – I first began corresponding with Nancy in 2019, and I've been pushing for her to write a pastiche for this collection ever since. (*Nancy: You're still invited!*) I was able to meet her in person at the Sherlock Holmes Birthday Celebration in New York City in January 2020, and found that she's just as nice as she'd been by way of email.

    In mid-2021, as this book was being prepared, she stepped up and agreed to write a wonderful foreword rather late in the game, showing what a truly consummate professional she is. Even though I haven't convinced her to write a Holmes adventure yet, I'm thrilled that she's part of these books. Huge thanks!

- *Steve Emecz* – Some people have a picture in their minds of a publishing company with several floors on some skyscraper, hundreds of employees running around like ants, with vast departments devoted to management, marketing, editing, production, shipping, etc. That is not always the case. Those old giant dinosaur publishers are still around, and they might squeeze out a Sherlockian title or two every year, but they don't represent the modern way of doing things. MX has become the premiere Sherlockian publisher by following a new paradigm. And they manage to get all of this done with a truly skeleton staff.

    Steve Emecz works a way-more-than-full-time job related to his career in e-finance. MX Publishing isn't his full-time job –

it's a labor of love. He, along with his wife Sharon Emecz and cousin, Timi Emecz, *are* MX Publishing. In addition to their very busy real every-day lives, these three sole employees take care of the management, marketing, editing, production, and shipping, and they absolutely cannot receive enough credit for what they accomplish.

From my first association with MX in 2013, I've seen that MX (under Steve's leadership) was *the* fast-rising superstar of the Sherlockian publishing world. Connecting with MX and Steve Emecz was personally an amazing life-changing event for me, as it has been for countless other Sherlockian authors. It has led me to write many more stories, and then to edit books, along with unexpected Holmes Pilgrimages to England – none of which might have happened otherwise. By way of my first email with Steve – *Only eight years ago!* – I've had the chance to make some incredible Sherlockian friends and play in the Holmesian Sandbox in ways that I would have never dreamed possible.

Through it all, Steve has been one of the most positive and supportive people that I've ever known.

Many who just buy books and have a vague idea of how the publishing industry works now might not realize that MX, a non-profit which supports several important charities, consists of simply these three people. Between them, they take care of running the entire business – all in their precious spare time, fitting it in and around their real lives.

With incredible hard work, they have made MX into a world-wide Sherlockian publishing phenomenon, providing opportunities for authors who would never have had them otherwise. There are some like me who return more than once to Watson's Tin Dispatch Box, and there are others who only find one or two stories there – but they also get the chance to publish their books, and then they can point with pride at this accomplishment, and how they too have added to The Great Holmes Tapestry.

From the beginning, Steve has let me explore various Sherlockian projects and open up my own personal possibilities in ways that otherwise would have never happened. Thank you, Steve, for every opportunity!

- *Brian Belanger* – Over the last few years, my amazement at Brian Belanger's ever-increasing talent has only grown. I initially became acquainted with him when he took over the duties of creating the covers for MX Books following the untimely death of their previous graphic artist. I found Brian to be a great collaborator, very easy-going and stress-free in his approach and willingness to work with authors, and wonderfully creative too.

Brian and his brother, Derrick Belanger, are two great friends, and five years ago they founded *Belanger Books*, which along with MX Publishing, has absolutely locked up the Sherlockian publishing field with a vast amount of amazing material. The dinosaurs must be trembling to see every new Sherlockian project, one after another after another. Luckily MX and Belanger Books work closely with one another, and I'm thrilled to be associated with both of them. Many thanks to Brian for all he does for both publishers, and for all he's done for me personally.

- *Roger Johnson* – I'm more grateful than I can say that I know Roger. I was aware of him for years before I timidly sent him a copy of my first book for review, and then on my first Holmes Pilgrimage to England and Scotland in 2013, I was able to meet both him and his wonderful wife, Jean Upton, in person. When I returned on Holmes Pilgrimage No. 2 in 2015, I was so fortunate that they graciously allowed me to stay with them for several days in their home, where we had many wonderful discussions, while occasionally venturing forth so that they could show me parts of England that I wouldn't have seen otherwise. It was an experience I wouldn't trade for anything.

  Roger's Sherlockian knowledge is exceptional, as is the work that he does to further the cause of The Master. But even more than that, both Roger and his wonderful wife, Jean, are simply the finest and best of people, and I'm very lucky to know both of them – even though I don't get to see them nearly as often as I'd like, and especially in these crazy days! In so many ways, Roger, I can't thank you enough, and I can't imagine these books without you.

And finally, last but certainly *not* least, thanks to **Sir Arthur Conan Doyle**: Author, doctor, adventurer, and the Founder of the Sherlockian Feast. Honored, and present in spirit.

As I always note when putting together an anthology of Holmes stories, the effort has been a labor of love. These adventures are just more tiny threads woven into the ongoing Great Holmes Tapestry, continuing to grow and grow, for there can *never* be enough stories about the man whom Watson described as *"the best and wisest . . . whom I have ever known."*

David Marcum
September 8th, 2021
A most important day,
for all kinds of reasons

Questions, comments, or story submissions
may be addressed to David Marcum at

thepapersofsherlockholmes@gmail.com

Foreword
by Nancy Holder

Sherlock Holmes and Christmas: Two fixed points in a changing world. The Great Detective, cracking the case with a dramatic flourish (and, often, a somewhat lengthy explanation). His faithful Boswell, marveling at the genius of Our Mutual Friend. Roasting chestnuts, glittering Christmas trees, carolers in hoop skirts and bonnets. A Victorian Christmas in all its holly-and-ivy splendor.

We who know and love The Canon – the fifty-six original stories and four novels written by John H. Watson (with an assist from Sir Arthur Conan Doyle) – wax nostalgic for the traditions of a time and place we will never see. At least I do, and I have spent the majority of my Christmases in Southern California, where guys in flip-flops spray artificial snow onto the windows of taco shops and sushi restaurants, and we watch *A Christmas Carol* with the air conditioning on – as do, I assume, my many friends in Australia, Hawaii, Florida, and so many other pleasant climes. Simply going by the cards I receive in December, Christmas as celebrated in late nineteenth century Britain and Ireland is the Ur of winter celebrations, and we perpetuate its hold on us with wholehearted devotion.

As a dedicated Sherlockian, I usually crack open "The Adventure of the Blue Carbuncle" to usher in Holmes at Christmas. This is the only story in The Canon that takes place at (or very near) Christmas. A review of the beloved tale is pretty much *de rigueur* at any December Sherlock Holmes cookie swap and/or Christmas jollification. How many of us have debated the various fine points of the story – (Why leave John Horner in the clink overnight? Does Peterson reap the reward for the gem?) – while sipping tea, brandy, or mulled wine and munching gingerbread? Nearly all of us – no matter if we celebrate Hanukkah, Diwali, Kwanzaa, or as is the case at my house, more than one winter holiday. For the duration of this one story, we happily transport ourselves to a Victorian Christmas.

But while "Blue Carbuncle" may be the only Christmas story in the Canon, it is, of course, not the only Christmas story featuring Holmes and Watson. MX Publishing, who published a lovely, hefty Christmas assortment in 2016, have done it again – a Santa sack brimming with Yuletide pastiches sure to please the traditionalists among us. Hewing close to the Canon, with no supernatural or fantastical elements, these are the kinds of stories sure to warm the heart (even if it's 98-degrees

Fahrenheit outside) and take us back to where we want to be for our winter holidays – with Holmes and Watson, wrapped in gas lamp frost, where it's always (or close to) 1895. Dozens of talented, clever, careful authors have penned wonderful stories tailored to this season of joy, wonder . . . and Sherlock. Whether it's Christmas in July where you are, or snowy with a chance of sugarplums, I urge you to unwrap and savor. What lovely gifts await you.

Nancy Holder, BSI
Near Seattle
July, 2021

"It is the Season of Forgiveness"
by Roger Johnson

In our minds, what do we associate with the stories of Sherlock Holmes? Crime, naturally, and mystery. Observation and deduction, leading to solutions, certainly. Gaslight and fog, yes. The mighty metropolis of London too.

But Christmas? There is, as we all surely know, only one Canonical investigation that takes place at Christmas time – it's "The Adventure of the Blue Carbuncle", and Dr. Watson's narrative famously begins: "*I had called upon my friend Sherlock Holmes upon the second morning after Christmas, with the intention of wishing him the Compliments of the Season.*" Not Christmas Eve, then. Not Christmas Day itself, nor the one immediately following – Boxing Day – but *two days* after Christmas. One might be tempted the dismiss its credentials (I mean *two days*?) but of course the whole account is imbued with the spirit of the season, and that spirit casts its benign shadow over our mental image of the Detective and the Doctor.

Last year Belanger Books published an appealing little book called *Sherlock Holmes: A Three-Pipe Christmas*, edited by Dan Andriacco. At its heart are "The Adventure of the Blue Carbuncle" by Arthur Conan Doyle, "The Adventure of the Unique *Hamlet* " by Vincent Starrett, first published in 1920, and "The Adventure of the Unique Dickensians", an exploit of Holmes's disciple Solar Pons, written by August Derleth and first published in 1968. The stories are accompanied by essays, whose authors include the editor of this volume and the author of this foreword. How entertaining the essays are, you must judge for yourselves, but the stories are excellent and the book as a whole is delightful.

Starrett was one of the immortals of Holmesian scholarship. So was S.C. Roberts, whose charming one-act play "Christmas Eve" you'll find in his classic *Holmes and Watson: A Miscellany*, first published in 1953 and now available in a new edition from the British Library.

The combination of Christmas and Holmes continues to appeal, to authors and readers alike. A notable recent novel, for instance, is *Sherlock Holmes and the Christmas Demon* by James Lovegrove. And the association is strong on stage and screen as well. It's a rare Christmas in Britain when theatregoers don't have the choice of a new or old Holmesian comedy, or more rarely a drama, among the seasonal fare. In recent years we have enjoyed *Sherlock Holmes and the Warlock of Whitechapel*,

Tweedy and the Missing Company of Sherlock Holmes, Sherlock Holmes and the Hooded Lance, Potted Sherlock, Mrs. Hudson's Christmas Corker, Sherlock Holmes and the Case of the Christmas Carol, The Adventures of the Improvised Sherlock Holmes, and any number of riffs on *The Hound of the Baskervilles*.

Mention of that particular classic reminds me that one of the better aspects of the 2002 TV film *The Hound of the Baskervilles* was the decision to set the story around Christmas time, and make the legendary Hound a character in a seasonal Mummers' play. And the last of the classic Granada Television series with Jeremy Brett as Holmes, "The Cardboard Box" broadcast in 1994, also relocated its narrative to Christmas to good effect.

Young Sherlock Holmes and the Pyramid of Fear (1985) begins with a decidedly weird Christmas episode and ends with a sad but hopeful one. More than thirty years earlier, an entertaining episode of Sheldon Reynolds's television series *Sherlock Holmes* was "The Adventure of the Christmas Pudding". Like *Young Sherlock Holmes*, it can be enjoyed today. And we mustn't forget the outstanding TV dramatisations of "The Blue Carbuncle", in 1968 with Peter Cushing and Nigel Stock as Holmes and Watson, and in 1984 with Jeremy Brett and David Burke. Two different interpretations – compare Madge Ryan's performance as the Countess of Morcar with Rosalind Knight's, for instance – but both excellent.

Sherlock Holmes and Christmas – inseparable? The stories in this book suggest that they are. And, as always, editor and authors won't get a penny from it, because all proceeds will go towards the maintenance of Undershaw, Arthur Conan Doyle's former home in Surrey, which now houses the Stepping Stones School for youngsters with special educational needs.

Roger Johnson, BSI, ASH
Editor: *The Sherlock Holmes Journal*
August 2021

An Ongoing Legacy for Sherlock Holmes
by Steve Emecz

Undershaw
Circa 1900

The MX Book of New Sherlock Holmes Stories has now raised over $85,000 for Undershaw, a school for children with learning disabilities, and is by far the largest Sherlock Holmes collection in the world.

Undershaw is the former home of Sir Arthur Conan Doyle, where he wrote many of the Sherlock Holmes stories. The fundraising has supported many projects continuing the legacy of Conan Doyle and Sherlock Holmes in the amazing building, including The Doyle Room, the school's Zoom broadcasting capability (including Sherlock themed events), The Literacy Program, and more.

In addition to Undershaw, our main program that we support is the Happy Life Children's Home in Kenya. My wife Sharon and I have spent seven Christmas's with the children in Nairobi.

It's a wonderful project that has saved the lives of over 600 babies. You can read all about the project in the second edition of the book *The Happy Life Story*.

In 2021, we are working on *#bookstobooks* which sees us donating 10% of the revenues from *mxpublishing.com* to fund schoolbooks and library books at Happy Life.

Our support for our projects is possible through the publishing of Sherlock Holmes books, which we have now been doing for over a decade.

You can find out more information about the Undershaw at:

https://undershaw.education/

and Happy Life at:

www.happylifechildrenshomes.com

You can find out more about MX Publishing and reach out to us through our website at:

www.mxpublishing.com

Steve Emecz
September 2021
Twitter: *@mxpublishing*

The Doyle Room at Stepping Stones, Undershaw
*Partially funded through royalties from
The MX Book of New Sherlock Holmes Stories*

Undershaw:
Eliminating the Impossible
by Emma West

Undershaw
September 9, 2016
Grand Opening of the Stepping Stones School
(Photograph courtesy of Roger Johnson)

I am delighted to share the news that Stepping Stones School has a new name. From 1st September, 2021, we will bear the name *Undershaw*, inspired by the building that houses our school. Stepping Stones has such a strong legacy as a school full of life, dynamism, and hope for a more inclusive future for our children. Undershaw is that school. Our staff, students, and families are proud of our community and excited for what the next stage holds.

> We stand for aspirational education free of discrimination.
> We stand for specialists supporting each young person their way, at their pace.
> We stand for our students developing the life and work skills necessary to navigate their adulthood and secure fulfilling and lasting careers.

We stand for breaking down barriers and creating a cultural shift in how workplaces of the future view diversity and inclusion so that they recognise the true talents and abilities of our learners.

These attributes run at the heart of everything we do, and I am thrilled that we are about to embark upon a new chapter in our story.

Sir Arthur Conan Doyle built Undershaw as a place of convalescence for his wife. It had an honourable purpose then, just as it has now. Together we have reignited the passion of Undershaw, firstly in 2016 by renovating the building as a state-of-the-art specialist centre for our students, and lately as an inspirational name for our school, as we take our philosophy forward and find our place in a wider societal conversation. Undershaw encapsulates our essence as we take the very best from the past and use it as the landscape for framing our future.

You have partnered with us for many years. Thank you for sharing our passion and ethos. Thank you for your benevolence. Above all, thank you for your good company. We could not do it without you. We have loved having you with us on the journey and hope you are excited to join in on our next chapter as we take Undershaw into 2022 and long into the future.

Emma West
Acting Headteacher
September 2021

"Undershaw" Hindhead, Conan Doyle's House.

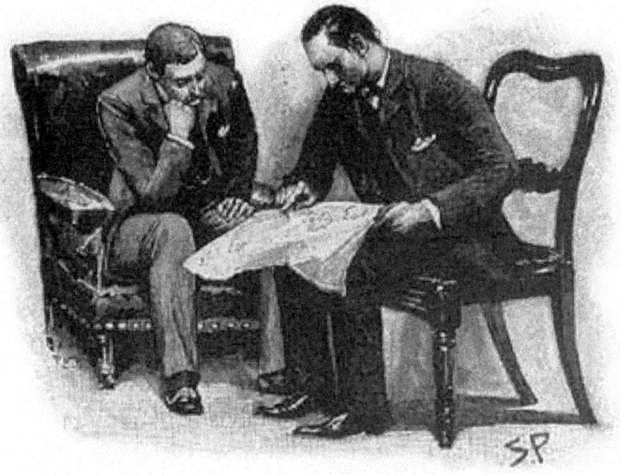
S.P

Sherlock Holmes (1854-1957) was born in Yorkshire, England, on 6 January, 1854. In the mid-1870's, he moved to 24 Montague Street, London, where he established himself as the world's first Consulting Detective. After meeting Dr. John H. Watson in early 1881, he and Watson moved to rooms at 221b Baker Street, where his reputation as the world's greatest detective grew for several decades. He was presumed to have died battling noted criminal Professor James Moriarty on 4 May, 1891, but he returned to London on 5 April, 1894, resuming his consulting practice in Baker Street. Retiring to the Sussex coast near Beachy Head in October 1903, he continued to be associated in various private and government investigations while giving the impression of being a reclusive apiarist. He was very involved in the events encompassing World War I, and to a lesser degree those of World War II. He passed away peacefully upon the cliffs above his Sussex home on his 103rd birthday, 6 January, 1957.

Dr. John Hamish Watson (1852-1929) was born in Stranraer, Scotland on 7 August, 1852. In 1878, he took his Doctor of Medicine Degree from the University of London, and later joined the army as a surgeon. Wounded at the Battle of Maiwand in Afghanistan (27 July, 1880), he returned to London late that same year. On New Year's Day, 1881, he was introduced to Sherlock Holmes in the chemical laboratory at Barts. Agreeing to share rooms with Holmes in Baker Street, Watson became invaluable to Holmes's consulting detective practice. Watson was married and widowed three times, and from the late 1880's onward, in addition to his participation in Holmes's investigations and his medical practice, he chronicled Holmes's adventures, with the assistance of his literary agent, Sir Arthur Conan Doyle, in a series of popular narratives, most of which were first published in *The Strand* magazine. Watson's later years were spent preparing a vast number of his notes of Holmes's cases for future publication. Following a final important investigation with Holmes, Watson contracted pneumonia and passed away on 24 July, 1929.

Photos of Sherlock Holmes and Dr. John H. Watson courtesy of Roger Johnson

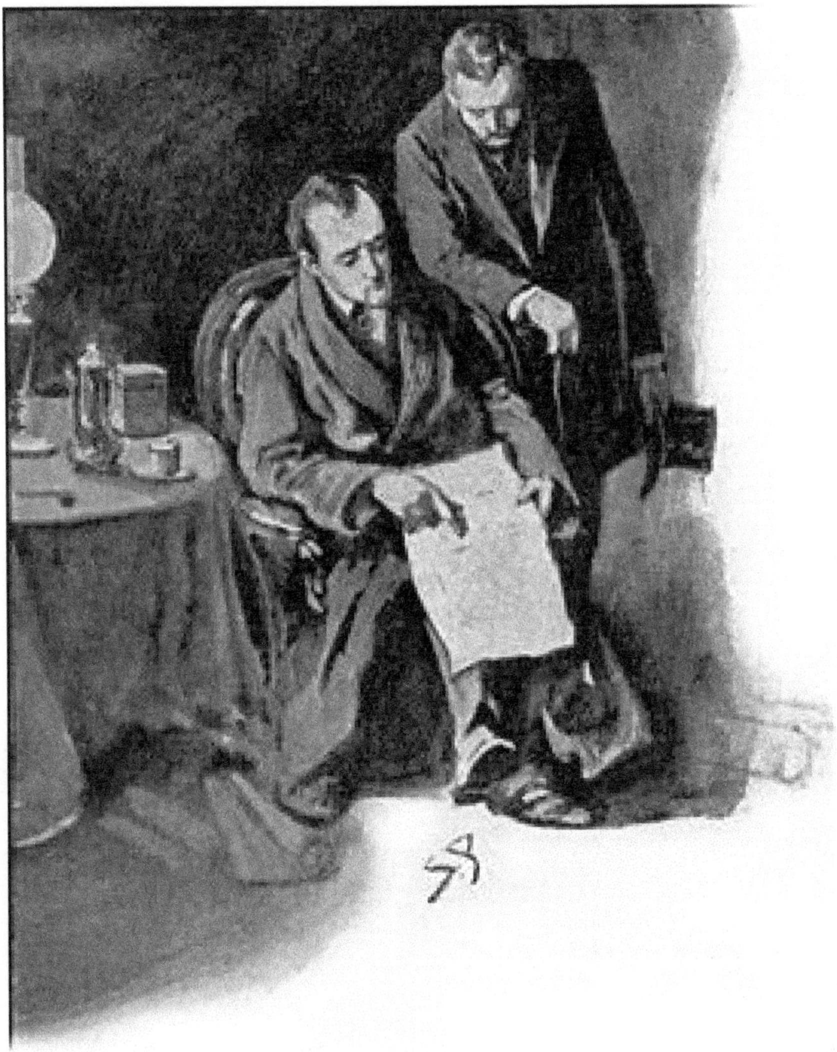

The MX Book of New Sherlock Holmes Stories

Part XXIX
More Christmas Adventures
(1889-1896)

Baker Street in Snow (1890)
by Christopher James

Nothing is so still as the street in snow.
The sills are heavy with it, the streets
are deep in it. The ghosts rest themselves
against the walls listening to distant carols
and whispered prayers trapped in the stone.
A drift by the archway is like a wedding veil
snagged on a railing, left trailing all winter.
Now the snow dusts the walls and shrouds
the rooves. Not even the blackbirds trust
their feet on the cobbles. At the window,
Holmes peers out and wonders whether
anyone will dare to make their petition today.
Each step is a slab of glass they must somehow
cross if they are to reach Holmes in snow.

The Sword in the Spruce
by Ian Ableson

When I reflect on the numerous cases on which I have joined my friend Sherlock Holmes, I am constantly astounded by their variety. Holmes and I are no stranger to London's seedy underbelly, and we have undoubtedly dealt with many of the most despicable folk to be found therein. But Holmes is, at heart, a problem-solver, and not all problems need be quite so grim and grueling to solve. At time of this writing, Christmas is fast approaching, and so in the interest of holiday cheer, I have it in mind to put to paper one of the more light-hearted tales that I rediscovered in my notes, which happened to take place at this same time of year.

The client that arrived on Holmes's doorstep this particular wintery evening was of the humbler variety, though certainly not the humblest, as his trade brought with it a good measure of respectability. It was a few days before Christmas Eve, and I had stopped by to visit my old flatmate for a bit of holiday cheer before returning home to Mary. As we sat reminiscing and sharing a bottle of burgundy, there came a knock at the door.

The man who entered was extremely tall and lanky, almost scarecrow-like in appearance, with a hawklike nose and protruding ears. He appeared to be in his early thirties, cleanly shaven and warmly dressed against the winter's chill. I offered him a glass of brandy as an extra layer of warmth, but he politely declined.

"I apologize for interrupting, 'specially so late in the evening," said the man, "but are you Sherlock Holmes?"

"I am."

The man stepped forward and grasped Holmes's hand tightly between both of his. "Mr. Holmes, a pleasure to meet you. My name is Robin Alder, and I am in desperate need of help. Something has happened in my home, and I'm not sure I want to approach the police just yet – not until I'm sure exactly what happened. A friend of mine has mentioned your name before, and I thought perhaps you'd be willing to give me some advice."

"Hmm," said Holmes noncommittally, casting a critical eye over our visitor. "And might this friend be a Mr. Leonard Phillips?"

The man's mouth hung agape in shock, and he seemed momentarily distracted from his predicament. "Why, yes! How on earth could you know that?"

Holmes smiled and sipped at his wine. "In my experience, lamplighters such as yourself tend to be a rather tight-knit group, prone to the sort of fierce camaraderie that one normally expects from soldiers. I helped Mr. Phillips with a rather peculiar problem just last month, and so I thought it logical that you might be a colleague of his."

"But I never told you my trade, Mr. Holmes!"

Holmes took another lazy sip of his burgundy. "Your complexion and the slight hints of weathering on your face speak of a man who works outdoors, in all manner of weather conditions. And yet you are well-dressed, and seem to have put some effort to make yourself look respectable. Given the status of lamplighters as a sort of unofficial night watchmen, it seems an appropriate conclusion when faced with an outdoorsman who has striven to ensure that he looks trustworthy to the rest of the community. Additionally, the calluses on your fingers and the inside of your thumb speak of a great deal of time spent climbing up and down ladders. And – I do hope you'll forgive me for saying so – your entrance brought with it the slightest whiff of gas."

"Astonishing," Alder murmured. "You read marks on my hands like a holy man reads the scripture."

Holmes smiled and drained his wine, placing his empty glass on the table. "In truth, even without the evidence that I have listed, I would know you nevertheless, Mr. Alder. My trade, like yours, requires a significant amount of activity at dawn and dusk, and I have observed you lighting and extinguishing the lamps along Piccadilly on several different occasions. So what, pray tell, might a lamplighter need of a detective on this fine evening?"

"It's the sword!" he blurted out. The words exploded from the man's mouth as though propelled by a force that he did not himself control. He was nearly shaking as he said it, and he ran his fingers through his hair in his agitation. "I don't know where it came from! It isn't mine, it isn't my wife's, and my son is but a lad of four years old. It's far too dear for me to own, and if I go to the police they'll think me a common thief. I'll not have such slander against my family, nor my fellow lamplighters!"

Holmes's eyebrow shot up. Without another word, he rose, retrieved a glass, and poured the man a few fingers of brandy. Despite his previous hesitation, in his agitated state the man readily accepted the refreshment. He took a healthy swig from the glass, and he lost some of his fidgetiness.

Having thus placated his client, Holmes sat back in his chair and steepled his fingers. "Start from the beginning, Mr. Alder: Of what sword do you speak?"

Alder laughed morosely. "If only I knew, Mr. Holmes! Maybe then I wouldn't need your help quite so desperately." Alder swilled the brandy in his glass half-heartedly, drinking from it occasionally as he spoke. "Don't know much about swords, myself, or anything militaristic for that matter. I come from a farming family, and since moving to the city and picking up the lamplighter's profession, I haven't had any cause to educate myself on armaments. Nevertheless, I find myself suddenly and unintentionally in possession of a sword that, to my untrained eye, appears to be of fairly decent quality."

Holmes's eye twinkled. "Many would consider such sudden possession to be a windfall in their favor and thank their lucky stars for the opportunity. And yet you seem to view the matter quite differently."

"Well, I wager you'd be distraught too, if the sword in question appeared unannounced in your Christmas tree! But even worse, I haven't the slightest idea what its sudden appearance might mean! Is it a threat? Did someone break into my house and place a sword in the tree as some sort of bizarre means of intimidation? I can't think of anyone I've angered enough to generate that sort of response! But if not a threat, then why? Who breaks into a man's house, steals nothing, places a sword in their Christmas tree, and leaves?"

"*In* the tree? Well, 'tis the season, I suppose," Holmes murmured. "I think you'd best start from the beginning."

"That I will, but I'm afraid there's little enough to tell," said Alder. "I live an uneventful life, all things told – hence my utter confusion at this turn of events. There's only three in my household: Myself, my wife, and my son, who just turned four last month. We live in a simple but comfortable home near my lamp route along Piccadilly."

"Now, I'm not an ostentatious man, Mr. Holmes, but I do like Christmas, and as such I make a considered effort each year to try and get a respectable Christmas tree. Truth be told, this quirk of mine causes my wife, Lucy, some degree of consternation, as every year I try my best to outdo my previous year's efforts. And so every year she is forced to sacrifice a little more of her living room to the coniferous beast that I bring home, but she always puts up with it with good spirits. This year I thought I'd reached a pinnacle – an elegant, beautiful Norway spruce, with a trunk straight as an arrow, wonderfully healthy green needles, and a mess of boughs that are practically a forest unto themselves. It's important you understand the boughs, for never before have I brought home a tree with limbs so densely packed along the trunk. I thought it to be a point in this particular tree's favor, as densely packed allows more support for ornamentation.

"Just an hour ago Little Joseph – that's my son – was laughing and shaking the limbs, an unfortunate habit that my wife and I sometimes have little choice but to temporarily allow as we complete chores around the house, when he grew suddenly silent. I don't know if you have any children yourself, Mr. Holmes, but when a child is at that age, the sound of silence can be very concerning indeed. After a few minutes, I pulled myself away from my task to go check on the lad, and to my shock I found him standing next to the tree, beaming and clutching in both hands a sword nearly as tall as he was.

"'Look, Papa!' he cried to me. 'I found an early Christmas present! It's a gift from the tree!'

"I think I now know how it feels to have your blood freeze, gentlemen. Once I'd gotten over my shock, I rushed to him and gently took the sword from his unsteady grip. I gave him some token explanation that the tree must have been mistaken, and that it wasn't yet the time for gifts, and gently prodded him from the room. I called Lucy, but she was equally shocked, and naturally she had no more explanation than I. It's a beautiful weapon, gents, and it's clearly been well taken care of. After some deliberation, we agreed that the best course of action would be to come to you at once."

"Well!" said Holmes. "What a curious problem to have." Despite his client's distress, Holmes himself seemed to be in good spirits. I, too, found myself to be more amused than disquieted, in a way that rarely happens at the start of a case. Nothing was stolen, no one had been injured, and despite Alder's anxiety to ensure his good name, it seemed unlikely that there was any true risk to him or his family. Should police involvement be required, I was confident that our testimony would be more than sufficient to protect his and his family's reputation. "When did you bring the tree home?"

"I put it up three days ago."

"Have you had any visitors to your home since that time?"

"Only a few. Two friends of mine – both fellow lamplighters, one of which was Mr. Phillips – came for a few rounds of cards yesterday. Lucy's sister stopped in as well, but she was only by for a short time to deliver a handful of baked goods and a present for her nephew. Apart from that, it's only been me, Lucy, and Joseph."

"I know something of Phillips, but what of the other man? I don't suppose he happens to have a military background?"

"No sir, not that he's mentioned, and it doesn't seem likely. Old Will Bisbee was born with a bum leg – he's limped his whole life."

"Any signs of a break-in? Anything else in the house out of place?"

"Ah, Mr. Holmes, it'd be tricky to say. No windows broken, and we certainly haven't noticed anything stolen, but little Joseph has started to explore the world with his hands more and more this past year. We give him little toys and bits and bobs to play with, but I've still found my boots on the wrong side of the room more times than I can count."

Holmes stood from his armchair. "Ah, yes, of course. Such exploration, while essential for a child's cognitive development, is unfortunately rather disruptive in a potentially criminal setting. Well, Watson, it seems to me that this case is going to require our presence at the location of the crime," said Holmes lightly. "If Mary won't miss you for a little more time, I would be delighted if you could join me."

"Of course," said I. "Allow me to grab the coats."

Relief flooded across Alder's face. "Gents, I can't tell you how grateful I am! The honor of the lamplighters of London is at stake!"

By this time in our partnership, I had developed a general sense of Holmes's methods, even if putting them to practice was typically beyond my own deductive capabilities. I predicted that Holmes's first inclination would be to search around the doors and windows of the building before any more time had passed, and in this I was proven correct. Holmes requested that Alder and I wait outside the door while he searched. He scowled as he looked at the ground, and I could immediately see why – the tromping of feet had destroyed any chance of footprints, and there was no indication how many people may have approached the house in the past few days. He didn't say anything when he returned from checking the windowsills, but from his expression I surmised that this search had proven equally fruitless.

We entered Alder's home to find Lucy, his wife, standing in the entryway with a mystified expression on her face, clutching an elegant sword in her hands. She was of a similar stature as her husband – tall and arrow-straight, with bright blonde hair. When she spoke, her words were tinged with a mild Welsh accent.

"This is Mr. Holmes?" she asked Alder.

"It is," he said.

"Well, sir, I hope you can help us with this strange little problem. I'm marginally less concerned than my dear husband for our reputation, but I can tell you that it will irritate me to no end if we are unable to discover its origin. To have such an item appear in our domicile is really quite vexing."

"Well, I will offer what help I can," said Holmes. "Although to begin, I will cede the first deduction in this case – that is, the state of the sword itself – to one who may well be more knowledgeable in the matter than I. Dr. Watson, would you kindly take a look at it? Your own military background could well make some detail obvious to you that would be less intuitive for me."

"Certainly," said I, gently taking the sword from Lucy Alder.

In truth, I was skeptical of my ability to offer any meaningful contribution based on the sword alone. As a medical man, arms and armaments hadn't been my specialty, and by the year of this case my time in the military had come to an end many years prior. It was therefore with considerable surprise that I realized that the anatomy and ornamentation of the sword did, in fact, resonate with an old memory.

"Why, I knew a man with a sword very similar to this one!" I exclaimed. "Look at the half-basket hilt and the double-edged blade. That sort of blade is called the claymore style. If memory serves, this is a Highland Field Officer's sword. The man I knew who had a weapon similar to this one was no longer a Highland Field Officer himself, but he'd taken the sword with him into Afghanistan nonetheless. He said it felt more comfortable than the new blade he'd been issued."

"Wonderful, Watson!" said Holmes, beaming. "You've far exceeded my expectations, notwithstanding my respect for your own branches of experience. From your knowledge I think we can draw a handful of conclusions. The owner of this sword is – or was – a military man, likely an officer, and almost certainly a Scotsman. Might I see it?"

I handed it over to him, and Holmes was silent as he carefully scrutinized the weapon. He took it lightly in his hand, moving it side to side a few times to test the balance. He peered closely at the hilt and pommel, twisting the sword this way and that so as to better view it from each angle. Finally he looked at the blade, gingerly running a finger up each side. His examination thus concluded, he turned to Alder.

"Might I now see the tree?"

Alder and Lucy led us into their living room. It was modestly filled with simple but sturdy furniture. Evidence of the consternation caused by the sword's appearance was clear. A plate and a dishrag sat discarded on the dining table, as though whomever had been working on the task had immediately abandoned it. A handful of children's toys were scattered around the room. These appeared to consist primarily of small balls and toy soldiers. Dominating the room – to the point that several pieces of furniture, despite having been pushed to the side to make way for the seasonal intruder, were caressed by the boughs – was a particularly massive Christmas tree.

The Norway Spruce is a handsome conifer, possessing both a stately bearing and robust appearance. Alder had stated previously that he had chosen this particular tree specifically for the density of its branches, and in this I had to commend him for his choice. The boughs overlapped and fell across each other like a hen's feathers. The overall effect created a thick umbrella of foliage through which it was impossible to see behind in any meaningful way.

I barely managed to suppress a muffled sound of astonishment at the tree's size. While it may not have felt out of place in a large country manor, or perhaps a hunting lodge, in a humble London tradesman's dwelling it dwarfed its surroundings to a degree that bordered on theatrical satire. Holmes, of course, maintained a carefully guarded expression. He walked slowly around the perimeter of the tree, quick eyes darting from bough to bough as he went. Once or twice he twisted one between his fingers, or bent it at an angle and let it spring back to a neutral position. His outward inspection complete, he turned to me, a twinkle in his eye, and handed me the sword.

"Dr. Watson, my friend," he said, affecting a disposition of grave severity, "should I fail to return from this excursion, I do hope you will write me a touching obituary." As Lucy attempted to hide her laughter, Holmes twirled around and disappeared into the boughs of the tree.

Alder had the grace to look ashamed as the tree rustled and shook. "Perhaps I might bring home a slightly smaller one next year."

A minute or two later Holmes emerged from the botanical umbrella, shoulders and hair covered with a light dusting of conifer needles. He brushed himself off as he spoke, creating a shower of needles to add to the ones already scattered on the floor.

"Well," said he, "I feel confident that I can offer you at least one reassurance: From what I have seen, I don't believe any stranger has broken into your house."

"No?" said Alder, a hopeful expression beginning to blossom on his face. "Can you be sure?"

"With all reasonable certainty. I saw no evidence of any forced entry on the windows or the door, nor has anything else appeared to be out of place."

"So was it one of our visitors?" asked Lucy.

Holmes shrugged. "A possibility, but overall I think it an improbable one. Based on your own description of your visitors, it seems unlikely that any of them would have any inclination or ability to place the sword in the tree, and the reasoning would be rather unclear. If it were a threat, it would be a needlessly obtuse one. Furthermore, I see no sign of recent breakage or severe bending on any of the boughs, which we could reasonably expect to find had one of them waded through the tree a few days ago as I just did."

"But how, then?" asked Alder with dismay. "Where in the heavens did the thing come from?"

"It appears that the sword and the tree have been one since before either ever became a part of your domicile. There is a very large gash in one of the boughs, about shoulder-height. Someone, by virtue of one mighty swing, intentionally stuck this sword into this particular tree. The little remnant spots of sap on either side of the blade confirm further confirm that the sword did indeed pierce the tree and wasn't simply balanced amongst the limbs. Did you cut the tree down yourself, Mr. Alder?"

"Well, yes! There's a forest perhaps half-an-hour's ride from town that my brothers and I always go to for our trees. My eldest cousin keeps a farm outside of London with a handful of horses and a large cart, and he lets us borrow them for the sake of hauling the trees home. We make a day of it."

Holmes smiled triumphantly. "Above the large cut, there are smaller cuts on the underside of several boughs above the one that held the sword. I believe that the blade cut these higher boughs while the tree was compressed – likely either during the cart ride, or else while it was being dragged out of the forest. The tiny, sticky droplets of sap on both sides of the blade – not just one side – make this scenario all the more likely. I imagine the journey in a bouncing cart shook it loose most of the way, and then young Joseph finished the job."

Alder spread his arms in jubilation and laughed, planting a kiss on his wife's cheek. "You hear that Lucy? Nothing to do with us at all!"

Lucy smiled as well, albeit less widely than her husband. "Well, I am relieved to know it was neither a threat nor some other act of mischief. However, I must admit that I am a little personally dissatisfied with the solution. While we know how it came to be in the house, it puts us no closer to knowing the sword's origins."

Holmes spread his arms in a gesture that may have been a shrug, a slight smile playing at the corners of his mouth. "To solve this mystery, we would need to travel to the source. But perhaps you'd be willing to lead us to the stump in the forest where you retrieved this magnificent tree, Mr. Alder? Call it professional curiosity if you will, but I've a mind to see this sword returned to its rightful owner."

Alder nodded, still grinning widely. "Not to worry Mr. Holmes, I'm about bursting with curiosity myself. Besides," he added, placing an arm around Lucy's waist, "my wife is right. It's a dissatisfying solution in the extreme. But it's late, gentlemen, and the forest won't be easy to navigate this time of night. I'll fetch the both of you on the morrow as soon as I've finished my morning duties."

The next morning I arrived at my old flat just as the sun was starting to peak over the crowded collection of buildings that lined Baker Street. Gray winter sunlight glistened serenely against the snow. Given the lateness of the season, the sun had taken its time to rise, and so I hadn't needed to rouse myself from bed quite as early as I might have at other times of year.

Just as I raised my hand to knock on the door, I was hailed from the other side of the street. It seemed my timing had been perfect – Mr. Alder strode towards me. The lamplighter's pole that so easily identified his trade swung merrily at his side, and his ladder rode on his shoulder, one arm looped through a rung. When I turned, he held the pole aloft in salute.

"Ho, Doctor!" he called. His good cheer from the previous night's revelations was clearly still in full swing, and he clapped me heartily on the shoulder. We exchanged brief pleasantries, and he gave me an interesting report of the morning's observations along the Piccadilly. Our conversation must have been louder than we'd realized, for just as I turned to knock upon the door it swung open, and Holmes appeared dressed in his winter gear.

"Gentlemen," he said in way of greeting. "Mr. Alder, would you like to leave your pole and your ladder in the hall? I can't imagine we'll need them in the forest, though I will confess that cases have surprised me before."

Alder looked startled. "Thanks very much for the offer, Mr. Holmes, and I think I'll accept. In truth, I'd rather forgotten I was carrying them – the equipment becomes a part of you."

"Understandable, completely understandable. To keep your hands from feeling empty, perhaps you'd be willing to carry the sword in their place." With Alder's equipment thus settled, the three of us took a carriage past the outskirts of London.

The forests of England are varied in character, and even though I am no botanist, my adventures with Holmes have taken me to a wide variety of woodlands. While plenty of the country's forests are old, with large trees and a variety of ferns and wildflowers growing along the forest floor, there are also many that are filled with younger trees and shrubs. Many of these are old fields and pasturelands fallen into disuse and reclaimed by woody vegetation. Despite its relative proximity to London, the forest to which the lamplighter led us appeared to be an old-growth forest, dominated by a variety of large conifers. I judiciously decided not to ask Alder if he knew whether some private interest might have ownership of the land – and if the same question had occurred to Holmes, he too chose to keep his silence.

The trail that we followed into the woods may have been a path intended for human use, but it could just as easily have been a well-travelled deer trail. We only walked a couple of minutes – trees are rather heavy, after all, and even with the assistance of a collection of relatives and horses they aren't easily dragged far – before we arrived at the very impressive stump.

"We are lucky for the wet snowfall a few days ago and the exceptionally cold weather over the past week – the snow has maintained much the same shape for the past three days or so. We may get lucky in our search for tracks," said Holmes. He asked Alder and me to stay where we were so as not to disturb the snow around the stump. The path that we'd taken to our present location was already obliterated, trampled down by footprints and drag marks. Holmes therefore started on the other side of the stump, moving in a wide semicircle around the opposite side. He called out only a moment later.

"It would seem that fate is with us!" he said. "Come here." When Alder and I joined him, he pointed triumphantly at a track in the snow. The two of us stared in silence for a moment, which Alder hesitantly broke.

"Erm . . . Forgive me, Mr. Holmes. It's not that I doubt your methods, but when you called us over I was expecting to see a bootprint or the like. This one seems to belong to . . . some sort of animal, I s'pose."

"A canine," I said, noting the five toes and slight claw impressions (absent on a cat, which retract their claws when they walk). "Do you think it might be a fox, Holmes? We are in their domain, after all . . . ."

Holmes shook his head. "A fox would be much smaller. This print could only belong to a wolf or a large breed of dog. Seeing as wolves have been extinct from England for some four-hundred years or so, I think the dog to be the much more likely option. Furthermore, the creature appears to have been moving fairly quickly – look at how deeply the imprint rests in the snow. Ah! And it appears that our mysterious dog wasn't alone." Holmes pointed to another track, perhaps five feet away from the first. "That one appears to have been its companion. I'd be willing to wager that were we to fan out from here, we may find a few others as well."

"A pack of ferals, then?" said Alder. "There aren't many this close to London, but I'd be willing to wager there may be a few."

"It's possible," said Holmes. "But on the whole, I rather think not. In fact, I believe that we may well have found the key to our mystery. If you'll humour me, gentlemen, would you kindly follow along behind me? I think it may benefit us greatly to see where these dogs might have come from."

Confounded but intrigued, Alder and I paced silently behind Holmes through the forest's serenity. His strategy was immediately clear – we were following the dogs backwards through the forest. The prints were truly remarkably clear – occasionally a handful were obscured by the tracks of rabbits, squirrels, or other wildlife, but never so many that we lost the trail. Only a few feet from where we had started, the tracks of the dogs began to converge, such that it was clear the dogs had all followed one another along the same path for the majority of their run. Occasionally I thought I could see the outline of another footprint, mostly crushed beneath the rush of dogs, but still occasionally partially visible. I said as much to Holmes.

"Well spotted!" he said, a gleam in his eye. "Those prints, obscured though they might be, fit well into one particular branch of thinking regarding this unique little problem. But come along now – I'm afraid that I have no hints as to how far we may have yet to travel."

Perhaps a quarter-of-an-hour later, we emerged from the forest, blinking a little at the sudden brightness of the sunlight reflected off the snow. We had followed the dogs from the stump clear through the entirety of the woodland – though whether we had gone more or less straight from our point of entry or wandered off in some other direction I wasn't sure – and emerged into a field. Although the blanket of snow made it impossible to be sure, it appeared to be an unused agricultural field of some sort, apparently left to lay fallow. Tall grasses, brown and dry with the lateness of the year, struggled to poke through, accompanied only by a few leafless shrubs. But the tracks were just as clear as they had been before, and we picked our way through the snow and vegetation alike. Eventually we came to a fence, which Holmes leapt without hesitation. Alder and I, both with a little hesitation brought on by thoughts of trespass, eventually climbed it as well and followed behind.

We walked perhaps another ten or fifteen minutes when there came a shout and a man appeared atop a small berm. He was young, perhaps seventeen years of age, with deep-set brown eyes and a shock of blond hair. He stood firmly atop the berm and held a pistol loosely in his right hand. While it wasn't yet aimed at any of us, the implication was clear. He called out to us with a voice that likely shook a little more than its owner would have wished.

"That's far enough! I'll kindly ask you to turn around and remove yourselves from the premises at once. There's been more than enough chaos here for one week. Now it may be that your intentions on this land are harmless, but I'm afraid you've come at a bad time."

"Apologies, good sir!" called Holmes. "My friends and I will leave momentarily, but I'd like to ask you a question first. We came this way following a trail of some fairly large canines who came this way a few days ago. Do you know the animals?"

"Of course. They came from my household."

"Excellent!" said Holmes, beaming. "In that case, I have another question. Mr. Alder, would you kindly show this young man the sword? Hilt first, I think, lest our intentions be misconstrued. Does the weapon in my companion's hand look at all familiar to you?

The young man nearly dropped his pistol in shock. Caution forgotten, he ran down the berm to us, practically shaking in excitement, and took a closer look at the sword in Alder's hands. Then he burst into excited laughter and took the sword from the lamplighter's unresisting hands.

"Why, this is my father's sword! I cannot express how pleased he will be to have it back. Who are you all, and where on earth did you find it?"

"I think those are questions better answered out of the cold and the wind," Holmes answered. "And seeing as I believe you are in possession of the first half of the story anyway, I suggest that we discuss it all somewhere a little more sheltered."

"Of course, of course!" said the young man. "Please, follow me."

Our new host – whose name, we learned after some hasty introductions, was Peter Wright – led us a short distance until we came across a large house. Given the rural setting, the house bordered on manor-like in size and stateliness, although it wouldn't have held a candle in comparison to the intricacy of similar-sized houses within the city limits. There we were greeted by a much older man. Apart from his age, receded hairline, and gray walrus moustache, he bore a great deal of resemblance to young Peter, and it didn't take Holmes's considerable deductive talents to conclude that this must be his father.

The man stood tense at the doorway, every muscle poised for a fight, but he relaxed a little when his son waved to him. His tension melted away into shock, and then transformed into laughter as Peter held the sword aloft in gleeful salute.

The older man – Henry Wright was his name – quickly welcomed us into the house and sat us around the dining table. As we introduced ourselves, he took the sword from his son and with great aplomb placed it in a prominent position on the center of the table, that we might all be able to look at it. When he spoke, a strong Scottish accent tinged his words.

"Well, gentlemen," he said. "I would like to apologize on behalf of my son and me for what I'm afraid was a very cold initial reception. We saw your approach from a window on the second floor and thought you may be the villain returned, or perhaps his associates, but I see now that nothing could be further from the truth."

"Villain?" asked Alder. "Have you had a crime take place here?"

"Aye. A burglary, I'm afraid. We reported it to Scotland Yard a few days ago, but we've heard nothing from them since. We'd rather abandoned hope on hearing any follow up."

"Did they take anything else in addition to the sword?" asked Holmes.

Alder turned to Holmes, a bewildered expression on his face. "You knew the sword had been stolen, Mr. Holmes? For how long?"

"I suspected it as soon as I saw the way that the sword had been embedded in your Christmas tree. Not casually tossed or dropped, but buried with considerable force into a branch very close to the trunk – very difficult to do by accident, so it had to be purposeful. Hidden, then, with the intention of eventually returning to retrieve it. Now, there are a handful of other reasons that one might desire to hide a weapon, but I thought theft to be a likely solution in this particular case. When we searched by the stump and found the tracks of the dogs, I felt that to be reasonable confirmation of the theory."

Now it was the Wrights' turn to look bewildered. "Pardon me, but did I hear that correctly? My sword was in your Christmas Tree?" Henry asked the lamplighter.

"Why don't you start from the beginning, Mr. Wright," said Holmes. "You are in possession of the beginning to the story, we have the end of it, and unless I'm very much mistaken, I believe we'll be able to surmise much of the middle by the time we're through."

"Very well, sir, although I'm not sure I'm quite as confident as you," said Henry. "First thing you must understand, gentlemen, is that we are a small household. Despite the size of the house, you see before you its only two inhabitants. I served in the military most of my life, but after injuries in Afghanistan left me with limited movement in my left leg, I was forced to retire. Thankfully, my long career and thrifty spending habits left me with more than enough to get myself, my wife, and Peter situated here on the outskirts of London. I am not a city man, and the serenity of life outside of the city proper appealed to me immensely. Sadly, my wife died a few years back, and since then it's been only Peter and me in the house.

"I suppose the burglar thought us to be relatively easy prey – just an old Scotsman and his son far away from any protection by police or any possibility of intervention by neighbors. I've no idea how he came to find the house in the first place. I can only guess that he received a tip from one of our few visitors. He came around midnight four nights ago, prying open one of our windows and slipping in like a serpent.

"Thankfully, it would seem that our burglar somehow managed to be unaware of the nonhuman members of the household. I have a great fondness for dogs, gentlemen, and I have taken to breeding guard dogs as a way to keep myself active in my retirement. The burglar hadn't gotten very far when the household was filled with a cacophony of thunderous barking. Although they couldn't reach the man – the dogs stay in another room during the night, with the door closed – they apparently deemed his presence to be highly suspect nonetheless. Peter and I awoke instantly and came down the stairs from our rooms to find a rough-looking man standing in the living room. Peter shouted and charged down at him while I ran to my room to retrieve my service revolver.

"The thief, apparently having chosen to conduct this burglary with no weapons of his own, leapt to the mantel and tore my old army sword from its honored resting place above the fireplace. He swung at Peter a few times, but a sword isn't so easy a weapon to wield as it may first appear, and his offense was very clumsy. The moment I emerged at the top of the stairs, pistol in hand, he turned tail and fled back out the window at once, sword still clutched in his hands. Once I ascertained that my son was safe, I released a few of my most loyal dogs to chase after the villain. Unfortunately I fumbled a few times with the lock as my hands shook, and as such they weren't able to follow behind him as closely as they might have. All the dogs returned unharmed, but the burglar appeared to have somehow eluded them. Then again, they are guard dogs, not bloodhounds. Perhaps they simply lost his trail."

"Perhaps," murmured Holmes. "Well, I cannot tell you where your burglar disappeared to, but I am glad to hear that he didn't abscond with any great amount of wealth. I can tell you that he appears to have made a beeline for the forest to the west, and that at some point your burglar chose to hide the sword in a large spruce tree – perhaps so that he would be less easily identified as a thief should he come across someone else during his flight. You can see little specks of sap on the blade from where it was driven into the wood. It may be wise to give the blade a thorough cleaning before you rehang it. That same spruce tree was then cut down three days ago by Mr. Alder here to serve out the remainder of its life as a Christmas tree in his home in London, where his young son accidentally dislodged the sword yesterday."

"Astonishing," said the elder Wright, shaking his head, and apparently unconcerned about the taking of one of his trees. "Hard to believe that my sword managed to travel into the city without me. I do hope it didn't give your son too much of a shock, Mr. Alder."

Alder laughed. "The lad was right pleased with himself, I think. By my reckoning, young Joseph will pull twice as hard on next year's tree, and be mighty disappointed when that one doesn't produce a sword as well!"

Henry Wright chuckled and picked up the sword, turning it over in his hands. "Well, gentlemen, I can't tell you how glad I am to have this back. It may be nothing but a sharpened piece of steel, but it served me well for many years and I am quite attached to it. I would have been willing to pay a fair fee to anyone who could return it to me, and I most certainly still am."

Holmes lazily waved a hand to brush off the offer. "Appreciated, but unnecessary. I am fresh off of several large-profile cases that have my needs well-covered for some time, and my efforts today have hardly been arduous work. A brisk winter's walk through the forest was really quite refreshing. Consider this a favor in keeping with the spirit of the season."

Alder nodded, a grin stretched across his face. "I already have my reward – I have gained an astounding tale for the pub, one that will last me many years, and I am more than content with that."

Henry opened his mouth, perhaps to press the matter further, when Peter leapt out of his seat. "I have an idea! Give me just a moment, please." The young man disappeared up the stairs and reappeared minutes later carrying a covered box. He placed it on the table and opened it up to reveal a plethora of children's toys – toy soldiers featured the most prominently, but there were also marbles, zoetropes, spinning tops, kaleidoscopes, and even a skittles set. "Perhaps you don't need a reward for yourself, Mr. Alder, but your son was just as instrumental in retrieving my father's blade. I have long outgrown these toys, sir, and it is nearly Christmas. He may not get to keep his Christmas sword, but maybe if you put these under the tree for him they might serve as a replacement."

Henry's eyes gleamed with approval for his son. "Now that's a fine idea, very fine indeed."

Alder hesitated for but a moment as he looked into the box. His grin widened further. "Well, young Peter, that is exceptionally kind of you. I will accept your offer on behalf of my son. I think you've made little Joseph a very happy lad indeed."

Holmes laughed. "I think we'll all be keeping a very close watch on your son, Mr. Alder. After all, at a very young age Joseph has pulled the sword from the spruce – it may not be enough to qualify one as king of all England, but it must be a step in the right direction!"

The Adventure of the Serpentine Body
by Wayne Anderson

When December of 1889 began, my life was still in a happy state of matrimonial bliss, every day enjoying the company of the finest of women, my wife Mary. My medical practice was thriving. In all, the only thing standing between myself and complete happiness was the fact that I was sorely lacking for time spent with my dear friend, Mr. Sherlock Holmes.

The final month of that year, though, was marred by something far more sinister than any villain that Holmes and I ever faced. With the lightning speed of modern travel, steamships and railways carried an invisible passenger from Russia all over the civilised world – the disease known as the Asiatic or Russian Influenza. This dreadful immigrant came to English shores in mid-December, sweeping like wildfire through rich and poor with no regard for station, vice, or virtue.

Indeed, on the European Continent, the Tsar of Russia, the King of Belgium, and the German Emperor had all fallen ill, though it had slain none of them. Half of the population of Berlin was said to be infected, and sixty-per-cent of Sweden was sick, recovered, or dead of it.

The first symptoms were similar to those of a cold – headaches, chills, fever, and a sore throat, and many suffered nothing more than that. But some – especially small children, the elderly, or those weakened by other debilities – faced a mortal threat, as it sometimes led to pneumonia, by which point it often resulted in death. Modern medicine could find no effective treatment. Of those it infected, it killed one in twenty-five.

As a practising physician, I had a closer look than most at this plague, and more than a passing acquaintance with the worst of it. Lacking any efficacious treatment, I was forced to witness the decline and passing of several of my patients.

Whether it was Sherlock Holmes's robust health or sheer luck that seemed to confer a fortunate immunity, to the best of my knowledge he was never touched by that scourge. Others at 221 Baker Street did not all share his good fortune, and among those who took sick shortly before Christmas of that year was Emily, one of the housemaids working for Mrs. Hudson.

At the tender age of sixteen years, this poor girl fell grievously ill and was confined to her bedroom, racked with chills or burning with fever. Mrs. Hudson, bless her, was more like a mother than an employer, and doted upon the poor girl even as I tried in vain to enforce a quarantine. The best I could do was to persuade her to sterilise everything again and again with carbolic acid, and to wash both her hands and the bedclothes incessantly.

I know not whether it was I who carried the germ home from one of my patients – as I never felt any ill effects – but on the nineteenth of December my own dear Mary complained of headaches and a sore throat. By the following morning she suffered chills and nausea. I attended her night and day, and her health was strong, so that by the twenty-second of December her fever had broken, and two days later she seemed as hale and sound as any of the fairer sex.

Emily seemed more frail, and was bedridden all through the approach of Christmas. On the afternoon of December 24th I visited her room below-stairs at 221 Baker Street, with a vigilant Mrs. Hudson hovering outside the open doorway of her room, unconsciously wringing her hands. The landlady had adorned the door with a wreath of holly in an attempt to impart some Christmas cheer, and the rich, warm smell of baking filled the air in a way that I never recalled rising to the upper stories.

"How are we today, my dear?" I enquired, taking out my stethoscope.

"I think I'm feeling better, Doctor," the pale blonde girl replied. "My breathing is easier, and I haven't suffered an attack of chills in two days." I noticed that the shakiness of days before was gone from her voice.

I pressed my stethoscope to the girl's back and ordered her to breathe slowly and deeply. "Your lungs sound much better. No pneumonia there," I reported happily, and applied my hand to her forehead. It was still clammy with sweat, but she was no longer burning up. "I do believe Mrs. Hudson's ministrations will pull you through. Do you feel like eating?"

She nodded slowly, and I looked at the landlady in the doorway. "Give her a light broth in small amounts. Also small portions of brandy may be beneficial. If her stomach tolerates it, she can have more food, but nothing heavy."

"Thank you, Doctor." Mrs. Hudson noticed her wringing hands, but seemed at a loss as to what to do with them.

"No, thank *you*," I said. "Honestly, you deserve the credit for this girl's care and recovery more than I do." I crossed to the washbasin, where I cleansed my hands with a cloth and a solution of carbolic acid. "I shall visit Holmes now, if you've no more need of me here."

He was in a contemplative mood when I entered, absently scratching out on his violin an improvisation combining bits of several Christmas carols. "Halloa, Watson!" he greeted me, lifting the bow for a moment. "I see that your patient downstairs recovers apace."

I knew better than to be surprised by his perceptions. "The dear girl has great fortitude, and I believe that she's past the worst. She'll miss the festivities of Christmas and Boxing Day, but should be up and about soon after."

"Splendid!" He played a little musical flourish. "Once again, you prove how invaluable you are!"

I brushed this aside. "I thank Mrs. Hudson for much of it. Tell me, have you any pressing cases at present?"

"None at all. It seems the English criminal element is either taking off for the holidays, or down with the influenza. Were it not for my work upon a monograph or two, I should find myself falling into a black humour for lack of stimulation."

"Ah, we can't have that, especially during Yuletide." My eyes strayed to the brown morocco case containing his syringe. His eyes followed mine, and I knew he divined my thoughts. "As your physician, I prescribe diversion and stimulation. Tell me – what do you know of the effects of immersion in near-freezing water?"

"Upon the living or the dead? I have heard tales of Esquimaux and Vikings swimming in the waters of the frozen North, but have seen no studies of scientific merit. Upon the dead, I should think it would help to keep a body preserved, almost as if frozen in ice."

I smiled at his turn of mind. "We can witness for ourselves its effects upon the living, at least. Have you heard of the Serpentine Swimming Club, in Hyde Park?"

"I've seen the name in the papers occasionally. Apparently they swim in the Serpentine year round, and claim it's beneficial to the constitution."

"So they say. They have an annual swimming race, one-hundred yards, on Christmas morning. My dear Mary has expressed an interest in observing this, and I have some interest myself in the physiological effects of such cold water. Would you care to join us?"

Holmes lowered the Stradivarius, thinking. I would have considered this invitation a long shot, for Holmes's instinct runs strongly against any social activities when he can possibly avoid them. But this was, perhaps, counterbalanced by my status as his dearest – or only – friend, and the scientific appeal seemed to decide the matter.

"What time is the race?" was all he said.

"It begins at nine o'clock."

"I shall meet you in Hyde Park at eight-thirty, near the bridge."

I nodded. "Capital! And now, I must make an early night of it, for Father Christmas has plans for my bride."

Holmes snorted cynically but good-naturedly as I bade him good-bye. I descended the steps, followed by renewed violin music, sounding vaguely like some sort of folk dance. A light snow was already gently dusting the streets of the city.

Christmas morning dawned clear, with pale sunlight brightening a blanket of fresh snow. The sun cast long grey shadows across the ground. As I helped Mary down from the cab on Hyde Park's Carriage Road, we heard deep, booming drums from within the park. Snow crunched under our feet, but on the Carriage Road it was already plowed into a melange of sandy ruts. Music burst upon us as we crossed by a neat row of trees and progressed toward the man-made lake called the Serpentine. Nearby runs the broad fashionable riding path called Rotten Row, normally topped with a smooth surface of sand. On this morning the snow was already churned into a slush by countless hooves.

Elsewhere, most of the grass also bore a lovely white sheet of snow, drifted against the trees and marked with many footprints of both human and beast.

Alongside Rotten Row we saw the mounted band of the Royal Horse Guards – the Blues, as they are called, based in the Knightsbridge barracks facing the park. Some twenty cavalrymen, resplendent in their blue uniforms, sat their horses in a precise line facing the lake, striking up a brassy rendition of "Good King Wenceslas".

Others of the Royal Horse Guard, not part of the band, took advantage of the holiday to proudly ride their great black warhorses along Rotten Row, there to see and be admired. Some remained at the Serpentine, their curiosity evidently piqued by the apparent madness of swimming in the gelid waters.

Arm in arm, Mary and I strolled toward the bridge, our breath making clouds of vapour in the chill air. I picked out Holmes's lean form near its southern end. Upon seeing us he waved and approached. "Good morning and a Merry Christmas to you, Mrs. Watson," he said, raising his stick to his top hat in salute. "You are looking quite well."

She smiled sweetly and looked at me with glowing eyes. "Thank you, Mr. Holmes. Thanks to John, I'm feeling so much better." I returned the smile with a nod, not mentioning that it was almost certainly through my profession that she had come into contact with the dreaded germ.

Holmes took out his watch. "It's quarter-of-nine now," he said. "Shall we proceed to the race?" Mary took his arm in her other, and the three of us found a place in the smallish crowd on the south shore. It pleased me immensely to see Holmes being so uncharacteristically social, and I knew that he did it for my sake.

The race was set up parallel to the shore, proceeding a hundred yards toward the southern end of the Serpentine. A narrow platform extended into the water, and the intrepid swimmers were gingerly gravitating toward it, barefoot in the snow. A few brave men among them were already on the platform, some dipping their toes into the near-freezing water. This, I imagined, would help reduce the shock when they must actually enter and swim.

"Merry Christmas, Mr. Holmes!" A uniformed constable approached us rapidly.

"And the same to you, Barclay," Holmes replied tolerantly. He obviously knew the man, though I did not. Holmes made introductions, but it was clear that he would have preferred to quietly observe the race.

Oblivious to this, Barclay began talking quite amiably about anything, while Holmes nodded absently, his eyes on the assembling swimmers. At length he raised a hand. "It's time," he said, and Constable Barclay fell silent.

The mounted band, too, had stopped their music. The swimmers took their starting positions, lined up closely upon the platform.

The club Secretary raised a stopwatch. "Ready!" he shouted. "Steady! *Go!*" As the first two swimmers dove into the freezing lake he started the stopwatch and began calling out seconds. Each swimmer had been given a handicap time, and as the count progressed they entered the water in turn.

As I understood it, the slowest swimmers started first, and the swiftest last, so that in theory they might all finish at the same moment. In reality, some were clearly ahead of the pace, and others behind it, but none of them seemed hampered in any way by the freezing water.

Mary squeezed my arm. "John, it's amazing that they can swim at all in such cold water. If I fell in I should freeze and drown!"

"As I understand it, my dear, these men are all accustomed to it, and their bodies have adapted."

Holmes spoke up. "I confess to some disappointment, Watson. It looks very like an ordinary sporting race. These men swim as if it were summer."

The leading swimmer, a handsome ginger-haired young man with a neat moustache, crossed the line, then stood in chest-deep water, shoulders heaving.

"The winner is Mr. Arthur Hester!" proclaimed another race official, stationed at the finish.

Mr. Hester raised one arm in triumph, took a step toward the shore, and recoiled, gasping. "There's something down here!" he cried. "I stepped on it!"

At this, Holmes, the constable, and I all moved forward. Mary's grip on my arm tightened, halting my advance. She looked at me breathlessly. "What can it be?"

Another swimmer cried, "It's a body! There's a dead man here!"

"Best you stay here, my dear," I said. Detaching my arm from Mary's grip, I hurried forward.

"He's wrapped in chains!" announced Mr. Hester, which explained why the body wasn't floating. The cold had almost nearly frozen it, so that it wasn't bloated with the usual decomposition gases.

Constable Barclay quickly took charge of the situation. "Bring 'im ashore!" said he. Four of the swimmers, muscular men all, bore the body gingerly below the water's surface, holding it by the chains that wrapped the torso. None wanted to touch the chilled flesh.

The man's arms and legs floated freely, the chains serving only as weights. He wore trousers and a shirt, but neither coat nor shoes. His head lolled loosely, mouth and eyes both open in the water. The cause of death was obvious: His throat was cut deeply.

"Support his head!" Holmes cried, not wanting the body to suffer further damage before examination.

"Bring a blanket!" Mr. Hester called. One was duly brought, and the swimmers together contrived to pass it beneath the unfortunate man. By this means they carefully set him on the shore.

The departed man was of medium stature but powerfully built, with thick arms and big hands. He wore black trousers and a fine white shirt, which bore copious rust-brown blood stains below the open throat wound, still visible even after being submerged in the water. He was clean-shaven, somewhere around forty years of age, with fair hair thinning on top. His naturally pale complexion was white as paper in death.

"Obviously," Holmes said, "he wore this shirt when his throat was cut, and the bloodstains were allowed to dry before ever he was put in the water – most likely some hours at least. Note that the edges of the stains are distinct. The cold water has preserved them for us."

"Not that we need the stains to determine the manner of his death." I knelt at the dead man's right side, and we immediately set to examining the body, while the constable sent for the police surgeon and a wagon. The victim's skin was soft and puffy, his extremities wrinkled and puckered in places.

"Right-handed," Holmes observed, half to himself. "Walked with a limp, favoring the right foot – probably carried a cane. Bespoke shirt and trousers, Savile Row, but he comes from a poor upbringing. Several front teeth missing, the others show considerable defects. This man was poorly educated, but tried to project an upper-class image. Former military. Non-commissioned. Probably a sergeant. Most likely served in India or Afghanistan." He looked up at me. "Your *milieu*, Watson."

I didn't question Holmes on these observations. I knew every one would be soundly based. "His lungs are full of water, but that would surprise no one," I remarked. "Otherwise I find no recent injury or trauma other than the obvious throat wound." Feeling a lump in the lower right leg, I rolled up his trouser. "And here is the cause of his limp, Holmes: This bullet scar shows where he was shot some years past. It broke the bone, which was poorly set, twisting his leg slightly." I grimaced. "That would be after his military service. My Army colleagues are better than that."

"There is nothing in his pockets to give any clue as to his identity," Holmes continued. "In fact, nothing at all – no watch, no money, no papers. His killer most likely removed everything."

"Completely exsanguinated," I noted. "If he hadn't lost all his blood from the killing wound, what remained would surely have dissipated into the lake."

"Is there any way of telling how long he's been there?" Constable Barclay asked, standing behind me.

"I fear that's nearly impossible," I responded. "The cold water has preserved him, almost as if frozen. I am not familiar with the effects of freezing water on the onset and passing of *rigor mortis*, though I find none. He could have been put there last night or several days ago."

Holmes looked up at the crowd gathered round the grim spectacle. "I fear he may be drawing attention away from Mr. Hester's swimming triumph." Mr. Hester, standing foremost in the circle around us, nodded at this and moved to lead the swimmers and their audience away.

At that moment several more policemen arrived, along with a wagon and Dr. Creswell, a police surgeon, as well as Inspector Athelney Jones of Scotland Yard. Dr. Creswell, who knew us well, knelt to join in the examination, and I quickly recapitulated the known facts.

"Check his right shoulder," Holmes said. The dead man's white cambric shirt was all but transparent from immersion, and some mark were visible beneath. I opened the shirt while Constable Barclay gave Jones a *precis* of what was already known. On the victim's shoulder was a tattoo, of a design quite familiar to me: A golden sun, surmounted by a British crown proper. The sun lay across two crossed blades, which should have been straight swords, but instead were broad, bent blades.

"British Indian Army!" I announced. It was the ensign, slightly simplified, omitting the ribbon and motto but still recognisable. "Save that these two blades should be swords in the Army ensign. These aren't swords, but *kukris*."

Holmes bent to examine it closely. "The traditional blade of the Gurkhas of India and Nepal," said he. "This man is no Gurkha – obviously an Englishman. Doubtless this tattoo came from military service in India."

He stripped the shirt away from the dead man's other shoulder, and there revealed another vivid tattoo of a grapevine, with green leaves and several grapes showing – but from each of the grapes fell a drop, bright red, as of blood. At the bottom of that tattoo were the initials: *SM*.

"MacDonald," Holmes muttered. He quickly and deftly sketched both tattoos in his notebook. "I shall have to pay a visit to Piccadilly Circus. Care to accompany me?"

"Piccadilly Circus? What's there?"

"The Hammam Turkish Baths at 76 Jermyn Street."

"And what's at the Turkish Baths?"

"Mr. Sutherland MacDonald," he replied. "Probably the foremost expert alive on tattoos – as well as the inventor of green tattoo ink. This grapevine, at least, could only come from his hand."

"Tomorrow, then," I responded as I opened the man's shirt further. "It's Christmas Day. I should think he'll be closed."

The man's chest and abdomen revealed further scars, some from blade cuts, others that appeared to be long-healed bullet wounds. "This man has lived quite a violent life," Dr. Creswell remarked.

"And died a violent death," said I.

"If you've naught better to do tomorrow," said Dr. Creswell, "you're both welcome to join me in a complete examination of the body." He looked at the circle of remaining bystanders, which included my wife Mary. "At the Yard," he concluded. "It isn't proper to make a spectacle of this."

Holmes and I met eyes and both nodded, accepting the invitation. Indeed, he would have been hard-put to keep us away.

Whilst the constables lifted the blanket and body onto the waiting wagon, I spoke to my Mary, giving her money for a cab ride home. She understood completely. "Go ahead, John," said she. "Do what you must. But please, you must promise to take the greatest care for your safety – and tell me all afterward!"

I promised as she asked.

"So you found nothing else of note?" Mary asked me as we rested after our excellent Christmas goose.

"Nothing that I could see, at least on first examination. I should imagine that Holmes found subtle clues, but if they were significant, he didn't share them with me. Tomorrow we shall know more."

Mary, no shrinking violet herself, nodded. Her curiosity was tempered by acceptance that a *post mortem* is no place for a woman. "I'm sure you will," she said. "And I have no doubt that Mr. MacDonald will be able to shed light on the poor man's identity."

"If," I said, "he keeps the names of his clients. And if, indeed, the man had even given his true name. This man's scars told of a violent life, and he may have been one to conceal the truth."

I saw the momentary hesitation in my wife's clear blue eyes as she considered this possibility. Years of association with Holmes have made me something of a sceptic. "Come, my dear," I said, changing the subject. "It's Christmas, and I hear carolers at the Hamiltons' house. Shall we go see?" I rose, she took my hand, and we went outside to hear the singing at the next house down.

The 26th of December dawned crisp and cold, with a light breeze from the south that stirred, but didn't quite dissipate, a fog in the air. Frost limned the cobblestones and kerbs, rendering footing treacherous. What snow remained in the shaded places was topped with a crisp shell of ice, causing it to crunch underfoot. Boxing Day has been a bank holiday since 1871, but as it fell on a Thursday, many businesses were open.

Mary and I began the day with gifts for our own staff, and set them at liberty to celebrate. After taking breakfast with me at a small restaurant down the street, Mary insisted that I must join Holmes in his investigation. I do believe she was as curious as I about the Serpentine body.

The streets were wet with melted frost by the time I arrived to take part in the Christmas boxes for Mrs. Hudson's staff. Holmes and I each gave a sovereign, along with chocolates and other small treats, for Billy and each of the housemaids. I no longer lived at Baker Street, but I had known them for many years, and still often spent a night in my old rooms.

I took the opportunity to check on Emily, my patient below-stairs, and was pleased to find her alert and in good spirits. Her fever had broken, and her lungs sounded clear. She accepted her Christmas box with heartfelt gratitude, but I advised her not to go out yet to celebrate Boxing Day. "I shall ask Mrs. Hudson to give you another day off soon," said I. "We mustn't imperil your recovery with a chill. Still, I think we can dispense with the bed rest." She gave me a bright smile and promised to be good.

The fog, mercifully, was a clean fog, not one of the sulfurous "London particulars" that affected one's lungs. Since the servants were given the day off, Holmes breakfasted at a cafe down Baker Street, and I joined him for coffee.

Our next stop was the morgue at Scotland Yard, where the chill of the unheated basement was enough to slow the processes of putrefaction. There we were able to examine the body in clinical conditions and compare notes with Dr. Creswell. The horrific cut that ended this man's life went so deeply into his throat that it notched the cervical vertebrae. Holmes remarked that the killer must have been quite a strong man. He further observed that, while the cutting instrument had indeed been sharp, resulting in a relatively clean cut with little tearing, the compression at the edges of the gash suggested a chopping motion, rather than the type of drawing cut one might expect from the movement of a blade like a sabre.

"Similar to what one would expect from an axe," I suggested.

"Except for this – the blade curved forward, where an axe generally curves back from its centre."

Dr. Creswell and I both leaned in to look closer. "Show me," said the police surgeon.

"Observe," Holmes said. "The cut on the left side of the neck goes deep, about two-thirds of the way through. On the other side the same cut goes just as far. In both cases they extend beyond the spinal column that stopped the blade. As I said, this blade curved forward on either side from its centre." He gestured toward the man's tattoo. "Like a *kukri*."

Dr. Creswell looked at Holmes, then carefully examined the cut where it curved around both sides of the unfortunate man's neck. "Indeed it does," he murmured, his breath forming a cloud of vapour in the cold room. "Can you think of any other sort of implement that might create a cut like this?"

"The *jambiya* of Araby is deeply curved, with edges on both sides," I remarked, "and usually devilishly sharp. It might fit the profile of this cut."

"In shape, yes," Holmes said in a quiet voice, fingertips probing the edges of the bloodless cut, "but the *jambiya* is a lightweight weapon, with a ridged spine along the center of the blade. It would probably lack the chopping power to cut a man's neck straight in as deeply as this."

"I say," said Dr. Creswell, "could not a man on horse, with a sabre, create a similar cut? At first cutting far across the neck, almost to the ear, but then, as the horse passes, bringing the blade across the nearer side? I've seen such cuts before, in my time in the Army – and the Knightsbridge barracks are right there, beside the park. There are many cavalrymen there who would be skilled wielding a sabre from horseback."

Holmes considered this for a moment. "Unlikely, Doctor. Such a cut, done by a right-handed swordsman, would angle downward from the nearer side – that is, the victim's right side – to the further side. This cut, by contrast, angles upward from here – " He touched the cut's edge. " – to here." He held his hand above the cut, aligned as a blade would have been, and demonstrated the angle. "This rising angle indicates a right-handed man on foot, chopping into the victim's neck while facing him. Since there are no other fresh cuts or defensive wounds, this was a surprise attack – possibly by someone the victim trusted."

"It would be possible for a skilled cavalryman to lean down from his horse, while passing, to gain greater reach and an element of surprise," Dr.

Creswell objected. "That might result in such an upward angle."

"What about a left-handed swordsman on horse?" I asked.

Holmes stepped around the table, thinking. "Possible, but again unlikely. There are very few left-handed cavalrymen – especially as cavalry formations are based on all the men wielding their sabres on the same side. A left-handed cavalryman would actually prove a danger to his comrades, with his sword interfering with that of the man beside him – while his right side goes undefended." He met my eyes. "No, I believe we have an image of the killing weapon right here." He tapped the tattoo. "This was done with a *kukri*."

"Where would one get a *kukri*?" Dr. Creswell asked. "Does that mean that the killer was a Gurkha? I still believe a sabre more likely."

"Many British soldiers who have served in India have encountered the *kukri* there," said I. "I saw them myself. Once they see one, Englishmen remember it, for nothing else quite matches its shape or terrific cutting power."

"I have seen *kukris* for sale in curiosity shops," said Holmes. "I imagine they were brought by soldiers returning from India, who may have fallen on hard times and been forced to sell them."

I nodded. "Some soldiers were quite keen to get their hands on one. The Gurkhas generally refused to sell them, as they hold them sacred, but I recall seeing a few in British hands."

"And of course," said Holmes, "there is nothing that would prevent a skilled bladesmith from fashioning a copy. I'm certain there are dozens, if not hundreds, of men in Sheffield who could make such a blade. All it would take is a drawing."

"Or a tattoo," said Dr. Creswell, gesturing toward the victim's shoulder.

"Whatever the source, I am certain this man was killed with a *kukri*, most likely by a trusted associate."

"Whatever you believe," Dr. Creswell said, "I still think a sabre cut is the more likely. There must be a thousand sabres in London for every *kukri*. I shall ask the investigating officer to question the Blues at Knightsbridge."

"Beyond the question of *how* this man was killed," I said, "there remains the greater question of *why* and *who* killed him. And indeed, *who was he?*"

"Quite so," Holmes nodded. "The Turkish Baths await us. Shall we go?"

It was nearing noon, and the streets were mostly dry in the pale December sunshine. I waved down a cab. "Take us to 76 Jermyn Street, off Piccadilly Circus."

"Oh, I know where Jermyn Street is, Guv'nor," said the driver.

Traffic was thick, with many of the serving classes given Boxing Day off and money to spend. Our progress was slow, and Holmes made idle conversation about pagan holidays like Yule and Saturnalia. At length our hansom turned from Piccadilly Arcade into Jermyn Street, and we rattled past the shops of mens' clothiers. We rolled to a stop at Number 76, the expansive Hammam Turkish Baths.

On entering we turned toward a small side door, beside which stood a sign that said, in large capital letters, *"TATTOOING"*. This showed a drawing of a tiger's head, surmounting a photograph of a man's heavily tattooed torso. The sign also spoke of *"the Patronage of the Highest Imperial and Royal Personages in Europe"*, which I took to be hyperbole. At the bottom it advertised, *"Any Design"* and *"Fixed Prices"*, concluding with the name of *"Sutherland MacDonald"*.

I must confess that I was impressed, as the quality of the artwork was far above that of any tattoo I had ever seen, and I had seen many as an Army surgeon.

Holmes seemed to know exactly where he was going. "I say," I ventured as we proceeded down a narrow staircase, "have you sought out information about tattoos here before?"

"A knowledge of tattoos is essential to the criminologist. There is no identifying marking so indelible, so unique, and so widespread. And Mr. MacDonald," he concluded, opening the door at the bottom of the stair, "is the greatest authority alive on tattoos."

We entered into a room of wholly unexpected Oriental splendour, festooned with tapestries and cloth hangings, art and scrolls of sundry types. Animals and mythology joined in riotous celebration – tigers, Chinese dragons, serpents and mermaids and unicorns. A hookah rested in one corner, surrounded by cushions. Deep Persian rugs softened the hard floor underfoot. I recognised decorative arts of India and Turkey, Egypt, and Araby. Silks from China and pottery from Japan, as well as other pieces I couldn't identify.

The wall near the door was decorated with printed photographs at which I could only gaze in wonder. His customers, assembled, would have formed a walking museum.

Bright electric lights illuminated centre of the room. Several tables stood near a chair, which in turn faced a large divan. On the tables were glass phials in a rainbow of colours, more than I had ever dreamed could be used in tattoos.

I don't know exactly what I expected a tattoo artist to look like – perhaps a great bearded, one-eyed piratical type with a parrot on his shoulder – but Mr. Sutherland MacDonald surprised me. He was a dignified, well-dressed gentleman with military posture and a handlebar moustache. At our entry he looked over and smiled, but I thought I detected a hint of annoyance when he spoke.

"Mr. Holmes," he declaimed, looking up from mixing something in a small bottle. "Don't you ever knock?"

Holmes glanced at the sign on the door. "It says you are open for business."

"For business, yes, I am," Mr. MacDonald replied. "You, sir, have been here many times, and have never yet proven to be 'business'."

On the divan rested a man, stripped to the waist, his arms folded over the end. His bare back, facing us, was covered with an outlined scene that appeared to represent Eros and Psyche. The Eros resembled the young man's own face, and the Psyche, as far as I could tell, was a portrait, finely drawn, of a young woman depicted in a photograph resting on a work table.

Holmes set a gold sovereign on the table beside the artist. "I am business now," he said.

"Oh, splendid!" Mr. MacDonald's sarcasm seemed good-natured. "What's it to be, then? A magnifying lens across your back – perhaps with a distinctive cigar ash, greatly enlarged? I'll give you a special rate."

Holmes smiled grimly. "It is a business of death, Mr. MacDonald."

"Don't you mean life and death?"

"Death only. The life of one of your clients has ended."

"I'm sorry to hear that." The artist rose and carried the small bottle of liquid – evidently ink – to the table beside the prone man. "And who is this unlucky patron of the arts?"

"That's what I've come to find out."

"Then how do you know he's one of my clients?"

"His skin bears your work. Green ink, and your initials."

"Ah." Mr. MacDonald spread some blue ink on his customer's back, delicately shading the figure of Psyche. His skill, I noted, was exquisite. "Keep your money," he said. "Someday I'll ask you for a favour."

"You say that every time, yet you've never asked."

Mr. MacDonald chuckled without looking up. "Then someday you'll owe me a very big favour."

"I have a sketch of his tattoos," Holmes said.

"Let me have it." Without turning his head, MacDonald extended his left hand. Holmes set the paper in it, and the artist regarded it for a moment. "Not a bad representation," said he. "You might have some talent for art, Mr. Holmes."

"Can you name the man?"

"Jenkins. His friends call him 'Gurkha Jim'. So Mr. James Jenkins." He looked at me. "Who's your friend?"

Holmes gestured toward me. "Mr. Sutherland MacDonald, may I present my colleague, Dr. John Watson? Watson, this is Mr. MacDonald, possibly the finest tattoo artist alive."

I shook his hand. "A pleasure, sir."

"The pleasure is mine, Doctor," he said amiably, and returned his attention to his work.

Holmes turned to me. "The sign about royal and imperial personages," he said, "doesn't exaggerate."

I thought briefly of the various aristocrats and kings who had come to our rooms in Baker Street. "Most impressive," I said. "But this looks like a good place to catch the influenza."

Mr. MacDonald shrugged without looking up. "I don't want to get sick, no more than anybody," said he. "I interview all my clients regarding their health before I begin. I don't know what more I can do."

"That's quite reasonable," said I. "We quarantine the sick. Shall we quarantine the healthy as well?"

"What can you tell me about Mr. Jenkins?" asked Holmes.

"I believe he has criminal connections, and from the scars I've seen on his body he has a dangerous trade. Also, in keeping with his nickname, I have seen him wearing a sheathed *kukri* knife." He shot Holmes a quick glance. "I always took that to relate to his trade."

"His violent life has ended violently," Holmes said, "and it may have been by his own knife. His body was found yesterday in Hyde Park. Weighted down with chains in the Serpentine. Throat cut wide open."

Mr. MacDonald's eyebrows shot up. "I'll not rejoice at a man's death, but from what I've seen I can't say it surprises me." He handed the sketch back to Holmes. "Can I help you in any other way?"

"Do you know where he lived?"

"From his conversation, I should say the Stepney area."

"Conversations with you? Or whom?"

"Sometimes he came in alone. On some occasions he came with friends or associates."

"He came in many times?"

"Tattooing is a slow process, Mr. Holmes," said MacDonald, suiting his action to the words. "You can't do it all in one day. Besides, he would come in for additional bits from time to time. Especially the grapes – from his talk with his friends, they commemorated something."

"Could you describe his friends?"

"As I said, they seemed criminal types. Rough, some ex-military. Some of them received tattoos as well. Many also showed scars or other signs of violent living. One has a tiger tattooed across his chest, with swords below. Big, burly man, with fair skin but a dark moustache. Scars on his forearms, like a knife fighter." He paused. "I didn't do the tiger."

"Do you have a name for that one?"

"Jenkins called him Tommy. I never learned his surname."

Holmes wrote in his notebook. "Any others?"

"There was another, a tall, thin one in his fifties, whom he called 'the Vicar'. Heavily tanned, spent a lot of time outside. I never believed he was really a man of the cloth. I did a Pegasus on his right shoulder. As far as I know that's his only ink.

"Once he brought in a woman, called her Meg. Maybe thirty or thirty-five years old. Voluptuous figure. She got a small tattoo on her right shoulder, a heart surrounded by flowers. She was quite pretty, and expensively dressed, and seemed possessed of a native intelligence despite a clear lack of education. Curly red hair, freckles, Celtic type. She tried to put on a posh accent, but I could hear the Cockney underneath it."

"Where might I find this Tommy, or Meg, or the Vicar?"

"I think they were all from the same area, knew each other – at least professionally. Meg flirted with Jenkins – but then, she flirted with me as well. Bold as brass, she was."

"Could you possibly sketch her tattoo for me?"

Mr. MacDonald looked at him and smiled. "Ah, that's my professional work, Mr. Holmes."

Holmes nodded. "Would half-a-pound be fair?"

The artist nodded, again stirring his ink. "For half-a-pound, I'll draw you Tommy's tiger, too. But it'll take a while. You'll have to come back for it." He gestured toward the man in the chair. "I have a paying client now."

"Of course," Holmes agreed. "I'll come back for the sketches tomorrow. Might I ask you another question or two while you work?"

The artist nodded. "You may." He set the ink on a table, then took up an apparatus unlike any I'd ever seen. It comprised what appeared to be a needle with an electric cord and motor, and a large housing above. He closed a switch, and the machine began to buzz in his hand.

"This is a prototype," he explained to me. "Once it's perfected, I intend to apply for a patent."

"Do you have any idea what this Meg does?"

"Isn't it obvious, Mr. Holmes? I took her to be a – lady of the evening."

"And Tommy, with the tiger tattoo?"

"Tommy's a big man, much taller than Jenkins – taller than yourself, and powerfully built. Dark hair, lots of it. He has a handlebar moustache, much like my own, and dresses well, but his speech is coarse. From the conversation, it seemed he and Jenkins worked together."

"How about the Vicar?"

"Posh accent – speaks like a toff. Educated. Well-dressed. Not as coarse as the others, but . . . ." he let his voice trail off.

"Criminal, you think?" Holmes paused his writing.

"Let's just say, for a Vicar, he might not enter into the Kingdom of God." He began applying the buzzing needle to his client's back. "Is there anything else I can answer for you?"

"Not at this time, thank you," Holmes closed the notebook. He proffered a half-sovereign. "You've been quite helpful, sir. Let me know if ever I can return the favour."

The artist waved it away. "Pay me when you come back tomorrow. If I need a favour I will come to you."

We left the studio and climbed the narrow stairs. "Where now?" I asked.

Holmes hailed a cab. "Pall Mall. I shall ask my brother to open some doors for me regarding military records."

We spent well over an hour in the government offices, with Holmes's elder brother Mycroft sending notes to certain functionaries in the Army records. It was late afternoon when we emerged again into the chilling London winter. It took only moments to get a cab, which I directed to my house.

In the hansom, I gazed out at the snowy, muddy city. The pale December sun was low in the sky, and the chill breeze bit at any exposed skin. Evening was drawing near. Mary would be expecting me home soon – and bursting with curiosity as to what we had learned.

Holmes sat quietly for a time, as was his wont. Then, as we approached my home, he suddenly turned to me. "Watson," he said, "Tomorrow I must go out alone and undertake some delicate investigations."

I chuckled. "I was about to say that tomorrow I have several patients to see, and will be occupied much of the day. I may come by in the evening to see how you got on."

He nodded. "I may be there, I may not. Some of the people I must speak with are – unpredictable, at best."

I nodded as the cab rattled to a stop. "Well, then, best of luck, and I shall hope to see you on the morrow."

Friday morning found the muddy streets of London whitewashed and frozen under a fresh coat of snow, making the city look like something from a Dickens novel. The sky was a bright overcast, the clouds diffusing the weak sunlight into a pale, directionless illumination. There was no fog, but the rime on the sidewalks and streets required careful steps.

After a hearty English breakfast with my wife, fortified with two cups of hot coffee, I advised her that I might be late coming home. I bundled up heavily, took my medical bag, and began my rounds. The day passed quickly and uneventfully – two of my patients suffering from the Russian flu were recovering well, but the third – the widow Mrs. Bellows, in her seventies – had developed an ominous rattle in her lungs. As with the other flu patients, there was little I could do besides tell her servants to keep her comfortable and warm. I feared she wouldn't live to see 1890, but a few days away.

Remembering that Holmes might be quite late, I saved my visit to Emily for last. The sun was a grey glow in the west, and the gaslights made halos in the gathering fog when I climbed the familiar steps. Mrs. Hudson greeted me warmly. "Mr. Holmes isn't in yet, Doctor, but Emily is fair bursting to tell you how well she feels! I've a supper for you if you haven't eaten yet, and I'll bring it up if you like."

"Mrs. Hudson, you are an angel," I beamed at her. "Let me see the girl first, and then I'll be up."

Emily was as Mrs. Hudson had said, lively and without a sign of illness. Her eyes sparkled as she spoke quite animatedly, telling me all about how good she felt and how she was ready to get back to work. I checked her thoroughly and happily pronounced her fit as a fiddle.

I was about to leave when she put her small hand on my arm. "Doctor?"

"Yes?" I returned my stethoscope to my bag and waited.

"Do you remember when I first came here?"

I nodded. "'Twas the winter of '83, wasn't it? You were about ten years old, and Wiggins brought you in."

She nodded slowly, her eyes shining. "My Pa was a sailor. He'd gone away and would be months at least. Me mum – she was, was . . . ." She trailed off, not wanting to admit how her mother had earned her food and a corner in a tiny, filthy room in Spitalfields.

I nodded. "I understand."

She pressed on. "But me mum 'ad just died. I don't even know as 'ow – just that she'd been sick. I'd nowhere to go, and Mr. Palfrey wanted to take me to 'is 'ouse, but I'd 'eard tell of 'im from the other gels . . . 'ow 'e's not right wi' them . . . ." Her speech, long refined under Mrs. Hudson's tutelage, was reverting back to her origins.

"And that's when Wiggins brought you here?"

"Aye, sir. Wiggins, 'e's a good boy, 'innie?"

"He is, dear lass, he is."

"An' so 'andsome!" I tried not to betray my surprise, for I'd never thought of Wiggins that way. Her eyes gazed earnestly into mine. "I'll never see me Pa again, will I? 'E won' even know as where to look fer me."

I patted her hand where it rested on mine. "There's always hope, my dear. I rather think Mr. Holmes could find him, if you ask."

She shook her head. "Me Pa used ter beat me – me an' me mum both, when 'e 'ad a belly full o' gin. 'E'd get so mean . . . ." She looked away for a moment, then back into my eyes. "I don't want ter be 'is daughter any more, any'ow." A long pause, heavy with emotion. "I wish you were me Pa, Doctor."

I was, for once, at a loss for words. I fear my mouth dropped open, then closed and opened soundlessly.

"Oh, now I've gone an' done it, ain' I? I've ruint it!" She squeezed my hand desperately, fighting tears. "I'm so sorry, Doctor. I'm so sorry! I shouldna' said anyfing!"

Gathering my wits, I managed to squeeze her hand back. "No, my dear, you haven't ruined anything . . . I'm so honored . . . but, but . . . I can't be your Papa."

"You wouldn't have to do anything!" she said quickly, her diction returning. "Just . . . maybe someday, when I get married . . . could you walk me down the aisle?"

At this I had to blink back tears of my own, lest she see how deeply she had touched me. "My dear girl – it would be my greatest honor." I leaned forward to kiss her forehead. "I give you my solemn promise: When that day comes, I shall be there for you. Now get some rest."

She leaned back against the pillows, shining like the sun, wiping happy tears from her eyes. "Thank you, Doctor."

"No, dear Emily – thank you." I rose, trying not to appear hurried, and took my leave. I needed a snifter of good brandy and a pipe before Holmes got in.

Mrs. Hudson stood in the hallway, and the door was open. There was no way she could have missed the conversation. "Doctor . . . ." She touched my arm, her own eyes looking at me brightly.

Victorian society allows men many privileges, and women very few. Of the few, perhaps the greatest one denied to men is display of the softer emotions. I managed to give Mrs. Hudson a thin smile. "I'll have that supper now, thank you." I could feel her eyes on my back as I turned to climb the stairs.

Some hours later, after a fine meal, two pipes, and several

newspapers, I finally heard Holmes's familiar tread on the steps. He hung up his coat, hat, and heavy winter muffler, and collapsed on the settee, charging his cherry-wood pipe.

"I say, Holmes, have you eaten?"

He waved a dismissive hand. "Soon. I have tobacco and I have data."

"What have you learned?"

"Our body from the Serpentine was Sergeant James Jenkins of the British India Army. He served under a Major Sebastian Moran, who is a crack shot and a famous tiger hunter. This is the same man later promoted Colonel, whom I suspect in – well, other things. We have crossed paths before.

"Jenkins was discharged dishonorably after a court-martial for his mistreatment of the natives, which nearly led to a small armed rebellion. Others included Corporal Thomas Boyce and a chaplain, Lt. Peter Garber. There were indications against Moran, but not enough to charge him."

"Corporal Thomas Boyce," I mused. "His friend Tommy. And the Vicar would be Garber?"

Holmes lit his pipe, nodding. "I'd wager so. The records mentioned Boyce's tiger tattoo for identification."

"What's the next step, then?"

"I want to track down Boyce, and Garber – the Vicar. And Meg as well. Now that we have names and descriptions, if they're in London – as I believe they are – it shouldn't be too hard. I've set the Irregulars to combing Stepney. I expect we'll have some answers soon. In the meantime, some food and sleep wouldn't be amiss."

Answers came early the following morning, in a report from one of the Irregulars, a lad of about fourteen named Gus. He had ginger hair, tattered clothes that had once been colorful, and shoes that showed the toes of his socks. As I entered 221b he was talking to Holmes, cap in hand, and his eyes alertly darted in my direction. Moments later he slipped past me, quickly and quietly, clutching several shillings.

Holmes turned to me as I poured my coffee. "Tommy Boyce has been located, with Meg. The Irregulars followed them, by relay, from a pub to a lodging house near Shoreditch. They seem to be something more than friends. I have the address of the lodging house."

"Do you intend to beard the lion in his den?" My coffee was barely warm.

"Outside it, rather. Mr. Boyce seems to be quite a dangerous man, and I'd sooner not give him that advantage. Would you and your revolver be so kind as to accompany me?"

I set down the coffee cup. "We'd best get moving if we're to catch him."

As he often did, Holmes talked of anything but the matter at hand during the ride. He had the jarvey stop two blocks from the lodging house, and we walked the remaining distance at a brisk pace.

The lodging house was shabby outside, though it would have been expensive fifty years before. The wrought-iron porch railing was hung with icicles, and a man's footprints in the snow descended the steps from the door. Holmes pointed out one smeared footprint that marked where the walker had slipped. His sudden grip on the railing had broken loose several icicles, which lay in the snowbank below.

As the footprints suggested, we were too late. A young pedlar, selling bread from a cart, knew my friend instantly, and reported that "Tommy Boy" had hailed a cab but a few minutes previously, telling the driver to take him to the Anglo-Indian Club.

"What was he wearing?" Holmes asked.

"A heavy dark grey overcoat, green trousers, and a dark grey top hat. Carried a black stick."

"Well done!" Holmes gave the pedlar some coins, and he promptly rolled his cart away, his mission completed.

"Shall we go to the club?"

"Are you a member of the Anglo-Indian?"

I smiled. "I can certainly become one – or at least make enquiries to that end."

"Good old Watson!" He clapped me on the shoulder, then thought for a moment. "Here we shall part ways. You go to the club, and watch for someone meeting his description, but be discreet. The club wouldn't admit me. I shall see if I can speak with Meg. I expect that she is substantially less dangerous than 'Tommy Boy'."

"Do have a care. Women can be dangerous as well."

"I shall endeavour to keep that in mind." He climbed the steps and I turned to hail a passing cab.

In truth, I had no idea exactly where the Anglo-Indian Club was located, but luck was with me, as the driver did know. He drove me to a large Georgian building in Mayfair, and I pretended that I knew exactly where I was going.

Once inside the door, I enquired about membership. I affirmed that I had indeed served in India, giving my regiment and the name of my commander, and mentioned the Jezail bullet that I received at the Battle of Maiwand. With this established, the secretary for membership agreed that I was eligible and offered me a tour of the premises. Among other things, it included a large room filled with card tables and smoke. There were far too many men for me to hazard an effective guess, so I tried a long shot.

"I say! Is that Boyce over there?" I tilted my head generally in the direction of the far wall.

"Boyce? Yes, that's him, partnered with Colonel Moran in the corner. Do you know him?"

"I've met him once or twice," I said quickly, "but he probably wouldn't remember me." Now knowing where to look, I focused on a corner table near the fireplace, where a tall and burly dark-haired man sat at whist across from a heavyset, balding man with a ferocious ginger moustache. I made a quick note of Boyce's green trousers and wine-red waistcoat.

We completed the tour without further incident, and I asked if I might buy a drink and consider my options. The secretary was only too happy to leave me in the card room, lingering over my brandy, and return to his duties.

A short time later there was a triumphant cry from the corner, and Boyce and Moran shook hands across the table whilst their defeated opponents gathered their dignity and left. Moran seemed eager for another rubber, but there were no takers, so he and Boyce sat and talked.

Figuring that they could very well spend the remainder of the day and night at whist, I took my leave of the club and returned home.

I didn't see Holmes again that day. It was well past midnight, and I was asleep in my own bed, when I heard a noise from downstairs. Knowing that our servants should also be abed, I took my revolver from the bedside table and, in my dressing-gown, crept quietly down the stairs.

The scent of familiar tobacco notified me, even before I saw him, that the intruder was Sherlock Holmes. He was calmly having a pipe in my sitting room, apparently awaiting my arrival.

"But why are you here now?" I asked.

"I believe I was followed upon leaving Stepney. I didn't wish to return to Baker Street immediately."

I creased my brow. "So you led them here?"

He smiled. "No – I'm certain that I eluded my tracker. I came here because they would expect me to return to Baker Street. I would rather let them enjoy a fruitless vigil in the cold, watching in vain for my return." He chuckled. "It is one of my maxims that one must never do what one's enemy expects one to do."

With this I smiled and relaxed. I stoked the fire, and apprised him of my success in locating and identifying Boyce, as well as his apparent partnership with Colonel Moran.

"Capital!" he enthused. "We now have his daytime haunt – or one of them – as well as Meg's location, where he seems to spend at least some evenings. Should we lose him, I'd wager we can pick up his trail at one location or the other. And Moran's involvement – it may be the reason for my follower," he finished mysteriously. Then he looked up suddenly. "Have you anything to eat? I'm quite famished."

I brought a plate of cold meat and cheese from the kitchen and opened a bottle of wine while he filled me in on his own discoveries. "I was able to meet with Meg, and we had a rather tense conversation. Her full name is Marguerite Collins. I introduced myself as Mr. Justin Smithers, a solicitor representing Jenkins. I learned as much from what she didn't say as from what she did. Her story was badly organised, inconsistent, and full of clumsy lies."

Between bites he continued. "I shan't repeat her lies, as that would be a waste of time. Instead, this is what I have concluded:

"Meg was orphaned at a young age, and like so many poor but pretty girls she turned to the only trade that paid her well. She was known as 'Kerbstone Meg' when she began, but quickly left that name behind. She was smart enough to avoid too much gin and opium, and formidable enough, in her own way, that she remained her own person. She met both Tommy Boy – as she called Boyce – and Jenkins shortly after their return from India, and was introduced to the Vicar – Garber – not long thereafter. She is a very comely woman, and it seems both Boyce and Jenkins were quite taken with her charms. As she isn't one to limit herself, she shared her favours with both of them. They seem to have accepted this, knowing her profession."

He finished his wine and refilled the glass. "Both Boyce and Jenkins made their living within the criminal underworld since returning from India. They fit into places in a vast puzzle I have been assembling, bit by bit, for years – as does Colonel Moran, who is incidentally an extremely dangerous man.

"It seems, also, that Garber – 'the Vicar' – had animosity toward Jenkins and Boyce, though I haven't learned the cause.

"She hadn't heard of Jenkins' fate, and was quite distraught when I informed her. Rather than sorrow at the news, she showed signs of fury. Her fists clenched suddenly, and she said something under her breath that I couldn't make out. I would wager she has some idea who killed Jenkins, but I could elicit no more information from her after that. Even her lies stopped, and I excused myself and left, advising her that I would return at a more opportune time." He paused, wiped his mouth with a napkin, and pushed the tray away.

I cogitated on this briefly. "So 'Gurkha Jim' Jenkins worked for a criminal organisation."

"Hardly surprising, eh? Perhaps several. MacDonald was correct. He seems to have been available on contract to anyone who would pay his price – though 'Tommy Boy' has apparently chosen a team – which may be why Jenkins is dead and he isn't."

I nodded. "Live by the sword, die by the sword. Or the *kukri*. You mentioned Garber's ill feelings. Do you think Garber killed him?"

"It's possible. I haven't enough data yet to be certain. I have set the Irregulars on the hunt for him this time." Holmes filled his pipe. "One more thing you should know about Meg: She is sick, very sick. Coughs, and her breath rattles. If I were a medical man, I should say she is suffering from the Russian flu, like so many."

"Good God, Holmes!" I said. "You must go and sterilise your hands immediately with carbolic acid!"

He waved it away, lighting his pipe. "Never fear! I stopped at Barts on the way home to do exactly that. It's a good job that a hospital never closes, eh?"

"Indeed," said I. "So what do we do now?"

"As there is probably someone watching my Baker Street rooms, with your permission, Watson, I shall spend the night here. I will be perfectly comfortable in this chair. You should probably return to your lovely wife, who may be awake and worried about you."

I hadn't thought of this, being too distracted with the story of Meg and Tommy Boy. Leaving Holmes gazing into a low fire, I took my revolver and returned to my bed, where Mary was still fast asleep.

When I woke on Sunday Holmes was gone, leaving never a sign of his nocturnal presence. Indeed, I almost thought I had dreamed the whole conversation, when there came a ring at my door. It was a boy delivering a telegram:

Watson: New development. I shall pick you up at 10 a.m. sharp. Bring your revolver.

S.H.

As it was after 9:30, I hurried through my morning ablutions and downed a hasty poached egg and cup of coffee. By ten a.m. I was on my doorstep, gazing at the freshly-fallen snow, when a hansom rattled up almost on the minute.

Holmes greeted me. "I got a wire from Inspector Jones at the Yard. There is a dead body in Stepney, outside the address where I met Meg."

"Is she dead?" I asked.

"Not she," he replied. "The police haven't yet identified the victim, but I believe it to be Tommy Boy."

Due to the fresh snowfall, the ride took longer than usual, but Inspector Athelney Jones had taken charge of the scene and managed to keep the crowd at bay. Any usable footprints had been long since trampled into slush by both the police and the civilians who had summoned them.

The body, at least, was still *in situ*, and Holmes muttered something about small favours. Still in his green trousers and grey overcoat, the dead man lay on his back in a splash of bloodstained pink slush. I held back whilst Holmes examined the scene, and on his signal moved forward to examine the body itself, which was stone cold. I confirmed his identity by opening his shirt – revealing the tiger on his chest as described by Sutherland MacDonald. "Definitely Boyce. From the temperature and the *rigor*, he has been dead at least six hours – killed sometime after midnight."

The cause of death was quite apparent – his throat showed a broad and deep puncture wound, as if a spike had been driven into it.

"Curious," Holmes said. "Not a knife."

"No, not a knife – a knife would have made a flat cut, shaped like the blade. This is consistent with a spike instead. It entered from the left side, punctured the left carotid artery, and proceeded through the trachea. He clearly bled to death quickly, but his last moments would have been agonising."

Holmes looked up at Inspector Jones, who shook his head. "My men have searched the area, but have found no spike, nor knife, crowbar, fire poker, nor any other apparent weapon here. Maybe the killer took it with him."

I looked at Holmes. "Garber?" I asked.

He thought a moment. "Possibly," he said.

"Why?"

"For the same reason as Jenkins – if this is Garber's work. I suspect another, though." He addressed Jones. "Thank you, Inspector. Your men may remove the body now. I expect we can examine it later at the morgue."

"As you wish, Mr. Holmes," the inspector said. "Come, lads, let's take him away."

As the police loaded the body of Tommy Boyce into their wagon, Holmes looked at me brightly. "Now, Watson – have you had breakfast?'

"Barely," I said, somewhat taken aback.

"Join me for a quick repast, then," he smiled. "Let's let the police do their work."

We found a small cafe nearby and suffered through a meal of execrable quality. Even the coffee was odious – though it had the virtue of being inexpensive – and Holmes refused to tell me anything more about the killing. "All in good time," was all he would say.

Leaving the scene of a gastronomic crime, we retraced our steps to the site of the morning's murder, now devoid of police and spectators. Rather than spend any attention on the scene – marked only by a pale stain on the concrete – Holmes went directly up the steps and into the building. "Meg's flat is on the second floor," he said, and so we proceeded.

Though it was late morning, it took several knocks on the door before it opened. The woman inside had naturally curly red hair and an exquisitely heart-shaped face, and would have been quite fetching, even beautiful, had she not appeared sick near to death.

She took one look at Holmes. "Oh, Mr. Smithers," she said in a rattly whisper. "Do come in. I fear I'm somewhat worse than before." Her forehead was shiny, her eyes were glazed with fever, and her rooms had the familiar sick smell.

She gestured toward me. "Who's this?"

"I've brought a doctor," he said. "Will you let him examine you?"

Suddenly I felt unprepared. "Hol – um, Smithers – I don't need to examine this woman to diagnose her," I said. "She has a severe case of the Russian flu. Quite serious." Honestly, having avoided the disease myself, I was reluctant to approach her without my kit.

Holmes merely nodded. "Please, Miss Collins, rest yourself. I have just a few questions, if I may."

She almost collapsed onto a rose-pink velvet settee and we took chairs near at hand. I noticed that the room was expensively furnished in excellent taste. "If you can make it quick, sir, I should be grateful."

Holmes steepled his fingers. After a brief pause, he asked, "First, then – where is the icicle?"

I was puzzled by this question, but she gave a rattling laugh. "So you know it all, then?"

"In the main, yes. I should appreciate if you can help me fill in the missing details."

"The icicle is melted," she said, and almost cackled. "There's no murder weapon."

He nodded again. "I thought as much. Was this planned or impromptu?"

"Let me call it," she breathed, "a weapon of convenience. How did you know?"

"There is a row of icicles hanging from the railing of your steps," he said. "Some were broken off. The wound in Tommy Boyce's throat is consistent with a conical spike, which is exactly the wound an icicle would have made. Why did you do it?"

"Because Tommy killed my love – Gurkha Jim." Her breaths made her sentences short and broken. "How'd you know it was me, then?"

"I didn't, or at least I wasn't certain," Holmes said, "until you confessed just now. But it seemed quite likely. Why did Tommy kill Gurkha Jim?"

"He was jealous – of our love. Wanted me." She coughed violently, gasped for breath. When she regained her breath she continued. "There was more. Tommy worked for someone – named Moran. He's part of – a bigger organisation. Right bad 'uns."

"I am familiar with Moran," Holmes said quietly, when she stopped to gasp for breath. "Pray continue."

"Tommy tried to get – Jim to join – them. But Jim wanted to – stay independent. I found out yestere'en – Moran told Tommy that – Jim knew too much. That's why he did it.

"He thought I wouldn't – find him out. Thought I would turn to him – for comfort." She paused, bosom heaving. "It almost worked. It might have – if I weren't sick." She looked at me. "But the doctor can tell you – " And here she was racked with a sudden coughing fit. " – that I haven't the time to lose. I won't live long enough – to meet Jack Ketch." She coughed again, then weakly wiped her mouth with a handkerchief.

"She's right, Holmes," I said. "I've seen this in a number of patients. This woman would be lucky to live another twenty-four hours."

Holmes looked at me, then at Meg. "So knowing your time was short, you took your own justice. Avenged Gurkha Jim with an icicle."

Meg nodded, smiled weakly. "Call it – cold revenge."

"Watson, is there anything you can do for her?"

I felt Meg's shining eyes on me.

"Nothing. Even had I my kit, all I might do is give her some opium to ease her discomfort. I have seen too many patients in this condition this winter." I met her gaze. "I'm sorry."

"I'm not," she said. "I have my vengeance." She drew a rattling breath. "You gents should go – before you get sick."

I stood up. "She's right, Holmes. Every minute we spend here is a risk."

Holmes rose. "Thank you for your honesty, Meg. Would you like me to send a man of the church?"

She almost laughed. "Why? Murder is – a mortal sin. There is no – redemption for me." She shook her head slowly. "Just let me – die in peace."

"Let me assure you," I said, "that you are not a murderess. You didn't murder an innocent man. You executed a killer."

Something came over her face – something like relaxation – as she contemplated those words. "The Vicar – will pay me a call – later."

Holmes opened the door. "I shall send the police in a day or two – to look after you."

We stepped outside and he closed the door softly.

"What do you say to that, Watson?" he asked as we walked quietly down the stairs. "A strange sort of justice, isn't it?"

"Strange indeed," I replied. "But still it feels like justice."

He opened the outer door. "It's almost a new year, my friend. But Moran will bear much more watching."

"A new decade, Holmes. I wonder what the 1890's will bring. I would wish merely for this plague to be gone."

Snow was falling on the street as we walked outside.

NOTES

The author would like to gratefully dedicate this story to the current members of the Serpentine Swimming Club for their enthusiastic kindness and assistance with my research for this story, and to the memory of Mr. Arthur Hester, a fine tobacconist and cold-water swimmer, and Mr. Sutherland MacDonald, an extraordinary artist and inventor.

The photo and character of Mr. Hester are used by kind permission of his great-grandson, Bobby Baxter.

Arthur Hester

Sutherland MacDonald

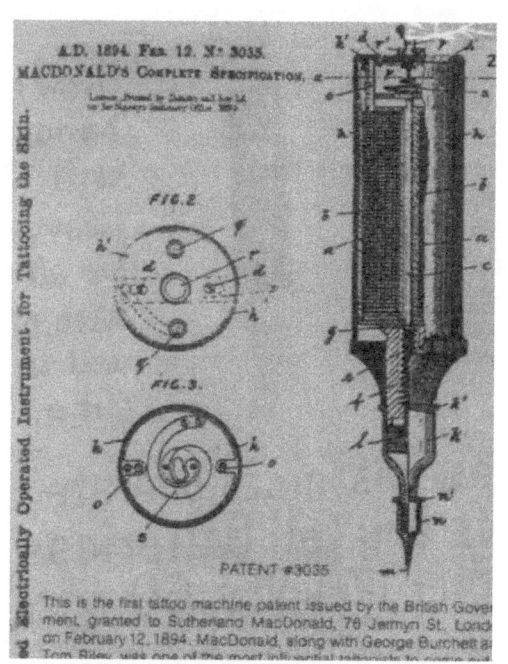

Sutherland MacDonald's 1894 patent for a tattoo machine:

The sign at Sutherland MacDonald's tattoo shop, 76 Jermyn Street

The Father Christmas Brigade
by David Marcum
for Marcia Wilson

"Mr. Holmes," said the young man, taking a sip of whisky and smiling, "if I'd had any sense, I would have asked you last Christmas to help me, but I tried to do it myself and muffed it, and I've had to wait a whole year for a second chance."

I considered this statement, and who he was, and hoped that he would soon explain what he meant.

I had stopped by about an hour earlier, late one afternoon, to wish my friend Sherlock Holmes the Compliments of the Season, and to catch up on those cases which were currently holding his attention. While I hadn't lost touch with him by any means after my marriage in the middle of the preceding year – my masses of notes and strained casebooks for 1889 and 1890 would easily attest to that – I had found that after the events of the recent autumn, as his ongoing campaign against Professor Moriarty's organization escalated, and also after an unexpected trip to Vienna in connection with Holmes's health which had threatened to shatter from the strain, it was a good idea to check on him, making certain that he was taking care of his body as well as his great mind.

I had been there some three-quarters of an hour, and our talk had ranged from his sincere interest in my growing practice and my wife's health to curious questions about aspects of my Paddington neighborhood, not far to the west (as he always wished to improve his encyclopedic knowledge of London). Finally we had caught up on a few of his more interesting investigations, and he smiled tolerantly as I jotted a few notes concerning the events connected to the Chamber Faith Swindle (of which I had read in the newspapers, not realizing Holmes's involvement), and the much more grim Healeyfield murders, where his examination of the murder weapon, an iron spike of ancient manufacture accidentally dropped by the killer, had led to a terrible confrontation in the Derwent Gorge with the man whom the newspapers called "The Writhing Watcher". I was sincerely disappointed that I had been unable to join him.

It was at that point in my visit that I began to think of departure, and of course Holmes noticed it. On past occasions when this point was reached, and he was in a garrulous mood, he might mention some other case, perhaps from his Montague Street days, tossed out as a conversational lure so that I might tarry just a bit longer. It was on such times as this that I'd heard of the last and most fatal disappearance of Able King of Crewe, and also the Seven Smiling Sisters – not pleasant women, as one might expect, but instead a series of seven turns and traps in a previously unmapped Yorkshire Cavern, where a Viking horde had been hidden long ago, and more importantly, where the two enterprising but ill-equipped brothers who had entered the earth to retrieve it had been rescued at nearly the last moment.

But today Holmes didn't tease any earlier cases, and I was preparing to rise with an eye toward walking back to Paddington when the doorbell rang. With a smile, I continued to my feet, crossing the room and refilling my glass at the sideboard. Holmes laughed and declined.

We both recognized Holmes's visitor, as he had been featured off-and-on in the newspapers for well over a year. It was John Oersted, the young heir to the Gravens fortune. It was a story that had captivated the public – and rightly so. Oersted had been an orphan, living on the streets of London after his parents had emigrated from Denmark to England in 1879 to obtain work, both sadly dying soon afterwards in a rail accident.

"They would sometimes leave me with a neighbor here in London," explained Oersted as he settled back in his seat with a comfortable measure of whisky, "while they traveled elsewhere, looking for work that suited them. Needless to say," he added with a sad smile, "we hadn't found the success we'd expected when we came here. Unfortunately, my parents had failed to carry out the necessary research before deciding to change countries. But we had no relatives left in Denmark, and they were seduced by the reports coming from England regarding the ever-increasing industrial successes."

His accent was a curious thing – more of a flat and featureless English than anything that reflected his original Danish upbringing, his years in London, both as a child and now, and the considerable time he'd more recently spent in America. It was as if he consciously and carefully monitored his speech so as to give no clue to his background. And yet, his story was so well known that it would certainly be rare that he might meet someone who didn't know who he was.

"It was on one such trip, to Liverpool and the surrounding areas, that my parents were killed – in the Burscough Junction collision, when the train to Ormskirk hit the Liverpool-to-Preston line. From what I've been able to learn, they died immediately. However, it was a number of days before I learned about it, as they weren't expected back home for a week or more. It was only when a man from the railway came to our lodgings that I heard anything. I was able to discover in later years that my parents weren't immediately identified, and by the time they were, they had already been buried in Burscough.

"The family who had been watching out for me was generally sympathetic, but the father – a hard and dark-tempered man – made it clear that he couldn't afford to feed another mouth, so I was turned out of both his home, and my parents' rooms as well, only able to carry a change of clothes. I watched as the landlord locked the door behind me, with all that we had brought with us from Denmark. He planned to retain it to pay the back rent – or so he claimed, but my parents had never been late with the rent. So at age eleven, I found myself living on the streets of the East End."

It was a fascinating story, especially knowing as we did what happened next, but I was unsure why he felt the need to explain it to us, instead of immediately telling Holmes why he was there. However, as Oersted continued to speak, it gradually became clear.

"In those days, as both you gentlemen know, the East End was not quite as terrible as it became – and fortunately I was long gone before the Autumn of Terror a couple of years ago. As you can imagine, I followed the story very much in the American newspapers, and when I was able to return to England, that area became the focus of my work." By which he meant his altruistic charitable efforts where he used his inherited fortune to try and improve the abominable conditions facing the residents of the East End. Some had tried to say that this was as fruitless as Canute attempting to command the waves of the sea, but in fact young Oersted was making a difference, his wealth and resources having arrived at a time when there was a sincere interest in improvement in that district, following the awareness that came because of the Ripper Murders.

"As a young boy living by his wits, I didn't do half badly. I worked small jobs throughout the East End when I could find them – unloading for the merchants, running errands and messages, and so on. Once or twice, Mr. Holmes, I was on the periphery of a couple of your investigations – Oh, we never met, but I was friends with one of your Irregulars, and he recruited me as something of a day laborer. His name was Joe Mancot. I believe that he died in the mid-eighties, after I'd gone to America."

Holmes nodded, his expression grim. I'm afraid that I'd never heard of that particular lad, but I suspected that there was some tragic story related to the boy's passing which Holmes might or might not ever share.

"It was through Joe that my life changed, gentlemen – and that's also the reason that I'm here tonight."

He finished the last sip of whisky, declined a refill, and continued.

"It was Christmas 1883, and by then I was fourteen, and not doing too badly. I had a room in the back of a small mission for the poor, run by a brother and sister. I had a friend – Joe – whom I'd met that fall, and there was talk that I could join him again at some point on one of your investigations, Mr. Holmes – possibly even become one of the Irregulars – although truth be told, I kept myself busy enough with the small jobs that I found and what help I gave around the mission.

"It was seemingly like any other day, but Joe asked if I was going that night to the Father Christmas party, held at the back of The White Hart. I'd never heard anything about it, but he insisted that I accompany him. He explained that we were a little old to attend, but that it would be good fun. And fun, gentlemen, was rare enough in that quarter that I was willing to go out of my way to find a little.

"As you both certainly know, a walk through the East End at Christmas-time looks nothing like a similar stroll down Oxford Street. The decorations in the West End, and the efforts that the stores make – the window displays, the foods, the ostentatious gifts! – Why, it's enough to make a man wonder if some of us will ever recognize the random inequities that are visited upon each of us. When I see the difference between the two Londons, so different and jammed side-by-side, I am amazed and dismayed. 'There, but for the Grace of God' I want to tell everyone – for I have seen both sides, and I know."

His voice drifted off for a moment, as if the work that he had taken on, in trying to help the downtrodden of the capital, was sometimes overwhelming and discouraging. But then he returned to his tale.

"Joe and I went to the pub, and it was a break in the daily routine that we each faced. The front was filled with its usual patrons, but at the back were crowded about two-dozen children, all quite poor, and many of them immigrants, as I had been – some looking frightened, and a number of others having no idea what was happening, as I doubt that they could even speak English. Around the periphery were their parents, some adding to the forced festivity of the moment, and others looking suspicious, or as confused as their own offspring.

"A man – I took him to be the owner of the pub – made a little speech, and then he called forth from a back room a tall man dressed as Father Christmas, who lumbered out, laughing loudly and crying 'Happy Christmas! Happy Christmas to all!' Then he set down a heavy sack which had been slung over his shoulder, bent over, and began to distribute little wrapped gifts to the children surrounding him.

"It was all sincerely for the best, but of course the children were more puzzled than anything, and a few looked as if they might cry. But after the gifts were distributed – and not a child made an effort to open his or hers just then – Father Christmas again delved into the sack and brought forth a number of treats, consisting of candies of all colors and flavors. This the children understood, and from their initial tentative response, they quickly progressed to smiles and laughter, having more of that type of thing in their hands that night than they'd probably ever held before in their entire lives.

"Joe and I were too old for such things, and we stayed at the edge, just watching and enjoying what was happening. I wanted to remember what I'd seen so as to tell Mr. and Mrs. Mullingar, who ran the mission, all about it, thinking that if a few spare coins could be saved back, something similar might be done for the children that we saw on a regular basis.

"Although we hadn't intended to do anything but watch, Father Christmas came our way and pressed a few pieces of candy into our hands as well. I felt that he gave me something of an extra look then, but thought nothing about it. Then, seeing as things were winding down, Joe and I stepped outside, where we stood under the gas-lamp and continued to eat the treats while we talked about what we'd seen. As you may remember, Mr. Holmes, Joe had a good heart, and if he hadn't been killed, I wonder if he might not have found a way into the ministry.

"'Oersted,' he said, for he always called me by my last name, 'tell me the truth – aren't you glad that you joined me?'

"Before I could answer, however, someone behind me said, 'Oersted? What's your first name, lad?'

"I turned to find that Father Christmas had come up behind us without our knowledge. I strangely felt no threat, and by then my instincts were quite good, so I answered his question.

"'John, sir. Originally Johannes, before my parents brought me here. To England.'

"'Would that have been in '79?'

"'Yes,' I replied, now becoming a bit puzzled, if not outright suspicious.

"'Were your parents Agner and Lise Oersted?'

"This time I simply nodded.

"'Then,' Father Christmas said, 'Some friends of your parents have been trying to find you, lad. After their deaths, you vanished. Do you have any objection to meeting them?'

"Dumbly I shook my head, and when asked, I informed him that I could be found at the Mullingar's mission, near the Boy's and Girl's School in Hanbury Street. Father Christmas said he knew of the place, and he would let my parents' friends know where to find me.

"Well, gentlemen, you probably know what happened next – it has been featured enough in the newspapers. The next day, Erling Gravens and his wife, Vada, came to the mission. They were a childless couple who had long before gone to America, where Erling made a fortune. They had no living relatives – except for me, the child of Erling's distant cousin, the late Agner Oersted. They wished to adopt me. And so, with the amazed encouragement of the Mullingar's, I barely had time to pack my meager possessions before I was in a room at the Langham and being outfitted with clothes for the journey to the United States. I never had a chance to see or say goodbye to Joe, and within days we were at the coast, and just a few weeks later, I was installed in their home along Fifth Avenue in Manhattan.

"To make a long story short, Erling had no hesitation at fully accepting me as his heir and adopted son. Both he and Vada were as good to me as they could be, and I loved them nearly as much as the true parents that I'd lost. Erling set about involving me in all the aspects of the management of his fortune, and it turned out that I had an aptitude for it. And when they were both unexpectedly killed two years ago in the Tariffville train disaster, terribly mimicking the type of tragedy that took my parents, I unexpectedly found myself as the heir to the Gravens fortune, and all that went with it.

"I had been trained well, and in truth with good managers, much of the affairs take care of themselves. During my time in America, I realized that many of the great fortunes were maintained and curated in this way, with the rich allowing a pilot to steer their financial ship while they lived off the proceeds in all sorts of manners, ranging from essentially harmless to detrimental and dissipated. As my life there seemed to be fencing me into such an existence as well, my thoughts turned more and more to the work of the Mullingars, and others like them. So in the middle of last year, I returned to England.

"It's nothing for the owners of the great American fortunes to jump up and travel the world, so I haven't been missed over there. But while the rest of them rotate between their main New York residences and similar gargantuan palaces scattered elsewhere in the United States, or make grand tours of the European capitals, I've rather vanished from their circles, staying quite busy here in London.

"I have been in the newspapers more than I'd like, but it's been useful enough in its own way, calling attention a bit to the charitable work that we're hoping to accomplish. And I must report that so far, things have been moving along quite well. But there is one thing that I've wanted to accomplish, and last year when I tried, I failed."

"You wished to identify Father Christmas," said Holmes.

"Exactly, and to do so in a way that will not spoil what he is doing by throwing bright light on it before I understand who and what it's all about."

"And he is still up to the same business as before you left?"

"He is, as I confirmed before I went looking for him last Christmas. When I returned to England in the middle of '89, I stayed busy setting up the various programs that I'd been planning, but as the weather turned colder, I began to recall that Christmas of 1883, and how the unexpected intervention of Father Christmas had so changed my life. Naturally I was curious as to his true identity – I've never stopped wondering about that. But I also recalled that little gathering in the back of the dark pub, and those small children who had no idea what was happening, somewhere between confusion and fear, and then the shared joy on their faces when the good Father started distributing candy. I want to help his work, small in scale as it is, but I can't just burst in and unmask him, and offer a vast amount of money for him to buy more and more candy. That would spoil it somehow, and that's the last thing I want to occur. No, this is a small but precious thing, and I want to do it right – or, if I learn what I can and determine that my involvement would ruin it, I want to slip away and allow it to continue without it ever being known that I have any interest."

"And you said that your efforts didn't go as planned last year," said Holmes, crossing his legs.

"I did." Oersted smiled. "Last year, my first Christmas back. A few weeks before Christmas, I went alone to The White Hart, to ask if Father Christmas still gave gifts to the children a few days before the holiday. Of course, I've learned to disguise myself somewhat as I go about the East end, as a man wearing the habiliments of the Graven fortune's heir attracts too much attention.

"I learned that indeed Father Christmas did still visit each year, and the word had already started to spread for the parents to have their children there on the twenty-first – but the pub owner became reticent when I seemed too curious, particularly about the man's true identity. Next I asked around amongst some of the people that I've met since my return, and some were aware of Father Christmas's visits to the pub, and others were not. Curiously, I also learned that there are a few other pubs in the district that also have visits by Father Christmas on the same night.

"Last year, on the night of the twenty-first, I was at The White Hart when the children and their parents began to arrive. As they gathered in the back, I drifted that way too. To those watching, I might have been a curious patron, or a relative. After a few minutes, the scene played out almost exactly as it had in 1883 – Father Christmas arrived, and there was some suspicion and confusion. Gifts were passed around, and then candy and treats, which seemed to be the universal language wherein any concerns were removed. I found that my eyes had filled with tears as I looked to the wall where Joe and I had stood then. I was filled with regret that I'd never had the chance to see him again, or let him know what his friendship had meant to me, or that he'd been unable to fulfill his own potential – for he always had a good heart.

"I said that the scene was almost exactly like the small party I'd attended before my own life changed, but there was one difference: Where before Father Christmas had been a tall man, he was now much shorter, but no less jolly. From what I've heard and read, Mr. Holmes, I have no doubt that you could have identified much from him that I missed, but all I could see was a man in a costume, his face thoroughly obscured by a thick, white, false beard.

"When Joe and I had attended the affair in '83, we had left before it was entirely over, but this time I stayed to the end, as Father Christmas displayed his empty sack to the children, wished a Happy Christmas to everyone, and then retreated to the rear room from whence he'd initially appeared. I finished my beer and stepped outside to wait for Father Christmas, but when he didn't appear – either in costume, or as a man of the same height who might likely be him – I realized that he must have gone out the back entrance. I made my way quickly around the block into the mews in time to see him, still in costume, making good time along Osborn Street. I tried to follow him for a few minutes, but I lost him. I wondered afterwards if he suspected that he was being followed and intentionally took turns down side streets and alleys in order to disappear.

"In the following days, I asked more questions, both at The White Hart and other Whitechapel pubs where I'd heard that Father Christmas also gives gifts to children. Nothing could be determined. Either they don't know who the fellow is, or they're deliberately obfuscating his identity.

"As my daily tasks continued to take up my time, I gradually stopped trying to track him down – and then the weather turned cool again, and eventually as thoughts turned to Christmas, so too did my interest in identifying Father Christmas, both to assist in his work if possible, and also to thank him for the intervention in my own life that led me to where I am now."

"But you said that it was a different man last year," I said. "Do you intend to thank him, whomever he might be? Before he was tall, and now he is short."

"That's true – or I believe it to be true. But then again, I was much shorter myself in 1883, so perhaps my perspective changed. The only way to know is to speak with him, but to do that he must be found, and then I must decide if my asking and potential involvement will perhaps spoil something good that should not be spoiled."

He looked back toward Holmes. "As I said, Mr. Holmes, I was one of your irregular Irregulars on a couple of instances – Oh, we never met, but I knew from Joe that the man we were following was important to one of your investigations. That's why, when I returned to London, I remained interested and aware of the work that you do, and have followed what mention there is of you and your investigations in the newspaper. It was with great enjoyment, then, that I read of your investigation into the stolen Indian treasure and the river chase, which was published earlier this year."

I glanced at Holmes to see his reaction, as he hadn't been overly pleased with either that volume, *The Sign of the Four,* or the previous narrative that had been published in late 1887, *A Study in Scarlet.* However, in spite of the comments that he regularly shared with me, the author, about his dim views on the subject, he chose to withhold them while conferring with his client.

"I especially enjoyed the segment," continued Oersted, "where you and the doctor, along with the dog, trailed the one-legged man across London and down to the boat-yard. Recalling that, I realized that you were both exactly whom I needed to follow Father Christmas, hopefully identifying him to the point where I can speak to him and see if I can provide any assistance."

Holmes shifted in his seat. "And it is your intention to assist this Father Christmas in his work?"

"I assure you that is my purpose, should that prove to be the best help to him," Oersted replied. "But first he must be found – and I'm convinced that you should do it instead of me."

"What additional information have you gleaned? I cannot imagine that a man of your resources simply gave up after last year's attempt."

"All that I've been able to ascertain is that Father Christmas meets the poor children at a half-dozen pubs throughout the East End – here is a list . . . ." And he fished a folded sheet from his pocket, handing it to Holmes, who glanced at it and placed it on the small octagonal table beside his chair.

"And the next meeting?" Holmes asked.

"It will be tomorrow night – the twenty-first, as it always seems to be, based on my limited experience. I've confirmed that date with the different pub owners, but they – all of them – become quite cagy and reticent when I press as to who is playing the part of Father Christmas. Most of them don't recognize me, but one of them does know who I am, and he's as secretive on the subject as the others."

Holmes glanced my way. "What say you, Doctor? Shall we be at The White Hart tomorrow night at – ?"

"Seven o'clock," replied Oersted.

I nodded. "I wouldn't miss it." What I didn't mention was that I would certainly have my service revolver with me, as I had long ago learned never to leave home without it. I felt its comforting presence in my coat pocket even then as I was sitting there, pressed between me and the arm of my old chair. While this sounded like a story of good Christmas cheer,

I knew that, when joining Holmes on one of his investigations, anything might happen before things were settled. For instance, once he and I had been taken captive by a cabal of deaf men soon after buying a Christmas present for Mrs. Hudson.

Oersted seemed satisfied and provided us with an address in Holborn where he might be reached with our findings. Then he stood, shook our hands, and departed.

We listened until we heard the front door shut. Then we conversed, while still keeping our voices low – for just a few weeks before, a man had supposedly departed before slipping quietly back up the stairs, attempting to hear our discussion from the landing outside the sitting room door. We'd since verified that, with the transom shut as it usually was, nothing of a normal conversation could be heard through the thick door and walls, but it had still made us more careful.

As I sat back down, Holmes rose and stepped across to the shelves where his scrapbooks were placed. These commonplace volumes contained a mass of clippings, notes, and other curious ephemera, often exhaustively cross-referenced, providing very useful information about individuals and incidents related to Holmes's work. He devoted a significant amount of time toward their upkeep, but it had proven worthwhile upon countless occasions. At this time, however, nothing further was learned.

"I have no additional notes about Oersted's personal story – the death of his parents and the transformation into a fabulously rich young man – beyond what is already popularly known," Holmes explained. "That was certainly him – I've seen him in passing more than once – although I have no memory of ever hearing of him before he went to America in connection with any old cases. Since his return last year, he has done exactly as we've heard – devoted himself to bettering the conditions of those in the East End, and using his substantial funds in responsible and effective ways."

"Then his efforts to find Father Christmas are mostly likely sincere."

"Almost certainly. I can't imagine that we'll lead Oersted to the man's true residence and introduce them, only to have our client pull a pistol from his pocket while crying aloud about some grievance of a decade past which has culminated in this moment of vengeance."

"He doesn't seem the Count of Monte Cristo type," I confirmed. In earlier years, I might have withheld that comment and its literary reference, literally believing Holmes's statement not long after we met that he had no use for such references in his "brain attic", but I had since learned that he had been misrepresenting himself to a certain degree when we first met, and that in fact he was much more knowledgeable about things, including literature, than I had first credited him, believing then that his knowledge about such was "*Nil*". (And I specifically knew that he was aware of the Monte Cristo reference after one of our early cases when a very old man, whom we later identified as one Edmond Dantès, sought Holmes's help to rescue his great-granddaughter from the influence of a particularly vile lesser member of the Royal Family.)

After replacing the scrapbook, Holmes remained standing. "You see the obvious question, no doubt?" he asked.

I nodded. "How did the Father Christmas of 1883 so easily recognize Johannes Oersted."

"Indeed. Perhaps learning that will help us discover the true nature of *this* Father Christmas, or possibly we'll learn it at the other end, when we've unmasked him."

I smiled. "Now you sound as if he's a villain in a music hall drama."

"One never knows – as you well know yourself." He took a step forward. "I know that you need to get home to your good wife. Shall we meet here tomorrow at five o'clock? Of course, wear something shabby."

I stood and agreed, and then walked home, crossing into Paddington and arriving on time for dinner, where Mary was quite interested to hear of my encounter with the famed young heir whose reputation was rising every day as the public's fascination with his history was matched only by their admiration of his charitable endeavors.

The next day was carried out like many others since I had married and gone back into active practice. My offices took up the ground floor of our modest building, but in spite of the general separation between the rooms where I saw patients and our quarters upstairs, Mary had gone out of our way to give the practice a sense of Christmas celebration, decorating the tabletops, windows, mantels, and other such places as she could find with colorful and seasonal ribbons and trimmings. When I went upstairs for lunch, I could hear that she was humming a lively carol, but she stopped when she heard me approach, and then ordered that I remain waiting on the stairs until such time as she accomplished some mysterious task – most likely the wrapping a gift. I had been forced to be just as careful downstairs several days earlier when taking pains to prepare *her* gifts, so I completely understood.

Although dealing with some of my patients' sad situations tended to dampen the good feelings associated with the season, in general there was a sense of joy and anticipation in the house that marveled me, and I was very happy indeed to count my blessings.

As the day passed and I completed my tasks, my thoughts were more and more occupied with thoughts of Oersted's request that we locate and identify the mysterious benefactor of the East End children. The previous night, Mary and I had discussed it from several angles, and like me, she couldn't perceive any way that the situation might turn out badly – but experience had taught me that absolute prediction of the path to any conclusion was impossible, and that it was better to be safe than full of later regret, so as usual, I made sure that I had my service revolver as I departed for Baker Street.

Mrs. Hudson was just returning from a shopping excursion, and I complimented her regarding the fine wreath upon the door. We stood outside for a moment, reminiscing about past Christmases when I had been one of her two tenants. We laughed at some of Holmes's adamant frustrations about how decorations would not be tolerated, for she had simply ignored him as one would a petulant child who issued ultimatums while stamping his feet and holding his breath as she went about the business of fixing up the sitting room nearly as nicely as her own festively adorned rooms. She'd had somewhat less success now that I'd moved away, but she hadn't given up.

We were still discussing her latest campaign when Holmes joined us, and I told her goodbye when he'd secured a hansom. Then we were off to Whitechapel.

I was in the worn clothing that I saved for such occasions, having learned to keep a few sets of such for these expeditions. The entire outfit probably wasn't as filthy as it should have been, but Mary, with a wary eye, refused to let anything truly dirty hang in the allotted space in my closet. But perhaps, I thought, the grime and sourness emanating from Holmes's own much-more-authentic disguise would suffice to mask my unhelpful cleanliness.

Our route found us working south and then east, along Oxford Street, and then through Holborn and into the City. Although I was already aware of the drastic differences in wealth and privilege between the residences of different parts of the capital, I saw what Oersted had meant about decorations. Most of the shops and houses that we passed had something of the sort, ranging from a simple sprig of holly to a fully contrived window display. And all around us, people seemed to step along with a great deal of bounce and good cheer. Yet I knew that in just a few miles, all of this would vanish as we entered the area with much less reason or opportunity to celebrate.

As we progressed, I debated whether to mention something that I'd wondered about since yesterday, during Oersted's visit. Finally I did so, knowing that Holmes would either answer, or he wouldn't.

"Yesterday," I began. "There seemed to be something tragic about your former Irregular, Joe Mancot. If you don't mind, might I ask what occurred?"

Holmes's eyes tightened, but not angrily. "I expected that you would ask. It's an unfortunate situation. As Oersted said, Joe was a good lad who was trapped in bad circumstances – an orphan living with a true rogue of an uncle. One night, this uncle had been drinking even more than usual and, having been thwarted in his attempts to start trouble at a nearby pub, he returned home to try the same on his family. Joe was there, and when his young cousin, a boy of just four, was the target of the father's cruelty, Joe intervened. While it was certainly an accident, the uncle swung a great sweeping blow toward Joe, who ducked away. But his feet slipped and he crashed to the floor, breaking his head open upon the hearth. He died immediately. The uncle was sent to Pentonville, where in less than a year he had a seizure in his isolated cell and passed unnoticed and unmissed."

Strangely at that moment, we rounded a corner where a street musician was playing "God Rest Ye Merry, Gentlemen" upon his fiddle to an appreciative crowd.

"I'd had hopes," continued Holmes, "that Joe would soon be able to begin studies that I'd arranged for him with a clergyman for whom I'd recently performed a modest service – locating a misplaced vital document. I greatly regret that I didn't make the effort sooner, to remove Joe from that house."

He sighed. "Such disappointments are part of my trade, Watson – or so I've come to believe. Because of that, I need some good news. Too often lately I've encountered various setbacks – losing ground for every step forward. I do wish that the solution to this Father Christmas business falls on the pleasant side of the scales."

"I'm sure that it will." And in truth, I hoped that it would, for I knew that of late he'd been using himself up quite too freely in his escalating efforts to place various counter-moves in answer to each of Moriarty's actions, gradually fencing in the wily academic and criminal – but I hadn't realized until then that his spirit was being so affected. I would need to make a better effort to assist him when possible as the situation reached a crisis.

But it was not at that point yet, and I turned the conversation to less grim shadings. I asked questions about locations that we passed, or made comments about people going about their business, allowing him to elaborate – or correct me – based upon his own observations. He knew what I was doing, but he was in better spirits by the time we disembarked in Whitechapel Road.

We walked the short distance to The White Hart, a small building not more than twelve or fifteen feet wide, and only four stories high. I had no idea what occurred upstairs – if there were rooms to let, or if the owner himself lived there, or if those upper floors served as meeting space for bar patrons. I'd been inside the ground floor on any number of occasions, one way or another, and most recently during the autumn of 1888, when I'd been summoned from a patrol through some of the more evil nearby streets and alleys and passages to sew up a gash on a constable's wounded forehead, the result of a false accusation from one drunk to another that the latter was most certainly The Ripper – a charge which he most vociferously denied, with the aid of a broken bottle.

As I had improved my ability to change my appearance over the years, as taught by Holmes, I was certain that we wouldn't be recognized. We slipped inside the dark and poorly lit room, the winter sun having long-since set. Ordering a brace of beers, we found a pair of stools along the right-hand wall and waited to see what happened next.

As seven o'clock approached, more and more small families tentatively entered the building. The pub's landlord, Mr. Bledsoe, met them at the door with a gruff sort of bonhomie and shepherded them toward the back. A few extra lanterns had been lit there to augment the normal dim gaslight. At five or so minutes after the top of the hour, about two-dozen children were seated in a circle on the filthy floor while their parents were layered around and behind them. Then, without further delay, Bledsoe danced his way across the crowded floor to a door at the rear, opened it, and ushered in Father Christmas.

The fellow was rather short – around five-and-a-half-feet tall – and dressed as one might expect in the typical costume of the holiday's patron saint. His robe was green in the old style, and he had a matching cap which held in place an apparently wig of long white hair – the same too-white shade as the heavy false beard which hung rather awkwardly and sideways upon his face.

He had a large and bulky brown Hessian sack across his right shoulder, held by both hands. However, it seemed more awkward than heavy, and he swung it rather easily to the floor when he stopped to face the children.

The events were carried out as described to us by Oersted during his visit to Baker Street the night before: The wishes of holiday cheer in a falsely deepened and hearty voice, followed by the dispersal of the contents of the sack, consisting of a number of small but festively wrapped gifts, and finally the distribution of quite a bit of candy – which successfully served to brighten the spirits of both the children and the parents. Then, after only a few minutes more, the garbed figure waved a gloved hand, boomed "Happy Holidays!" and slipped away through the back door. Holmes, having left most of his beer untouched on the shelf where we had leaned, was already out the front door, and I was close behind.

By that time, I had known Holmes for almost ten years, and he had managed to teach me, a rather slow pupil at first, a number of useful skills that enabled me to more effectively assist him in his work. While we were good friends – in many ways he was much more my brother than the disappointing fellow who was actually my blood kin – I don't believe that he would have tolerated me quite so much or for so long if I'd been completely ineffectual at assisting him. After working together for so long, we functioned in some similarity to the way that a wolf pack can slowly approach and then gradually get around and in front of its prey. Without discussion, we separated outside the pub, Holmes more directly following Father Christmas while I moved ahead on a side street, picking up the trail while Holmes took the opportunity to advance to his next location farther ahead. Thus, we stayed with our subject as we crossed a good-sized piece of London.

The festively attired man didn't make it difficult. He first led us along the Aldgate High Street, moving at a steady even pace with his empty sack hanging at one side. On occasion he would stop and speak with a random passer-by, and several times he fished in his pocket to give a less fortunate figure a coin or two. Once, I saw from a distance when a drunk began to yell something his way in a mocking tone, but Father Christmas simply changed direction and went directly up to the man, who then abruptly changed his tone and slunk away. Then the green-garbed fellow resumed his previous pace.

I was beginning to have suspicions about the true identity of the man I followed, and wished that I could have conferred with Holmes, but he and I were taking separated routes so that one or the other of us wouldn't be spotted, and our thoughts would have to remain unshared for the present.

Down Leadenhall Street, and then along Cheapside we went. By the time we were passing through Newgate Street and then into Holborn, I would have bet a hundred pounds that I knew our destination – and I was sure that Holmes knew as well, although he had been there far fewer times than I had. By the time we veered left from High Holborn into the Little Turnstile, I felt that I could have gone on ahead and been waiting for Father Christmas when he arrived at the doorway his destination – the Ship's Tavern in Gates Street, just to the northwest of Lincoln's Inn Fields. In truth, as I emerged from the narrow passage, Holmes was already waiting at the door, alone.

"I let him go inside," he explained.

"When did you realize who it was? I think that I knew from the first time I saw the way he walked."

Holmes smiled. "Yes, that left foot of his with its inward twist is unmistakable. Shall we?" And with that, he held the door for me to enter.

Unexpectedly, for it was still rather early, the pub appeared to be closed, except for a small private gathering at some tables about midway back. I was rather amazed to see that the group, consisting a dozen men, were all frozen in some sort of curious *tableau*, looking in our direction. Some sat, while others were standing. Some held drinks, and a few were in the process of pouring their own. The most unique feature of the group was that all were dressed, in some form or fashion, in traditional green or more modern red, as Father Christmas. There were tall ones and short, thick and thin. And to a man they were turned to face us. Standing in front of them was the shorter fellow whom we had just followed from Whitechapel, and he was the first to break the illusion and step our way.

"Welcome, Mr. Holmes, Doctor Watson. I thought about stopping and inviting you to walk with me when I realized that you were both following, but as we would all get here in any case, it was more fun to draw you along."

"Good evening, Inspector," said Holmes, stepping forward into the better-lit part of the room. "*Inspectors*, I should say. Season's Greetings to all of you."

"And to you!" came their hearty reply, in tones high and low, from various parts of the island.

The shorter man stepped further forward, peeling off his white wig and beard. "I suppose it was young Mr. Oersted who hired you," commented Inspector Lestrade of Scotland Yard.

We nodded. "Yesterday," I said. "He knows something of your charitable work, and wishes to learn more."

A taller Father Christmas broke from the group and approached us, revealing himself to be our old friend, Inspector Bradstreet. "We knew he'd keep after it – several of the pub owners who help arrange this each year said that someone was asking questions, and Bill Parrott at The Boar knew that it was him."

"Was it you, Bradstreet, that identified Oersted back in '83 at The White Hart and directed Mr. and Mrs. Gravens to find him?"

Bradstreet nodded. "It was. The Gravens had come to London just a few days before. I was one of the officers who met with them. It was just coincidence – or a Christmas miracle, I suppose – that I noticed he matched the description, and not long after I heard the boy's name spoken outside the pub, and I was able to make the connection."

"But you didn't reveal yourself then," I said, "because you didn't want to explain the connection between Father Christmas and the Force."

"That's it," Bradstreet explained. "This is something that we do, and it's between us – for us. We don't even tell our colleagues about it – constables or superintendents. If I'd identified myself to Oersted that night, he would have either mentioned that Father Christmas was an inspector, or if I'd have taken him to the station while still in my Christmas suit, I would have had to explain to the lads on duty. Better to send the Gravens to find him at the mission the next day."

By this point, the other Father Christmases had joined us: Lanner, and the Jones brothers – Athelney and Peter. There was MacDonald and Youghal and Morton, and of course Gregson, standing at the rear, with a silent nod in my direction.

"Oersted wants to help what you're doing," I explained.

"I have no doubt of it," said Lestrade. "But as Bradstreet explained, this is something just for us. Of course, we trust you two, as friends, to keep our secret."

"Certainly," agreed Holmes. "We will not report a word of what we found here tonight – and hopefully it will be explained in such a way that Mr. Oersted will stop trying to discover who you all are. But perhaps you might agree to his financial support, even if he remains unaware of who is receiving it?"

The question remained open-ended at that point, but as the evening progressed, it was discussed several times, and by the end of the festivities, the inspectors' secret Christmas party, it was decided that if John Oersted wished to donate funds to their cause, they would gratefully accept them.

It was a jolly time, and I cannot remember when I had so much actual fun in the company of the Yard's inspectors. I was honored, as I know Holmes was as well, to be included in the party, and it was a most unique experience to be surrounded by a dozen or more Father Christmases.

Later, after Holmes and I had shared a cab as far as Baker Street, and then I rode on alone in the gaslit darkness to my Praed Street home in Paddington, it all began to feel like a distant Christmas dream, and even more so when I described it to Mary before falling into a deep sleep.

The next year was one of great emotion. As 1891 commenced, Holmes's struggles with Professor Moriarty escalated as he was finally able to head off the criminal's schemes, in one direction after another, leaving the only path forward one toward inevitable destruction of the illegal organization – but not without great cost.

On the fourth of May, Holmes was thought to have perished at the Reichenbach Falls, locked in combat with the Professor as both tumbled to their terrible deaths at the base of the nearly nine-hundred-feet tall cascade into the raging torrent below. I returned to London in despair, and it was Mary who reminded me of how fortunate that I still was. I had a wonderful wife, a growing practice, and friends, many of whom were inspectors with the Yard. I was more honored than I could express when they invited me to be a part of their Father Christmas Brigade the following December.

I had been taking on work throughout those months as a police surgeon, and my ties and friendship with the inspectors continued to grow. It was to them that I turned for strength when Mary, never in the best of health, had passed away in the spring of 1893. It nearly broke me then, but they were my firm and fast friends and they made sure that I survived.

In April 1894, Holmes returned to London, having never, in fact, gone over the Falls to his death. Instead, he had roamed the world for three years, carrying out a number of delicate tasks for his brother Mycroft, and also looking for the opportunity to bring Moriarty's prime henchman finally to justice. After that task was complete, I – having no reason to stay there by then – sold my practice and moved back to Baker Street. What followed were many months of investigations and adventures, keeping us both extremely busy as the year passed.

As Christmas approached, we had visitors – Lestrade, Gregson, and Bradstreet. They ranged themselves throughout our sitting room in a loose semi-circle in front of the fireplace, with the mantel very much decorated for the holiday, courtesy of our landlady.

"We really won't take no for an answer," explained Lestrade. "Through the financial arrangement you worked out with Mr. Oersted, and his happy willingness to let us remain anonymous – even to him – the amount of good that we've been able to accomplish at Christmas – with Dr. Watson's assistance – has grown ten-fold in just a few years. Now it's that time of year again, Mr. Holmes, and we want you to join us. To be part of the Brigade, as the Doctor started calling us."

Holmes started to speak, but Gregson cut him off, raising one of his large hands and leaving my friend sitting there speechless for one of those rare occasions in his life, his mouth open for a moment like that of a codfish.

"There will be no debate, Mr. Holmes," said the flaxen-haired detective, his fingers wide. "Your suit has been ordered, and it will be delivered tomorrow. The day after that we'll gather at The Ships and spread out across the city. The doctor can explain further. Afterwards will be the celebration. You've been there before. You know what to expect."

After that, there was really nothing that Holmes could do to say no, and so he didn't. He and I were there at the pub two nights later, where we separated to give out toys and treats to the young children in some of the worst parts of the city who didn't have much else to look forward to. Later, as we returned to the small bar for the policeman's own celebration, I don't think that anyone enjoyed it more than Sherlock Holmes – and he has continued to do so in all the years since, right up to the time that I've set this account down on paper. He's returning to London tonight from his retirement villa in Sussex, and as he told me when I confirmed his attendance the other day on the telephone, "I wouldn't miss it for the world!"

JHW
21 December, 1909

The Adventure of the Fugitive Irregular
by Gordon Linzner

Chapter I – Holmes at Home

The winter of 1890-1891 was the coldest one England had endured in Sherlock Holmes's memory. It would, in fact, later prove the most severe of his lifetime. His last case of even moderate interest had wrapped up just as the cold spell began. Now, a month later, on arrival of the Winter Solstice, there was still no sign of warming. Due to constant cloud cover and freezing fog, most of London had gone for days – weeks – without a hint of sun.

The hour was well past noon when Holmes finally rose from his bed. Draped in his mouse-colored wool dressing gown, he stared out his window at the bleakness of Baker Street below. A handful of heavily bundled Londoners wandered the sunless pavement with unusual haste. The world continued to bask in a perpetual twilight.

At least the Russian Flu epidemic that first struck England the previous winter seemed to have subsided.

With no new cases in sight, Holmes regretted letting his friend Watson wean him off cocaine. After a near-crippling binge three years earlier, he'd been forced to admit the good doctor had a point and promised to cut back on its use. Not entirely, though. Of late he felt again drawn to his desk's bottom drawer.

Stacks of file folders, newspapers, and clippings from agony columns lay strewn across the desk, overflowing onto the floor and chair alongside. Atop one stack were his notes for an all-but-completed monograph on malingering. His violin case sat in a corner of the room. The Stradivarius, untouched for days, was likely out of tune. The detective had to admit that neglecting his favorite instrument was not at all like himself.

Holmes started sorting through his syringes when he heard a familiar stately tread on the stairs outside his rooms, along with a more eager set of footfalls. Even as her first hesitant rap fell upon his door, Holmes called out, "Yes, Mrs. Hudson?"

"You have a guest, Mr. Holmes. A young boy. The new one, Simpson. Are you decent?"

Holmes shut the drawer with its drug paraphernalia and moved to sit by the fireplace. "As best I can be at this hour, Mrs. Hudson. Please, show the lad in."

The landlady opened the door. Before she could step forward to make a proper announcement, however, a rough-clad boy of twelve or thirteen years, wearing a thick jacket, torn but serviceable, rushed past her.

"Mr. Holmes!" he shouted.

Mrs. Hudson was not pleased with the child's dress and deportment, but she had learned over the past decade to deal with such issues with more decorum and less disdain than Holmes's sometimes-flatmate, Doctor Watson. At least, this one didn't need to be constantly reminded not to bring the rest of the Irregulars with him.

"Ah, Simpson, my boy! Good morning!"

"It's afternoon, Mr. Holmes," the boy corrected. He could at times be as cheeky as his predecessor.

Holmes glanced at the brass clock on his mantel. "So it is. Judging by your pale skin, and the stiffness in your fingers, you've been out in that bitter cold far longer than I should recommend. Come sit by the fire and warm yourself. You may toss those papers aside."

"The boy called earlier today, Mr. Holmes," the landlady explained, "but I knew you were still abed, and requested he return at a more convenient hour."

Holmes arched an eyebrow. "You knew I was asleep how?"

Her lips twitched in a rare smile. "How long have you been my tenant? You're not exactly subtle once you're up and about."

"*Touché*. That's right, Simpson, pull the chair closer. Mrs. Hudson, would you be so kind as to bring us some tea? Something strong and hot? And perhaps some curry chicken, and a couple of your Cornish pasties, if any are ready? This young man seems a bit famished."

"I am, always," Simpson affirmed.

"I'll see what I can do." Then, as discreetly as she'd arrived, the landlady disappeared down the stairs.

Holmes turned his attention back to the boy. "I'm afraid I haven't any jobs for you and the other Irregulars at present. It's been a slow month."

"Perhaps the cold is discouraging London's criminals," Simpson suggested.

"The interesting ones, at any rate," Holmes agreed.

Simpson looked around warily. "Doctor Watson isn't about, is he? He doesn't much care for we Irregulars. What did he call us in print? 'Half-a-dozen of the dirtiest and most ragged street Arabs that ever I clapped eyes on'."

"I'm afraid the good doctor is a bit of an elitist. To answer your question, no, he hasn't been here for a while. He's married now – to the former Miss Morstan, if you recall. The woman he met during Wiggins' last job for me."

"That doesn't prevent him from hanging about from time to time, though, does it?"

"True. For him to intrude today is unlikely, however. He's been extremely busy this year, between the flu epidemic and the recent uptick in cold-related cases."

The boy nodded. "Well, then, Mr. Holmes – " he began.

"I see by your boots you've been spending some time at the stables. Those stains are much higher up than one would expect from simple street muck."

"I have been helping out in Hyde Park for an extra bob or two, yes, but – "

"You've also had a recent altercation with another boy, and one taller than yourself, because that bruise is oddly high up on your forehead."

"You should see the other boy," Simpson began again, a little firmer. "But, Mr. Holmes – "

"Not a serious injury, thankfully. The result of some simple rough-house shenanigans, no? That isn't surprising. The necessity of confining oneself indoors for long periods in this weather naturally leads to short tempers – "

"Mr. Holmes!" Simpson shouted.

"I rest my case." Holmes sounded more pleased than offended by the lad's pluck. "Indulge me in one last observation, if you will. This is no ordinary social call on your part. You have been fidgeting in the pocket of your jacket, which you have not removed, since your arrival, though you should be warm enough by now. I take it you have something for me?"

"Finally," Simpson replied with a sigh. He withdrew a square brown envelope from his right coat pocket, then thrust it at the detective.

Holmes held the envelope up to the gaslight, narrowing his eyes. "I note that this envelope is not sealed."

"That's how it was given to me, Mr. Holmes. One of our younger members got it from Wiggins, who insisted it be passed it on to you before he ran off. That lad gave it on to me, since you made quite clear I am now the leader of the Irregulars. Ever since Wiggins got a proper job."

"As I was pleased to hear. He's too old to pass for an idle youth these days. He is of course welcome here any time."

"I think he didn't feel it safe to call on you in person."

Holmes did not like hearing the young man might be in danger. He turned his attention back to the envelope, fingering the flap. "With long enough exposure to freezing temperatures, a sealed envelope can be opened without damaging the flap, although anyone going to that much effort would likely re-seal it afterwards. Was your fellow Irregular curious?"

"Unlikely, Mr. Holmes. I'd rather not say his name, but his reading skills are, shall we say, more limited than mine."

"And you undoubtedly took a peek yourself."

Simpson tightened his lips.

"Relax, Simpson. It's perfectly natural. I do pay your group to observe." Holmes opened the flap and withdrew the holiday card enclosed.

An elaborately lettered greeting along the bottom of the face read "*A Merry Christmas to You*". The illustration above the words showed two frogs. One lay on its back, in a pool of blood, a knife protruding from its heart. The second was slinking away with a bag of cash.

"I see our card makers haven't lost their dark sense of humor," Holmes opined. "At least it's not Krampus stuffing some errant child into a sack while Saint Nicholas calmly looks on."

Opening the card, Holmes found the same warm greetings repeated, sans the deceased amphibian and his killer. To the left flap was added a trio of crude pencil sketches. He held the card up for his visitor to see.

"Do you know what these mean, Simpson?"

"No idea, Mr. Holmes. That looks like a steam launch on the left, and the wavy lines on the right might be waves. The stick figure in the middle, waving a white flag . . . is he giving up?"

"It's a clue to his location. You don't need to know more, or even that much. Ah, Mrs. Hudson! Your timing is impeccable! Eat up, Simpson, but be quick. You may take mine as well, for later. I will have to be off as soon as I assemble a few necessities and finish getting dressed."

His mouth half-filled with warm pasty, Simpson mumbled, "May I tag along? Wiggins bragged about seeing you operate in person more than once."

"As much as I would appreciate the help and the company, I believe it's safer for Wiggins – " And yourself, Holmes added silently, knowing the warning would only do the opposite of dissuading the lad. " – if as few people as possible know where he is hiding. In any case, my activity will be primarily mental – quite boring to any observer."

"Can't be worse than when you had me hang about that cripple's house last year."

Holmes covered his smile with a hand. "I promise to explain all once the situation is resolved. Unless Wiggins himself beats me to it."

Chapter II – Jacobson's Yard

The docks at Jacobson's Yard were unusually quiet, even for a Sunday afternoon. Shipping, like every other business in London, had been sorely affected by the unending cold. Eleven miles upstream, at Twickenham, the Thames had even frozen solid. The few workmen visible in the shipyard were mostly clearing away ice and snow.

Into this unnatural calm shambled the figure of an elderly, stoop-shouldered man. He used a crooked walking stick to help balance the heavy cloth bag flung across his shoulders like a shabby version of Saint Nicholas. A casual observer would assume the man was homeless, seeking some warm refuge. Many of Britain's poor had already fallen victim to the brutal weather in the past month.

The stranger paused at the yard's gate, shifting his bag for better balance. His gloved right hand clutched the metal fence, while the left used the stick to brace his stooping body. Grey eyes peered from beneath heavy brows, toward the line of sheds within.

No one inside the yard approached to chase him off. Given the frigid wind off the river, the workers preferred spending as little time outdoors as possible. Why bother to harass some harmless beggar? He'd likely move on soon.

Outside the yard was a different story.

"You! Old man!" A harsh Northern Irish accent echoed from behind him.

Using his walking stick as a fulcrum, the man with the bundle slowly turned. He responded in a high, reedy Irish accent of his own. "Would you be addressing me, sir?"

Two beefy thugs with thick, unkempt beards, clad in heavy jackets and workman's gloves, approached their target.

"I'll not be seeing anyone else about." These words came from a different voice than the first, resonating with a thick Yorkshire accent. The speaker stood a good three inches shorter than his companion, with an annoyingly smug grin.

Sherlock Holmes adjusted his grip on his walking stick, prepared to employ it quickly should he need to defend himself. He stared blankly past his two inquisitors, then blinked twice before focusing his attention on the taller man.

"That's the point, Sean," the Irishman whispered to his associate. "No one about. Leave this to me." He seemed the brighter of the pair, and his face would be familiar to anyone who frequented local alehouses. Holmes regularly made such rounds to keep his observational skills keen, and so had no difficulty identifying Conan Jamesson. The man was used by various gang leaders, one in particular, for odd jobs.

"We're looking for a young man, eighteen or twenty years of age, near six feet tall, dark hair," Jamesson continued. "We're told he works these docks. Sound familiar?"

Holmes blinked again, raising a gloved hand to rub his eyes absent-mindedly. The action concealed a further tightening of his grip on the head of his walking stick.

"As to that," the detective replied, "I could not say. The cold air's badly affected my eyesight. I came down here in search of shelter. Heard there might be a couple of discarded shipping containers. You two seen any?"

"There's a quid in it for you," the second man interrupted, ignoring Holmes's question as he reached into his pocket.

Jamesson gripped his companion's arm, stopping him and turning away from Holmes. "It's no use, Sean," he whispered. "The old man is practically blind. Let's find the others, see if they've had more success."

Without so much as a goodbye, the pair moved on.

Holmes's face went grim in the revelation that these two were not the only ones seeking his former agent.

No one was about for the moment to notice Holmes's return to scanning the sheds beyond the fence. Thus, there was no one to be startled when a short sharp laugh escaped his lips. Holmes even briefly rose to his full six-foot-plus height.

Roughly chalked against the side of the nearest shed, facing the street, almost invisible against the dark wood, was the stick figure of a squatting man. It blended so well with the background even a man of Sherlock Holmes's observational skills might have missed it, if not for the blotch of bright red paint topping the head. Stylistically, it otherwise appeared a perfect match for the figure in the Christmas card, the one that represented a boy signaling the departure of the steam launch Aurora from these very docks two years earlier.

"Well done, Wiggins," Holmes muttered, rapping his walking stick against the pavement in appreciation. "Well done, indeed. I, too, thought these docks too obvious a meeting place."

The detective left Jacobson's Yard at a slightly faster pace than one might expect for a man of his apparent age. He knew where next to go.

Chapter III – Wiggins Underground

"I'd feel more comfortable if you stood at your proper height, Mr. Holmes."

The voice came from a shadowy corner to his left as Holmes entered the basement of Wilson's pawn shop, near Saxe-Coburg Square. The detective gave a rare smile at being recognized. He had not had time to change since leaving the shipyard.

"Excellent observation, Wiggins. I've fooled Watson with far less elaborate disguises."

"To be fair to the Doctor, you were expected."

Holmes turned to fully face his former Irregular, pleased to note the quality of Wiggins' heavy coat and trousers. They were a small step up from the rags that made up Simpson's outfit, the kind Wiggins himself had worn when running the detective's errands. A wooden cudgel swung casually in his right hand, though not in a threatening manner.

"We haven't spoken in over a year," Holmes continued. "I trust all is well with you. Apart, that is, from being stalked by a criminal mastermind?"

Wiggins had been tall for his age even as a pre-teenager when they'd first met. Now he stood nearly as tall as Holmes himself. His features otherwise were youthful enough that he could still have passed for sixteen or seventeen, if he adopted Holmes's crouch. Only the concern lining Wiggins's features fully gave his age away.

"Well enough," the young man answered. "As you know, I've a real job now, at the docks. At least, I hope I still have one, when this is over. And a girlfriend. We plan to marry. My apologies for the runaround. I'd planned on hiding out near Jacobson's Yards, being familiar with the area, but had second thoughts after handing off that card. I dared not be seen by either my fellow workers or my bosses. Leaving you that second clue was risky enough. Also, the basement of this pawn shop is warmer than the sheds."

"How did you know I was involved in the Clay case, by the way? My name wasn't in the newspapers."

"All of us Irregulars know Inspector Jones is not the brightest member of the force. He may have gotten credit for capturing that thief, but if I haven't learned to see your hand in such matters, then half my life has been wasted."

Holmes let loose another short, sharp laugh. "Perhaps you should take up my occupation. London could use a few more consulting detectives."

Wiggins shook his head. "I've seen some of the dangers you face, heard of others. No, thank you. I would like to enjoy a few normal, happy years after growing up the streets. Unfortunately, perhaps because of my association with you, it seems I can't count on that. Have you learned who's after me, and who I supposedly crossed?"

"I have strong suspicions, and at least one lead. I hope to confirm matters shortly."

"I trust my stalkers failed to notice the sketch on the shed, or if they did see it they missed its meaning, even if they know of our connection."

"It is likely so. That fact does not preclude possible discovery by more astute trackers. Their leader is one of the cleverest criminals in England. Let us not take any chances. I have a bolt-hole set up not far from here, unconnected to any of my cases. It has proven quite useful when I need to change personas without returning to Baker Street, or even hide out for a day or two. I'm planning to establish more throughout London. Admittedly the place isn't as warm as this basement, but it is stocked with thick blankets, as well as canned goods and fresh water. You may safely shelter while I conclude my investigation."

"You don't need my assistance?"

"Were you not just now concerned about the danger? No, Wiggins, I promise to let you know if and when I require you. I've already encountered two rather rough gentlemen looking for you. I recognized one and will seek him out presently, in a different guise. In the meantime, in the unlikely event someone has managed to decipher the figure you sketched, and is waiting nearby, I brought another costume for yourself." Holmes rested his cloth bag on a shaky wooden table and indicated that Wiggins should look inside.

The young man's eyes widened as he removed the contents. "This must be a mistake. A woman's dress?"

"With that grey wig and bonnet, you will be unrecognizable, even to your former fellow Irregulars."

Wiggins frowned as he fingered the garment's coarse fabric and stiff lace collar.

"I've used this outfit twice to date, myself," Holmes assured him. "Each time it proved quite useful. We are of a similar height and build, so there's little need to modify it."

"A woman's dress," Wiggins repeated, his tone flattening.

"If any stranger can pass less noticed than a crippled old man, it is an elderly woman. Change quickly, and I'll give you a quick lesson in moving like one. None of those eager long strides you're so fond of."

Wiggins's frown deepened further.

"Come, now," Holmes encouraged. "It's at most an hour's walk to my bolt-hole – less if we find a hansom, though most drivers are wisely keeping their horses safe in their stables."

The young man sighed. "My own coat should help conceal most of it, I guess."

"Capital, Wiggins! Let us make haste. Once you're settled in place, and I've upgraded my disguise, you'll be on your own. I need to follow my lead before it grows cold."

"As cold as this winter air?"

"Worse than that, my young friend. Far worse."

Chapter IV – An Unlikely Duo

"Open up, Belwether!"

The voice of Conan Jamesson echoed throughout the wooden building's narrow hallways. His thick fist pounded on the door of Roger Belwether's flat with such ferocity Holmes half expected it to give way. Fortunately, in this kind of building, neighbors kept to themselves.

The detective took a step back, letting his new partner take the lead. For now.

This area of Stepney, just off Mile End Road, hosted some of the most unsavory rookeries in all of London. The poorly maintained building they'd entered was at least a century old. Rotted wood had creaked under their weight when the pair made their way up the narrow stairwell to the second floor. Two battered privies behind the building served the score and more occupants but, in view of the extreme cold, their bedpans were getting more use than usual. A man of lesser constitution could easily lose his dinner from the stench.

Holmes had located his Irish quarry an hour earlier at the Gargoyle's Nest, the third venue he visited, an undistinguished alehouse with a line of mismatched stools running along the bar in the main room and a dozen tables lining two walls.

Jamesson had been sitting alone in a side room, next to a roaring fireplace, nursing a porter. His colleague Sean was nowhere in sight, as Holmes expected, having observed their earlier interactions. After ensuring the cold wind had not weakened the glue holding his thick black moustache and goatee in place, Holmes strode to the man's table and introduced himself as a Mr. John Nichols.

True friends were few and far between for the solitary detective, but Holmes could project a friendly, open, trustworthy attitude when necessary. He bluffed his way through what little he knew enough to convince Jamesson to reveal the name of the victim, and that he, too, was searching for the man who stole the blackmail documents, and furthermore he would be a far more capable partner than the surly Sean.

An hour – and three pints – later, he persuaded the Irishman they should speak to that man directly.

"I've done nothing wrong," squeaked a voice on the other side of the door. "You can't arrest me!"

"We are not the police." Holmes's tone was softer than Jamesson's. "We've been hired to look for the thief who stole that document. Some crucial details need clarifying."

"Who sent you?"

"You know who sent us!" growled Jamesson. In fact, they acted without orders, but Belwether needn't know that. "You know me – Conan Jamesson!" He started to pound the door again.

Holmes lifted a finger in a silent request for patience.

The reluctance with which Ronald Belwether finally undid the door latch was palpable.

Belwether's one-room crib was lit only by a single gas lamp on a table and the flickering glow of the fireplace. Even by day, little natural light could enter the narrow window from outside. Thin sheets streaked with dark brown stains were draped over the daybed in one corner. The wooden table and a lone straight-backed chair made up the rest of the furnishings.

Belwether had fallen on hard times, indeed, even discounting multiple purplish facial contusions and cuts on his hands. The ring of hair around an otherwise bald head hung unevenly on either side. Obviously he'd attempted trimming it himself. His sunken chin trembled. Watery blue eyes darted from one visitor to the other and back again. Holmes felt a momentary pang of compassion.

Which quickly faded, as this was the man who'd put loyal Wiggins in fear for his life.

"Did you find the document? The thief?" Belwether's tone was anything but hopeful.

"Not yet," Jamesson grumbled. "Nichols here and I are still searching."

To the latter's surprise, Holmes added, "Yet we grow close. As for the man responsible for your bruises . . . ."

"He's an elusive fellow," Jamesson put in, re-establishing which of the pair was in charge.

At least, which one Jamesson *believed* was in charge.

"No question of that," the heavyset man continued. "Oddly, the few people who recognized his description also insisted such actions were out of character."

"Yes," agreed Belwether, picking nervously at a scab on his lip. "Well. We all have our desperate moments, don't we?"

Holmes moved toward the fireplace, removing his gloves, ostensibly to warm his hands. The action allowed him to secretly remove a long cigar-shaped roll from his left coat pocket. This ruse would have benefitted from some outside help, as in the past, but Jamesson's distraction and Belwether's general ignorance should serve.

"Good heavens, man!" Holmes abruptly shouted, flapping his arms. "Don't you ever clean this fireplace?"

Belwether's eyes widened. "I beg pardon?"

"These sparks, man! The dry wooden floor! Look at the smoke! The place could go up in flames!"

Jamesson scooped up the bedpan beside the head of the daybed. Holmes retreated a pace to avoid being splashed with the foul liquid, but kept his attention fixed on Belwether. The nervous minion had bent to one knee to retrieve a badly dented metal file box from under the daybed.

By the time Belwether noticed Holmes staring at him, it was too late to replace it.

"What prank is this, Nichols?" Jamesson bellowed. "There's no fire! Just a harmless plumber's smoke-rocket."

"Which sufficed to get Mr. Belwether to reveal himself." Holmes turned back to their subject. "What exactly is in that box you were so eager to rescue?"

Belwether's fingers drummed nervously on metal. "Personal family papers. Irreplaceable. Of no value to anyone else."

"Ah. I have a fondness for family histories. As does Mr. Jamesson, I expect. Pray, let us see."

"No. I can't. As I said, they're personal." Belwether's fingers whitened. "I find your harassment highly inappropriate. I must ask you both to leave at once."

"Nichols is right," Jamesson responded. "I, too, would be interested."

In a burst of bravado, surprising even himself, Belwether snapped, "I don't take orders from lackeys."

A Webley .450 Bulldog revolver appeared in Holmes's right hand. "You may find this persuasive, then. Hand the box to my associate, Belwether."

Face pale, hands twitching, Belwether reluctantly held out the storage box. Jamesson snatched it and, finding the lock broken, immediately began rifling through the papers within.

"You know what to look for, I trust?" Holmes asked.

"I have a rough idea." Jamesson dumped the contents onto the daybed.

Holmes returned to his interrogation. "You were never attacked, were you, Belwether? Those facial bruises are inconsistent with an ambush from behind, in both location and severity. They resemble what one would expect from pounding your own head against a hard surface, such as this mantel, where I detect a few flecks of dried blood. Similarly, the unbandaged cuts on your left hand are deeper than those on the right – some more shallow than others, indicating a certain hesitancy. Were you truly defending yourself against a knife, those cuts would be appear surer, and equally deep on both hands."

Belwether cringed.

"This looks like it," Jamesson announced, waving a folded sheet. "Better paper. Lots of big words."

"May I see?" Holmes took the paper in his left hand, while holding the Webley steady with his right. "Ah! Did you recognize this name?"

"A member of the House of Lords, I think. Don't know him."

"He's also a friend of my brother. As much as my brother has any friends. An acquaintance, at any rate. For anyone else, the details in this document would seem trifling. Given the gentleman's status and reputation, however, such revelations would be disastrous. I see why blackmail might pay handsomely – though only with this physical proof."

Holmes turned back to Belwether. His grey eyes seem to bore through the shaking man. "Anything you'd care to add?"

Belwether took a deep breath, then sighed. "You've got me dead to rights. I can only rely on your mercy." He slumped into the room's sole chair. "After the incident that cost me my teaching assistant job, a momentary lapse I assure you, I have not done well. I reached out to several colleagues in similar situations. The government clerk who'd secured this incriminating document, knowing he'd be considered a prime suspect, needed to quickly pass it on to a go-between. I was in the best position to act. However, once I realized the contents of this document, and how much could be gained from it . . . Well, you see my circumstances here. I pretended to be attacked and robbed, planning to wait a fortnight or so before approaching the gentleman myself. Really, it would have been to the victim's benefit. Our employer would demand far more money."

"Why accuse an innocent man? Why not make up a description?"

"I'm not very imaginative under pressure. I described a random young man I'd noticed near the docks earlier that day. I had no idea you'd be able to track him down."

"Random, you say? You had no idea of the fellow's past?"

"None at all. You likely know more than I. Is he also involved in some criminal operation?"

"The opposite. Your inability to see that connection doesn't mean your superior can't."

"We have what we came for, Nichols," Jamesson insisted.

Holmes ignored him. "Tell me, Belwether: How did you expect to achieve your own blackmail without being found out?"

"I, um, hadn't worked out the details. Please, Mr. Nichols, Mr. Jamesson. I admit to giving in to an unfortunate impulse. Take the thing. Tell the people we work for that the thief had a change of heart and returned it. Or you beat it out of him. I beg you, leave me out of it. I'll make it worth your whiles."

Jamesson looked around the shabby room with a sneer.

"In the future," Belwether continued. "Once I'm more established in the organization."

"That won't be happening," Jamesson snarled. "You had your one chance. That's all this organization allows."

"Should we not give him the benefit of the doubt?" asked Holmes, grey eyes twinkling.

"Absolutely not." Jamesson was firm.

"Agreed." Holmes tossed the document into the fireplace.

Jamesson lunged forward, hands outstretched, then froze as Holmes turned the pistol on him.

"Who the devil are you, Nichols?"

From the corner of his eye, the detective watched the paper curl into a tiny black cinder. "The name is Sherlock Holmes. Your employer knows me. Our paths have crossed, though not in person, several times in the past year, and undoubtedly will again. Now, if you gentlemen will excuse me, I have not eaten all day, and I do have other chores to catch up on."

Webley Bulldog in hand, Holmes backed out of the flat, down the stairs, and into the foggy, bitterly cold night.

Chapter V – Christmas Karma

Despite the chill air, and a hard layer of ice covering the streets, Holmes clearly heard carolers and revelers from his first-floor flat. They moved on quickly, but it would have taken more than a few repetitive choruses of "Annie Rooney" to distract the detective, now that his concentration was fully engaged on a mission.

He retrieved that morning's *London Standard* from the stack of newspapers on the corner of his slightly more organized desk to skim a particular article one more time. Given his memory, Holmes didn't need to reread the column. In fact, he softly repeated the words as he did so. Nonetheless, he found the act satisfying, if admittedly petty.

Earlier that day, shortly before dawn – not that the fog and cloud cover allowed a decent view of the sun – the body of former teaching assistant Roger Belwether was discovered floating down the Thames amid blocks of ice. The police report indicated the man had been badly beaten, showing fresh bruises mingling with older, lesser ones.

Holmes felt little sympathy for someone who risked the life of an innocent young man with a casual lie, especially since the accused had been a valuable asset, associate, and, yes, to some extent even a friend over the past decade. He also recognized the real danger had come not from Belwether, but the man for whom he worked, a figure whose evil grip over London's criminal enterprises had been spreading far too quickly of late. Having no other pressing cases to hand, Holmes determined he would dedicate the full power of his observational and deductive skills toward taking down this criminal mastermind. The consulting detective had little doubt he could have the man behind bars within six months, and possibly less.

"You have bestirred your personal Krampus, Professor," Holmes muttered, "whether deliberately or no. Enjoy your Yuletide, for it shall be the last one you spend outside a cell."

His Irregulars had helped to focus his resolve. Sherlock Holmes could hardly have asked for a more perfect Christmas present.

The Incident of the Stolen Christmas Present
by Barry Clay

On Boxing Day in 1890, my practice being closed and Mary engaged in good works as befitted the season, I decided to pay a visit to my friend, Sherlock Holmes. As a confirmed bachelor and without relatives save one brother whom he rarely saw, I suspected London's only consulting detective might benefit from an hour's company, though he would quite rightly object to being an object of charity and declare such a visit unnecessary on that grounds. But that was of no matter. Does one need a reason for visiting his friends? The truth was, I often found a visit to Sherlock Holmes stimulating and, as on this day, one that provided unexpected returns.

When Mrs. Hudson announced me, Holmes was lounging with pipe and tobacco, dressed in his unique purple dressing gown. He was twirling his revolver in a desultory manner, as if attempting to decide if he should engage in indoor target practice or if the effort was too much bother. Mrs. Hudson, if she noticed it, gave no sign as she left. She was well used to his eccentricities. To my surprise, for to Holmes one day was like another and I had never known him to bother with decorations in observance of a holiday, there was a very small pine tree in a pot, decorated with a string of popcorn and some tiny ornaments.

"Good morning, Watson." As he greeted me, and to my relief, he set the revolver down on table in front of the roaring fire.

"It's good to see you."

"And I you. By the way," Holmes informed me, "Mrs. Hudson insisted."

"I don't follow you. Insisted on what?"

"The tree, if one can call such a small example of Douglass fir a tree. I saw you glance at it, and the look on your face was quite instructive."

"I was surprised to see you showing the holiday spirit," I admitted.

"She found it while shopping and insisted on decorating it and putting it there. She claimed it would put me in the mood."

"And did it?"

He smiled. "Hardly, but the scent is welcome." That question out of the way, he asked, with a twinkle in his eye, "Come to see if you can cheer me up?" I began to protest, but Holmes waved my words away. "If a little guilt will provide a motivation for you to visit an old friend, I will consider the results happier than the reason."

"You well know that guilt doesn't motivate me to visit!" I told him.

"Indeed I do, and I apologize for the remark. You are one of the few men whose friendship I know to be genuine, and his regard unfeigned." When I settled down in my accustomed chair, he asked me, "Did Mrs. Watson enjoy her necklace as much as you did your tie pin?"

I didn't need to ask how he knew the present my wife gave me, since I was wearing it, and Holmes's observational skills were amazing. And I had told him of the pearl necklace that I had purchased for Mary. "Yes, she did."

"I still have some of your wife's biscuits left, and I hope you'll join me in tea."

"With great pleasure, though," I added with regret, "I may have already eaten too many this season."

Holmes, who never seemed to gain an ounce of weight, smiled. "The dangers of marriage, Watson. You'll recall that I tried to warn you."

"That you did, though I assure you the benefits far outweigh the perils." This was an old debate between us. Holmes considered marriage to be a kind of self-inflicted wound and often wondered aloud why men voluntarily engaged in it. I attempted to explain the happiness that connubial bliss can mean for a man, but I fear my efforts again fell on deaf ears.

But we weren't to have tea that day. At that moment, we could hear Mrs. Hudson's feet on the stairway, and she soon entered at Holmes's call.

There was an expression on her face that I couldn't remember having seen before. "Begging your pardon, Mr. Holmes, but Master Wiggins and a Master Christopher Baker are here to see you."

"On Boxing Day?" I couldn't keep myself from asking.

"Wiggins, I know, of course," said Holmes, "but who is Master Baker?"

"I couldn't say, sir." Her expression was bemused, as if she were enjoying a private joke.

"Well, there's only one way to find out. Give me five minutes to dress and send them up."

"Very good, sir." She closed the door.

Holmes disappeared into his room. Wiggins was the leader of the unofficial Baker Street Irregulars, boys whom Holmes used from time to time to run errands, but I was unfamiliar with the name Christopher Baker. Could he be a new boy added to the Irregulars? Well, as Holmes had remarked, we would soon find out.

When Holmes returned, he was dressed to receive visitors. After the time allotted, we heard feet on the stairs and a knock on the door. "Come, Wiggins," called Holmes.

Wiggins was, by my estimation, nearing adulthood at that time, and almost as tall as I was. He was dressed, as always, in patched pants and a thin jacket with a cap he must have found in a dustbin. He was handsome in a jaunty sort of way, though his hair was long and could have stood cutting. Dressed as he was, he should have been cold, but if he was, he wasn't going to admit it to any man, woman, or child.

Beside him was a far younger boy who I placed at eight or nine years of age, wearing a heavy coat and holding a cap in his hand. He was dark-haired and very thin. He wasn't malnourished, but perhaps one could say he was undernourished. Despite the possibility that he wasn't eating his fill, he had outgrown what appeared to be his Sunday best pants, for his socks peeked out underneath the hem.

"Well, Wiggins," asked Holmes, "what do we have here?"

"This 'ere is Christopher Baker, Guv'nor. I brought 'im 'cause 'e is in need of 'elp."

I had noticed before during those times when he was exposed to children that Holmes wasn't at his best. Such was the case now. He looked at the boy in front of him as if he wasn't quite sure what to do with him.

So I intervened. "You did the right thing, Wiggins." Holmes raised an eyebrow at me, but said nothing.

"Then I will just step out and wait for 'im down below, so's 'e can tell you 'is business." And Wiggins left us.

"Please take off your coat and take a seat, Master Baker," I said, indicating the chair most often used by clients. He shrugged off his coat and took the chair, his feet dangling over the edge, making his pants look even shorter than they were. Holmes and I sat in our usual spots.

"Are you Sherlock Holmes," the boy said to me.

"No. I'm Dr. Watson," I said, indicating my friend. "This is Sherlock Holmes."

The boy looked squarely at Holmes. "I would like to hire you, Mr. Holmes, sir, if you are willing to take the case." His grammar was proper – certainly better than Wiggins's.

"Indeed," said Holmes.

"Wiggins says you are the smartest man in London."

Holmes was amused. "I dare say several men, including my own brother, might take exception with that description, but it is certainly flattering. How may I help you?"

"I can pay your fee."

"I am glad to hear it."

"I can prove it," the boy said as if Holmes had challenged him, and he proceeded to dump a pile of pence from his pocket. They clattered noisily on the table. "That's two shillings and five pence," he said proudly.

Holmes's mouth twitched. I knew that he often waived his fee if a client couldn't pay or a case interested him, but I also knew that when he charged a fee, it was considerably more than two-shilling-and-five-pence.

Holmes rearranged his face to show that he was impressed. "How did you manage to assemble such a princely sum?"

"I do odd jobs for the grocer nearby my house. I was saving for a football, but as I got one for Christmas, I don't need the money now."

"Well, since you have so admirably established the fact that you can pay me, how may I help you?"

"I want you to find my sister's dolly," he told us.

Whatever Holmes expected, it certainly wasn't this. "Did she lose it?"

"No, sir. Someone broke into our home on Christmas Day while we were all asleep and stole it from underneath our Christmas tree."

Holmes suddenly leaned forward. I could see that while I found Master Baker's statement unbelievable, he found it interesting. "That is most unusual. How did you know a dolly was stolen?"

"Because it wasn't there under the tree, and I knew it should be. I was with Father when he bought it. The box was there, but not the doll."

"Was anything else stolen?"

"No, but they unwrapped some of our other presents."

"Only some of them?"

"Yes, sir."

"What presents were unwrapped?"

He thought about it. "There was a watch and gloves for my father, and a new hat for my mother."

"How many presents were left wrapped?"

"My football and a new coat for me. A hat pin for my mother. A new pair of shoes for my sister." He thought about it. "There were a couple of others, but I don't remember them all."

"You have done splendidly," said Holmes approvingly. He sat back and peaked his hands under his chin.

The boy interrupted his thoughts. "Will you take the case, Mr. Holmes, sir?"

"Yes," he replied. "There is a facet to your account that interests me considerably. Yes, I will take your case."

I had been worrying about something since I had seen the boy, and I could no longer prevent myself from asking, "Do your parents know you're here, Christopher?"

At this, he looked uncomfortable. "No, sir. When I told my story to Wiggins, and he suggested I tell it to you, I decided to come myself. I didn't want to disappoint Amelia in case Mr. Holmes wouldn't help us."

"Amelia is your sister?"

"Yes. She is my younger sister. She's five."

"And how old are you?"

"I'm eight, sir, if it pleases you."

"Master Baker," said Holmes, "please join Wiggins below and ask him to wait for us. We will accompany you to your home and speak with your parents and examine where the theft occurred."

"Thank you, sir!" He turned to leave, but stopped himself. "Oh, and one other thing, if I may ask."

"Please do," said Holmes.

"Amelia still believes Father Christmas delivers our presents. You won't spoil it for her that Mother and Father are doing it, will you?"

Gravely, Holmes replied, "She will never learn it from me."

And then he left us.

When he was certain that the boy was downstairs and out of earshot, Holmes did something that was rare for him: He burst into laughter. When he was done, he said, "Certainly, this is the youngest client who has ever engaged me!"

"Thank you for taking the case, Holmes."

"I'm not an observant man, but even I draw the line at someone stealing Christmas presents from a child. The criminal element has sunk rather low this year. Nor do I think I have ever been paid so much in relation to a client's income than I have been paid just now."

"But you aren't going to take the money, are you?"

"And rob this boy of his pride by returning it and treating his obvious sacrifice as if it was of no account? It would be hurtful to the extreme. Certainly I will take it!"

I wasn't happy with this decision. I understood what Holmes meant, and he was probably correct, but it still made me uncomfortable. "I daresay, this is probably nothing."

His expression sobered. "On the contrary. I am very concerned."

I was puzzled. "Really? Why? It seems very straightforward."

"It is that, but not as you mean."

"How so?"

Holmes began explaining. "Assuming that the information we have been given is accurate, a thief broke into Master Baker's house on Christmas morning and began opening presents. Normally, even the criminal element is inactive Christmas morning, so the timing of the robbery is interesting in itself, but that is of no account. The thief opened several packages, including a watch, which should certainly be worth more than a doll, and yet the watch was left behind. Only some presents were opened, which suggested the thief stopped as soon as the package with the doll was opened and he had it in hand. What does that suggest to you?"

"Well . . . that the doll is valuable in some way."

"And yet, you saw Master Baker. His coat is heavy and hat new, and he told us that his sister received new shoes, which demonstrates that his parents love them, but his pants are too short, which indicates that his parents have insufficient funds to immediately replace them. They are husbanding their resources to provide for their children, supplying for their children's needs in order of importance, not the least of which is schooling for their son. You no doubt observed that his manners and speech are far better than one might expect from a lower middle-class family as his appears to be."

"And what does that tell us?"

"They could never have afforded an expensive-enough doll that, upon unwrapping its package, the thief delightedly abandoned the watch and a further search and left with his find. No, the doll wasn't valuable."

"Then?"

"Do you remember the case with the Blue Carbuncle?"

"Of course! You think something was *in* the doll! Something equivalent to the Carbuncle?"

"Perhaps, or perhaps something equally of value. We need to get to the bottom of this, for I expect it's something more sinister than the theft of a doll. Will you join me in accompanying Wiggins and the boy to his home?"

"With pleasure. I'm interested in seeing this through."

"Then let us take our coats and hats and join our unlikely client."

The air was cold and the wind more than a little blustery, but Holmes and I were bundled against both. As I thought, Wiggins pretended to be unaffected by the icy air, as did our client. Perhaps it was my age in addition to my stint in the Army that I seemed to feel the cold more. The wounds I'd received in Afghanistan unfailingly ached in the cold, sometimes severely, and they did so now. After a half-hour's brisk walk, we arrived at Christopher Baker's home.

It was a humble affair, but not penurious. The front had been whitewashed, and there were boxes in the windows that, I presumed, would be bright with flowers during the spring. I assumed the upper rooms were bedrooms, and the downstairs for living – suppositions that were confirmed when Christopher let us in.

"This is where I leave you, Guv'nor," said Wiggins. "Good luck!" He tipped his hat to Christopher, somewhat ironically, I thought, and sauntered off.

When we entered, Christopher called out, "Mother! Father! There is someone here to see you!" A presentable Christmas tree was standing opposite the fireplace, with unwrapped presents still under the tree. A young girl with blond hair, obviously Amelia, was sitting in front of a low table with a child's tea set and, as a companion, a stuffed rabbit that had been well-used. She was a fetching child, and she looked up as we entered with interest on her face.

I heard a woman's voice. "On Boxing Day?" She and I might have been reading from the same book.

Almost together, she entered from the kitchen, and a man descended from the stairs. Mrs. Baker was as blond as her daughter, with an oval, handsome face, currently looking quizzically at Homes and myself. Her husband was a strong-looking man with hair as black as his son's. His beard was closely trimmed.

"Here now, Christopher" he asked, "who is this you bring visiting?"

Proudly, Christopher said, "This is Mr. Sherlock Holmes and Dr. Watson. I've hired them to find who took Amelia's dolly. I hired them with my football money!"

"Oh, Chris, you worked so hard for that!" said his mother.

The look on Mr. Baker's face – or I should say the looks – were what one might expect from a father on hearing such a pronouncement from his son. He showed first disbelief and surprise, followed by the embarrassment of what it meant that complete strangers had been hired by his son for a childish problem, followed by disapproval that his son had done so without permission from him, and then, finally, understanding of his son's laudable motivation and pride in his sacrifice. He arranged his face.

"Chris, you ought not to have done that. These men are sure to have had plans. It's Boxing Day!" But the remonstrance was mild, and as much for us as his son.

"On the contrary, Mr. Baker," said Holmes, "Dr. Watson and I were doing nothing but relaxing, and we both rather welcomed an opportunity to be of service."

Amelia spoke. "Are you going to find my dolly?"

I bent down to speak to her. "Mr. Holmes will do his best." As I did so, I surreptitiously removed a pound piece from my pocket and placed it under the table that stood between us. "Mr. Holmes is very good about finding things."

"Oh, I am so happy. Her box was all empty." Soberly, she said, "Someone kidnapped her."

"Dastardly," I told her.

"I asked Father Christmas for her," she informed me. "I saw her in a store window, but she isn't there now, so he got her for me, but some bad man kidnapped her." She didn't cry, for she was obviously attempting to be brave. "All I have left is her box!"

Her mother went to her. "There, there, Amelia. These gentlemen are here to help." She cast a look at us as she said the words, a look that was as much hopeful as it was a little anxious.

"We can make no promises," I explained, "but we will do our best to return your dolly to you." I stood. As I did so, I caught a look from Holmes that told me he'd missed nothing of what I had done.

Mr. Baker came and took our hands, one at a time. "I am Jason Baker, and this is my wife, Clarissa."

"Sherlock Holmes and my associate, Dr. Watson. I was hoping you could answer a few questions about the doll and what happened yesterday morning."

He hesitated and looked at Amelia. "Can we do it outside?"

Holmes nodded. "Of course. We have no desire to intrude."

"I'll get my coat," he said, but before he could do so, his son cried out.

"Father, look!" He reached down under the table and stood, holding in his hand the pound-piece I had placed there.

"My lands!" said Mrs. Baker. "Where did it come from?"

"Perhaps Father Christmas brought it," I suggested.

So that only I could hear, Holmes murmured, "Shameless, Watson."

I could feel myself redden, and more so when I saw the master of the house looking at me suspiciously. I tried to appear innocent, for indeed, I had done nothing wrong.

Slowly Mr. Baker said, "I'll take that then, Chris." Without a trace of regret, he handed it to his father. "I think I'll hire Mr. Holmes myself. Would that be alright? And I can give you the money for his hire." Christopher's face fell. His father saw it. "Or perhaps not. We can put this to good use. It was a good thing you did, son, hiring Mr. Holmes for your sister." The boy looked relieved and glowing at the praise. "And now, let me get my coat."

He left the room, returning shortly as he donned it.

"May I come, too, Father?" asked Christopher.

After a moment's hesitation, he said, "I don't see why not, Chris." And so, we left the warmth of the house for the blustery winter air outside it.

Once out of his daughter's hearing, Mr. Baker said, "I am sorry that you've come all this way for nothing, for we have found the dolly already."

"You found it, Father!" said Christopher.

Holmes said, "Your daughter seems unaware of it."

"This is why." From inside the coat, he pulled out a doll. It was a rag doll with a porcelain face and hands, and dressed quite finely in a yellow silk gown with lace and a matching hat. But the doll's face was cracked on the left side, and down the middle of the doll was a long slit in the dress that revealed her cotton stuffing to the world. "I couldn't let her see the doll like this. I found it outside yesterday morning. I guess the cat got it."

"May I?" Holmes took the doll from him as he nodded. He examined it. "No cat did this, Mr. Baker. There is no indication of the shredding that a cat's claws would inflict on cloth. No, this was done by a sharp knife. And it isn't the first such injury the doll has sustained. Look here. There is another rent in the doll's body, but rather badly sewed up. It was probably done with the doll's dress removed. The second incision was more hastily done and through the dress."

"But, who would do such a thing? It makes no sense."

"It does if something was first hidden inside the doll and then retrieved."

He was bewildered. "But what would be in the doll?"

"That is what we must discover," responded Holmes. "You handled the doll when you bought it. Was its body soft? Hard?"

He thought about it. "Now that you mention it, her body was lumpy and hard in places. I thought it was how she was made."

Holmes mused, "Seeing she is completely soft now, whatever was in her had been hard." He pointed. "The damage on the doll's face doesn't appear new. The crack in the porcelain isn't bright. That would suggest it isn't a recent breakage."

He signed. "It is not. It was like that when I bought it."

"You bought a damaged doll for your daughter?" Holmes's tone wasn't accusatory, only intrigued.

"Aye. She saw the doll in Uncle's window." From my association with Holmes, I knew that the owners of a pawn shop were often called "Uncle", and I assumed that was what he meant. "She took pity on it. 'No one will buy her,' she told me. 'She is all broken. She must be very lonely. May I have her?' She is such a tender-hearted thing. I told her that I hadn't the money, but perhaps Father Christmas would bring it on Christmas Day. I returned later with Chris and purchased the doll."

"I'll wager Uncle was surprised."

"That he was, Mr. Holmes. 'I never thought I would sell her,' he told me."

"Did he tell you how he came to have her?"

"No, nor did I ask."

Holmes returned the doll. "It is interesting. Although damaged, it appears to have been originally of high-quality manufacture. It's hardly the kind of doll that one would expect to find in the hands of someone forced to use it as collateral for short-term money. How such a doll come to be in a pawn shop is an interesting line of inquiry. I think we need to speak to Uncle."

"Is it really that important?" he asked. "It is only a doll."

"As you have remarked, the situation surrounding it makes no sense. What was in the doll? Why hide something there? And why, if having hidden something of value in the doll, was she put in pawn? And why, having left it so long in the shop that it was offered for sale, did he then return to rob you of it? There is a mystery here that speaks of something more important than the theft of a Christmas doll." Holmes finished by saying, "So, yes, Mr. Baker, this is really that important."

"Well, I cannot argue. I can take you there," he said. "It's only a short way."

The three of us followed Mr. Baker down the street. After several turns, we found ourselves at "*Odds and Ends*", a medium-sized establishment painted with green trim above which were the expected three golden balls identifying the building as a pawn shop. I was uncertain if it was going to be open, but it was. Holmes, approaching the shop, remarked, "This door has been forced."

Several items that hadn't been claimed were displayed in the windows, but to my eyes, they seemed badly jumbled and hardly set up at their best effect. The inside of the store was worse. As we entered, the bell suspended above the door jangled, and a middle-aged man with a beard and a sallow, sunken face, but bright, intelligent eyes, looked up from his work. In a reedy voice, he said, "Mr. Baker! What are you doing here again? Did your daughter like her Christmas doll?"

"To be true," said Mr. Baker, "that is why we are here."

"I will be with you in a moment. Please excuse the disarray. I am afraid that someone broke in to my shop while it was closed."

"So was our home, on Christmas morning no less! And they took and damaged Amelia's doll. These men have come to help." He introduced us.

"I am Phineas Gittleman, but I am often called Uncle," explained the proprietor. "How odd that we have both experienced thievery on a day set aside for peace and goodwill. And of a doll, no less!"

Holmes asked, "Was anything stolen from your shop?"

"Now, that is the odd thing. Many things were moved. Quite a mess he made of it. Even my account ledger was opened, but from what I can see, nothing was taken." His eyes twinkled. "In fact, not only was nothing taken, something was left!" He gestured to the counter, on which were several coins. "It won't quite pay for repairing the damage to my door, but it's a good start."

"Interesting," declared Holmes. "Hardly what one might expect from a hardened criminal. This puts these thefts in an entirely different light."

"But you said the doll was taken and damaged. Might my intruder have been after the doll, and when he didn't find it here, went to your place?" His mind was working quickly. "Yes, that would explain the ledger being opened." He went to the counter and looked at an account book opened on it. "Yes, it's open to the sale of the doll to you. But whatever for?"

"Do you remember who pawned the doll, Mr. Gittleman?"

"Not his name, but him I certainly remember. We normally get more women than men, and we never get someone dressed so well." He leafed through his book. "Ah, here it is. The doll was pawned on 27 October by John Smith."

"Not very original," commented Holmes, dryly.

The proprietor smiled. "No. But I don't care about their names. All they need is the claim ticket. As I said, we don't get many men, and those that come are somewhat embarrassed. I assumed at the time it wasn't his true name." He shrugged. "As I said, his name was of no matter to me."

"What do you remember of him?"

"He was well-dressed in a blue tailored suit. I was astonished to see him, for he didn't look like someone who needed a loan. He asked me how much for the doll. Well, the doll had at one time been a rich girl's doll, but the dress had lost its luster and was stained, and her face was cracked. I told him, 'Not very much. She's broken.' He said, 'But how much?' I said, 'A pence.' I could hardly go lower. He said he would take it. And then he said an odd thing. He said I wasn't to sell her. I said, 'Not much chance of that, broken as she is!' But I also told him that anything that was not claimed within a month would be sold or thrown out. He said again that I shouldn't sell her or throw her out. He was very . . . firm about that."

"I assume he didn't come back."

"Well, not right away. It happens sometimes. I waited for a bit, but he never returned. It was no great concern. I was only out a pence, and such losses are the cost of doing business. I almost threw her out, but my wife was able to clean her dress. That made her look better. She told me with Christmas coming, some poor soul – I do beg your pardon, Mr. Baker – might buy it for his little girl because he couldn't afford a new doll, and you did."

"But the seller did come back?"

"Yes, that he did. The day before Christmas. He told me he had been sick and that was why he hadn't come earlier. The truth was, he did look as if he had been ill. He presented the claim ticket and said he must have the doll now. I explained that he hadn't come in the allotted time, and I thought he no longer wanted her, so I sold her. He was very upset. He wanted to know who had bought her, and I told him that was none of his business. He demanded the name. I refused." He shrugged again. "He left when I threatened to call the constable."

"Would you recognize this man again if you saw him?"

"Oh, I daresay."

"Can you describe him?"

"Not very tall. Thin. Both times he was dressed well. His hair was a light brown and thinning a little, and his eyes dark brown. He was perhaps in his twenties. He spoke with a posh accent."

"Mr. Gittleman, let me commend you on your powers of observation and recall."

"Very kind of you, but in my line of work, a good memory is rather necessary."

"You have been most helpful. If it's necessary, would you be willing to repeat to the police what you have told us?"

"The police?"

"I suspect it may not be necessary, but it could be."

"Well . . . I suppose so, but it seems to me quite a lot of bother about a doll."

"Yes, it is that," agreed Holmes.

When we left, Mr. Baker asked us, "Will that be all?"

"I think we will continue our inquiries," said Holmes, "but you and your son may return to your home. We can proceed without you."

"If I may," I interrupted, looking at Mr. Baker.

"Yes?"

"Would I be able to take the doll? My wife is a very good seamstress. She might be able to repair her. I could then return it to you."

He hesitated. "That is very good of you, Dr. Watson." He turned to his son. "Chris, could you run back home and tell Mother that I am on my way? And not a word about the doll to her or Amelia."

"Yes, Father," and he darted off.

When his son disappeared around the corner, he turned to me. "I would be willing to let your wife try her hand at the doll, Doctor, but I would want to pay her. I have in my pocket an unexpected pound piece delivered rather mysteriously by Father Christmas." I was forced to conclude that I hadn't fooled anyone but myself with my clumsy attempt to reimburse Christopher Baker for the money with which he hired us.

I balked. "A pound is too much! And your son has delivered his life savings to Mr. Holmes."

"Aye, and the proud bugger wants to pay you." He considered. "How much was your fee?"

"Five-shilling-and-two-pence," I said, knowing full well that young Christopher Baker only given us only two-shilling-and-five-pence. I tried not to let the fact that I was exaggerating the sum that had been given us by his son, but I feared that I wasn't completely successful. Despite the chill in the air, I abruptly felt very warm.

Mr. Baker was surprised. "He had that much?"

Holmes said, with a heavy trace of irony, "He appears to be uncommonly thrifty."

"Well, then," returned Mr. Baker, but suspiciously, "would Mrs. Watson accept payment of fourteen-shilling-and-eighteen-pence for her work?"

"I still think it is too high."

"I'll not pay a pence less," he warned me.

"Very well," I said reluctantly. "Fourteen-shilling-and-eighteen-pence."

"I'll have it for you when you return the doll." He handed the doll to me, tipped his hat, and started after his son.

Holmes looked at me with a bemused expression. "And what will you do, Doctor, if he asks his son how he managed to acquire such a large sum?"

"Oh!" I replied. "I hadn't thought of that." What could I say? "Perhaps I can say that five-shilling-and-two-pence is the lowest fee you charge for services."

Holmes became stern. "You will kindly leave me out of your subterfuge."

I was a little indignant. "I am only trying to help them. It is Boxing Day! It is obvious that they could use a little extra."

Holmes's expression softened. "You have a kind heart, Watson. I'm certain you are right. I suspect they didn't just happen to be in front of Mr. Gittleman's shop by chance. You may be unaware of it, but many people actually pawn their Sunday best on Monday and, after the breadwinner is paid on Friday, redeem their clothes on Saturday so they may be worn to church, and no one the wiser. But be that as it may, they appear far better off than many, and disinclined to take charity."

"In my mind, that makes them all the more worthy of it."

The corner of Holmes's mouth turned up. "The point is well-taken. And, as you say, I'm sure they can put it to good use."

I was rather glad that topic of conversation was exhausted. "How will we continue our inquiries?"

"I thought a visit to Scotland Yard might yield more information. I suspect they might be involved with this, but we will only know for sure if we ask."

When we arrived, Holmes asked if Inspectors Lestrade or Gregson were in. Lestrade wasn't, but Gregson, we were told, was in his office and would be able to see us. Gregson was a big, solid man, with fair hair and a square face. He greeted us cordially. "Good day, Mr. Holmes, Doctor. Good to see you both. I assume this isn't a social call."

"We may be in a position to help you solve a case, assuming that the Yard is involved."

"I'll welcome any help you can give me. What case?"

"There is where I need your help. The case would date back two months, though probably just after that date, possibly a couple of days earlier, though that's unlikely. It would involve something lost or stolen of relatively small size. It would have no intrinsic value, like rare coins or gems would. Or I should say, it is unlikely that it would. More likely, it would be something of little monetary value but important for legal or sentimental reasons. The summons for help would have come from an upper class, wealthy home. The case would have remained unsolved. Do you have anything like that?"

Gregson looked sharply at Holmes. "It's all a little vague, but, yes, we had an odd request that fits your bill. We had a call from a Charles Hawtrey – man in his sixties. His family made money in manufacturing. Claimed that his family seal had been stolen. Normally, this wouldn't have been a case for the Yard, but Hawtrey is connected by marriage to Lord Pennington, and the Yard was instructed to provide all possible assistance."

"And did you?"

"I went out myself. Hawtrey is approaching seventy. Looks more like twenty years older than that. Death warmed over and all. He insisted that someone had stolen his seal. I tried to explain that there was no reason for a seal to be stolen, and it was probably just mislaid. After all, it's of no value to anyone but the man whose seal it is. His butler said that a thorough search had been conducted of the entire house and grounds without success, but at Hawtrey's insistence, I commandeered no fewer than ten constables and we made another search."

"But didn't find it," finished Holmes for him.

"No."

"Why was he so insistent on the seal?"

"He wanted to change his will."

"I wasn't aware that a family seal is necessary for validating a will."

"It isn't, but he had a bee in his bonnet about it. You see, his previous will had left everything to his wife. When she passed away, he refused to change the will without the seal."

"But given the fact that you didn't find the seal, did he change his will?"

Gregson shrugged. "I couldn't say. We were unable to find it, and that was as far as I could justify the Yard's involvement."

Holmes said, "Perhaps I can provide you with more justification." And quickly and succinctly, he related to Gregson all that we had learned. When he had finished, Holmes said, "It might be instructive to see if Mr. Hawtrey's seal has recently been found."

"You think it was in the doll?"

"I think it likely. And it relieves my mind. I feared this case might involve something for which someone might resort to desperate measures. But a seal, stolen by a thief who leaves behind him money to repair the damage he has caused? I'm hopeful that this case is less dire than I first feared."

"Well, it's Boxing Day, and a little slow here at the Yard. Would you care to visit the Hawtrey estate with me?"

As Holmes had predicted, the estate was a grand edifice, ornately carved, three-stories tall, surrounded by grounds that – even in a month that wouldn't display them to their best effect – were impressive, with tall pines and even taller oaks. A butler answered the door.

"Inspector Gregson of Scotland Yard to see Mr. Hawtrey."

"Very good, sir. I will see if he's in."

In a very short time, we were shown into a small, richly appointed office. Mr. Hawtrey sat at a large desk, behind which was a window to let in the light of the day. His hair was completely white, but still plentiful. His face was lined, and there was an unhealthy pallor to his skin. He rose with difficulty to greet us, and his voice, though cracked with age, was still robust.

"Inspector Gregson, I appreciate your diligence, but I regret to inform you that I have wasted your time in coming here. I have found the seal. It was in my desk drawer the entire time."

"This is Mr. Sherlock Holmes and Dr. Watson. Mr. Holmes is a private inquiry agent, and he was working on a case that, I believe, has a bearing on the loss of your seal."

"But, as I say, I didn't lose it. It was here. I don't know how I missed it."

Holmes asked, "Were you the only one who looked in your desk, Mr. Hawtrey?"

Hawtrey was startled. "No." His features sharpened. "No. I know Graves did, and I think some of my children did, too. It's where I kept it, and I thought at first that I must have overlooked it."

"So we can be certain that with so many people, the seal was, in all probability, *not* in the drawer at that time."

"Yes, I see that. But then, how did it come to be there now?"

"It was returned by the person who first removed it."

"But who would do such a thing? And why?"

"My understanding, Mr. Hawtrey, is that you were going to change your will but were prevented when you couldn't find the seal." The old man's face lit up with comprehension. "Is that true?"

"Yes. I wanted to wait until we found the seal."

"But you had announced your intention to change your will, did you not? Perhaps you even said who would be included in the will and who would not. Is that the case?"

"It was."

"Did you perhaps decide recently to revise the changes you intended to make?"

He looked at Holmes with astonishment. "Yes! How could you possibly know that?"

"Because it's the only thing that accounts for the seal's return. What was your original intention for your new will?"

Hawtrey looked embarrassed. "I had intended to leaving small bequeaths to the staff and stipends for my children, but I intended to will the bulk of the estate to the Orphanage of St. Paul, from where I was adopted by my parents as a child."

"And now?"

"The bequeaths remain the same. The remaining estate is split five ways in equal allotments between my children and the orphanage."

"Why did you change your mind?"

"I realized when talking with my children that they would be unable to maintain this home and grounds with only the stipends I intended to provide them, and I wanted this house to remain in our family. I simply hadn't thought through the finances. Perhaps later, if our business continues to expand in the hands of Lysander – he's my oldest son – he can purchase the house outright from the others, assuming they are willing to sell, but right now, he couldn't do it. And my younger children still live here."

"They are unmarried?"

"Lysander and Vincent are married. They have their own homes, but they are here with us for the holidays. Rosamund and Benedict are single and live here with me."

Holmes said, "Do I correctly gather that this new arrangement for your will meets your approval?"

"Absolutely. As I said, I hadn't thought through the financial aspects surrounding my previous intention. The results of that will would have been most unsatisfactory. The house would have needed to be sold, and our staff let go."

"Then the loss of the seal was, in some ways, providential?"

"Yes, I suppose you could say that."

Holmes glanced at Gregson, then back at Hawtrey. "Then, I see no reason to trouble you further. Though I have a request. May I speak with your children?"

Hawtrey was puzzled. "I'm sure you may, but why do you want to speak with them?"

"I was investigating a small case for a family, of importance to them but to no one else. I believe your children, quite by accident, can shed light on that affair if I can speak with them."

"Will you need me?"

"I think not."

"Then I will ask Graves to arrange it."

In short time, we were in a larger sitting room with the rest of the family: Lysander Hawtrey and his wife Beryl, Vincent Hawtrey and his wife Irene, Rosamund Hawtrey, and the youngest, Benedict Hawtrey. From Mr. Gittleman's description, it was evident upon meeting Benedict Hawtrey that he was the man who had pawned the doll. He looked apprehensive.

Gregson introduced us. Upon the conclusion of the introductions, he told the family, "Mr. Holmes has been working on an unusual case. This isn't Yard business, but the Yard would appreciate your cooperation."

Beryl Hawtrey said, "This is exciting. Like a Christmas puzzle!"

Holmes was amused. "It's a very small puzzle, but it is of importance to my client. We have already spoken with your father."

Lysander Hawtrey frowned. "Just who is your client, Mr. Holmes?"

"Normally, I wouldn't divulge that information," replied my friend. "But in this case, I believe it would serve the cause of justice to tell you that I was hired by an eight-year-old boy, Christopher Baker, to find a doll, a Christmas present for his sister that was stolen from their home on Christmas morning."

Vincent Hawtrey gawked at him. "You're here on a holiday because of a doll?" His voice was filled with incredulity.

Holmes permitted himself a small smile. "I agree it is outlandish, but to this family, and especially the children, the doll was important." He turned to me. "Show them the doll, Watson."

I pulled her from my coat pocket and Rosamund Hawtrey exclaimed, "Why, it's Caroline!"

Holmes said, "I thought you might recognize it, Miss Hawtrey."

She took the doll from me. "Of course I recognize her! She was my favorite for many years, but then I dropped her, and she broke. Even then, I slept with her, but . . . well . . . I grew up. I thought she had been consigned to the dustbin years ago."

Vincent Hawtrey said, "And this was the doll this family is concerned about? Who buys a broken doll for his children?"

Holmes's voice hardened. "A working-class man who, even on Christmas day, cannot afford a new doll. I understand that his daughter saw the doll for sale in a window and took pity on her because she was broken, and specifically asked for her."

Vincent Hawtrey looked ready to speak again, but his wife put a hand on his arm. "Don't be difficult, Vincent. I think it's touching. Poor little waif."

Rosamund asked, "But how did my doll come to be in a shop window?"

"As to that, I believe Mr. Benedict can provide the most comprehensive explanation. Am I correct, sir?"

"I . . ." began the youngest son, "That is . . . I . . . well – "

"Perhaps it will help if I begin the story. After the death of your mother, your father revealed his intention to change his will, leaving the bulk of his estate to the Orphanage of St. Paul."

Lysander, the oldest said, "That's correct Mr. Holmes. It wouldn't have affected me or Vince, but it would certainly would have meant that Roz and Ben would have had to find a new place to live. I could never have maintained two homes, or even one this size."

"Mr. Benedict agreed with you. He knew, as I suspect you all did, that your father wasn't wholly himself, and that he would regret his decision later. Of course, a will can be changed, but your father is in poor health. He might not have lived to do so. I presume his previous will, leaving everything to your mother, was more in line with his current plans."

"If she predeceased him, the estate was to be divided equally among us," said Lysander.

"But his intention to bequeath the bulk of the estate to the orphanage would, you felt, ultimately be contrary to your father's real desires. Mr. Benedict agreed. Knowing his father's desire to use the seal to certify his actions, he removed the seal from your father's drawer. Is that correct, Mr. Benedict?"

The younger Hawtrey replied, "It is, Mr. Holmes. I thought it would give him time to . . . well . . . to regain his senses. But then he ordered the search. I wasn't anxious about that at first. But when he insisted on calling the police, I worried that the seal would be found in my room. And how would I explain it? I could hide it somewhere else in the house, but what if it were found? He still might change the will. So . . . I hid it in my sister's doll which I had come across by chance some years ago and kept. I thought then to repair it and surprise Roz with it, but I never got around to it. At first, I thought hiding the seal in the doll would be enough, but I became anxious. What if it were found there?"

"So you pawned the doll."

Miss Rosamund said, "You pawned Caroline!" Her distress was real.

Benedict was embarrassed again. "I did. I thought no one would buy her. She was broken. Once Father came to his right mind, I would redeem the doll and return the seal to his desk."

"It was quite ingenious," commented Holmes. "It was safe from a search in the house and grounds, and yet accessible to you. Even if someone found the pawn ticket, it would have no meaning."

"And then I took ill."

"And for quite some time, I assume."

"Yes. It was three weeks. The doctor said inflammation of the lungs. Father had already changed his mind, but I was too sick to retrieve the doll. Finally, on Christmas Eve day, I was well enough to return to the shop, but the proprietor told me she had been sold. I would have happily bought her back, but he refused to tell me who had bought her."

"And so?"

If Benedict had been embarrassed before, he was absolutely mortified now. He spoke, almost whispering. "I broke into the shop."

His family reacted with dismay. "Oh, Benedict!" said Vincent's wife.

His sister said, "You didn't!"

"I did. As you know, I told everyone I was still recovering and wanted to retire early, and then I slipped out and hailed a cab to the pawn shop. I had to break into it. I first searched it, hoping the owner was wrong and the doll was there. But he was right. I couldn't find it. But I found his ledger and obtained the name and address of the purchaser. I left what money I had, less my return fare, to cover the damage I had caused. That night, I waited outside their home until it was dark. It was so cold! I worried that I might become sick again. But I stayed – I had to! When I thought it would be safe, I entered the house."

Holmes asked, "The door was open?"

"Yes."

Holmes shook his head. "Too many people are far too trusting of their fellow man."

"I opened presents until I found the doll. I took it outside, opened it up, and retrieved the seal. I left the doll there."

Rosamund said, "Oh, poor Caroline! What a way to treat her!"

"And that poor family!" echoed Irene. "Imagine, coming down to a Christmas with the presents already opened!"

Gregson cleared his throat. Severely, he said, "Mr. Benedict, no doubt your father will not press charges, but you have broken into a pawn shop and burgled someone's home. I'm afraid I must take you in."

The dismay that went around the room was as loud as it was expected after such a pronouncement.

"Surely not!" objected Lysander.

"It's Christmas!" his brother observed.

Gregson was unmoved. "Even on Christmas, ransacking shops and theft aren't condoned by the Yard."

"If I may, Inspector," interrupted Holmes, "don't you think this was more a case of poor judgement rather than criminal intent?"

"Be that as it may, these are still crimes."

"Agreed, but may I suggest that if Mr. Benedict were to add to the money he left for repairing Mr. Gittleman's shop door, with a little extra for his trouble, and if he were to compensate the family for the intrusion into their home and the shock his actions brought them, this would serve the cause of justice far more than bringing Mr. Benedict before the Assizes. After all, very little harm has actually been done."

Lysander Hawtrey readily agreed. "It is more than fair."

Benedict nearly spoke at the same time. "I am deeply ashamed of what I did. I'd be happy to pay."

Gregson looked reluctant. "Well, it isn't strictly legal."

I pointed out, "But it is Boxing Day, and the Christmas season. Perhaps a little forgiveness at this time wouldn't be amiss."

Gregson relented. "Well, very well." And then he wagged a finger at Benedict. "But let's not be stingy about it!"

And he wasn't. The amount that Benedict Hawtrey gave us to provide to Mr. Gittleman was such that the gentleman said, "Please tell whoever it was that he may break into my shop at any time if he intends to be this generous after."

When my wife learned of the doll, she found additional stuffing for her and sewed the body up tightly. She found a contrasting but complementary blue silk to hide the rent in the doll's dress, and embellished her outfit with the same material. When she was done, the doll was even more grand, I thought, than it would have been when first purchased.

"But what do we do for her face?" my Mary asked me.

"We do nothing," I told her. "It was the doll's injured face that first prompted the child to want her."

Holmes and I delivered the doll the next day. Amelia's delight lit up her face.

"Oh, thank you!" she said. "She is so grand!"

Seeing that Holmes and I had a story to tell, Mr. Baker sent her daughter to her room with her new treasure. When she was gone, he carefully counted out fourteen shilling and eighteen pence to me in the presence of his wife and son.

"This really is unnecessary," I protested.

"It's only right, Dr. Watson."

Holmes said, "But it is also only right that the man who broke into your home repays you for the trouble he caused you." And, without mentioning names, he relayed the story to them.

Christopher was pleased. "Wiggins was right! You are the smartest man in London!"

Holmes smiled at the compliment. He then handed an envelope to Mr. Baker. "From your intruder to compensate you for the trouble he caused you."

When he opened it, he paled. "It's too much!" he said at last.

"Not at all," said Holmes seriously. "The man broke into your home on Christmas Day and upset your family. He is quite well-to-do and can well afford this as recompense. In fact, he insists on it. If you refuse it, you reject his heartfelt remorse."

"We're rich!" declared Christopher.

"Hardly that, son," said his father, slowly. "But it is a goodly sum. Husbanded well, we can send your sister to school as well as you." He glanced at his wife. "And perhaps other brothers and sisters that may come along."

Mrs. Baker began to cry. "Oh, who would have thought anything good would come of this!"

Her husband said to his son, "And with this money, I will now repay you for your hire of Mr. Holmes, and I'll hear no quarrel about it. We aren't rich, but you can let that man reimburse you for your generosity."

Christopher's eyes widened. "I'll get all two-shillings-and-five-pence back?"

His father glanced at me, then returned to his son. "Well, I thought five-shillings-and-two-pence would be about right, for the man would want you to know how sorry he is." And then he looked back at me. "Don't you agree, Doctor?"

And, of course, I did.

The Man of Miracles
by Derrick Belanger

The sky and the land had become a conjoined blanket of white, making it feel as though the few dots of people congregating in the street were walking in a blank canvas, searching for the landscape that would give them their setting and purpose. Unlike the locals who had complained of the miserable December bleakness, Sherlock Holmes enjoyed such weather. It made him want to spend time indoors, away from the slight distraction of taking a stroll, hiking in the hinterlands, or travelling along the nearby coast, as much as his body might need the physical exercise. It gave his brain full attention to his study at hand, his research into coal tar derivatives. He had been away from London for years now, voyaging from one discovery to the next. He had studied with the Head Lama in Lhasa, had traversed Europe in the disguise of a Norwegian, and now found himself settled, at least for a time, in the French city of Montpellier.

Holmes had begun to ready himself for the day's work. In the large two-room flat that served as his bedroom and laboratory, he'd arranged his beakers, lit three Bunsen burners, and adorned a lab coat. With tongs in hand, he was about to place his first concoction of the day onto the flames when he was interrupted by a rapping on his door. Very few people knew of Holmes's location, and maybe four in France knew of his true identity. The last time he was interrupted was three days before when he received a delivery of milk and fresh bread which he had ordered from the Boulangerie. He had no such delivery scheduled for this morning.

"*Bonjour*, Monsieur," Holmes was greeted warmly by LaPerle, the squat grey-haired inspector from the National Police.

"*Bonjour*, LaPerle. What brings you to my humble domain on this chilly morning?" Holmes asked kindly, hiding how perturbed he felt to be distracted before he even had a chance to begin his experiments for the day.

"May I enter?" the inspector asked.

Holmes's lips tightened in a thin line. He didn't want to seem unfriendly, but he also wanted to be allowed to work undisturbed. The inspector was handpicked by Mycroft to be one of the few who knew of Holmes's true identity. He didn't want to coldly turn the man away. Holmes gave a nod of assent and stood to the side so that LaPerle could enter his domicile. He would find out what the inspector wanted and try to get him to leave as soon as he could. Most likely LaPerle had a knot in a case which he wanted Holmes to untie for him. With the lack of crime mentioned in the papers, and nature's deterrent of frigid weather, Holmes thought the knot would most likely be a single one – perhaps he'd only had to tug at a lace to unravel.

"To what do I owe the pleasure?" Holmes asked once he and the inspector were seated in some cushioned wooden chairs around a side table in the lab. "I'd offer you a drink, but in a laboratory . . . ."

The inspector shook his head at the suggestion. "I have an engagement at nine this morning and will have my fill then. A bit of early holiday cheer with some chums at the tavern." The little man looked up at the detective and gave a genial smile.

Holmes was pleased to hear that, for it meant the inspector would need to leave within a half of an hour. The detective had noticed the wreaths people had begun to hang on their doors and the decorated trees appearing in windows. To Holmes, though, Christmas was but another day of the year, no more special than any other.

"I will get right to the point, my friend," the inspector answered in a heavily accented English. Holmes had tried to get the inspector to speak to him in French at their last engagement, but the inspector insisted on English, even though his mastery of the language was rudimentary. "I need to . . . how they say . . . pick at your brain a bit. I have an unusual case. I'm not sure if it is even a case, and I'd like your advice on how to proceed."

It was just as Holmes thought. Nothing more than a mere puzzle missing a piece or two. The inspector was a direct fellow who got to the point. Holmes admired that in LaPerle and was glad that Mycroft chose LaPerle as one of the men in which he confided. This might only take a quarter-of-an-hour, perhaps even as few as ten minutes to solve.

"There is a man," the inspector began, "a German who has come to our fair city in November for the last three years. During his time here, the man is said to perform miracles."

Holmes let out a loud harrumph at the inspector's words.

"I know, but it isn't as unbelievable as it may sound. This fellow, a Nikolaus Kringle – " (Holmes let out another harrumph at the name.) " – provides solutions to the most difficult problems faced by people. It is said that he has healed the sick and saved many lives."

Holmes shook his head. He was upset that his experiments were being delayed by this fairy tale. He held his tongue though for fear if he objected, it would only make the inspector's story drag on.

"This man – some call him 'The Man of Miracles'. Others call him 'Father Christmas', and a few even refer to him as 'Saint Nikolaus'. Anyway, he doesn't charge for his advice. He merely asks for people to give what they can or what they deem is fair. Most of his visitors are the city's poorest, so he doesn't make a lot of money. However, one day last week, we received a complaint from Monsieur Toussaint, a noted banker whose wife brought their ill son to see Monsieur Kringle. He was able to solve the boy's breathing problems which had been plaguing him since he was born. Madame Toussaint returned to the small church where Kringle resides and gave him five-thousand *francs*. As you can imagine, Monsieur Toussaint was livid. He demanded that the police arrest Kringle for being a fraud."

"Ah," Holmes said, hoping that the inspector's story so far had just been an introduction to the real problem, "so you arrested him."

"No, my friend, we did not, for Toussaint dropped the charges against him."

Holmes raised his brow, "Dropped the charges?"

"*Oui*, he dropped the charges, and because Kringle not only returned the money but also saved young Toussaint's life, Monsieur Toussaint emphasized that he expected the police to leave him alone, to let him go on healing the weak and helping the poor"

"And may I surmise," Holmes said dryly, "that since Toussaint has said the police must leave this Mister Kringle alone, then you must leave him alone."

"*Oui*, you are correct. Toussaint has, shall we say, given much to the Force. Unless Monsieur Kringle commits a serious crime such as bank robbery, or the people who see him become a public nuisance, then we will leave him be."

"That's why you've come to me," Holmes said with a sigh of resignation. "You want me to do what you cannot: Investigate this 'Man of Miracles' to see if there is any sinister motive behind his free advice."

"You understand perfectly, my friend." The inspector stood from his seat and Holmes joined him. "I must away to my appointment. Please, take your time in your detective work. I shall be away for a few weeks, spending Christmas with my family in Paris. I find myself, a man of but forty-two years of age, a grandparent, and I have yet to see my grandson. I hope you understand."

"Of course. I shall look into the matter. I'm sure it will take but a day or two to draw my conclusions. I shall see you in the New Year, Inspector."

LaPerle gave Holmes a warm goodbye and then departed.

Sherlock Holmes spent the next few hours working on his latest coal tar derivative formula, calculating the right amount to assist people suffering from severe psoriasis. Holmes had the idea when he saw one of his neighbors, a factory worker named Gus, with bright red, blistered skin that was flaking off his arm. Holmes had asked the man if he'd be willing to be the test subject for his research. "Bless your heart, Monsieur Girard," he said to the detective, using Holmes's current alias. "Anything you can do to help my condition would be greatly appreciated." After working all morning, Holmes delivered a sample to him in hopes that it would show better promise than the last three treatments, which left him still in agonizing pain.

Once the tincture had been delivered and the dose applied, Holmes decided he would take the afternoon to learn about Nikolaus Kringle. He wanted to end his assignment as soon as possible. His time away from London wasn't meant to be spent on menial tasks for local police, and yet at every place on his sojourn from Tibet to Norway, he'd been compelled to help fill the deficiencies of the local law enforcement agency on at least one occasion per location. It seemed it was now his turn to do so in France.

Holmes's first stop on his investigation was at the Toussaint home. The estate house was a four-floor mansion that took up a city block. Its wrought-iron gate was adorned with festive garlands, and in the front window Holmes saw a tree decorated with electric lights. Toussaint was clearly one of the city's scions. Holmes knew full well that if he tried to gain entry to the home to speak with the husband or wife then he would be denied, so he wandered the grounds in the guise of a reporter writing a story on Nikolaus Kringle.

The stable boy he encountered knew nothing, but the cook who was returning from the produce stand had much to say. "That man's a blessed saint, he is!" the buxom woman told Holmes, her wide mouth forming a toothy grin. "Young Master Gerard always had trouble breathing. He'd go into fits, gasping for breath, but the missus took him to good ole St. Nick, and now the boy runs around everywhere with nary a wheeze in his chest."

Holmes pressed the woman to explain how the "saint" cured the child. "He's a wise one, he is. He just looked at the boy and asked him some questions, then, believe it or not, he asks his mum if he can keep the boy for the afternoon. She's nervous, of course, but she allowed it. She come back to get him, and he was a new lad. Now, he does these exercises every day."

"Exercises?" asked Holmes.

"Yes, he stretches out his body. He also sits up and crisscrosses his legs like a Hindu every morning for fifteen minutes. Don't quite understand it, but that St. Nick used his magic on the boy. That's the only way it makes sense to me."

Holmes knew the "miracle" advice that Kringle had provided to the boy. Holmes, himself, had spent two years in Lhasa perfecting such breathing exercises. It helped him improve his own health immensely and wean himself off his less-savory habits. He asked the cook if she knew of others who had been helped by Mr. Kringle. "Of course – Mr. Fontaine, the butcher. You pay him a visit, now. St. Nick cleared up his belly aches. He'll tell you all about it."

The detective thanked the woman and did as she suggested, finding Fontaine in a bloody apron behind the counter at his shop, eyeing a list of orders for Christmas dinners. "I wouldn't say that he's a saint like a lot of his followers do," the plump clean-shaven man said, "but I will say that he knows things, and the fellow does a lot of good. He cleared up my stomach, he did." The bald-headed man's eyes got wide as he told Holmes. "He just looked at me when I saw him. I was holding my sore belly, in a lot of pain, and he just looked at me and asked, 'Do you eat a lot of meat?'

"'Why yes,' I replied. 'I am a butcher.'" Fontaine slapped his belly for emphasis, and then continued.

"His eyes squinted as he stared at me for a moment, and said, 'You are fond of ale.'

"'Course I am,' I tells him.

"Well then, he gives me the strangest advice. He tells me for every cup of ale I drink, I'm to drink two cups of water. He also tells me to eat green vegetables with every meal. I thought it was most peculiar, but if it was going to ease my pain, I thought I'd give it a try. So I started eating mustard greens, kale, and spinach as much as I could, and guzzling down water. Sure enough, it cleared me right up, and I've felt good ever since."

Holmes spent the rest of the afternoon in his reporter guise interviewing those who had met with Kringle. One man was saved from gout by eating fruits, drinking vinegar, and soaking his feet in cold water. A young woman was helped with her sore gums by swishing salt water and drinking peppermint tea.

There were a number of similar people with whom Holmes spoke who were aided by Kringle, but there were also plenty of people who did not take his advice. "Man's a fool," said one waiter in a cafe where Holmes stopped for a baguette. "He advised me to give up drinking. Can you imagine?" the mustachioed man lamented furiously, clenching his fists and shaking slightly at the absurdity of the notion. "A Frenchman who does not drink wine? Impossible!" Holmes noted that the waiter was bloated and slightly jaundiced. He also yawned several times and swayed slightly from his outburst. Holmes knew that he was not long for this world.

Several farmers complained about Mr. Kringle's insistence that they boil milk before serving it. "Ridiculous!" one farmer in a tavern roared. The other farmers at his table toasted him in agreement with his conclusion. "Boiling milk ruins the flavor. I never heard of anyone getting sick from drinking milk." But Holmes had. He'd read about the method being used to kill typhoid fever and tuberculosis. It wasn't common in the world yet, but the process was growing. A number of other farmers that Holmes encountered had started boiling their milk on St. Nick's advice. All had said they'd noticed that their families rarely got sick anymore.

That evening, Holmes returned to visit Gus, his test subject, in his rooms. Holmes inspected the arm where he had applied the ointment and was disappointed in the results. The coal tar derivative treatment was showing improvement in Gus's skin, but not enough to cure him of his pain. "Cheer up, Monsieur Girard. You are doing more for me than anyone ever has." Holmes frowned at the compliment. He also took note that Gus only had one chair in his entire flat.

Frustrated with his progress, Holmes returned to his own rooms. He was tempted to take out his beakers again, but refrained from doing so, thinking it would be best to give his mind a break from the experiments, a chance to focus on other subjects, and then return to the matter resharpened. Holmes let out a sigh and thought about the research he'd conducted on Mr. Kringle. The detective leaned over his desk while puffing at his pipe and reviewed his notes for the day. It was clear that Nikolaus Kringle was helping the people of Montpelier. All of his advice seemed sound. Some of it wasn't based on current scientific knowledge, but Holmes himself had made breakthroughs which didn't follow from accepted beliefs and principles. Perhaps this Kringle chap was a fellow researcher and scientist, spreading his knowledge in hopes of helping others. That wouldn't be unlike Holmes, who used his knowledge of the criminal mind to help make London, and now the world, a safer place.

Still, there were aspects of the man that Holmes found unsettling. Why was he providing his knowledge in such an unusual way? Was he using it to make money? It appeared that he was, and yet, he could make so much more money by taking in rich clients and asking exorbitant fees for his advice. Perhaps he just wanted to help the poor. If that was the case, then why charge money at all? Holmes saw several possible explanations that would be reasonable. He also saw a few that could have sinister motives. Without actually meeting him, Holmes couldn't draw any final conclusions.

The only one he knew for certain was that Nikolaus Kringle was not a man of miracles. He was a knowledgeable man, but all of his magic was from the mundane. Holmes would spend the next day visiting Kringle. He would have all of his questions answered in less than two days of work. *A nice distraction,* Holmes thought to himself. *I've hit a block in my research. A few days away will give my brain time to examine my errors and make corrections. I'll return to my work on coal tar derivatives with a new-found vigor.*

Kringle's church was on the eastern border of the city. It was a small single-story stone structure that had some boarded-up windows where the stained glass had holes or was completely shattered. Holmes could tell that the derelict structure hadn't been used regularly for a while and would probably have shown much worse wear had it been made of less-sturdy material.

The detective chose the guise of a rag-picker to complete his work for the day. His hair was dirty and disheveled, a fake wart adorned his chin, and Holmes had found a puddle of sewage to roll in to add a nauseating smell to his torn and tattered clothes. When he arrived at the church, Holmes was surprised that the street and entryway were empty. There was no line to see the supposed saint. A few people loitered in the snow outside the building. They were dressed in patchwork coats and threadbare pants and dresses. These were the city's poor that LaPerle had spoken of being Kringle's main clients. Holmes considered entering the church and directly confronting him. However, he opted to spend some time conducting more research before making a personal visit. He wanted to speak with some of the church's other visitors to see why they were drawn to Kringle.

Holmes wandered the grounds, his eyes darting to-and-fro, taking in all of his surroundings. There were shanty structures – small shacks for the huddled masses that were trying to keep warm by fires. On the edge of the property was a row of steaming cauldrons. A few women were going around, stirring the contents. A man came around with a bin of vegetables which the woman took, kindly thanking him.

"They're making stew," Holmes said aloud to himself.

"Soup actually."

Holmes turned to see who had addressed him. He was a sorry-looking fellow, the skin of his face as rough as a boulder. There were barely any teeth in his mouth, and his left eye was dull and useless.

"Compliments of the Season to you."

"And to you as well. Do you live here?" Holmes asked.

"Aye," answered the man. "I'm Jean-Luc. You are welcome to stay for dinner."

Holmes learned from Jean-Luc that the riff-raff had formed their own little community around the church. They pooled what resources they could collect, made sure that everyone had food to eat, and a roof over their heads.

"This is all St. Nick's doing," explained Jean-Luc. "He makes sure everyone treats each other kindly. If everyone just showed a little brotherly love, there'd be enough to go around the world."

After spending an hour on the grounds of the church and speaking with the poor who were the happiest citizens he'd met in their condition, Holmes decided it was time to meet Mr. Kringle. As he walked up to the festively decorated church door, he thought of how impressive it was in the way the poor people took care of one another. While they were destitute, they had full bellies and were surrounded by friends. Holmes felt a pang of sadness. He realized how much he missed Watson – how it'd been years since he'd had a conversation with a genuine friend.

Holmes opened the door to the church, which gave a loud creak as it swung. When he entered, he found more people, the elderly and infirm, sleeping in the pews. It was part of the church society – allow the weakest to sleep inside where they have more shelter from the cold.

At the front of the church, sitting in a rotted wooden chair, was a very old man. He wore a brown robe like that of a monk. His head was bald, but his beard was long and touched the ground. He was sitting at a slight angle, propped up by his bony left hand. A book was open in his lap, his knobby fingers of his right hand holding the pages in place.

The elder lifted his eyes at seeing Holmes approaching him. "Just a moment, my friend," he said as his eyes darted over the pages. He paused and then closed it. "I had to come to a good stopping place. I read this book every year at Christmas." He held it up to show the title to Holmes. It was Dickens's *A Christmas Carol*.

"Now, what can I do for you?"

"I understand that you are a man who can perform miracles," Holmes said in a nasally voice, getting into the character of the rag-picker.

"You may understand that, but perhaps I can persuade you otherwise," was the answer. There was a pleasant friendliness to him. The softness in his eyes and rosy cheeks, the cheeriness despite the squalor he lived in, made him come across as that rarity: A truly content man. "Please, come closer."

Holmes did, and the man, upon seeing him, leaned in and squinted. "You, my friend, are not from these parts."

"Neither are you, I perceive."

Nick let out a jolly chuckle. "With my thick accent, it is hard to miss. No, I am German. Though I have traveled and seen much of the world – such as yourself, I'd imagine."

"I'm just a humble collector of rags which I sell to make what I can," Holmes answered sadly, playing his part to perfection.

"I say, with your grey eyes, long nose, and aquiline features, you remind me of a Norwegian I've read about named Sigerson. Have you heard of this man?"

"Oh, no, sir, I can't say that I have."

"There's someone else you remind me of. A British fellow. A Londoner to be precise."

"Who is that?" Holmes asked.

"His name is Sherlock Holmes. Like me, he is a man who knows things."

"I heard of him. Didn't he die?"

"Yes, supposedly he fell to his death alongside a master criminal. He sacrificed himself in order to save London. At least, that's the story that was in the news. I've learned over the years that what one reads in the papers is often not the full truth."

"Ah, and you are a man of knowledge."

"Yes, I am. For instance, I know why you are here."

"You do?" Holmes asked, truly curious as to the reason he would be given.

"You are here to listen to a story."

"A story?"

"Yes, because the story will give you all of the answers that you seek."

Kringle invited the rag-picker to take a seat beside him. Holmes took the least worn, most stable chair he could find and pulled it up next to the man, who then began his tale . . . .

A long time ago, in a village on the side of a cliff, there lived a librarian named Perro. He lived with his young brother and his mother. His father had died in a logging accident when he was just ten years old and his brother was six. Since that time, it had been Perro's responsibility to work and supply food for his family.

Perro had first worked as a delivery boy and a stable boy, but while he did these menial tasks, his brain, like a sponge, absorbed knowledge. He remembered everything that he read as though each page was etched into his brain. He loved learning languages, and when he would converse with travelling foreigners who kept their horses at the stable while they were in town, he would often have a rudimentary understanding of their language before they left. So impressed were the townsfolk at Perro's abilities that when Mr. Griswold, the town librarian, finally expired at the age of ninety-five, all knew that the position should be offered to young Perro. At the urging of his mother and brother, he accepted the job.

The town was only a village of a couple-thousand people, so their library was limited in its capacity. Still, Perro had the job of his dreams. He loved being surrounded by books, by old dusty tomes and by new books he bought from collectors who stopped in the village on their way between cities.

Though he loved his job, over time a great sadness grew in him. The limits of his library began to gnaw at him. He had mastered all of the languages that he'd read in the library's books and heard from foreigners. It had been years since Perro's ears heard a language that he hadn't fully mastered. He had memorized every page of every book contained on his shelves, knew the history of the world from the last thousand years, and he had full comprehension of the scientific knowledge contained in the few dozen books he had on that subject.

While he did get the occasional new book, within a day his mind had memorized its contents. He needed so much more stimulation. His library was beginning to feel like a prison. The job of his dreams was becoming a nightmare of stagnation. He longed to escape the village – to see the world, learn new languages, study more cultures, learn all that life had to offer. But that was an impossibility, for to leave the village would mean to leave his mother and brother in destitution. Perro could do no such thing. And so, he was stuck in a routine where if it weren't for the changing of the seasons, all days would feel precisely the same.

One particularly nice Tuesday in October, when the weather was unusually balmy, Perro took a walk around the edge of a cliff in the hills just outside his village. He enjoyed walking in nature, away from people, the solitude giving his brain time to reflect on his knowledge, string together facts that no one had thought to string together before, and draw new conclusions. He was reflecting on the cadence of the Yei language, concluding that it was so similar to that of the Zulu that the two must have split from a common tongue, when he looked out at the horizon and saw an odd shape in the sky. At first he thought something must be wrong with his vision, for he saw a little black dot ebbing and gybing between the clouds. Perro had never seen anything move that way, and he continued to watch as the shape got closer to him and began to come into focus.

It was a carpet, Perro perceived, a flying carpet as he had read about in *The Arabian Nights*. The carpet was red with a zig-zag pattern in orange and white around the edges. When the carpet was quite close, Perro could see that it was quite old and dusty. Yellowed stains were splattered across its back, the front left corner was ragged and torn, and what was left of the fringe was stringy, soiled, and frayed.

"Hello, Perro," said the carpet in a voice like that of a dented doorbell. It had a melody to it, but it was warped and off-putting.

"Hello," the librarian responded. Then he added, "You seem to have the better of me, for you know my name, but I do not know yours."

"Carpet," the carpet responded, and its dirty weaves fluttered in the wind.

"Ah, Mr. Carpet," Perro responded.

"No," the carpet corrected. "Just Carpet." It shook some dust from its body and Perro saw a moth flutter out from between a tear in the carpet's weaving. The creature fluttered off into the woods, away from the daylight, its flight pattern not unlike that of the carpet.

"I have been sent here to retrieve you," Carpet explained.

"Retrieve me?" asked Perro.

"Yes," the carpet replied. "You have been called to The Library of the Gods. The celestial beings who rule over all have observed your skills, your longing to escape the mundane, and your thirst for knowledge. They have agreed to answer your prayers, and so they have sent me to retrieve you." The carpet gave a lopsided bow.

"I see," said Perro, much impressed that the gods would take interest in a small-town librarian such as himself.

"In The Library of the Gods," continued the carpet, "you shall spend all of your days reading an endless supply of books, imbibing all knowledge that has come before, and mastering all the languages which are no longer spoken. You shall be free of distractions as you shall be the only living person there."

Perro was impressed. "Just how big is this library?"

"Its size is unmeasurable. It is so enormous that you can fit your entire village in one corner of one room. The stacks reach from the floor to the ceiling, and the ceiling is past the clouds in the sky. The walls are lined with every book ever written. So complete is the catalog that when a book is written, it automatically appears on the library's shelves."

Perro was practically salivating at the carpet's description of the library. It was so vast that his brain would never run out of information to soak up. "And it is all for me, Carpet? I can learn the languages of the ancients, the knowledge of those that have come before – all of it?"

"Yes," the carpet answered in as lofty a tone as it could muster. "You can learn it all. You can learn the language of the people who came before the Sumerians, of the Zhada people who spoke in odd buzzing noises, or the clicking language of the dreaded Cho-Cho people. All of these languages that are no longer spoken may be yours. All you need to do is sit on my back when I spread myself upon the ground, and I shall take you to The Library."

With a trembling hand, Perro reached out to the carpet, wanting to touch it, to make sure it wasn't an illusion – that the carpet, and therefore the offer, was for real. This was a miraculous dream come to life. He could have infinite time to learn infinite knowledge. He could spend the rest of his life as the only living soul in a land of books, learning languages no one still speaks. And yet, as tempting as it was, his mind went to his mother and younger brother. They both still depended on him. It was his job as a librarian that paid their bills. If he were to leave, they both would starve. And so Perro had to refuse the carpet.

"I cannot abandon my family," he explained gloomily.

"Very well," said the carpet. "Then I shall return and return again until you are ready to accept my offer. When that time comes, I shall take you to The Library of the Gods where you shall have all that you seek." And with that, the ratty carpet flew away, back into the sky.

Perro was devastated at his decision, even though he knew it was the right one to make, but being a reader and researcher, he spent much of his time in his mind asking critical questions. By the time he had made his way back to the village, he realized how little he knew of flying carpets and wondered if anyone had heard of The Library of the Gods. There were few in the village who could answer his questions. He started with the old blind weaver woman, who was said to be nearly five-score in age.

"Carpets," she spat in her croaky ancient voice, "are meant to stay on the ground. There's nothing natural about those that fly. I'd say that's the work of a genie – or worse, a wizard. Take my advice: Next time you see that carpet, take a torch and set fire to it. You'll be killing that which is evil." She had never heard of The Library of the Gods and thought the idea of it showed that the carpet was an unholy force looking to snatch Perro away.

The rest of the afternoon and into the evening was spent asking the other town elders about the flying carpet and The Library of the Gods. No one had ever heard of such a place, and there was universal agreement for Perro to stay away from the carpet, for such a creature must be evil. He was surprised that the only person who had a positive response to the flying carpet was his mother.

She hugged him tight after he had told her the story, and said to him in a soft, comforting voice that only a mother can make, "You have adventure in your soul, my dear boy. You always have. This village cannot contain those who must wander. You have the responsibility of your family for now, but there will come a time when that responsibility shall be lifted. Wait a few years, and you shall be rewarded with freedom and a clean conscience for your patience. Whether you ride off on a carpet or use your own feet to venture, you shall quench your inner thirst and see that which lies beyond our borders."

Perro thanked his mother and he did as she suggested. He patiently waited, working in the library, itching to escape his life, but holding steadfastly to his family duty. So it went for the next ten years. At least once a year, the moth-eaten carpet would return and ask Perro to join him, and every time, Perro refused. Over the years, the man felt more and more despair at being trapped in his village with languages he had already mastered and books he had already read.

Perro took every opportunity that presented itself to ask about the magic carpet, hoping to learn more about what it was and where it came from. He would approach any foreigner that wandered through the village. If the foreigner was a book seller, Perro would practically interrogate him. He'd inquire if they had any tomes on flying carpets or even The Library of the Gods, and if not (they never did), whether the man could supply any information about them. Their responses were always the same: Either they had no such knowledge, or they only had heard terrible things about magic marpets and Perro should keep his distance. "Never trust anything miraculous," they warned him. "Carpets are meant to stay on the floor, not ride in the air."

Over the years, despite the warnings, Perro's desire to leave upon the carpet only continued to grow more and more, at times overwhelming him. But as he led the same dreary life, and felt the same itch to escape, he failed to see that a change came to his family. Perro's brother grew stronger and taller. He left the village, went to school, and learned to be a doctor. Unlike Perro, his brother had no lust for adventure and was content to return to the town. He treated the villagers who were more like family members than patients. Perro appreciated his brother, and as he gained medical knowledge to share, as often happens as siblings age, they became good friends. The two spent many nights staying up late after their mother had fallen asleep discussing the brother's medical practice, or the latest words Perro had learned from new books that were delivered to the library. All was good with the two, but as life changes, so do human needs. While Perro's thirst was for an adventure outside the village, his brother thirsted for a family of his own. Soon, he married a nurse and moved away to his own house several streets away.

It was almost a year to the day after his brother left that the final block to Perro leaving the village was removed. His mother, who over time had shriveled up like a fruit left out in the sun, fell asleep with a content smile on her lips and passed on to her next adventure in the afterlife. Two days after his mother's funeral, despite the warnings he had received from all of the elders and foreigners – Perhaps even because of them – Perro returned to the cliff where he had encountered the magic carpet and called out for it to return. Once again, he saw the little black dot appear in the sky and then come more into focus as the carpet ebbed and gybed and eventually landed in a cloud of dust at his feet.

"Carpet," he told the miraculous device, "I am no longer needed in my village. My brother has married and is expecting a baby. My mother has died."

"Do you accept my offer?" the carpet asked.

"I do."

"Very well, then sit on me, and I shall take you to The Library of the Gods."

Perro climbed on the carpet's back. He considered that it was even more threaded and tattered than before and wondered if it might tear in two under his weight while they were soaring into the heavens. If that is to be my fate, thought Perro, then so be it. But it was not. Once he sat upon the carpet, it lifted into the sky, and together they flew on until they arrived at The Library of the Gods.

It was more impressive than he had imagined. It looked similar to the images Perro had seen in books of the Taj Mahal, but even grander. It was a glorious white marble building with spires so tall that they were hidden by the clouds. The structure's intricate designs were so detailed that it appeared that the gargoyles might spread their wings and fly away. So large was the building that he could see that a thousand thousand villages could fit inside a corner of it.

The carpet flew through one of The Library's open windows, taking Perro inside. He gasped at what he saw. Endless rows and rows of bookcases that reached from the floor up so high that their tops were beyond his vision. And every shelf was full of books in all shapes and sizes from all parts of the world, every book that had ever been written. And they were all for him – *Him!* – as he was the only living soul in the building.

"Thank you," Perro managed to gasp in a hoarse whisper. They were all the words he could form with his tongue, so taken was he by the splendor of the library.

"This is all yours, Perro. You shall have this library all to yourself," the carpet said in its dull chime voice. It glided down and landed upon the marble floor. Little clouds of dust poofed up which made Perro sneeze.

"I apologize for my condition," said Carpet. "I didn't mean to make you sneeze."

Perro shook his head. His eyes were trying to take in the sights around him, and even with all of his mind working at full speed, he couldn't comprehend the wonders around him. "Do not apologize for anything. You have taken me to Heaven itself."

The carpet pulled itself off the ground and bowed as best as a carpet could. "There may come a time when you wish to leave the library. Should that time come," Carpet explained, "simply call to me from an open window, and I shall return. Know that once you leave, you may never return, for The Library will then be granted to another living soul." The carpet then said goodbye and flew off, up into an open space of the library. Perro watched it rise up and up until it was a dot, and then disappeared out a window. He couldn't imagine ever wanting to leave such a miraculous place.

"It is Paradise," Perro gasped, and so it was. He went to the shelf and pulled out a handwritten book on the language of the ancient Babylonians. He opened the book to the first page, and began to read. Thus began Perro's study of the dead languages. He spent years studying the language of the people who came before the Sumerians, of the Zhada people who spoke in odd buzzing noises, and the clicking language of the dreaded Cho-Cho people, and many, many more forgotten tongues.

While Perro was the only living soul in the library, he wasn't the only soul there. A number of ghosts roamed The Library's halls, reading books from their own time period or those that came before. He spent his days studying the language of the ancients, but also having discussions with spirits from all time periods in history. That is how he learned to actually make the correct clicks to speak the language of the Cho-Cho, though he shuddered when those dark eyed spirits shared their secrets with him. He mastered the buzzes of the Zhada people, a gentle race that still had simian hair upon their brow. The language of the pre-Sumerians he found oddly similar to his own language and therefore was the easiest to speak.

Perro spent year after year in The Library of the Gods, conversing with the dead in dead languages. He never slept, nor ate, nor drank – such was the sustenance of the knowledge contained within the building. He may well have stayed in that Heaven forever, conversing with ghosts and uncovering more forgotten languages, if fate had not intervened.

One day, Perro wandered through the stacks as he was wont to do when he came upon the newest section of the library. This section had the newspapers of the world, displayed out on racks that stretched on for close to a mile. These racks changed several times each day as suns rose across the lands of the world. They also changed over as the evening editions went to press. There were no ghosts in this section of the library for they were only concerned with their own lifetimes and the times that came before them.

Walking through the rows, watching as some papers magically disappeared while new editions formed in their place, Perro thought it might be fun to read the little weekly newspaper published from his own village. It took him an hour to walk far enough down through the alphabet to find the newspaper. It was an old-fashioned, large single sheet newspaper. The type that required being spread over a table like a cloth for one to be able to read all of the articles.

The news, he discovered, was rather grim. The village had been subject to an outbreak of a plague, a dark disease that turned the skin chalky white and filled the lungs with dust. Many in the town had succumbed to the dreaded illness. Perro thought of his brother, the doctor, and worried that he may have contracted the disease. He read through the list of the dead in the newspaper and was relieved that his brother's name wasn't there. However, he knew that the list was probably at least a few days old. The librarian felt a pang of sadness and concern that he hadn't felt in years. He had to return to the village to see if his brother was well, even if it meant leaving the Library of the Gods forever.

Perro made his way to a window and called out to the carpet. Within moments, he saw the familiar dot appear in the clouds. The carpet bobbed about in the wind then spiraled downward and landed on the floor beside him. The carpet was even more moth eaten and threaded than before. Holes were poked throughout its body.

Perro thanked the carpet for returning and told him he wanted to go back to his village.

"Very well," said the carpet. "You do know that you shall not be able to return here, once you leave – at least you shall not be allowed to return while you are alive."

Perro thought about all he had learned and yet, he'd probably only read less than one percent of one percent of the wonderful books in The Library. Was he willing to give up all that he had left to learn? Was he really willing to walk away from such knowledge? He decided that he must for his brother. He had glimpsed more of Human History and learned more than possibly anyone who had come before him. That would have to be enough to sustain him.

"I understand," said Perro soberly, "but I have no choice. I must leave."

"Very well," agreed the carpet.

Perro climbed onto the carpet, whose form sagged a bit from his weight. It teetered, but then flew off into the sky.

"You must get repaired, my friend," Perro advised the carpet. "You are unraveling."

"I cannot be repaired," the carpet explained. "I have been living for hundreds of years, but now my time grows short. Your voyage shall be one of my last."

"But surely," Perro argued, "it would just take some patches and thread to make you live a bit longer."'

"When a carpet is brought to life by magic, that same magic must be used to make repairs. The wizard who brought me to life has long passed from this world, and he left no such magic threads to make repairs."

"But surely a different wizard could save you," Perro practically pleaded with the carpet. He didn't wish to see the miraculous creature perish. "Once repaired, you could last forever."

"Nothing lasts forever," the wise carpet reminded the librarian. "I have had a good life. I have enjoyed transporting people throughout the world. I have enjoyed getting to know you, but I also look forward to my time after this. And now, my dear Perro, I leave you for the last time."

The carpet had reached Perro's village. It landed with a dull thud on a grassy field just outside the houses. He stepped off and said, "Goodbye, Carpet."

"Goodbye, Perro. I hope you enjoy your time with the living as much as you enjoyed your time with the dead." The carpet then lifted up, and fluttered off into the sky. Perro watched until it was a dot and waited until it had completely disappeared from his vision. Even then, he waited a few moments more before moving on toward his village.

When he entered, he could see the devastation that the plague had brought. Houses were boarded up with warning signs painted on doors: *Plague – Do Not Enter*. The streets were deserted. Perro went to his brother's house only to find it boarded up and abandoned. He had hope, though, for there was no warning painted on the door. He then made his way to the hospital. It was more like a cemetery than a house of healing. Bodies were piled out front. The halls were filled with those suffering, spewing chalky dust from their lungs. As he wandered the halls and saw the suffering people, a memory tugged at him. There was something familiar about this illness afflicting his former village, but yet he couldn't place it. At one point, he came across a nurse who was leaning against the wall, exhausted. She was taking a moment trying to regain her composure from her nonstop work treating patients who were likely to die.

When she saw him, her eyes widened in horror. "What are you doing here?" she sputtered. "You must stay away! You might get sick!"

Perro explained that he was looking for his brother and told the nurse his name.

"I didn't know he had a brother," the nurse explained, and she told him of her brother's fate. He had been one of the first to die from the plague when it infected the town. His wife and son succumbed to the illness soon after. "They were a caring family," the nurse lamented. "There isn't a family in this village who doesn't owe a debt of gratitude to your brother and his wife."

Perro thanked the nurse for her time. After walking the halls, he stumbled, fell against a wall, and slid to the floor. He was suddenly overcome with grief. He lost his brother, sister-in-law, and nephew. He'd had a nephew he had never met, he thought to himself, and now never would. He looked down at his wrinkled hands and knew he had been away in the Library of the Gods for decades. Time did not exist in The Library, but it was catching up to him here. He thought back to that Heavenly place, to the knowledge in its shelves, to the beginning when he first started speaking with the ghosts . . . *Ghosts!*

Perro shot up, memories flooding back to the forefront of his mind. Of course! He remembered speaking with one of the Cho Cho about a plague like this that devastated their community, and the cure! The cure was here! It was a mushroom that was uncommon in their land, but grew wild in the forest outside his village. It was considered useless as it was poisonous in large doses, but in small bits . . . .

And that was how Perro saved the rest of his community from the dreaded plague. With his guidance, the townsfolk each ate a small piece of the mushroom, its spores counteracting the ills of the plague. That wasn't all that he brought with him, for he had a plethora of information that held the cures to many ills. Perro spent time helping his village just as his brother would have done, spreading his knowledge and helping to cure all sorts of sicknesses.

But he didn't stop at his village. He knew he had a responsibility to share what he knew with the rest of the world. So he did. He spent his days wandering in loops, going from village to village, from city to city, sharing his understanding, helping to save those that were afflicted with pains, doing his best to heal the world. He spent three years in the same pattern going from the same village to the same city, planting seeds, nurturing them, and then once they sprouted, going to new villages and new cities.

Thus, Perro, who had spent decades living with the dead, determined that he should spend the last decades of his life with the living, helping them as best he could, sharing his knowledge, and helping all who sought his aid.

"That is my story," the Man of Miracles said to Holmes, and he slumped back into his chair. "I believe that, in telling you this, I have answered all of your questions."

Holmes, in the guise of the rag-picker, contemplated all that he had heard from Nikolaus. After some time of quiet contemplation, Holmes softly responded, "I believe you have."

The detective turned and began to walk away. "You are welcome to stay," Kringle called to Holmes. "Of course, a man like you is a man of knowledge. This is not your place – at least it won't be for long. Still, you are welcome to stay for as long as it pleases you."

Holmes had paused, listening to the man's words. After Kringle finished, Holmes didn't respond, he simply headed back to his home.

When Holmes returned to his rooms, he took out a pad of paper and began making several sketches. He then wrote letters to a number of people he had met over the last few years during his Hiatus. Once done, Holmes took some envelopes and added a sketch and letter to each one. The next day he would send them out in the mail to different parts of the world and await his recipients' responses.

Once Holmes finished up the letters, it was rather late. He thought a glass of sherry would be nice. The detective didn't go to get a glass though. Instead he left his flat, walked three doors down, and knocked.

"Why, Monsieur Girard, I didn't expect to see you tonight," said Gus. "Did you need to give me a new treatment?"

"No," Holmes said, smiling kindly. "I wondered if you might join me in having a drink."

Inspector LaPerle never expected to hear jolly laughter come from the door to Holmes's flat, but that is precisely what he heard when he returned from his Parisian vacation and followed-up on Holmes's investigation into Nikolaus Kringle. The laughter was good natured, from multiple voices, and LaPerle hesitated before knocking, not wanting to interrupt the morning fellowship that a part of him longed to join. Outside the door to Holmes's room was a receptacle filled with brightly colored paper waiting to be picked up by the trash collector. Could the detective have celebrated Christmas?

LaPerle wavered, fist in the air for a few seconds before swinging down and knocking loudly upon the oak door. There was the noise of chairs scraping across the floor and a distinctive apology from Holmes. "Sorry, my friends, duty calls." This was followed by, "You will have to come by this evening, Mr. Holmes."

"*Mr. Holmes!*" LaPerle gasped out loud. The inspector stepped back, and shook his head. It was as though an invisible hand had slapped him hard across the face. Who else in Montpellier, besides himself, knew of Holmes's true identity?

His question was answered as the door to Holmes's rooms was opened and a trio of men waved goodbye and said their pleasantries. One man, a small fellow with a slight hunch to his back, reminded Holmes that they had a card game scheduled for the evening. "I shall be there, Francois," Holmes assured him.

With a pleasant wave the men headed past LaPerle, who they gave a friendly nod to as they passed. The trio continued chatting about as they walked down the hall. The inspector saw that none of the men was wearing a jacket.

"They are my neighbors," Holmes told the inspector. LaPerle watched them go and then turned back to Holmes who, he was surprised to see, had a glow about him, the kind one gets after spending a day in the company of good friends. "Can you believe that they have lived in this building for ten years and only just this Christmas spoke to one another for the first time?"

"That is surprising," LaPerle answered meekly. It really wasn't, for in flats many people aren't as neighborly as those who dwell in houses, but LaPerle didn't come to have a debate with Holmes about social graces. He wanted to know if there was anything to concern him about Monsieur Kringle.

Holmes invited LaPerle into his lab and walked over to his small table in the corner. "Please, excuse the mess," Holmes said. He collected the dirty glasses from the table and moved them to the sink.

While Holmes was tidying up, the inspector said, "I am surprised to see you entertaining in your laboratory." LaPerle remembered how Holmes refused to offer him a drink for fear it might taint the area. "But I am even more surprised that your guests called you by your true name, Monsieur *Holmes*."

"Oh, that," Holmes said. The glasses chimed a bit when they clanged together in the sink. "I decided that there was no need to be incognito in my own home." The detective returned to the table and offered the inspector a cigarette. He thanked Holmes, and the two men took a seat at the table. While LaPerle took a drag, he saw that Holmes didn't join him.

"The men who live here are carpenters, factory workers, mechanics, plumbers, and chimney sweeps. I really have no fear that they will spread my identity far. Besides, all but one had never even heard of me."

"Well, I must say," the inspector admitted, "I was surprised to see you taking a break from your work to socialize."

Again, that beaming smile. "There is more to life than work, Inspector. I got to know one of the men here, Gus is his name, who I've been helping with my experiments. We ended up having Christmas dinner together, and then soon after, I got to know my other neighbors. Socializing gives my mind a break and when I return to my experiments, I look at them with fresh eyes. I've made great progress in the last two weeks. Plus," Holmes confided, "I do enjoy the company."

The inspector agreed with Holmes and was happy to hear that the detective had settled into his life in the city. Perhaps he would stay.

"But you have come to hear what I have discovered about Mister Kringle."

"*Oui*, Monsieur."

Holmes leaned forward, drawing the inspector into his eyes to hear his research. "I went to see Mr. Kringle at his church. I had spent a day speaking with those who he had helped and those who he tried to help but had ignored his advice. I quickly surmised that Kringle was a man with a great understanding of science and medicine. Some of his ideas are well known, some are currently unknown to science, and others are in their infancy, just beginning to be studied.

"I went to see Kringle to learn how he came to such knowledge and also if his intentions were for good or for ill."

LaPerle perked up at this, "And what did he tell you?"

"He told me a story."

"A story?"

Holmes gave one of his odd little silent laughs. "Yes, a story, one that was a fairy tale but contained all the clues I needed to find out for myself the true identity of the Man of Miracles."

"And what did you discover?"

"It took me a few days to gather the information I needed, but what I learned was this: His true name is Johann Richter. He was a librarian from a small town in the hinterlands who was known for his wisdom. It was said that he could look at a person and explain his or her life story simply from the clothes that he or she was were wearing that day."

"Sounds like you, Mr. Holmes."

"Indeed, it does," agreed Holmes. "We are like-minded in many ways." Holmes gave a nod and then continued on his story, "I don't have all the details for the next part of the story. I know that Richter left his village and travelled abroad, studying at various museums, universities, and libraries throughout the world. I'm not sure how long he was away. It seems as though it was for at least twelve years, but possibly as many as twenty. When he returned to his village, he found it ransacked by a cholera outbreak. His one relative, his brother, perished in the epidemic. Richter was devastated, but he had learned from his studies how to treat those suffering from cholera. He had the afflicted replace their fluids by drinking water that had been purified by boiling it in advance.

"Once the cholera plague had passed, Richter decided to spend his life sharing his knowledge with the world and helping to better humanity. He took on several different guises and travelled to different towns and cities, giving advice to help the poor and afflicted. Richter returned to each of his locales three times. The first time he would establish himself as a man of knowledge, the second time, he'd spread his knowledge to more people in the town, and by the third time, he'd ensure that the knowledge he had provided had become common enough locally that it would spread beyond him. He also charged a nominal fee for his advice, so he could provide food for the poor, and in time, a residency.

"Richter has been doing this for over thirty years. Thus, he has ensured that much of his knowledge has spread into journals of science and medicine, yet he receives no credit for it. He is an old man, but I wouldn't be surprised if he continues spreading his knowledge for another three or four cycles. The world has much to learn from him."

"I see," LaPerle answered thoughtfully. He squinted his eyes for a moment as he pieced together all that Holmes had told him. "So . . . if it is true that he comes to a village or city three times, then he has come to Montpellier for the last time."

"*Had* come," Holmes corrected. "He left shortly after the start of the New Year. He bought the church and its grounds for the poor, made sure the community could run on its own, and disappeared one evening. I don't think we shall ever see him again."

LaPerle took a final drag from his cigarette then ground it out in the ashtray before him. "This is good," he admitted. "So he wasn't a man of miracles after all."

Holmes looked offended at LaPerle's conclusion, and the inspector told him so.

"I believe you err in your deduction," Holmes explained. "Mr. Kringle, or Richter, or whatever name he chooses to go by, was not a man of magic, but I would say that the knowledge he spread was nothing short of miraculous. He is a man of science with a plethora of information that has saved countless thousands of people. While his work is grounded in reason, I would argue that it took his mind to puzzle it all together and draw the correct conclusions. There are so many paths a mind like that could take. It could have gone to self-serving and even sinister purposes. The fact that Kringle has taken his gifts and used them to selflessly serve humanity is a miracle in and of itself."

Absent Friends
by Wayne Anderson

Some time ago, with a weight pressing heavy on my soul, I took up my pen to record the last story of Sherlock Holmes that I shall ever write, which I titled, "The Final Problem". My pen and my heart are today heavier still, if that is possible. I fear I shall never publish this new narrative, and belike none shall ever even read it – save perhaps my heirs, going through my papers, in some distant future in the coming century.

In truth, I cannot even say with any certainty why I am writing this. Perhaps because I have already set down so much of my life that it seems a way to fix it in time, to make it permanent. Yet the moments I record herein might not be ones that I should want kept green in memory, so I cannot say how I gain thereby.

Perhaps it is a catharsis, a way to purge my soul of the pain and sorrow therein. By pouring it out on paper I can let it spill from where it burns darkly in the depths of my heart. If you, dear reader in some distant year to come, can feel for the sorrow of *this* year, then it may be that my own sorrow is diminished in some small way.

This year, 1893, should have been the happiest of my life. Yet two years past, at a distant waterfall in Switzerland, I lost the dearest friend and best man I have ever known, and that loss still weighs heavy on my heart.

My sorrow of that day was diminished in no small part by the happy presence of the finest of women, my beloved wife Mary, who brought into my life joy hitherto unknown. Her announcement that we were to have a family in the autumn of this year lifted the clouds, and a bright ray of hope shone upon me.

Alas, it was not to be. Would that it had been a bullet aimed at her heart, for then I could have stepped in front of her and taken it unto myself. Even this chance was denied me. When came the time for the birth of my daughter – for daughter she was indeed – instead both were taken from me, in the worst and hardest day of my life. All my medical knowledge was for naught, and in vain I struggled to my uttermost to save her life.

When our daughter was born – with a terrible loss of blood on my wife's part – I cut the cord and placed her in her mother's waiting arms. Mary smiled weakly, and kissed the tiny face, and looked up at me. "Amelia Elizabeth," she said in a breathless voice. "Name her Amelia Elizabeth, and love her for me."

"You shall – " I began, but bit off my words, unable to continue.

"My dear John," she said, her voice faint and unsteady, almost a whisper, "You still cannot lie to me, even now, can you? We both know my time is short. I entrust her to you after I'm gone." She faced her death with a courage and an honesty that would have done many a soldier proud.

Unable to speak, I nodded mutely, then bent to kiss her clammy forehead, and then our daughter's. Finally I mustered the strength to give the promise she asked, the one time in my life that I spoke untruth to her. Were I to tell her the truth, that our daughter had already passed, I should have robbed her of her departing hope of happiness.

Mary was gone in minutes after that, following our daughter into the Hereafter. If there is a bright hope, than perhaps I shall see them both again someday, but such is not given to men to know.

Numbly I wrote the birth certificate with the name Mary had spoken, with one change: Mary Amelia Elizabeth Watson. Then I signed two death certificates with shaking hand.

I shall not bore you, nor torture myself, with a recounting of the funeral. Suffice it to say that Mrs. Hudson was there, and Holmes's brother Mycroft – somehow informed of the grievous events – attended as well. So, too, was Inspector Gregson, to represent Scotland Yard. He informed me that Lestrade and the others were committed to urgent duties, and he brought with him their sympathies.

Unless you have lost one, you cannot fully imagine the sorrow, made all the greater as it was a reversal of anticipated joy. I am not a man given to despair, but it rested heavy on my shoulders, and even now it casts a shadow upon my future. For weeks I sat alone in my silent house, turning away patients, barely eating, my only solace tobacco and whisky. The nursery that I had prepared waited empty, a physical manifestation of the vast hollow in my soul, both destined to remain devoid of childish gurgles and happy hours.

I viewed the approaching Christmas with dread. How can a man, alone and bereft through the holidays, find cheer in them? How can one pick up the pieces of a shattered life and rebuild it, when two – nay, even three – of the largest pieces are missing, with never a hope of finding them?

Englishmen do not weep. Weeping is for women and for willows, and perhaps drunken Irishmen. We Englishmen keep a stiff upper lip through thick and thin, through sorrow and terror, and through those lips we imbibe alcohol. Should any tears escape our eyes, we can ascribe them to the liquor. This is, perhaps, both the strength and the weakness of the English race.

Thus it was that I was drowning my sorrows, and almost myself, in the middle of December, when a messenger rang at my door. I made my way with less than half a heart, to be handed a sealed envelope of a fine, rose-pink paper. By long habit I gave it a cursory glance, prepared to toss it into the cold and cheerless fireplace, when the return address caught my eye: 221 Baker Street.

This is some kind of a cruel joke, thought I, and with a flash of weary anger I discarded it unopened in the fireplace and returned to my chair and my whisky.

It was some hours later when I awoke. The chill of December outside had penetrated the walls, and the house was cold and dark with the evening. Vaguely I thought I must light the fire and find some sustenance. I noticed the envelope where I had thrown it, resting among the cinders, and, with a somewhat clearer head, I plucked it out to at least open it and see what was inside.

Doctor Watson, [I read]

I understand how you must feel, for I have felt that myself, when my husband passed long years ago. I can say with confidence that the pain is softened with time. Your other loss I share with you. I would dearly like to invite you to join me for a Christmas repast, that we might toast and celebrate the life of the man that we both miss so much.

I shall hope to see you around five in the evening on Christmas Day. You need bring nothing but your memories.

Yours faithfully,
Mrs. Hudson

This brought a realisation to my mind: I wasn't the only one who had suffered a loss. Mrs. Hudson had known Holmes as long as I had, if not as closely. Mary, also, she had met upon a few occasions, and I believe each had liked and respected the other.

I wasn't the only one grieving. Instead I was being selfish – self-indulgent in my grief, as if it was mine alone. Those of us who knew Holmes well were all devastated by his passing. Mycroft, somewhere in his office in Pall Mall, must be missing his brother.

Perhaps, rather than wallowing in solitary misery in the dark, we would do better to cheer each other up for the holidays.

I took a pen and wrote at the bottom of the note:

My dear Mrs. Hudson,

I should be delighted to accept. I look forward to seeing you again. Thank you ever so much.

Yours truly,
John H Watson, MD

I would post it to her at on the following morn.

In the days that followed I began, gradually, to feel reborn after a fashion. Yes, we suffer our losses and take the bruises that life delivers, but sooner or later we must gather what remains to us and go on – or else lie down in despair and follow our beloved into oblivion.

I had danced with oblivion for weeks, drinking myself into a stupor over and over. The time for pitying myself was over. A proper amount of grief shows respect for the departed. An excessive show of grief is self-indulgent and, indeed, unmanly.

To this end I let it be known that I would begin taking patients again. And in the days that followed, I discovered that the pain is assuaged when others need us. Helping my patients was, indeed, a balm on the wounds of my spirit, and reminded me why I had chosen the practise of medicine in the first place.

As Christmas drew near I felt myself considerably uplifted from my former depths of despair, all thanks to Mrs. Hudson and her letter. To my considerable surprise, I found myself now eagerly awaiting the holiday that I had dreaded but a few days before.

The day finally arrived, with a thick overnight snowfall to mute the endless sounds of London. The virginal white of the snow seemed to tell me of new beginnings and, perhaps, new hopes.

The familiar step at 221 Baker Street had been swept clean of snow by the time I arrived in the late afternoon. Despite Mrs. Hudson's letter, I was determined to bring her something, and I carried with me two bottles of fine brandy – one to share, perhaps, and one to leave with her for later.

As I expected, the landlady herself greeted me at the door, though her sudden embrace came as a surprise. "Merry Christmas, Doctor," she said, and her voice had lost none of its warmth. "Come in and join us."

As I entered I muttered some platitude about her looking well, and it was true. By long habit I almost began the seventeen steps to our old rooms above, but I consciously turned away. Instead, I followed her into her own drawing room, wondering who comprised the "us" she mentioned. To my surprise, two of the chairs were already occupied – one by Inspector Lestrade, who raised a glass to me and nodded. In second chair sat a young man of familiar aspect, but it took me a moment to recognise him as Wiggins, formerly leader of the Baker Street Irregulars, now grown to a handsome young man in his early twenties. He, too, saluted me with a glass.

"I felt 'twould be better for more of us to remember Mr. Holmes together," Mrs. Hudson said, taking my coat and hat. "If you'll have a seat, Doctor, I'll bring you some mulled wine, or whatever else you fancy. We are still awaiting one more to join us."

I set down the bag with the two brandy bottles and took an open seat before the fire. I gratefully accepted the wine, and as it warmed me within, and the fire warmed me without, I wondered who the last person might be.

As it turned out, we didn't have long to wait. The bell rang again, and she came back leading the improbably ponderous figure of Mycroft Holmes, Sherlock's elder brother. Since he could rarely be found apart from either his offices or the rigid silence of the Diogenes Club, I wondered what it must have taken to pry him from his shell.

I winced as the answer came to me unbidden: The death of Sherlock Holmes.

He looked at the small assemblage as he doffed coat and hat. "Good evening, all, and Merry Christmas," he began, removing his fine kidskin gloves. "Doctor," and here it was my own turn to raise a glass. "Inspector. And young Wiggins."

I was startled as Wiggins, former street urchin and Baker Street Irregular, rose, for he had become tall in the few years since I'd seen him last – something I had never imagined. Mycroft shook his hand graciously, before settling his vast bulk into the large chair the landlady had set for him. "A pleasure to see you all again."

"Thank you, Mr. Mycroft, sir," Wiggins answered.

Mrs. Hudson rejoined us, settling in the last open chair, and all eyes turned toward her. "Christmas dinner will be ready soon," she said, warming to her unaccustomed role as hostess. "I thought, since we are all united by our affection for Sherlock Holmes, we might do him honor by remembering him together."

There was a murmur of general assent. Our chairs formed a loose arc before the fire, with Wiggins nearest the door. Beside him, in the largest chair, sat Mycroft, then our hostess. My chair was fourth, with Lestrade on my further side.

Mrs. Hudson turned toward me. "Doctor, forgive me if I have taken the liberty of informing Mr. Wiggins of your recent loss, I wanted to avoid any unintended *faux pas*. The other gentlemen present already knew."

"Thank you, Mrs. Hudson," said I, and indeed I was grateful for this action on her part.

Beside me, Lestrade cleared his throat. "Doctor, you are as versed as any in Mr. Holmes's methods of detection," he began, seeming uncertain. "I have a little conundrum that seems his type, and I know it isn't your business now, but I'd be grateful if you could give it consideration."

"You overestimate me, Inspector," I replied. "I was never the detective that Holmes was, but I'm willing to offer any modest ability I may have. If you want the true thinker present," I continued, nodding across the arc of chairs, "then Mycroft here is your man. A better mind may not exist in all the British Empire."

Mycroft, never one for false modesty, simply looked interested, as Lestrade addressed him. "Sir, if you could also lend your powers, I should be much obliged."

The elder Holmes nodded. "Whatever I can do for you, Inspector, is at your disposal."

Wiggins leaned forward, saying nothing, but his eyes were bright and attentive. Mrs. Hudson excused herself to check on the kitchen.

Lestrade, too, leaned forward, addressing himself to both Mycroft and myself. "Are either of you familiar with the recent difficulties of Sir Cedric Owlsby?"

I, of course, had been consumed with other things, and had paid no attention to the news. Mycroft, on the other hand, was as well-informed as any man in Britain. "I presume you are referring to the kidnapping and ransom of his prize dog? A trivial affair."

Lestrade nodded. "So one would think, I agree. Yet there are puzzling aspects about it. Sir Cedric, you see, claimed that he knew beyond a doubt who was responsible – a doctor named Harry Westcott. The tale goes that they were friends until recently and were hunting together when Sir Cedric's dog attacked Dr. Westcott's dog. Before they could be separated, Dr. Westcott's dog, which was the smaller, had been severely mauled, and had to be destroyed."

"How unfortunate," I said, and Mycroft merely nodded. If his brother's behavior was any measure of Mycroft's, I would have said that nothing yet had taken his interest.

"Unfortunate, yes, and that was the story both parties put out. Yet the dogs in question weren't hunting breeds – they were both English bulls. I did some investigating after the fact, and it seems they weren't hunting at all – these gents were involved in dog-fighting."

This unexpected news brought a collective response – Mycroft's eyebrows rose, and I heard an intake of breath from our hostess, who had returned from the kitchen. Had Wiggins been a dog, his ears would have stood up and turned forward at this. As it was, he was watching and following the conversation alertly.

"Dog-fighting has been outlawed in Britain since the Humane Act of 1835," Mycroft said, his fingers steepled in a way eerily reminiscent of his brother.

"I'm well aware of the law, sir," the inspector replied. "Yet, paradoxically, that law seems to have made it more popular."

Mrs. Hudson found this hard to fathom. "How could that be?"

Lestrade turned to her. "'Twasn't just dog-fighting that the law banned, but bull-baiting and bear-baiting as well."

"Barbarous sports – if they could even be called sport," I interjected. "We're well rid of them."

"Aye, Doctor," Lestrade continued, "and those required large spaces. With the space, the noise, and the spectacle, 'tis well-nigh impossible to open a bull or bear ring without drawing notice. But dogs are much smaller, and no one notices if one keeps a dog. Them as previously went to bear-baiting and bull-baiting now go to dog-fights, which can be held in a basement, and kept secret."

To my surprise, young Wiggins spoke up. "I know several places where dog-fights are held," said he, "and cock-fights as well."

Lestrade pointed a judicious finger at him. "Then I should like to have a careful talk with you sometime, young man." Wiggins flushed bright red, but nodded. Lestrade went on. "Sir Cedric claims that after his dog fought with Dr. Westcott's dog, the doctor swore revenge upon him. He made no secret of it.

"Hence, when the dog was taken, he had no choice but to pay the ransom. The ransom note was handwritten, and signed by a man calling himself '*Mr. E.*' He described the man taking the ransom as of medium height and build, wearing a heavy black cloak and a cloth mask that covered his face, save for his eyes. He spoke with a voice artificially hoarse, to disguise it. Almost nothing to distinguish him, really. Sir Cedric said his height and build matched those of Dr. Westcott, but so do a quarter of the men in London. The ransom was paid, and the dog released unharmed. Afterward, Sir Cedric came to us, demanding that we arrest Dr. Westcott for the crime. It made no sense – Could Sir Cedric be certain that Dr. Westcott wouldn't implicate him in dog-fighting as well? But he did it anyway."

I held my peace, as it seemed neither of the men in question had any moral standing to speak of.

"So you arrested the doctor?" Mycroft asked.

"We did," Lestrade said, "but we were forced to release him. As it turned out, Dr. Westcott had an unimpeachable alibi – he was at his club, both when the dog was taken, and when it was ransomed and returned. He has dozens of witnesses who vouch for his presence – including some men who don't like him at all.

"I have here the ransom note, signed by '*Mr. E.*' An obvious pun, but the note is in a hand that closely resembles that of the doctor." Lestrade took a small sheaf of folded papers from his pocket.

"And do you have a sample of the doctor's hand as well?" Mycroft asked.

Lestrade handed two papers over, and Mycroft scanned them quickly, then handed them to me. The first was a quick and remarkable note scrawled and signed by the doctor on an ivory-colored paper of high quality. Holding it to the light, I discerned the watermark of a prominent London papermaker.

The ransom note was written in an unsteady hand on ordinary foolscap, available from any stationer. I immediately noticed some points where the ink had smeared slightly across the words.

> *If you want to see your dog again, you will bring £100 in gold to the alley behind the ruint Opera House, Haymarket, an hour after midnight. Come alone. Do not inform the police. If you do not comply I will kill your dog.*
>
> *Mr. E*

"The ransom note was written with the left hand," said I, "by a right-handed man."

"Indeed it was," Mycroft responded, "A rudimentary attempt to disguise one's hand. The formation of letters, though, is a habit which carries through as long as the same mind is directing that hand. These letters are clearly formed quite similarly. There are a few variations which might be deliberate. I judge it quite likely that Dr. Westcott wrote both notes."

"That was our judgement as well," Lestrade said. "Yet, as I said, the doctor has an airtight alibi. And there's more."

"Can it wait, gentlemen?" Mrs. Hudson had quietly returned to the drawing room, and was standing behind her chair. "If you'll excuse me, the goose is ready, and I should hate for the gravy to congeal. If you will join me in the dining room, it's almost time for dinner to be served."

Lestrade put his papers away, and we agreed to continue the discussion after our repast.

Thus we found ourselves seated at her table – myself at one end, with Mycroft at the other. Lestrade was on the side at my right, and across from him were seated Mrs. Hudson, nearest me, and Wiggins, nearer to Mycroft.

I nodded toward our hostess. "With your permission, I should like to begin by proposing a toast." I rose and lifted my wine glass. "To absent friends," I said quickly, before my voice could shake.

They each faced me, raising their glasses, and echoed: "To absent friends." We all drank.

With a grunt of effort Mycroft ponderously rose and faced me. "And family," he added, raising his glass.

Of course, Sherlock had been his brother, but his statement put me in mind of my Mary, whose loss was still an open wound in my heart. "And family." I joined the chorusing response, and that time I'm afraid my voice did break. A moment later I mentally added my lost daughter, Mary Amelia Elizabeth, whom my wife Mary had lived long enough to hold and kiss.

I took another drink from my glass and we resumed our seats. Glancing at Mrs. Hudson, I could see that her mind was, for a moment, far away, doubtless remembering her husband of long ago.

I looked to my right at Lestrade. His fingertips were playing idly with the stem of his glass. His eyes faced across the room, unfocussed, gazing perhaps at a distant thought, and he seemed to be remembering someone else, someone other than Holmes. I knew that his wife and children were out of town, while he'd had to remain in London. I understood how he must be missing them.

Last my eyes sought out Wiggins, the youngest of our number. Was he too young to have suffered such a loss? I chided myself mentally. His life had possibly been the hardest of us all – orphaned at an early age. How much did he remember of his mother and father? Who had cared for him in his tender years – an aunt or uncle? Grandparents? Strangers?

Perhaps Holmes had known, but if so, he had never discussed it with me. To me, Wiggins had simply been the leader of the Baker Street Irregulars. Active, smart, quick, ambitious – all the things an orphan needs to survive. And yet, also a leader, able to organize his troops, inspire loyalty, and to care for them when they needed it.

He should join the army, I thought. He could be a leader of men, rather than of just children. He had already overcome so much. The fires of adversity had burned off the slag, and forged a strong and resilient core in that young man.

I drained my glass thinking on him, and Mrs. Hudson refilled it. Then I was distracted when she stood and raised her own glass. All eyes turned to her.

"To present friends as well," she said in a clear and steady voice. Her gaze moved from left to right, taking us all in. "We are none of us alone. We were united by our love of Sherlock Holmes. Let us united stay."

There were nods as we all repeated, "To present friends," and I drank to that without hesitation. A fine and uplifting sentiment was exactly what I needed to force the shadows out of my mind.

Lestrade stood next as Mrs. Hudson resumed her seat. "They say you can measure a man by his enemies, and Sherlock Holmes certainly earned a distinguished lot of those," he began. "I say you can measure a man by his friends and his legacy. You are, all of you," and here he paused, meeting the eyes of each of us in turn, "among the finest people I have ever known. Sherlock Holmes was a lucky man, and we are all the luckier for having known him." He raised his glass. "To the friends and family of Sherlock Holmes!"

We nodded and murmured assent, and drank again. Then, inevitably, our eyes turned toward young Wiggins.

For a moment he seemed taken aback, but then he gathered himself and rose. "I'm not used to makin' speeches," he said, and his diction was somewhat clearer than the street patois I expected. "But Mr. 'Olmes was in many ways the father I never 'ad. 'E was the one we turned to in our hour of need – not just me, but all the Irregulars. I say 'e was family to all of us, and that makes all of us a family, even now, without 'im. So for me, I'll drink to family, whether by blood or no." He raised his glass, and looked about, seeming almost to ask if he had been presumptuous.

I raised my glass. "To family," said I, and I drank. Mrs. Hudson followed suit, then Lestrade.

Mycroft paused, but then nodded and smiled. "Sherlock's family has always been mine own, from birth," said he, "and so it remains." He drank solemnly.

I knew that Mycroft had no other relatives remaining, after the loss of Sherlock. He honored us all by accepting us, even Wiggins, as family.

A silence descended on the group then, with each of us lost in thought. Mrs. Hudson's serving-maid, Emily, entered carrying a platter bearing the Christmas goose. Mrs. Hudson broke the silence with a clap of her hands. "Well, everyone, 'tis Christmas dinner, and we've a fine goose! Let's tuck in! Mr. Holmes, will you carve it, please?"

Later, with our bellies pleasantly full, we returned to the drawing room. Unlike our old sitting room one floor up, where Holmes and I had lived for years, Mrs. Hudson's abode was decorated with doilies and antimacassars and paintings of flowers, and there was a distinctly feminine aspect to its decoration, as one might expect – yet it pleasantly functional.

I brought out the two bottles of brandy I had packed. Our hostess graciously encouraged us to smoke, and provided snifters that the brandy might be properly appreciated. I poured brandy for all the gentlemen present, even Wiggins. Mrs. Hudson poured herself a small glass of a dessert wine.

There was an awkward silence after Lestrade and I lit our cigars, and Mycroft his pipe. Wiggins, to my surprise, preferred to abstain from smoking.

Our hostess began the conversation. "Mr. Holmes," said she, with a twinkle in her eye that bespoke unexpected depths in her character, "I think it's safe to say that you knew your brother better than anyone else present."

Holmes's elder brother waved it away dismissively. "I should say, rather, that I knew Sherlock in his youth. In more recent years, I would defer to the doctor, here, who spent many years in his company, and shared a number of adventures with him."

I was about to modestly attempt to deflect attention, but the landlady spoke up again. "But I knew him during those same years as Dr. Watson. I should like to hear of Mr. Sherlock Holmes in his youth. Please, sir – tell us a story from his younger days."

Mycroft again demurred, but I joined in the request. "That is a capital idea! Please, Mycroft – tell us something of your brother when he was growing up." When Lestrade and even Wiggins added their voices, Mycroft at last conceded.

"Did you know," he began, "that Sherlock almost did not become a detective? There was a time, when he was ten or eleven years old, that he had decided to become a naturalist. Our father actually encouraged this idea. He felt it a splendid way for a young man with Sherlock's prodigious intellect to advance science.

"As you may know, we grew up in Yorkshire, (though father was determined to keep our diction free of the common Yorkshire dialect). We traveled extensively, both on the Continent and within the British Isles, and everywhere we went, father would put to us what he called 'exercises of the mind'. He would ask us questions – first simple ones, then progressively more difficult, often involving both factual knowledge and deductive reasoning. Mother, too, joined in this game, making it a competition, and often demonstrated knowledge we would have never guessed." He paused. "I credit both of them for developing, in both my brother and myself, the habits and the pleasure of deductive thought.

"One autumn day in the early Sixties we were in the west Midlands, father seeking out Roman ruins between towns, when our horse developed a limp. Father stopped the carriage and found a sharp stone lodged against the frog in the horse's hoof. This he duly removed with a hoof pick. This would barely merit mention, save that, by mischance, the horse unexpectedly shied to one side, and, quite by accident, stepped on father's left hand, breaking some of his metacarpal bones." He tapped the back of his left hand, indicating the bones in question.

I winced at hearing this, well able to imagine the pain.

Mycroft continued. "Father gave me the reins, and mother insisted that we find a doctor in the next town to tend to his hand. The nearest town was a small village called Puddleby-on-the-Marsh, of which you have probably never heard. The only medical man in the whole village was an eccentric veterinarian named Dolittle. As it turned out, he had actually taken an M.D. before he turned his attention to veterinary medicine, and he was able to render the assistance father needed.

"The chap was quite peculiar, and possibly daft, with queer ideas, but he was a wonderful storyteller and there was no faulting his medical skills. Whilst he patched up father's hand, he began telling stories of animals, some quite fanciful, and I almost believe that he believed them. Sherlock, in particular, was enchanted by his talk of the language of bees. I haven't studied the creatures in any detail, but for a time Sherlock was determined that someday he should learn to understand them."

I spoke up. "He had mentioned to me that he still hoped, someday, to retire and become an apiarist."

Mycroft nodded. "That comes as no surprise. I think the old chap's stories found fertile ground in Sherlock's brain. As it was, once he had finished with father's hand, the doctor insisted on examining our horse, which he pronounced healthy and happy. I admit he had a wonderful way with animals. In the end we had to cut short our planned journey, but Sherlock spent much of the following month studying everything he could about bees.

"In later years, when I occasionally mentioned the old veterinarian, Sherlock merely dismissed him as a harmless eccentric – which I am certain he was."

We all chuckled at this, and I privately wondered what might turn a physician away from practicing on humans. This turned my mind to my own recent experiences, and I thought perhaps a tragic case might be the cause.

With this reminder my thoughts took a melancholy turn. The others seemed to notice this. Quietly I filled and lit my pipe, and Mycroft took out his own.

"Inspector," Mycroft addressed Lestrade, "before dinner, you were describing your conundrum. Pray continue."

"Aye, sir." Lestrade lit a cigar. "As I said earlier, we were unable to connect the kidnapping of Sir Cedric's dog to Dr. Westcott, because of his alibis, even though he was the clear and obvious suspect."

"Might he have hired someone to do it for him?" Mrs. Hudson asked.

Lestrade shook out the match and threw it into the fireplace. "That possibility occurred to us as well. If he did, we could find no connection to anyone to actually do the crime for him. And indeed, there's more to tell in the crimes of Mr. E.

"About a fortnight ago he surfaced again, and he isn't satisfied with taking a dog. The two-year-old daughter of a cabinet official was taken this time – from a pram in the park, with the nurse chloroformed and no witnesses to be found. Again, there was a ransom note from Mr. E. The same man, cloaked and hooded, was at the exchange of the ransom for the child."

Mycroft was watching Lestrade alertly now, taking in every word. "You are referring, of course, to the daughter of Jonas Ogilvy."

"Aye, that I am. It seems you're familiar with this case." Lestrade again took out his sheaf of papers, unfolded another piece of foolscap, and passed it to Mycroft. Mycroft regarded it critically for a few moments, then handed it on to me.

> *If you want to see your child again, you will bring £100 in gold to the alley behind the Rose Tavern in Flowerydean at midnight tonight. Come alone. Do not involve the police. If you do not comply you shall never see your daughter again.*
>
> *Mr. E*

"Clearly the same hand, and the same man, as the first note from Mr. E." Mycroft drew on his pipe, then exhaled a cloud of blue. "I expected this to come up next. There is very little that happens in the government – or to government men – that does not cross my desk. Once again, the mysterious Mr. E cannot possibly be the obvious Dr. Westcott." He handed the note to me.

"Indeed, sir. At this time, during the kidnapping, he was in his medical practise, as patients have attested. And, when the child was ransomed – and returned unharmed, I hasten to add – he was at a party at Lord Southwick's home, seen by dozens. Yet the 'Mr. E' who did the exchange was again described as of a similar height and build as Dr. Westcott, with the same dark cloak and cloth mask as before." Lestrade paused. "There was one additional detail mentioned: Mr. Ogilvy noted that Mr. E limped, favoring his left leg as he walked – something possibly overlooked by Sir Cedric."

"And Dr. Westcott, of course, walks without a limp – but that's an easy thing to imitate, to throw the police off the scent." Mycroft looked upward, drawing on his prodigious brain. "Yet Dr. Westcott has a grudge against Mr. Ogilvy – are you familiar with the circumstances?"

Lestrade fixed Mycroft with a penetrating glance. "No, sir. We were unaware of that. Can you elucidate?"

"This is little known outside the offices of the Government," the elder Holmes said. "I will expect you – " We looked around at all present. " – all of you – to keep this to yourselves. Even you, Mr. Wiggins." He pointed his pipe-stem at Wiggins, who nodded. "Mr. Ogilvy has a gambling habit. Not that he runs up debts – on the contrary, he seems to be quite a successful gambler. So successful, in fact, that there are murmurs of him cheating, though it has never been proven. Shortly before the kidnapping, he had spent an evening at cards in his club, and again he was profitably victorious. Dr. Westcott was among his opponents that night.

"It seems – from what we were able to reconstruct – that Dr. Westcott confronted Mr. Ogilvy outside the club as he was waiting for a cab. The doctor called him a cheat, and demanded a full refund of his moneys. Mr. Ogilvy naturally denied it, and they came to blows. Unfortunately for the doctor, Mr. Ogilvy also seems to be as skilled at fisticuffs as he is at cards, and the doctor found himself lying on the kerbstone, while Mr. Ogilvy climbed into the hansom and drove away.

"The doctor didn't file a formal complaint against Mr. Ogilvy in the club, but he did speak to many people, and there were a number who heard him promise revenge. I interviewed Mr. Ogilvy after the kidnapping, and the amount of the ransom – two-hundred pounds, far less than one might expect for a wealthy man's child – matches the amount lost by Dr. Westcott almost exactly."

Lestrade stroked the stubble on his chin, nodding slowly. "Mr. Ogilvy failed to mention that to us. More evidence – a clear motive – pointing to Dr. Westcott, yet still circumstantial. Of course he could have asked more – 'tis almost as if he were mocking us."

"Or, more likely," I ventured, "mocking the victims, wanting them to know he was taking his vengeance, yet untouchable by the law." I handed the second ransom note on to Mrs. Hudson, who had been looking curiously over my shoulder. "There is little to be learned from this second note."

"But," said Mycroft, "there is a great deal that can be inferred from these notes together. Yet very little of it is useful. The writer is clearly educated, and I should say attended one of our finer universities, most likely Oxford or Cambridge. From the way the numbers are formed, I would say he has had a scientific education, and the size of the capital letters indicates a considerable ego. Again, this comes through even with a right-handed man writing with his left hand."

"All of which could still point toward Dr. Westcott," I put in.

"And that is why there is little useful. Evidence that points to a man who cannot have possibly committed the crime is of little use indeed."

"And there is still more from Mr. E," said Lestrade. "This one, even you, sir, might not have heard of, as it involves a very common man."

"Indeed?" Mycroft's eyebrows shot up. "That is unexpected. Sherlock would have said that criminals rarely change their patterns, especially when that pattern is producing the desired results. There is some logic in kidnapping people – or dogs – who are unable to describe their captor or situation. In addition, a 'very common man', as you describe him, seems less likely to have much money for a ransom."

"True, Mr. Holmes, but the money seems to be almost peripheral to the crimes. You will note that in both the kidnappings the ransom demands were relatively modest. Indeed, Sir Cedric seemed far more outraged at the audacity of the kidnapper – whom he still believes was Dr. Westcott – than at the amount of the money.

"Last week there was another kidnapping, and another ransom demand from Mr. E. Unlike the other victims, this person has no apparent connexion to Dr. Westcott at all. This involved the infant son of a pawnbroker, Mr. Thaddeus Harris. Here is the note." Lestrade passed Mycroft a third piece of foolscap. He read it briefly, then passed it to me.

> *If you want to see your child again, you will bring £100 in gold to the alley across from the Church of St. Michael in Whitechapel at midnight tonight. Come alone. Do not involve the police. If you do not comply you shall never see your son again.*
>
> *Mr. E*

"The same hand, the same verbiage, the same *modus operandi*," Mycroft murmured. "In each case the ransom demands are modest – in this one, perhaps, to ensure that a man of moderate means can actually meet the demand. And in each case the rendezvous is late at night, in a neighborhood of, shall we say, dubious aspect."

"A neighborhood where a man takes his life into his hands," I said, "to be caught out alone late at night."

"I believe that is what I said, Doctor," Mycroft replied. "Doubtless intended to deter pursuit, once the precious hostage has been recovered. Do you know if Mr. Harris is involved in any obvious illegal work, such as fencing? Pawnbrokers often are."

"Of course they are," Lestrade replied. "But in this case, as far as we could determine, Mr. Harris is an honest pawnbroker."

I snorted. "A species new to science!"

Mycroft chuckled. "And this Mr. E was again as described before?"

"He was, and Mr. Harris also mentioned the man favoring his left leg. We had arranged to wait a block away, to ensure his safety. We also stationed officers at street intersections nearby, but we were unable to find Mr. E after the exchange."

Mrs. Hudson spoke up. "Did you ask Mr. Harris if he was acquainted with Dr. Westcott?"

Mycroft looked at her approvingly.

"We did, and he stated clearly that he had never heard of the doctor. Instead, he felt he knew who Mr. E was."

"And who was that?" Wiggins could barely contain his curiosity.

"He told us of a man he knew, a Mr. Hubert Gormley, who had threatened him last week – some disagreement over a debt, an item of jewelry that he had pawned with Mr. Harris. Yet when we questioned Mr. Gormley, he was able to produce an alibi – he had been in the custody of the local constabulary at the time, having made of himself a drunken public nuisance."

"Another obvious candidate for Mr. E, also obviously not your man," Mycroft murmured, setting down his pipe. "Have you any connexion between Mr. Gormley and Dr. Westcott?"

"None that we can find," Lestrade replied. "We have searched their clubs, their social circles. They live in different parts of London, and move in different levels. Mr. Gormley served in the Navy. Dr. Westcott was never in the military. Dr. Westcott is an educated professional, plays cards at his club, and secretly bets on dog-fights. Mr. Gormley is a common man of the working class, keeps accounts for a haberdasher, plays billiards in a pub, and loses money at horse races. He has no family, is unmarried, and rents a room in a boarding house. The only commonality is their both being suspects in the Mr. E cases."

Mycroft tapped his steepled fingers against his chin. "Where did you question Mr. Gormley?"

"In his office at the haberdashery."

"Was he seated behind a desk?"

"Yes, as it was his office." Lestrade seemed puzzled by the question.

"Did he ever get up?"

"Not while I was there."

Suddenly Wiggins spoke up. "Does Mr. Gormley 'ave any distinguishin' features? Anything unique about 'im?" This question surprised us all, sounding like something Sherlock Holmes might have asked. I reminded myself that Wiggins had been trained for years in observation by Holmes.

Lestrade smiled. "Yes, he is fairly recognisable. I noticed that he is missing the last two fingers on his left hand, though it seems to hamper him little, being right-handed."

"That argues somewhat against his having written the notes by Mr. E," Mycroft said. "It would still be possible, but more difficult. Did Mr. Harris notice Mr. E having any missing fingers at the exchange?"

"No, but he wore gloves, in addition to the cloak and mask." The inspector looked from Wiggins to Mycroft. "Also, his face is badly pocked. He seems to have had smallpox long ago. Of course, the mask would have hidden that."

"Does he 'ave a 'abit of squeezin' 'is eyes shut when 'e blinks?" Wiggins asked. "An' a moustache that droops 'longside 'is mouth?"

Lestrade paused, looking at Wiggins intently. "Now how did you know that?"

"Because I've seen 'im," Wiggins replied flatly. "There couldn't be two like 'im, even in all o' London. And," he added, "'e limps, favors 'is lef' leg."

"And where did you see Mr. Gormley?" Mycroft asked.

Wiggins paused, biting his lip. "At the dog-fights. Las' month."

"You go to dog-fights?" Mrs. Hudson was clearly surprised, but seemed less than scandalised. Long years of meeting Holmes's associates have hardened her sensibilities to realities of modern life.

Wiggins appeared slightly abashed, reddening a little. "Aye, ma'am, sometimes I do. Long ago, when I was workin' for Mr. 'Olmes, we was followin' a certain bloke, an' 'e was a dog-fightin' gent. I got me a job with one o' the gents what arranges the fights, so's to watch 'im for Mr. 'Olmes, an' it's proven a useful source o' knowledge – an' a few quid in me pockets besides. So I kept with it, a few times a month."

"Do you know of Dr. Westcott?" Lestrade asked. "Have you seen him there?"

"Them bettin' gents never use names, Inspector. Can you describe 'im?"

"He's a gent of medium height, maybe five-feet-nine-inches, sturdy build, dark red hair and whiskers. Muttonchops. He fancies he cuts a dashing figure. Carries a white walking stick, usually wears a light grey suit and matching top hat. Quite a noticeable chap."

Wiggins pressed his lips together in thought, then nodded. "Yes, I know the bloke. I've seen 'im talkin' with yer other chap, Mr. Gormley, after the dog-fights."

Mycroft suddenly snapped his fingers in triumph. "That's the connexion, then! We have them!"

Lestrade was clearly baffled. "'Them', sir?"

Mycroft's face, so like that of my departed friend, showed patient amusement. "Don't you see? It isn't one of them or the other."

At this point the truth burst upon me. "By Jove, it's both! Isn't it?"

Mycroft nodded. "They are both your mysterious 'Mr. E', the kidnapper. They collaborated on this, sharing the same disguise, each freely casting clues in the direction of the other, knowing the other had a perfect alibi. Dr. Westcott wrote the notes for both, confident that his alibi would rule him out of consideration. Individually neither of them could have escaped justice, but by working together on this, they almost did."

"So Mr. Gormley was Mr. E for Dr. Westcott's cases, and Dr. Westcott was Mr. E for Mr. Gormley's case!" Mrs. Hudson sounded triumphant.

"That's the way of it." Mycroft gestured toward the youngest guest at the table. "Thanks to Mr. Wiggins here, and the skills he honed under Sherlock's tutelage, for finding the link that solves this conundrum." He raised his glass toward Wiggins, who looked quite abashed. We all joined in the salute.

Lestrade drained his glass, looked round the room, then at Mycroft, amazement written clearly on his face. He rose from his chair. "Gentlemen – and lady – " He nodded toward Mrs. Hudson. "pray excuse me. I have to get back to the Yard and prepare arrest warrants. Your combined knowledge has found a solution where none of us, individually, had all the pieces of the puzzle. Mrs. H.," he continued, "I must also thank you for a most extraordinary Christmas dinner."

Mrs. Hudson beamed. "Inspector, you are invited to join us at the same time – next year, if you would. As are you all," she added.

Lestrade shrugged into his heavy overcoat and donned his hat. "May all our meetings prove this successful," he said. "Goodbye, and a Merry Christmas to you all." With that he took up his stick and left the room, and we heard the front door open and close.

Wiggins chuckled. We all looked at him. "I've just declared meself family wif a rozzer," he explained. "Never thought that'd 'appen."

"Well, dear boy," I said gently, "that was always the side Holmes was on. And you and the Irregulars chose that side."

"Yes, well, 'twas excitement, adventure, and a little extra money," he responded. "We didn't even think about the fact that we was workin' for the law."

"Yet," said Mycroft, "your work, such as it was, was sometimes instrumental in ensuring justice."

"'At's good to 'ear, Mister Mycroft," Wiggins said. "Betimes on the streets, the crushers are counted enemies. More'n once I feared the bad'uns'd come after me or some o' mine."

"'Twas a dangerous game you played," Mrs. Hudson said. "It took courage and cleverness."

Wiggins actually blushed at this unexpected praise. "Thanks, Mrs. H.," he said. "'At means a lot, comin' from such as you."

Mrs. Hudson again lifted her wine-glass in salute to the lad, and Mycroft and I joined in this silent tribute.

"'Twas Mr. 'Olmes what made it 'appen," Wiggins said. "We was already friends, survivin' together. 'E gave us money, but 'e also give us sumfin' important to do. It brought us together, made us stronger. Mr. 'Olmes made us what we are."

"He had an impact on all our lives," Mrs. Hudson said. "The good that he did outlives him."

We all drank to that as well.

Mycroft took out his gold hunter, compared it to the clock above our hostess' fireplace, and rose with a visible effort. "I must beg your indulgence," he said, "but I have an early day tomorrow, and must excuse myself from this – " Here he smiled and nodded, looking specifically at Wiggins. " – worthy company."

He accepted his hat, overcoat, and stick from Mrs. Hudson, and I rose and shook his hand at the door. As we clasped hands, his eyes – grey like those of his brother – met my own.

"I know this year has been onerous for you, Doctor," he said, placing a large and heavy hand on my shoulder. "Let me assure you that next year will be better."

I nodded. "Because I've nothing left to lose," I said glumly.

"No." He shook his head. "Because things will get better. Keep the faith, Doctor." Then he turned and was gone.

As I sit here writing in my empty house, and the year 1893 draws to a close around me, I can only wonder how that man – whom I have never known to be wrong – can say that in full confidence.

The fact that he does gives me some hope.

The Incident in Regent Street
by Harry DeMaio

Father Christmas Kidnapped! Held by Anarchists! Bold Demands for Release of Bomber!

This blaring headline in *The Daily Mail* was followed by a short but sensational narrative relating the daring abduction of the Father Christmas at Hamley's "world renowned" Toy Store in Regent Street.

> The Daily Mail *is in receipt of a copy of a letter sent to Scotland Yard demanding the release of the notorious Serbian anarchist bomber, Miroslav Petrovic, in exchange for the return of the beloved Father Christmas employed by Hamley's Toy Store. Few details are available on how this criminal act was carried out, other than he was seized and carried away while traveling home from his day's service.*
>
> *The letter follows:*
>
> Season's Greetings. We are holding as prisoner the living symbol of England's ridiculous Yuletide tradition – your Father Christmas. He will be returned unharmed only upon the release of Miroslav Petrovic from Scotland Yard custody and permission to safely leave the country. Upon your agreement, we will issue further instructions on how the exchange is to be carried out. Failure to comply within two days will result in his dead body being deposited at an appropriate location. For the sake of your children, we strongly urge your conformity.
>
> The Commission.
>
> *How did this happen? Who is "The Commission"? What will Scotland Yard do? Who is in charge? How will the Public react? We will continue to provide timely coverage of this outrage. Stay with us.*

Three years after his plunge and disappearance from Reichenbach Falls in 1891, Sherlock Holmes unexpectedly returned from his "Hiatus".

The explorer Sigerson vanished and Sherlock Holmes resumed his practice in 1894 with renewed energy.

I was simultaneously delighted, puzzled, and – as I had pronounced him dead, after all – embarrassed by his reappearance. Still devastated by the death of my devoted wife, Mary, I rejoined Holmes it Baker Street. Mrs. Hudson had restored our rooms to us, and we strove to pick up where we had left off.

During Holmes's long absence, I had resumed my medical practice, mourned my deceased wife, and committed a few more unpublished stories to the tin dispatch box I keep at Cox and Company. At odd moments, I had worked with Inspector Lestrade of Scotland Yard, offering medical opinions, and I even boldly took on several clients who had sought the missing Holmes's services. I was now readjusting to our former mode of operation.

So it was on a bleak London morning in mid-December '94, as we were finishing breakfast, that I read that disturbing article aloud to my companion. Although I despaired of its sensational journalism, Holmes insisted that we subscribe to *The Daily Mail* as one way of keeping tabs on the less-attractive aspects of London's activities.

After I finished reading, he asked his typical question: "What do you make of that, Watson?"

I was appalled at the consummate gall of this so-called "Commission" and said so. "This Petrovic is a vicious villain. Fortunately his bombing attempt failed, but he should still stand before the bar of justice. The threat is surprisingly literate. Usually they are barely understandable. I'm certain that Scotland Yard, as is their wont, will refuse to negotiate, but the Serbian anarchists have put them and – no doubt – the Home Office, in an untenable position. Can you imagine trying to explain to your little ones that Father Christmas has been abducted – or executed? Not I, thank you! Do you propose to get involved?"

"I'm not sure I would be welcome on this occasion. I shall wait a short period and see if I'm approached by the authorities. Who knows – my brother may deign to participate."

Mycroft Holmes was hardly a Yuletide enthusiast, but this event was clearly an embarrassment for Her Majesty's government. We would see shortly.

That afternoon, we received a visit from Lady Sybil Fairbrother, wife of the Earl of Seldon. She had sent a message in the morning requesting an audience, but gave us no indication of the issue she wished us to pursue.

At the agreed upon hour of one, a well-appointed brougham adorned with the Seldon crest and pulled by a lustrous black horse stopped in front of 221. A tall young footman descended, opened the carriage door, and assisted an attractive woman in fashionable travel dress to the pavement. He then rang our doorbell, waited for Mrs. Hudson to respond, and retired to the vehicle.

We heard the familiar sound of our landlady ascending the steps to our rooms, followed by light footfalls behind her. I turned to look at Holmes, who waved me to the door. I opened it at the first knock and Mrs. Hudson announced, "Lady Sybil Fairbrother to see you, gentlemen." She held out a silver tray with the noblewoman's decorative calling card on display.

The Countess swept into the room, and if she took account of its general untidiness, didn't react. She was quite striking: Dark of hair, light of complexion, and fair of visage. Her figure, while full, was graceful. Her posture and attitude radiated nobility. Her voice was surprisingly low and melodious. I judged her to be in her late twenties or early thirties. She turned to my companion.

"Mr. Holmes?" He nodded. "And Doctor Watson, author of those thrilling stories?" I bowed. "Thank you so much for agreeing to see me on such short notice. I hope you can assist me."

"Please be seated, my Lady," I said. "May I order up some tea?"

"No thank you. I shall get to the issue immediately. It is my daughter, Lucinda."

"Has something befallen her?" I asked.

"Oh, nothing of the dire nature to which you gentlemen are accustomed. I assure you she is well, unthreatened, and still her very willful self, as only an eleven-year-old can be."

I could tell Holmes was becoming mildly impatient, although he was successfully hiding it from our prospective client.

"May we know what the issue is?" he asked.

"Father Christmas! Lucinda wants you to find him, and I have agreed to commission you to do so."

"My dear Countess," he replied, "I assume you are aware of the unfortunate event that has taken place with the Hamley's Father Christmas."

"Precisely. Lucinda is a very precocious young lady who is quite capable of reading and of outrage. Somehow, she became aware of the article in *The Daily Mail*. I think one of our servants had it. She met this same Father Christmas at the toy store and was summarily charmed. She has reached an age where she's doubtful about Father Christmas, reindeer, elves, and other Yuletide sprites – until, that is, she met this particular individual. I know not how, but he managed to convince her that he was the real thing. She is now adamant that Father Christmas *does* exist. But he has been stolen. He is missing, and she wants him found and returned."

It was clear that Lady Sybil acceded to her spoiled daughter's every demand. I fully expected Holmes to gently but forcefully persuade the Countess to seek help elsewhere. This abduction was serious business, and not for children to be involved. But as is often the case with Holmes, I was wrong.

"Can you provide us with any more particulars, my Lady?" He asked. "I may be able to persuade your daughter to leave the problem to the authorities. if such is your desire."

She frowned. "It certainly is *not* my desire. She is very much disturbed. She knows all about you and Doctor Watson and will settle for no one else. She can surely be obstinate, but I agree with her. I have little confidence in the police in this instance."

"Then I'm afraid we can be of no assistance. It is a matter of personal ethics. I will not accept a commission and spend the money of a client, no matter how wealthy, on what I believe to be, forgive me, a wild goose chase. It is a police matter."

"I appreciate your frank honesty and your ethics, Mr. Holmes. That is why I have come to you. But Lucinda has read several of Doctor Watson's stories and will have no other person in this matter. May I ask you to take on this case with an open mind and come with me to meet my daughter? She can indeed be very persuasive, and her narrative of how she met her Father Christmas is – let us say – *unusual*. If, after an interview, you still wish to withdraw, I shall reluctantly accept your decision. If you can join me now, I shall wait in the brougham." She accompanied this with what is usually described as a winsome smile. She rose, smoothed her skirts, adjusted her hat, and headed for the door.

To my surprise, Holmes agreed to her proposal. Whether it was curiosity to meet someone I suspected would be a little hellion, the spirit of the oncoming season, his shared outrage at the anarchists, the lady's attractiveness, or the fact that we were in short supply of cases, he acquiesced and agreed to join her in the stylish carriage waiting in the street. He invited me to come along, and I confess my interest had been piqued. I decided to join him.

As we descended the stairs, I said. "I am amazed. With the exception of your Irregulars, you don't even like children."

"That was in the past, Watson. During my recent travels, I adjusted a number of my previous attitudes. I met some extraordinary individuals, many of a tender age, especially in Tibet. They can be most enlightening, The pejorative term 'childish' should often be replaced by the more complimentary 'child-like'. Anyway, we are about to discover the nature of eleven-year-old Lady Lucinda Fairbrother."

We had reached the brougham. The footman opened both doors and we joined the Countess. Holmes sat next to her and I took an extension seat opposite. She produced that same smile and said, "Gentlemen, thank you for accepting my invitation. The Earl's property is in Kensington. We shall arrive in due course and I'll introduce you to Lady Lucinda and her governess and companion, Mrs. Peterson. Lucinda is our only child. Of course, Henry is quite eager for us to add a boy to our family, but he dotes on our daughter." She laughed. "As, I suppose, do I. Oh, where are my manners? You are both most welcome to stay for tea."

I accepted before the abstemious Holmes had an opportunity to decline. Perhaps many things about him had changed during his wanderings, but not his eccentric eating habits. While engaged in unravelling a case, I've seen him go without nourishment for several days. I could not.

Our trip through the London streets and lanes was sporadic. Traffic usually increased during the Christmas season, and December 1894 was no exception. Our footman and driver took some unusual side routes that enabled us to avoid some of the congestion. We finally arrived at the Earl of Seldon's estate. The grounds were not that extensive, but the edifice itself was quite impressive. As we pulled up to the covered portico, a pair of large ornate doors opened and an individual that I assumed to be the butler emerged. He opened one of the doors of the brougham, and taking her hand, assisted the Countess to the ground.

"My Lady, welcome back. Lady Lucinda is in the drawing room, anxiously anticipating your return."

She flew up the stairs and into the extensive foyer, removing her hat as she went. Obviously the child wasn't to be kept waiting. Holmes and I extricated ourselves from the carriage and moved to the steps where the butler stood.

"Mr. Sherlock Holmes and Doctor Watson?" We nodded. "Gentlemen, welcome! I am Edwards, Seldon Estate Butler to the Earl, the Countess, and Lady Lucinda. Please follow me. We shall be serving tea shortly, but first, I'm sure you wish to get acquainted with the young lady."

The foyer shouted wealth, as no doubt did the remaining rooms in the elaborate establishment. The usual portraits of the usual ancestors flanked the walls of the passageway. A large formal staircase stood at the end of the hall, and a smaller set of several steps led off to the left. Edwards led us up this minor elevation and into a nicely appointed drawing room. The Countess had settled on a chaise longue and was engaged in animated discussion with a diminutive version of herself. Lady Lucinda was Lady

Sybil in miniature, at least in appearance. As we entered, the conversation stopped and before Edwards could announce us, the girl shot out of her seat and ran over, shouting. "Mr. Holmes! Doctor Watson! I'm so glad you have come. Thank you, thank you, thank you!" She reached out both her hands and grabbed ours. The butler turned and left the drawing room.

We shook the child's extended fingers and she raced back to her mother. "Oh, Mama, I am so glad! Now we will surely find Father Christmas!"

The Countess motioned toward another woman who had risen from a straight-back chair and walked in stately fashion in our direction. "May I introduce Mrs. Peterson, Lady Lucinda's governess and companion."

She was tall and slender with greying brown hair. A *pince-nez* framing brown eyes balanced itself on her Roman nose. Her complexion was fair, and some lines surrounded her eyes and mouth. She extended her hand and said with a slight European accent, "Welcome gentlemen. I do hope you can solve this terrible problem."

Holmes issued one of his brief and inoffensive smiles and responded, "I hope so, Mrs. Peterson, but first we must understand exactly the nature of the situation. I haven't yet spoken to the police. I gather, Lady Lucinda, that you are quite taken with Hamley's Father Christmas." He turned to the young girl who seemed completely eager to launch into her story.

"Oh, he doesn't belong to Hamley's, Mr. Holmes. He just has a throne there. He lives in Lapland and has reindeer and elves. He is quite real."

At that moment, Edwards returned, coughed gently, and announced tea was being served in the adjacent parlor.

Lucinda stamped her foot. "Oh, bother. Now I shall have to wait to tell you about Father Christmas."

Lady Sybil smiled that smile and said, "Nonsense, Lucinda. We have taught you how to speak and eat at the same time. Come, let us go to the table."

The girl ran into the parlor and, ignoring the butler's offer to assist, seated herself at the center and proceeded to unfold a serviette on her lap. Lady Sybil took up her position at the head of the table with the butler's support. Mrs. Peterson sat next to Lucinda, and we placed ourselves at the remaining places. It seemed the Earl was not going to join us.

Lady Sybil nodded to us. "The Earl is taken up with affairs at the House of Lords today, but he is most eager to make your acquaintances. He is, as they say, a great admirer. He was devastated, as were we all, at the news of your demise, Mr. Holmes. Imagine our elation to find that it wasn't true and, after all these years, you have returned to Baker Street. He suggested that he call on you tomorrow morning. He wishes to meet you *in situ*, as it were. Would that be agreeable?"

Holmes smiled, looked at me, and we both concurred, although I was astonished that he was going to continue this engagement.

A maid and a footman entered with an array of sandwiches, scones, and pastries and set about laying plates and cups before us. The Countess poured and then began to eat, a signal that we should do likewise. Lucinda swiftly demolished a jam and cream-covered scone, looked at Holmes and myself, and in a loud voice proclaimed, "He was at Hamley's on his throne!"

"The Toy Store?" I asked.

"The largest toy store in the world. That's where I met him. Father Christmas."

Holmes put down his spoon and said, "That is hardly surprising, Lady Lucinda. Hamley's employs several Father Christmas actors every year during the entire month of December."

"Oh. I know that, but they are *actors*. My Father Christmas is *real*. Tell them, Winnie. You've met him."

Winnie was Mrs. Peterson. It was clear that none of us were going to have our tea in peace.

She looked at us and in a clear, aristocratic voice, said, "Well, he certainly was unusual."

"Pray, Mrs. Peterson, in what way?"

She turned to the girl. "I shall let Lady Lucinda describe him. Perhaps you should tell your story from the beginning, dear."

The young lady was beside herself with excitement. "I have a collection of Queen Victoria dolls. On Tuesday, Winnie and I made our annual visit to Hamley's to see what new ones they had for this season. They have several, Mama. I would be ever so pleased if you and Papa got them for me for Christmas."

She laughed. "Perhaps Father Christmas will see to that."

"We must find him and I will ask. Anyway, after we looked through the doll department and the rest of the displays on the Girls' Floor, we went down to the Main Lobby where Father Christmas sat on a throne, surrounded by several small children. They were talking to him. One little boy pulled his beard. It was real. So was his white hair. He looked very much like the pictures in the catalogs and books. Fat and jolly with big dimples. He wore a green velvet robe and a matching cap.

"I let go of Winnie's hand, marched up, and stared at him. He shooed the little ones off his lap and platform and turned to look at me. I said, 'You're a fake. You're not real. I don't believe in you.'

"He looked sad for a moment and said, 'I'm very sorry to hear that, Lady Lucinda. I was hoping you would believe in me.'

"I was startled. 'How do you know my name?'

"'I know all about you, my Lady, and your mother and father too.'

"I turned to Winnie. 'Did you tell him about me?' She shook her head no.

"'How do you know my parents?'

"'I'm Father Christmas. I know these things. I know you live in a splendid house with this lady here – Mrs. Peterson. You're an only child. I know your parents want you to have a brother. I know you have a doll collection and want more of them. And I know you are a very willful little girl.'

"I stamped my foot. 'I am not little. I am eleven, and I am not willful.'

"'Perhaps. After all, you will be twelve in January, but you certainly want your own way.'

"Mrs. Peterson laughed. I frowned. 'It's not funny, Winnie.'

"She laughed again. 'But it's true, my dear.'

"I turned back to him. 'You know so much about me. I don't know much about you except what is in the books.'

"'Oh,' he replied, 'There is so much written about me that is inaccurate. Can you imagine me sliding down chimneys? I'd get stuck on the first try. But I do have a sleigh and reindeer. They are all girls, by the way, with one exception. My home is in Lapland. That is where we make the toys and keep track of the boys and girls. And I do travel at great speed on Christmas Eve, Christmas, and Boxing Day bringing joy, good tidings and gifts.'

"I sniffed. 'I don't believe a word of it. I think you're a stage actor hired on by the shoppes to help sell their goods.'

"He smiled. 'I'm sorry you feel that way, Lady Lucinda. I believe in you and have such hopes for you. Please stand aside and let some of these other children who do believe in me have a chance.'

"Winnie and I turned and left the store."

Holmes had listened to her tale with rapt attention. Lady Sybil and Mrs. Peterson looked quizzically at the two of us. I'm sure the Countess was about ready to accept Holmes's refusal to pursue the search. Instead, he turned back to the precocious young lady and asked, "What caused you to change your mind? Why do you now want to find him?"

Lucinda caught her breath. "He said, 'I believe in you and have such hopes for you.' What did he mean by that, Mr. Holmes? Doctor Watson? Do you have any idea?"

"I don't know, my dear. But now he's missing."

"Yes, Winnie and I went back to Hamley's yesterday and he wasn't there. Was he really kidnapped?"

"We think so. There was a letter to Scotland Yard."

"I saw it in the newspaper. I read very well, you know. We asked the store manager. He said he had expected him, but he never came in. They have an obvious fake playing the part, with a false beard. Nobody seems to know where Father Christmas is. I want you to find him, Mr. Holmes. Please!"

"And if we do, what then?"

"I want to tell him that I do believe."

The footman and maid entered the room and began to clear the table.

"I can't believe you intend to go on with this, Holmes. These anarchists have no qualms about doing away with this actor. You are giving false hopes to this child. And what are you going to say to the Earl when he arrives?"

We were seated at the table, finishing another one of Mrs. Hudson's excellent breakfasts.

"What is the Earl going to say to us? I have the impression that he dotes on his daughter just as much as his wife does."

I nodded. "She is a very spoiled young lady, but appealing, nonetheless. I was stricken by her sincerity when she said she now believes in Father Christmas. Her rapid change of heart is most remarkable."

Holmes raised an eyebrow. "Like so many members of the gentle sex, she is led by the emotions of the moment. I feel certain she will sustain another change of heart when we discover his whereabouts and bring him back."

"So you *are* taking the case. I hope you don't disillusion her in the process. Even if he is found, he will be discovered to be a talented actor."

"No, it's up to him to let her down gently. It seems he has an aptitude for soft words. I plan a visit to Hamley's shortly after we meet the Earl. And then we'll go to the Yard. Are you free to accompany me?"

I consulted my pocket calendar and found my afternoon was open. I poured another cup of coffee and we awaited the arrival of Lord Henry Fairbrother, Twelfth Earl of Seldon.

At precisely ten o'clock, I observed the same brougham and splendid black horse stopping outside. The same footman dropped gracefully to the pavement and opened the door of the carriage. An archetype of nobility stepped from the brougham, straightened his morning coat, took up his silver headed cane, and strode past the driver to rap on the door.

We had alerted Mrs. Hudson that the Earl would be coming. While she was somewhat accustomed to people of consequence entering her premises, I would imagine that she would nonetheless feel a flutter of excitement as he arrived. Opening the door, she would drop a curtsey, place his card on a silver tray, and lead him up the stairs to our rooms.

I had opened the door and she thrust the tray at me. "His Lordship, the Earl of Seldon, to see Mr. Holmes and yourself, Doctor." She stood sideways, allowing the Earl to stride into our quarters.

"So this is where it happens, eh? I congratulate you, Doctor. In your stories, your description of these digs is most accurate and complete. This all feels very familiar to me. I should tell you that I avidly consumed each one of your tales. I hope there will be more."

Lord Henry stood a trifle over six feet. His sturdy build and ruddy complexion, matched with his russet locks and minimum moustache, reminded me of one of Robin Hood's Merry Men. He was otherwise clean-shaven and attired in morning clothes of the latest fashion. His appearance made it clear that here indeed was a wealthy individual, no doubt willing and capable of responding to his wife and daughter's every whim.

He turned. "Mr. Sherlock Holmes. I am honored, sir, to meet the world's greatest detective face-to-face. I must tell you how greatly relieved we all were to hear of your return, and I hope to know the story someday. We hoped against hope that you had not succumbed. Can you now perform the same miracle and bring this Father Christmas back to life and console my daughter?"

Holmes directed the nobleman to our sofa and signaled me to pour the coffee that Mrs. Hudson had left for us. "My Lord, welcome to our humble abode. Thank you for your good wishes. My post-Reichenbach adventures are too extensive and complex to bear telling at the moment. But tell us: What makes you believe this Father Christmas is deceased?"

"Isn't it obvious?"

"That conclusion is quite premature. The Hamley's Father Christmas has been missing for just a few days. I understand his replacements are hardly up to the store's high standards, and I am certain management is making every effort to assist the police to reinstate him on his throne. I plan to go to Regent Street this afternoon, and then to Scotland Yard. I hope we will overcome these anarchists and find this Yuletide paragon still alive and well."

"Jolly Good!" He sipped the coffee and munched on a biscuit while we conversed. "I don't suppose you believe this individual is the real Father Christmas."

"I'm afraid I don't share your daughter's belief that such a person exists. However, if necessary, I am prepared to construct a scenario that will let her down gently. I'm somewhat surprised at how rapidly she switched from disbelief to belief."

"Lucinda, like her mother, is impulsive. She responds to first impressions. I must confess that we have catered to her whims, but dash it all, she is my only child, and I have the wherewithal to respond to her desires. That applies to Lady Sybil as well. Perhaps one of these days there will be a male heir to carry the Seldon crest. We are both young and healthy."

As I speculated that the Earl was no older than forty, if that, he added, "Well, I'm quite satisfied to meet your fee in this matter, Mr. Holmes. On my daughter's behalf, I'm pleased to be your client. Perhaps you may even find a story here to record, Doctor: 'The Father Christmas Adventure', or some such."

He laughed, picked up his carefully brushed hat and cane, shook our hands, and headed for the door.

Down in the street, the door to the brougham opened and closed again with a hefty thud. The driver took his seat on his bench and urged the beautiful horse into motion. I turned away from the window as Holmes asked his usual question: "What do you make of that, Watson?"

"He's a great admirer of yours, and an adoring father. I'm inclined to think he would actually like you to prove that this Father Christmas *is* the real thing, if for no other reason than to please his daughter, and possibly his wife. But first, he must be rescued."

"Lady Sybil didn't have the opportunity to meet this Father Christmas. She has had to rely on the word of Lady Lucinda and Mrs. Peterson. As have we. I propose to remedy that condition posthaste. Are you ready for a journey to Toyland?"

Regent Street was suitably bedecked with Yuletide adornments. The merchants sought to outdo one another with immense wreaths, garlands, heavily decorated trees, and figures galore. Hired carolers entertained on the pavement. Pictures and sculptures of Father Christmas dotted the commercial landscape. But none were as ornate or delightful as the windows and sidewalks at Hamley's. Each window showed samples from the seven floors within: Stuffed animals, dolls, prams, mechanical sets and trains, lorries, and other vehicles. Puzzles, sports equipment, and games, games, games.

We entered the Main Hall where stairs and newly installed lifts promised to bring us to the wonderlands of our choosing. Midway through the heavily bedecked displays sat Father Christmas' throne. It became immediately apparent that the current incumbent was not up to Hamley's usually exacting standards. Wearing an obviously false beard and a robe far too voluminous for his scrawny frame, he was listlessly attending to the cries and squawks of the children surrounding him. This was not Lucinda's idol. A group of mothers and nannies were struggling unsuccessfully to maintain order. Several young women dressed as fashionable elves were trying to keep a queue intact.

Holmes turned to me and said, "Clearly, there is more impact from this abduction than we imagined. Let us seek out the store manager and make inquiries."

We were directed by a commissionaire to an isolated lift that only rose two floors to the executive offices. Once there, the name of Sherlock Holmes again worked its magic and we were escorted into a large but sparsely decorated office – sparsely decorated, that is, except for the wild array of toys that took up every available inch of floor and table space.

A portly individual in a business suit that barely fitted him peered at us over his spectacles, looked at our cards, and broke into a smile. "Sherlock Holmes and Doctor Watson! Imagine you being here at Hamley's Toy Store! I am Reginald Small, Manager-in-Chief. Welcome back to London, Mr. Holmes! Glad to see you are still in the land of the living. Are you here to satisfy some craving by the little boy that dwells inside all of us? Often carefully hidden, mind you, but there, nonetheless."

Holmes's little boy was more-than-carefully hidden. It was buried. I, on the other hand . . . I looked around the room in awestruck wonder. Clearly, Mr. Small's little boy was right at the surface. He smiled again. "How may I help you?"

"We're hear about your Father Christmas."

"Oh, I am mightily embarrassed. As we speak, I have several agents out scouring for acceptable actors to fill our needs. The substitute we are using now is beyond the pale and will be removed shortly. Unfortunately, all the good candidates have been snapped up by our rivals. We had a most exceptional individual who fit the image perfectly. Unfortunately, he is now the subject of a kidnapping investigation. Anarchists, if you can credit it.

"We are endeavoring to effect his rescue. At the moment, I'm not yet working with the police. A private client is most anxious to bring him back. Tell me about him."

"He goes by the name of 'Chris'. Not sure where he lives. He gave us a false address and references when he took employment with us. Normally, I would have rejected him outright. But he had a perfect Father Christmas image. Pure white hair and beard. Twinkling eyes. Rosy cheeks and dimples. Plump! He even had his own costume. And his way with the children was delightful. He was such a total fit that I chose to overlook the deception."

Then he paused. "Wait, you don't suppose that *he* has anything to do with this Serbian anarchist crowd, do you? He did have a slight foreign accent. I certainly hope he doesn't! But then, if he were one of them, why would they abduct him? No, that doesn't make sense. I've spoken to the police, and considered hiring a detective myself. I suppose I have no need for a detective if you are on the job."

Holmes ignored the remark. "Where was he when he was taken?"

"As best we can tell, at the end of the day, when he was emerging from the loading dock at the back of the store. That's where most of our employees enter and exit the building. One of our costumed 'elves' saw him being hustled into a growler. She could only remember a partial cab number. She spoke with the police. An Inspector Gregson and several constables have been here and gone. I assume you will be dealing with them. If you find Chris, bring him back. He was the best Father Christmas we've ever had. The kiddies will all be so disappointed if he doesn't return."

I nodded. We knew of one already.

Armed with those small fragments of information, we headed for Scotland Yard, but first made a detour to Whitehall, arriving unannounced at the office of Holmes's brother, Mycroft. The elder Holmes was hardly a Yuletide enthusiast, but would, no doubt, be concerned by the public embarrassment to Her Majesty's Government and the well-being of the "Jolly old elf".

Surprisingly, we were immediately ushered into his office and unceremoniously seated. "It takes no great insight on my part to know why you two are here. You have decided to involve yourself in this Father Christmas imbroglio. Good! The Home Office and the Foreign Office are under pressure from the Prime Minister to bring these Serbian scoundrels to book. The House of Commons has initiated a debate on whether to accede to their demand. The press is baying at full throat. The Queen has expressed her horror that such a barbaric thing could happen in her realm – especially in London in a season when peace and joy are supposed to be rampant. The Church has spoken out, although they are relieved that it was not a religious attack. Could you imagine if the Archbishop of Canterbury were spirited away?"

I was about to remark that there would probably be less of a fuss than about Father Christmas, but decided to hold my tongue.

"Anyway, your presence here is quite fortuitous. I was just about to send for you. Inspector Gregson is on his way here as well. Scotland Yard has had further communication with this Commission gang. They wish to negotiate. Sherlock, I would like you to be our hostage intermediary."

Holmes looked at Mycroft. "Why me? I am not a disinterested party. I have a private client who has engaged me to seek out his rescue."

"They don't know that. They refuse to deal with Scotland Yard or Her Majesty's government. Given your fame and reputation, I believe they'll see a further publicity angle to this that they hadn't anticipated. They will believe that you have influence to effect Petrovic's release and offer safe conduct out of the country – which we have no intention of allowing to happen."

"In other words, any agreement we reach will be breached by you once our hostage is recovered."

"Yes. I realize that may strike you as dishonorable, but this Petrovic is a wild fanatic and cannot be allowed to roam freely over the landscape. We will either renege, or we will set about recapturing him."

"I'm sorry, but I cannot agree to that. You must at least allow us to live up to whatever agreement we make. Otherwise, they will feel betrayed and retaliate. At a minimum, Watson and I will be in peril, to say nothing of renewed attempts on Father Christmas. Remember, these are desperate people. "

Mycroft simply shrugged.

I rejoindered. "What do we know about this Commission? Who are they? Are they a large organization? Are the members known to us? Are you setting us up for retribution from a bunch of fanatics?"

"They are new on the scene, Doctor. We know very little about them except by inference. We know Miroslav Petrovic is a Serb and is wanted by the Belgrade government. They wish to extradite him. He obviously does not want to return there. Our interviews with him have been fruitless. He is clearly insane and blindly motivated by vengeance on all governments."

He went on. "We aren't sure how many of his fellows are equally unreasonable. We think they are a small group. They hadn't appeared in any incident reports until the attempted bombing, and now this current entanglement. They are clearly innovative and daring, but they don't seem very competent. Witness the bungled bombing in Trafalgar Square."

"But competent enough to pull off a sensational kidnapping!"

"*Touché, Mon Cher Medecin*! Well, what say you, Sherlock? Are you up to salvaging Christmas for London's little mites?"

"I am more interested in rescuing a beloved old man from a threatened death."

Mycroft coughed, "Of course, of course! Ah, here is Inspector Gregson. Have a seat, Gregson. You, of course, know these two worthies. Bring us up to date."

"Good day, Mr. Holmes, Mr. Holmes, and Doctor Watson. We've received another missive from our fanatic friends. This time they didn't send a copy to the press. Thank goodness! They want to negotiate. I think they are concerned that they have bitten off a bit more than they can chew, or there's some conflict among the members. Killing off Father Christmas would spell doom for them, but they do want to get Petrovic out of England. They are fervent anarchists. They categorically refuse to deal directly with the Yard or any other representative of the government. 'No politicians! No *aristos*! No royalty! No Church members!' We need a disinterested intermediary to deal with them."

"Exactly the task I have been attempting to get my esteemed brother to take on."

"A fine idea! They may not entirely trust you, Mr. Holmes, but I think they would deal with you. You are clearly an independent soul who will not be dictated to by the bureaucracy – or so they will believe."

"You are correct, Inspector. I will not be dictated to by the bureaucracy. What do you think, Watson? Are you up for some diplomacy and hostage swapping?"

"There don't seem to be many alternatives. Let's remember that Lady Lucinda is depending on us."

Mycroft and Gregson stared blankly. "Who is Lady Lucinda?"

Holmes smiled. "Another story for another time. Very well. How do we approach this Commission?"

Gregson frowned. "We leave notes at places they designate. They have an articulate spokesperson who has been writing their communications. Not at all like a foreign thug or roughneck. We have yet to make any direct contact with him."

"Or her," added Holmes.

The inspector gawked. "A woman? I hadn't considered that."

"Why not? This whole circumstance has some definite female touches. The Father Christmas image has always had a very strong influence on women, especially little girls. It is highly possible that an ingenious distaff member of this Commission saw the social, sentimental, and political impact of Father Christmas in peril and decided to use it to great advantage. Don't dismiss the feminine Yuletide viewpoint. Much of the relevant Noel literature involves young ladies, Tiny Tim notwithstanding."

"That was Scrooge."

"Thank you, Watson. All right, Gregson. We reluctantly agree. Make your contact and we will set the negotiations in motion."

Later in the day, we received a wire from Gregson. The Commission was demanding free and unobstructed passage to the Continent for Miroslav Petrovic and certain Commission members on a fishing vessel they would hire. Only when the boat exited British jurisdiction would they release Father Christmas. We could then pick him up. Any attempt to board the boat would result in him being thrown overboard, bound and weighted.

Many details needed to be worked out before we could accept their terms. More remote negotiation took place. We finally settled on a plan through a clumsy exchange of messages. The boat, *Vanessa G.*, was tied up at a remote quay at the London Docks at Wapping, prepared to sail on tomorrow's tide. Holmes and I were to proceed to the boat where we would be allowed to see Chris and determine his state of health and relative safety. As a physician, I would determine his physical condition. If all was well, we would proceed. Holmes would then stay on the boat as a temporary hostage until Inspector Gregson arrived unarmed with Petrovic in custody.

I would join Gregson in transporting the anarchist to the boat. Holmes, Gregson, and I would then disembark and the *Vanessa G.* would cast off, being followed at a half-mile distance by a Royal Navy Patrol Boat down the Thames, out into the outer Channel, and onto the open sea. Once in international waters where the Navy lacked jurisdiction, Father Christmas would be lowered to a dinghy and cast off. Presumably, he would be immediately picked up by the Navy boat and returned safely to London. The *Vanessa G.* would not be followed or intercepted. Its destination was unknown.

Scotland Yard, the Home and Foreign Offices, and Mycroft Holmes all grudgingly acquiesced to the arrangements. The Prime Minister and presumably Her Majesty were also informed.

There were conflicting messages from the conspirators as to whether the press should be present. Several members apparently wanted the publicity, but caution won out, with too many opportunities for the escape being foiled by over eager reporters or amateurs. Secrecy was key. The Government, Holmes, Gregson, and I agreed.

Next day, the high tide at Wapping was predicted at 2:30 p.m., and thus we arrived at the remote quayside an hour earlier to begin the complicated procedures. A cold December wind blew off the Thames and I was glad of my heavy overcoat. Holmes was, as usual, more lightly dressed. The *Vanessa G.* was moored as predicted, but no indications of life were obvious. I had expected to see crew members engaged in final preparations. Of the passengers-to-be, there was not a sign.

Holmes looked at me and asked if I had my service revolver hidden away in my voluminous coat. I nodded. He said, "Good old Watson! I can always rely on you."

He walked up to the gangplank and called out, "Ahoy, the *Vanessa G.* Sherlock Holmes and Doctor Watson here. Permission to come on board?"

There was a brief pause and we could hear the sound of doors sliding along the forward cabin. Two guards holding revolvers stepped toward the gangplank followed by . . . *Mrs. Winifred Peterson.*

My mouth dropped open.

"Good afternoon, gentlemen. Right on time! I assume the inspector will be along with Miroslav in as prompt a fashion."

"Good Lord!" I muttered.

She looked at the two of us with a supercilious smile. "Yes, gentlemen. I am the voice of the Commission. I am also the wife of Miroslav Petrovic."

It dawned. Peterson . . . *Petrovic*! Obvious when one thought about it.

Holmes decided to play to her ego. "So you developed this clever, almost bizarre, scenario to get your husband released from a virtually certain term in prison."

"Yes, Miroslav is a man of action. I am the subtle planner. There was a bit of serendipity involved. It was only when Lucinda and I visited Hamley's that I saw the impact Father Christmas had on the children, their parents, grandparents, nannies, aunties, and uncles. He was such a natural. When I slipped him a note with details regarding Lucinda and the Earl's family, he played it back effortlessly. If he could do that so convincingly, he would have all of London at his beck and call. It was then that I realized what a marvelous opportunity his kidnapping would represent. What a loss it would be! You have witnessed the result: Public uproar! Calls for the man's rescue from all quarters. Our demands would be met."

"Tell me, Mister Holmes, would the Prime Minister have responded so vehemently to a member of the House of Lords being apprehended? I originally thought of Lord Seldon as our victim – he and his vapid wife. I even thought of capturing the brat, but that would have pointed too early and obviously to my involvement. My God, I hate them!"

"No, Father Christmas was our ideal target, and he was so easy to grab. He offered some futile resistance to our men, but was promptly sedated. I suppose you want to see him. He is bruised, but otherwise unhurt. We do have some honor, as I hope you do too. Come, Doctor Watson. Form your medical opinion. We want the world to know he has not been harmed. You will find him below, tied up with the ship's Captain and his three crew members. They are unnecessary. My men are skilled sailors."

"So you have added nautical hijacking to your list of crimes."

"None of that matters as long as Miroslav is released and we are gone. Now come. Let us not waste any more time talking. The inspector should be arriving with my beloved any minute now."

I was led below by one of the armed guards. He neglected to check my clothing. They were not the most intelligent of men, in contrast to the *femme fatale* we had been facing. I found Father Christmas – Chris – lying unconscious on a packing case. The ship's crew were writhing, trying to free themselves from their bonds. The tough who brought me down waved his gun threateningly at them and then at me. "Hurry up!" he growled. I checked the victim's vital signs, looked for bruises and breaks, and I noted his sedated condition. If they dropped him in a dinghy in his current condition, he might not survive. I was about to make that point when I heard a shout from the deck above. Gregson and his prisoner had arrived.

I emerged from the cabin to behold the revolutionary breaking free of the inspector's hold. "You are all oppressing swine! I'll kill you all!" He snatched a guard's revolver and lunged at Holmes, firing a shot in his direction. His wife screamed and grabbed at him. "Miroslav, stop! Give me the gun!" Holmes then grasped him with a baritsu hold and flipped him over, causing the gun to fire again – this time hitting Mrs. Peterson squarely in the chest!

I fired my revolver at his kneecap, causing him to collapse. He screamed. "Freddi, Freddi! No, No! It cannot be!" He crawled to her side and held her in his arms. "It cannot be! It cannot be!"

But it was! She looked up at him briefly, sighed heavily, said nothing, and expired. Petrovic was wracked with heaving sobs. Gregson seized him roughly and pulled him to his feet. Holmes assisted. The guards ran down the gangplank only to be surrounded by a contingent of River Police who had been hidden in a boat on the opposite side of the quay. Scotland Yard was taking no chances.

I returned below-decks, untied the captain and his crew and, with their assistance, helped the semi-conscious Chris to his feet. The River Police had summoned an ambulance and he was transported to Barts for observation.

Holmes was standing on the deck staring out at the Thames. I approached him, but said nothing. He simply shook his head and said, "Hardly a Happy Christmas. Let's go home."

The press had a proverbial field day. *Father Christmas Rescued. Anarchist Wounded. Scotland Yard Triumphs. Happy Christmas to All!*

There was no mention of Holmes's or my involvement, which is exactly the way we wanted it. We heard from Mycroft and Gregson. The powers-that-be were settling back into their holiday torpor. Petrovic was back in custody facing an array of new charges. No extradition was forthcoming. To all intents and purposes, the Commission had disbanded and the Yard was in pursuit of the fugitives. Little or no comment was made about the untimely death of a professional governess who was accidentally shot in a mysterious dockside conflict. Christmas was fast approaching. Other issues captured London's attention.

Several days later, as December 25th rapidly approached, Holmes and I met the Earl, his wife and daughter, on the main floor of Hamley's Toy Store, where we'd been invited to witness her reunion with Father Christmas. The two parents and the young girl stood patiently (*well, maybe not*) in a queue of mothers, fathers, nannies, and their charges. We made polite conversation, but when the Earl quietly mentioned the governess, Lucinda heard and asked, "Where is Winnie? She left without saying goodbye."

"Winnie has gone back to Europe, dear," said her mother. "We don't know if she'll be back."

The Earl, changing the subject, said, "I also asked you here to settle your fee, Mr. Holmes."

"There is no need, my Lord. Her Majesty's government has seen to it."

The Countess glanced down the line toward Father Christmas and asked, "Why did they keep him in hospital, Doctor Watson?"

"He is an old man. They were just holding on to him out of a sense of caution and until the pandemonium died down. He doesn't want any of the publicity, although the store was salivating at the prospect."

I looked around us. The throne area was packed to capacity. The store manager was beside himself with glee. Two "elves" tried mightily to maintain order and a group of carolers strained to be heard above the noise. The young people of London were descending on Father Christmas en masse. Shouts, cries, and wails galore! As the line moved forward, Lady Lucinda Fairbrother turned to her mother and father and, adding to the tumult, cried out, "It's him! I knew it would be! Mama, Papa, it's him! He's back! I told you so!"

"Yes dear," Lady Sybil said. "I'm sure it's really him. Our turn is next."

We stepped out of line as they mounted the steps to the throne and took a closer look. It was the same real white hair and beard, the same ruddy complexion and pudgy face, and the same charming smile. There were no sign of bruises, but a bandage peaked out from under his velvet cap. His capacious robe was immaculate except for a spot where some excited child had thrown up. He reached out his hand. "Lady Lucinda, Lady Sybil, Lord Seldon – Merry Christmas! It is so nice to see you again."

"You remembered us!"

"How could I forget?"

Lucinda interrupted (*as usual*), "Are you all recovered? We were so afraid for you!"

"Yes, I am quite well. Still have a bruise or two." He pointed at the bandage. "Tell me, Lucinda: Do you still want those Queen Victoria dolls to play with?"

She hesitated. "I . . . I think so."

The old man glanced toward the girl's parents. Unseen by Lucinda, her father nodded slightly. "I think that might be arranged," was Father Christmas's answer.

Then he glanced my way and gave a small wink, his eyes twinkling. Throughout the time I'd treated him following his rescue, he'd never revealed any more of his name than "Chris". *Could it be?* I wondered. *Could he really be Father Christmas? Could Holmes possibly find out the answers?*

I decided that I didn't really want to know for sure.

The Baffling Adventure of Baby Jesus
by Craig Stephen Copland

December 1894

"The only people, Watson, who attend a Methodist nativity pageant are hypocritical poseurs who never darken the door of a church at any other time of year . . . with the possible exception of Easter. Why, in the name of all that is holy, should I even think of attending?"

"Because, my friend, the congregation may be full of hypocrites, but some of them could be your future clients. And may I remind you that having only returned from the dead a few months ago yourself, you still need more clients. Your calendar has been empty for the past two weeks and your bank account is still recovering."

"Blessed are the poor, for theirs is the kingdom of heaven."

"That isn't quite what it says."

"Perhaps not, but it was all I could think of."

"Holmes, your brother has ceased paying for your rooms, and you are at risk of falling behind on your rent to Mrs. Hudson. You cannot leave her short at Christmas time."

That got to him. He tossed his newspaper on the floor, smacked his pipe to empty the bowl, and stood up.

"Fine. Then let us go, try to be conspicuous, and get out of there as quickly as possible."

He pulled on his overcoat and hat and I did the same. Before we started down the stairs to Baker Street, I handed him a flyer that advertised the Living Nativity Celebration at the Hinde Street Methodist Church.

"Here. This is the program for the evening. It will only last an hour. You will thank me later when several of the attendees accost you and request a private audience to discuss the problems besetting their lives. At least one or two of them will have promising criminal connections. Now, let us be off. A seat near the front of the church would be advantageous."

"Wait."

He was looking at the program. He stuffed it into the pocket of his coat and started down the stairs.

"Come, Watson. No time to lose."

I caught up to him on the pavement of Baker Street.

"Merciful heavens – what came over you?"

"Did you not see the name of those who were playing the role of the Virgin Mary and Joseph?"

"Yes. It says that Lord Arsfasten will play Joseph and his wife, Mary, will be the Virgin Mary. He's the richest member of the congregation. What else would you expect?"

"A few days before we departed for Switzerland three years ago, his former wife came to me and asked for my services. I would have helped her, but that damnable professor interfered."

"Did I not read that she died not long after that? A terrible accident. Her carriage overturned, or something like that."

He had started to walk even more quickly. I could see that his fists were clenched and his arms swinging in time with his rapid steps.

It was a week before Christmas in December of 1894, and Baker Street was in darkness except for the glow of the streetlamps. A light dusting of snow was descending, and in the distance, I could hear a band from the Salvation Army playing Christmas carols. I would have been a delightful Yuletide stroll had it not been for the forced march Holmes was inflicting upon me.

"I doubt it was an accident," he said. "She told me she was in fear of her life. When I read about her death whilst I was in Tibet, it was already several months past. I have been suspicious ever since."

"Why? Carriage accidents do happen. What was wrong with that one?"

"I don't know, but what she told me of the way her husband had treated her, especially since the death of their son, was horrifying."

We had crossed Marylebone and were continuing south on Baker Street toward the church. Every ten or twenty yards, we excused ourselves as we pushed past clusters of people – families, couples, and a few young men and a young woman walking by herself – who were enjoying a more leisurely pace. They were on their way to celebrate the birth of Christ. We were hurrying because Holmes suspected that Saint Joseph was a killer.

"He can't have been all that bad," I said. "He was in the society pages not long after. He remarried, and to quite the beauty. And now they have a son. Didn't you see that in the program? They've given him the role of Baby Jesus. Seems to me like the happy little holy family."

"We shall see."

Hinde Street Methodist Church, at Hinde and Thayer, was an impressive building that had been erected only a few years earlier and was one of the first places of worship in London to be equipped with lamps powered by electricity.

By the time we arrived at the church, the first of the attendees were entering the building. We found our way to one of the front pews and took our seats on the center aisle, the better to be seen by the over five-hundred members of the congregation who were expected for the performance.

The lights were lowered and the organ began blasting out "Hark the Herald Angels Sing", which, if my memory served me correctly, was written by Charles Wesley. The choir filed into the loft and, on a signal from the choirmaster, erupted into a loud rendition of the same carol. Once through all the verses, the choirmaster turned around and gesticulated to the congregation that we were to stand and join in.

After several more Nativity Hymns written by Wesley, the lamps in the sanctuary were lowered and the organ sounded with yet another carol. As the lamps were then raised again and a glow suffused the room, a cluster of actors shuffled their way onto the platform. The first four were dressed in shabby dressing gowns, with tea towels tied around their heads. Each of them had a hand on the corner of a substantial cradle, which they laid on the platform. It was filled with straw and served as a replica of a manger.

They were followed by a woman dressed as an angel who stood on an elevated platform behind the manger, and three older chaps wearing turbans and satin robes who were carrying wrapped Christmas presents in one hand and leading an ox, a cow, and a small camel, likely rented for a day from the London Zoo.

The choir sang quietly, and all the cast gesticulated toward the center aisle. Slowly, plodding from the back all the way to the front, was a man leading a donkey, upon which sat a lovely young woman. Joseph was richly dressed and seemed to me more pompous than dangerous. Mary was in blue, as required by tradition, but her garments were very fine-looking satin and silk.

Once all were assembled in front of us, the lamps were dimmed until the church was in total darkness while the choir sang "Joy to the World". When the light returned, Mary was sitting beatifically behind the manger, holding an adorable baby boy in her arms. As a medical man, the thought crossed my mind that we had witnessed the fastest and least painful birth of a large infant ever recorded.

With the choir and the organ filling the hall with music, Mary wrapped the baby in a lovely silk cloth and laid him in the manger. The shepherds came forward and bowed, and the wise men presented their Christmas presents, one of which was wrapped in gold paper, but we were left to guess which was which of the other two.

Holmes leaned into my ear. "Lord Arsfasten has to be at least forty years older than his young wife."

"*Holmes!* Please," I whispered back and added an elbow to make my point.

The pageant continued with music and readings of the Christmas story from St. Matthew and St. Luke, and concluded with several more rousing Christmas hymns. The lamps were again dimmed and the sanctuary became entirely dark whilst the choir and organ sang "O Come All Ye Faithful". When the lamps were turned back up, the stage was empty, and the splendid live Christmas pageant was over.

Reverend Hodson Helliwell stepped into the pulpit and asked for complete silence so that he could deliver the final orison of praise and thanks to the Almighty. With his face lifted and his arms outstretched, he was about to announce his benediction when a woman's voice shrieked from the doorway through which the nativity procession had made its exit.

"Where's Augie? Where's my baby?"

Her shouting continued and carried to the back of the sanctuary. Then a crescendo of murmuring erupted.

"Where is my child?" We could hear fear and panic in her voice. A cacophony of talk and shouts now sounded from the hallway the actors were standing. One of the young shepherds leapt out and onto the platform and furtively looked under the chairs and furniture that had been pushed aside to make way for the manger.

"Who has Augie?"

The congregation was now voicing their concern at full volume. Reverend Helliwell shouted above the din.

"We have had a bit of a disruption. It is being attended to. So please all, relax and chat with your neighbors, exchange greetings of the season, and then make your way out in an orderly manner. God bless all of you. Happy Christmas!"

There were now at least twenty people clustered on the platform and in the hallway to the back of it. All were loudly barking instructions and orders to the others as the chaos of an incoherent search swept the building.

The baby, Augustus Purifoy Arsfasten, was nowhere to be found. The adorable little tyke had vanished.

Two hours later, Holmes and I were sitting in the same pew we had occupied during the service. In front of us and turned around to face us was Inspector Lestrade of Scotland Yard.

"Right," he said. "So just what was it that Mr. Sherlock Holmes, the dead-and-alive-again detective, was doing at the site of the kidnapping of the child of one of the richest men in London?"

"Observing the nativity of Our Lord, Inspector."

"That I doubt, but since you're here anyway, Mr. Holmes, you can get to work. Here's what we know so far from their statements to my men: When the lights went out, the wise men all exited. They had their

Christmas presents in one hand and the leash of an ox, cow, or camel in the other. Next were the four shepherds. All young and handsome and strong lads. They each picked up a corner of the manger. It's two-hundred years old and solid oak, an heirloom borrowed from one of the church families who has been showing it off every Christmas for the past decade. It weighs a ton."

"What do you know about them?"

"So far, all good families. All members of the Methodist Youth organization. None of them even smoke or use tobacco and probably fear eternal damnation if they were ever to utter even a mild curse word."

"And what about Lord Arsfasten?"

"You mean the toff who was in the carpenter's robe tailored in Savile Row?"

"Yes. He is – "

"I know who he is, Mr. Holmes. He was first off the stage and his wife, the Virgin Mary, was right behind him. Frankly, I don't like him. Amongst the police, he is referred to only by the first syllable of his name – but don't you let on I said that."

"Your clever wit is safe with me, I assure you, Inspector. The minister and the organist were occupied, so that leaves the angel who was hovering above the scene."

"The angel," said Lestrade, "is a dear soul named Mrs. Loretta Winterburn, and she is the nursery maid to Lady Arsfasten. She was up on a stepladder spreading her wings when the lights went down, and she had a hard enough time getting down herself. She was the last one off the stage and well-behind the manger."

Holmes sat back in the pew and absent-mindedly reached for his pipe. I gave him an elbow.

"You're in a church."

"They smoke the place up every mass with their censers. What's the difference?"

"Not the Methodists."

"Indeed? Pity them. Very well then, Inspector. What most likely took place is that someone – one of the shepherds perhaps – scooped the infant out of the cradle and handed him off to an agile accomplice who had managed to leap up to the platform in the dark, take the infant from the shepherd, and run off all before the lights came back on."

"And just how probable is that, Mr. Holmes?"

"Not very, but everything else about the evening was improbable, beginning with Lord Arsfasten pretending to be Saint Joseph. Speaking of whom, might I have a word with him and Her Ladyship?"

"They're all back in the Sunday School room. She is utterly distraught, as you might imagine. He's as mad as a wet hen. We've already taken their statements, but you're welcome to have a chat and see if there's something we might have missed."

A half-dozen police constables stood in strategic locations around the perimeter of the room. The various parties to the nativity pageant sat in clusters according to their roles. The four shepherds were in one corner and, being all young men, they could be overheard chatting about rugby and cricket and trying to keep their laughter muffled. The wise men were likewise sitting together and muttering to one another.

Lady Arsfasten, sobbing loudly, was beside her maid, Mrs. Winterburn. The older woman had her arm around her young charge and was attempting to comfort her. His Lordship was strutting around the room, glaring alternatively at the shepherds and the wise men. The Reverend Helliwell was sitting across from Lady Arsfasten, his Bible open on his knee, and appeared to be reading words of succor and comfort from the Psalms.

"My dear Reverend," said Holmes, "kindly forgive the interruption, but I have to ask Lady Arsfasten a few more questions."

His Lordship was standing within earshot of Holmes and barked a question in reply.

"Who the deuce are you?"

"My name, sir, is Sherlock Holmes, and Scotland Yard has requested my assistance in helping to find your missing son and heir."

"Are you that famous amateur detective?"

"I am a consulting detective, sir. It is not up to me to declare whether or not I am famous."

"Whatever you are, you're hired! So get busy and find my son."

"Perhaps you could join Her Ladyship and answer my questions," said Holmes.

"I've already spoken to the police. That should be enough."

An excessively large police constable who was standing nearby walked over until he was close beside His Lordship – a full head taller and almost a foot wider.

"My Lord, shall I bring you a chair so you can sit beside your wife?" he asked the smaller man.

Arsfasten glared up at him but nodded. "Yes, do that."

He sat down. "Fine, now ask whatever questions you want."

Holmes positioned himself in front of the couple. "I appreciate that this is a very trying time for both of you – "

"Cut the feigned sympathy," snapped His Lordship. "I told you to get on with your questions."

"Very well, sir. I shall do that. Permit me to give a brief note of context. There are two apparent motives for someone's stealing a child of a wealthy noble family: The first and most common is illicit financial gain. The second is to inflict injury and pain upon the family. If whomever took Baby Augie – "

"His name is Augustus Arsfasten the Third. You will refer to him that way and not by any sobriquet given by his mother or nursery maid."

"Of course. If whomever took your son and heir intends to hold him for ransom, we have no immediate alternative but to wait for a demand. We may, however, begin straight away to investigate the alternative motive. Someone may be trying to cause you pain . . . for revenge, perhaps. Is there anyone you can think of who bears an animus against you?"

"Not a one. I strive valiantly to exude goodwill toward all, and in return I receive the same. I don't have an enemy in the world."

His young wife lifted her tear-stained face from her hands and gave him a rather hostile look. "Oh, Gus. Our son has been kidnapped. For pity's sake, don't mislead the police! Nobody likes you. The staff, our neighbors, and half the House of Lords despise you. Most of your family would happily see you dead."

Lord Arsfasten's eyes went wide with rage. "Silence!" he shouted, and he hit her in the face with a violent blow from the back of his hand. She shrieked in pain.

Before any of us could say anything, a fist the size of a small anvil swung down from the excessively large police constable and clobbered His Lordship across the jaw, sending him toppling backward off his chair.

Arsfasten twisted himself out of a crumpled heap on the floor and shouted at Lestrade.

"Inspector, arrest that man this instant!"

Lestrade put on a bewildered face. "What man?"

"That monstrous ape. Arrest him!"

"Constable Higgs? What for?"

"What for? You saw what he did. He struck me."

"He did? I didn't see that. All I saw was you falling off your chair. Here, let me help you up."

Inspector Lestrade leaned down and offered an outstretched hand to Arsfasten. As he did so, he quietly added, "And I am warning you that you will fall off your chair even harder if any of my men ever see you do that again to your wife."

His Lordship's face was red with rage, but he sat down and looked furiously in all directions.

He did, however, answer Holmes's questions. Once done with him, Holmes moved around the room and briefly questioned everyone who had been on the platform. Their answers were consistent.

"There are no discrepancies," Holmes said to Lestrade and me after he had completed his interviews. "Every one of them agrees that when the lights were shut off, the child was in the manger. When they arrived in the hallway after passing through the door at the far-right corner of the platform and re-entered a lighted area, the child was gone."

"That's what my men learned without your help," said Lestrade. "What are you going to do now?"

"I have asked Lady Arsfasten to make a list of the people of whom she is aware who hate His Lordship the most. I shall begin with those at the top of her list and make inquiries concerning their reasons for not liking her husband. It is possible that none of them will become suspects for the kidnapping of Baby Jesus, and that the motive will be to hold the child for a ransom. If that's the case, we shall have no alternative but to wait for a ransom note to arrive."

"We have everyone's name and address. Shall we send them all off to their homes?"

"I would be concerned for the safety and well-being of Her Ladyship. Would it be possible to send a constable with her? Perhaps a large one?"

Lestrade smiled and winked at Holmes. "Constable Higgs! A word."

The excessively large police officer grinned from ear to ear on being given the assignment.

"Happy to do my duty as always, Inspector, sir. May I suggest you assign Constables Hood and Brough as well, and we can arrange a rota of our shifts?"

He indicated two of the other constables who were almost the same size as he was.

"Excellent suggestion, Higgs," said Lestrade, and he dismissed all the people who were simultaneously witnesses and suspects.

I saw nothing of Holmes the following day and spent the time writing brief notes of Yuletide greetings and mailing them off to the limited list of friends and family I had in England. I was finishing off the last of them when Holmes entered, climbed the stairs, and shook the snow off his hat and the shoulders of his coat.

He strode immediately to the sideboard and poured himself a glass of Bristol Cream sherry I had set out for the Christmas season. Then he dropped his lanky frame into his armchair and began to sip. He was smiling.

"What are you so jovial about? Did you find the missing Baby Jesus?"

"Not yet, but I have had a most informative day. Shall I regale you with my findings?"

"I am all attention."

He set his sherry on the end table, lit his pipe, and leaned back in his chair.

"Where shall I begin? Ah, yes, with His Lordship. His wife was utterly correct. Nobody likes him. Nobody in all of London has even a kind word to say about him. He is a member of the hereditary wealthy but hasn't an ounce of the condescending manners and suave behavior that make the members of that class passably bearable to the rest of us. However, in as much as they would all be happy to see him dead, none appear to be sufficiently motivated to either murder him or to steal his child. They all spoke of their deep sympathy for Lady Mary Arsfasten, whom they universally like and would never wish to injure."

"That's good to know, I suppose. He will pass into 1895 still alive."

"He will," said Holmes. "Although I should mention that he did receive condolence cards and a few days of human kindness when his first son died in Her Majesty's service several years ago. He was shot by the Ashantis whilst serving in the Gold Coast. He was the only child in the family, and Lord Arsfasten was left without an heir."

"Which led," I said, "to your suspicions about the death of his first wife."

"A position, I discovered, in which I was far from alone. She was beyond the age of child-bearing, and her family are convinced that even if he didn't murder her outright, he arranged her death so he could find a younger wife and generate a new heir."

"Which now leads you to the current Lady Arsfasten."

"Indeed it does. Would you like to guess where she came from?"

"Haven't the foggiest," I said.

"The London Palace Theatre. She was a Tiller Girl."

"Was she on the hunt for wealth and a title?"

"The opposite. *He* was on the hunt. I had a fascinating chat with John Tiller himself, who told me that immediately after the death of the first Lady Arsfasten, His Lordship began to attend the fancy precision dancing shows regularly and had a reserved seat in the front row. After seeing that all of the girls on the stage were uniformly pretty, contoured in the same proportions, and superbly athletic, he approached Mr. Tiller and asked which of them was the brightest."

"On a quest, was he, for the best choice to breed his heir?"

"Precisely," said Holmes. "Mr. Tiller immediately identified Miss Mary Smithers, who had joined the troupe whilst it was performing in

Liverpool. She had remarkable native intelligence, was an outstanding autodidact, and had an unusually good head for business."

I refrained from any of the customary unkind comments Londoners reserve for Liverpudlians and acknowledged the prudent choice of His Lordship.

"He wooed her for a week," said Holmes, "and married her the next week. In short order – but not unacceptably so – she became pregnant and six months ago delivered a baby boy, to whom you have already been introduced. Augustus Purifoy Arsfasten the Third entered the world back in June, and it wasn't long after that when, according the staff of the Arsfasten house, who see all and know all and who don't display a speck of loyalty to their master, the marriage began to deteriorate."

"He has a history of striking her?"

"Of that and of constant verbal insults. He regularly berates her for the way she is caring for their son. They no longer dine together as a married couple. He usually sleeps over at his club and his man, a decent chap named Derwan Fairbanks, let me know that he frequents the high-priced courtesans who patronize the better shops on Regent Street."

"That poor young woman."

"*Poor* she is not. *Unhappy*, she most definitely is. If he were to die tomorrow, she would be extremely wealthy. She began to seek the solace of religious faith for the first time in her life after the birth of her son, and it was she who volunteered the three of them to serve as the Holy Family in the pageant. His Lordship was not pleased with the prospect until he was told he could play Saint Joseph and accept the gifts of the Magi on behalf of his incarnate offspring."

"Is he blaming her now for what happened at the pageant?" I asked.

"Yes. Mind you, the presence of the constables in the house has forced him to be restrained. Otherwise, I would fear for her well-being."

"Are you suggesting that her life might be in danger?"

"That is a remote possibility. Her utility as a mother is still acknowledged. But given what I suspect about his first wife, I would caution her to be very careful once her son is sent off to school."

"Assuming he is still alive and well."

"I'm sure he is. He is much too valuable to let anything happen to him."

He had only spoken these words and taken another sip of sherry when the bell rang. A minute later, Inspector Lestrade entered the room.

"A ransom demand arrived, just as we predicted, addressed to His Lordship," he said as he walked past us and over to the sideboard. He poured himself a glass of sherry and sat down on the sofa. "Here it is. Read it. Your analysis and deductions, please, Mr. Sherlock Holmes."

He handed Holmes the note, which he read carefully. After doing so, he took out his glass and looked at every line of it under magnification.

"A masculine hand, though not a strong one. Young. Not particularly well-educated. Right-handed – that can be seen by the absence of any small smudges to the right of the down-strokes of the letters. Clever but utterly amateurish in the practice of kidnapping and securing a ransom."

"How can you tell that?" I asked.

"By the arrangement he demands for the payment. He suggests a reasonable amount. I am certain that His Lordship has £5,000 sitting in his safe and can obtain the funds without having to sell any of his assets. Very clever. But he asks for it to be left in a watertight sack behind the south edge of the Shaftsbury Memorial in Piccadilly Circus after midnight tomorrow. Terribly amateurish."

My having mentioned the Criterion Bar in the first story I ever wrote and published about the adventures of Sherlock Holmes endeared me to the owner of the establishment forever afterward. He happily acceded to our request to be allowed to sit at the window on the second floor beginning at eleven o'clock the following evening. From there, Holmes, Lestrade and I all had a commanding view of Piccadilly Circus and the recently installed Shaftsbury Fountain.

As midnight approached, I watched as the streets and pavement emptied of decent, upright citizens, instead becoming populated by certain ladies of ill-repute who were being accosted by certain men of limited self-respect. We were a day away from the solstice and the night was dark, cold, and still. I felt a pang of sadness for those who were engaging in transactions of the world's oldest profession. The Christmas season may be a joyful one for those of us who are blessed with friends and family, but it is incurably lonely for those who aren't so fortunate.

As the minutes passed, all three of us trained our spy glasses on the designated side of the fountain. The ladies came and departed and were replaced by others. It all appeared to me to be an entirely usual December night in the center of London.

"Here he comes," said Lestrade.

At exactly one minute past midnight, a police constable approached the fountain. He ascended the few steps and sat down on the edge. Acting as if he did the same thing every night, he lit a cigarette and took several puffs. After flicking the stub of his cigarette behind him and into the water, from under his greatcoat he extracted a small sack. In an almost undetectable motion, he put it around his back and dropped it into the water.

"Well done, Snidley," said Lestrade. "Very smooth. Just as you were told. Now, get up and saunter off."

As if he had heard his inspector's instructions, the constable stood up and moved away, stopping to say a word to several of the ladies as he walked unhurriedly in the direction of Leicester Square.

"Now what?" I asked. "We wait for some chap to come and pull the sack out and run off?"

"Precisely," said Holmes.

We waited . . . and waited.

"Are you sure he will come?" I asked Holmes.

"Give him credit. He's being patient."

In the distance, I heard the clocks tolling one o'clock and was thankful that I was sitting inside a heated building. Looking out, I could see that all the prostitutes were now bundled in their winter coats, hats, and muffs. One of them, appearing weary and chilled, ascended the steps and sat in the exact spot the constable had an hour earlier.

"Oh dear," I said. "She's going to be in the way when our man comes to fetch his money."

"My dear Watson," said Holmes. "*She* is our man."

"I beg your pardon. Are you saying he sent a woman to fetch the money for him?"

"No, Watson. *She* is *he*."

I fixed my eyeglass on the woman and could see her feminine hat, hair, powdered face, and even her rather provocative cleavage that was exposed by her unbuttoning her coat and flaunting her bodice. As I looked at her, not believing what Holmes had said, I saw her stand up and raise her foot and place it on the edge of the fountain. She leaned down to adjust her laces and, in doing so, lowered her body far enough to allow her hand to dip into the fountain.

"Well done, my darling," said Lestrade. "Now, let's watch what happens next."

She, or maybe *he*, had retrieved the sack and had laid it directly beside her boot, allowing the water to drip off. Ever so deftly, she then lifted the sack and slid it under her coat and stepped down off the fountain.

"She's getting away," I said. "Isn't someone going to stop her?"

"At ease, Watson," said Holmes.

I watched as she-or-he walked away from the fountain toward Haymarket. As she passed another of the few remaining prostitutes, the second woman put out her foot, tripped her, and dropped to her knees on top of her.

"Goodness gracious! That woman is trying to rob her," I exclaimed.

Holmes laughed and Lestrade guffawed, slapping his thigh as two more prostitutes joined in the assault of the would-be villain. By the time the four of them were back on their feet, the first lady had been relieved of the sack of money and was now in handcuffs and being led toward a police wagon.

"Ha! That's my girls," said Lestrade. "Weren't they fabulous?"

I was shocked. "You had your men dress as prostitutes and wait for him?"

"I did. I asked for ten volunteers to dress up as scandalously as they could imagine, and a dozen came forward. Most of them thought it a grand excuse for a giggle. Mind you, there were a couple who seemed just a bit too eager. But they all stood there in the cold in their stockings and corsets. They'll be laughing about it for weeks. Come now – they're taking the wretched fellow down to the station. We can hold his feet to the fire."

Upon entering the headquarters of Scotland Yard on the Embankment, I heard gales of male laughter coming from somewhere in the interior. The desk officer rolled his eyes and nodded in the direction of the hall. Lestrade marched off, and a moment later the laughter stopped. But by the time he returned, it had started up again.

He was shaking his head and grinning.

"The lot of them are getting out of their dresses and changing back into their uniforms. They seem to think it is hilarious to flirt and tweak and pinch and pat and compliment each other on certain bits of anatomy and irresistible allure. I best let them have a laugh about it. It's the only time in their lives they'll ever have a chance. Well, enough of that. Let's go chat with our culprit."

In a room used for interrogations, there were two constables in their full uniforms standing over a terrified fellow sitting on a bench. His wig and dress had been removed, and he was clad only in his underwear with a blanket wrapped around him. His facial cosmetics were still all over his countenance, and he looked profoundly pathetic.

"State your name, your place of residence, and of your employment, if you have one," said Lestrade.

He couldn't have been more than thirty years of age and was somewhat on the scrawny side. He spoke in the direction of his bare feet.

"Darrel Brewster. I live at 434 Shoe Lane. I'm a reporter for *The Evening Star* and I swear, I had nothing to do with the kidnapping."

"That will be for us to decide," said Lestrade. "Now, we can make this easy for you, or we can make it difficult. It will be easiest for you if you tell us straight away where the Arsfasten baby is."

"I don't know! I don't know!" he said to his toes, and then he raised his head. He was white with fear. "I swear, I don't know."

"You knew enough to demand the ransom, and now you're telling me you had nothing to do with the crime. I do not believe you. Now, the truth."

He shook his head and seemed humiliated beyond description. "I was at the paper yesterday afternoon when the report of the kidnapping came in. We all know that whomever gets there first gets the story. I guessed it worked the same way with being paid the ransom, so I sent a note off asking for £5,000, thinking if I didn't ask too much and did it quickly, I might score myself a few quid. I would never have kept it. It was a lark. It would have made a great story for the weekend edition. But I was nowhere near the church when it happened. I can prove that."

"Good," said Lestrade. "Prove it."

"I was having supper with my parents. Please believe me and don't ask them. I don't want them to know about this."

"A bit too late for that, Mr. Brewster," said Lestrade. "Where did you get the clothes?"

His answer was almost inaudible. "My sister's closet."

Then he raised his head. "But it weren't no crime. Playing a joke is no crime."

"Jokes? No. Extortion? Yes. You will be charged, and you can explain your joke to a magistrate. Now get dressed, and if I ever hear of you trying a stunt like this again, I'll hand you over to a boatload of Russian sailors."

One of the constables handed him the winter coat he had been wearing. He pulled it and his boots on and was led down the hall where he would be formally charged.

Lestrade sighed. "Where do they come from?"

"When five-million people live in one city," said Holmes, "it is inevitable that some of them are pitiable. However, we best bid each other *à demain* and get a good night's sleep. It is late, and there is far too much left to do."

We didn't sleep well. It may have been undisturbed, but it lasted less than five hours. At half-past seven, Lestrade was at our door and, a few minutes later, in our sitting room. He sat down at the breakfast table and poured himself a cup of coffee.

"This one looks more serious. Take a look."

He handed Holmes a note. He read it over several times and examined it with his glass. Then he handed it on to me.

It had been typed on high-quality notepaper with an expensive typewriter. The language used was educated, bordering on erudite. It demanded that £15,000 be transferred to a bank account in Switzerland within one week and concluded with the words: *Your son's life is dangling by a thread and I assure you, I hold the razor in my hand.*

"Well, Mr. Holmes," asked Lestrade, "what do you say this time?"

"Another young male who – "

"Come, come," remarked the policeman. "That is impossible to know. There isn't a word of handwriting in it. It has been typed."

"Had it been typed, my dear Inspector, by a woman, it would have been done so in the manner used by professional women typists. Women have a light touch, and professional typists use an even pressure. If you examine the back of the note, you will see that some of the letters have been hit so hard, they have come close to puncturing the paper. Most have given the surface a significant bump, and a few of them caused no embossing to the surface whatsoever. Only untrained men type in this manner, and only young men punch the keys one at a time with their index fingers instead of typing with all their digits."

"So it's from a young man. What else?"

"Highly educated. Look. His grammar, syntax, and punctuation are all flawless. The commas he missed whilst typing have been inserted by hand. Our man is a university graduate who has had sufficient introduction to the world of commerce and finance to arrange a secret bank account in Switzerland. It is likely that this one is *not* a hoax."

"What are you going to do about it?"

"Please have the shepherds rounded up and brought in for questioning."

Unlike the Church of England, the Methodist Church attracts a wide cross-section of believers from all classes of British society. So it wasn't unexpected that two of the lads who had served as shepherds during the nativity pageant were from working-class families and had jobs at Paddington. The other two were students, one at each of the nation's better two universities.

Out of consideration for the working lads, the meeting with the four shepherds did not take place until six o'clock that evening when they had finished their shifts with the station.

The four of them were brought in and were sitting at small tables in one of the rooms in the Scotland Yard. Holmes met briefly with Lestrade and me in the hallway outside the room.

"Mr. Holmes," said Lestrade. "You've got four of them in there. How are you going to tell which grabbed the baby?"

"The left-handed one. The odds are that only one of them will be."

"That note was typed," said Lestrade. "Don't tell me you can tell a dexterous typist from a sinister one. That's impossible."

"Correct, Inspector. But you can distinguish one who makes minor edits to his typing. In the fifth line of type, there were two slight errors, those missing commas that he inserted with his pencil. The one nearest the left side of the page had a tiny smudge to the right of the error, caused as the writer slid his left hand across it so that he could fix the second error. Quite elementary, I assure you. Shall we proceed?"

Inspector Lestrade smiled warmly if not altogether sincerely at the four young men who were sitting nervously in front of him.

"The Metropolitan Police apologizes for the inconvenience we have to put you through, but some legal requirements are necessary. The written statements you submitted after the incident at the Methodist Church were all quite acceptable, but my lads – your handwriting was horrible. We had to have our secretaries type the statements, and now we have to ask you to sign them. That is all."

Grins of relief spread over their faces, and they exchanged a few semi-humorous comments amongst themselves while Lestrade handed out the copies of their statements.

"Read them over carefully, lads, and if you are sure that this is what you wrote yourself, then sign at the bottom. And no, you cannot fix your grammar or commas."

Again, they responded with boyish murmurs, picked up the pens provided, and signed. Lestrade collected the papers, again smiling.

"Have a fine evening, lads. Straight home now. Oh, Mr. White, could you wait behind for just a minute?"

The tallest of them, a strapping, good-looking young man who must have been at least six-feet three-inches in height, and with a torso shaped like an upside-down pyramid, stopped as requested. He had signed with his left hand.

"Is there anything wrong, Inspector, sir?"

"Not at all, not at all. You are Geoffrey Winston White, correct?"

"Yes, Inspector."

"A student at Cambridge?"

"Yes, sir. Reading philosophy, sir."

"When will you graduate?" asked Lestrade.

"I already did, sir. Two years ago. I am now working toward my Doctor of Philosophy, sir."

"And what will you do once you have that behind you?"

"I hope to do philosophy and to teach it, sir. Why?"

"Have you published anything yet?"

"Just a few short critiques," said the erstwhile shepherd.

"What did you write?"

"Uh . . . my first was called *Why Kant Can't*, and the second was *Tom Was Not A Great Man*. It was a critique of some of the work of Thomas Carlyle."

"Carlyle? Yes, I've heard of him," said Lestrade. "Are you familiar with him, Mr. Holmes?"

"Who?" asked Holmes. "Cannot say as I am."

"You might like him, even if Mr. White here does not. So, tell me, young man: How are you going to support yourself after you finish your studies? Scribble away in a cold cottage somewhere? Paid a shilling or two by your students?"

"Well, no sir. I am fortunate to have been born the only son of a gentleman, and I receive a remittance of five-hundred quid a year, sir. I shall be free to read and write and teach . . . and enjoy the sporting life."

I could almost hear the wheels turning inside Holmes's brain. The only left-handed shepherd obviously had no need of financial gain. Lestrade must have reached the same conclusion and changed his tack.

"Just a quick routine question about the incident at the church," said Lestrade.

"Of course, sir. I tried to put everything in my statement. Was there something I missed?"

"That manger you moved. Rather heavy from what I could see."

"A bit, sir," said White. "But not too bad. No more than what we have to lift in the gymnasium thrice a week, sir."

"But you needed two hands did you not?"

"Not really, sir. Can't speak for the other lads, seeing as it was pitch dark, but all I needed was my left hand as I was on the back right-hand corner of it. So, that was all I used."

"Ah, so your right hand was free. Which means, Mr. White, that you could have grabbed a few more pounds with it. Right?"

"Usually, sir, but I was doing a round of boxing last week against a chap from Oxford. I gave him a jolly good thrashing, but I sprained my thumb whilst doing so. They say it'll be fine in another two weeks, but I have to give it a rest until then."

He stretched out his right arm and pulled back the sleeve of his sweater to reveal a flesh-colored cast that was wrapped around his lower wrist and hand, immobilizing it.

Lestrade stood and stared at the hand for a moment and then looked over to Holmes. He shrugged and waved his hand toward the door.

"No more questions, Mr. White," said Lestrade. "Hope that's all better soon."

"Oh, thank you, sir. We have a game against some Scottish boys right after the New Year. I need to be back to playing form by then."

"All right, Mr. Holmes," said Lestrade. "It wasn't the pathetic reporter, and it wasn't the left-handed shepherd. So, who was it?"

"At this precise moment, I do not know. Ask me tomorrow. I expect to by then."

Without speaking to me, Holmes walked out of the Scotland Yard building, crossed the road in front of it, and stood looking out over the Thames. It was a clear, cold winter night, and the stars, the streetlamps along the Embankment and the lights from the far side of the river gave the evening a feeling of being detached somehow from the quotidian turmoil of everyday London.

I waited for him.

He lit a cigarette and did not move, except to take it from time to time from his mouth and blow out a long, slow stream of smoke mixed with the vapor that a man's breath creates in a night near to the solstice.

I continued to wait. I knew better than to interrupt him.

After ten minutes, he turned to me.

"It is time to pay another visit to His Lordship's home."

Without waiting for me to reply, he hailed a cab and gestured for me to get in.

"Would you mind terribly," I said once I was in the cab, "telling me why we are going there? What can you learn from him?"

"Nothing."

"Holmes?"

"We shall learn nothing because he isn't there. He spends almost every night at his club. Now that his son is no longer at his home, he is sure not to be there."

"So who are we going to talk to?"

"His wife and the nursery maid."

"And would you mind telling me why them?"

"They are the only two left who were on the stage. The three old duffers who pretended to be wise men were leading the animals and carrying their presents. Saint Joseph was first off and wasn't carrying a baby. The only left-handed shepherd was incapable of picking up a six-month-old child and handing it off if he had one hand on a heavy manger and the other covered in a bandage. That leaves the two women. As I have said before, when you eliminate – "

"Yes, you've said that a thousand times, but you cannot possibly be thinking that *they* stole the baby. That's absurd."

"Indeed it is. However, I have no alternative but to question them closely and have them recount every second that passed from the time the lights were turned off until Lady Arsfasten saw that her son wasn't in the manger. There must be something that happened that was out of order in some way. Discerning what it was could open up an entirely new line of reasoning."

He lapsed into silence until we reached an elegant terraced house on Gilbert Street in the northern reaches of Mayfair. The clocks were tolling eight o'clock in the evening when we knocked on the door.

"Derwan Fairbanks was the chap I spoke to about Lord Arsfasten," said Holmes. "I expect it will be he who greets us."

He was wrong. The door opened to reveal and an attractive young woman in her early twenties.

She looked at us, somewhat bewildered for a moment, and then smiled. "Mr. Holmes and Dr. Watson, do come in. But I'm very sorry, His Lordship isn't present. Shall I let him know you came by? Or would you like to enter and have some hot cider and Christmas shortbread? Her Ladyship always enjoys visitors. Shall I tell her you are here?"

"Such a kind invitation of the season," said Holmes. "We can catch up with His Lordship tomorrow, but your offer of Christmas cheer and a chat with Her Ladyship would be most welcome. And, forgive me, but I don't know your name, miss."

"Oh, I'm Primrose Winterburn. You've met my mother, Mrs. Loretta Winterburn. I help her out with the duties here. We're taking shifts at the moment. Mine has just started. With all that has happened, we don't like to leave Her Ladyship alone."

As we were walking down the hallway, a very large body appeared at the other end of it.

"Well, best of the season to the two of you!" the bass voice of Constable Higgs resounded down the corridor. "Thought I recognized your voices. Anything wrong?"

"Not at all, Constable," said Holmes. "Glad to see that you are still here and standing guard."

"It's a plum assignment, sir. Nothing has happened. His Lordship has only come by a couple of times, and meanwhile the lady and the staff are treating me as fine as I could ever ask for. Feeding me right generous too, they are."

"What he means," said Miss Winterburn, "is that he's eating us out of house and home." She laughed and so did he, and I caught a wink exchanged between them.

We were led into the parlor, wherein was a decorated Christmas tree standing immediately to the right of the hearth. Such trees had become very popular in the years after the Queen and Prince Albert released an illustration of the two of them and their children standing beside one. We sat on the small sofa on the other side of the crackling fire.

We were alone for a minute, and Holmes whispered to me. "A pleasant-enough young woman. Interesting perfume. I had forgotten that Higgs would be here. That may complicate my plan."

"What do you mean, it – "

I was cut off by the entrance of Lady Arsfasten. She was elegantly dressed and, with her thick auburn hair all in place, she looked more like the beauty she was reputed to be.

She greeted us in a friendly way, and I couldn't help but remark on how much better she appeared to be compared to the last time I had seen her.

"Thank you, Doctor," she said and added a weary sigh. "You are very kind to notice. These past few days have been terribly difficult for all of us. My poor husband is beside himself with distress and I am worried sick. But we are all English, and it seems we must keep the stiff upper lip and try to carry on."

"And doing a splendid job of it," I said.

"Thank you. But please, please, tell me that you have come with some news of my son. Have you been able to find out anything? I heard about the two ransom demands. Has whomever kidnapped Augie let you know he is still alive and hasn't been harmed?"

I glanced at Holmes and he answered. "Not yet. But I need to advise you that whomever has committed this crime appears to be exceptionally capable and devious. Scotland Yard and we will continue to investigate the case until the criminal is hauled before the bar, no matter how long it takes. However, it is conceivable that your husband would be better to pay the ransom and get your son back now. I am sure His Lordship has more than sufficient funds available to do that."

She sighed and gazed up at the portraits of Arsfasten ancestors. "Oh, he has more than enough money to do that, and in the long run, he may have to agree. That is what I told him when Augie was taken. I told him again when the second ransom note came. But he hates to lose. He thinks that Sherlock Holmes and Scotland Yard are going to catch the culprit, and he will get his son back without having to pay a farthing. Can you speak to him, Mr. Holmes? Please, sir. Maybe if it comes from you, he will listen. We could get my son back and we'd all be better off."

"Like hell we will!"

This outburst came from Miss Primrose. I was shocked to hear her speak like that to her mistress but she continued.

"Don't be a fool, Mary. You know bloody well that he'll blame you for it. He'll hire governesses for Augie. You will never get to see him, and you'll spend your life shut up in some country estate and never get out to anywhere . . . *ever!*"

I was stunned, and so was Holmes, but it was immediately apparent that there existed a depth of friendship and familiarity between the two young women that hadn't started recently. Lady Arsfasten stood, walked over to Miss Primrose. and put her arms around her.

"You're right, dear cousin. That is exactly what he would do."

She turned to Holmes and spoke in pleading tones. "Please, Mr. Holmes, keep looking for my son. If I can help you, just say the word, and I will do anything I can. Anything."

"If that is your wish, My Lady," said Holmes, "that is what I shall do. Now then, Watson, we need to be on our way. We have already upset Her Ladyship more than we should have. Perhaps, My Lady, we can return tomorrow to chat further?"

"My husband has made demands on my time tomorrow. The day after would be better."

"Until then," said Holmes, and he turned and headed for the door. I was in a complete fog as to what had happened and followed him blindly.

Once out on the pavement, he walked quickly from Mayfair to Oxford Street and marched along until he came to a pub that was sufficiently to his taste.

"A pint. Watson? And you must be hungry? Let me order something for the two of us."

He returned to our table bearing two plates of fish and chips and mushy peas. There was a twinkle in his eye, and he seemed to be suppressing a smile.

"Holmes, what was all that about?"

"Doctor, I shall want your co-operation."

"I remember your saying those words to me before. As always, I shall be delighted."

"You don't mind breaking the law?"

"You asked me that before as well. If the cause is good, my response is the same."

"Oh, the cause is excellent! Better than ever. We are about to re-unite a loving mother with her child."

"Then I am your man, if you will tell me what you plan to do."

He told me. I was amazed beyond words. And thrilled.

Our first stop after supper was 221b Baker Street. Holmes remained outside and blew a special sequence of blasts on his police whistle. Within five minutes, six of his Irregulars were gathered in front of him. He chose two whom I recognized as being the most likely to act somewhere on the border between courageous and devil-may-care reckless.

Next, we returned Oxford Street, and he sent the two of them into a working-man's restaurant with a shilling, and they returned with a hot meat pie each and a cup of steaming cocoa.

"You will be outside for a half-hour, my lads," he said to them. "Best get some food and drink into your bellies before you set out."

The next stop was Carnaby Street in Soho.

"Is this where she lives?" I asked.

"It is. As soon as the clocks have struck ten, my boys will pound on the front door. She will come, and they will give her a long tale of woe that she will see through, and she will shoo them away. Northrop, the taller of the two, will reach his long arm inside the door and steal one of her umbrellas, and then they will run away. She will give chase and scream for the police. Meanwhile, you and I will enter from the back door. The lock will be easy to pick."

"And you are quite sure of this based only on – "

"The way her daughter smelled. If you would read the commercial announcements in the newspapers, my friend, instead of wasting your time on the sports pages, you would have seen the news of the arrival last year from America of Johnson's Talcum Baby Powder. It has become quite the rage amongst the mothers of England, and the scent of it on Miss Primrose Winterburn was unmistakable. She had been holding a baby not more than an hour or two before we spoke with her."

"And you are certain he is here?"

"Nothing about this case has been certain. If I am wrong, we will have lost a shilling on food for my boys and nothing more."

"Unless we are caught."

"You made it out of Afghanistan alive. Soho is much easier. Come. It is almost ten."

Mrs. Loretta Winterburn's house looked out on Carnaby Street, but there was a lane behind it that we slipped into by way of Ganton Street. At five minutes before ten, Holmes was kneeling in front of the back door, his locksmith's tools in his hands.

The bells of St. George's in Hanover Square rang out the tenth hour of the night and we waited. Before the full round had sounded, we heard a commotion at the front of the house.

"Now," said Holmes. Within two minutes, he had picked the lock and opened the door. We entered in silence and tiptoed our way to the bedroom. Shouts from the front entrance of the house suddenly got much louder, and I could hear Mrs. Winterburn screaming some rather nasty words at our two lads.

We couldn't turn up the lamps, but I opened the curtains just an inch or two, enough to let in a few rays from the streetlights outside. Then I saw it. In the corner of the room, lying on the floor, was a small cradle. Without making a sound, I knelt down and slid my forearm under the sleeping body of a six-month-old baby. Ever so slowly and gently, I lifted him up and then grabbed all of his blankets with my other hand.

"I have him," I whispered to Holmes. "Let us get out of here before he wakes up."

As we moved back out of the house, I could feel a chilly breeze sweeping through from the wide-open front door. Mrs. Winterburn was shouting for the police. Holmes and I stepped out the back door and closed it behind us.

"We have to hurry," said Holmes. "We need to get back to Mayfair and deliver our prize before she sees he is gone."

It was two blocks out to Regent Street, and I dared not run, but walked as quickly as I could, carrying Augustus Purifoy Arsfasten in my right arm, much as I would a rugby ball. They fit in somewhat the same manner.

A cab stopped and we entered. Holmes shouted the address and off we sped. I was all prepared to lean back and enjoy our successful adventure when the little tyke started to make unhappy sounds. Then he began to cry. By the time we reached New Bond Street, he was howling, and no amount of bouncing or rocking would shut him up.

He kept it up all the way to Gilbert Street. As we pulled up to a stop in front of the Arsfasten house, Holmes turned to me.

"Tomorrow, my dear Doctor, please enlighten me as to why any rational human being would want one of these noisy things in their lives. And why would anyone pay good money to get one of them back?"

I didn't answer. We stepped out of the cab and knocked on the door. As the hour was nearly half-past ten, no one came for several minutes. The harder Holmes knocked, the louder the child screamed. Finally, the door opened, and Miss Primrose Winterburn opened it.

"And a good evening to you, miss," said Holmes. "Please call your mistress to the door and tell her that Sherlock Holmes is returning her baby to her."

The look on the girl's face was beyond priceless. She took two steps back into the vestibule and then turned and ran toward the stairs. If anyone else in the house was trying to sleep, Augustus Purifoy Arsfasten made sure that they couldn't continue to do so.

"Ah, Lady Arsfasten," said Holmes to the woman descending the stairs. Some combination of fear and confusion were written all over her face. She approached us and looked at the still-screaming child and gasped. I spoke before she had a chance to.

"This young man wants his mother much more than me," I said and didn't exactly toss the child into her arms, but I came close to it. She had no choice but to take him from me. Within a few seconds, the wailing had stopped.

"Might I suggest, Madam," said Holmes, "that you take your son up to his nursery and put him down in his own bed, and then we need to have a chat, don't we? Miss Primrose, would you be so kind as to organize a pot of tea and some Christmas shortbread?"

"And some brandy," said Lady Arsfasten over her shoulder as she ascended the staircase.

Ten minutes later, with tea, shortbread and brandy on the coffee table in front of us, Holmes, Lady Arsfasten, Miss Primrose and I sat in the parlor, looking at each other.

"Well done, Mr. Holmes," said Lady Arsfasten. "Yes. I kidnapped my own child. What are you going to do with us?"

"Madam, that depends on – "

He was interrupted by a thunderous banging at the front door of the house.

"I will answer it." said Miss Primrose, "That must be my mum."

She went to the front door and as it opened, we could hear someone rush inside and a trembling voice.

"He's gone! Someone stole him. He isn't there anymore. I . . . I . . . they distracted me and they took him . . . ."

"It's all right, Mum. Baby Augie is upstairs in the nursery. Come in and sit down."

She didn't come into the parlor. Instead, she took off up the stairs, taking two steps at a time. A minute later she returned, entered the parlor, and sat down.

"How did you know?" was all she said to Sherlock Holmes.

"Thank you, my dear Mrs. Winterburn, for asking," said Holmes, "I am always more than happy to explain what to me had become obvious."

"Holmes," I said. "She asked for an explanation. Don't gloat."

"I would never think of it, my friend. Are you taking notes? Well then, as always, there is seldom any one clue that in and of itself reveals the mystery. It is a combination of evidence that accumulates and is then synthesized. In no particular order, I shall elucidate. Perhaps a round of brandy would be in order whilst I do so."

Mrs. Winterburn poured and handed around generous snifters of brandy to all present. Holmes carried on.

"Having eliminated the wise men and shepherds, I was forced to investigate the less likely suspects. Learning that you had been a Tiller Girl, my Lady, was useful. That meant that you were fit and nimble on your feet and accustomed to entering and leaving a stage in complete darkness, as any theater troupe must do several times a performance. Your reaction to the vanishing of your child was wonderfully theatrical but highly unrealistic."

"In what way?" said Lady Arsfasten, sounding like an offended actress who had just read a critical review of her performance.

"My dear lady, when a normal mother sees that her child has disappeared, she doesn't fall into hysterics and loud sobbing. Those actions are useless. She immediately starts to search. She takes command and begins to shout orders to all and sundry, getting them to join her in looking. Your performance was worthy of the National Theatre, but not what I would have expected of a mother."

She shrugged. "It was the best I could do for my first time in that role without an experienced director. I will have to work on my lines."

"And, my dear, your 'stiff upper lip' routine was entirely too early and eager. Tut-tut. With the life of your son at risk, you should have been wan and exhausted. Instead, you were lovely and radiant earlier this evening. And then we come to Miss Primrose."

"What did I do wrong?" asked the young woman.

"You entered the church at the same time that Dr. Watson and I did. A detective learns to take a close look at any young woman walking by herself after dark on the streets of London, and I took note of you. And, my dear young lady, a little talcum is always welcome, but you powdered Baby Jesus' bottom with rather generous amounts, and I suspect you liked the sensation so much you may have added some to your own anatomy. Whatever you did, your scent can be detected yards away."

"Who," asked Mrs. Loretta Winterburn, "were those scallywags who stole my umbrella?"

"Two of London's finest young spies. Ah, but I must compliment whoever it was that typed the ransom note. Wonderfully disguised. Well done."

"That was me," said Lady Arsfasten. "You learn how to do a great many things when touring with dancers all across Europe. I just copied some of the big words Gus likes to use when he writes letters and then typed it the way I had watched some of our male dancers pound a typewriter."

"Brilliant. Then please tell me, all of you, why you did it? Kidnapping is a terribly serious crime, and you could be facing years of imprisonment. If there is some justifiable reason, it is possible that the child could suddenly turn up here back in his bed with no explanation, but you will have to convince me that there was no criminal intent."

"If he stays here, I will take him again, and we will never be seen," said Lady Arsfasten.

Holmes and I both looked at the young mother, stunned by what she had said.

"Madam," said Holmes, "you had best explain yourself, or I shall have no choice but to call straight away for the police. Speaking of whom, what happened to the large constables who were stationed here for your protection?"

"Inspector Lestrade told them that as His Lordship was staying at his club, they did not have to remain here. I told Constable Higgs that I should miss his protective presence," said Miss Primrose Winterburn, "and he promised to return on New Year's Eve and take me out dancing."

"A mutually beneficial agreement, no doubt," said Holmes. "Now then, back to my question. Why?"

Lady Arsfasten didn't immediately answer. She stood up and walked over to the large window and looked out toward the street and her neighbor's houses, all sparkling with their Christmas candles.

"Mr. Holmes," she said, looking up at the night sky, "my husband is a vile and horrible monster. He was a concerned and solicitous gentleman up until the day my son was born. After that, he withdrew from all affection. If I offend him in any way, he beats me. I am called no end of vulgar and insulting names. I have no money of my own to spend, and I am confined to this house except to attend church once a week. When you were here earlier, Miss Primrose told you what we expect will happen to me as soon as my son is of school age. Several of the household staff have already warned me that the death of his first wife was highly suspicious. When the opportunity of participating in the nativity pageant was offered, I volunteered. My plan was rash, but it was the only chance I would ever have to escape from his clutches."

"Now, Mary," said Mrs. Winterburn, "let us give credit where it is due. The kidnapping wasn't your idea. It was mine. It wouldn't do just to run away with your child while penniless. You wouldn't last long if you did."

"Yes, of course, Auntie Lori. It was a brilliant scheme, and we pulled it off rather well, the three of us, didn't we?"

"Please explain, my Lady," said Holmes.

"It was all quite brilliant. I had secretly opened a bank account in Switzerland – something else one learns to do when touring the Continent – and all we had to do was have the money transferred and we could run off to anywhere we wanted in the world. When our chance came, as soon as the lights went out, quick as a wink I jumped up and lifted my son out of the manger and handed him up to my aunt on the ladder. She passed him up and over the curtain to my cousin, Primrose, who spirited him out of the back door of the church before the lights came back on. Unfortunately, we hadn't counted on having Mr. Sherlock Holmes present for the occasion. So that is what happened, Mr. Holmes, and why. You had best have me thrown into prison, because I will try again until I succeed in escaping from that ogre . . . with my son."

"My dear lady," said Holmes, "please know that I sympathize with your deplorable predicament, and there may be a way in which I and the police can protect you from your husband's cruelty. Nevertheless, you simply cannot rob a man of his son, no matter what his station in life. Augustus Purifoy Arsfasten the Third must be returned to his father, and you must never attempt to abduct him again."

Lady Mary Arsfasten said nothing for a full minute and then answered quietly.

"That isn't my son's name. His name is David Anthony Owen . . . the same as his father's."

Now it was Holmes's turn to be shocked into momentary silence.

"Madam, are you saying that Lord Arsfasten, your husband, isn't the father of your child?"

She sighed. "That is exactly what I am saying."

"Would you mind explaining?"

"I am the only child of aged, impoverished parents. Two years ago, I fell in love with and married a prince of a man, a lieutenant in the Welsh Guards. Mr. Tiller doesn't accept any married women into his troupes, as he is a firm believer that a married woman should never be separated from her husband and children. I wasn't prepared to give up my dancing, and so we kept our marriage a secret until David was promoted to captain and we could afford to live on his salary. Fifteen months ago, he was killed whilst on duty in the Sudan. That very day, I realized I was with child. There was nothing I could do. I kept dancing. The show must go on, as they say. We were performing here in London and on the third night of our run, His Lordship asked to speak to me following the performance. What can I say? I was desperate and not thinking at all properly. I married him the following week, and I brought forth a son somewhat prematurely eight months later."

"That does cast the events of the past few days in a somewhat different light."

"Yes, Mr. Holmes. It does. We didn't abduct His Lordship's son and heir. We rescued *my* son from *his* clutches. If Lord Gus becomes aware of this, I would be cast out of the house within the hour, and I would fear for my life. So now, Mr. Holmes, what are you going to do with me and my aunt, my cousin, and my son?"

"Will His Lordship return to this house before Christmas?" asked Holmes.

"No, but he will be back here on Christmas Eve so that he can bestow gifts on his son on Christmas morning. He likes to keep up appearances."

"Then it would be best to keep your son in secret with Mrs. Winterburn until the twenty-fourth. I will see what I can do."

Midnight found Holmes and me standing on the Mayfair pavement. He was puffing on his pipe, and I was shivering in the deep, still, winter cold.

"Well," I said, "that wasn't what you expected. What are you going to do now?"

He didn't deign to answer me until he had finished his pipe.

"My dear Watson, a few hours back, I asked if you would mind breaking the law. Are you still of the persuasion?"

"As long as the cause is good is what I said. I haven't changed."

"Wonderful. I knew I could rely on you."

"What are we going to do?"

"We are going to go home and get a good night's sleep. We are going to need it starting tomorrow morning."

"Holmes, I haven't even started my breakfast. What is the rush?"

"The Albemarle Club serves excellent coffee and pastries. I cannot recommend them highly enough."

"The Albemarle? That place is nothing but a den of cads, rakes, rogues, and immoral poseurs. I cannot think of a single respectable citizen who would belong to it."

"I can."

"Who?"

"Lord Augustus Arsfasten. He will be expecting us in twenty minutes. I told him we would have fresh news about the abduction of his son and requested that he have refreshments served."

I never did learn what plan Holmes had concocted in his creative mind, nor what fresh news he intended to impart to His Lordship. For as soon as we met Arsfasten at his club, it was he who delivered news to us.

"Before you go slopping into your coffee and devouring the house pastries like a couple of hungry dogs," said His Lordship in the breakfast room of the Albemarle Club that morning, "pay heed and listen to the news I have for you."

"We are all attention, sir," said Holmes.

"Good. You should be. Well then, get this straight: I decided yesterday that I didn't have the patience to wait any longer for you or Scotland Yard to find and return my son. I want him there with me on Christmas morning. So I sent off the money off to the Swiss bank account last evening. It will be deposited by noon today, Swiss time. Frankly, I shan't miss it. I expect to see my son by this evening. By Christmas Eve at the latest."

I was aghast, and I could see that Holmes was as well.

"Your Lordship, was that wise?" said Holmes. "You have no idea with whom you are dealing. We have no guarantee they will honor their promise. How do you know they will not now come back and demand another £15,000?"

"A gentleman knows another gentleman. I re-read the letter I was sent, and I knew I was dealing with one of my own kind. The elevated vocabulary, the precise syntax, the perfect punctuation . . . they are indisputable proof that I am dealing with an English gentleman. He may not have blue blood in his veins like I do, but he is certainly a gentleman none the less. And an English gentleman never goes back on his word. His word is his bond. I am not the least in doubt. So you may as well be on your way, Mr. Holmes. And do have a Happy Christmas."

Once again, Holmes stood out on the pavement, puffing on his blessed pipe whilst I waited and listened to carolers strolling up and down Piccadilly.

"Well, what this time? Weren't expecting that either, were you?"

""No, I most certainly was not. But one must always be prepared to adjust one's strategy to meet with the unexpected. What I never expected was that she would receive all the money she needed for a decent life somewhere abroad. Now she has it. All I have to do now is find a way to get her and her son and relatives out of England before he catches on."

He puffed for another ten minutes whilst I shivered. Then I watched as that familiar twinkle came into his eye, and the barest hint of a smile came over his face.

"Watson, I shall need a few hours. Please meet me in Mayfair at four o'clock. Enjoy the day. And my warmest best wishes for the season."

He hailed a cab, hopped in, and sped off, leaving me in the middle of the Burlington Estate. I walked down to Piccadilly in search of my breakfast.

At four o'clock, I was on time. Holmes was running late, but when he arrived, he was looking like the cat that ate the canary. We entered the

Arsfasten house and took our seats in the parlor while Miss Primrose served a round of decently adulterated eggnog and Christmas cake.

Lady Arsfasten was bouncing a jovial Baby Augie – or David or Jesus – on her knee. I was sure that he would break into frightful screams at the sight of Holmes and me, but he refrained. All three women sat and waited for Holmes to announce the purpose of the meeting he had called.

"Fifteen-thousand pounds has been sent, my Lady, to your account in Switzerland. It is yours to use as you wish, and I am sure you will use it wisely for the care of your son and your family."

Three mouths dropped open.

"Now then," he continued, "you will have to move with great alacrity as soon as Dr. Watson and I depart. You must pack everything you need, for you are departing England tomorrow on *The Empress of Japan* from Southampton. Here are your tickets. They are only second class, but under the circumstances that should suffice, and you don't want to draw attention to yourselves."

Three jaws nearly hit the floor.

"You're sending us to *Japan*?" gasped Primrose.

"No, I am sending you by way of the Suez, Hong Kong, and Tokyo to Canada. If you have your funds transferred from Switzerland to the Royal Bank of Canada in Vancouver, they will be waiting for you when you arrive. Your new life in the new world should be much more to your liking. Perhaps you can start a school for precision dancing, but you will have to move to Montreal if you hope to do so. The entire rest of the country is altogether too dull and Protestant to support such titillating culture. Any questions?"

"What about Gus?" asked Lady Arsfasten. "He isn't going to put up with this. He'll come after me just out of spite and vengeance."

"I think not. We shall pay him a visit tomorrow and, I assure you, he will be glad to see you gone. And now, we must take our leave and you must get busy and pack. The train to Southampton departs tomorrow from Victoria at five o'clock in the morning. *Bon voyage* and happy Christmas."

Yet again, I confronted Holmes as we stood out on the pavement.

"Where in heaven's name did you get the money to buy those tickets? You shouldn't have to bear the expense, and you will not get a farthing from either Arsfasten or Lestrade for this case."

"Elementary. Banks are fair-weather friends to any customer they deem credit worthy. I arranged a loan with the expectation that Her Ladyship will repay as soon as her abundant funds are made available to her. Now, if you will excuse me, I have some arrangements to put in place before we meet Lord Arsfasten on Christmas Eve."

At four o'clock in the afternoon of Christmas Eve, Holmes and I met on the pavement of Gilbert Street. Darkness had already fallen, and many of the houses had arrangements of candles lighting up their windows. It seemed an ideal time to celebrate the incarnation of Our Lord. Unfortunately, we were about to be agents of the Last Judgement, visited in some singularly devious way upon the execrable Lord Augustus Arsfasten.

"Come in please, gentlemen," said Derwan Fairbanks. "I shall let His Lordship know you have arrived. I must warn you, he isn't in a mood appropriate to Yuletide."

"I should hope not," said Holmes. He was rubbing his hands together, and it wasn't because they were cold.

"Where are my wife and son?" a voice descending the stairs bellowed at us. "And what is the meaning of *this*?"

He was holding a piece of notepaper upon which a short letter had been typed. Holmes read it with feigned interest and handed it to me. It ran:

Dear Lord Arsfasten:

Permit me to share some news with you, from one noble gentleman to another. Your transmission of £15,000 is duly acknowledged and we extend our gratitude.

I assure you that not a farthing of your donation will be used for any personal gain. All of it, in its entirety, will be distributed to the branches of the RSPCA through Great Britain. The Christmas season is such a busy time for all of us who are members of the human species, and it is far too easy to forget our little furry friends. However, because of the generosity of gentlemen such as yourself, they will all have a few extra treats on Christmas morning.

We regret the rather disturbing method of implementing our annual Christmas appeal, but the letters we sent out last year delivered a less-than-satisfactory return, and we had to try something more creative this year. A dozen wealthy members of England's aristocracy were selected for generous donations, and all have responded as we had hoped, except for one, who shall remain unnamed, that is demanding that we pay him before he accepts the return of his somewhat obstreperous son.

With all best wishes for the season,
Happy Christmas

It was not signed.

"My congratulations, sir," said Holmes, "on your generosity. You are a lover of animals, are you not? Such a fine act of human compassion at this time of year."

"How I feel about animals has nothing to do with how I am feeling now! Let them have their money for the mangy mutts. Where are my wife and son?"

"Your son, sir, was returned to your home yesterday afternoon. Unfortunately, he and his mother have now departed from England to seek a new life in Europe."

The miserable old lord was speechless . . . for about ten seconds, and then exploded, using a string of words that I have chosen not to record, but ended with a demand that Holmes, Scotland Yard, and police forces on the Continent were expected to find her and bring her back. He would see that she was charged, tried, convicted, and thrown into prison.

"My Lord," said Holmes, donning a face of human sympathy, "that isn't advisable. There are a few things that, in your haste to marry her, you didn't learn about your wife."

"What?"

"To begin with sir, her true name wasn't Miss Mary Smithers. It is Maria Smerdyakova."

"A Russian? Say it isn't so."

"It is. Her family immigrated to Liverpool when she was a schoolgirl and changed their name to sound English. Her uncle and his family remained in Sergivev Posad, and he now holds quite a senior position in the Okhrana. I assume you have heard of them."

"They are the Czar's secret police. You horrify me. What an awful way to taint my family name."

"It is worse than that, sir. She had written to her aunt and told her about every time you beat her or otherwise mistreated her. The aunt showed the letters to her husband, and it made him rather furious. Family honor and all that. He has, as you know, agents throughout London, and they were given orders to murder you and toss your body in the Thames, leaving your entire estate to your wife."

A pallor emerged on the face of the detestable lord. "Surely, you cannot be serious."

"Entirely, sir. You may thank your wife that you are still alive. Out of consideration for your son, she persuaded her uncle to spare your life if he would arrange to have her come and live in Russia, along with your son. They departed last night from Southampton on the *Grand Duchess Anastasia,* bound for St. Petersburg. The good news, if we can call it that, is that with your connections at Westminster, you should be able to have an act passed within a few weeks granting you a divorce. You are still a vigorous man, and there is more than enough time to start over."

Lord Arsfasten entered a near catatonic state for a full minute before shaking his head and nodding.

"Derwan!" he called down the hall. "Here. Now!"

His man appeared immediately. "Yes, my Lord. What is it?"

"When do the Tiller Girls perform next?"

"Immediately following the New Year, my Lord, at the Palace."

"Get me a ticket for the first performance. Front row as always."

"Of course, sir. But if I may say so, sir: Are you sure you are up to another round?"

One final time, Holmes and I strolled through Mayfair on our way home to Baker Street. A light snow was falling and we passed a group of carolers singing "God Rest Ye Merry, Gentlemen" as we crossed Marylebone.

"Good heavens, Holmes.," I said. "The RSPCA? Russia? What in the world – "

"I have a friend in Minsk who breeds wolf hounds. It was all I could think of at the time. Happy Christmas, my friend."

The Adventure of the Second Sister
by Matthew White

Chapter I – A Visitor and a Problem

It was during the first Christmastime after Sherlock Holmes's dramatic return from the long absence which followed the events I have previously recorded under the heading of "The Final Problem" – December 23rd, 1894, to be exact – and he and I were walking back to Baker Street after lunch. A light snow, crisscrossed and stained by the footprints of pedestrians, blanketed the pavement, and the streets had been rendered into a brown sludge by the busy London traffic. On the rooftops, however, the snow was white and virginal, and the diffuse light of the sun glittered gayly on the icicles which hung from every roof and lamppost.

"I fear, Watson, that I have been too successful in my chosen profession," remarked Holmes.

"What?" said I, incredulously. "Too successful? Can there be too little crime?"

"No doubt you are right, from society's point of view," Holmes replied. "But consider – if your own medical skills rose to such a height that you could rid England of all but the most trivial ailments to which any housewife might know the remedy, you would quickly find yourself without work. Likewise, I have been so successful in capturing criminals, and in exposing the network of criminality that once ran through London like malignant roots of an evil tree, that soon I shall have no work left, and be forced to retire and rusticate in the country."

"But that is ridiculous!" I laughed. "There will always be more crime, just as there will always be more sickness."

Holmes sighed.

"Perhaps. But I fear the best days of my career are behind me. There is nothing so invigorating for me as the opportunity to apply my special skills, my singular faculty for observation and deduction, to a problem worthy of them. Therein lies my difficulty. There are no Moriartys, no Morans – not even the likes of a John Clay to set myself against. I have beaten them all, and in their place there are only petty problems which are so simple, and their solutions so predictable, I need hardly leave my chair to solve them. The days of the great challenges are over. Yes, I fear I have been too successful."

"I think you are being a bit selfish," said I. "These triumphs which you are so eager to lament have made England a better, safer place. The country, and indeed Europe, may now sleep easier because of you. Really, how can you regret that?"

"You are right, of course. Hullo! What could this be, I wonder?"

Ahead of us, a small shape darted and weaved down the crowded street toward us like a little monkey dashing through an overgrown jungle, forcing pedestrians to leap out of the way, glaring and shouting as it passed. Billy, Mrs. Hudson's page boy, came to a halt before us. Red-faced and gasping after his exertion, his breath rose in great billows of steam above his head. He gripped an envelope tightly in his fist and held it out to my amused friend.

"Urgent, sir," he said between heavy breaths. "Said it wouldn't wait, sir."

"Who said so?"

"The commissionaire who delivered it, sir."

Holmes examined the envelope minutely.

"Very fine quality, expensive ... address written by a woman ... wax seal stamped with '*V.R.*' – Ha! I think we may safely assume this missive was not sent by the person who first comes to mind, however."

He took a letter from within and read it quickly before passing it to me. It said:

Dear Sir,

I beg that you will meet with me at once to advise me on a very serious and deeply personal matter. I hope very much that it will be convenient for me to call this afternoon at two o'clock.

Once I have explained the facts, you will understand the urgency of the matter. In the meantime, please do not disclose my visit or this letter to anyone.

Yours sincerely,
Violet Reynolds

"This may be something," said I.

"She has lost her little dog, perhaps," said Holmes sardonically, "or wants help choosing between two suitors. Well, we had better get home at once and prepare for our guest, for it seems she means to call whether it is convenient or not."

We wasted no time in procuring a four-wheeler for the purpose. Billy, for whom cab rides were a novelty, looked out the windows with delight as we rattled down the street.

We arrived at 221b Baker Street with only ten minutes in which to prepare our sitting room to receive company – a task which was complicated by Holmes's reluctance to move any of his papers or books, or to put away any of the strange objects which he had accumulated and placed in inconvenient spots. Though he was fastidious when it came to personal cleanliness, Holmes and I had quite different ideas about the sort of environment which was fit for human habitation. At last we managed to get the room into a more-or-less orderly state, just in time for the ringing of the bell and the sound of feet on the stairs which told us that our visitor had arrived.

"Please come in, Madam" said Holmes to the lady who entered the room, escorted by Billy. She was a lovely young woman, richly dressed, with luxuriant dark hair, noble features, and intelligent eyes which regarded each of us in turn. It was easy to imagine her pleasant mouth smiling, but at the moment it was set in a disapproving frown.

"Which of you, please, is Sherlock Holmes?" she asked. Her voice, though soft, possessed that steely character characteristic of the strong-willed woman. Billy closed the door behind him as he left the room.

"I am," said my friend. "Allow me – "

"Mr. Holmes, I had expected, after my letter, that you would meet me alone. I was told I could rely on your discretion."

"You may rely on it completely, Miss Reynolds. This is Dr. John Watson, my colleague, who has aided me on many of my most important cases. He is a man of the utmost integrity."

She turned a searching gaze toward me, then nodded.

"Very well. I hope, sir, that you are not offended by my caution. It is most necessary that my visit here should be kept secret."

"I quite understand," said I.

"Please, be seated," said Holmes, inviting our guest to the sofa. Holmes occupied his usual chair by the fireplace, while I seated myself in my own and readied my notebook and pen. Miss Reynolds looked down at her hands. The confidence with which she had addressed us only a moment ago seemed to have melted away, and she now appeared not to know what to say.

"Your letter mentioned that you wanted advice," Holmes prompted her. "Please, tell me how I can be of assistance."

After a moment's hesitation, the young lady spoke.

"To begin with, I must explain my family's situation," she said. "My father is Sir Edmund Reynolds, whose name is no doubt familiar to you."

I could see by Holmes's face that it was not.

"A well-known philanthropist," I explained. "The considerable profits from his Birmingham factories have been used to finance a number of projects for the benefit of the poor and infirm. He has had a seat in the Commons for a number of years, and I understand that he is seeking a position on the Cabinet."

"Thank you, Watson. You are a veritable encyclopedia of society."

"You are quite correct, Doctor," said our young visitor. "As you may imagine, his position places him under a great deal of public scrutiny. Furthermore, his success in life has aroused the jealousy of a number of the old families who resent that a commoner has risen so far in the world while their ancestral fortunes dwindle, and would welcome the opportunity to discredit him. He is quite conscious of all this, and therefore makes every effort to conform himself to the highest standard of propriety. He expects the same from his family, of course, since our behavior reflects upon him."

"I take it, then, that something has happened which might disgrace him and jeopardize his future career?"

She grimaced and nodded.

"Does he know you are here?"

"No, Mr. Holmes. I came to you without his knowledge. But once I have explained, I am sure you will understand that I couldn't do otherwise."

"Tell me everything and leave out no detail, however small." Holmes closed his eyes and drew his fingertips together as he listened to her singular narrative.

"I am Sir Edmund's eldest daughter. After me came my brother and then two sisters. The youngest is seventeen, and a very bright and proper young lady. My other sister, Beatrice, is twenty-one years old, and it is is concerning her that I have come to see you. I shall tell you everything exactly as it happened.

"Betty, as we call her, was always a willful sort of girl. She quarreled awfully with our parents, and seemed to delight in flouting propriety just to make them uncomfortable. She never got on with any of us, really, for she preferred the company of our cousins. When my uncle emigrated with his family to New York the trouble started, for being deprived of her customary companions she befriended, well . . . people of a certain character, if you understand. Oh, not criminals, at least not violent criminals, but actors, musicians, and artists of the most vulgar sort. There was nothing artistic about that crowd, and you may take my word for it.

But she was quite taken with them, and was often seen in their company. It was a terrible embarrassment to Father, of course. Three years ago, in March, she had one last quarrel with our parents, during which she said the most dreadful things. She left the house, and we have had no word from her since."

"Did she take anything with her when she left?"

"Some clothes and money, as well as all her valuable jewelry and other possessions."

"Could not she have gone to her relations in America?" I asked. She shook her head.

"We have not heard from Uncle Henry or our cousins for many years. Between ourselves, their departure was precipitated by some rather hard feelings between my father and his brother. We have had no notion of where they might be or how to reach them for quite a long time."

"Do you recall the names of your sister's friends?" Holmes asked.

"Now we come to it, Mr. Holmes! I did my best to avoid making their acquaintance, but there was one whom she would speak of constantly – an artist, if you can call him that, named Mr. Catesby, who I understand has been before a judge more than once for some outrage or other. I am quite convinced that he knows where she is, or at least where she went."

"Why do you think so?"

She produced an irregular scrap of paper, blackened at the edges and handed it to Holmes, who examined it with interest.

"It is a telegram, or rather the remains of a telegram," he remarked. "Much of it is no longer legible, and it is no longer possible to see the names of the sender or the intended recipient."

"It must have been sent to Beatrice, for it was found in the grate in her room the day after she left."

Holmes showed me the burned sheet on which I read:

is ready. Will meet at dock. Remem

your father.

C

"The 'C', then – you take to be Catesby?" Holmes asked our client.

"Who else?"

"Quite so. But please, continue your account, for I observe that you have several more papers with you."

"Certainly. The maid who found that paper brought it at once to my father, who sent a letter to Mr. Catesby demanding to know where Beatrice was, only to receive an offensive reply denying any knowledge of her whereabouts. Father didn't wish to go to the police for fear of scandal, and because there was no positive proof she was in danger. So he waited, hoping she would come to her senses and return. As you may imagine, the situation caused him a great deal of anxiety. As if that were not enough, this September past we began to receive strange letters in the post purporting to be from Beatrice, intimating that she was staying at an unnamed hotel and in want of money, making it plain that if it was not forthcoming, she would see to it that the business found its way into the papers. Can you imagine the scandal? All Father's ambitions would be dashed."

"These are the letters which you have brought with you?"

"Yes, I have them here," she said, drawing out a small bundle of papers which she handed to Holmes. "Five letters in all, each containing a demand for money. The fifth arrived just this morning."

"They are in her handwriting?"

"Very like it."

"But not exactly?"

"I'm sure I couldn't venture to say exactly. It is near enough to put us in doubt either way."

Holmes took the letters over to the table and laid them out before him. Over his shoulder, I read the most recent one.

Dear Father, [It said]

I am getting married the day after Christmas to a fine young man of my acquaintance. I would be obliged if you would send me one-hundred pounds as a wedding present. If you will not, I understand the papers pay for interesting gossip about public figures.

Your daughter,
Beatrice

"It is a pity you did not bring the envelopes. They would have been most informative. I don't suppose you recall the postmark?"

"London. Answering letters were to be left at the Commercial Road Post Office."

Holmes studied each of the letters in turn with a magnifying lens.

"They were certainly written by the same hand. The author is right-handed and writes sloppily, with her hand touching the paper. She overindulges in drink, is untidy in her habits, of limited means, and keeps an animal – a cat, if I'm not mistaken."

"You said 'her'," I interjected. "You are certain it was a woman?"

"How can you possibly know all that?" Miss Reynolds asked.

"I observed and deduced. As to her sex, there are marked indications of femininity which a student of graphology could hardly fail to notice." He lifted the envelope and sniffed it. "It is just possible to detect a faint trace of perfume – a common, inexpensive variety. The ink and paper are also of poor quality. The ink has been smudged in several places – and see how her hand left streaks of it on the right side of the page? It is also possible – particularly here, and here – to see where her hand shook as she was writing. She seems hardly capable of making a straight line in this letter. This is characteristic of a hand impaired by drink. And look – " He pulled a short, straight hair from where it was stuck to the dried ink. "This is no human hair."

"Remarkable," said Miss Reynolds.

"Is there anyone you know who might answer the description I have given?"

"No one."

"An impostor, then."

"Whomever this person is, she certainly knows a great deal about our family. She uses the nicknames Betty had for us. My brother Theodore, for instance – she always called him 'Teddy', because he hated it. In one letter, you will see, it says 'Teddy'. They also allude to arguments she had with Father, and what they were about. We have always kept such things very private."

"That is suggestive. What did your father do after receiving the letters?"

"After the first letter came, he went immediately to the post office to see if he could learn who had posted the letters, but they were most unhelpful. But then Father, who is really very clever sometimes, went there and left a letter for Beatrice. He'd brought a disguise with him, and he put it on, went back inside, and waited."

"To see who would appear to claim it?" I ventured.

"Exactly. He bought some shabby clothes, and wore a false beard and thick glasses."

"That is a very bad disguise," interjected Holmes. "A beard and glasses? I can't imagine anything more obvious than that."

"It is hardly his specialty," Miss Reynolds replied with some little irritation. "He waited three days in the post office, from morning to evening, not daring to leave even for a moment. But no one came. So

Father had me go and ask for any letters being held for Beatrice Reynolds. But there were none!"

Abruptly, Holmes began to laugh, but quickly regained his composure.

"Forgive me, Miss Reynolds, for I don't mean to make light of your problem. Indeed, I find it quite stimulating."

"I am glad to hear that it stimulates you, sir," the young lady replied coldly, "for we shall not sleep easily until the matter is resolved."

Holmes rose from his chair. "You may leave the matter in my hands. And now, if there is nothing else, I intend to start my inquiries at once, for there are still many hours left in the day."

"Thank you. Please, let me know the minute you have news."

"How shall I communicate with you?" he asked.

"Write to my maid, Bess Saunders, and she will deliver your message to me." She provided her address. "She is a trusty servant, and discreet."

"How many servants do you keep?"

"Why, let me think," she said, a little surprised by the question. "There is the butler, the housekeeper, father's valet, two maids, the cook, and her son who is our page boy. There are also a groom and a gardener, but they don't live in the house."

"Could any of them have written the letters?"

"They are all trusty servants!"

"I understand your hesitation, Miss Reynolds, but please think carefully. Is there any possibility at all that the writer of these letters could be among your staff?"

"I am quite certain they could not, Mr. Holmes," she said firmly. "All have excellent characters, and none have ever been known to drink immoderately, and there is no cat in our house."

"Have any servants departed or been dismissed in the time since your sister left home?"

"No."

"Very well. Good day, Miss Reynolds."

"I beg you to spare no effort, Mr. Holmes. You are our only hope."

"You may rest assured," said I as I showed our guest to the door.

Chapter II – A Warning and an Investigation

"Well," said Holmes once Miss Reynolds had left, "this promises to be an interesting little diversion, after all. I don't know that I have ever received a more congenial Christmas present."

"Where shall we begin?" I asked. He stood gazing thoughtfully out the window for a little while.

"That name she mentioned – Catesby, the artist. I know that I have heard it before."

Holmes walked over to the shelf where he kept his index, a collection of notes and newspaper cuttings related to every subject which was likely to be useful to him. He pulled down a volume and began flipping rapidly through the pages.

"Ah, here it is. Arthur Catesby. He's quite notorious in certain circles."

"I've never heard of him."

"His isn't a name likely to appear in the society papers. He has indeed, as Miss Reynolds said, been before the magistrate's bench a number of times, usually in relation to some manner of public indecency, or the display of his very questionable art works. Despite this, he is a charmer – the kind of dashing, swaggering fellow who never fails to make friends. He has made a career of insinuating himself into the company of dissipated sons of the aristocracy and gaining the confidence of young women with wealthy families. Some of their money then finds its way into his pockets. Inevitably, a scandal of some kind emerges, which is suppressed, with varying degrees of success, and Mr. Catesby, having exhausted any good will toward himself, is soon looking for another fool to take advantage of."

"The scoundrel! The wedding that the letter mentioned – Could he be – ?"

"My dear Watson, if we go on the assumption that the writer of these letters is not our client's sister, then I think it very unlikely the wedding is anything more than a fabrication meant to frighten her father into compliance."

"Hadn't we better confront him, and be sure?"

"In good time. As yet our data is incomplete. I sense, however, that you have formed a definite opinion on the case?"

"It does seem rather plain to me," said I. "This villain Catesby has taken advantage of the young lady's confidence and convinced or coerced her to furnish information which he can use to blackmail her family."

"And how do you account for the mysterious woman who wrote the blackmail letters?"

"Some ally of Catesby's, no doubt."

Holmes shook his head.

"This is an excellent illustration of the error in attempting to reason with insufficient data," said he with the tone of a professor lecturing an errant student. "While your reasoning is coherent in itself, you have not availed yourself of all the available facts, and so you fail to take into account two points which call your conclusion into question."

"Those points being?" said I with some asperity.

"Firstly, blackmail is a much more dangerous game than Catesby is known to play. He practices on his victims more subtly. Secondly, as a rule Catesby associates himself only with the wealthy or people whose social position might offer some advantage to himself, if he were to gain influence over them. He would have no use for a poor woman such as our letter-writer appears to be."

"When you put it in that light, I do see what you mean. But if Catesby is not involved, who is the '*C*' who sent the telegram to Miss Beatrice? And if all you say of him is true, is she not precisely the kind of girl he would prey upon? I find it difficult to believe he is not involved in some way."

"I do not deny the possibility," said he thoughtfully. "On the contrary, I have a notion that he's involved in some way. The question is *how*."

"Have you no theory, then?"

"I have three. Now I must test them."

Holmes replaced the book on the shelf and retired to his room, leaving me to puzzle over the mystery our young client had brought us. After some minutes he emerged again, transformed by his formidable powers of disguise into the very image of an English laborer in woolen working clothes and a flat cap, and had convincingly applied long, dark whiskers to the sides of his face.

"I am going out. No, it would be best if I were on my own at present, but no doubt I shall call upon your assistance soon enough. Kindly ask Mrs. Hudson to have dinner ready at six o'clock. I fear she is still cross with me after my last chemical experiment spoiled her tea party and caused the house to smell like sulfur for three days."

After Holmes had gone, I sat down in my chair by the fire and tried to interest myself in the latest edition of *The British Journal*, only to fall asleep. I awoke some time later, surprised to see Billy enter the room escorting yet another visitor. This was a young man in his early twenties, tall, clad in evening dress with a silver-handled cane in his gloved hand. He had a proud, gentlemanly bearing, and his bright, intelligent eyes swept over every detail of the room before coming to rest on me.

"Forgive the intrusion," he said. "My name is Theodore Reynolds. I believe you are already acquainted with my sister, Violet."

"Dr. John Watson," said I, rising groggily. "How may I be of service?"

I put out my hand, but he declined to accept it.

"I understand Mr. Holmes is out, but that you are his colleague and collaborator?"

"I have that honour, sir."

"I should have liked to speak with him as well, but I have a pressing engagement and cannot wait. I trust then, Doctor, that I may depend upon you to convey a message to him?"

"Certainly."

"Very good. I will be brief. I know that my sister has been to see Mr. Holmes, and I know why. Let me be clear: She didn't have, and would certainly never obtain, our father's permission to consult with anyone about our private affairs. On the contrary, he is determined that absolutely no one should become involved in this business, or learn about it. That cannot be helped now, of course, but I urge you and Mr. Holmes in the strongest possible terms never to speak to anyone of what she told you or act on it in any way. I will, of course, pay reasonably for any trouble which you have already taken, but you must both stay clear of the matter from now on. Do you understand?"

"Once Mr. Holmes has agreed to take a case, he will not withdraw, save at the request of the client who engaged his services."

"My sister had no right to engage him in the first place. You should know also that she cannot possibly pay, having no money of her own. No doubt she expected that Father would pay, but that will never happen. We aren't in the habit of rewarding people who meddle in our private affairs – quite the contrary, in fact, I can assure you."

"Are you threatening me, sir?"

"Threatening you? No, sir. I am warning you. Stay clear of my family's affairs. I shall not warn you a second time."

"You aren't the first man to come to these rooms to frighten us off a case," said I, "and far from the most intimidating. You shall not be any more successful than they were. Now, if there is nothing else, I must ask you to leave."

The visitor's face reddened, and he tightened his grip on his stick. Instinctively, I squared my shoulders, ready to receive a blow and to return one if necessary, but it didn't come to that. Without another word, he turned and left, slamming the door behind him and stomping loudly down the stairs. When I heard the front door open and close, I relaxed. A moment later, I heard the front door again, and Holmes's familiar tread upon the stair.

"Who was that fellow leaving the house just now?" he asked upon entering the sitting room. "And what in Heaven's name did you say to him, to put him in such a fury?"

"That was our client's brother," said I, and I gave him an account of our conversation. To my surprise, he laughed heartily.

"This adds some colour to our investigation, don't you think?" he said. "In any case, I have made significant progress toward resolving the case. I know the name of the woman who wrote the letters."

"You amaze me!" I cried. "How on earth did you discover it so quickly?"

"Let me first clean these whiskers off my face, and then we may share a smoke while I tell you all about it."

"There is a kind of fraternity amongst domestic servants," said Holmes after lighting his pipe. We were relaxing in our armchairs by the fire, and I was listening eagerly to his account.

"Generally, they are close about their employers' affairs – if not out of loyalty, than at least to preserve their positions – but amongst their own class they can be quite garrulous. If you can draw them out, they will tell you anything you might wish to know about their employers. I made some inquiries in Park Street, where Catesby's house is situated, giving out that I was a gardener looking for a position and that I wished to know which houses are managed well and which to avoid. A kindly cook invited me to warm myself by the oven as she worked, and was only too happy to tell me what she knew about Catesby's domestic arrangements.

"'You'd do better to look elsewhere,' said she when I asked about Catesby. 'No one stays on there more than a year.'

"'Does he pay so poorly?' I asked.

"'I can't speak to that, but it's no secret he's got an awfully sharp temper. Why, they say he once chased his maid out of the house with a riding crop! That would be Annie Parker, who's still there now after two years – longer than anyone else I can remember.'

"'Why does she not leave, if she is so ill-treated?'

"'I think she'd like to. One look at her face, and you'll see how miserable she is. I suppose she needs the money.'

"'Who else works there?'

"'Oh, they come and go so quickly that I can hardly keep track. A new cook started in September, but I've seen little of her.'

"A pity she had nothing useful to tell you," I said.

"As a matter of fact, she was extremely helpful, for she led me to the maid, Annie Parker. Miss Parker feared to say too much while her employer was home, but with the offer of a five-pound note and by appealing to her hatred of her master, I secured her promise that if I came tonight she would tell me anything I wished to know."

"He will not be at home tonight?"

"According to Miss Parker, he will be spending the evening at a Christmas party at the home of Thomas Ackroyd, the nephew and heir of the Earl of Courtenay."

"And how can I help?"

"By standing watch on the street and alerting me in the event that Catesby should return unexpectedly. Your assistance would really be invaluable."

"Then I shall certainly come."

He smiled and rubbed his hands together.

"Good man! You need not bring your revolver. I don't think we shall be in any danger. It wouldn't hurt to bring a stout stick, however, just to be sure. And now, I fancy that is Mrs. Hudson bringing up our dinner."

Chapter III – A Diversion and a Confrontation

The afternoon shadows lengthened in the street and the too-short daylight hours were nearly done when Holmes and I had finished our meal, bundled ourselves in our overcoats, and walked out into the London night, leaving the warmth of 221b behind us and exchanging a crackling fire for bitter cold and gently falling snow. We were quickly able to secure a cab and rattled away, moving slowly due to icy condition of the streets as darkness fell like a curtain over London.

"Here we are," said Holmes as our hansom turned suddenly off of a busy street into a tree-lined lane of elegant houses. "Number 34 is down there, on the other side of the lane. We will walk from here."

We alighted and Holmes ordered the driver to wait, and on no account move for anything or anyone. Together we walked until Number 34 was across the street and to our right, so that we had a clear view of a gate which opened onto a little paved drive. The house was bounded by a seven-foot red-brick wall topped with iron bars to prevent intruders from climbing over. We strolled in a leisurely way down the street, observing the house in a disinterested manner. We came to a dark little alley between houses which afforded a view of Number 34's gate, and here, hidden by shadow, we began our vigil.

We waited, standing in the biting cold for what felt like an hour but was probably really no longer than thirty minutes or so, before we saw the first sign of activity. A youth unlocked the gate and ran briskly toward the thoroughfare from which we had come.

"As I thought," Holmes said. "They are sending for a cab. I must go now, while the gate is open and unwatched."

"How will you come out?"

"It will be easier to open from within than from without," he answered and dashed across the lane, remarkably sure-footed on the icy pavement. No sooner had he slipped through the gate and into the shadows than a four-wheeler came down the lane and rolled to a stop in front of the house. The page who had summoned it leaped down and ran inside, and moments later two gentleman in lavish evening dress stepped into the light of the street lamp. One of them, whom I supposed must be Arthur Catesby, was in his thirties, with a strong chin, fair hair, and ostentatious dress. The other, however, I was shocked to recognize, for he was none other than Theodore Reynolds!

At once, the possible implications sprang into my mind. Did this mean he was in league with Catesby, and perhaps party to his sister's disappearance? Had he attempted to warn us off the case, not out of concern for his family's honour, but for fear that his own crimes would be exposed? If so, the young lady might be in terrible danger, for if her captors knew that Sherlock Holmes was on their trail, it might drive them to desperation.

As the two men climbed into the carriage, I was in some doubt as to what I should do, for though Holmes had asked me to watch the house, I felt sure he couldn't have foreseen this eventuality. Chance had placed in my hands a thread that, it seemed to me, might lead directly to the solution we sought. There was no sight of Holmes and I was loathe to allow such an opportunity to slip away. The driver whipped up the horse and the cab lurched forward.

At that moment I was struck with inspiration, for I remembered a trick Holmes had once employed in a similar situation. I ran toward the receding cab as fast as I dared, slipping a little on the ice, and upon reaching it, pulled myself onto the back end of the carriage, hoping the sudden addition of my weight wouldn't alert the occupants. I felt a sort of giddy satisfaction at my success, but it was short lived, for as the cab rolled away I realized the absurdity of my position. I had been so preoccupied with getting myself onto the carriage, I had given no thought to what I might do when it reached its destination, or how Holmes might find me again. But it was now too late for second thoughts, and I determined to make the most of my situation, for I considered that I was now acting as a scout gathering reconnaissance from enemy territory.

After twenty minutes or so of travel, the four-wheeler turned onto a gravel drive and deposited its passengers outside a large Georgian house. Light shone through the windows, and music and sounds of frivolity could be heard within. Once the cab had pulled away from the light and into the shadows of the drive, I slid off and onto my feet, relieved to be on solid ground again. Reynolds and Catesby were standing outside conversing with another man and his female companion, whose dress and hat were decorated with so many different kinds of colorful feathers that she looked more like a giant pigeon than a woman.

I observed them for a few moments, not daring to step into the light, for I didn't doubt that Reynolds would recognize me as easily as I had spotted him. I watched them enter the house and tried to think of what Holmes would do in my situation, eventually concluding only that Holmes wouldn't have been so impulsive as to put himself such a situation at all. But there was nothing to do but go forward. With a boldness with which I would hardly credit myself, I adopted a sort of indolent swagger in imitation of Catesby and approached the door.

Inside was such a din of noise and raucous merrymaking that it was a wonder the party-goers could hear one another speak. It was clear at once that this wasn't the sort of function a respectable person would attend. Liquor and uncouth conversation flowed freely, and though I trust that I am neither a snob nor possessed of particularly delicate sensibilities, I was quite taken aback by the vulgarity and tastelessness on display. A servant approached me, offering a glass of what I took to be champagne, which I accepted so that I might appear more at home in the odd company in which I found myself.

"Catesby, dear," a woman called in a laughing voice. "Do come here! I have someone you must meet!"

Doing my best to look nonchalant, even bored, I followed the sound of that voice and found Catesby in conversation with Reynolds and several others. I attempted to move closer without being noticed, hoping to overhear their conversation.

"Doctor Watson! I say, Doctor Watson!" called a voice from behind me. I was horrified to hear that I was recognized in such company, and didn't turn around, hoping that the person calling would believe they were mistaken. Reynolds had evidently heard my name, however, for he looked over and stared at me in bewilderment for a moment before his expression hardened into barely-suppressed rage. He muttered some apology to Catesby and stalked off. I felt a hand on my shoulder.

"How wonderful to see you here, Doctor Watson!"

I shrugged the hand off without looking at its owner.

"I'm sorry, you are mistaken," I said curtly, and extricated myself from the circle of people in the direction Reynolds had gone. Though I was still determined to follow him, I knew that he would be watchful and felt that it would be best to disguise myself. I looked about, hoping to find some source of inspiration, when my eyes rested on someone's coat and garish velvet hat, left on the back of a nearby chair. Did I dare take them? I hesitated for only a moment, for I was in it now, and felt I had to pursue my quarry by any means necessary. Quickly, I exchanged the coat and hat with my own and stalked off in the direction Reynolds had gone, weaving through the crowd and doing my best to avoid attracting attention to myself. At that moment, someone grabbed me by the arm and I was whirled around to find myself face to face with a gentleman with a waxed moustache and an angry expression on his face.

"Pardon me," he said, "but I believe you are wearing my things."

"Oh," said I, "I beg your pardon! My mistake, I'm sure. A little too much to drink, you know."

"There you are, old boy!"

Sherlock Holmes, carrying my own coat and hat, emerged from a group of amused spectators.

"Oh, old chap, there you go again!" Holmes helped me out of my borrowed clothes and tossed them to their bewildered owner. "A thousand apologies. No harm meant, I'm sure. He gets like this, you know."

Holmes took my arm and led me toward the door.

"Not to worry, we'll be home soon enough. Oh, you will feel dreadful in the morning, don't you know?"

As I was led away, I looked behind me. My eyes met those of Theodore Reynolds, glaring hatefully.

Holmes and I made our way out to the road, where our cabby from earlier was waiting to take us back to Baker Street.

"I suppose you deserve some credit for your initiative tonight," laughed Holmes, as the carriage lurched forward. "I had anticipated a number of possible eventualities, but I must confess that you took me completely by surprise."

"Well, I learned it all from you, Holmes," said I modestly, but really feeling quite proud to have so confounded my old friend.

"It was all very impressive," he said, lighting a cigarette and offering one to me. "It was also, I am bound to say, entirely unnecessary."

"Did you not see Theodore Reynolds there with Catesby?"

"I did indeed," he returned. "Another unexpected development, the significance of which will, I expect, become apparent very soon."

"How so?"

"Our client's unpleasant brother following us from the house. It is no doubt he in that four-wheeler trailing us so closely."

"What do you suppose he intends?"

"Some mischief, no doubt. Let him think himself the hunter! We shall catch him in a trap of our own. We will get out just ahead. There is a yard in that alley which will allow us to get the advantage over young Mr. Reynolds."

We got out of our cab at the point Holmes had indicated. Once Reynolds was close enough for us to be sure he could see us, we turned into a dingy little alley which ran behind a row of houses. Before we had gone very far, Holmes turned left and walked through a gate in a high wooden fence which would hide us from anyone walking in the alley. It was fortunate for us that the snow had frozen over, so that our footprints wouldn't so easily give us away. Our pursuer's footfalls became louder as he approached the gate, and his shadow passed across the dark opening. Holmes tightened his grip on his stick and slipped back into the alley as silently as a spirit. I followed as quietly as I could. Reynolds stopped and seemed to listen for a moment before he began to turn around.

"Perhaps you are looking for us, sir," said Sherlock Holmes.

Reynolds started and stumbled backwards, raising his stick in one hand. The other was in his coat pocket. His back was to the wall, and even in the dark alley I could see his eyes glinting like a trapped tiger's.

"I understand you wished to have a word with me, Mr. Theodore Reynolds," Holmes said. "I would be very interested to speak to you as well, and I suppose this is as good a place as any. What exactly is your business with Arthur Catesby?"

Reynolds gritted his teeth. "You think you can trap me in an alley and interrogate me?" he said, defiantly. "I always heard you caught criminals, Mr. Holmes, but I see you are nothing but a common thug yourself!"

"Interrogate you?" Holmes replied in amusement. "*I* didn't follow *you* into a dark alley with a loaded revolver in my pocket. Kindly do me the courtesy of handing it over, until our interview is concluded."

The young man glared at Holmes. He took his hand from his pocket, and I could see that he was indeed gripping a short-barreled revolver. With sudden determination, he raised it and pulled back the hammer. With the quickness of a striking viper, Holmes's stick struck Reynolds's wrist and the pistol clattered to the ground. At once I snatched it up and emptied the cylinder, shoving the cartridges into my pocket.

"I must say," said I, "you seem quite eager to prevent your missing sister from being found."

"How dare you!" he growled. "You know nothing whatever of the matter."

"What we do know," said Holmes. "is that she is missing, and her family is being blackmailed in her name, and you seem determined to deliberately sabotage an investigation into her whereabouts. One might be forgiven for thinking you preferred her not to be found."

"You are wrong!"

"Then tell us the truth."

"Why should I owe you an explanation?"

"You don't. But I have been engaged to find your sister and put an end to the blackmail, and though I will endeavour to accomplish this with or without your help, hindering me can only increase the danger to her and to your family's fortunes. If that is an outcome you wish to avoid, it would be in your interest to tell me all you know."

"And how am I to know you can be trusted?"

"My young friend, do you suppose I got what little reputation I have by cheating my clients?"

"If, indeed, you wish to preserve your family's honour," I urged the young man, "you would do well to avail yourself of Holmes's assistance." I saw hesitation in his eyes.

"I suppose . . . I suppose you are right. But surely you understand, if any of this were to come out . . . ."

"I assure you, the situation has been fully explained to us," Holmes replied. "Is that why you were with Catesby tonight?"

He nodded.

"Arthur Catesby was one of her closest associates – I hesitate to call him her friend – and I felt sure that if anyone knew where she is, he would, whatever he may say to the contrary."

"Did you learn anything?" Holmes asked. The young man shook his head despondently.

"Nothing at all. Catesby always took a liking to me, though of course his feelings of camaraderie weren't reciprocated. I therefore thought that I had a fairly good chance of convincing him to let me in on any schemes he may be hatching, for he's a loose-lipped braggart. But all his talk was of the girl Margaret Ackroyd, or else his own disgraceful 'art', as he calls it."

"I commend your effort," said Holmes, "though I cannot do the same for your methods."

"What have you found then?"

"Well, for instance I 'm firmly convinced that Catesby has nothing whatever to do with the blackmail."

"That seems incredible to me, Mr. Holmes! Who else could it be?"

"It happens that I now possess both the name and whereabouts of the blackmailer."

Both Reynolds and I were caught off guard by this pronouncement.

"What! Tell me!" cried young Reynolds.

"That I will not do just yet," replied Holmes. "It will not do to act rashly. But if you and your sister will join us in Baker Street at eleven o'clock tomorrow, I expect I shall have good news for you."

"I suppose I must do things your way, Mr. Holmes. It has done me no good to distrust you so far. It isn't easy for me to admit I've made a mistake, but I think now that Violet had the right idea, after all. I certainly owe her an apology."

"The ability to admit one's mistakes is the beginning of wisdom," said Holmes. "Do not berate yourself. Instead, examine your actions and learn from them. This the key to perfection in art, science, and life. And now, gentlemen, we have been standing in the alleyway long enough. There is nothing more to be done tonight. I propose we return to our respective homes and gather our strength for tomorrow."

There were many questions that I wished to ask during our return to Baker Street, but clearly Holmes was deep in thought, and I learned no more that night.

Chapter IV – A Conclusion

Christmas Eve dawned as white and lovely as one could wish, and even the London clouds were unable wholly to blot out the deep, exquisite blue of the sky. After I completed my toilet, I went down to the sitting room to find that Holmes had evidently risen quite early, or had simply not slept at all. He was bright eyed, however, with the cheerful attitude which came upon him when he foresaw a solution near at hand.

"Good morning, Watson!" said he with aplomb. "You are just in time for an excellent breakfast before the conclusion of our little drama."

"And yet, you still have not told me what occurred at Catesby's house last night, or how you were able to find me so quickly."

"As for how I found you," said Holmes, "when I left the house and saw you were not there, a quick glance at your boot prints disappearing where they met the cab's tracks told me what had happened. You had already been gone for a quarter-of-an-hour, but I knew the cab would be going to Thomas Ackroyd's address, which is no more than two miles from Catesby's. For a four-wheeler to travel between the two points, it would of necessity have to cross at least two busy streets or go out of the way by another half-mile. Either would cause a significant delay. Meanwhile an active man on foot, if he knew the route, could cut through yards, back alleys, and mews in more or less a straight line, and so reach his destination in half the time it would take a carriage."

"Wonderful!" I ejaculated.

"It was no difficult feat for a man who has made a special study of the city," he demurred. "I told our cabbie where to meet me and set off."

"And your interview with Catesby's maid?"

"Come now, Watson, we've no time for more lengthy explanations. The sooner you finish your breakfast, the sooner you will witness the conclusion of our investigation. After, if any questions remain, I shall happily answer them."

Holmes himself ate nothing, for when occupied by a case he seldom spared the time and energy for food, regarding it as an imposition rather than a necessity. After I had finished and we had fortified ourselves against the bitter winter air, we summoned a cab and set off for our final destination. The hansom carried us ponderously through the icy streets, past the snow-covered lamps and rooftops, and the joyful throngs who passed excitedly by on their way to see their loved ones. I felt a pang of grief then, remembering my dear Mary and the too-few blessed Christmases we shared, and thinking of joys which I felt would never be mine again. I thought also of the strange chance by which, while millions of teeming souls would enjoy a day of rest and simple pleasure, we should be on our way to confront a blackmailer and discover Beatrice Reynolds's uncertain fate.

At length, we alighted onto a dirty street lined by unkempt row houses. I followed Holmes as he strode purposefully down the street, looking at the house numbers as he passed. Finding the correct door, he knocked upon it sharply with his stick. It was opened by a short, plump woman who could not be much older than forty, but who had been aged prematurely by a lifetime of drink, self-neglect, and ill usage. She blinked at each of us in turn.

"Can I help you, gentlemen?" said she, slurring her words slightly. I detected the distinctive scent of strong spirits as she spoke.

"My name is Sherlock Holmes," said my friend, "and I presume I'm addressing Mrs. Dorothy Peasley?"

She nodded.

"Mrs. Peasley, we would like to speak with you. May we come in?"

"Depends what you want to speak about."

"As a matter of fact, we were hoping to discuss the current whereabouts of Miss Beatrice Reynolds."

The woman started and hurried to slam the door, but Holmes stepped forward and barely kept it from closing with his boot.

"Mrs. Peasley, we are not the police. We only wish to speak with you."

"I don't know nothing about it, I tell you! Leave me be!"

"Holmes," I cried, "listen!" On the other side of the door, there was a gasping sound and then a thud as of something heavy hitting the floor. Holmes pushed the door open, and we saw that Mrs. Peasley had collapsed. I hurried to her side and examined her.

"She has only fainted," said I. "The sudden shock was too much, no doubt. Help me raise her up."

Together, we propped her into a sitting position. I drew out my brandy flask, though I had doubts about its efficacy on one so inured to alcohol. It did revive her a little, to my relief, and we kept her propped up as she returned to her senses.

"I'm a doctor," said I, attempting to soothe her. "Stay calm, give yourself time to recover."

"What . . . what do you want with me?"

"We're looking for Miss Reynolds, as we said," answered Holmes, as I helped her into a chair.

"Don't know any Miss Reynolds."

"I am afraid it is no use," said Holmes, firmly but not unkindly. "There is very little about the business I do not know."

"And what is it that you think you know?"

"I know that you were formerly employed by Mr. Arthur Catesby as a cook. I know that despite the fair pay earned through that employment, you were so much in want of money that you resorted to begging from your acquaintances, and when they refused to help you, you began stealing from your employer. You were caught looking through his private papers and summarily dismissed. But you managed to take some of those papers away with you, didn't you?"

She looked defiantly into his eyes and read there the hopelessness of her position. She sighed heavily and hung her head.

"Lord in heaven, sir," said she, too exhausted to protest, "I see there's no use denying it. I won't say it was right of me, sir, but I had no choice. You must understand."

The pitiful creature began to weep, with great tears streaming down her red cheeks. She reached for a bottle on the nearby table, but I picked it up and withheld it, lest further drink should render her insensible.

"Help us understand," I urged.

She opened her mouth to speak, but at that moment I heard floorboards creak above us and a man appeared on the stairs. My eyes were drawn at once to the medical bag he carried. He looked curiously at us before addressing Mrs. Peasley.

"Ma'am, I've finished my examination. You may summon the undertaker."

Despite the woman's crimes, I was horrified to discover that we had intruded at such a delicate time.

"My sister," she explained between sobs after the coroner had departed. "She's been sick for a year, and I've been helping her take care of her little ones. Her man up and left, so I'm the only one who could work. But my wage wasn't enough to feed four and buy medicine. What was I to do? Let my sister go without medicine? Let her children starve? When I asked Mr. Catesby for help, he laughed at me! You see, I had no choice."

"But what use would his papers be to you?" I asked.

"I took some of the master's papers with me, thinking to sell them, for I've heard there are people who'll buy such things. But when I looked at them, I found these letters from the Reynolds girl, complaining about how hard it was to live in a big house with her rich family, and servants to look after her wants, and how it was all so terrible that she was going to run away. So I got the notion to write those letters, for why should folk be so rich they cannot appreciate their luck, while my poor sister's children go to bed hungry?"

"How did you know the real Beatrice would not interfere with your scheme?"

In answer, Mrs. Peasley rose and walked over to a cupboard from which she pulled a bundle of papers. She looked through them a moment before picking one out and handing it to Holmes.

"It says she has arrived safely in New York," said he. "Your intuition does you credit, Watson. She's staying with – Ha!" He gave a cry of exaltation.

Mrs. Peasley retrieved an envelope from the cupboard, from which she pulled a number of banknotes.

"You'll want these too, I expect," said she, holding out the notes for my friend. He looked at them thoughtfully.

"Your sister had three children?"

"Yes, sir. Though I suppose they're mine now."

"How old?"

"Six, four, and three, sir."

Holmes reached out and gently pushed the woman's hand away.

"It's a pity that I was unable to recover the money my clients have already lost," said he. "They will have to be content with the recovery of these letters, and my assurance that the blackmail letters will cease. Permanently."

"Yes, sir," said Mrs. Peasley, whose eyes once again welled with tears.

Holmes looked at her for a long moment. Then he took a little lead pencil from his pocket and wrote something on the back of one of his cards.

"If you can muster the strength to put down the bottle for good, go to this establishment in Whitechapel. Tell them you have experience as a cook, and that Sherlock Holmes sent you. You have been given a reprieve. For the sake of your sister's children, do not squander it. Happy Christmas."

Without another word, he turned, and I followed him out into the snowy lane.

"I understand why you did it," said I as our cab carried back to the warmth of our Baker Street rooms, "but don't you think that Reynolds family will want to pursue their money?"

"They will have to do it without help from me," he answered. "I was retained to find Miss Beatrice and discover the source of the blackmail letters. I have fulfilled my commission."

"And made yourself accessory to a crime."

He smiled.

"Yes, I shall have much to answer for, if I am ever put in the dock."

"I assume that it was Catesby's maid who told you about Mrs. Peasley's dismissal?"

"Quite so. She confirmed the suspicion which had been growing in my mind that a servant was responsible for the blackmail."

"What gave you that idea?"

"It was clear that the blackmailer possessed intimate knowledge of the Reynolds family's private troubles. How might a woman in her position gain such knowledge? From Catesby? A distinct possibility, but as I mentioned before, our letter writer would be an unlikely ally of his, and to involve a servant in such a scheme would be to put himself in that person's power. From Miss Beatrice herself? Possibly, but that would not account for the close imitation of her handwriting, which indicated either a high degree of familiarity with it or access to sufficient examples to reconstruct it. It would not be difficult for a clever servant to learn her handwriting from her correspondence, so I took the possibility quite seriously. Our client's insistence that the letter writer could not be a member of their household staff didn't completely rule out the possibility, for I knew that Beatrice was in frequent correspondence with Catesby, and samples of her writing would be at his house as well. My reasoning proved to be reasonably correct, though I couldn't be sure until I spoke to the maid."

"That didn't take so long to explain. Surely you could have told me over breakfast."

Holmes burst out laughing.

"I prefer to do things in my own way, as you know well. Here we are! And by the footprints outside our door, I judge that Mr. Reynolds and his sister await us upstairs."

"Mr. Holmes," said Miss Reynolds after he had related, with several omissions, the conclusion of our investigation, "I must confess that this ended better than I dared hope. The nightmare over, and Beatrice safe in

New York! Whatever mischief she gets into now, it is unlikely to embarrass Father from across the Atlantic. You and Dr. Watson have both deserved well of our family, and have my personal gratitude."

"And mine," concurred Theodore Reynolds. "Send me your bill, and I will pay it myself."

Holmes gave a little bow. "I am pleased you are satisfied with the outcome."

"There is one thing more I should like to know," said our client. "If Catesby was not the blackmailer, then who was the 'C' who sent the telegram to Beatrice?"

In answer, Holmes produced the letter Mrs. Peasely had shown us that morning. Miss Reynolds frowned as she read it, then her features suddenly changed and she smiled broadly.

"Of course! It was Cousin Calvin! Why did it not occur to me before? Good day to you, Mr. Holmes, Dr. Watson, and Happy Christmas!"

"And now, Watson," said Holmes once our guests had left, "let us enjoy a well-deserved day of rest by the fire, and the promise of Mrs. Hudson's Christmas pudding tonight."

The Twelve Days
by I.A. Watson

The Twelfth Day of Christmas my true love sent to me:
Twelve lords a-leaping,
Eleven ladies dancing,
Ten drummers drumming,
Nine pipers piping,
Eight maids a-milking,
Seven swans a-swimming,
Six geese a-laying,
Five gold rings,
Four colly birds,
Three French hens,
Two turtle doves,
And a partridge in a pear tree.

Traditional Folk Song
Version from Robert S. Salmon,
Notes & Queries v. 12 (July-Dec. 1855) [1]

Christmas of 1894 seemed likely to be a melancholy time. On the one hand, Holmes was alive, returned after three years from seeming destruction over the Reichenbach Falls in his death-struggle with Professor Moriarty. We were reunited in our cosy familiar rooms on Baker Street with Mrs. Hudson as if he had never been torn from our lives. On the other, I was only back in my old bachelor digs because of the passing of my wife Mary, and Holmes understood how the shadows of that brief, sweet marriage must crowd in on me during the festive season.

We determined to pass the time quietly. Holmes was still catching up on his researches, amending and updating certain monographs for republication. I had again taken up my pen and was revisiting several of his old cases whose accounts I had previously not had the heart to complete.

Nor did the weather encourage us to venture out much. The winter of 1894 brought with it "the great snow" that had Britain at a standstill, and in the first months of 1895 closed the streets and port of London, but as the feast of Yule approached the weather had not yet become a national phenomenon and was confined to simply framing the city as a quaint Christmas painting. Warm log fires seemed more attractive than bleak trudges over snowscapes.

Holmes and I weren't entirely sedentary. There had been some unpleasantness regarding the 'Boulevard Assassin' Huret and his legacy, and an investigation into the odd cargo of the *ZM*[2] *Freisland*. But for once Holmes was content to be home with his books and his odious chemicals, and I found solace in our customary routine.

The Feast of Our Lord's Nativity passed quietly, save for one curious matter. That morning Mrs. Hudson discovered on our doorstep a weather-sealed waxed package addressed *"To all at 221b"*. It contained a rather battered second-hand copy of the compiled *Monthly Chronicle of North-Country Lore and Legend* for 1888, a doorstop-thick six-hundred-page collection.[3] There was no sender's address. Preoccupied with coal-tobacco stains, Holmes set the book aside.

The day after Christmas, when regular postal services resumed, Holmes received a second package with no return address, this time a small carton, a three-and-a-half-inch cube wrapped in festive red paper and tied with gold thread. He examined it carefully and drew conclusions. "Shop-wrapped with a clerk's assured technique. The label is written with good regular penmanship from someone taught at one of the better council schools in the last thirty years – possibly the same clerk who made up the parcel."

Holmes sniffed and shook the box, then reached for a letter knife and neatly sliced open the bottom of the wrapping paper to remove the three-inch red cardboard cube within. This proved to be a crepe-paper-stuffed toybox, containing a small but exquisite clockwork monkey in the figure of a gentleman with top hat and tails, complete with monocle. When wound up and set off, the tiny toy would clap its hands and perform a somersault.

I set down my pen and looked at the object. "Who might send you such a thing, and why?"

"The figure is a quality item," Holmes commented. "The manufacturer's stamp on the base provenances it as the work of Mssrs. Hoopin and Shanderwig of Newcastle-upon-Tyne. The quality of the packaging suggests its purchase at one of the superior toyshops. The mechanism works perfectly, but I don't discern by the movement or appearance of the simulacrum any further indication of why it should be sent to me."

As Holmes and I discussed the matter, Mrs. Hudson sent our page up with another package that had just arrived by courier. It proved to be a second, identical simian gentleman, save that the box and packaging were blue.

"We are to have a parade, then," Holmes declared when a third, purple-boxed clockwork model arrived a quarter-hour later.

All in all, the Feast of Steven brought us no less than a full dozen of the tiny wind-up monkeys, but no explanation at all.

That was but the start, however. The 27th of December saw the delivery of different presents, in the form of a series of three-inch high cut-crystal nymphs frolicking on their coloured-glass stems. They had originated from a rather exclusive glassware shop on the Champs-Élysées. Throughout the day we received ten of the objects. An eleventh and last arrived broken, snapped into three pieces.

"Now you *must* explain what is going on, Holmes," I insisted. "Why should we suddenly be swarmed with mechanical monkeys and frolicking nymphs?"

"I'm not yet sure," Holmes confessed. He fingered the damaged figurine that I had assumed had suffered from postal transit. "This statuette was deliberately snapped at neck and knee," he noted.

"But why?"

"I believe we're being set a puzzle."

I rather expected a twelfth nymph to arrive to match our previous collection of metallic monkeys, but no such gift was forthcoming.

On the 28th, I rose to discover that Holmes had distressed Mrs. Hudson by covering our dining table with pieces of dismantled mechanical monkey. The hop-frogging top-hatted figures were each carefully disassembled on separate sheets of foolscap as carefully as a watchmaker might lay out the components of a timepiece.

"I made an error," Holmes confessed to me. "Not yet understanding the nature of our presents, I didn't take proper note of the order in which these springing mechanicals were delivered to us. Careless of me."

"All the leaping monkeys look the same," I objected. "Well, six have black bases and six green, but otherwise identical – "

"But they are not!" my friend told me triumphantly. "See, Watson!"

He held his jeweller's lens for me to observe the tiny letters engraved on the inner mechanism. The moulded tin cowl of the little simians had covered the marks, but each device bore a single character, some different from others.

"Four *E*'s, two *L*'s, two *T*'s, an *O*, an *R*, an *S*, and an *M*," I noted.

"An anagram," Holmes speculated. "Added after manufacture, to convey a message to us. I might have made this simpler for myself if I had only detailed the order of arrival of our engraved toys."

I tested out a few letter combinations, though there must have been thousands. "'*Let Eels Metro*'," I tried. "'*Lore Settle Me. Emotes Retell. Toll Tree Seem. Melee Lets Rot . . . .*'"

Holmes shook his head. "You are forgetting the origin of the second set of gifts. Our prancing nymphs were dispatched from a nation where English does not rule."

"From Paris, yes, so . . . the message is in French?" That seemed rather like cheating to me.

My friend passed over another of his foolscap sheets, on which had had simply written '*Elle est morte.*' She is dead.

"Who is dead?" I demanded, baffled. "The broken glass nymph?"

"We haven't yet been told that. Ah – there is the post," Holmes advised me, hearing our page thundering to the letterbox downstairs. "Let us see what drummers await our attention."

"Drummers?"

Holmes kept his counsel as our mail was brought to us.

That day we received five calendars, card-backed with ribbon loops to allow wall-hanging. These particular and identical gifts were rather useless though, since they were for the year 1891. They were evidently old promotional items for a music garden in Cologne. The right hand side of the landscape sheet had the days and months printed in German, whilst the left contained a schedule of fixtures, below a drawing depicting some operatic event in which a fellow in doublet and feathered cap was jumping onto a table, presumably to begin his solo.

The whole layout was indeed flanked by full-length drawings of two Negro drummer boys, figged out in Oriental costume, standing at the ready to offer a salute.

"Why we should want five out-of-date advertisements for the Claudian Musikgarten on Gartenstraße?" I puzzled.

Holmes examined the envelopes in which the calendars had arrived. "These were postmarked from Germany. Additional local postage has been added and the packages re-addressed. The original address handwriting is Teutonic – note also the use of *M.* rather than *Mr.* as the salutation. A second hand has added the new label and directed it to us in such a timely manner."

"You have evidently seen the pattern and understood the message. How did you know to expect drummers?"

Holmes ventured a smile as he reached for his tobacco. "We are having our noses tweaked, Watson. I shall make a prediction: Our next gifts tomorrow will be trumpet players, bagpipers – wind musicians of some sort – and there will be nine of them." He indicated the cloth where he had arrayed his store of gifts. "We are being treated to a Christmas mystery, old friend. Or should I say a 'Twelve Days of Christmas' mystery?"

"The Twelve Days?"

"You recall the old children's memory game?" Holmes checked with me. "Each player sings a round of the song, adding a new line at the beginning and repeating each line that has come before. There are forfeits if the previous content is not correctly recollected."

"'*The first day of Christmas my true love gave to me* . . .'" I hummed.

"That's the fellow! Now bethink the countdown of the lines. Twelve Lords a-Leaping . . . ."

"The clockwork monkeys with the toppers!"

"Eleven Ladies Dancing, and now Ten Drummers Drumming. Nor did our mystery begin on the Feast of Steven. You recall Mrs. Hudson's book on Christmas Day?" Walter Scott's *Monthly Chronicle of North-Country Lore and Legend* still lay atop the book-stack beside Holmes's chair. "Refer to pages 41 and 42, the article by Mr. John Stokoe entitled 'A North Country Garland of Song'."

I did as bidden and discovered that the entire folk-song was printed out there, with music. "We were sent warning of the conundrum to come!"

"And of the variation of the song which seems to be chosen. There are several versions extant, but this is the most prevalent. The folk-song is believed to have originated in the area around Newcastle-upon-Tyne, where it was first recorded, and from whence Hoopin and Shanderwig, our clockwork monkey manufactures, also hail."

"Someone is playing a joke upon us, then?"

Holmes frowned. "Possibly. But it is a very elaborate jest."

"What else could it be?"

Holmes fingered the anomalous ballerina figurine that was snapped in three. "Ten pristine statuettes and an eleventh deliberately shattered. What harm has befallen the last? What has she to do with Cologne's Claudian Musikgarten in 1891?"

"For that matter, why the lords and drummers?"

My friend turned back to our growing collection with an odd enthusiasm, but shadowed by a frown.

"I am concerned that this is more serious warning than a festive game. Tomorrow I shall know."

I thought back to childhood rounds of the children's chorus and calculated that it would next be the turn of Nine Pipers Piping.[4] "What shall we know tomorrow?" I wondered.

"We shall know whether we are investigating a murder."

The 29th of December saw the delivery of more packages, nine tins of Edinburgh toffee, the strong sticky jaw-breaking type so beloved of the Hibernian people. Indeed, these particular confectionaries came in handsome containers decorated with a picture of a kilted bagpiper on the walls of Edinburgh Castle. The name "*McArgus's Highland Taffy*" was printed on the lid with the motto, "*Will ye nae ha'e a chew?*"

I tasted the confection once Holmes assured me there was no poison involved. It was good, but terribly chewy.

"We have our pipers, then," I mentioned as Holmes examined the containers and contents in his more forensic manner. "Perhaps you might expand upon your speculation yesterday that these odd gifts somehow presage a murder?"

"I shall certainly know tomorrow, when I receive the results of certain enquiries I have set in hand. In the meantime I shall summarise what I have discovered through wiring to the Continent."

"I should welcome it."

Holmes had commissioned research from colleagues and correspondents in Europe. He unsealed a packet of documents wrapped in brown paper with several foreign stamps upon it. This proved to be a collection of clippings and document facsimiles, most of them German and French, collated by Holmes's overseas correspondents, hastened to us by express mail.

"You know that I occasionally use local investigators to extend the reaches of my investigations. I sent an agent round to the Claudian Musikgarten in Cologne regarding its former programme."

"The 1891 calendar," I understood.

"And to ask about the plume-hatted swain who is illustrated thereon. My correspondent informs me that he is meant to represent Don Giovanni, from *Il dissoluto punito, ossia il Don Giovanni*, 'The Rake Punished'. The Claudian put on a performance of Mozart and De Ponte's famous work in February of '91, as you can see from the itinerary on the calendar itself. Enclosed with these documents is a programme of the actual production."

I accepted the small deckle-edged brochure but it told me little.

"You will note the cast," Holmes suggested. "In addition to the significant soprano roles of Donna Anna, Donna Elvira, and Zerlina, there are eight girls credited in the chorus, singers, and dancers."

"Three plus eight. Eleven Ladies Dancing?"

"Indeed. Here is a lithotype of the company, dressed for the opera. Our attention is being drawn to those chorus dancers – or to one in particular."

"Whom you suspect to have been murdered?"

"Perhaps. I predict that it is this one, fourth from the left, on whom our attention should be focussed."

I looked at the tiny blurry face of a sweet-looking young ingénue in a feathery ballet costume. "Amelie Cornemuseur?" I read from the subscripted text. "Why her?"

"Come, Watson. The young lady's stage name, *Cornemuseur*. Where is your French? A *cornemuseur* is a piper."

"Pipers piping?"

"And might we insult your Scots relatives by confusing a braw piper's kilt with a knee-length ballet skirt? May we indulge in some schoolboy punning and infer from our present of toffee that she got into some sticky situation?"

"So the mystery centres upon that girl. On the basis of one fractured glass statue, you believe some harm has come to her?"

"On the contrary. My basis for such a hypothesis is now strengthened by the fact that she hasn't been seen for two years, and her whereabouts are presently unknown."

"Ah."

Holmes had anticipated the pipers. Of course he had made additional enquiries. "I am awaiting the results of further researches."

Holmes was up before first post, and when I joined him at breakfast he had already stacked up the day's correspondence in the toast rack and was perusing the first of it.

"Milk-maids?" I enquired.

"More ladies dancing first," Holmes told me. "My agents have afforded me with such background information and present whereabouts of the Claudian's chorus as may be quickly discovered. I haven't yet come across any sinister difficulty that has befallen other cast members."

I looked with sympathy at the bright young dancer in the smudged foreign print – the missing Amelie Cornemuseur.

There was one obvious item in our post pile that Holmes hadn't yet addressed. "Are you not going to open the card-reinforced package with the French postmark?" I suggested.

"Once I have finished with these notes I shall. You have time to assault the kedgeree and kippers, and then we shall assay the envelope together."

Once my toast-and-seafood needs were assuaged and Holmes had caught up on his correspondence, we made such an exploration of the letter from Marseilles.

This time Holmes had been sent a small framed art picture, the sort of cheap block-printed smears that are sold for a few Francs to tourists on the Left Bank and end up on coffee house walls to give them a supposedly-sophisticated veneer. In bright primary impressionist strokes, it depicted three semi-clad dancers doing the can-can dance that is so popular in the French music-halls, with a pair of top-hatted, evening-suited, monocle-wearing admirers proffering banknotes in adulation.

"Maids a-milking," I concluded, seeing the cynical meaning of the message. "But shouldn't there be more of them?"

Holmes examined the picture closely, then opened the frame and removed the back. Five postcards fell out and scattered over our breakfast table.

These were postcards of the French sort, which are found in officers' messes and company barracks everywhere. They featured young women who have had difficulty with their wardrobe but have overcome their shyness to pose for a photographer all the same. I need not describe them further. Now we had eight maids, though likely not maidens.

"A-ha," Holmes said, sadly rather than triumphantly. He tapped his finger on one of the tinted images. "Amelie Cornemuseur. Perhaps she is found?"

A telegram to the Marseilles printer of the postcards elicited the information that the pictures were now more than eighteen months old. Other poses of the same model were now sold out. Only the tamest remained. Perhaps sir might be more interested in a fresh collection of new art images featuring the latest examples of nubile loveliness? Alas, he couldn't now place sir in contact with the particular girl in that photograph, nor with any of the other four in the similar images, but he would be delighted to make introduction to any number of sprightly young Marseillaises who would be pleased to meet a generous English gentleman. Or, if sir already had a particular model with whom he enjoyed a special arrangement, then a private sitting to sir's requirements could be conducted, depicting any number of intriguing scenarios. Such had been the case with the *jolie jeune femme* who had arrested sir's attention previously.

"It's disgusting, Holmes," I fumed at the greasy chap's response. The fellow was lucky he was across the Channel from me.

"The information that Miss Cornemuseur was *brought* to the photographer is relevant. I shall need to seek more clarification from this unpleasant fellow on that issue."

"If it requires going to France to take the fellow by the collar and shake him like a puppy, then I'm for it."

"I think for now we shall confine ourselves to the telegram. We have other lines of enquiry to also pursue."

"And our presents are being delivered here," I conceded. The weather wasn't conducive to a visit to the Continent, or anywhere else.

Holmes soberly regarded the sad cheap postcard of the lost girl. "It seems as though Amelie fell on hard times. I have traced some of her history. She was sixteen at the time of the *Don Giovanni* production, and had been in the chorus at the Claudian Musikgarten for three months. In June of '91 she moved to another position, as part of a travelling troupe that toured through Belgium and Northern France. In May of '92 she left the chorus for a position at the Théâtre de la Faubourg Saint-Denis in Paris."

"She was doing well, then?"

"Until four weeks later, when she was dismissed for theft. I am waiting to hear from the management about the details of the charge, but they seem reluctant to discuss it. The police weren't involved. That is the last record of Mam'selle Cornemuseur – except for the postcard."

I stared out of our window at a bleak and snow-choked street. "What can we do now for that poor soul, after so long and so far away?"

"That is the mystery. Why are we being involved, and why now? Why in this manner?" Holmes joined his fingertips together and pressed them to his lips, intrigued.

At least he was enjoying his Christmas presents. I said as much, and he had to confess it.

"I have been making some enquiries about the origins of our strange packages. I contacted the toy shop on Bond Street that dispatched the leaping monkeys, and the china and glass shop on the Champs-Élysées from which the dancing nymphs were commissioned. In each case, the purchase and precise delivery instructions were made via letter and postal money order. The client signed himself *K. Kringle*, which is probably pseudonymous. A kringle is a knotted Scandinavian pastry, but in this context is more likely drawn from the American tradition of the Pennsylvanian '*Kriskinkle*', the jolly gift-giving avatar of Yule who rewards deserving children in the tradition of Clement Clark Moore's poem." [5]

"You cannot then trace the person who is sending these packages, these clues?"

"He has so far gone to a good deal of trouble to prevent it. However, we might infer that our benefactor knows, or thinks he knows, something of a crime which has taken place. For an unknown reason our correspondent doesn't wish to lay information directly to the police or to speak plainly to us. Fear of reprisal? An accomplice's guilt? Conflict between betrayal of a loved one and outrage at his deed? For whatever purpose, we are being fed pieces of a puzzle which we are now challenged to assemble. And we shall."

"Is this all some cunning ploy to make a fool of the great detective?" I worried. "Or might the murderer himself be taunting you?"

"Either are possibilities," Holmes allowed, "but I think . . . I cannot put a reason to it, disturbingly, but I *feel* . . . as though the gifts are well-meant."

He shook his head to overcome his weakness of reasoning. "We shall perhaps know better tomorrow, when he receive our Seven Swans a-Swimming."

There were no parcels delivered on New Year's Eve, but instead we first received a postcard from Paris, mailed first class the previous day for delivery via the overnight mail boat.

"Addressed in an elderly woman's hand who learned her letters late in life," Holmes determined from the handwriting.

Fortunately, this card didn't contain any *risqué* print unsuitable for the post, but rather an image of the Statue of Liberty – or so I thought until I saw the Eiffel Tower looming behind it. Holmes identified the casting as the quarter-scale replica of "Liberty Enlightening the World" on the Île aux Cygnes that protects the Pont de Grenelle in the River Seine.[6]

"I thought we were to expect seven swans. '*Île aux Cygnes*' means '*Isle of Swans*' in French, of course, but we have only one picture and no actual birds."

"We may receive additional examples of *Cygnus cygnus* in further deliveries. We are being taught patience – and anticipation."

"And the message on this card?" I pondered, "'*Wish you were here*' – in English."

"We shall add it to our stack of conundrums."

At noon we had a response from that Marseilles printer regarding the arrangements that had been made for Amelie's modelling session. Evidently she was one of a number of "special commissions" which he had received from the same source over the last four years. He couldn't identify the lady who arranged them, except that she was "a woman of experience" from Paris, which we decoded as meaning a madam of a house of ill repute. There had been eight such commissions, all of delightful free-spirited *ingénues*. Certain postcards from some of the series were still available in stock if sir would care to purchase copies.

Evidently mistaking Holmes's enquiries as interest in such services, his message went into lurid detail about the kind of photographs that he might similarly arrange for a model of our choice. Decency forbids me from outlining the appalling possibilities that he suggested, to which Miss Cornemuseur and others brought to him had been subjected.

By return, Holmes contacted the Gallic enquiry agent Le Brun, whom he had engaged in Continental work before, to take train to Marseilles and make personal enquiries about the seedy printer.

"And give the blaggard a thump from me," I muttered additional instruction.

Last post brought another Christmas-wrapped gift through our letterbox. It turned out to be a leather note-case wallet, sent from Maidstone. Instead of banknotes, the contents were the other six anticipated swan pictures, unstamped, unwritten postcards of various places in Europe. For my satisfaction, each of the images included an actual swan or cygnet, however small.

Even Holmes's copious store of information might have been taxed to identify the scenes on these other cards, but fortunately the locations of each picture were printed on the backs. Hence we were treated to views of Lac d'Aiguebelette in Savoy, of the River Marne near Charenton outside Paris, of the Canal du Midi where it runs through Toulouse, of Argenat on the Dordogne, and engravings of the River Loire and of the shore at Bremerhaven in the German Empire.

All the places were in France save for one.

"What are we to make of this?" I fretted.

"Why firstly, that though collected internationally, these cards were assembled and sent to us from the Thames Valley. The parcel was addressed by a fellow of middle years with a flourish to his penmanship, but not the regularity of a clerk or academic and not school-taught, I would estimate. Postage was affixed rather carelessly. The stamps are set unevenly. The parcel is sealed with spirit gum, an unusual choice. I might venture a theatrical gentleman?"

My friend regarded his new clues with his magnifying lens. "The wallet is of fine quality. It bears the mark of Smythson's of Bond Street. [7] I shall pursue the purchase, but I suspect Mr. Kringle might have made another cash or postal order payment."

"The swans, though. What do they mean?"

"That will require additional telegraphy, I fear." Holmes frowned at the cards, as if worried that he might be missing something. "What is different about the Isle of Swans postcard, that it doesn't contain an actual swan? Is that card, which came first and separately, of special significance? The key to the rest? And the wallet, which contained postcards rather than money . . . Is it more than a container and actually part of the clue? Why does our correspondent wish me to be there? What might I discover if it were possible? Or had once been possible?"

He lost interest in speculative conversation and bent to pen the telegrams he needed to urgently send to overseas correspondents and to his newspaper-story clippers.

New Year's Day brought heavier snow, delaying the post and making travel in the capital difficult. Yet we still received an article, delivered by an heroic courier on a sledge. Never doubt the versatility and ingenuity of the common Londoner, nor the hardy determination of the humble postman. I tipped the fellow generously.

We had scarcely received the heavy brown-papered book-parcel up to our rooms when Holmes broke off from his examination of the outer wrapper to say, "We are about to have a visit, Watson! A solicitor and his clerk."

Holmes had a view of the slush-choked street and had evidently observed the brave carriage that had negotiated the banked snow to deliver passengers to our doorstep. I had witnessed Holmes's instant deductions about our callers before but it always impressed.

"The older gentleman in the snow-frosted top hat is accompanied by a subordinate who carries his legal briefcase. Small hairs from a peruke have stuck to the elder's coat where he habitually stuffs his legal wig into his right pocket. His strides are long but irregular. He is unhappy to be dragged from the comfort of his home for the journey. His boots are new but ill-suited for the weather and his left heel is leaking. His assistant is wary of his master's temper and fearful for his position."

Our bell rung. Our page brought up the calling card of Mr. Brunor Cassoway Q.C., of one of the superior Grey's Inn legal firms, who required to speak with us without delay.

"On January 1st," I commented. It was an odd time to receive a visit from a silk. [8]

"Indeed." Holmes agreed. "Let us face the onslaught of the law, shall we?"

Our visitors were shown in. "Mr. Holmes," Mr. Cassoway began, before we could even make him welcome or proffer a drink, "I am instructed by my clients to insist that you forbear from your present impertinent investigations into the matter of the late Amelie Cornemuseur."

"Ah." Holmes sat back in satisfaction, delighted at the implied threat. "Mr. Cassoway, perhaps you might unfold the urgency that brings a man of business such as yourself to our door on the first day of the year, in such inclement conditions?"

"The message I impart is grave, sir!"

"Grave and ill-advised, sir. Name your clients. Outline the basis on which they might issue such insistence, and adduce the reasons for believing that such will deter my curiosity."

"My clients value their privacy. However, they are quite willing to make themselves known if you continue with your mischief in these enquiries. They have sufficient resources to make you regret it."

Holmes's eyes twinkled with delight. "What do you imagine will happen, sir, if I don't desist in discovering the young lady whom you name?"

Mr. Cassoway's own eyes narrowed unpleasantly. "I *imagine* that you will face *consequences* – legal, social, financial, reputational, possibly even physical. Do not underestimate the severity of my caution, Mr. Holmes. You are not untouchable."

"Now see here – !" I began, but Holmes lifted a finger to curb my ire.

"I have been threatened before," my friend observed. "Here I remain."

Cassoway's jaw tightened. Finding that Holmes didn't shy from his imperious stare, he instead produced a folded sheet of paper from his pocket and handed it across. "Here is a list of names that you wouldn't wish to disturb," he said coldly.

Holmes received the list and perused it.

"There is nothing more to say about the dead girl that you have made enquiries about," the solicitor instructed us. "She was a sad *putain* who took her life, as so many girls of that quality eventually do. Do not expect to profit from stirring up artificial scandal about her."

"If Mam'selle Cornemuseur is indeed dead," I bristled, "then Holmes and I will determine the how and why of it without the permission of you or your arrogant paymasters! And if there is aught has occurred which shouldn't have, be quite sure that we shall not rest until truth is revealed and justice done!"

Cassoway wasn't impressed with me. He sneered and gestured to the list. "There are five names on there. Any one of them could break you at a word. Any of them."

"Five interesting names," Holmes agreed. "I thank you for bringing them to my attention."

He turned the note over and added five more names on the back. "I'll see your five names and throw in five of my own. Only three are crowned heads of Europe. Another is premiere of a foreign power. The last such name . . . well, God bless Her and send her victorious. I have assisted a number of illustrious clients in my time, Mr. Cassoway. Many of them were quite satisfied with the results of my interventions. If there are questions of legal, social, financial, or reputational natures to consider, I shall certainly bear them in mind."

The legal representative blanched a little at Holmes's returned list.

"Good day, sir," Holmes told him. "You have been most helpful in our enquiries."

"I'll be pleased to show you and your clerk out, Cassoway," I added.

I was delighted to assist the fellow onto the icy street, leaking boot and all.

I returned to the warmth of our chambers after seeing Cassoway from Baker Street. "What was that about, do you think?"

"I surmise that somebody has been arrogant and has miscalculated," Holmes replied. "However, I grow more and more convinced that this is a dangerous business. It's certainly no holiday game."

I indicated the book parcel that we had set aside at Cassoway's interruption. "Do you think he saw that there? Or watched as it was delivered?"

"I imagine so. There have been a few odd layabouts grubbing about outside. It's a chilly business for the fellows trying to keep a watch on Baker Street in this kind of weather. An idler can hardly stand around credibly without it being obvious why he's there. Dark clothing stands out against white snow. Carriage traffic has been higher than I might have expected too, in such inclement conditions."

The parcel was bound up with string – household twine, square-knotted and wrapped in common greaseproof paper suitable for winter delivery, with a return address from a Charing Cross bookstore. The package contained six brand-new French copies of the well-known *Histoires ou contes du temps passé, avec des moralités* or *Contes de ma mère l'Oye* (that is, *Stories or Tales from Past Times, with Morals*, or *Mother Goose Tales*).

The top volume had a feather inside as a bookmark – a rare black swan's feather. [9] It kept a place with a handsome full-page illustration plate of the story that began on the opposite sheet: the story of *"Barbe bleue"* - Bluebeard.

"Six geese a-laying," Holmes observed, seeming amused. The ominous visit from Mr. Cassoway had put him in fine spirits. "We are directed then to Mother Goose's morality tale of the woman-murdering nobleman. Interesting."

"Holmes . . . The names of the powerful men who want you to cease puzzling this enigma name . . . Do you believe that one of them might be Amelie's murderer?"

"Perhaps. But we need not jump to conclusions. There are five more days before Twelfth Night, and I have enquiries in hand that will perturb the gentlemen on our visitor's list more than our rattling of a seedy pornographer in Marseilles."

I regarded the identical volumes of Charles Perrault's 1697 collection of literary fairy tales. The narratives hadn't originally been intended for children – as their gruesome content perhaps illustrated – but for a courtly Parisienne literary salon audience. Bluebeard was the sixth of eight tales in this edition. The story describes the eighth marriage of the titular murderer, of his new wife's discovery of the bloody corpses of her seven predecessors, and of her rich noble husband's attempts to slay her for her inquisitiveness.

The newspapers were delayed the next morning by the inclement weather. There was speculation about whether the Thames Basin might freeze for the first time since 1814.[10] Reportedly, many Londoners had braved the snowfall to skate on the frozen Serpentine in Hyde Park.

I ventured no further than a brisk constitutional that left my boots soaked and me grateful for the hearth and hot posset prepared for my return by our excellent landlady. There was no sign of a watcher following our investigations. Indeed, any man who kept sentinel or spy on our premises in this kind of weather would soon succumb to the vicious sleet, but Holmes was unconvinced.

A special messenger ploughed his way through the snow-banked streets to deliver Holmes a package from his brother in government service. A chilled liveried post office courier braved the young blizzard that gusted down Baker Street to bring return replies to Holmes's telegrams.

Least pleasant of our deliveries was a plain brown packet of more French postcards, including additional prints of two girls whom we matched with a pair of the four that came with the framed can-can picture, each in less salubrious poses with unsavoury companions. The printer further included cards for the three other models brought to him at different times by the experienced Parisienne lady, depicting similar images. Now we had all of our maids a-milking.

Holmes received the additional data with a grunt of enthusiasm and added them to the clutter that had now escaped our dinner table to additionally colonise his laboratory bench, two sideboards, a sofa, three occasional tables, our green bough-decorated mantelpiece, our guest chair, and a proportion of our carpet.

"Have you even been to bed?" I asked, noticing my friend's rumpled and unshaven appearance.

"Why should I wish to sleep when I have such a fascinating conundrum?" he answered me without looking up. "Kindly pass me that stack of newspaper cuttings from the regional newspapers of the Loire Valley. It is under the biscuit tin. No, the other folder, with the green ribbon, pressed against the cuspidor from the Crosby incident. Ah, thank you."

"May I enquire as to the reason you have elected insomnia over sensible sleeping habits? This time?"

I had to admit that Holmes betrayed few signs of weariness. Indeed, he was bright and animated despite his long cerebration. "I begin to see that patterns, Watson! The puzzle is unlocking."

"Might it be productive for you to summarise what you perceive? I would certainly find it helpful, and might then be able to clear my armchair for its customary use."

Holmes reached out to the corner of the table where Mrs. Hudson had ventured to leave a toast-rack amongst the strewn papers and scattered clockwork monkeys. He absently folded a slice into his mouth without seeming to notice it. "We are sent a message, in a dozen parts, with layered meanings," Holmes began between chews. "I am now convinced that our benefactor is a person of significant wit and subtlety who wishes to avoid the attentions and malice of the powerful men on Mr. Cassoway's list. In presenting what our gift-giver knows in puzzle form, he or she is correctly convinced that I will not be able to resist uncovering the facts for myself."

"And you are unlikely to back down from intimidation, whatsoever it is," I recognised.

"Naturally – although I have set in place certain precautions since yesterday. We need not review them now, but . . . messages have been sent." Holmes didn't specify whether those might be to his allies or to adversaries – quite possibly both.

He returned to the figurines, toffee tins, and opera calendars. "The glass nymphs and the anagram '*Elle est morte*' indicated some singular unpleasantness to a young woman. The primary purpose of our presents of the 28th and 29th were to direct us to Amelie Cornemuseur and her unfortunate decline, which with these telegrams today I can verify terminated with her death by apparent suicide."

He handed me an index card to which was pinned a newsprint cutting in French, along with a helpful translation by whichever of Holmes's newspaper researchers had uncovered the item. It was a brief, stark death notice mentioning that a young woman had been fished out of the Seine at the Île aux Cygnes on the ninth of March, 1894. She had been identified as former dancer and music hall hostess Amelie Cornemuseur. A verdict of death by suicide had been pronounced.[11]

Holmes further handed me a transcript and summary of the very cursory coroner's examination that had passed for a final investigation into the girl's end. I couldn't say that I admired the diligence or sensitivity of the police doctor's work, but he had recorded the needle-marks suggestive of serious opium addiction and the signs of advanced syphilis that the deceased had exhibited. She had also been thirteen-weeks pregnant.

Holmes was unmoved by the poor girl's plight, engaged as he was in the cerebral challenge before him. "The Bluebeard motif suggests that Mam'selle Cornemuseur was preyed upon, perhaps murdered, by some gentleman of supposed quality. Our mystery gift-sender may know this person to be able to direct us towards him. But remember the French postcards? Eight fallen angels were depicted in those photographs. Several had been concealed. With the material delivered this morning from my researchers, I can prove that the five I can so far identify are all dead. All by suicide in water – swans a-swimming. All taken up in the last three-and-a-half years from the various bodies of water illustrated in the seven postcards showing scenic views."

Holmes passed me two more sets of news cuttings. "Furthermore, at the two sites that do not match with our known girls, I have reports of similar discoveries of unidentified drowned young females that exactly match the circumstances."

"So this killer has struck more than once? He is preying upon women in reduced circumstances?"

Holmes wasn't yet willing to confirm his hypothesis, but he did note that the postcards of the places where the bodies had been dredged up had come enfolded in a rich man's wallet. Had such "suicides" been paid for?

He offered another disturbing possibility. "Eight maids were photographed by the unpleasant Marseilles photographer, but only seven drowned girls were discovered."

"Might one still be *alive*?" I wondered. "Do we race against time to somehow assemble the knowledge to save her?"

"If so, then it is one of the three young women from these art cards whose real names are yet to be established."

"What is to be done?"

Holmes gestured to the stairs, where the ungainly thump of our page on the treads indicated that he was racing up with another package. "That will be our daily delivery, Watson: Five Gold Rings."

He was correct. The presentation flip-cases each contained a man's signet. The bands appeared to be gold but were actually of an alloy which only made them appear so. Each bore a crest, intended to be used as a seal for imprinting upon wax, such as was the fashion in our fathers' time.

"Shall I tell you the owners of the heraldry?" Holmes asked me without bothering to look at the motifs.

"Will it equate to the five eminent men with whose names you were threatened yesterday?" I ventured, and was gratified to discover that I was correct. "Five suspects, then?"

"Or collaborators. But where is the sixth eminent man?"

"Sixth?" I echoed. "Why . . . ?"

Holmes slapped his hand down on the six volumes of Mother Goose under the tantalus. "Only one of these had the black swan's feather trapped in its pages. And six of the clockwork Lords-a-Leaping had black bases, perhaps reflecting their morality. There are more messages yet to come."

Despite the weather, on Thursday the 3rd we took a trip out.

Our departure from Baker Street was extraordinary and notable. "We must be ready to leave at thirteen-minutes-to-ten," Holmes instructed me that morning. "Timing is everything."

"I feel compelled to enquire why," I replied.

"Even though you know that I delight in surprising you."

As we opened the front door and stepped across the salted threshold, there was a disturbance in the street. The slow progress of a hansom slipping its way past our house was halted by the sudden influx of two-score urchins barrelling along the snow-clogged highway, engaged in the grandest and most glorious of snowball fights. It was an epic confrontation, carried on remorselessly despite the complaints of pedestrians, and it brought what little traffic there was to a halt.

Indeed, when the hansom-driver dared to venture a rebuke at the street-Arabs who had impeded his progress, to raise his buggy-whip at the rogues in reprimand, he was instantly beset from all sides by icy missiles. A particularly accurate shot took him on the nose, toppling him back off his perch to sprawl in the snowbank below.

Nor did the two passengers cosseted inside the carriage fare any better as they emerged. The mischievous snow-fight that has spilled across our thoroughfare continued without abate, locking the whole traffic of the street in shrieking chaos.

During that time, Holmes and I quietly slipped into another cab on the opposite side of the street and proceeded to vanish from view. Almost immediately, the rascals who had caused such disruption melted away like the snow-forts they had constructed.

"Those ruffian ragamuffins who caused that affray," I mentioned to Holmes as our carriage struggled on through half-cleared routes, "I thought that I recognised several of them."

"Some few of them may have done me various small services in the past," my friend conceded.

"It seemed to me as if those young jackanapes were at pains to detain and distract the vehicle which was driven by that unfortunate jarvey."

"The one that has driven past Baker Street no less than one-hundred-and-forty times in the last two days, to my own counting? Yes. It and two other carriages with similar habits all suffered some inconvenience just now, as did a number of half-frozen itinerants with a strong fascination for trudging past number 221."

"We have avoided a watch that was set, despite the difficulties presented by the winter."

"Indeed, my friend." Holmes's eyes twinkled, delighted at his jape. "And what is more traditional for snowy London that a juvenile snowball match?"

I rather thought that I recognised our present cabbie too, one of those whom Holmes called upon when he required a reliable driver who could maintain discretion. "Where are we going?"

"I have arranged a visit to a young man in the legal profession. We are going to deliver an offer of employment."

"Why would we need to retain such a specialist?"

"The job isn't with us. It is a chance to article with one of the pre-eminent Chambers around the Old Bailey, an opportunity that few ambitious young men would wish to decline. He will need new employment, you see, if he reveals to us what it is his present employer is up to."

"Brunor Cassoway's clerk!" I realised. "The fellow who trailed after our legal visitor of the day before yesterday."

"Indeed. I read in him several useful traits. Despite his employment he is impecunious. His present employers don't treat him well. His maintained-but-shabby clothing and shoes told all, along with the state of his chewed fingernails and the way he held himself in relation to Mr. Cassoway. He is conscientious – his pens are well cut and his writing neat and organised. But he has a troubled conscience. That much became evident from his reactions, expressions, and glances during our confrontation in our rooms as Cassoway spoke. I suspect he also noted the French postcards that I left out."

"A young man of limited experience might well be shocked by them," I pointed out.

"He didn't blush, but blanched. He recognised one or more of the images. He kept silent because he is bound to keep his employer's confidentiality. However, since then he has had two days to fret and speculate, to gnaw upon what he knows and what he suspects. He has had opportunity to consider the line between professional discretion and moral responsibility – and legal culpability. Hence, I have arranged for us to meet him in his digs, and I have an alternative for his future well-being should he decide to put righteousness before Mr. Cassoway and partners."

Mr. Herbert Oster chose righteousness. After some coaxing, he was even relieved to unburden himself of the doubts and fears his employment had raised in him.

"We have a contract, a partnership agreement, with a Paris attorney firm," he explained. "Paquet, Royer, Morel, and Mercier. They are very exclusive. They represent only the oldest and most wealthy of European families. Mr. Cassoway acts on their behalf when their clients require litigation or business affairs in Britain. They are often . . . very stern in their requirements."

"You mean that they try to break their clients' enemies," I surmised. "As Cassoway threatened with us."

"There are . . . sometimes people who have offended the clients of Paquet, Royer, Morel, and Mercier come into *problems*. They are overwhelmed with lawsuits, or exposed in some scandal, or they lose significant parts of their income – broken contracts, failed investments, and the like. S-sometimes . . . sometimes family members suffer illness or disgrace."

Holmes nodded, as if this merely confirmed his opinions. "You recognised a photograph at my chambers, I believe," he challenged Oster.

"Perhaps," the clerk conceded. "I could not be sure. I only glimpsed . . . and she was so changed . . . ."

Holmes produced the French postcards. Oster identified one for us, a name we hadn't so far discovered. "Miss Lilibeth Beale, I think. She was in the ballet chorus at one of the Drury Lane theatres. I don't remember which."

"When?" Holmes pressed. "And how do you come to know of her?"

Oster flinched. "I was obliged to send out correspondence regarding her. A letter to the manager of the troupe with which she was employed, disclosing information about her character – I don't know the truth of the allegations, but they were serious – and a threat of compensation demands upon the management. That was sufficient to obtain her dismissal."

"Do you have any idea why?" I demanded, outraged that a girl's reputation and future might be smirched with such slander.

"There were other letters of a similar nature. I am not the only clerk and do not always issue all the correspondence. It did seem as though Mr. Cassoway was intent to blacken Miss Beale's name and to ruin her career. The last time I saw her image before last Tuesday when I glimpsed those cards at your flat was on a publicity photograph of the sort that would-be artistes submit for consideration to a theatrical company. She had applied for a place with some touring troupe going to France, and I sent off a letter from Mr. Cassoway to its impresario instructing that she be given a place. I thought . . . perhaps the persecution was over and she was forgiven."

"Forgiven for what?" enquired Holmes.

"Forgiven for denying one of Paquet, Royer, Morel, and Mercier's rich clients whatever he had wanted from her," Oster suggested. "I assumed that she had reconsidered his demand."

Thursday's post brought only letters, but one of them contained a soiled, crumpled, and much folded piece of second-hand correspondence with the letterhead of Paquet, Royer, Morel, and Mercier. It was dated *Juin* 1894 and addressed to Mlle. L. C. Beale at a cheap hostel in Pigalle, Paris.

In terse legal terms, it gave her seven days to repay a sum of one-hundred-and-fifty francs which she was alleged to have stolen from their client Eneas Clovis Marrok Brodeur, le Marquis de Gambaiseuil et Rambouillet – that would be around fifteen pounds sterling, a significant sum and probably impossible for a young woman in straightened circumstances to afford. [12] The threatened alternative to the legal demand was arraignment in civil court, distraint of assets, and imprisonment for bankruptcy.

It wasn't a pleasant letter, and one against which a defenceless, impoverished girl in a foreign country had no chance of defending herself.

"I'd like to meet this Brodeur and have a chance to exchange views with him on this," I told Holmes, again ready to consider a voyage across the Channel, now to vent my spleen on Paquet, Royer, Morel, and Mercier and their illustrious employers every one.

"Well," Holmes considered, looking at the names on the legal firm's embossed letterhead, "we have our four colley birds." [13]

"Black vultures, more like, preying upon a helpless young woman like that. Even if she did steal something of this . . . Marquis's, then there is . . . ."

Even as we spoke, Holmes was lifting one of his reference works from the shelf behind him. It was the rather foxed second-hand edition of a history of French nobility that he had resorted to before to identify the seals on the faux-gold rings. I knew it to be summarised from and based around the forty-six-volume *Nouvelle Biographie Générale* from the 1860's, [14] a sort of French attempt at *Burke's*, [15] somewhat updated in what Holmes described as "a gossipy and ill-researched manner". The French have an odd, uneasy relationship with their peers.

"Ah, here we have the de Gambaiseuils et de Rambouillets," Holmes noted. "The family has long been in decline. They were disfavoured by Louis XVI in the eighteenth century, stripped of many of their lands and revenues, and never recovered. The present Marquis is indeed Eneas Brodeur, born in 1851, and evidently draws his income from Caribbean tobacco. I shall need to look more closely at His Lordship."

"What about Miss Beale?" I enquired. "Can she be found? Might we render her assistance, or is she amongst the poor drowned swans you mentioned before?"

Holmes returned to his writing desk, clearing space. He lifted carefully to one side the photograph of the adventurous and memorable Miss Adler, a memento of one of the few cases where he was matched. He took up pen and began to write several letters, including missives to the Chief of the Paris Police, to Mssrs. Paquet, Royer, Morel, and Mercier, and to the Marquis de Gambaiseuil et Rambouillet himself.

There was a disturbance in the night, some kind of affray behind our house. By the time Holmes and I had donned boots and gone out to investigate, the scuffle was done. Three enterprising ruffians were laid out in the snow beside their crowbars and coshes. Four of Holmes's boxing acquaintances were also present, pleased that they had "just happened to be passing" at two o'clock when they had discovered louts of felonious ill-intent loitering. They had dutifully and loyally undertaken enthusiastic citizens' arrests.

A constable was summoned, then several, and eventually the unlucky loiterers were carted away to make statements at Marylebone Police Station.

Holmes invited his pugilistic partners into 221b and had Mrs. Hudson supply them with hot soup, mince pies, and a tot of whisky before they departed again into the bitter cold.

"Fortunate that those chaps happened to be passing," I noted, not believing it for a moment.

"Our investigation is scaring somebody, Watson. Precautions have been laid."

"I don't suppose those ruffians will name the fellow who set them on?"

"I doubt they'd know his name. But I know *them*, and where they drink. In the morning I might brave the elements down to their watering hole in the persona of weather-shored seaman and make some enquiries about their recruitment. It depends whether I shall have time given other developments."

"Other developments?"

"Yes. We are expecting Three French Hens, are we not?"

There was more excitement on the street the following morning, when two unpleasant foreigners were arrested for attempting to interfere with the Royal Mail. Their efforts to seize the postman's sack as he made deliveries along Baker Street were thwarted by two plain-clothed policemen and their superior, whom I thought I recognised as Inspector Lestrade.

"My Christmas present to him," Holmes told me when I mentioned it. "It is the season for gift-giving. Two mysterious post-thieves attempting to seize a mail-sack in plain day on a public London street is sure to garner a few lines in the papers, with some approbation from the Commissioner of Police for the officer who masterminded their arrest."

"Might we perceive the hand of Brunor Cassoway? He has decided that we are getting too much information about his clients' clients."

"Ah well, he may be right," Holmes agreed. "Take this letter here, one of several abstracted from Cassoway's correspondence file for me yesterday by the ambitious clerk Oster before giving his two-weeks' notice. It was hand-delivered by one of my Irregulars just now, whilst the fuss was occupying the street. This is the odd correspondence from Paquet, Royer, Morel, and Mercier that set Mr. Cassoway on his visit to us, requesting and requiring him to bribe, intimidate, or otherwise warn us off investigating 'the Brodeur affair', authorising him to name the powerful men whose ire might otherwise be invoked."

"Here is surely evidence!" I exclaimed.

"Not if it was stolen," Holmes pointed out. "Tomorrow Mr. Oster must return it from whence he abstracted it, so that it may be found there by a court-ordered search in due course. But to the point: These unsavoury pieces of correspondence from the French attorneys have offered us yet more excellent data. One piece is of particular interest."

He had the borrowed letters pegged out across our sideboard, and he showed them to me with an enthusiast's fervour. "You remember the affair of Mary Sutherland and her odious stepfather Windibank?[16] You may recall from that case that I have a special interest in identifying typewriters by the unique character imprints of their keys."

The correspondence from Paquet, Royer, Morel, and Mercier was all typed, laid out in formal French style under printed letterheads. The typeface all seemed identical to me.

But not to Sherlock Holmes. He gleefully passed his magnifying glass over chipped *T*'s and misaligned *V*'s and spoke of carriage returns and ribbon ink. The summary of his lecture was this: All the letters had been typed by the same machine of provincial French manufacture, and were probably done by the same typist. Save for one: The letter that had recently set Cassoway on.

"This," Holmes told me gleefully, "is a forgery. It is typed using an American Remington machine on an American ribbon, by a typist of less experience using more forceful strikes. The notepaper, however, is genuine."

"How do you know that it isn't simply a new secretary on a new piece of office equipment?"

Holmes tapped on the circulation list subscribed to the letter, with initials of those to whom carbon copies were to be distributed. One was '*For file*', another for '*N.P.*' (probably for *Paquet*), and a third listing mischievously added for '*S.H.*'

"Imagine for a moment that the message sent us on January 1st was *not* the half-dozen Perrault volumes. After all, we were given only one goose, in half-a-dozen copies. What if the other five fat geese were herded to our door to lay themselves before us in other ways?"

"That was also the day that Brunor Cassoway revealed his list of men who might crush us for our investigations," I recalled. "Five names. Five plus Bluebeard, all served up for us as a New Year dinner."

Holmes looked as satisfied as if he had indeed sat down to a six-course repast. He tapped out his pipe and refilled it, and in that time his thoughts moved on. "A secretary at the French attorneys, appalled at the treatments given to one or more of Brodeur's victims? Privy to some unscrupulous plot by what he or she types? It almost fits, but . . . No."

He lit his tobacco and took three pondering puffs. "Some relative or friend of one or more of the deceased? Amelie most likely, since our focus was first directed there. Or some woman who has escaped similar persecution and degradation? Perhaps, but . . . not quite."

Another long draw. "Somebody capable of co-ordinating a timed international post campaign, erudite enough to formulate clues, mobile to acquire postcards, able to reach into the very offices of Paquet, Royer, Morel, and Mercier and extract information, as well as notepaper. Somebody who wishes to remain anonymous, invisible to spiteful revenge, but recognises in me a kindred spirit that need not fear such malice."

He slid his pressed pointed fingers up to his thin, sensitive lips and almost smiled.

"Five shabby gold rings representing five faded noblemen of jaded appetite, but six predatory plotters before that. One was eliminated before our investigation could start? By whom? For what? And how?"

We waited for second post.

Despite the thwarted postal thieves, it was a day of much correspondence. There were more information packets from Holmes's foreign researchers, including a report from Le Brun and a long letter from M. Dubugue of the Paris Prefecture of Police. A score of sealed telegrams arrived from all across Europe, and two from the United States of America. A discreet package from Marseilles delivered yet more *risqué* photography. A second similar parcel from a specialist collector's shop in London added some missing images to our postcard pile.

There also arrived a long epistle of legal warning from Paquet, Royer, Morel, and Mercier that seemed to delight Holmes the more threatening it became.

And there were Three French Hens, all arrived in one package by the noon delivery, in a thick padded envelope from no further than Covent Garden. It included a framed coloured line-drawing of a hen, which Holmes identified as the being of the ancient French breed La Fleche from the Loire Valley, noted for its delicate flesh. The forest of Rambouillet is in the Loire Valley.

The second item was a tintype of a prize-winning hen at some kind of rural show. Holmes instructed me that the bird's beard, muffs, feathered feet, and five toes per foot marked it as a Faverolles, a utility fowl bred in the sixties and named after the village whence it originated. In the last decade it had become a popular breed in Britain.

"Holmes," I demanded, amazed. "how can you possibly be expert in typing hens?"

"Knowing what kind of puzzle would be handed me today, and with some spare hours overnight, how could I not?" my friend answered, as amazed perhaps that such diligence hadn't occurred to me. "Anyhow, Faverolles is also in the Loire Valley, near Brodeur's vestigial estates. I have a list of his properties there on the mantel, under General Gordon's portrait."

The third hen was less literal. A last photograph was of a well-dressed plump woman of middle-age, expensively but gaudily garbed in an outfit perhaps better on a younger woman. She was posed outside, with an old-fashioned steepled church in the background. Of special interest to Holmes was the coat-of-arms engraved on the side of the belltower.

It took only a few minutes' work with magnifying lens and heraldry reference to describe the arms as "Vert, a crescent Argent set in base debruised by a stem of three broad bean pods, or within chief two stars Gules." In plainer English, that was a three-stalked beanplant, with a red star on either side above it, and a sickle crescent at its base, on a green background: The blazon of the village of Faverolles.

"I wish I could see that woman's hands," Holmes told me. "But her clothing is modern and Parisienne. I may well be able to identify her by her milliner. And she clearly has some association with a village or nearby estate in Eure-et-Loir, which is some twenty-five miles into the country from the capital."

"We are being directed to some specific place associated with the Marquis?" I wondered.

Holmes nodded, thoughtfully.

"I, um, I may be able to help with identifying this woman," I was forced to admit. "This isn't the only image that we have of her."

To assist in the case, I had been reviewing the new stock of postcards forwarded by that Marseilles printer who had supplied the images of the lost girls, and the supplemental material from the Soho specialist. Holmes had ordered other images that featured the same girls in other poses. Several of the portraits included two women, though never more than one of our "eight swans" at a time. One older female appeared in three of the set boxed from France, and now she occurred again in a photograph sent to us today.

I indicated this connection to Holmes.

"Well done, Watson! What an eye!" my friend remarked. "This woman is a madam, likely the procurer who lured the missing girls into her profession, quite probably the 'experienced lady' who arranged the Marseilles modelling. I shall set enquiries in hand with Dubugue to put a name to her, and have her taken up by the police for further questioning."

I added it to the stack of evidence that was now threatening to overwhelm me. Holmes, however, was in his element.

His cogitations were disturbed again when the three p.m. post returned his first-class letter to the Marquis, with a covering note coldly informing him that Eneas Clovis Marrok Brodeur, Marquis de Gambaiseuil et Rambouillet, was dead. He had passed away on 1st August of last year, of a hunting accident.

"*Careless!*" Holmes exploded, accusing not the negligent hunter but himself. "I should have checked the obituaries!" This he now did, verifying the demise of Lilibeth Beale's accuser.

I tried to make out some kind of chronology for the unfortunate young women in our case. Mam'selle Cornemuseur had met her end before Miss Beale had really got into difficulties. Had Lilibeth been able to escape and vanish because of her accuser's death? Or was there a closer cause and effect?

I wondered if Holmes and I were a pair of the wind-up monkeys that had set our case going, primed and then set to leap somersaults for our correspondent's amusement.

"You are concerned that we are being abused," Holmes noted. "Do not fear. We are on the trail now. There shall be justice for Amelie and the others."

"But what of Miss Beale?" I fretted. "Is it also too late for her? Your reports say that she also disappeared, about the time that the Marquis died, and – "

"I can tell you some things about Miss Beale," Holmes conceded. "She was a talented young performer who had hopes of rising in her profession. She was also a rather blameless girl, a Sunday School prizewinner who nursed her ailing mother through a long final illness. She was hardly the sort of *ingénue* who might be amenable to liaisons with rich patrons, exchanging her favours for advancement or wealth.

"However, she certainly came to the attention of the Marquis de Gambaiseuil et Rambouillet. I have some accounts from her chorus-mates, who were rather envious of his regard and who wouldn't have been so reticent to earn his good opinion. Miss Beale, however, denied his advances.

"This seems to have invoked the involvement of those French attorneys, who contracted some of their dirty business to Cassoway since the girl was then working in England. Matters were contrived to end her employment and to offer her an opportunity in France, thus separating her from home, family, and friends. Once in Paris she was prey to false accusations of theft, to career ruin, to threats of imprisonment, and, ultimately, she was presented with the choice of acceding to Eneas Brodeur's demands or being destroyed in even worse ways.

"We may suspect that the seven other women to whom we have been directed, who were driven to suicide or who were murdered in such a way as to seem like self-termination, were placed under similar pressure. Certainly Amelie Cornemuseur appears to have been a blameless girl at the time she joined the Claudian Musikgarten, and yet a year later she was posing for filthy pictures in a seedy Marseilles bawdy house. A short time after that, she was dead in the Seine.

"Miss Beale, however, seems to have avoided such a dire end. My American enquiries inform me that she arrived in New York on August 28th last, on the passenger packet *Toronto*, listed as personal companion and maid of a Mrs. Cooper of Bridgeport, Connecticut. From that disembarkation, both Miss Beale and Mrs. Cooper vanish entirely."

"And who is this Mrs. Cooper?"

Holmes spread out his hand in a gesture of good-natured bafflement – or so I thought. "There is no further record of the lady. She saved young Lilibeth then disappeared, Watson – like Saint Nicholas up a chimney."

Holmes and I were up early on Saturday morning. We had scarcely finished breakfast and answered correspondence when our visitor arrived.

Mr. Cassoway entered in some agitation, more snow-bedraggled and far less confident than at his previous visit, and lacking his attendant.

Holmes was on his violin. He ignored Cassoway until he completed his rendition of *Questo è il fin di chi fa mal* – "This is the end that befalls evildoers." I am told it is from *Don Giovanni*, the part where devils drag the miserable sinner down to hell.

"What have you done?" Cassoway demanded in a trembling voice when Holmes finally attended him.

Holmes set aside his Stradivarius and regarded the lawyer coolly. "*I do not make threats. I take action.* Yesterday I passed a line on to the Parisian police, who arrested and questioned one Mme. Lucrece Caron. She is a notorious procurer and brothel-keeper who has previously evaded police attention because of the influence of . . . shall we say five powerful men who found her services useful? At the counter-influence of certain other figures on the European stage, M. Dubugue of the Paris Prefecture was finally allowed to stage a raid and acquire her for interrogation."

Cassoway frowned. "I don't know – "

"Mme. Caron was an agent of Paquet, Royer, Morel, and Mercier. Certain correspondence was brought to light that she had hidden away as an insurance, or perhaps as a nest-egg. These documents outlined a number of unpleasant instructions regarding certain young women whose demises had previously been assumed as suicides. Reviewed in that way, and with support from some circumstantial material I had forwarded to Paris as a contingency, M. Dubugue acquired a court order to seize the attorneys' offices and inspect certain files for further evidence of conspiracy to commit murder."

"Paquet's . . . " breathed Cassoway, even paler than before.

"Around five this morning, officers of the Prefect of Police entered the premises and uncovered accounts and instructions given to Paquet, Royer, Morel, and Mercier from six notable clients of theirs, rich men of international stature. I am sure you know their names. One is already dead. The other five now stand exposed."

"They could not be!" the lawyer breathed. "They are untouchable. They know too much. They own too many."

"Alas, the allegations have somehow become known to the gutter press," Holmes continued inexorably. "The broadsheets will be full of it by tonight. It will now be more politically embarrassing to attempt to cover over these significant indiscretions than to admit them. Other powerful people will consider these five men fair sacrifice to maintain their own standing."

I had read Dubugue's hastily-sent report less than an hour ago, which is why my breakfast was unsettled in my stomach. "An alliance of idle cads," I snarled at Cassoway. "Their sport to select some virtuous young woman and organise her absolute downfall. To use poverty, fraud, blackmail, and violence to drag her into the vilest of slavery, and there to torture her with every degradation until she is done to death. All for the amusement of villains who thought themselves untouchable! Well they shall be touched now – and so shall you!"

Cassoway flinched as if I had struck him. I was tempted to knock him down where he cowered.

"They have come to *my* offices," he bleated. "The police! Scotland Yard! They are there now! You must . . . you must help me!"

"I doubt that I must," Holmes assured him.

"I can tell you much," he offered. "People, places – the estate in Rambouillet Forest where the revellers met for their pleasures – the men who took bribes to assure the victims' downfalls – the contacts who provided the suicides – the servants who covered up what happened to the Marquis that night at his villa, when he was . . . I can supply all, if only you save me."

"This is Sherlock Holmes," I observed to the worm. "He doesn't need you to tell him anything."

"True," the great detective agreed. "Also Mr. Cassoway, I doubt you will survive the day to speak. Your five powerful men will be working frantically now to silence those whose testimony might indict them. Only those in police custody may be safe – I say *may*, for they are as you noted powerful. Fortunately, the chain of written evidence and the confessions so far obtained are quite sufficient to put a noose around the necks of those wicked murderers. Amelie Cornemuseur and her sister-victims shall be avenged."

Brunor Cassoway stared at Holmes and I in abject horror.

"You may go now," Holmes told him, and rang the bell for our boy to show him out.

The last post that day brought us a small packet containing one of those antique lockets shaped like a heart, which when split open contain miniatures of a pair of lovers. Holmes examined the sterling silver piece with some amusement.

"Are you not going to open it?" I asked him. "Surely it contains some further clue to the mystery around Amelie and Lilibeth."

"That mystery is solved," Holmes assured me. "The rest is merely a matter of assembling the evidence and bringing the prosecutions. Concerns for the police of three nations, not for us. We have played our part, drummed our drums, piped our tobacco pipes long into the night, remembering riddle-games. The rest of the orchestra may complete the piece."

"There is still the question of Kringle, and the fate of Miss Beale with the unknown Mrs. Cooper. There may be more detail inside the necklace to further those queries."

"I already know what is inside the locket, Watson. I can guess the future of Miss Beale – or whatever name she chooses to take in the New World, her new world – and I am confident it will be a good one."

He spun the locket on its chain. "Surely you apprehend that our gift-giver, becoming aware of the downfall of Amelie, a friend she had once known in Germany, and comprehending that cruel game played by cruel men, intervened to rescue Lilibeth and saw her safe away. For this purpose and to inform us of the additional unpleasant characters involved in wider plotting she utilised a number of old contacts from across Europe, several in the theatrical profession. If she also acted directly to terminate the deeply unpleasant Eneas Brodeur, then I cannot condemn her. It was an act of public good."

"Then we have merely been this Kringle's agents in exposing the rest of that ugly network of vice."

"It is the season of goodwill, Watson, when light prevails over darkness. I am pleased and privileged to have played a part."

"But – "

"Consider: this could have been a melancholy time for you and me. We both have our ghosts of Christmas Past. Instead, we have been diverted with useful party games that have avenged some young women and saved others who might in future have faced vicious destruction. I deem us most fortunate to have received season's blessing from . . . *Kringle*."

"You will not tell me who is in that locket?"

Holmes pocketed the gift. He gave me a rare, beaming grin of a smile, such as I have seldom seen on his craggy face.

"Why, Doctor," he answered me, "it is Two Turtle Doves."

On the Twelfth Day of Christmas a plain legal envelope appeared from America, stamped Hoboken, New Jersey, and marked "*Personal*". It contained some official certificate of the kind that are issued for births, marriages, and deaths, but Holmes carried it off into his room and I never saw it again. [17]

NOTES

1. This version is almost identical to the song's first appearance in *Mirth without Mischief* (1780) and to several nineteenth-century recorded versions. By the time of our present story, 1894, the most recent printing of the folk-song that cleaved to the earliest version was in "Old Songs and Airs: Melodies Once Popular in Yorkshire", *Leeds Mercury Weekly Supplement*: 5 (10th January, 1891), compiled by Frank Kidson. Frederick Austin's best-selling arrangement of the song, published by Novello in London, 1909, introduced the now-well-known tune, standardised the verses in a different order, prefixed "On" to the first line, and changed "colly birds" to "calling birds".
2. That is *Zijner Majesteits*, "His Majesty's", the old Dutch prefix for a naval vessel, equivalent to the British *HMS* or the American *USS*. The modern prefix is *HNLMS*: "His/Her Netherlands Majesty's Ship".
3. An online version of the copy of this volume retained by Harvard University is available at:
https://archive.org/details/monthlychronicl02unkngoog
4. Actually, the "North Country Garland of Song" version uses "pipers playing".
5. *A Visit from St Nicholas* is now better known by its first line, '*Twas the Night before Christmas*. Originally published anonymously in the Troy, New York *Sentinel* on 23 December, 1823, authorship was later claimed by Moore. Some scholars prefer to attribute it to Henry Livingston, Jr., but Holmes had a very limited knowledge of much popular literature and was probably uninterested in the question.
6. This miniature Statue of Liberty, raised to commemorate the raising of the original in New York, now faces west, away from the Eiffel Tower, from its inauguration by President Marie François Sadi Carnot on 4 July, 1889, but was turned round in 1937 when Paris hosted the World Fair.
Île aux Cygnes, the Isle of Swans, is a 2,789-foot long, 36-foot wide artificial island in the Seine, created in 1837 to reinforce the Grenelle Bridge.
7. Frank Smythson Ltd. was established in 1887 as a manufacturer of luxury stationery, leather goods, diaries, and fashion products, and is still a brand today. It is credited with selling the first "featherweight" diary, *i.e.* a portable pocket diary.
8. *Q.C.*, meaning *Queen's Council*, or *K.C.* for *King's Council* if the British monarch is male, is a Crown-conferred merit-based office for a senior legal counsel who undertakes significant court cases. Members receive the privilege of sitting within the inner bar of court and wearing distinctive silk gowns, for which reason they are sometimes colloquially called "silks". Becoming a Q.C. is called "taking the silk".
9. Red-billed and mostly black-plumed *Cygnus atratus* is mostly found in the southern regions of Australia, but was introduced to various countries as an ornamental bird in the 1800's, whereupon it escaped and formed small wild populations.

10. Many climatologists mark the winter of 1894-1895 as the last great event of the "Little Ice Age" that had affected Europe since the Thirteenth Century. Low temperatures were unmatched again until 1940-1941. London had previously experienced a killing winter in 1881-1882, and before that in the long snows of 1814, when the Thames last froze entirely and hosted the last of the Frost Fairs on the ice.
January 1895 was also notable for the appearance of thunder-snow over Britain, a rare form of lightning storm in which snow or sleet, not rain, pelts from the sky.
11. This was not an uncommon find in the Seine. The most famous young woman taken from that river in the Nineteenth Century became known as *L'Inconnu*, "the Unknown", after plaster masks and busts of her face became popular wall-decorations. L'Inconnu's many likenesses were commonly held to be echoes of the muse. By 1899, they were famous enough to form the central theme of a novella by Richard le Le Gallienne. In *The Worshipper of the Image*, a young poet gains inspiration from the moulded face, but its evil influence eventually drives him to madness and death. For a fuller discussion of L'Inconnu's remarkable life after death as an art icon, as the face on many life-saver practice dummies, and for a Holmes plot regarding her, see I.A. Watson's novel *Holmes and Houdini* (2017).
12. A French franc had roughly the consumer buying power of U.S. five dollars today, but amounted to two days' income for a working-class labourer (who might earn as little as a twelve centimes, or a sterling shilling a day), albeit in an era when food and rent were significantly proportionally lower. An undistinguished chorus girl might expect a weekly stipend of ten shillings a week, which assuming continuous employment might mean a salary of up to £20 per year. Miss Beale was therefore being expected to repay a sum equivalent to nine months of her income.
13. These are probably blackbirds, using the old Newcastle slang term "colley" or "colly" for "black". Older versions of "The Twelve Days of Christmas" published in *Mirth Without Mischief* (1780) and Angus, Bodleian Library (1774-1785) both include the term "colly birds". The 1842 Halliwell and 1846 Rimbault publications substitute "canary birds" before most subsequent nineteenth-century versions revert to "colley", with the exceptions of Hughes's 1864 "ducks quacking", Henderson's 1879 "curley birds", and Clark's 1875 "colour'd birds". More modern versions, especially in the U.S. where the slang "colley" is not well-known, now substitute the term "calling birds", but that version was unrecorded at Holmes and Watson's time.
14. *Nouvelle Biographie Générale, depuis les temps les plus reculés jusqu'a nos jours, avec les renseignements bibliographiques et l'indication des sources a consulter* ("New General Biography, from earliest times to the present, with bibliographic information and details of sources to consult", 1852-1866), compiled by French physician and lexicographer Ferdinand Hoefer.
15. Burke's *Genealogical and Heraldic Dictionary of the Peerage and Baronetage of the United Kingdom* (from 1826), renamed *Burke's Peerage*,

Baronetage, and Knightage (from 1847 to present) is an annual listing of the present nobility of the United Kingdom and their genealogy.

16. The mystery of the disappearing Mr. Hosmer Angel and his jilted fiancée's appeal to Holmes form the substance of "A Case of Identity" (1891), collected in *The Adventures of Sherlock Holmes*, 1892.

17. This account from Dr. Watson's dispatch box was presumably never sent for publication in his lifetime because of the risqué nature of certain pieces of evidence, the sordid nature of the crimes, and mostly due to the unsatisfying lack of a full solution to the identity of Holmes's mystery gift-giver.

    However, amongst the unsorted personal documents left in trust by Mr. Sherlock Holmes's estate to Dr. Watson's executors in 1957, which are only now being fully catalogued, is a faded State of New Jersey birth certificate for a boy weighing 10 lb 13 oz., born to a Mrs. I. Adler. The father's name is not filled in.

The Dilemma of Mr. Henry Baker
by Paul D Gilbert

An unusually wet Christmas Eve had found me floundering along a wild and windy Baker Street, while juggling with a pile of brightly wrapped parcels, a holly wreath, and an umbrella that had hardly been worth the effort in such atrocious conditions.

By the time that I had reached the door to 221, I was drenched through, and any sense of the spirit of Christmas had long since deserted me. However, the sight of a most sympathetic Mrs. Hudson standing by the open door renewed my energy, and I clambered up the stairs to the rooms that I shared with Sherlock Holmes with the promise of a hot pot of coffee ringing in my ears.

"Oh Watson, my dear fellow, I really wonder if the prospect of making merry is actually worth such extraordinary efforts." Holmes could hardly suppress his amusement at the sight of my predicament and I expressed my annoyance by hurling the sorry and distorted remains of my umbrella violently to the floor.

"For all of the appreciation that you show, I would say most certainly not!" I barked while hanging my sopping coat onto the stand by the door.

I moved urgently over to the fire and stood there rubbing my hands together by the welcoming flames, while awaiting the arrival of our landlady. Once the coffee had been poured and I had sat comfortably in my usual armchair, the entirely understandable resentment that I had felt towards my friend began to ease somewhat. It had been rather disconcerting to find Holmes still attired in his purple dressing gown at this time of day, and the sight of his dishevelled hair hanging over his tired red eyes filled me with still further concern.

Holmes had evidently sensed my mellowing mood.

"It is good of you to have gone to such extremes on our behalf," he conceded and he poured me a glass of warming Cognac from the decanter by way of a further recompense.

I temporarily abandoned my coffee cup in favour of the glass of glistening golden nectar that Holmes had just thrust into my hand. I sipped slowly and appreciatively while appraising the extent of my friend's personal neglect. Holmes responded to this as if he had acquired the power to read my innermost thoughts.

"You shouldn't judge me too harshly, friend Watson, for as you will most certainly know by now, assumption is the arch-enemy of the truth and logical deduction. You will surely have observed how my humble practise has been suffering from a dearth of stimulating and worthwhile cases of late. In such circumstances, as you have mentioned so often in your tawdry little tales, I have occasionally lapsed into those dark and insidious little habits of which you wholeheartedly disapprove. However, you should be cheered by the revelation that my time has been more gainfully employed, in the study of this."

Holmes immediately reached into his dressing gown pocket and then threw across to me a medium-sized manila envelope. He laughed once he had observed the facial expression of my surprise and consequent intrigue, and I removed the contents of the envelope with care.

Inside I discovered nothing more startling than a humble Christmas card, a not uncommon bounty at the time of year. However, it was the name inscribed at the base of the card that caught my attention at once: *Mr. Henry Baker*!

For those not familiar with some of my earlier attempts at providing my friend's work with a worthy showcase, I should briefly describe the circumstances that had surrounded our previous encounter with the man. Mr. Baker had first entered our rooms in answer to an advertisement that Holmes had placed in all of the London evening papers, on the second evening after Christmas a few years previous.

The items that Baker had come to reclaim, namely a battered old felt hat that Holmes had examined with meticulous care and surprising enthusiasm, together with a fine fresh goose, had led us to the recovery of the fabulous jewel known as the Blue Carbuncle, the theft of which Baker had been entirely ignorant. The scholarly gentleman had clearly fallen on hard times, as the condition of his hat had attested, but the great gusto with which he had reclaimed his missing items told us still more of his sorry situation at that time.

Aside from the usual greetings of the season, Baker's card had contained nothing more intriguing than a request that he be granted an interview with my friend at a time of his convenience.

"By Jove, it is odd to hear from that venerable gentleman after all this time. Only a matter of some concern could have lured him out of doors on so foul a Christmas Eve." I speculated.

"We shall discover that in but a moment or two, for I have suggested an appointment in precisely five minutes, and he strikes me as being a man of punctual habits." Holmes jumped up and rushed into his room to attend to his attire.

Just five minutes had gone by before I heard the sound of the bell pull. I barely had time to fetch my notebook and pencil before Mrs. Hudson had shown our guest through. Holmes came out of his room just as she was opening the door

The alteration that had manifested in the appearance of Mr. Baker, since our previous encounter, had been as dramatic as it had been unexpected. His tired and threadbare overcoat had been superseded by a smart covert coat in navy blue, and that instructive old hat had been replaced by one of the finest crushed felt and bereft of wax stains. His shoulders were still rounded by his scholastic habits, and he moved with an uncertain shuffle that his new situation hadn't improved. However, his white mutton chops were now well groomed and his wispy hair was rich with pomade, and there was a confident twinkle in his eyes that hadn't been there previously.

Holmes responded to our guest's resounding season's greetings with an outstretched hand and a welcoming smile, and before long Mr. Henry Baker was seated by the fire with a warming glass of cognac cushioned within his appreciative hand.

"I am exceedingly grateful for your agreeing to see me on so auspicious a night, Mr. Holmes, but I remember most fondly the kindly and gracious manner with which you bestowed on me so great a bounty, all those years past." Baker smiled.

"Mr. Baker, surely you exaggerate, for it had been a matter of the merest trifle," Holmes responded in a most off hand manner.

"To you perhaps, Mr. Holmes, but I assure you that the goose had been something of a peace offering to my wife, and in that it proved to be remarkably successful. Unfortunately, Mrs. Baker had found it difficult to adapt to the beleaguered nature of our circumstances at the time, and I fear that I had lost not only her affection, but more poignantly, her respect. That goose went some small way towards repairing that rift and for that," Baker concluded before taking a small sip from his glass, "I shall be eternally grateful to you."

Holmes acknowledged Baker's outpouring with the briefest of smiles and a barely discernable nodding of his head.

"As gratifying as that is to hear, I'm certain that a humble goose hasn't led to the most obvious change in your circumstances that we see here tonight, and that this Christmas you have a bird already being prepared for the morrow." Holmes pointed towards Baker's hat and coat while he made his observation.

"Oh yes, indeed, Mr. Holmes, and a very fine specimen it is too! However, as you have already correctly surmised, it is the manner of my advancement that is the crux of the dilemma in which I now find myself, and upon which I now seek your good counsel."

"Ah, to that you are most welcome, Mr. Baker, but I beseech you to be as concise as you must be precise in laying your problem before me. Dr. Watson here will take notes, and you can rely on his discretion as surely as you can upon my own." Holmes lit up a pipe and, as he closed his eyes and leant back into his chair, he took down a deep draw of his pungent smoke.

I had noticed that Baker's ruddy completion of his previous visit had lightened somewhat, no doubt due to an abstinence of the alcohol that had once plagued him. However, his cheeks now reddened as he primed himself to present the nature of his problem to us and he shuffled awkwardly in his chair.

"Now now, Mr. Baker," I smiled encouragingly, "you are amongst friends here."

By now the roar of the wind and the lashing of the rain upon our windows had calmed discernibly, and the melodic strains of "Deck the Halls" rose up towards us from the carolers on the street below. Baker glanced towards the window and then smiled back at me.

"Of course, although I hesitate to set before you a problem that will, in all probability, seem dull and mundane to you both."

"Have no fear, Mr. Baker," I assured him, "for I can promise you that some of our most fascinating and intriguing cases have been born from the most inauspicious of beginnings."

"Very well then, although I fear that your expectations might yet culminate in disappointment. As you have probably already deduced from my complexion, my consumption of alcohol, which had been at the root of most of my problems, has dramatically reduced in recent times. Consequently you will be surprised to hear that the inception of my current dilemma actually took place within The Alpha Inn public house, the very same establishment that supplied me with that propitious goose.

"Despite my abstinence, I occasionally call in to my old haunt to reacquaint myself with my former companions at the bar, over a single pint of ale. It was during one such visit that I found myself being summoned over to a corner table by a waving arm and a most enthusiastic voice. As I drew closer I recognised a former colleague of mine at the British Museum – namely Mr. Arthur Connolly of the Roman Antiquities Department.

"A short while after I last saw you, I decided to better myself, and I was fortunate enough to have found a more gainful form of employment at a local library. Although my remuneration hadn't vastly improved, the increase had been sufficient for me to regain the respect of my wife and to afford the laying on of gas at our home. Consequently, it had been some considerable time since Connolly and I had last spoken, and I joined him at his table with great eagerness.

"I had been a little surprised to find him there, for despite The Alpha's close proximity to the Museum, it hadn't been an establishment that Connolly cared to frequent. Nevertheless, we enjoyed reminiscing about our time together at the Museum, and before long my old colleague began to tell me of his recent promotion to the head of his department.

"There and then, gentlemen, and to my great joy and surprise, he asked me to fill the vacancy, which had been created by his own promotion!"

Holmes opened his eyes immediately and then strode over to the fireplace where he relit his pipe with a set of tongs and a piece of burning coal.

"That is indeed a most fortuitous coincidence – would you not say, Mr. Baker?" Holmes declared.

"Oh, indeed it was sir, but it was certainly not a piece of good fortune that I had a mind to refuse. My new duties involved the collating and cataloguing of the museum's latest acquisitions – primarily those belonging to Mr. Connolly's department, although not exclusively. It proved to be a job for which I was eminently qualified, and for once I was able to put to good use the vast array of knowledge that I have gleaned from my beloved books. I must admit that the remuneration is beyond anything that I anticipated or experienced before, and our lives have changed beyond recognition as a result." Baker sighed deeply and regretfully before taking another sip from his glass.

"Mr. Baker, with all seemingly set so fair, I fail to see what use I could possibly be to you." Holmes suddenly seemed to become disinterested in our guest and he turned his attention towards the window and the street below.

"Ah, I see that the rain has begun to turned to snow. You should make your return journey with all speed, Mr. Baker, lest it sets in for the night" Holmes suggested.

"Oh, but Mr. Holmes, I fear that my new life may shortly come crashing down about my ears!" Baker suddenly exclaimed.

"You had better tell us about the rest," Holmes said calmly while returning to his chair.

"If I may, although on the surface it might appear to be a rather trifling matter: The Museum has recently acquired a substantial haul of Roman coins, the majority of which date back to the First Century A.D. – more specifically to the age of the Julio-Claudian Dynasty of the earlier part of that century. Of these, I must confess, the majority were either in very poor condition or so common that they were of very little worth and of even less interest.

"Nevertheless, I was given the rather thankless task of cataloguing each and every one of them, while Mr. Connolly sifted through my lists with an air of indifferent disdain. Mercifully there were a few diamonds in the rough, most notably a silver *denarius* depicting the Emperor Galba, dated 68 A.D., and a similar coin of the Emperor Claudius that is nineteen years earlier. Both were in near perfect condition, and therefore of immense importance and great value.

"To my great surprise, Mr. Connolly expressed neither interest nor delight in these discoveries, and to my dismay, both coins found their way into the box reserved for those artefacts deemed unworthy of further examination and display. He waved aside my protests, and before long I was reassigned to a rather dull batch of Ottoman armour that had recently been acquired."

Holmes interrupted our guest by raising his hand. "Did Mr. Connolly offer any explanation for his apparent lack of interest in these coins? After all, it seems to me that you should have been congratulated for these exceptional finds rather than dismissed and reassigned."

"No, Mr. Holmes, his reaction was in fact quite the opposite, for he became quite agitated and almost offensive when I proposed an alternative home for these coins. So I decided to bite my tongue and turn my attention towards my next task. Over the succeeding weeks, I thought about the incident of the coins less and less. Consequently, it came as some surprise when one of the senior curators asked me if I had any suggestions for a private exhibition that he was arranging for a wealthy sponsor who had a specific interest in Rome of the First Century. As you can imagine, my thoughts immediately turned to those silver *denari*.

"I knew the coins in question would easily stand out from the rest, by virtue of their silvery gleam and quality, so my dismay upon discovering that they were no longer in the box might easily be understood. Initially I hadn't the time to dwell upon the matter, as I was still faced with the task of putting together the display that the curator had requested. I had no great difficulty in accommodating him, for our department possessed a plethora of suitable items, even without those coins, and the curator congratulated me upon my choices.

"However, once my day at the museum was done, I made my way to The Alpha in order that I might evaluate the situation over a quiet pint. I could only arrive at one inevitable conclusion: My colleague and benefactor, Mr. Connolly must have removed the coins for questionable reasons of his own!"

"You seem to have come to this insight with very little hesitation and with great certainty." Holmes remarked.

"What other conclusion could I possibly have reached? After all, Mr. Connolly and I are the only keepers of the key to that safe in the entire building, and I knew that I hadn't removed the coins. Believe me, Mr. Holmes, when I tell you that it hadn't been a result that I'd reached lightly, for I have known Mr. Connolly over many years, and the prospect of his being nothing more than a common thief filled me with dismay.

"However, as I sat there in my quiet niche, I began to recognise the awful ramifications of my discovery, should the fate of those coins come to light. There was no question in my mind that the years of faithful service, performed by Mr. Connolly, would weigh heavily in his favour, should our superiors feel obliged to choose between we two. After all, I have no proof that it had been he and not I who had done the deed, and even you, gentlemen, cannot be certain of my integrity, save for my presence here today."

"I suppose that it has now occurred to you that Connolly's arrival in The Alpha Inn hadn't been mere coincidence and that he had seen in you the perfect scapegoat for his crime," Holmes suggested, but with uncharacteristic sympathy. "A gentleman like yourself, loyal beyond reproach, but also indebted to him for your sudden rise in fortune, was hardly likely to betray him for something as trifling as a pair of old coins."

"It saddens me to admit that it has, although I cannot in all good conscience let the matter lay. I seem to remember that Connolly once had a reputation for liking a flutter or two upon the horses, to his great detriment at times. If that has been his motivation for implicating me in his crime, then I shall have no qualms about seeing justice served upon him!" Henry Baker had become more animated at this moment than I would have thought him capable of.

"Please calm yourself, Mr. Baker, although I can understand how unsettling this dilemma of yours might appear to you. You do realise that it is almost impossible for me to instigate the recovery of these trinkets without implicating either yourself or Mr. Connolly?"

"Perhaps it is asking too much, but if you can find a way to help, I assure you that I'm able and willing to recompense you for any trouble and expense that you might incur."

Holmes rose to his feet once more and he lit a cigarette whilst on his way back to the window. Ironically, the melancholy strains of "Silent Night" pierced the eerie stillness that had descended upon Baker Street now that the snow had set in, and my friend gazed down upon this scene while contemplating the problem at hand.

He walked determinedly over to the desk, upon which he hurriedly inscribed two of his inscrutable notes.

"Mr. Baker, I cannot subject our long-suffering landlady to the prevailing conditions outside. Therefore I would ask you to place this advertisement with all of the prominent evening newspapers and despatch this wire with as much urgency as you can muster." Holmes thrust two sheets of paper into the scholar's mitten-clad hands, assured that the destination for each would be obvious to him.

"If you return at this time on the day after Boxing Day, I will inform you of any progress that I might have made." Holmes's rather dismissive tone seemed to unsettle our guest and he rose to leave with more uncertainty than he might have hoped for.

"I am exceedingly grateful for your time, Mr. Holmes, and I wish you both the greetings of the season."

I reciprocated, of course, but my friend had already returned to the window and his thoughts.

"Holmes," I asked quietly once I had shown Mr. Baker to the door, "while I understand the reason for and the nature of the advertisements, I cannot, for the life of me, identify who the recipient of the wire might be."

"I've made an inquiry of the one man I know who might be able to guide me through the murky underworld into which we will now be required to descend. I am, of course, referring to Shinwell Johnson," Holmes added with a mischievous smile. "However, we may have to be patient, for he does like to celebrate most heartily at this time of year."

Johnson had indeed been invaluable to us on more than once occasion, for he possessed a vast knowledge of London's darkest passageways and anterooms, while at the same time being able to rise above its despicable allures. He had, therefore, proven to be a most steadfast ally and associate.

"I understand, although knowing of Johnson's propensity for celebration," I suggested, "we could be in for a long wait."

To my surprise, Holmes clapped his hands together joyously before making his way over to the port decanter.

"So there is nothing else for it, Watson. We shall have to celebrate ourselves, although in our own quiet manner, of course."

I couldn't offer a single word of objection, and the next two days passed very pleasantly indeed.

By the morning of the second day after Christmas, the snow had long ceased its steady fall and a slight thaw had started to set in, while Holmes's mood had heated up somewhat. The long wait for replies to his advertisements and wire had taken its toll upon his serenity over the past two days, and he spent much of his time in pacing up and down within our small sitting room while waiting for the sound of Mrs. Hudson's footsteps upon the stairs.

Mercifully, the reply from Johnson arrived somewhat sooner than the answer to Holmes's advertisements, and when that was finally delivered, my friend became galvanised once more. He despatched me with his response, and a short while later he was pulling on his overcoat and grabbing his hat. Curiously, he placed a bundle of blank sheets of note paper into a buff envelope which he then stuffed into the inside pocket of his coat.

"What say you to a visit to the Black Lion Tavern, of dark and dubious repute?"

"I should be delighted."

"Excellent," Holmes called out as he made his way down to the street. "And don't forget your gun,

Needless to say, the short journey from Baker Street to Bloomsbury didn't allow Holmes sufficient time in which to describe his machinations in any detail, although the reasons for this visit were soon to become apparent. Suffice to say that Shinwell Johnson had suggested the Black Lion as being a venue commonly used for meetings of a decidedly dubious nature, and one doubtless familiar to Holmes's respondent.

The interior of this ancient establishment had been so poorly illuminated that the dark swirls of tobacco smoke rendered a few isolated corner tables as almost imperceptible. In view of the tavern's questionable reputation, I was certain that this effect had been deliberately created and was certainly not a flaw in design or decor.

Holmes took to a table in the furthest and darkest recesses of the saloon bar and then indicated a table within sight of his own, although not obviously close by, whereby I should take my position. My instructions had been simplicity itself: Upon his signal, Holmes required that I should move my hand towards the pocket containing my revolver, although the weapon wasn't to be removed, except under the most extreme and urgent set of circumstances.

Our wait proved to be a long and tiresome one, only tempered by a good cigar and a glass of whisky that Holmes had ordered from the bar. As the evening wore on, the saloon gradually began to fill and it became increasingly difficult for Holmes and me to maintain the exclusiveness of our respective tables. One particular ruffian became quite aggressive when I suggested that he try another place, and I had been on the point of moving on myself when I glanced across to see Holmes engaged in an earnest conversation with a thick-set, middle-aged gentleman who took a seat opposite to that of my friend.

Their conversation had been drowned out by the rising hubbub of the rowdy clientele, but I could detect that a heated form of negotiation had been taking place. I saw Holmes remove and then replace the buff envelope that he had hurriedly put together, and the man opposite to him seemed to become quite agitated when Holmes refused to let him examine it. Suddenly the man's mood and attitude seemed to alter, as if Holmes had said something to him that shook him to the core.

At this juncture both Holmes and the man, who I was now certain had been none other than Mr. Connolly, looked towards me with some intensity and upon Holmes's signal I moved my hand towards my revolver. This action left Connolly both defeated and deflated and, without another word being exchanged, Connolly brought out an envelope of his own, albeit a considerably smaller one than that produced by Holmes.

After a brief though undoubtedly satisfactory examination, Holmes pocketed this other envelope and then dismissed the man with a sharp nod of his head and a brief, triumphal smile. Connolly shuffled dejectedly towards the door, only pausing to gaze longingly towards the contents of the bar. Holmes jumped up immediately and roused me to my feet with a sharp clap across my shoulders.

"Come, our return to Baker Street is long overdue and we must spare Mr. Henry Baker even an extra minute of his long and anxious vigil." Holmes called cheerfully. I drained my glass hurriedly and followed my friend to the door.

A fast cab made the return journey in no time at all and, as we burst through the door to our rooms, we could see that Mr. Baker's nerves had been shredded to the point of despair.

"My dear Mr. Baker, I owe you a thousand apologies for having subjected you to such a long wait. However, as you will shortly discover, it will not prove to have been in vain. Please, let me first calm your nerves with a festive glass of port." Before Baker could raise any form of objection, Holmes had the drink poured and he then thrust the glass into the man's reluctant hand.

Holmes smiled as he watched Henry Baker sip nervously from his drink. At the same time he slowly removed the smaller of the two envelopes from his inside pocket.

"Please put your drink down, Mr. Baker." Holmes suggested while replacing the glass with the envelope.

Baker's hands were visibly shaking as he tore feverishly at the envelope, before tipping the contents out into the palm of his hand. He sank back into his chair with a deep sigh of both relief and great wonderment and in hand sat the two coins which had been at the root of his awful dilemma.

"My dear sir," Baker asked breathlessly, "by what miracle have you caused this to come to pass?"

Holmes laughed sympathetically.

"I can assure you that there was nothing remotely miraculous about this night's work. An associate of mine, who shall remain nameless, furnished me with the perfect location for such a surreptitious transaction, and I then allowed man's most ignoble vice to do the rest of the work for me. Knowing only too well that the valuation I had placed on these coins in my message had been greatly inflated, Mr. Connolly decided to add deception to his crime of theft. Of course, I couldn't guarantee that your former colleague would rise to the bait, but I was certain that the financial lure that I had placed within the original newspaper notice would have been sufficient to bring him out into the open.

"Your assessment of the man had been a correct one, Mr. Baker, for I saw nothing but desperation in Connolly's eyes, from the moment that he took up his seat opposite to mine. Gambling, I assure you, is as much of an addiction as is alcohol or the intake of tobacco, and your former colleague had surely fallen into its darkest and most forbidding depths. Why else would he deceive and then implicate you in such a deplorable manner?"

"By what means did you manage to coerce the coins from him?" Baker asked.

Holmes produced the other envelope at once and he could barely contain his laughter when he observed Baker's look of astonishment upon discovering the torn sheets of paper.

"In his desperation, Connolly firmly believed that there was enough in there with which to satisfy all of his debtors. However, I refused to hand it over until the coins were firmly on the table before me. Upon my signal, Dr. Watson placed his hand upon his revolver and Connolly knew that his game was up. He never discovered the true nature of the contents of that envelope, and he slipped away into the night a broken and defeated man."

"Yet you did allow him his liberty." I stated, not with a little disappointment.

"Yes, but only on two conditions. That he would move away immediately, never to return, and that he would recommend Mr. Henry Baker as his successor in his letter of resignation to the Museum. He agreed to both without a moment's hesitation. Mr. Baker, I take it that you will be able to return the coins to their rightful place without the fear of detection or discovery?"

"Oh indeed, Mr. Holmes. In the absence of Mr. Connolly, I will be the only remaining key holder."

"In that case," Holmes proclaimed proudly, "you should hear nothing more of the matter, save for a very handsome promotion in the New Year!"

"Are you that certain that Connolly will carry out your exact instructions?" I asked.

"Watson," Holmes answered disdainfully, "invariably greed and fear go very much hand in hand, and I recognised both within the eyes of Mr. Connolly."

"Mr. Holmes, I have taken up far too much of your time, but how can I ever thank you enough for this great bounty?" Baker asked as he rose slowly from his chair.

"Perhaps if you have any further problems in the future, you might present them to me at a different time of year. Furthermore, Mr. Baker, I beseech you to stay away from The Alpha Inn!"

The Adventure of the Injured Man
by Arthur Hall

The past few days had been, as I recall, a Christmas that was quiet and without incident. My friend Mr. Sherlock Holmes and I had done nothing but converse, smoke, and read, with no disturbance or distraction other than our good landlady producing her excellent fare at mealtimes. Holmes refuted my suggestion that we should leave our lodgings for a walk through the nearby streets of the capital, reminding me that he deplored exercise for its own sake, and drawing my attention to the dark clouds that had hung over London for many days past.

"You expect that we will have snow then?"

He blew out a final smoke ring and knocked out his old briar. "I am certain of it, and before long. This persistent bitter cold can mean nothing else."

"I have probably presumed unjustly," I confessed, "since I had imagined that you wished to remain here for no other reason than to receive an unexpected client. Your growing restlessness since your success in the Justice Master affair has not escaped me."

"You know me too well." He replaced his pipe in its rack. "But my ordeal, I think, is over. My client of this morning isn't unexpected, but the appointment was arranged in response to his letter of Christmas Eve." He took out his pocket watch, but the door-bell rang before he could open it. "Mr. Fitter is prompt," he said with approval.

Our landlady showed in a tall young man with a sallow face and thin moustache. "Mr. Linus Fitter to see Mr. Holmes."

"Thank you, Mrs. Hudson. Kindly bring a fresh pot of tea and an extra cup."

Our visitor held up a hand. "Not for me thank you, sir. My work will have accumulated significantly during the holiday, and I must return to it at the earliest possible moment."

"Very well, then," said my friend as our landlady withdrew. "Pray be seated. I think you will find the basket chair comfortable as you explain your difficulty. This," he gestured in my direction as I rose in acknowledgement, "is my friend and colleague, Doctor John Watson. Be assured that you can speak as freely before him as you would to me. He has been instrumental to the success of many of my past cases."

I felt slightly embarrassed at this exaggerated praise as I shook hands with Mr. Fitter, a very brief experience as he withdrew his hand rather hurriedly. When we were settled, I saw that Holmes was drawing his conclusions from our client's appearance, though he revealed but one.

"You may, if you wish, partake of your usual snuff, Mr. Fitter, provided that you don't object to the aroma of strong tobacco."

"Not at all, Mr. Holmes, for I am accustomed to it from my business partners." His expression changed to one of curiosity. "How, may I ask, did you know that I am in the habit of taking snuff?"

"The tiny amount remaining upon your moustache led to that unmistakable conclusion."

"Of course. Quite an obvious observation, really."

Holmes shrugged. "In my profession, it is as natural as breathing."

"As I would expect," Mr. Fitter replied in a slightly arrogant tone. "The matter which brings me here, is one that you have doubtless met before. It is a case of blackmail."

"And what crime or indiscretion have you committed, that could allow such a situation?" Seeing our client's hesitation, my friend prompted, "I must know this, sir. If you have been subjected to blackmail, I must be aware of the reason. I cannot begin an investigation blindfolded."

The reply came reluctantly. "A week ago, I rode my mare in Hyde Park. Somehow I struck a man in passing, although I recall no sense of the impact. He lay upon the ground, dead I thought, and I looked around me and saw no other soul. My horse appeared not to have suffered any harm, or even to have become alarmed, so I urged her into a fast trot and left the place quickly."

"You didn't attend to the fellow?" I said, my tone a mixture of disgust and dismay. "I am shocked at such deplorable conduct, sir."

"I'm not proud of my actions, but at the time I felt they were appropriate. You see, gentlemen, by profession I am a lawyer, a junior partner at the firm of Lenstrom, Fitter, and Parker, and any legal repercussions from the incident wouldn't sit well with our reputation."

I started to further express my strong disapproval, but was silenced by a gesture from Holmes.

"But you have stated that the unfortunate man was dead, and that no one witnessed the incident."

"That is how I perceived the situation, and I endeavored to put it out of my mind. However, I was at home in Hampstead Heath, no more than two days afterwards, when a surly ruffian called upon me and demanded money in exchange for his silence regarding the affair."

"Did he offer any proof of what he knew?" Holmes enquired.

"He related the incident as if it had taken place before his eyes."

"How much did he demand?"

"Five-hundred pounds."

"No doubt he claimed that you would hear no more of it, after the payment of such a large sum. In fact, it would have been the first of many demands. I take it that you refused?"

Mr. Fitter produced a shiny new snuff-box, breathed in some of its contents, and blew his nose loudly into a handkerchief.

A few moments passed while he resumed a respectable posture, in silence except for the faint sounds of passing vehicles along the street and the occasional sigh of the wind.

"Excuse me, gentlemen. This is something of a habit, which I have entertained for years." He returned the snuff-box to his pocket. "I told the blackguard that I would require some little time to withdraw the money, and that he should call again this very evening, but he was too astute. He said that I should acquire the amount, but he would choose his time for another visit."

"You intended that he should call again, but after you had consulted me?"

"Exactly that. I thought that we could lie in wait."

Holmes leaned back in his chair. "That wouldn't be practical now, since the date of his intended return is unknown to us, and he may be keeping your house under observation. Did he give you any indication as to how he traced you to your address?"

"None. I have since wondered about that."

"Can you describe him?"

Our client pondered for a moment. "Short, unshaven, and not too clean, as you would expect from those of his class. His hat was pulled down almost over his eyes, and a thick muffler obscured much of his lower face. I could make little of his looks."

"The man you injured," Holmes said after a short silence. "What of his appearance?"

"That is much easier. He was short and muscular. His head was completely bald, and tattooed with the figure of a bird."

At this, I saw Holmes's expression change.

"I think that is all I need to ask, for now." he said in conclusion. "Mr. Fitter, kindly give Doctor Watson your address. If you hear any more from this blackmailer, or anything else of this incident, you must not fail to inform me at once. You will hear from me, I think, in the very near future. Good day to you, sir."

Holmes turned abruptly and strode over to the window. He looked down on Baker Street as our client produced an engraved card before leaving.

When we were alone again, I remarked to my friend, "Objectionable fellow, don't you think? I didn't like the arrogance of him, nor could I approve of any man who would abandon someone to whom he had caused injury."

"My dear Watson," he shook his head and smiled, "how many clients would I never have had if I dismissed them because of their peculiarities or because of some annoying trait? I have mentioned before now that I regard each as a unit, a conduit to the little puzzles that illuminate my life, and nothing more."

"When Mr. Fitter described the injured man, I saw recognition in your face."

"Yes, indeed. Unless I am much mistaken the victim, if I may call him that, is one Milos Narvik, a Hungarian émigré who has retired from circus life and makes his living in ways as yet unknown to me. He is often seen in various districts of the capital."

"Not any more, if Mr. Fitter's account is accurate."

He nodded. "Our client's caller who proposed blackmail was undoubtedly Silas Norris, a common figure in the London underworld and a known associate of Narvik."

"So," I said lightly, "the case is all but solved."

"Perhaps, but I think a little excursion to Lambeth, where Narvik most often plies his trade, might settle some doubts that I have developed. Mrs. Hudson will serve luncheon within the hour. After which we can set off."

I spent the next while perusing an issue of *The Lancet*, but curiosity as to Holmes's intentions dominated my thoughts, so that much of what I read was lost to my memory. Luncheon was over quickly and my friend jumped to his feet and handed me my hat and coat the instant that I drained my coffee cup. We stood in Baker Street under persisting dark clouds, our faces reddened by the keen wind, until a hansom appeared and the driver responded to my signal. He nodded silently in acknowledgement Holmes's direction and the horse took off at a fast trot.

We had passed through Charing Cross when, having failed to understand his reasoning, I enquired as to our purpose.

"There is something which disturbs me about Mr. Fitter's accident, Watson. It could be the instinct I have which often warns me when I am not hearing truth, or perhaps that he mentioned no visible injury, such as a spreading pool of blood, to Narvik after he collided with the horse. If it is nothing, then we have had a pleasant journey after our recent confinement to our rooms, and no harm can come from it."

Nothing more passed between us until the hansom left us in Lambeth High Street. We were surrounded by folk going about their daily business, but Holmes strode through the crowd with clear purpose.

"Where are we bound?" I asked him.

"I have a notion to visit some of Narvik's local haunts. We may encounter someone who has seen him recently."

We turned a corner, and I chanced to look back. "Holmes, surely that is the man whom Mr. Fitter described?"

As we watched, a fellow conforming exactly to our client's description sauntered along the pavement and studied the passing conveyances carefully, as if expecting a particular carriage. A landau approached at speed, and at that precise moment he stepped into its path. The impact flung him down, and the coach came to a halt at once. A crowd gathered quickly, and the landau's occupant and the coachman stood near with faces full of concern.

Holmes stood silent and very still, peering at the spectacle before us. Then a slow smile crept across his features and he gave way to a fit of mirth.

A few faces among the crowd glanced at him in annoyance and disapproval, and I found myself totally astonished.

"Holmes! There is no humour in this. I must go and do what I can for that poor fellow. He evidently survived his encounter with Mr. Fitter, but I doubt he has done so now."

I would have rushed to push my way through the crowd, hadn't my friend grasped my arm while struggling to contain his laughter.

"Oh, that was superb! He timed it beautifully! I don't wonder that our client was deceived, but I see it all now. Do not trouble yourself, Watson, for he has no need of you."

I stared at him in disbelief. "Do you mean because you believe he is beyond help?"

"No, old fellow, that isn't it at all. Come, let us find a hansom and return to Baker Street. Trust my judgement, I beg you, and I will explain the situation."

We were more than halfway back to our lodgings, in the company of a cabby who sang Christmas carols to himself or to his horse constantly, before Holmes had collected himself sufficiently to satisfy my intense curiosity.

"I would be grateful if you would elaborate on that disgraceful exhibition that I have just witnessed," I said when I was certain that he had calmed himself, "and your reason for preventing me from doing my sworn duty and attending to that stricken man."

"Watson, let me tell you at once that I am innocent of that charge, for the reason that there was nothing for you to do."

I shook my head in perplexity. "What can you mean? I saw the man who you have called Narvik lying there, probably severely injured."

"Lying there, yes, but no more injured than you and I are at this moment."

"But . . . I confess to being completely bewildered."

"That is because you have likely never seen that trick before now. It was an acrobatic somersault, a backflip I believe is the correct term, executed at the precise instant necessary to produce the effect of being struck by the horse. You will recall that Mr. Fitter stated that he felt nothing when his mare struck Narvik. That was because Narvik wasn't struck."

"Then this, and the incident of Mr. Fitter, was all a trick?"

"Indeed it was, and an ideal opportunity for extortion, in one way or another. Heaven alone knows what Narvik intended to hold over his victim just now. Doubtlessly he studied and selected his prey carefully, always choosing men whose reputation was precious to them. Why, I even glimpsed Silas Norris, Narvik's accomplice, among the crowd. There can be little doubt that Narvik performs this feat regularly, perhaps even daily in various places."

I sighed, both at my own lack of observation and my failure to trust Holmes's judgement when he had responded so.

"Then we can tell our client that he has nothing to concern himself with, after all. Should we not inform the official force of this?"

He nodded. "It would be as well to send a telegram to Lestrade a little later, so that he can put an end to Narvik's tricks. I doubt if Mr. Fitter will care to be a witness in court, though."

This proved to be unnecessary. We returned to Baker Street to find the good inspector awaiting us in our sitting room, Mrs. Hudson having had standing instructions to admit him in our absence.

"Good afternoon, gentlemen," he greeted us, beaming as we entered. "I do hope you have no objection to my calling on you unannounced."

Holmes gave him a wry smile. "None at all, Lestrade. After all, you have visited us many times before without warning. However, you don't usually make a point of mentioning it. Would you care for tea, or a cigar perhaps?"

"Thank you, no. I am here only to convey my appreciation. Immediately afterwards I will be on my way to Edmonton in a police coach which will shortly present itself. A local burglar has at last been apprehended."

We settled ourselves around a blazing fire.

"I am exceedingly glad to learn of that," my friend said, "but what, pray, are you here to thank us for?"

"For your assistance in the Justice Master case, of course. It is true that I would have had the fellow behind bars quickly enough had he not met with the end that he did, but you were a great help during the investigation, and The Yard is grateful."

"Thank you, Inspector," Holmes replied with a straight face. "It is good to know that my enquiries sometimes produce useful results."

"Indeed they do, sir. Incidentally, just as I was leaving my office, I chanced to meet Bowman, one of our more observant constables. He told me that he saw you in Lambeth earlier, as he was on his way back to The Yard. There's nothing in this that I should know about, I suppose?"

Holmes nodded. "I was, in fact, about to send you a message. Milos Narvik, of whom you are aware, seems to have adopted a new trade. I know of two instances when he has feigned injury after falsely appearing to be the victim of an accident. He then arranges to blackmail the unfortunate who believes himself responsible."

For the second time that day I found myself astonished, for Lestrade's response was as unforeseen as Holmes's had been earlier.

He looked at my friend with an incredulous expression, which after a moment became a superior smile.

"I am afraid, Mr. Holmes, that this time your conclusions are way off the mark. What you suggest is quite impossible. Whomever is responsible for these crimes, it cannot be Milos Narvik."

Holmes raised an eyebrow. "You seem very certain of that, Lestrade."

"Oh, but I am, sir. You see, the body of Milos Narvik was discovered yesterday morning, beneath a pile of rotten vegetables in an alley near Waterloo Bridge. He had, by my estimation, been dead for a few days. Someone put a knife in him, it seems."

"How very curious. I would like to visit the scene of his unfortunate demise."

"The body has been removed to the mortuary, naturally."

"As I would expect. But I would like to examine *the place* where he died."

Lestrade adopted a surprised look, but conceded. "Very well, but my men have already been there and found nothing."

"Nevertheless."

The inspector produced his notebook and riffled through the pages. "It was the north end of Needler's Alley, near a house with a broken-down garden fence."

"Thank you, Lestrade. I do believe that your coach has arrived near our front door. I wish you well with your enquiries in Edmonton."

Having declared that the lack of light at this late hour would hinder his investigation, Holmes postponed our visit until the following morning. Dinner, our evening, and breakfast were spent with him in a largely morose frame of mind, doubtlessly brought about by this unexpected turn of events.

We left our lodgings early, and I was glad to see the sun emerge at intervals from the heavy clouds as we neared Waterloo Bridge. The hansom having left us, we found ourselves confronted by a street of dilapidated terraced houses, and Holmes amazed me once again by striding to the entrance to Needler's Alley without hesitation.

At the entrance we hesitated, for the smell of rotting vegetables lay thick in the air.

"Hold a handkerchief to your mouth if you must. Ah, we are fortunate. It's unnecessary to venture very far into this odious place for there, if I am not mistaken, is the damaged fence that Lestrade described."

I did as he suggested, although he seemed unaffected. As I watched, my friend peered along the walls of both sides of the alley before pacing further in and returning several times. He scrutinized some muddy imprints before making a hopeless gesture.

"If only Lestrade and his men had refrained from dancing all over this patch of ground, what might we have learned from it?"

I was about to reply with some conciliatory remark when he knelt suddenly to retrieve a small object from a stagnant pool near the fence. The ray of wintry sunlight that had weakly penetrated this dismal corridor shone briefly upon it, before Holmes dropped it into his pocket without comment.

I sensed that this wasn't the time to ask questions of him, but I imagined his find to be a ring or brooch, although what part that such baubles could play in our enquiry I couldn't imagine.

After a further few paces, during which he several times poked at little piles of rubbish with his stick, Holmes shrugged and turned away abruptly.

"I can see nothing more of interest here. Let us hope that it will not be too difficult to procure a hansom."

Holmes proved to be more cheerful during luncheon, from which I gathered that he had learned something of significance from our morning excursion. I had hardly finished my blackberry-and-apple pie, and noted with surprise that he had consumed all of his, when he hurriedly left the table with the air of having come to a decision.

"Perhaps you would care to accompany me again, to Fulham this time. There is someone whom I wish to see who may be able to throw some light on this matter."

I rose and put on my greatcoat. "I wonder whether Lestrade will discover the identity of Narvik's killer."

"If he doesn't, then I must remember to point him in the right direction when we see him next."

"You know this now?"

He smiled grimly. "I do. It was elementary. I'm more interested, however, in ascertaining how Narvik performed the feat we saw yesterday, while apparently lying in the mortuary. There can be only one solution of course, but I must have other aspects of my theory confirmed before I share it with the inspector. We're about to visit a man who I believe can assist us."

We had almost arrived in Fulham when our conveyance was delayed by an overturned cart. Two young men were frantically attempting to retrieve vegetables that had been scattered across our path from burst sacks, while a third calmed a frightened horse.

I was about to use this opportunity to ask Holmes about our destination when he looked at me thoughtfully, as if he had defined my intention.

"Mr. Piotr Kavanski is a retired circus ringmaster, Watson," he began. "I wonder that it didn't occur to me before, that he might be useful in our enquiries. After all, who else would know more of those skilled in acrobatics than someone such as he? Ah, but I see that the way has now been cleared, and we can now proceed."

We alighted in a side-street before a red-brick house that was almost completely covered in ivy. I paid off the hansom while Holmes rapped upon the door with his stick, and received a response as I approached. An elderly man, slightly stooped, stood before us. He regarded us with a blank expression, fingering his untrimmed moustache before recognition dawned and his face lit up with a broad smile.

"Why, it is Mr. Holmes!" he exclaimed in a voice tinged with an accent that was unfamiliar to me. "I hadn't thought to see you again, but I am exceedingly glad to renew our acquaintance. Come in, please, with your friend."

We removed our hats and entered, to be led into a room with walls that were decorated with posters depicting circuses performances in bygone years in half the countries of Europe,. Two large and overfull bookcases stood near several armchairs and a low table.

"Be seated gentlemen, please," invited our host, settling himself opposite us. He offered glasses of a clear spirit, but both Holmes and I refused. His pleasure at my friend's visit was obvious.

"After so many years, I'm glad to see that you are still in good health," Holmes said after he had introduced me.

Mr. Kavanski brushed a lock of grey hair back from his brow. "I'm most fortunate. I suffer from occasional indigestion, but that is all. It is good to be retired when you have some years left to you, although I still miss the circus. Pavelli the tightrope walker, Valentini the juggler, and a few others come to see me when the company is in this country, and it is enough. I spend my time reading and among my many memories."

"There speaks a man who is content." I remarked.

"Indeed I am, and that is no small thing as the end of one's life grows nearer. How long is it, Mr. Holmes, since you helped me? Were it not for you, that scoundrel Morgandahl might still be continuing with his sabotage. More of my people would have been killed, and I could easily have been ruined!"

Not having heard of this before now I turned to my friend questioningly, but received no response.

"It was a simple matter," he assured our host. "Concluded long ago."

"There can be no connection, surely, to your visit today?"

"None. We are here because we need information regarding a performer who may have appeared in the circus during your travels, or you may know of him from others. He features in an affair which I am currently investigating."

Mr. Kavanski leaned forward in his chair, his eyes bright. "Of course I will help, if I can. Who is this man?"

"We know him as Milos Narvik."

"Oh, yes. He is an acrobat who once worked for me for a time, and for many other circuses. I am not so surprised that it is he that you seek, for he was always the sly one. I will tell you all that I know of him, but little of it is pleasant."

The time for dinner was fast approaching as we left Fulham. Holmes bade the cabby to wait at the first post office we passed, and was gone for a short while.

"Telegrams, I presume?" I ventured when he had resumed his seat and we were once more on our way to Baker Street.

"You presume correctly."

"To Lestrade?"

He nodded. "And to our client."

"Ah. You have told him that Narvik still lives?"

"I have invited both of them to visit us, this evening."

We regained our rooms in time for a warming glass of brandy before our meal. A bleak cold had settled upon the capital and, as Holmes had predicted, it seemed certain that we would see snow soon.

Holmes barely touched his trout, being unsettled and full of the enthusiasm that was typical of him as a case drew to its close, but I did justice to mine and to the dessert that followed.

He said little as we ate, but his eagerness was apparent. He left the table the moment our meal ended, and we seated ourselves around the fireplace as Mrs. Hudson cleared away our plates.

"I'm expecting Inspector Lestrade and two others very soon," he informed her and rose impatiently to look out of the window. "In fact, I see the inspector passing beneath the lamp across the street."

"Very good, Mr. Holmes. I will show him in."

She withdrew, carrying the laden tray, to reappear after a few minutes had passed looking bemused. Lestrade was announced, and he entered handcuffed to the acrobat whom we had seen in Lambeth.

"Good evening, Lestrade," Holmes said as our landlady withdrew once more.

The little detective removed his hat. "Good evening, gentlemen. As you can see, Mr. Holmes, I have acceded to your request to arrest Narvik. We have him for blackmail, and Silas Norris will shortly be joining him in the cells, but you hinted that there is more to this."

"Indeed there is, and if you will both be so good as to conceal yourselves there in my bedroom, I think I can promise that you will hear a confession to a more serious crime. You will leave us tonight with two prisoners, which isn't a bad night's work I think you will agree."

"Yes, Mr. Holmes, and thank you, but – "

"The door-bell has rung, and I hear Mrs. Hudson rushing to answer it. Retreat if you please, Inspector."

Appearing incredulous, Lestrade looked at his sullen prisoner. "If you know what's good for you, stay silent."

They disappeared into Holmes's bedroom before footsteps sounded upon the stairs. Our door swung open.

"Mr. Linus Fitter, to see Mr. Holmes," our landlady announced.

When all three of us were seated before a crackling fire, greetings having been exchanged, our client stared at Holmes expectantly.

"As you have summoned me here, I imagine that you have something to report."

"Indeed we have. There are several things, in fact, that must be brought to your attention. The first of these is the murderous attack that you made upon a man in Needler's Alley – the man whom you believed was blackmailing you."

The effect on our client was dramatic. His body went rigid in his chair, and all colour drained from his face. His mouth fell open, as he fought for breath.

"What . . . What are you saying?" he spluttered. "Did I not consult you to put this matter straight?"

Holmes nodded. "Indeed you did, doubtless with the intention of concealing your actions, since it would be considered unlikely that a murderer would set in motion enquiries in pursuit of his own crime. Oh, don't bother to deny your guilt, Mr. Fitter. Your response to my accusation was sufficient to convince me, even had we not acquired further evidence."

"What evidence?" His voice was a croak, his face ashen.

Holmes took something from his pocket and set it down on the coffee-table. "Your snuff-box, I believe – left at the scene of the murder, and completely ignored by the police. I noticed that you were using a shiny new replacement during your original visit. If Scotland Yard were to examine the contents of the old one, would they not find them to be an identical mixture to that in the snuff-box you currently use?"

"There are hundreds of snuff-boxes, and many who use them in London."

"Quite so, but there is more. I have determined that your snuff mixture is unusual, probably your own invention. Again, comparison with the box that I recovered should be revealing. And there is yet more evidence to come." Holmes gestured towards his bedroom door. "Watson, if you would be so good . . . ."

I got to my feet, opened the door, and stood aside to allow Lestrade and his prisoner to pass. Our client half-rose from his chair, then fell back into it as if he had swooned.

"This is impossible," he gasped, in a voice that was little more than a whisper.

"Not at all," my friend assured him. "This is Inspector Lestrade of Scotland Yard. The other is the man who attempted to blackmail you, Milos Narvik."

Narvik looked at his former victim, scowled and remained silent. Our client trembled visibly.

"No, you aren't in the presence of a ghost," Holmes continued, "nor of a man who has returned from the dead. Earlier today, Watson and I visited a man who has spent his life in the circus. His information regarding this man and his identical twin, Janos, was most illuminating."

"You seem to have murdered the wrong twin," Lestrade informed Mr. Fitter.

"Precisely," Holmes confirmed. "They were born to a half-gypsy woman whose function within the circus was to ride an elephant, and a clown with an outrageous act that appealed to the lower classes. From the first, not even their parents could tell the twins apart, until their rather insensitive mother had a blue swallow tattooed upon the head of Milos, and a red one upon that of Janos."

We all turned to look at Milos Narvik's bald head, to confirm that the bird was blue.

"As well as their appearance, they also shared the unfortunate peculiarity of never growing any cranial hair. After leaving circus life behind, the brothers settled in Lambeth. They lived apart and pursued their different illegal professions independently. Janos became a professional card cheat, it is true, and Milos derived his income from his acrobatic skill followed by blackmail such as you have experienced."

Our client sat slumped in his chair, his hands covering his face. "No, no, no!" he wailed.

"I am aware," said Holmes after a moment, "that your irresponsible actions in the past have several times brought the legal practice in which you are a partner near to disrepute. This additional incident, had you been genuinely at fault, could scarcely have avoided a scandal for them. That you became suspicious about the 'death' of Narvik, possibly because of a slip of the tongue by Norris, and made use of agents known to you through your position to discover whether he still lived, I have no doubt. But they identified the wrong man."

Milos Narvik leaned towards Mr. Fitter, so that Lestrade had to restrain him by means of the handcuffs.

He glared hatefully at our client. "So now I know why I haven't seen my brother recently. You better hope they hang you, Mister, because if they don't you'll be a lot sorrier. I have friends in prison who'll be glad to meet you, but if you ever get out I'll be waiting."

"That's enough out of you," said the inspector.

Holmes rose and went to open the window. "I see that you have brought others to assist you as I suggested, Lestrade. Capital!" Wherupon he called out before shutting out the cold blast.

Moments later heavy footfalls on the stairs preceded our door being opened to admit two burly constables.

Lestrade took out a key and unlocked the handcuffs before handing his prisoner to the tallest of the officers. "Take him straight to the Yard, Simmonds. I want him in the cells by the time I return." To the other constable, after indicating Linus Fitter, he spoke also. "This one, too. I presume that you have arranged for the police coach to meet you here?"

"It has arrived, sir."

"Good. Get on with you, then."

Both officers saluted and, with their prisoners, were quickly gone.

When the protests of the prisoners and the rattle of the conveyance had faded from our hearing, Holmes addressed Lestrade, whose expression was one of satisfaction.

"The arrest of those two should add, I think, to your already formidable reputation, Inspector."

"Again, I am in your debt, Mr. Holmes."

"Not at all. You really must not feel obliged." My friend smiled warmly. "You could, perhaps, consider our contribution as a sort of belated Christmas present. But for the moment, I am sure that you will not be averse to taking a glass of brandy with Watson and me."

The Krampus Who Came to Call
by Marcia Wilson

Chapter I – A Cold Question

"I have a simple question to ask of you, Mr. Holmes," began Inspector Lestrade, "and if you could answer it without laughing?"

"A challenge! I have no choice but to do my best. Sit, Lestrade."

"I've been at the most baffling murder scene half the night," the little policeman growled. "It wasn't so bad until you could hear the pressure drop when it hit. I had to send one of my men back to the station. He thought he was fighting the Marri when the roofing-tiles started to break." It was a rare British soldier who could adjust from war abroad to the more restrictive life of a policeman, but the Old Guard, such as Lestrade and Gregson, quietly advocated their difficult transitions. Holmes was eternally amused at how they could "manage their ethics without sullying their enmity a jot".

"I gather your murder scene centres around your simple question."

Lestrade took a deep breath. "You've travelled abroad and across the Continent. You have experience with . . . matters that are . . . ."

We watched in fascination as the little detective struggled through invisible layers of words, almost visibly picking through and discarding the vocabulary in his mind for something suited for his strange account.

". . . perhaps not . . . English." Lestrade managed at last and drank his tea in open relief that the worst was over.

Holmes pursed his lips. "One of London's attractions is the unique recipe of its melting-pot, Lestrade. One might argue that quality and quantity are at war with each other. But yes, I am known to dabble in the refugee's boroughs. As for travelling, I have been a guest through much of the Continent, even when it was most inconvenient for me to be a stranger unannounced. What is your question?"

"Does a Krampus normally kill people? Are deaths ever attributed to the Krampus? I don't . . . well, this is a dirty mess! Mr. Holmes, we have a dead man, and a Krampus was seen at hand. Some fool mentioned Fenians, so now of course they sent me the case as though I have any experience with them, but I can tell you there's a better chance of an apple-tree being this killer than a Fenian!"

"Tell me what you do know."

Lestrade took a deep breath, and I reached for my notebook.

Chapter II – An Unkind Man

"Arthur, or *Artur* Ross when he was an Austrian citizen, was a successful pawnbroker in the City. He was also one of the most formidable, and as for his friends, the police found none. It wasn't that he was cheap, for his services were dear. He had the nerve to hold valuable items owned by clients of the highest discretion, and none could use the honours of their name, title, or military achievement to sway him. It wouldn't work. Nothing mattered but the collection of numbers in his ledger. He had come into some wealth in his middle years, the sort that makes gossips talk about a swift and short marriage (That was from his clerk, a Patrick Snuff, who promised to answer any questions we may have). We know he lived on Godolphin Street, but in bad weather he would come in through the back of his house by the tradesman's entrance because it was less exposed. That street, if you can call it that, is short and mean and called Serving Walk from back in the days when only the staff in service lived in there. It is narrow, pitted, and badly kept.

"It was Mr. Ross' ritual to attend services at the Church of Helvetia after work, and he was heading home from the December 6th Liturgy at seven o'clock at night. The weather had been mild during the day, but with the temperature dropping, it was miserable for a soul to be out. A pocket-lamp was Ross' only means of illumination, outside of the rare scraps of light escaping the heavily shored windows and doors of the humble quarters. He was last seen alive by PC Barrett, who is familiar with Godolphin Street. The old man was walking quickly against the cold, his walking-stick tapping loudly against the pavements, hasting out of the chill. A rented cab was pulled up to the side as it waited for its client, and they were still there when Barrett finished his turn at the end of the street and headed back.

"He was surprised to see a Krampus walk out of Serving Walk. If that weren't enough to give a grown man a turn, seeing that in London! It was the odd, lopsided gait of the man in costume that puzzled his eye. The man walked as if wounded, and long, gasping breaths made an infernal steam from the mouth of the mask. Off the man lurched, swaying from side to side and into a cab, which clicked up and departed at a leisurely stroll. Barrett decided it was better safe than sorry and made a note of the license before detouring down Serving Walk with his lantern. It was there he found the crumpled body of Mr. Ross. The man was lying against the low picket-fence that girdled the back of his house, and he had fallen – or been flung – with enough force that the cold-softened iron latch and hasp had broken from impact. The roads and sidewalk paving were frozen taut with sign made to indicate Ross had encountered someone at his back gate: Ice-glazing was broken from the weight of their feet as they struggled, and as far as we can tell, there was no one else."

The account was passing strange, but there was a continuous twist of distaste on our guest's face that I thought suggestive of things unsaid, and Holmes voiced my thought directly.

"Tell us what you're thinking."

"It is nothing."

"Let me be the judge. You are consulting me. This is part of my fee to you."

Lestrade sighed. "Rumours of ill-feelings against our two Swiss Churches. Mr. Ross left the first to join the other."

"And the originators of the rumours?"

"Well, if I knew that, it wouldn't be a rumour, would it?" Lestrade retorted with some heat. "Twenty years ago, the Swiss Church grew a little too large in number, or perhaps the congregation found their own company too crowded. This new church is called the Helvetians for sake of clarity. I really can't see how this could be attached to the crime – presuming it is a crime because nothing about this case is straightforward.

"I know how you feel about speculation, Mr. Holmes, but I'm working with my constable's report, a single shoe-imprint with a hoof for the left sole, and a broken bell we usually see on a Krampus's belts. And," he added, "the Krampus left his cow-tail whip in the gutter where the cab had been waiting."

"Cause of death?" Holmes wondered.

Lestrade spluttered. "Have you ever been struck with a cow-tail whip? The bones are still in those tails! Being hit with a truncheon hurts less, and I know from personal experience it can cause less damage! He was an old man, quite fat around the middle, and unsteady. It sent him flying into a small fence and – if we are to believe the blood-smears – he struck his head against the iron hinge with enough force to break it, causing a fatal concussion."

"Were there no witnesses?"

"None found."

"Have your men finished eliminating the evidence with their feet yet, or shall I have anything to inspect?"

"Mr. Holmes," Lestrade said with what was for him an admirable patience, "it should amaze me if an army of bobbies could damage the marks. As I said, the barometer dropped. You might find a welder capable of cutting through the trail-signs, but I shouldn't like to ask him to come out in this weather."

Holmes chuckled. "Then by all means, let us examine."

Chapter III – A Return to Godolphin

Godolphin Street had changed very little since our last visit, * for it would take more than mere time to alter the old-fashioned houses. Some had been slyly changed, and portions were carved into smaller, separate homes for servants until one must wonder if they slept standing up or hung themselves on wall-hooks. It was one of these that the unfortunate Mr. Ross had taken for his London address. I studied the modern changes with new eyes, for experience had taught me to see a little better into the purpose of the planners. London often has an ill-deserved reputation for anarchy amongst its architectures, for it is no more immune to grandiose miscalculations than any city. Most of this, I suspected, would dissolve with time.

Our police cab took us slowly across this street, whittled into a splinter from development. The facings had the gloss of respectability for anyone with the appropriate amount of money and taste. The obverse real estate was a completely different world: The back-gates, short alleys, snickets, and connecting mews, where servants and tradesmen could enter without being seen. I admit this poorer facet was slightly more cheerful, for the washer-women were taking full advantage of the freezing dry air in hanging up the linens for a freeze drying, and here the children played rough games with icicle swords.

Our cab pulled up to a patient bobby standing on the front-step of a sober black door, trying to speak to an agitated little man wrapped like a bear for hibernation in an expensive Russian dogskin coat and hat. Tufts of wild white hair popped over his temples like the ears of a lynx, and his voice was shrill and piping as he lifted a gleaming mahogany walking-stick with enameled knob in the air, a strange conductor orchestrating the matters of the day to his liking. Lestrade groaned under his breath before sticking a pleasant smile over his lips.

"Hallo, Mr. Octavius. I've returned swiftly, as promised."

"And how will that help me?" peeped the man. "The rent was due this morning at seven o'clock! How is a decent businessman to survive if you prevent me my livelihood?"

Lestrade stopped smiling. With his hands on his hips, he glared at the righteous fellow. For all that they were of a height, the smaller man swelled up with propriety. "A crime has been committed, and if a decent businessman is unconcerned for what happens on their own lease, then we must disagree on the definition of 'decent'. I have brought experts to this matter, which with their help I expect us to finish without delay.

"However," he growled as the other made to speak, "any hindrance to our work can be seen as interfering with the law. If you persist in this, you may go to the Home Office and complain in person, or you can stay here, and I can escort you there at my own discretion." For effect, Lestrade dangled a set of derbies which had appeared in his hand as if by magic.

Holmes coughed. "You are the landlord, I presume? Did you know Mr. Ross?"

The bewildered man twisted from professional to amateur, a man truly out of his depth before responding. "He paid his rent without fail for two years, never damaged my property, nor broke my rules for guests or frivolity. These rooms are for respectable servants and bachelors. I can hardly risk my reputation for their extraneous comforts."

"Too true. I would like to speak with you after I'm finished here, but I would be remiss of interfering with your business if I kept you now." With that he took Lestrade's elbow and propelled the two of them inside the door.

The quarters were dully Spartan. Outside of a foyer that could be crossed in a single step was a room that held a crotchety old stone fireplace with a muddy painting of a primitive morality theme on its throat. Above it and touching the ceiling was another small painting, this one of a Black Madonna and Child, the sort often seen in the older parts of Europe. A table was set for a single person before this fireplace, and no signs of a second chair could I see, nor any newspaper, books, or even a writing desk for a gentleman's business. A small box rested on the table with the dead man's effects collected out of his pockets. Lestrade often resisted Holmes's advice, but he had taken to heart the idea that a murder victim's possessions shouldn't leave the location of the crime before a thorough examination.

The walls were dark-panelled wood and wainscotting of bottle-green varnished with age. Nary a drugget decorated the floor. Lestrade showed us the rest of the rude rooms. Up a stairwell that pinched even Holmes was the one single room for sleeping. A standing wardrobe of the same materials as the wall and wainscotting stood beside the bed. The bed was in a cabinet, built inside the wall. The lamps were small and stingy of flask, with no modern gaslights to bring cheer.

"The attic and cellar?" Holmes wondered as he peered up the stairwell.

"Both locked from tenants. He keeps it for his own use, which, if my men have collected the right gossip, he uses for farming mushrooms, or storing dynamite for a war against the Fenian, or burying pirate treasure."

Lestrade sniffed. "We had to investigate as soon as we heard the word 'Fenian', worse the luck."

The remains of a long-cold fire sat in the grate as the winds moaned in the top stack. Through this room I could see a small kitchen and a narrow door that presumably led to the outside.

"We have to go through the kitchen to get to the yard and back-gate where the murder took place," Lestrade grumbled, and I could hardly blame him his low spirits. Holmes's smile for his task only annoyed him, and I could see why Inspector Gregson enjoyed riling the little professional as much as he did. Lestrade's single-focussed attack on crime left much space for surprise, and he hated surprise.

"A moment first."

Holmes lined up the contents of the box on the table. There was a thin wallet rendered soft as silk from years of use, a pocket-watch that had stopped in the cold, and a small coin-purse, the sort a gentleman would use to tip a driver. Holmes was slowly plucking money and notes out of the wallet when he suddenly looked up and stopped.

"Hmmph! Now that is a little out of the ordinary."

We followed his gaze but saw only the painting. I found it exceedingly strange. It featured a stout man with barely an expression as he watched a fierce stranger walking into a room, terrifying the children about the table. The figure pointed to the windows where lightning flashed.

"Very well. I should like to see the body."

We passed through the kitchen. The yard, originally set aside for the labours of servants, was even harder than the streets. Someone, perhaps Mr. Octavius, had paved over every thread of green years ago with what appeared to be old firebrick. The result was a dangerous, glazed surface marbled and pitted into whirlpools, waves, and waterfalls from frequent freezing and thawing. Our walking sticks were indispensable, and our pace slowed to a crawl before we could reach the shivering bobby on the end of the yard. Just past his guard we could see the darkened form of a man in a rich black wool coat trimmed with musquash. Less than a yard from his outflung left arm was a cow's-tail whip, the hairs at the end splayed like dark, frayed wool and the grip-end wrapped tightly with stout packing-string.

"Begging your pardon, Mr. Lestrade." The constable tapped his gloves to his brim as he spoke. "Clancy thought he might ask the neighbors, as they were coming up with the milk, and I told him I would stay guard."

"All right, Barrett," Lestrade nodded. "I suppose they couldn't recall anything?"

"Too soon to tell, sir. The man's deaf and the wife's blind and their grandson speaks for them both, but he be a tyke still. They just went just as the bells rang the quarter-hour. Shall I fetch them?"

"Not yet," Lestrade said as Holmes gave an almost imperceptible shake.

The dead man had begun to freeze almost as soon as his body had sagged to the earth. As Lestrade had said, he was elderly and plump about the middle and that, along with his coat, was at odds with the meanness of his address. After years of stubborn training, the police had learned not to close the eyes of the dead, and we could see they had naturally slit half-shut, the eyes rolled up as unconsciousness descended. A trail of dark red marked the slide of the back of his skull from the broken fence to the earth. His left hand was gloved and clutched still around his stout stick. As a former military man, my attention was sorely distracted from the dead man's left hand. It was bare. Within its palm rested one of the tiniest hand-revolvers I had ever seen, the sort glamourised in sensational novels with gamblers and frontier fighters.

Holmes knelt carefully on the hardened lumps of snow, black with age and soot. "He hit the iron hinge hard enough to break it," he muttered. "It was only thirty degrees at supper yesterday. Lestrade, what was the temperature in the night?"

Lestrade flipped through his notebook. "Recorded at twenty-one degrees at nine. Gone up to twenty-nine since then." He glanced up to the sky uneasily to where the clouds were gathering in a yellowish-brown billow. "We'll have snow if it keeps warming up."

I understood his fears. Snow could easily hide the small clues required to solve this case.

Holmes sat back on his heels in thought and then carefully leaned over to examine the soles of the shoes, which seemed to be perfectly ordinary black leather and wooden-soled gentleman's half-boots, the sort worn for formal occasions.

Lestrade knelt carefully on the painful-looking lumps of frozen snow and tapped him on the shoulder. "That left hand concerns me for several reasons. Why was his glove off? We found it in his pocket."

"Ah, but Lestrade, how could he fire this dainty pistol with a glove on that hand?"

"He was a madman to walk around with his hand primed for shooting in his pocket. He must have been expecting trouble."

"I hesitate to agree without further news."

Lestrade and I saw nothing, but Holmes's sharp, grey eyes narrowed. A frown crossed his brow.

"Your Krampus is innocent of murder, Lestrade." Holmes pointed to a portion of the iron gate where the bars were clean of the thick glaze of ice elsewhere. At the bottom of the spikes were shattered ice. "Herr Ross' stick is a formidable weapon, and one to avoid." With his own stick he pointed to the bottom of the man's shoes. "Those wooden soles are completely unsuitable for this rude path. He was unsteady on his feet and this altercation, whatever its nature was to him, caused a fatal imbalance."

"Are you saying the gun and the Krampus have nothing to do with this?" Lestrade exclaimed, his outrage smoking the air about his face.

"Oh, of course not. We have ourselves a mystery, Lestrade, and if I am correct, a crime."

"Be that as it may, I must still look over all possibilities. Do you want to know when we find the cab driver?"

"Of course," Holmes said cheerfully, which promptly turned the policeman a shocking shade of purple.

"Mr. Lestrade?" PC Barrett poked his head out of the door. "The large painting's starting to crack apart from the cold, and when I said that, the landlord told me he doesn't want to bring the heat in to save it."

"My day continues its blessings," the inspector said under his breath. "I suppose I shall have to remind him of his duty to the law – Eh?" for Holmes was plucking at his sleeve.

"Bring the painting to our rooms, Lestrade. I daresay it's cozy enough to preserve the evidence, and I can sign a covenant promising not to tamper with it."

"As can I," I added stoutly.

Lestrade smiled wryly. "When you have a thought in your head, no matter how outlandish, I've learned to let you take your lead. You're worse than a cold-nosed hound in a pack of lurchers, Mr. Holmes."

"A compliment, I am sure."

"Oh, it is." Lestrade's expression was a little strange. "You think the painting is important, eh?"

"I shouldn't like to speculate at this point, but if it is damaged, we'll be forced to work ever harder. And more holidays are coming up."

"Very well. Tell me how you want it wrapped and we'll deliver it – Oh," Lestrade coughed at the bright anticipation that had illuminated my friend's face. "You want it now."

"It can be delivered directly. In the meantime, I should like to see our victim's place of business."

The solitary clerk in Mr. Ross' employ was a sad, lean man with a beard grown as thick as fashion would permit against the office chill. He shook hands with us as a workman and met our eyes as a gentleman. Even PC Barrett received the same respect.

"Thank you for seeing me at this hour," he began. "I ought to unlock the doors in an hour, and this gives me time to collect my thoughts. I am Patrick Snuff, and I have worked for Mr. Ross over thirty years."

"That is a long time," Holmes observed.

"Enough wages for my roof and a meal a day. Someday I shall retire to a place with fewer stairs and more hot water bottles." He smiled painfully and leaned upon a homemade crutch before sitting down. "Have a seat, do."

"Did you know your employer well?"

"I couldn't say, for I don't know how well one could know him. He was remote – remote as an alp, and those were his own words, recited often with satisfaction. I don't think he cared much for anyone. They didn't matter to him as much as the numbers he totted up at the end of the day. Oh, he could be a poet when he spoke of numbers, for he thought them beautiful . . . but people? No. He was quare, sir. Quite quare."

"Did he have interests? Passions?"

"He was a believer in the Swiss Church until twenty years ago, and he moved in with the new church – they call themselves Helvetians, the Church of Helvetians. They are a bit revivalist, leasing a place a year at a time. I understood the old church thought respectable businessmen should tithe, and he felt singled out, though on occasion some of the old congregation would come and plead with him to return to their fold, claiming it was but a misunderstanding. Last night was the eve of the sixth, and he never missed a service. First one to arrive, last one to leave. He loved to watch the Krampus."

"That isn't a common sentence."

"No, and I mind there precious little of that foreign nonsense in London! Yet among their own people they would come. I saw it myself once or twice. The Krampus would come out of the shadows, a-frightening the children and weak-minded, and I hear there's quite a collection of funds taken after he's driven off." The old fellow chuckled suddenly. "He used to be a Krampus. His suit is still in the back. Would you like to see it?"

I once saw several Krampus in character when I was abroad with Holmes, but there is something off-kilter about seeing one during the light of day. Their garb is meant to be appreciated under the wild, flickering firelight, for it brings out a savage element that taunts the power of the intellect against fear. Here under the electric lamps, the hulking shape on the corner coat-rack was sorely out of place and time, its effect a pale shadow of its true nature.

The Ross Krampus was a collection of goatskin pelts, sewn in patches over the tops of a rough wool suit. The mask was heavily lacquered thin wood wrapped around a dangling red tongue, sharp white teeth, and bulging, mocking eyes. A lump of black wool was its hair, mane, and tangling beard. The ram's horns were large, but surprisingly well balanced on their headdress. On the wall rested a thick leather belt clotted with rumble bells. The boots and trouser legs were wrapped in more wool to look like the hairy legs of a sheep or goat.

To the complete surprise of myself, Lestrade, and Mr. Snuff, Holmes suddenly dipped his nose into the costume and breathed deeply. "An interesting perfume, wouldn't you say?"

"No," Lestrade answered bleakly. "I shan't. Because my nose will not go near that."

"Not a costume for an old man," Holmes commented.

"You'd be surprised," was Snuff's answer. "Those heavy bells are placed in the back for a reason. They counterweight that heavy mask in the front. Once they are suited, they can move surprisingly fast. Still, it is an adventure for younger men to run, and old men to walk."

"You seem to know a bit more of the custom than your humility conveys."

"One can learn a lot by accident in thirty years. Mr. Ross had some pride in this thing and said that every village had its own special way of doing their Krampus, and that you could tell them apart from the very style. I think it meant more to him because he couldn't be one anymore, you see. He had bad lungs."

I nodded to Holmes to show I agreed. The cyanic tint about the dead man's mouth and nails had been darker than expected from his cause of death.

"Barrett?" Lestrade turned to the younger copper. "Did the Krampus you saw look like this?"

"I thought so, sir," the young man answered. "But now that I see it closely, no. It looks very much like it, but the mane on that Krampus was very pale and grey, like what you'd see on an old mountain-sheep."

Lestrade's hopeful expression fell. "Ah, well," he muttered, tapping the rumble-bells on the broad leather belt. "Mr. Holmes, I'm back to work. I have more threads to gather. Do you wish the news as it comes?"

"Of course. Thank you for your patience in this, Lestrade. This isn't an ordinary matter, and it has my attention. You, Mr. Snuff, have been a great help."

We parted ways in the wintry streets. Holmes scribbled a note and folded it over a coin. A sharp whistle soon brought over a little street-urchin wrapped in many layers.

"Do you know where the Church of Helvetians might be, my lad?"

The child sniffed. "Course I do."

"Can you run this to the minister at the church?"

"Course I can."

Holmes laughed as the lad ran off with breathtaking speed. "They are their own priceless depths of knowledge. There is no inkling of prayer or sermon that can soak into the heads of such children. They are too interested in filling their bellies and sitting by a warm stove, but they can quote you book and verse everything you say to them – It is a game they play with respect for the rewards."

"Do you think Lestrade was wrong about Ross leaving the Church?"

"Oh, no. Merely incomplete."

Chapter IV – Portrait of a Crime

The duties of my profession demanded that I part ways with Holmes. I tended my patients for the rest of the week and barely saw Holmes or Lestrade. Both men orbited around Baker Street for news or a sandwich before returning to the case on hand. In the late hours I would find Holmes staring at the painting that now lived in our rooms. As the days passed, I caught crumbs of intelligence: The cab's license was forged, the true identity unknown. Ross's clerk had confessed to a misspent youth in petty crimes after Lestrade had found him in old records but had, he swore, lived honest since. Less could be said of his employer, who had been suspected of the disappearance of several liquidated estates in Austria.

At the end of the week, I came to breakfast and found that Holmes had moved the painting to his chemistry table, his glassware perilously arranged about the floor. He was completely absorbed in study with a long-cold pipe between his teeth. I recognised his prized olive-wood. He treasured it for its effortless draw when he couldn't remember to keep it lit, and I think the bowl existed unsmoked as much as smoked. Still, Holmes's moods were diagnosed with acuity if I checked his choice of smokery as seriously as I did any patient's colour, weight, and pulse. This an encouraging sign.

"Holmes?" I asked with some reservations, as such broad questions can be taken quite literally.

He didn't look up from the canvas. "This isn't a fine work or art, nor was it meant to be, but I should think it worthy all the same."

"Come eat and tell me about it. Also, can you tell me why you said Lestrade's information was incomplete on the morning of the seventh?"

Holmes snickered. "He didn't think to ask *why* the church had closed at the hour it did."

"How would that matter?"

"Because the Church of Helvetians closes much later by custom – nine of the clock at the earliest. Pipes had burst and the cold had pulled the gas to dim flickers, forcing the elders to close outside of their schedule. Mr. Ross wasn't expected by the Krampus when they met. I believe it was a peaceful plot gone awry."

Holmes tapped his pipe thoughtfully. "Which itself could be invisible information. It's likely that the Krampus is the one who brought this painting and went through the trouble of hanging it up, and that he was strongly compelled to create this message without Mr. Ross being anywhere nearby. A strong message normally begs for the recipient of the message to be witnessed." He returned to the painting with a scowl.

"Why do you study this so? Has it revealed anything to you?"

"Even more than Herr Ross and his Krampus coat."

"I thought the costume interesting but not illuminating."

"That is because it was worn by the Krampus that night."

"What! But Barrett said it wasn't. The mane was completely different!"

"Barrett will have to learn to trust himself. The mane is detachable. You saw me lean closer to smell it."

"We all did. I thought Lestrade's jaw would hit his shoes."

"The mane smelt of mothballs and preservatives, but the rest of the costume, the robes and mask, still carried the scent of a cold night outside. I said nothing because I am still collecting my traces."

"There was a rumble-bell at the scene."

"And there was a rumble-bell with a new, hastily made stitch in the back. Surely you wouldn't expect a costume to be neglected? This is a point of pride. Who would own a Krampus guise and not keep a little supply for repairs?"

"Then Snuff is the killer?"

"I would be very surprised."

There were times when I felt complete sympathy for Lestrade. "Very well. This painting – what have you seen?"

"Much. It has taken several years to make it, and with pigments collected as they were made available. Likewise, the brushstrokes vary in skill, but I believe it was the effort of our painter to compensate from less-than-ideal materials. I even found an overpainted cat's-whisker in the corner."

"How sad for the artist to be so improvident."

"Perhaps not. A cat doesn't actually have whiskers, but *brissae*."

"It was habit," I responded testily. "As a man of science, I do know *brissae* from whiskers. They are stronger and more elastic."

"And since you are also a man of the arts, you would know a miniaturist makes much use of the *brissae* in felines, otters, and walrus. Thus, I think this artist isn't so mean as he pretends. Fine details weren't the focus of the portrait, but whatever effects could be made to startle the viewer."

I looked again at the painting. In the more familiar and warm light of our room, the work seemed less crude and clumsy, somehow, but powerfully emotive. "A rough peasantry style, I thought at first. Now I think it deliberate."

"It was likely begun in the '80's, and as you should know, there are few decades in civilisation where drama and discontent existed on such outstanding levels. We have ourselves an early Impressionistic student – a mongrel born of the unholy union of Realism with the morals of a Positivist permanently marred by exposure to Eakins."

I couldn't hide my distaste. "You are saying that this painter believes the subject of the painting is more important than the story behind the painting?"

"Not quite. I think the two are completely the one and the same, with little of that obfuscation too many artists employ, as if two-dimensional art must be converted into a multidimensional puzzle. Look hard, old fellow, and describe to me this work of art."

"I see a poor, rude room that is barely furnished with only a clock high in the wall for decoration. I wouldn't call the painting of the Madonna and Child a decoration, of course, but it is peculiar that this is one of the Black Madonnas. The curtains look cheap. It has a rough table, sufficient for dining but nothing more. The cloth is tawdry. The chairs are slightly more elaborate and may be older, from a different set. There is a small lantern for light for the Madonna, and a single candlestick on each end of the table. Were the room rich enough for proper furnishings, they would all be inadequate to the task."

"Very good, Watson!"

"The scene about the table is fear and discord. The Prayer Book or Bible is left open. Small toys have been cast to the floor in a tantrum, and upon this scene a Krampus has been called. He is tall, lean, elderly, and silent. I call him a Krampus because at the chair of the standing father I can read in German – '*Anti-St. Niklaus*'. The children are hysterical with fear at this image, one beseeching his father on his knees for pity. But the father isn't paying the least attention. He is watching and waiting with an odd expectancy, not upset that his children are about to be taken away by the Krampus."

"Excellent! What else?"

"This must be an older version of the Krampus. The word means 'claw', as in from starvation, and this being is thin indeed! There are no accoutrements that the tourist sees of this monster, just a menacing figure entering the room."

"You have seen a great deal, but not the most important thing."

"Then what did you see?"

"A monster among criminals."

"What!"

"The man of the house is the monster, not the Krampus! Remember that the Krampus is used as a weapon against naughty children, but no one – man, woman, or child – is free from his justice. Look at the chair's lettering! '*Anti-Nicklaus*'! It was on *his* chair and no one else's! The painter could have chosen any place in the painting, and if this were the traditional Krampus, would it not have been for a naughty child? No, this is for the man. He sits upon the throne of anti-Christmas fellowship.

"The house is meagre, yet the clothes are decent. The girl's hair nicely set, her stockings and shoes modern. The children wear velvet coats and new collars. And just look at the terrified infant – clutched protectively by a sibling. Hardly the act of a bad child. See how the older girl leans forward, placing herself between the threat and her younger loved ones? And what infant, I ask you, would deserve a Krampus? Yet the children seem to think he has come for them!"

"Good heavens!" I found myself exclaiming. "The toys are on the floor because they flung them *at* the Krampus? Go on."

"The father-figure thinks the Krampus has come for the children. Rather, the Krampus has come for him."

"This is a chilling thing."

"It was meant so. It is night – the clock confirms the late hour. It is a quarter-til-midnight, and yet the children are still up and awake at this farce. Yet look – the curtains have been drawn to expose the wintery storm. Lightning in the heart of the winter! And why, I ask you, are most of the children seated with their backs to the Madonna and Child? Why does this man with his pious stance and complacent expression with the open Bible before his belly set the children so they cannot look upon the veneration?"

"I don't like this at all. He has seated the children with their backs to the Holy Mother and Child."

"Exactly. He has cast them from the eye of Heaven."

"I am appalled."

"Study this Krampus well, Watson. See how his garb is rags and moth-eaten pelts, more in the style of the old Belsnickle who treated the good and bad according to their actions. His shoes are rude. And," Holmes pulled out a length of measuring-tape from his pocket and stretched it from the eye of the Krampus to the standing man at the table, "the newcomer's attention is completely on the man. The man isn't yet aware that *he* is the purpose of the visit."

It was true. A straight line could be drawn from the eye of the Krampus to the fatherly figure opposite the table.

"The question, is who planned this?"

Holmes aimed the stem of his pipe to the centre of the painting. "Who else but one of the cowering children."

"You are certain."

"As I am of anything. This is the only child separate and apart. He has been favoured from the others in some way, but you can see it gives him no comfort. He huddles in on himself, a position of cowardice as his brothers and sisters cluster together. At the same time, look at how he alone has the unobstructed view of the Madonna and Child! This child, for whatever reason, was singled out for punishment or praise, and either would be an endurable burden." Without taking his eyes from the canvas, Holmes pulled matches and made a fresh pipe. "This child is our painter, my old friend. See how the painter's point of view is almost the same as this poor boy. He is practically sentencing himself as judge and jury."

"But how are you to find this boy? Or if we are to rely on the painting, will he be an adult by now?"

Holmes suddenly smiled at me. "The answer has been written for me."

Chapter V – Well-Meaning Witness

"Do you know aught of this?" Lestrade asked me in way of a greeting and waved a clutch of note-paper in his gloves. "Mr. Holmes tells me to come here and listen to the witnesses of the events of the sixth." Lestrade grunted impatiently and threw himself before the fire. "Got word from the coroner," he grumbled. "The case may be thrown out for lack of evidence."

"Or proof of innocence?"

"My conscience should only be so fortunate."

We didn't have long to enjoy the fire, for Holmes's familiar stamp upon the stairs followed the clap of the front door and the heavier shuffle of a second man unfamiliar with our layout.

"Ah, Lestrade! Punctual as always! If I may," Holmes half-bowed. "I have a guest who would like to make our acquaintance, and yours in particular, Inspector." He stepped aside and let the other inside the room.

The man was tall and stooped forward, his shoes slightly scuffling on the carpet. He was lean with large hands and feet, and the pasty complexion of someone who spends long hours indoors at his craft. Instead of the usual fob on his watch-chain, I saw a fine brass loupe, its quality at odds with the common style of his watch and chain. Premature ageing had whitened his hair and the long, thinning beard trickling down his chest. In a moment I recognized the Krampus of the painting. My face betrayed me, for he smiled and looked down at his shoes.

"I used to put chalk in this to look older," he said softly, and stroked his beard. "I don't have to do that now." At that he turned to Lestrade. "Is it too late to confess? My name is Andrew Eder, and I don't want to cause any trouble."

Lestrade's face was nearly priceless with surprise, but his answer was calm. "Never too late, I should hope. But what, if I may ask," he scowled with his familiar skepticism, "is your confession?"

"Well, I thought it was from my father's death, but he," and he nodded at Holmes, "said I should confess with the truth and let you decide what it is."

Lestrade looked at Holmes, our guest, at me for clarification I couldn't provide, and to Holmes again. "We'll talk about this later, Mr. Holmes," he promised with a rather dark expression, and smoothed it back to gesture at the empty seats. "I would very much like to listen to what you have to say." The inspector lifted the papers Holmes had written up with an inquiring lift of the brow. "This is how you wish to explain it?"

"It is. Young Mr. Eder and our Clerk Snuff have agreed to meet with us, and – hah! There is the very man!" Holmes leaped down the stairs as a timid knock fluttered against the wood of our door. Before long, our room had a fifth man. The Clerk and Mr. Eder seemed ashamed of looking at anyone but each other, but Holmes dismissed this and threw himself into his favourite chair with a flourish.

"Gentlemen, this is Inspector Lestrade of Scotland Yard. He is here to listen to your accounts regarding the night Mr. Artur Ross, or Johannes Eder, met his unfortunate end. The gentleman in the corner taking notes is Dr. Watson, my esteemed colleague, and both men can be absolutely trusted with their discretion."

"Of course," I vouched, and Lestrade followed me a moment behind, for he was still wary in the manner of all policemen.

"Very well. I shall begin. First, we can agree that Mr. Ross was completely flawed as a human being, a father, and a provider. The extensive records the Swiss police have been happy to provide us describe a successful businessman at the expense of those who were kind enough to extend their trust. Do we not agree?"

"We agree," Mr. Eder and Snuff chimed together.

"His treatment of his young, half-orphaned son Andrew was poor enough, but things worsened when he took in his orphaned nieces and nephews, the children of his own sister, Anna, and her husband Helmut Oswold. The starvation and depravity were extended even though these children came with their late parents' inheritance, which was well enough for any large family. He brought them all to England, where there were no relatives within easy reach, and on one fateful December day, he abandoned them."

"He was going to leave my cousins behind," Eder corrected. "I refused to go with him, and he left me too. He said we could all starve together."

"Which you nearly did!" Snuff snapped. He glared at Holmes. "I had been his clerk for years and I'd already had my fill of him, but what he did .... He came to work and I asked about them, for they were good children. *Oh*, he said, *I have lightened my load. They are back with family in Vienna.* How much a fool did he think me, when I had to keep his own books and I knew there were no relatives left?

"I went cold all over, and I swear I imagined those children dead in the Thames, pushed over the dock or in a ditch. As soon as I could I left work and sought them out. I finally found them huddled in a corner at the King's Cross Station, frozen to the bone. Somehow, I got them to my bachelor rooms, but it were months before the youngest stopped coughing. I used my own money and put them up even though it was barely enough for a single man." Snuff took a deep breath. "I wasn't an honest man when I was young. I was in gaol and he had found out about it. I had no hope of finding work anywhere else for he made certain the world would know if I ever left his office." He dropped his head in shame. "I taught the children a few of the things that got me in gaol, just so's we could eat. We had to live in secret, always afraid of being found out."

"Ross paid you lower wages because of your past, I suppose?" Lestrade asked wearily.

"Much lower."

"Go on."

"He had no interest in ever coming to my rooms, so the children were safe enough. But little Annie, the baby – she was weak from the night he abandoned them and kept their money."

Eder choked. "It was better than live with Ross. By then he knew about us, and he found ways to make us suffer because he enjoyed it. Every Christmas we would look forward to Snuff giving us toys and a good supper, and every year we would only be allowed to enjoy them for a few hours. Ross would dress up like a Krampus in our family's suit and come in, demanding our new clothes and toys because of some false offense we'd supposedly committed during the year. We'd give him all of it just to keep the Krampus from getting us, and because we dare not make him angry at us or Snuff. Then, Ross would sell the toys for his own pockets. The joy that it gave him to do so was perverse."

Lestrade's face didn't change. "I've arrested parents for even worse, but drink was usually the cause. What happened the night he died?"

"I painted that." Eder nodded to the painting on the table. "We all have respectable work now, but I'm a miniaturist with very little free time, so it took me years . . . I was trying to burn him out of my soul and when I had a little paint leftover from a job, I worked on it, imagining him dragged to hell. At first it was by the old Krampus of my mother's village and eventually I painted myself into the Krampus.

"One day it was finished, and it wasn't enough to paint it. I wanted him to see it."

"I was worried about Andrew's health." Snuff coughed. "When he had the painting to think and fret over . . . he had focus. But it was done, and he told me he wanted it left where it could be found. I didn't think it would end so badly. Every December 6th, the old man would go to his church and be out most of the night, for they close late. I thought I would keep the lad out of trouble and deliver the painting myself, and he gave it to me. I'm sorry that I lost my nerve from the waiting, and finally it seemed a good idea to put on the Krampus robes and take the painting to his house that way . . . someone might see me, and they wouldn't see me under the mask and furs, would they?

"I went to the office, pulled on the robes and an old sheepskin to look different, just in case. I had the painting inside the large sack that a Krampus carries, I limped to the cab we had rented. Andrew was my driver and we had thought the night would be as it had been during the day – damp and dank. We hadn't thought the weather might change. Before long it was cold enough that frost was starting to fall over the canvas and the cobbles were turning slick and hard as diamonds, and I was afraid the whole bit would break apart before I even got there, or the horse would slip and ruin his leg. Somehow we got to the Walk where it met the regular road and I got out as planned. I kept Mr. Ross' key for him, for I had to deliver his things at odd hours. I used it to open the door, and I stepped in long enough to put the painting up on the mantel and lock the door on the way out.

"It is hard to see through those eye-holes, and after I closed the iron gate and turned three steps down the road, I found myself staring at Mr. Ross, his eyes bulging out of their sockets. He let out a yell like a man before a demon and grabbed at the cow-tail whip in my hand. His other hand raised it up to strike me, but the ground was hard and greasy with ice, and he slipped, so instead of hitting my throat, he knocked a bell off the belt. I heard it ring as it fell to the ice.

"He fell on his side, trying to swear at me and gasp for air at the same time, and I knew I must walk away or my own hate of him would be my undoing. I walked best as I could, but I never looked back at him. I didn't dare. It felt years, but I escaped to the cab and Andrew took us away. It wasn't until the next morning that any of us knew what had happened."

"It is my fault," Andrew spoke up. "The plan was mine. We didn't think he would break his skull open on the gate. I wanted justice, not murder."

"We all did," Snuff reminded him. "It was my work, my doing."

"A moment, please." Lestrade lifted both hands, and temporarily, his gaze to the heavens. "Just a moment please, both of you." He took a deep breath. "Mr. Holmes, the note you sent me implied you had read and agreed with the verdict of our coroner?"

"I do."

"Very good." The policeman's mouth twisted. "Would you like to share it?"

"Neither man is guilty. Ross slipped on the ice with his impractical Church shoes and his walking-stick wasn't able to compensate for his balance. He fell and met his own demise against the gate, most likely the second time he tried to get up and shoot Mr. Snuff in cold blood."

Andrew gasped, and Snuff clapped his hands over his mouth.

"You are both fortunate to be alive." Holmes said sternly. "Lestrade, I shall not give you the details that I've learned of this man. He was far more sinister than even you can imagine. You meted out a non-violent justice and meant nothing more, Mr. Snuff. Ross would have gone much further."

Snuff gulped hard. "Aren't we going to gaol?"

Lestrade sighed. "Mr. Snuff, the prisons are full of men and women who thought they were doing the right thing in confessing to more than what they did. My duty is to the law." He rubbed at his head. "You had the key to his house because you were his business partner, and you went into his house to deliver a gift, and it is the Christmas Season. You had the help of his only son and heir, so if I took this to the courts, I'm sure their laughter would keep me warm a month. I would, however, like to know the name of the man who rented you that cab, as the license number was an *excellent* forgery."

Some weeks later the winter turned foul and I found myself sharing an awning with Lestrade. We watched the storm over our heads in silence for some time before I finally spoke.

"I thought it fortunate that the coroner's decision coincided with Mr. Holmes's."

"Morelike the coroner agreed with what Holmes told him had happened." Lestrade said without looking at me, his attention on the rare winter levin. "He has a reputation at the Yard. Not to mention the luck of the very devil. The Office was so grateful that the Fenians weren't in the case they would have agreed if he'd said an elephant had trampled Ross. I was afraid they were going to do their own trampling and make a travesty of the law in their haste."

"Surely that was more than luck," I protested. "Holmes has laboured hard for his reputation."

"Which is what frightens them, from every corrupted beat copper to the Foreign Office clerk we aren't supposed to know about." Lestrade pulled up his collar moodily. "He can't be bullied, as you know. God help anyone who lies to him, be they high or low. If he hadn't been consulted from the start, I would have been forced by my own duty to bring in those poor gulls and it'd be a manslaughter charge and ruined lives. Thankfully he took my case and stopped a scandal before it started."

"Why, Lestrade!" I laughed. "You make my friend sound more formidable than a Krampus!"

"Oh, Dr. Watson." Lestrade turned away from the storm to stare at me. "Which one of the two would you rather face?"

NOTE

* A reference, however subtle, to "The Second Stain", and we should warn the readers who wish to date this story by Watson's own words: *It was, then, in a year, and even in a decade, that shall be nameless.*

The Adventure of the Christmas Wish
by Margaret Walsh

It was two days before Christmas when Lady Augusta Bellwether came to our rooms in Baker Street. Holmes, being the man that he is, gave little sign of the spirit of Christmas except for a wreath of holly and ivy that Mrs. Hudson had affixed quite determinedly to our door.

I put aside the morning newspapers that I had been reading. The theft of Lady Cottingley's diamonds was the major story in all the papers, alongside the annual wish for snow on Christmas Day.

Lady Augusta was a stout woman in her mid-fifties, with silvering hair drawn up in a simple bun. She surveyed us both with a forthright gaze. The lady took the seat offered to her as if it was her due before announcing, "Mr. Holmes, I wish you to find my grand-nephew. The imbeciles at the police station tell me the boy has run away. I ask you, what eight-year-old boy runs away into the cold and wet?"

"If you could begin at the beginning, Madam?" Holmes said, taking his usual chair and gesturing me to resume mine.

"Of course. Mr. Holmes, my eight year old grand-nephew, Simon Staines, is missing. His father, my nephew Augustus Staines, is currently in India. His wife, Simon's mother, died of some dreadful fever there, and Augustus thought it best to send the lad to me. He hasn't been here long, and the dear lad is dreadfully homesick, I will admit. But that alone is no cause for that stupid policeman to tell me the boy had simply run away. Simon knows no one else here. Where would he go? He may be only eight, but he is bright enough to realize that he cannot walk to India, which is the only place he would have to go to."

"From where did the lad disappear, and when?"

"My home near Hyde Park. His nurse discovered he was missing this morning. Naturally, I went straight to the police. When they proved to be distinctly unhelpful, I came to you."

"With your permission, we will visit and look for ourselves."

Lady Augusta smiled briefly and rose to her feet. "We shall go at once. My carriage is downstairs."

Taking our coats and hats from the stand by the door, we followed the lady down to our front door, where a fine coach-and-four stood at the curb.

Holmes handed Lady Augusta into the carriage before he and I joined her, sitting opposite as the vehicle pulled away.

The journey to Hyde Park was undertaken in silence. Lady Augusta clearly wasn't the sort of person to engage in idle chit-chat and, to be honest, neither was my friend. I contented myself with gazing out of the window at a dreary London that was cold and wet, but with no sign of the snow much longed for by the newspapers, and wondering what on earth had happened to the child.

Lady Augusta's home was an elegant Georgian townhouse situated in Albion Street. Hyde Park was clearly visible at the end of the road. A holly wreath bound with red ribbons was attached to the front door, which was swiftly opened by a smartly dressed butler. We followed Lady Augusta up the steps and into a house filled with warmth and light. For all that she was a grand lady, it was obvious that Lady Augusta was a great admirer of innovation. The hallway and surrounding rooms were lit with electric lights, at that time quite rare in private homes.

"You will be wanting to see Simon's room, I suppose. This way, then." Lady Augusta led the way up the stairs. Holmes and I followed meekly in her wake. At the end of a corridor, she stopped and threw open the door. "In here. I shall be downstairs if you should need me. Do ring for Donaldson to see you out when you have finished. And don't forget to send me the bill for your services."

I assumed Donaldson was the butler we'd seen fleetingly as we arrived. Lady Augusta swept away, leaving Holmes and me to look at each other with slight bemusement.

"That woman is quite the force of nature, eh, Watson?"

"Somewhat," I agreed.

"Now then, let us have a look at the lad's room."

It was pleasant enough. A comfortable looking bed with a green silk coverlet upon it sat with its headboard against the wall facing the door. A well-polished wooden blanket box was at the foot of the bed. A small fireplace was set into one wall to the right, with a firescreen decorated with images of wild animals in front of it. In the wall beside the bed was a window framed in soft drapes of a muted blue colour. Beneath the window sat a child-sized desk and chair. A piece of paper lay in the middle of the desk, with a pen resting upon it and an inkwell next to it. I walked over and picked up the paper, wondering if the boy had been doing schoolwork before he disappeared. The paper, however, proved to be a letter to Father Christmas. I read it, smiled sadly, and handed it to my friend. "A great pity Father Christmas isn't real," I commented.

The letter read:

> *Dear Father Christmas,*
>
> *All I wish for this Christmas is my papa. Please bring my papa to me for Christmas. I know it is an awfully long way from India, but that really is all I wish for. If you cannot bring papa to me, perhaps you could take me to him? Please? I do not want any toys, nor any –*

The writing, though extremely good for an eight-year-old, broke off at that point. "Young Simon was interrupted whilst writing this. Look, you can see where he put the pen down abruptly, leaving a slight trail of ink upon the paper."

"Was he snatched while writing it?"

Holmes shook his head. "Not snatched. The paper was left upon the desk and the pen laid down upon it. No, the lad was disturbed by something, and put his pen down briefly, expecting to return to it immediately. You notice that he hadn't wiped the pen, nor placed the cap upon the inkwell?"

"What could have disturbed the boy?"

"That, my dear Watson, is what we need to discover." He frowned and looked out of the window. I followed suit. There was nothing that I could see apart from a small patch of garden. Holmes opened the window and leaned out. He hummed thoughtfully to himself, before pulling the window closed and frowning at the floor. "Come, there is nothing to be learned in this room, but perhaps the one below will have something to say."

"The room below?"

"Something disturbed the boy. It wasn't at the window, for it was locked when I opened it. Therefore it likely came from either directly outside of his door, or from the room below."

Holmes grabbed the bellpull beside the door and gave it a sharp tug. It was a matter of but a few minutes before the butler, Donaldson, appeared in the doorway. "You rang, sir?"

"Yes, Mr. Donaldson. What room lies directly below this one?"

"That is the small drawing room, sir. It isn't usually in use, but Her Ladyship reopened it when Master Simon arrived. It is currently decorated for Christmas."

"May we see it?"

If the request surprised the man he didn't show it. "This way if you please, gentlemen."

We followed Donaldson down the stairs. He opened the door to the small drawing room. We saw a comfortable room with several well-upholstered armchairs gathered near a smallish fireplace. I could see why the room wasn't in general use, as the size of the fireplace meant that it would have been barely adequate to heat the space. In a nook to one side of the fireplace stood a respectably sized Christmas tree, decorated with strings of coloured crystal beads and shiny stars punched out of tin. A few gaily wrapped presents lay beneath it. The scent of pine sap filled the air. I noted that Lady Augusta was a practical woman. There were no candles upon the tree – combustible tree sap and fire not being a safe combination.

Holmes moved into the room and examined the window sill. To my amazement, the window was cracked open a little. Holmes looked at Donaldson. "It is a trifle too cold to leave a window open here, surely?"

"That was on the recommendation of the chimney sweep, sir."

"The chimney sweep?"

"Yes, sir. As I said, this room is rarely occupied. But once Master Simon arrived and Her ladyship decided to open the room for his use, the chimney needed to be cleaned before the fireplace could be used. The sweep advised us to leave the window open a very small amount for a day or two to allow excess smoke and soot to blow out."

I raised my eyebrows. I hadn't heard of a chimney sweep doing that, but I supposed that the size of the room and the narrowness of the chimney flue may had been the reason for the advice.

"Well," my friend said, "it appears to be working, as there is a small amount of soot upon the sill itself. Interesting."

Donaldson made a small tutting noise and hastened to straighten up a vase upon the mantelpiece which he had obviously just spotted. "Indeed, sir."

Holmes cast a thoughtful glance at the vase which was a vile pink colour, with handles shaped like the heads of elephants and with a scene of people wearing tricorn hats and indulging in some sort of bucolic pastime that I couldn't identify. The illustration was surrounded by a wreath of green-and-gold laurel leaves. It was incredibly ugly and gaudy beyond words. I could understand why Lady Augusta confined it to a room that normally wasn't in use.

Holmes turned to the butler. "We shall take our leave now. Donaldson. Please tell Lady Augusta that I'm hopeful of having Master Simon back by Christmas Day."

"Yes, sir."

"Meanwhile, there is something you can do for me."

"And what is that, sir?"

"Get me the name of the chimney sweep."

"Of course, sir." Donaldson didn't so much as bat an eyelid at the strange request.

He swept out of the room.

I looked at my friend in some confusion. "The name of the chimney sweep? What on earth does a chimney sweep have to do with the disappearance of the child? This isn't some novel by Dickens!"

Holmes gave a brief, wintery, smile. "I am aware of that."

"And why the interest in that ugly vase?"

"It isn't to your taste, my friend?"

"Most definitely not. It is quite the ugliest thing I have seen in years."

"Nevertheless, it is Sevres China, made around 1760, unless I miss my guess, and quite valuable."

I looked again at the vase. "Valuable? That?"

"Beauty doesn't equal worth, Watson."

I was still casting doubtful glances at the vase when Donaldson returned with a piece of paper, which he handed to Holmes. "Mr. Havering has an arrangement with his local tobacconist. A telegram sent to that address will reach him and he will come as soon as he can."

Holmes took the paper from Donaldson, read it, then folded it carefully and stowed it in his breast pocket. "Thank you, Donaldson. You have been most helpful."

"Anything to get Master Simon back, sir. He has only been here a short time, but we have all become quite fond of him."

Lady Augusta's carriage took us back to Baker Street, where Holmes promptly disappeared into his bedroom with a stack of old newspapers. I watched with a great deal of perplexity as he proceeded to light a fire in the fireplace in his room and methodically fed it with the newspapers. He watched the papers burning merrily for a while, then got to his feet and fished the paper that Donaldson had given him from his pocket. "Watson, could you please send a telegram to Mr. Havering at this address? Tell him I have need of his services quite urgently."

"What is so important that you need me to go and send the telegram?" I was frankly reluctant to go back out into the cold and the wet. "Can you not do it yourself?"

"I have a fire to feed." Holmes flapped a hand at me. "Off you go."

I sent Holmes's telegram and then took myself off to my club in something of a sulk, I must admit.

The next morning at breakfast, Holmes was pleased to inform me that he had received a reply telegram, telling him that Mr. Havering would be around that very morning to do the urgent cleaning of Holmes's fireplace. My friend turned to me with a serious expression. "Whatever I say this morning, I want you to play along with me."

I paused with my teacup at my lips. Then I lowered it and looked at Holmes across the table. I thought about it for a moment. Only one thing made sense to me. "You believe the chimney sweep has something to do with the disappearance of Simon Staines?"

"I do. There were certain indications at Lady Augusta Bellwether's house that led me to that conclusion."

"Will you share them with me?"

"Once we get the boy back, I will tell you all."

I nodded and returned to my breakfast. After several forkfuls of bacon and eggs, I paused and looked at Holmes again. "The lad is all right?"

"I believe so. For the moment, at least. No good can come from him harming the boy."

Holmes returned to his own breakfast without a word, and with that I had to be content.

It was mid-morning when a disapproving Mrs. Hudson showed a soot-besmirched individual into our rooms. Our dear landlady had a sweep that she preferred to use, and couldn't see why Holmes was insisting on someone else to clean one single chimney.

The man was of middling height and cadaverous appearance. Soot was ingrained into his hair to the point that he himself could probably not be able to tell what colour it was originally. He blinked at us with watery blue eyes. He seemed a little uncertain.

Holmes sprang from his chair and shook the man's hand briskly. "My dear fellow, so good of you to help me out! I have to go away for Christmas and I had forgotten to get the chimney in my room swept before I left." His voice took on a confiding tone. "I burn a great deal of correspondence in my grate and our landlady, dear soul that she is, insists that I pay for it to be cleaned myself. Isn't that right, Watson?" Holmes turned to me with a smile.

"Oh yes," I said. "Mrs. Hudson is most emphatic on the subject."

"When are you going away, sir?"

"This very afternoon, Mr. Havering. Typical of me, I forgot about the chimney until my friend reminded me yesterday."

"Let me 'ave a butcher's. If it ain't a big job then I can most likely do it for you now." Havering appeared to relax a little.

Holmes clapped the man on the shoulder. "Capital! Through here." He opened the door to his bedroom and showed the man in.

The bedroom was much as it always was, except a great deal tidier than normal. Something flashed in the light from the window, and I looked across to see Holmes's emerald tiepin sitting in its box which sat open on the mantelpiece. As I knew he usually kept it stored away in a drawer of his desk, I was a little bemused to see it sitting out so openly upon display. I opened my mouth to say something, but before I could, Holmes put a finger to his lips indicating I was to remain silent.

The sweep, Mr. Havering, knelt down upon the floor in front of the fireplace and peered up the flue. "It looks a simple enough job. Not too dirty, but you don't want to be leaving it. I'll just pop downstairs and get me tools."

"Much obliged to you, Mr. Havering."

The man disappeared and then came back with a cloth bundle and a carefully bound collection of wooden canes and a wheel-shaped brush. As we watched, he undid the bundle of cloth, which proved to be pieces of canvas, and draped it on the hearth and the floor, and on top of furniture close by the fireplace.

Next he placed the bundle of canes on the floor and attached the brush to the end of one of them. It occurred to me that I had never actually seen a chimney being swept before. Havering carefully inserted the brush into the flue and pushed it upwards, stopping to add extra pieces of the cane to the end. Once he was certain that the brush was the full length of the chimney and clearing the pot outside, he began to carefully raise and lower the brush, twirling it slightly in his hands as he did so. Soot and small pieces of burned wood and coal ash began to trickle down the chimney and onto the hearth.

Havering noticed my fascination. "You have to do this careful-like," he said. "If you rush it, then the room gets full of muck."

I nodded my understanding.

After about thirty minutes, Havering carefully removed the brush and peered up the chimney again. "That should do you. Leave your window open a bit for a day or two, to let any vapours out. Then it'll be as right as rain."

He removed the head of the brush and carefully wrapped it in one of the canvas sheets. He then proceeded to gather the other canvas sheets up closely, taking care not to let any soot or ashes escape. I was impressed by his care to avoid making a mess and said so.

The man laughed slightly. "People don't like it when you leave a mess. Besides, I sell the ash and soot and such to the dustman."

I blinked slowly. "Really? Why on earth do they buy it?"

"They sell it to the brick makers, and to them that sells fertilizer to the farmers." He got to his feet and walked over to the window. Casting a casual glance out of it, he carefully opened it a fraction. "There you go, sir. Just enough to let the vapours out. That'll be five shillings. It didn't take me long, and 'tis Christmas, after all."

"Very generous of you, Mr. Havering." Holmes took some money from his pocket and counted out five shillings which he gave to the man.

Havering carefully stowed the coins in his pocket, shouldered his bundles, and saluted us with a grubby finger to his forehead. "Nice to meet you, gents. Merry Christmas to you both."

"Merry Christmas to you as well," I replied for both of us. I stood at the window and watched him walk away up Baker Street.

Holmes disappeared into his bedroom, where I heard him locking up the tie-pin, and then he reappeared wrapping a scarf around his neck. "Come, Watson."

"Where are we going?" I asked as I reached for my hat and coat.

"To Scotland Yard. I need to talk to Lestrade, and after that a slice or two of good roast beef at Simpson's wouldn't go amiss."

Lestrade heard our story and was quite keen to assist us. "I have little on at the moment – unlike Gregson, who is desperately trying to discover who stole Lady Cottingley's diamonds and other valuables. He hasn't a clue."

"In my opinion," Holmes said drily, "Gregson is quite often without a clue."

That evening Lestrade and several uniformed constables came to Baker Street. Holmes bade them to wait quietly in the sitting room, whilst he and I repaired to his bedroom and hid behind his dressing screen.

It was boring, waiting in the dark – not to mention uncomfortable. Holmes showed no sign of discomfort, standing there like a statue. I had no idea how long we had been at it when there when the soft creak of the window being raised caught my attention. Holmes gripped my forearm tightly. We waited a moment or two, then Holmes hissed in my ear "Now!"

We thrust the screen aside as Holmes leaped for the intruder. I yelled for Lestrade as I joined him.

As Lestrade and his constables entered the room, Holmes was shaking Havering like a terrier shakes a rat, snarling into his face. "The boy! What have you done with the boy?"

Havering suddenly collapsed, bursting into tears as he did so. "I ain't done nothing with 'im! 'E's safe. 'Onest. I didn't mean to take 'im. But I couldn't let 'im go either. 'E saw me."

"He heard you enter the house and came down to investigate?" I asked.

Havering nodded miserably. "Must've 'eard me open the window. 'E come in just as I touched the vase. Nice piece of Sevres, that. Worth a few bob. 'E asked me if I was there to take 'im to 'is papa."

"And you said yes," Holmes said.

Havering nodded. "What else could I say? 'E'd have made a ruckus if I said anything else. Didn't want to get caught, did I? So I sneaked 'im out of the 'ouse. 'Ad to leave the vase behind. Would've looked a bit rum if Father Christmas's 'elper had 'elped 'imself."

"Where is the boy?" Holmes asked.

Havering looked shifty.

"What have you done with him?" Lestrade bunched his fists into the man's coat and slammed him against the wall.

Havering let out a squeal. "Nothing. 'E's safe. 'E's at the tobacconist shop. In an attic room there."

"And the tobacconist just lets you leave strange boys on his premises for safe-keeping?" Lestrade asked with more than a hint of sarcasm.

"Oh, I don't think he's doing this from the goodness of his heart, Lestrade," Holmes said softly, but with a great deal of anger. "I strongly suspect that the tobacconist in question also acts as Havering's fence. I also believe that once the hue-and-cry had died down, Simon Staines himself would have been sold like just another piece of stolen merchandise."

I gasped in horror. "He would sell the child?"

"Children are worth a good price in certain quarters, Dr. Watson," Lestrade said. "Boy or girl, it doesn't matter. But given the antecedents of the lad, he would have likely been sold to a house somewhere in Europe, never to have been seen again."

"Agreed," said Holmes. "And I think that the only reason that young Simon is still in London is the fact that at this time of year, few illegal cargos are being transported. Even the rawest of villains prefer to spend this time with their nearest and dearest."

Havering was handcuffed and lead from the room. I followed, with Holmes lingering just long enough to shut and lock his window, before he came behind me, shutting his bedroom door as he did so.

We accompanied Lestrade and his constables to Scotland Yard, where Havering was left with a sergeant to be processed and charged.

Lestrade rounded up some more constables and a second police brougham and we set off to the tobacconist shop, which was located in Southwark. The shop itself was seedy and somewhat rundown, as befitted the area. It was also hard by the docks, which would have made it simple for Havering's tobacconist accomplice to smuggle stolen goods, and the occasional human being, out of the country.

The tobacconist, a fat, middle-aged man by the name of Claude Brownlee, made a voluble protest, which ended only when Lestrade spun him into the wall and handcuffed him. Leaving the stunned man in the care of several constables, with others tearing his living quarters apart looking for stolen goods, Holmes, Lestrade, and I, hastened to the attic.

Soft crying alerted us before we reached the door to the small room in the eaves. Thankfully the key was in the lock. I suspected that if we'd had to go back downstairs and obtain it from Brownlee, a certain level of violence would have ensued. None of us particularly cared for those who abuse children.

The crying stopped as Lestrade opened the door. A small boy with a tear-stained, grubby face, peered at us out of the darkness.

"Simon?" Holmes asked softly, coming to stand at Lestrade's shoulder.

The boy nodded hesitantly, no doubt afraid that we had come to hurt him.

"I am Sherlock Holmes. This man – " Holmes patted Lestrade on the shoulder. " – is Inspector Lestrade of Scotland Yard. Out there is my friend, Dr. Watson. We've come to take you back to your Great-Aunt Augusta."

The lad blinked at us for a moment, then hurled himself across the room to crash into Holmes's legs. He began crying again. Holmes reached down and lifted the boy into his arms, where Simon buried his head in Holmes's shoulder. "Now, let us get you out of here," Holmes said softly.

Lestrade led the way as we headed downstairs, Holmes in the middle carrying Simon, with myself bringing up the rear.

As we came into the main body of the shop, one of the constables came up to Lestrade. The man was grinning like the Cheshire Cat.

Lestrade raised his eyebrows. "Something amusing, Evans?"

"More satisfying than amusing, sir."

"Oh?"

"Mr. Brownlee here keeps some very interesting stock for the 'simple tobacconist' he keeps trying to tell us he is."

"Get to the point, Evans. It's been a long day."

"Sorry, sir. Hidden away under a loose floorboard in the kitchen was an interesting hoard of rather expensive knickknacks – including Lady Cottingley's diamonds."

"*What?*"

"Well done, Lestrade!" Holmes chuckled. "In rescuing a kidnapped boy, you also broke a major jewel theft ring. I do hope the Commissioner gives you a nice bonus for Christmas."

"Gregson is going to be unhappy," I observed.

"I can live with my colleague's unhappiness," Lestrade replied as he dispatched one of the constables to Scotland Yard with the news.

The four of us then took one of the broughams to Lady Augusta Bellwether's house in Hyde Park. Donaldson, who opened the door at our ring, forgot his professional demeanour to the point that when he saw Simon in Holmes's arms, cried out in delighted shock.

This brought Lady Augusta into the hallway. She stood for a few seconds just staring at us, then her stern face broke into a warm smile. "Simon! Oh Simon. You have found him!"

A tall man whose likeness to Lady Augusta spoke of a kinship came out of the room behind her. Simon, upon seeing him, cried out, "Papa!"

Holmes set Simon on the ground and the lad ran to his father, who swept him up in his arms.

"Papa stay?"

"Yes, little monkey," Augustus Staines told his son. "I am staying."

"Good!" With that Simon snuggled back into his father's arms and promptly went to sleep.

"I shall get him bathed and settled into bed," Augustus said, signalling to a young woman in a blue dress and stiffly starched apron, who was no doubt Simon's nurse. She followed the man and his son up the stairs.

Lady Augusta insisted that the three of us join her in the drawing room for a warming drink and something light to eat. "My nephew and I both wish to know how you discovered Simon's whereabouts, Mr. Holmes. There seems to me to have been no clues at all."

"I wouldn't say that, Lady Augusta," Holmes demurred. "There were clues."

A short while later we sat sipping a brandy toddy and nibbling on caraway seed biscuits, as Holmes explained everything. Augustus Staines joined us.

"It was obvious that Simon hadn't been abducted from his bedroom. There was no sign of a struggle and nothing out of place in the room, except for the half-finished note and the unwiped pen and uncapped inkwell. That told me that Simon must have disappeared from somewhere else."

Lady Augusta nodded her understanding.

"When I examined the small drawing room, I noticed three things at once that alerted me to the fact that the room was where a crime had occurred: The open window, the soot on the window sill, and a vase which was out of alignment."

"The window I can understand," Lestrade said. "Havering needed it open to gain access to the house. But the soot?"

"From Havering's clothes as he climbed through the window?" I asked.

Holmes nodded. "Very good."

"But the vase?"

"It was obvious that the vase had been moved. Indeed, if you remember, Donaldson straightened it up while we were there. It became obvious to me that the thief had come in through the window, but was disturbed before he could take the vase. The soot told me that the man was most likely a chimney sweep. It could have been a dustman, I admit, but a dustman wouldn't know what small, expensive items would be available to take in the room, for he wouldn't have access. A chimney sweep, on the other hand – "

"That's why you asked Donaldson for the sweep's address," I said.

Holmes nodded.

"And you set a trap."

Holmes nodded again. "With my emerald tiepin as bait. I knew we had him when he said to leave the window open a fraction. I doubt Havering was stealing from every house whose chimneys he swept, but when he saw something he knew he could sell, he arranged for the owner to be his accomplice in the crime, by leaving him an easy means of entry."

"And Simon?" asked Augustus Staines.

"He heard the window being opened more fully and went downstairs to investigate. His head was full of dreams of Father Christmas and having you with him, and convinced himself that what he was hearing was Father Christmas or one of his helpers."

"But it wasn't Christmas Eve," I objected.

"Simon is perhaps a little young to understand the actual date, I think," Lestrade said.

"Indeed," said Holmes. "To a boy that age, with all the decorations and ongoing merriment, it never occurred to him that it was too early for a visit from Father Christmas."

"So when Simon entered the room, the thief panicked," said Lady Augusta.

Holmes nodded. "Simon probably babbled on about him bringing his Papa to him or taking him to his Papa. That is what gave Havering the idea to take the boy instead of the Sevres vase."

"Poor Simon," I said. "The lad has had quite an ordeal. Though it seems young Simon didn't need to write to Father Christmas after all," I observed.

Augustus Staines looked around at us and smiled slightly. "I set off from India some weeks ago – not long after I sent Simon back. It was odd. An elderly, white-bearded gentleman came into my office and advised me of the availability of a post back here in London – it hadn't even been announced yet. He even told me what ship would be best to catch. You can imagine how I felt when I arrived this afternoon and found the house in an uproar and that my son had vanished."

"So Simon has got his Christmas wish after all," I said softly.

Augustus smiled. "Simon did indeed get his wish. – especially since the ship wasn't supposed to arrive until the New Year."

A strange feeling came over me. "The white-bearded fellow – did he give a name?"

Augustus raised an eyebrow and nodded. "He just said his name was 'Nicholas', and he was delivering a message on behalf of a friend."

We took our leave then, and as we stood outside the house, about to enter the brougham, soft flakes of snow began to fall. Into the silence the bells from nearby St. James church began to toll midnight.

Holmes looked at Lestrade and me. "Merry Christmas."

"Merry Christmas, Holmes," we replied.

The Adventure of the Viking Ghost
by Frank Schildiner

It was a chilly, blustery day in late December when my friend Sherlock Holmes barked out a brief laugh that woke me from a light doze. I had been seated by the fire, having returned just before breakfast after assisting a colleague in a particularly difficult bit of emergency surgery that saved the life of a young girl. The child would walk, thanks to our efforts, and I entered our rooms at Baker Street drained, yet elated by the result.

"Watson," Holmes said, his eyes shining with amusement. "I present to you the very essence of the ridiculous nature of modern society. Please cast your eyes upon this missive which arrived by messenger this morning."

He extended a single sheet of creamy, stock paper with no heading printed upon the top. The inked words were written in a precise hand that reminded me of the teachings I received in my earliest school days.

"Inexpensive paper," I said before reading the brief lines.

My friend nodded quickly, rising from his seat and striding towards the front window. "Standard stock purchased in bulk by hotels of the middle grade. Based on the slight scent of plum I detected upon opening the envelope, I would hazard to guess Great Northern in King's Cross. Do continue."

"Handwriting is that of a man of classic schooling," I said, using Holmes's methods.

"Correct, though imprecise," he said, not turning my direction as he studied the street below.

With that, I read the letter:

Dear Mr. Sherlock Holmes,

Having heard of your skill in solving crimes, I would wish your assistance in the matter of the murder of the Yule Boar. This has caused unrest in our small community of Hoo Wulfhere, and I have seen a return of the ghost of Ivar the Boneless three times since the death of the Yule Boar.

With your permission, I shall upon you at two o'clock this afternoon after my business with the partners of Hoare and Company.

Lionel Ivarson
Lord of Digons Manor

I read the lines several times before saying, "How extraordinary and inexplicable. Yule pigs, ghosts . . . very strange."

"Quite," my friend said. "What does the note suggest about the writer to you?"

"A wealthy man from a small community . . . I believe there is a town called Hoo in Kent?" I asked.

"Two, both in that county," Holmes said, his voice little more than a murmur. "Hoo suggests a settlement on or near the Hoo Peninsula. Go on."

I read the words again and said, "A man who is quite traditional, based on his use of the title of Lord of the Manor. I believe such titles ceased being of any importance decades ago."

"A lordship of a manor is a traditional title which holds some small rights upon their land but are of little importance," Holmes said, turning and dropping into a chair near where I sat. "Some such titles, such as the Manor of Scrivelsby in Lincolnshire, hold the additional title of King or Queen's Champion. The Champion spoke words of challenge before the coronation of the King, though the practice has been abandoned by the previous and current monarch of our nation."

"I have heard as much of Scottish Laird titles as well," I said. "What is this about the ghost of Ivar the Boneless? I read of Ivar and the Great Heathen Army, but never anything of his spirit inhabiting the Kentish coast."

"True, true," Holmes said, reaching for his black clay pipe and busily refilling the bowl. "Anything else?"

"I've never heard of a Yule Boar in any of the Christmas tales I've read since childhood," I said with a small laugh. "Is this some unknown assistant to Father Christmas?"

Holmes looked up from his work upon the disreputable pipe. "As you are no doubt aware, Yule, as a point of fact, isn't the same as Christmas. It is the Northman celebration of the winter solstice, celebrated through the sacrifice of animals, as well as feasting. The word 'Yule' was subsumed by our ancestors and merged with Christmas as they converted the followers of the ancient religions. The sacrifice and feasting upon a prize boar is one of these traditions no doubt maintained by Hoo Wulfhere."

"How very interesting," I said, "and that does fit my statement that Mr. Ivarson is a man who holds strongly to tradition."

"Precisely," Holmes said and lit his pipe. "Based on the deeper indentations upon the word 'I' and his name, I would state our potential client is one consumed by tradition to the point of stifling. Based on his choice of hotel, I would add that he isn't nearly as wealthy as he believes, and holds some resentment towards those with greater economic advantages. He is younger than his words suggest, yet behaves closer to that of a Regency-era landholder than that of a modern man. We shall undergo a trial of self-control as we listen to his bluster and complaints at two o'clock."

"You're taking his case?" I asked. "He sounds like quite an unpleasant fellow, to say the least."

Holmes blew a long stream of smoke through his nose as he said, "I haven't committed to such a course of action. However, his letter does hold several points of interest that intrigue me enough to consent to a meeting."

Knowing my friend as I did, I didn't inquire further regarding these areas he found intriguing, knowing that they would emerge in the fullness of time. I did spend a brief period reading about the infamous Viking reaver, Ivar the Boneless, as well as the origins of the Yule festivals of days long past. The information was dry barebones stuff, and I still felt no further enlightened.

Mr. Lionel Ivarson, the self-styled Lord of Digons Manor, arrived on our doorstep at precisely two o'clock in the afternoon. He proved to be a broad shouldered, red-faced individual with nearly colorless blond hair, a narrow, precisely trimmed beard and moustache, and dark clothing more suitable for a clergyman of the earlier part of the century. His hat was an elderly beaver specimen that reminded me of the one my late uncle wore until he passed away in my youth.

"Mister Sherlock Holmes, I presume," he said, addressing me and ignoring Holmes, who stood near the mantel.

"A pleasure to meet you, sir," I said. "My name is Watson. Doctor John Watson. Mister Sherlock Holmes stands before the fireplace."

"Thank you, Watson," Holmes said as a taut smile crossed his thin lips. "Mr. Ivarson, I found your note of some slight interest. Please do take the seat beside Watson and explain your intriguing tale of Yule Boars and Viking spirits."

Lionel Ivarson appeared distressed for a moment as he glanced in Holmes's direction, seemingly preferring my company to that of my friend. I found this behavior discourteous to say the least, but remained silent as the man regained his composure.

"Well, Mr. Holmes, I am not in the habit of hiring private detectives. My brother Osbert is quite opposed to the notion. Despite that, I heard from several friends connected to my bank, Hoare's of course, that your abilities were rather useful with oddities. You see, my community, Hoo Wulfhere, is an ancient dwelling, one of the oldest in the entirety of England. My legendary ancestor, King Ivar the Boneless, ruled the location and placed one of his sons, Prince Wulfhere Ivarson, as Lord of the Land. Since that time, my family has led the community through many of the ancient traditions."

"Such as the keeping of Yule?" Holmes said, raising a hand as Ivarson opened his mouth. "Watson and I are aware of the differences between the festivals of Christmas and Yule, so you need not trouble yourself on that account. I would wish to learn more of the reason you hold to those customs and the methods used."

Ivarson harrumphed for a moment, looking slightly put out. He then straightened and said, "Well, sir, our community recognizes the Church of England as the true path of religion. We do consider Yule a tradition dating back to our founding in the same manner other communities perform Maypole dances and the like. Each year we gather the townsfolk, and the Lordship of Digons Manor of the Ivarson family kills the Yule Boar. The blood is captured in a heavy, ancient, clay bowl and poured across the grave marker of Prince Wulfhere. We then roast the boar and feast upon the animal, as well as grains and vegetables donated by the peasantry."

"I see," Holmes said. "And this year, you encountered some resistance to your ancient ways?"

"We did, Mr. Holmes, we did!" Ivarson said, thumping a heavy fist into the arm of his chair. "The new Vicar, Mister Wellesley! He just joined our community with the death of old Stephenson, who served in my late father's day. No less than a month after joining, he began sermonizing against idolatry and how Exodus says, *'Thou shalt have no other gods before me!'* and the like. He is lucky my brother Osbert was present and held me back, or I'd have given him a right hiding, I tell you!"

Holmes nodded with what I took as lax interest before saying, "I take it your conflict with Mr. Wellesley hasn't dissipated in time."

Ivarson's face turned a brighter shade of red and I wondered if he would expire of apoplexy at any moment. "You are correct, sir, quite correct. The young upstart appealed to the people, as well as the local authorities. They informed him that the ceremony is conducted on my land, and he has no say in how I conduct myself at that time. Do you know the foolish cretin threatened me with expulsion from the church? His bishop rejected that plea, I happily inform you!"

"Then the pig died?" Holmes asked.

"Murdered, my man, murdered!" our potential client cried. "My prize boar, Gullinbursti, sliced apart and left as food for the remaining swine. A true tragedy!"

"Will that prevent your ceremony?" I asked.

Ivarson shook his head, the scarlet shade draining from his cheeks. "It will not, sir. I immediately purchased a replacement and the creature sits under constant guard in case of a second attempt. The ceremony will commence in four days' time!"

"Tell me of the sighting of the ghost of Ivar the Boneless," Holmes said, dropping onto the sofa, crossing his legs, seemingly more alert now.

"As you may know, my legendary ancestor was a man of great passion and determination. He believed in the ancient ways and cursed the English church that murdered his father, Ragnar Lothbrok. As such, we appease his wrath through the yearly Yule Festival. The night after the death of the sacrifice, I was in my gun room, looking out the window, and spied King Ivar standing upon the hill overlooking my land. It was just before full darkness fell when he appeared, his mighty horned helmet glinting in the few remaining rays of sunlight. His great hand raised, he pointed a spear that crackled with lightning in my direction before he faded from view." His voice was hushed now. "I tell you truly, gentlemen, I was frightened to my very core. My heart nearly stopped in my chest. My butler, Jameson, had to help me back to my rooms."

"Horned helmet, you say?" Holmes said, his eyes narrowing. "Did you see this ghost again?"

"Once more," Lionel Ivarson said, his head lowering. "Just before my planned business trip to London. This time I was just finishing my account books when I heard the blast of a horn in the darkness. I ran to my window and there he stood in the distance . . . spear held high above his head. He vanished when the moon fell behind a cloud."

"Did you notice any other details of the ghost? His face? His helmet, and armor?"

"No sir," Ivarson said. "Just the same as last time. A tall horned helmet like great Ivar wore, and the spear. The darkness hid him from sight, for which I am eternally grateful."

Holmes rose and crossed to the mantel, plucking his cherry-wood pipe up while reaching for the Persian slipper where he kept his tobacco.

"Mr. Ivarson," he said, "your problem does interest me. Watson and I shall catch the morning train and join you in your town by early afternoon."

Our client rose, frowning. "You haven't spoken of your fees . . . ."

Holmes turned his back as he said, "My charges are upon a fixed scale and I don't negotiate them, sir. You shall receive the details upon the successful completion of your case."

Ivarson opened his mouth, apparently in protest. He then slowly closed his lips, nodded, and said, "Then I bid you a good day."

Holmes lit his pipe just as the downstairs door slammed shut, glancing my direction with a trace of amusement in his gaze. "I take it you are less-than-enamored with our client."

I snorted. "The man is a pompous jackanape. I am surprised you took his case."

Holmes lit the pipe as he said, "Oh, I have no compunction in saying the man is a fool and an ass. Despite that, I do believe that his life is imperiled in ways he doesn't comprehend."

Hoo Wulfere was precisely as I pictured the town, a small village with an elderly church, several municipal structures, and vast stretches of land. The land was, I later learned, mostly common space held by the town and used by the community in the ancient fashion. Such locations are becoming rarer in England, which was sad since there is a certain quaint charm in these hamlets.

Just outside the town proper lay Digons Manor, a stone structure that appeared a strange mixture of ancient design and Georgian additions. This was easily identifiable from a distance since it lay near a great rise and sat imposingly like some horrific Gothic monstrosity.

Our client didn't meet us at the station. Instead, he sent his dogcart and a bluff, hearty man named George Hulme as driver. He was a wide-shouldered fellow with a massive paunch, a heavy black beard streaked with gray, and bright blue eyes that shimmered when he lit a tiny briar pipe.

Holmes and I perched on the rear of the small conveyance, with Hulme driving the single animal, a tired, unenthusiastic chestnut mare that moved with a heavy dogged tread through the narrow country lanes.

"I'm the gamekeeper," Hulme said in answer to my friend's question. "Though in truth, I have little enough to do there these days. Most of the game moved back when my Da was a child."

"Do you know who killed the boar Mr. Ivarson named Gullinbursti?" Holmes asked.

"No," Hulme said. "Seemed a queer thing to do, if you ask me. Nobody but His Nibs takes the whole Yule rot seriously. They dress up in them silly old Viking helmets and yowl like cats' words none of us can understand. For the rest of us, it's just a community dinner where we share in a bit of pork. No reason to cancel it, though my Missus dislikes the pouring of blood on the stone. When His Nibs's Da was alive, they spattered some of the blood on the people. That ended when it got one of the parish council's ladies got the stuff on her new dress."

Hulme laughed uproariously at his story and began whistling off-tune as he steered us around a bend and back in sight of the manor house. The large hill I noted earlier possessed a gentle slope with several clusters of trees and thickets spread about a vast grassy plain.

"Does that hill possess a name?" I asked the whistling gamekeeper.

Hulme chuckled as he said, "Well, that's a source of debate in the parish. You see, Mr. Ivarson and his family own a good bit of it and want it called Ivarson Hill. Officially it was recorded some years back as Hoo Hill, and it rankles the family something awful."

I noted that George Hulme didn't appear upset that the name wasn't to Lionel Ivarson's liking. There didn't appear to be little malice in the gamekeeper's words, just a general dislike that I did find quite understandable.

"Did you see the ghost?" Holmes inquired, turning his head while watching the dogcart driver.

Hulme shook his head. "No, sir, can't say I did. I was at home when the hallooing started. I came out with my shotgun but saw nothing on the hill. I did see the pig and thought that was a blessed shame."

"How was that?"

Hulme shook his head and sighed deeply, reminding me of my nurse when I asked a particularly foolish question.

"Because Mister Holmes, sir, they ruined the meat. If you pierce the organs of a pig when killing it, the green stuff spreads all about and it becomes bitter and foul-smelling. The one who slaughtered Old G, the prize boar of the town, kept us from using most of the great beast."

Holmes pursed his lips briefly in thought at the response and said, "Thank you, Mr. Hulme. Your information has been most efficacious."

"If you say so, Mr. Holmes." Hulme replied and resumed his tuneless whistling.

A lanky man with a nearly bald head and a dusty butler's garb from my father's time greeted us at the door of Digon Manor. He bowed slightly, his disapproving, skeletal face gazing upon us with what I took as open disregard.

"My name," he said in a heavy, sepulchral tone, "is Jameson. I am the Lord of the Manor's personal butler. I recognize you as the private detective named Holmes. Your companion was identified to me by the Master as one Watson, a medical man. If you will follow me, the Lord of the Manor awaits your presence in the gun room."

He led us down a narrow corridor paneled with heavy dark wood. Candle sconces lay upon the wall, many filled but few lit. There were a series of indistinct portraits of stiff-backed men in different traditional forms of dress. The chamber we soon entered, the supposed gun room, was rectangular with rows of guns in cabinets along the far wall. The rifles were well-cared-for, their dark metal gleaming in the sunlight that streamed in from the bay windows.

Lionel Ivarson was upon an oversized wooden chair designed in the shape of a throne, with a smaller, rounder duplicate standing by his side. Seated in it was a man that I took this as his brother, Osbert Ivarson, given their similar countenance and the glare upon his face. Said brother glared in our direction, snorting as we approached.

"My brother dislikes the idea of hiring a detective, Mr. Holmes," our client said.

"It is a waste of time and money, Lionel!" Osbert Ivarson said. "We know who caused this nonsense and should just thrash the blighter and be done with it!"

"That would be a mistake," Holmes said, "if the individual you believe responsible is innocent."

"Ha!" Osbert said, the words exploding from his lips. "Everyone knows it was that psalm-singing fool Wellesley who killed the boar to stop the celebration!"

"How does Mr. Wellesley reply to your accusation?" Holmes asked.

Lionel Ivarson barked out a laugh lacking any trace of humor. "Claimed he was home, alone working on a book he is writing. A clear lie if I ever saw one! His own lady wife couldn't swear he was in his study the whole night!"

"And where were you when the pig's butchery occurred, Mr. Ivarson?" Holmes asked the brother.

"How dare you accuse me?" Osbert said, rising and stepping forward while lifting his fists. "How dare you!"

My friend raised an eyebrow as he asked, "Have I accused you, sir? I simply ask to eliminate your possible involvement."

Osbert lowered his fists, straightened his cuffs, and said, "Then I will have you know, I was home writing letters. My wife could swear to my presence both times, without fail. I hold employment as the Affeeror for the Parish. The second time our ancestor visited my brother, I was at home asleep since I had a particularly busy calendar the next day, and in my role as – "

"Thank you, Mr. Ivarson," Holmes said, turning towards the windows. "Tell me, sir. You first viewed the spectral personage here, in the gun room. Where were you the second time?"

Lionel Ivarson stood and walked across the room with us trailing behind. He opened a door, leading us into a small, cramped space piled high with books and papers, neatly arranged in precise angles. There wasn't a trace of dust visible. A slight smell drifted our direction and I immediately identified the scent as that of mouse droppings.

"Here," our client said, pointing at the chair behind a dark wooden desk with intricate carvings across the surface. "I was doing my accounts. I own several fishing vessels and the costs are higher than you might realize. You see, the number of fish is oftentimes – "

"I am sure you are correct." Holmes said, cutting off the explanation and studying the view from the desk to the window. "With your permission, Dr. Watson and I shall walk to the crest of the hill and spy the land where you spied the vision of the Viking. After which, with your permission, I should like to visit the site of the Yule Festival."

Ivarson appeared momentarily put out, but nodded, turned away, and waved towards the door. He picked up a small leather-bound book from the top of the nearest pile and quietly leafed through the pages.

Holmes pulled his deerstalker back upon his head before marching from the room, heading with long strides towards the nearby rise. I caught up with him and, when we were sufficiently away from the house, decided I must broach a question.

"Do you believe there was an actual ghost upon this hill?" I asked.

"Most assuredly not," my friend said. "I believe the evidence shall point towards a far more mundane answer to the problem at hand. Now, let us begin a search for the location where this false spectre stood."

Climbing the rise was more difficult than I anticipated because the grasses and weeds grew high and were untended by the owners. Though our step slowed, we trudged ever upward until reaching the crest moments later. Holmes waved that I should halt my progress before he knelt and examined the ground before his feet.

"Come here and gaze upon the evidence of the so-called ghost of Ivar the Boneless," he said, undisguised amusement ringing in his words.

Several feet down from the summit, near the edge of the crest, lay a clump of grass beaten down by what I took as footsteps. Several indistinct sets lay across the dry earth and the weeds appeared crushed as a result.

"How do you know this was the location the false ghost stood?" I asked. "It could be a visitor, or even Hulme going about his work."

"Nonsense," Holmes said, pointing down the hill. "From this vantage point, the study and gunroom are clearly visible. Should we reach the zenith of this hill, I should think we would be nearly out-of-sight. The costumed individual wished to be seen – that was the point of this ridiculous drama. I knew that from the time our client reported the incident in Baker Street."

Holmes knelt further and laughed. "And I think you shall find the footprints are from the same shoe. The size, shape, and depth reveal this individual being heavyset and wide in build. This, along with the weak comprehension of history demonstrated, rule out the presence of the supernatural."

"How do you know that last point?" I asked, astounded by this leap in logic.

Holmes straightened, clucking his tongue before chuckling with merriment. "That was the only interesting feature of our rather pompous client's tale. Come, let us return. I must view this bowl and sacrificial rock before meeting with the local vicar. I think both shall prove quite enlightening."

The grave marker of Prince Wulfhere proved a disappointment to me, having imagined a small monument to this unknown son of a legendary Viking warlord. The monument was a stone, less than a yard high and half that wide. The pale stone held several faded runes across the surface, none of which I could decipher.

Holmes appeared almost disinterested in the grave, circling the location once and studying the etchings for several seconds. Then he crouched for several seconds and performed a cursory inspection of the ground near the monument before standing.

"Thank you, sir," he said to our host who led us there. "I believe your man approaches bearing a small chest. Does this contain the bowl you mentioned?"

"Yes, Mr. Holmes, it does at that," Lionel Ivarson said. "We always keep the ancient bowl of my ancestor properly locked away until the time of the ceremony."

"I still see no purpose in showing an outsider!" Osbert Ivarson said, standing to one side. "What right does this gossip-monger have in demanding to see our family's treasures?"

"Oh, do be quiet, Osbert!" Lionel countered, the flush rising in his face again.

The supercilious butler Jameson approached, his step slow and filled with self-importance. Held between his pale palms was a wood-and-iron chest bearing a heavy lock made from a dark metal. He stopped before our client, bowed his head briefly, and extended the box.

Just as Lionel Ivarson removed a well-polished metal key from his inner pocket, Holmes stepped forward and said, "One moment, please."

My friend raised his magnifying glass for a moment, studying the lock with narrowed eyes. He then studied the outer edge of the key before stepping back.

"Scratches on the outer casing," he said, pocketing his instrument. "Hmm. Do go on."

Raising the key into the air in the manner I would expect from a monarch conveying a knighthood upon a kneeling subject, Ivarson placed it in the lock. It slowly turned, and he bowed his head as he opened the lid. A red silken pillow covered the bottom of the case, the fabric shimmering in the sunlight.

The object was about eighteen inches long with a wide circular mouth that narrowed into a distinct, curved, point. The light clay that covered it was a dull, insipid shade of brown, and several deep carved letters ran across the surface.

"I believe," Holmes said, "'bowl' is an improper term for this object. 'Drinking horn' would be a better description."

"It has been called a bowl since the days of Queen Catherine," Osbert explained, "and we shall continue to do so."

Holmes ignored the man, pointed towards the horn, and asked, "If I may?"

"Please do," our client said. "We pass it around every year at Yuletide so that all participants get a bit of luck. Otherwise, it sits locked away in my study for the remainder of the year."

Holmes lifted the so-called Bowl of Prince Wulfere, studying the pillow where it lay for several seconds. He touched the pillow, pressing downward and watching the fabric slowly rise. Holmes performed that action several times and studied the various creases in the material. He then weighed the object in his hands for several seconds.

"A heavy piece," he said while raising the horn upwards and turning it slowly in his hands.

"They made things properly in those days." Osbert said, puffing his chest out as he spoke.

Holmes spent several minutes running his fingers down the surface, stopping near the tip. Rubbing his fingers together, a faraway look entered his gaze before he frowned and cocked his head in thought. Then he handed me the horn, and I must admit it did weigh more than I expected. It felt at least four pounds or more in my hands. I glanced at the object for a moment before returning it to our client.

"Very good," Holmes said. "If I may, I should require the use of the dogcart. I would speak to Mr. Wellesley regarding the incidents of the last several days."

Rejecting the use once more of George Hulme, Holmes perched in the driver's seat of the two-wheeled cart, gently steering the tired horse down the lane. I remembered something Osbert Ivarson said and a single word that I couldn't define despite my past education.

"Holmes," I said, "what is an 'affeeror'? Osbert Ivarson said that was his profession, and yet it is one that I've never encountered before."

"You have," Holmes said, releasing a quick bark of laughter, "though under the modern term of 'town clerk'. An 'affeeror' is a title once used in Manor Courts for the person who leveled fines against those violating the local rules. Such powers ceased being of any importance by the time Parliament ended the use of rotten boroughs as a means of seating members of Commons."

I had to chuckle, realizing that the use of the disused title fit the pompous demeanor of our client's brother. I didn't like the man, but that didn't mean he was behind the odd events taking place in Hoo Wulfhere. If there was anything I learned from my time with Sherlock Holmes, it was that just because a fellow is unpleasant does not make him a criminal.

Moments later, he reigned in the horse beside a stone church built in the pre-Gothic fashion. It was a sturdy rectangular building with a new wooden roof and simple carvings across the outer walls. The wooden doors were heavy wooden portals held together with massive metal strips. The lush scent of grass and charcoal wafted from near the house of worship, though I attributed that to a clay chimney I spotted down the lane. There was a quiet majesty about the place, and I found myself admiring the antediluvian simplicity.

"May I help you, Mister Sherlock Holmes?" a man asked, stepping from around the corner of the building. "Oh, do forgive me. My name is Wellesley. Howard Wellesley. I am the recently appointed Vicar of this parish."

Wellesley was a man of medium height whose short muddy-brown hair lay in some disarray across his wide forehead. He possessed a round, smiling face and a slight paunch under his black robes. There was a boyish air about the man, reminding me of the kind rector who ran the church for several years back home in my childhood. He rubbed his hands across the cuffs of his shirt as he stepped closer.

Holmes hopped from the dogcart and extended his hand. "A pleasure, sir. Since you know of me, I have little doubt you recognize my friend, Dr. John Watson."

"Oh yes, sir," he said, shaking Holmes's hand and then mine. "When I studied in Christ Church, a tale of your adventure in France was the talk of the school for several weeks. I remembered your etching in *The Times*."

"And you no doubt anticipated someone's presence investigating the events of Digon Manor," Holmes said. "Mr. Ivarson insists that you are opposed to the Yule Festival that he and his family conduct every year."

Wellesley nodded easily, his smile still in place. "That I am, and have said so publicly. However, why are we chatting in the cold? Do come inside my home. I always keep a pot of tea brewing if visitors come calling for any reason. My study has a pleasant fire, and I shall tell you all in relative comfort."

Holmes and I agreed, following the portly vicar as he walked in a rolling, waddling fashion towards the small cottage in the rear of the church. His wife, a pleasant thin-faced woman with ash blond hair and enormous eyes, looked up from a large picture book she held in her long, thin hands. A small boy of about two or three with Wellesly's physique and the wife's hair sat in her lap, and a small kitten lay curled next to the child.

"This is my wife, Margaret, and our dear little son, Gabriel. The cat is named Daniel," the vicar explained with what I took as amused fondness. "Gabriel's choice after he heard the tale of the Prophet and the lion's den. My dear, these gentlemen are the famous Mr. Sherlock Holmes and Dr. Watson."

"Good day, Mrs. Wellesely," Holmes said. "Pray don't rise. We shall not detain your husband for long."

"A pleasure, and I do thank you, Mr. Holmes," she said in a soft, slightly quavery voice.

The study proved to be the cottage's basement, a small chamber with a narrow clerk's desk, four wooden chairs, and several boxes of books. The vicar sat us down, left the basement, and returned a moment later with a silver teapot and three china cups. A small plate of biscuits, many still warm from recent baking, lay upon a dish between the saucers.

"Now," Wellesley said as he poured us each a cup. "You asked about the Yule Festival. I did object to it because it is quite against the First Commandment."

"How interesting," I said. "Mr. Ivarson said your sermon used the Second Commandment."

The Vicar smiled gently as he handed me my cup of tea. "That is a simple enough mistake. In the *Book of Exodus*, the First Commandment says '*I am Yahweh your God, who brought you up out of the land of Egypt, out of the house of bondage.*' That is the source of my dispute. The ceremony in question is a truncated form of a pagan worship, based in that of the worship of the ancient deities of the north."

"Is that so?" Holmes asked, accepting his cup, and sipping slowly. "Still, there is no harm in such local festivals, is there not?"

Mr. Wellesley sat down and shook his head with sadness. "I cannot but disagree with you, Mr. Holmes. The German chronicler Adam of Bremen wrote in the Eleventh Century how the Yule Festival consisted of nine males of every species sacrificed to these bloody gods. Such behavior, even in a far lesser form, is quite against the ways of the Church. Does not it say in *First Corinthians* 10:18-22, '*The sacrifices of pagans are offered to demons, not to God, and I do not want you to be participants with demons. You cannot drink the cup of the Lord and the cup of demons too. You cannot have a part in both the Lord's table and the table of demons. Are we trying to arouse the Lord's jealousy? Are we stronger than he?*'"

Holmes drank a little more and I tasted the tea, which was a bitter blend that tasted wrong in my mouth.

"How true, how true," Holmes said. "I take it, Vicar, that you are something of a scholar. What are you working on at this time?"

Unconsciously, the holy man dusted off his cuffs and said, "Oh, nothing particularly important. A simple history of the Hoo Peninsula and the inhabitants of the past – which returns us to another point against the local gentry's behaviour: The namesake of Hoo Wulfhere is a son of the infamous pirate king, Ivar Ragnarson, known as the Boneless. This is a doubtful lineage. Our neighbors in Hoo St. Werburgh are named after the princess and saint, Werburgh of Mercia. What Mr. Lionel Ivarson fails to realize is that her father was King Wulfhere of Mercia, a Christian-converted son of the Norse-worshipping King Penda. These men are directly connected by trade to the Danish kings such as Ivar Vidfamne. They lived approximately two-hundred years before Ivar the Boneless and were famed for their riches. Two of their gold vessels sit in museums in Denmark. I said as much to both Misters Ivarson, but they are fixated upon their belief they are the heirs of an infamous pagan sea king."

Mr. Wellesley then leaned back and laughed. "Do forgive me, I am becoming a bore. When I begin discussing history, I approach the subject in the same manner as a lecturer. You were asking me about my debate with the community. I freely state I did dispute the Yule Festival, but my resistance began and ended at my pulpit. I doubt the bishop would believe these activities worthy of notice. Though I believe they are against the proper order of Church, I would be a poor Vicar should I judge the members of my parish with such ingratitude. As it says in *Matthew* 7:1-3, '*Judge not, that ye be not judged. For with what judgment ye judge, ye shall be judged: and with what measure ye mete, it shall be measured to you again.*'"

"I find your explanation interesting," Holmes said, finishing his tea. "Mr. Ivarson said you threatened him with expulsion from the church. And that your attempt at excommunication failed when presented to your bishop."

Howard Wellesley straightened, placed his cup down, and shook his head emphatically. "Someone has been telling tales. No, Mr. Holmes, I have never and would never behave in such a boorish manner. I spoke to my parishioners before and after my sermon on the subject and stated that neither I nor my family would attend such a ceremony. I cited my reasons, and heard nothing more until someone slaughtered that poor animal."

"Yes, the boar. That interested me a great deal," Holmes said after we had risen and taken our leave of the man.

"It seems to me," I said, "We are no closer than we were when we arrived in Hoo Wulfhere. Other than establishing the ghost was a falsehood."

"Ah, Watson," Holmes said, "I think the scent of this town is quite refreshing and useful for consideration. Let us walk about the village briefly as I consider the details."

He said no more for several minutes, leading me through the small cottages while avoiding the shops. Occasionally he lifted his aquiline nose and abruptly changed directions. Eventually he stopped before a house, where he sniffed loudly and chuckled.

The house was a tiny cottage, smaller than the Vicar's dwelling. A one-story stonewalled structure with a thatched roof, the home appeared cramped and somewhat dilapidated. Black smoke emerged from the chimney, though the scent was the same lush, grassy, odor I had smelled earlier near the church.

"Watson," Holmes said, his eyes glowing, "I think the truth slowly emerges from the fog of misdirection."

"How so?" I asked.

"Inhale deeply and you shall have one piece of the puzzle complete." He said, nodding towards a cottage nearby, "Also, I think you will find this is the home of Mr. Osbert Ivarson."

I was about to ask him how he reached that final deduction when the angry face of our client's brother appeared in the doorway. Once again, he glared our direction before slamming the door shut.

"He was peeking from the curtains for some time as we approached," Holmes said, He inhaled deeply again and nodded, "Yes, very apparent."

Holmes turned away and we headed back towards the church and the dogcart. He pursed his lips several times in thought before lifting his fingers and sniffing again. This caused another bark of laughter in my friend and his stride increased.

"You have a question?" he asked as the dogcart came into view.

I nodded and said, "You mentioned the death of the boar. How does this fit with someone dressing up as the ghost of a Viking?"

"Quite well, I should think," Holmes said, "The death of the boar, the words of Mr. Wellesley, the history of the region, and the horned helmet of the so-called spectre tell the tale completely. Now, we must repair to the manner and speak to the most officious Jameson regarding the accoutrements used in the Yule ceremony!"

The irritating Jameson proved efficient as ever, bringing us directly to the closet where the devices used for the Yule ceremonies lay. Holmes lifted several tin Viking helmets from a shelf looking within each.

"A small stain of sweat lays within this cap," Holmes said in a murmur, handing it to me, "And I see a wooden spear with several specks of dirt upon the bottom inches. As I suspected. I believe we can bring this business to an end presently. Let us make a few arrangements . . . ."

It was nearly dusk when Holmes's final arrangements were in place. We met Lionel and Osbert Ivarson in the former's study, with my friend waving them into seats. Mr. Wellesley appeared several moments later, greeting the Ivarson brothers with the same cheerful demeanor I observed earlier.

"I think we shall bring this rather interesting puzzle to a conclusion," he said without preamble. "Please look through the window to your left and tell us what you see."

There, standing upon the hill stood the image of the Viking ghost – a distant figure in a horned helmet, face in shadows. Slowly he raised his hand and shook a spear over his head.

"The ghost! My ancestor, King Ivar!" Lionel Ivarson leapt to his feet, his face flushed, his breathing labored.

"Nonsense," Holmes said, pushed open the door and called out. "Mr. Hulme, please come here."

The spear hand lowered and the figure on the hill slowly trudged downward towards our position. Holmes whirled in place, his eyes narrowed, his thin lips a slash across his face.

"No, sir, no ghost. Simply a small demonstration as to what occurred and why," he said. "An act meant to bring about the end of the Yule festivities . . . Is that not correct, Mr. Osbert Ivarson?"

Osbert stood nearby, white faced and appearing frightened, "How dare you – ?"

"Oh, do stop your protestations," Holmes said. "You heard the words of Vicar Wellesley and believed there was a hidden treasure hidden in plain sight. His historical discussions brought about your actions and foolish attempts to end the Yule traditions."

"Mr. Holmes," Lionel Ivarson said. "I think you made a mistake. My brother never advocated the end of the Yule Festival, and there are no treasures in this village.

Holmes laughed and said, "Jameson, please bring forth the box."

Jameson strode into the room, stepping with the solemnity one would expect from a Royal Usher escorting the Queen's treasures into her person. He placed the heavy chest on the desk and stepped backwards and before the door.

"You will notice several scratches on the outside of the lock. Given the character of your manservant, I couldn't see him permitting any damage remaining upon this important item. Jameson keeps your home spotless and free of dust and damage. Therefore, I knew someone may have opened the box recently, evidently in a hurried fashion due to nervousness," Holmes said and watched as our client glanced at his brother before opening the case.

The drinking horn lay upon the pillow, the dark clay rendering the article barely visible in the dim study.

"The pillow beneath the horn retracts slowly beneath the touch. You will see several folds in the fabric laying several inches from the edges. This is because the item was replaced with some haste and not the precision I exercised early today. However, now we bring the true reason for Mr. Osbert's actions."

Holmes lifted the heavy drinking cup, wetted his fingers, and rubbed quickly upon the fine point at the end of the horn. Lionel Ivarson cried out in protest, with Osbert fleeing towards the door outside.

I was about to spring into action, when Osbert yelped in pain and fell back inside. George Hulme grinned, his head still covered by a tin-horned Viking helmet.

"Shoe polish," Holmes said, lifting his damp, darkened fingers. "I discovered this when I first examined the horn's tip. At the time, I wondered why that substance was in place. It could have been a simple decision in which the item received some damage. Then Mr. Wellesley mentioned the history of gold cups and such past events."

"You were right, Mr. Holmes," Hulme said, roughly dragging Osbert back into the chamber. "Tried to run past me like the manor were on fire."

"Thank you, Mr. Hulme," Holmes said and turned the tip of the article's tip up and into the light.

The drinking horn's point glimmered in the spare illumination, shimmering with a dull shine. My eyes widened at the sight and I shook my head in shock.

"My word," I said. "Is that gold?"

"Yes, Watson, that is precisely what it is," my friend said. "Suspecting, based on the weight of the horn, this one could be gold covered in clay, Mr. Osbert rubbed off enough to see for himself. Believing it was gold, he re-covered the revealed portion with shoe polish. We viewed his less-than-lavish lifestyle today and his unimportant position in the community. The drinking horn represented a rise in position, I should think. I believe, Mr. Ivarson, you shall find this of great value."

"Oh!" Mr. Wellesley said, eyes widening, "Such a find! Sir, with your permission, may I?"

The elder Ivarson extended the drinking horn, a smile of triumph upon his podgy face. This transformed a moment later to one of sheer, unhidden malice as his eyes fell upon his struggling brother. There followed a riot of noise, with the brothers berating each other and not listening to the other.

Holmes and I left, returning to the train station in time for the evening express to London. It was only then that I aired some questions remaining.

"How did you know it wasn't Wellesley that sought the drinking horn? He is evidently a scholar and would recognize the worth of such an item," I asked.

"Easily explained," Holmes said, leaning back in his seat. "He had no occasion to hold the item in question. He is a newly appointed Vicar and not welcome upon the Ivarson property."

"I see," I said, recognizing the fact now. "Then why was the boar killed?"

"I have not the precise details, but the facts point to another basic conclusion. Mr. Osbert, having learned of the cup's intrinsic value, wished an end of the Yule Festival. He killed the animal and planned on repeating the exercise, as well as appearing as a Viking ghost to his credible brother. Lionel Ivarson defeated further pig killings by having the animal placed under guard. He stated that at our first interview."

"One final point that still confuses me," I said, "You appeared inordinately interested in the odors surrounding Osbert's home. What did that signify?"

"A deduction based on the evidence of my nose alone. I suspect that, should Osbert's efforts in halting the ceremony have proven successful, he would have replaced the drinking horn with a clay simulacrum. The earth odor that wafted from Mr. Osbert Ivarson's cottage suggested as much – he was firing clay. Short of breaking into said gentleman's home, such information was unavailable. Had Lionel Ivarson proved truculent in his belief in his brother's innocence, I would have demanded such a search.

This proved unnecessary, so I didn't raise the information in the conference. There are times when a client should not be confused with every fact present in a case," Holmes said with what I detected as a twinkle in his eyes.

I nodded and said, "Quite impressive."

"Elementary," my friend replied as he pulled out his pipe. "Elementary."

The Adventure of the Secret Manuscript
by Dan Rowley

"Holmes, this goes too far!"

My friend stopped playing his violin and said, "Why, Watson, whatever do you mean?"

"You just said a potential client is here. What in Heaven's name led you to that conclusion? The sleet is hitting the windows so loudly as to cover any sound outside, and the accumulated slush outside muffles traffic noises. As if that were not enough, your violin playing drowns out all else."

Holmes smiled and replied. "My dear Watson, you have accurately captured what can be discerned by hearing. But you forget there are other senses."

"Well, you certainly cannot smell, taste, or touch this supposed client. And you are over there and cannot see outside through the window over here."

"Ah, but I can plainly observe *you*."

"I have known you for almost fifteen years and am familiar with your ability to read my clothes, how my hair is combed, and so forth. But I have just been standing here by the window. What do I have to do with this?"

He laid aside his instrument and bow on the sofa and explained, "There are any number of *indicia*. Since you sold your practice a year ago after Mary's unfortunate demise and moved back in with me, you have craved stimulation. It has been almost a month since the Bruce-Partington affair, with no other cases of interest in the interim. Your restlessness has been steadily increasing. You seem to have trouble concentrating on the newspaper or the book you have been toying with.

"Additionally, I have always felt that weather and holidays have an effect on people's moods. I contemplate a monograph on the subject at some point. While late November was foggy and dismal, the first part of this month was warm enough for flowers to bloom. But starting a few days ago, the weather turned dreary as you just stated. Those weather fluctuations, and the fact that Christmas is in two days, which probably reminds you of Mary, have exacerbated your mood.

"While I have been trying to occupy my time today, you cannot focus on any activity. You read, you fidget, you continue to go to the window. Just now, you clearly saw something. Your back became straight as if you were again in the army, you touched your tie and straightened your waistcoat, brushed your moustache. Your eyes seemed to gleam, and you glanced at me. The conclusion is obvious. Only a prospective client could cure your *ennui*."

Before I could reply, there was a knock at the door. Mrs. Hudson opened it and said, "There is a Mr. Mitton to see you." She handed him a card, which he in turn gave to me. It read:

Jonathan Mitton, Solicitor
London
Southampton Buildings, Room 409

Holmes told her to admit him.

A tall, slim, and rather haggard man came in. He looked to be in his late fifties or early sixties. His dark hair was streaked with white. He was dressed in a black suit and tie with a black overcoat that shone with moisture from the sleet. He was pale with grey eyes. Altogether, the term "colourless" would have fit him perfectly. Before he could speak, Holmes abruptly said, "Mr. Mitton, you have wasted your time venturing out in this horrid weather. I will not deal with a solicitor as a representative of a potential client. I must meet the client in person."

The man seemed flustered for a moment. Then he said, "No, no, I am the one seeking your advice."

Holmes examined the solicitor, considered for a moment, then nodded. "Very well. Hang your coat on that peg and pull up a chair by the fire here. Now, tell us why you have come." Mitton glanced at me, and Holmes said, "You may say anything with Dr. Watson present. He is the soul of discretion and assists me in my inquiries. Now proceed, and leave nothing out. I will decide at the conclusion whether to assist you."

The potential client sat down, cleared his throat, put on a pair of glasses, peered at us, and began. "Perhaps some background would be of assistance. I am the nephew of Thomas Mitton, who was a partner in the law chambers of Smithson, Dunn, and Mitton. All three of those gentlemen have passed away. I was apprenticed to my uncle and inherited what was left of their practice. They had chambers in Malton and London, but only the London location is active currently.

"Both my Uncle and Mr. Smithson were very close to Charles Dickens and handled his legal work. In fact, Mr. Dickens stood surety for my Uncle when he incurred debt to purchase his share of the firm."

"Do you mean Charles Dickens the author?" I asked.

Holmes nodded. "Of course. Dickens had a long-standing fascination with the law, as evidenced in several of his novels. I believe it may have begun when he worked as a junior clerk at a chambers here in London when he was a teenager."

I was a bit taken aback by Holmes's apparent literary knowledge, but I then realized it probably had to do with Dickens's portrayal of crime, not his novelistic prowess.

"Quite, quite," affirmed Mitton. "Well, to continue, I am here because a number papers were stolen from my chambers the other day. My Uncle collected documents of historical interest, which were kept there. The documents mainly had the holograph of various prime ministers. For example, he obtained a letter of the Duke of Wellington. He also had a memorandum on slavery legislation signed by William Pitt the Younger, and some notes for a speech in Parliament written by Robert Peel. There were approximately twenty of these type of documents, many fairly rare outside family, academic, and official collections. Some of these documents are rather valuable, perhaps as much as five to ten pounds each."

Reflecting that even half of such documents could pay the rent for a family for a year, I asked, "Have you gone to the police about this?"

Mitton again cleared his throat. "I am coming to that. It isn't just the holograph documents that were taken. Among my Uncle's collection was a manuscript copy of Dickens's *A Christmas Carol*. That too has been stolen."

"But wait a moment," I again interrupted. "Did I not read in the newspaper in the last year that a manuscript given by Dickens to his lawyer was purchased by the American financier, J. P. Morgan? Surely it is now in his collection in New York City? If that is stolen, what concern is it of yours, and what was it doing here in London in your chambers?" Although Holmes focused on crime news and the agony columns, my newspaper reading was more catholic in nature.

Holmes had been leaning back with his eyes nearly closed. He now leaned forward. "Is Watson correct about this manuscript purchased by Morgan?"

Mitton resumed, "After *A Christmas Carol* was printed in December 1843, Mr. Dickens had the manuscript bound in crimson goatskin leather. He then presented that to my Uncle. In 1875, five years after Mr. Dickens death, my Uncle sold that bound manuscript to a bookseller here in London. It passed through several hands over the following decades until, as the Doctor correctly notes, Morgan purchased it. That is *not* the manuscript I am here to see you about.

"Mr. Dickens gave my Uncle another, unbound manuscript of the story. It was an earlier draft. My Uncle entrusted it to me and enjoined that I must keep it always and never let anyone else see it. That is why I have come to you rather than the police, as I must have absolute confidentiality."

"But why did your Uncle require such secrecy!" I exclaimed.

"I am sorry, Doctor, but I cannot tell you, as it would violate my Uncle's trust." Turning from me he said, "Mr. Holmes, please help me. The thieves can keep the other papers for all I care. But I must have the return of the Dickens manuscript. I don't know how you charge for your services . . . ."

"We will discuss that later. Your matter has some items of interest. As an initial matter, I would like to examine your chambers. Do you have any employees?"

"Yes, I have a clerk, James Ashton. He started there as a youngster in my Uncle's time."

"Please see that he is there tomorrow morning. The Doctor and I will arrive at ten."

"Oh, I cannot thank you enough, Mr. Holmes!"

"Until tomorrow then, Mr. Mitton." With that, after our client retrieved his coat, I led him to the front door.

When I went back upstairs, Holmes was seated in his chair by the fire and smoking his favorite briar pipe. He clearly was deep in thought. "Do you want me to have Mrs. Hudson bring up some food for you?"

"Just tell her to leave it on the table. Anything will do. This will require at least two pipes, perhaps three."

The next morning, when I came down from my bedroom, I couldn't tell if Holmes had slept. The room was fuggy with the odor of tobacco, and he was still in the same chair. Although I ate heartily of Mrs. Hudson's kippers, eggs, and toast, Holmes merely consumed a piece of toast and had some coffee in silence. "Well, let us be on our way." We donned our ulsters and cravats and went down the stairs.

Outside the weather was no better. Luckily we found a hansom, which made its way from Baker Street to Oxford Street. I always enjoy traveling down the street at that time of year, but Holmes didn't engage in any of the normal Christmas traditions. We had no tree decorated with gingerbread, marzipan, paper fans, pine cones, dried fruits, or other trinkets that others put in their homes. No garlands or Christmas cards appeared on the mantel, as they would interfere with the Persian slipper for his tobacco and the letters pinned there with a jack knife. Mrs. Hudson wasn't allowed to scent the rooms with fir, cinnamon, or apples, nor could she hang mistletoe decorated with cranberries. Holmes usually relented and allowed Mrs. Hudson to prepare a special meal, and I wondered what she had planned for this year.

On Oxford Street, by contrast, one knew it was Christmas. While many viewed the rebuilding of the south side of the road to create more uniformity as "progress", I much preferred the north side with its Georgian houses, store fronts, and charming irregularity. The shops were beautifully decorated with garlands over the doors and windows. Some had trees or beribboned wreaths in their windows, while others had miniature pines in tubs flanking the door. Most had displays of Christmas ware in the windows, such as mufflers, work slippers, umbrellas, and cigar cases for men, and aprons, fans, handkerchiefs, pin cushions, and sewing accessories for women, and hair ribbons, music books, sleds, skates, toy animals, and marbles for children. Despite the dreadful weather, shoppers were beginning to appear for last minute purchases.

When we passed Tottenham Court Road and continued on toward High Holborn, I reflected we were somewhat near The Alpha Inn, which had featured in the Blue Carbuncle matter. We then turned right at the South Hampton Buildings just East of Chancery Lane and Lincoln Inn, the heart of London's legal fraternity.

We made our way through the maze of doors and alcoves and finally found Mitton's chambers in room 409. Upon entering, I was struck by the sight. There was an outer room with several chairs, and a clerk's desk and stool. The inner room evidently was Mitton's office, as it contained a roll top desk, swivel chair, and an arm chair apparently for a client. A small window looked out on an inner courtyard. The window appeared as if it hadn't been cleaned since Dickens's time. Both rooms had stoves to provide heat. But the truly amazing aspect was the innumerable bundles of paper. They were everywhere in both rooms – on shelves, the floor, some of the chairs – anywhere there was space.

Mitton and the clerk, Ashton, were waiting for us in the outer room. Ashton was a wizened miniature of Mitton, also dressed all in black, but shorter and stooped.

"Hello, Mr. Holmes, Dr. Watson. As you can see, I have had Ashton come in as you requested. Where would you like to start?"

"I would like to ask Mr. Ashton a few questions."

"Certainly. James, give Mr. Holmes your complete cooperation."

"Of course, Master Jonathan." Mitton then turned and went into his office and shut the door.

Holmes began, "I understand you have been here quite a long time."

"Oh, yes, sir. I came shortly after Master Thomas, Master Jonathan's uncle, began at the firm."

"So you remember Charles Dickens."

"He and Master Thomas were very close. Mr. Smithson also became friendly with him after he started using chambers for his legal work. In fact, Mr. Smithson used to say the Malton chambers were the model for Scrooge's office in *A Christmas Carol*. I suppose that is why Mr. Dickens gave that bound copy of the story to Master Thomas. I recall the day he brought it in. Master Thomas was beaming and murmuring, 'Yes, Charles, yes. A fitting way to tell the tale.'"

"Did you know about Thomas's other collections?"

"Well, I just tend to the legal papers. Master Jonathan cares for his Uncle's private things. He is very fond of them, often spreading them out on his desk to savor them. Especially does he do that around this time of year."

"I assume you have seen quite a bit of change over the years."

As do many people of his vintage, he warmed to the chance of reminiscing. "Oh surely. I am of course getting up in years. I used to live across the river in Southwark, but moved closer to chambers a few months ago. I miss the old neighborhood but have adjusted. And the practice here, in chambers keeps changing, which sustains my interest. In Mr. Dickens time we handled more civil work, like his contracts, estate matters, real estate, and so forth. Master Jonathan still does that sort of work, but he has built up some other cases that requires barristers. It is exciting to see the papers on those matters." He of course was referring to the English practice of dividing work between solicitors, such as our client, who weren't allowed to appear in court to try cases. Only a barrister could do that.

"Did you discover the theft?"

"No. Master Jonathan gave me time off for the holidays. He was the one to discover it."

"Thank you, Ashton. You have been most helpful. Come, let us look at the inner office." He knocked and opened the door, and we entered the room. Holmes turned to Jonathan Mitton. "Where was the Dickens manuscript kept?"

"Over there in my rolltop. I keep it locked. You can see where the thieves pried it open."

"Were the other stolen documents there as well?"

"No, they were over on that shelf."

Holmes nodded and, without saying another word, dropped to his knees. He commenced to crawl across the floor, giving it the most minute attention. He then gave a similarly careful examination to the desk, especially all the storage holes and where the pry marks were. He proceeded to the shelf where the other documents had been kept and peered at it for several minutes.

I was naturally accustomed to his methods, but out client had a look of astonishment. That only increased when Holmes curtly said, "That will be all for now. We will notify you when we need to speak again." Without another word, and leaving Mitton open-mouthed, Holmes turned and strode from the office.

Once we were outside, Holmes said to me, "Watson, I have something to attend to. Amuse yourself for the afternoon, but be back at Baker Street by four." Knowing it was useless to protest, I watched him walk away. I decided to spend the next few hours at the Reading Room so that I could make some notes and check a few facts related to Holmes's ingenious solution of the poisoned ink well.

Having finished that, I arrived back at Baker Street shortly before four. As I approached our residence, I noticed an odd looking character lurking there. He was short, wearing an old overcoat and trousers that were too short for him. His face had a long scar running from his ear to his chin, and his hands were gnarled and bent with arthritis.

"Here, what do you want?"

"I'se 'ere ta see 'Olmes."

"Mr. Holmes, to you. Wait out here while I see if he is in." As I turned, I heard the familiar voice. "I am quite sure he isn't in there." I turned and the man was taller, his hands were normal, and I could see the twinkle in his eye.

"All right, you have had your fun. Have you learned anything?"

"Yes, indeed. Let us go inside." At the top of the stairs, he entered his bedroom through the hallway door while I proceeded to the sitting room. Once he had changed out of his outfit and removed the makeup, he joined me. "Well, we should be on our way. We are going to Booksellers Row on Holywell Street."

"But some of those shops are rather disreputable. I have heard they sell salacious materials."

"Yes, some of them do. You should go get your service revolver, just in case." I went over to my desk to get it. We then put on our ulsters and went downstairs.

We hailed a cab and were on our way. As we were shortly pulling into Holywell Street, Holmes remarked, "I hear they are going to widen the Strand, which likely will eliminate this street. I presume some people think that it's an improvement, but human nature will not change, no matter the street layout. The material you deplore will still find an audience."

We came to a small shop with no identification other than a sign reading "*Rare Books and Oddities*". It being Christmas Eve, there were few shoppers about, and this shop certainly had no decorations like those that I had admired this morning. We alighted from our cab and entered a gloomy interior lit by a single gaslight. There were some shelves with indiscernible objects that may have been books. Several customers were furtively looking at us and trying to shield what they were examining with their bodies. One was a rather well-dressed man who seemed startled by our presence and hurriedly departed. Another was rather shabbily attired and seemed a bit under the influence. He seemed uncertain what to do, but decided he too should follow his fellow customer out the door.

At the other end of the room was a counter behind which sat a small man who was, if anything, even more ferret-like than Inspector Lestrade. He was clothed in a shirt that may have at one time been white, a moth-eaten cardigan, and a pair of baggy trousers. "Are you looking for something special," he leered, starting to reach under the counter.

Holmes replied, "No, we want none of that. We are here to see Jack Winslade."

"Never heard of him."

Placing a shilling coin on the table, Holmes smiled. "Does this refresh your memory?"

He snatched the coin and replied, "Wait here." He turned and went down a narrow corridor behind him. We could hear a knock, a door opening, and an impatient voice saying, "What is it, Kendrick? I told you Billy and I didn't want to be disturbed." The door shut and we heard nothing until it reopened, and the man returned and gestured for us to go down the corridor.

Reaching the door, which was open, we saw that there was an office there with a desk and two chairs in front of it. Behind the desk sat an extremely obese figure, with a thick moustache and a bald head shining with sweat. Behind him stood a man over six-and-a-half feet tall, very muscular and watching us carefully – presumably the "Billy" Winslade had referred to.

Holmes said, "I presume you are Jack Winslade. We are here to see you about a manuscript."

Winslade snarled, "We don't carry things like that."

"But I have it on good authority that you do carry such items, although their provenance wouldn't bear scrutiny by the authorities. We would rather not involve them."

"I have no idea what you're talking about. This is my office, and all the merchandise for sale is out in the room through which you entered."

Holmes began to move toward the desk. Billy began to move forward but Winslade waved him back. Holmes said, "I would prefer to talk openly and settle this amicably."

Winslade paused for a moment. "Well, let us just assume for a moment I have things like you're talking about. Do you have money with you?"

"My dear fellow, you don't expect me tell you how much money I have with me, do you?"

Winslade glanced at his companion and replied, "Well, what exactly are you looking for?"

"We are only interested in one thing that I understand came into your possession in the past few days – a manuscript of Charles Dickens's *A Christmas Carol*."

"Well, I might have something for you." Winslade reached into his desk drawer and pulled out a long, wicked-looking butcher knife. "I believe it's here."

Faster than eye or mind could comprehend, Holmes moved behind the desk. Using his baritsu skills, he numbed Winslade's hand through a pressure point on his shoulder, making him drop the knife. Simultaneously Holmes bent Winslade's other arm with such force that Winslade's face was pushed onto the desk top. While this was taking place, I was holding off the growling Billy with my revolver.

Holmes smiled at me. "Good work, Watson."

On hearing my name, Winslade gave a start. "What! Are you Sherlock Holmes? Why didn't you say so? Let me up and the manuscript is yours. We want no trouble with the likes of you."

After being released and massaging his arm, Winslade went to a cabinet on the side of the room and retrieved a sheaf of papers tied together with a black ribbon. "Here you are, Holmes. It's in the same condition as when we received it. Never opened."

Holmes nodded his head and we left the room, went down the corridor, passed the odious Kendrick, and went back onto the street.

"Let us return to Baker Street. On the way, we'll stop and send Mitton a telegram to meet us at eight this evening. Despite the impending holiday, I'm confident he will come."

Promptly at the time requested, Mitton entered our rooms, hung his coat on the peg, and joined us by the fire. "Oh, Mr. Holmes, I do hope this is good news. I have barely slept since this dreadful business started."

Holmes handed him the manuscript, and Mitton seemed about to cry he was so relieved. "I can never thank you enough," he said.

"It would have gone more smoothly had you been honest with me from the start," Holmes sternly rejoined. Mitton was startled and looked about to speak, but instead lowered his head to stare at the floor.

Holmes continued, "It was fairly certain that you were implicated in the theft of your Uncle's document collection, but not the manuscript. Your hesitations at our first meeting suggested you weren't being fully forthcoming.

"But what would induce you to do such a thing? Financial necessity was the most logical answer. Your clothes told a story. The elbows on your jacket are worn, and the knees of your trousers are shiny. And your shoes have obviously been resoled several times. Also, when you put on your glasses, it was clear that they were out of date because you had to squint to see properly, which also probably explains why you have missed patches of beard. That, and the fact your hair needs cutting, means you cannot afford a regular trip to a barber shop for a shave and trim.

"As we proceeded, there was corroborating evidence. The chambers are a shadow of its former configuration – one office instead of two, only one lawyer and a clerk, and the rather unused and run-down condition of the current rooms. The decline probably started twenty years ago when your Uncle apparently had to sell the bound manuscript – surely a prized possession.

"After you left here, I knew I had a few missing pieces to fill in. Once I met Ashton I had one answer. He mentioned that you now have occasion to work with barristers. Given the parlous state of the chambers, that suggests some criminal elements as clients. You likely went to one of your clients who had escaped punishment and inquired about petty thieves. Your training as a lawyer enabled you to question the client without him realizing what you were doing. You made contact with a thief and arranged for him or a confederate to steal your Uncle's collection and share the proceeds of the fencing with you.

"My inspection of the shelves in your office confirmed this. There was a clutter of papers everywhere, but the shelves hadn't been searched – not a mote of dust had been disturbed. The thief clearly knew right where to go. Who but you could have told him, as Ashton only took care of the legal papers."

"Yes, Mr. Holmes, you are correct about the decline of my chambers. To be honest, I'm not a very good solicitor. The practice had begun to decline as many of the clients started to pass away, as Mr. Dickens did in 1870. I have tried to rationalize that my Uncle didn't train me properly, but that is unfair to him. It really is my inadequacies. I'm not very good with clients, and my attention wanders while working on documents. I find history and literature far more interesting."

I asked him, "But why did you not go to a reputable seller of such documents?"

He blushed and replied, "I didn't go to such a seller because I was ashamed, and didn't want word to get out about my straightened circumstances. The legal community in London is rather small and close-knit – quite prone to gossip and rumor – and I was afraid what little practice I have left would dwindle further."

"Why not insure them and simply claim them stolen?" I had to ask.

Mitton could shake his head with a sad smile. "That would be wrong, Doctor – and in any case, insurance premiums, should the company choose to cover something so small – cost money that I do not have."

"Did you not realize Sherlock Holmes would discover your duplicity?"

"Yes, Dr. Watson, I have read your accounts and knew Mr. Holmes likely would figure out my involvement. For obvious reasons, I couldn't go to the man I'd hired about the theft or to the police, and Mr. Holmes was my only hope to recover the manuscript. My shame also held me back. I had to take the risk and rely on his reputation for discretion and good judgment of my greater objective. But if you both feel it is necessary to turn me over to the authorities, I will abide by your decision."

He turned back to Holmes. "The rest is just as you say. I found a willing accomplice, told him where the documents were, and was to split the money. But I swear I didn't tell him about the manuscript. I would never betray my Uncle."

"I believe you, Mitton. The inspection of your office confirms it. Unlike the shelves, your roll-top desk had been ransacked. Every storage hole and drawer had been rifled until the thief found what he was looking for."

"But how in God's name could he know?"

Holmes smiled. "Ashton once again provided the *indicia*. He clearly enjoys spirits, as it shows in his face – especially his nose. He surely spends his evening at the pubs. As he has grown older, he has become more garrulous, as he was with us. He mentioned you reading your Uncle's materials, especially at this time of year. He can see into your office and at some point probably noticed you retrieving the manuscript from your desk and not the shelf. An excellent tale to tell to the locals – very sentimental, especially when he can weave into it your Uncle's relationship with Dickens. Although he didn't know what it is, a careful listener might deduce some Dickens material might be involved.

"The final clue was that Ashton recently moved from Southwark. That of course is adjacent to Elephant and Castle, home to the Forty Elephants. They are one of the most widespread gangs in London and hold the distinction of being composed entirely of females. They have a network of informants throughout that area and the West End. It would be a simple matter for Ashton's pub gossip to reach the ears of that notorious group.

"After we left your chambers, I crossed the river in disguise. I pretended to have some stolen papers and was looking for a so-called fence. After visiting several pubs and buying some strategic rounds, I was approached by a minion of the Forty Elephants. She directed me to a bookshop here in the City, in return for a promise to send pickpocket work her way, as that is one of the gang's specialties. Watson and I went to the shop and recovered the manuscript. I didn't inquire about the other documents, and leave them to you and your confederates. I believe that, along with the grief and shame you have suffered, is sufficient punishment. I see no reason to notify the authorities."

"Mr. Holmes, that is amazing. You are everything and more that they say about you. I am greatly relieved, but am forced to say that I cannot pay you. So I insist you take this manuscript as a token. I know you will do right by me and my Uncle." He started to hand the manuscript to Holmes, who appeared reluctant. Mitton silently placed it on a table, got his coat, and took his leave.

"What an astounding turn of events. You were at your finest."

"Watson, as always you played an indispensable role. Let us have a sherry and turn in." As I went to the sideboard to pour our drinks, he got two cigars from the coal scuttle. We both sat quietly with our sherry and cigars, listening to the sleet still beating at our window.

Christmas morning, I was up first. As Mrs. Hudson brought in a splendid repast of eggs, bacon, and fresh baked scones, I asked her, "So what is in store for us later today?"

She smiled. "Well, I'm making a mince pie and a steamed pudding, as I know you like those. And Mr. Holmes allowed me to get one of those turkeys. I've been talking to some other cooks I know as to how to prepare it. It is much larger than a goose. I went to the market yesterday and bought some fresh vegetables and fruit to go with it."

"I cannot wait. You undoubtedly will do the turkey justice."

I was having another cup of coffee when Holmes, in his favorite dressing gown, entered the room. He had the manuscript in his hand, and there was a thoughtful look on his face. Accepting coffee, he sat for a few minutes.

"Did you read it?"

"Yes. I started to notice some differences from what I remembered my mother reading to Mycroft and me. I went to my bedroom and got her copy. Indeed, there were differences."

"One would expect that in an earlier draft. I've often worked over the narratives of our cases several times before I am satisfied."

"Here, the biggest difference is the ending. You will recall that the last place The Ghost of Christmas Yet To Come takes Scrooge is his own grave. Then, when Scrooge awakens, he has a change of heart and makes amends."

"Of course. Everyone knows that."

"In this version, there is no visit to Scrooge's grave. The last visit is to the Cratchit residence, where Tiny Tim has died. Then Scrooge wakes up, but dismisses the entire set of ghosts with his normal 'Bah, humbug'. He justifies his conduct and the English economic system. The last line of the story is: '*And so the vision of the Ghost of Christmas Yet To Come came to pass.*'"

"That's terrible. Why would Dickens write such a thing?"

"He had an abiding passion about the conditions of the lower classes. After a visit to Manchester, he said he wanted to 'strike a sledge hammer blow for the poor'. That seems what he was trying to do with this version, using Christmas traditions in an ironic sense."

"Why do you think he changed his mind?"

"Ashton said that when Dickens brought the bound copy to the chambers, Mitton's Uncle called it 'fitting'. The best conclusion is that Dickens showed Mitton this draft, and Mitton persuaded him to change the ending more in 'fitting' with the Christmas spirit. That also explains why Dickens bound the version we all know and gave both it and the earlier one to Mitton."

"But if Dickens changed his mind, why did he not destroy the manuscript? Or Mitton certainly could have done so after the story became so famous."

"An excellent question. Based on what we know, I believe both Dickens and Mitton had mixed emotions about the manuscript. Dickens still believed in the social message of the manuscript, as reflected in many of his later works. He may have worried he might be tempted to publish it. But that of course became increasingly difficult, given the popularity and commercial success of the story. I'm sure you as an author can appreciate being torn between releasing a message to which you passionately adhere or destroying it, further complicated by the financial benefit you receive from another version. So he decided not to make a decision and leave that to his good friend Mitton. It relieved him of having to make a somewhat painful choice.

"Mitton's motives are also mixed but slightly less complicated. As the story became more and more famous, the manuscript represented Mitton's role in changing the story into the beloved version we know today. He abhorred the idea of the manuscript becoming public, but couldn't bring himself to destroy the token of his involvement in English literary history. So he cherished his secret while he lived, and then entrusted it to his nephew. Our client may not be a good solicitor, but his Uncle correctly judged his character – at least so far as the manuscript is concerned."

We both sat without talking. I was pondering what an impact this unknown version would have when people learned that the familiar story could have had a far more somber conclusion.

As these thoughts went through my mind, Holmes rose from his chair, walked over to the fireplace, and threw the manuscript into the flames. Although seldom glimpsed, both the great heart and great brain were evident at that instant. As he watched it burn, I went over, placed a hand lightly on his shoulder, and said to the finest man I know, "Yes, a 'fitting' Christmas present for England."

The Adventure of the Christmas Suitors
by Tracy J. Revels

It was one of the coldest Yuletides on record. Holmes and I, being bachelors, celebrated Christmas Day by remaining close to our fireplace, enjoying a fine roast goose and two bottles of excellent wine. As a result of our little jollification, neither of us was particularly receptive to the idea of entertaining visitors on Boxing Day, but when Inspector Lestrade arrived at an early hour, so bundled in his coat, hat, and scarf that he was recognizable only by his dark little eyes, we felt it was our duty to be hospitable.

"What I want is assistance," the Scotland Yard man grumbled, holding his blue-tipped fingers toward the blaze. "It's a bad business, Mr. Holmes, in a house filled with spirits."

My friend gave me a wink behind the inspector's back. "Shouldn't all homes be spirited in this festive season?"

"Not with devilish cats and walking skeletons and ghosts of long-dead nuns! Nor, in my opinion, should any house, in any season, host a beauty contest with the prize being a husband."

I nearly spit out my coffee at this bizarre remark. Holmes merely sank into his armchair with a sigh.

"How many times must I instruct you, Lestrade? Begin at the beginning!"

The inspector turned, still shivering. "Only if you promise to return with me. I'm not too proud to say I'd like this affair wrapped up before New Year's. The missus is mad enough as it is that I was gone most of Christmas Day."

Holmes cast a quick glance toward the window, where the snow was falling so heavily that the world seemed suspended in a cloud. "You assure me this case is unusual?"

"It is."

"Very well. Carry on."

Inspector Lestrade dropped into a chair. "You've heard of Mr. Edward Dewar? Lives at Flaxen Hill?"

"One of the richest men in England, though originally from America, where he made his money in phosphate mining." Holmes replied. "Married to an Englishwoman who was herself the only child of a textile magnate. In his sixties now and long a widower. There was a tragedy in the family last year – the Dewar heir perished in a hunting accident, I believe."

"You are correct. Young Stanley Dewar was himself a widower, with two small children who now reside with their grandfather. Edward Dewar's remaining child and heiress, Maggie, is twenty-five years of age and a strikingly beautiful girl. For years now she has flitted about the social scene, turning down marriage proposals willy-nilly. She is one of these annoying 'New Women', I suspect, intent on some career other than what the Lord intended for the gentle sex to pursue. But this winter her father ordered her to settle upon a suitor. His health is poor, his days are numbered, and he is worried about the future of his orphaned grandchildren."

Holmes yawned. "What does this have to do with a 'bad business'?"

"And a house full of spirits?" I asked.

Lestrade favored both of us with an irritated scowl. "I'm getting to it! Dewar invited a dozen of his daughter's most likely mates to Flaxen Hill for the holidays. Maggie Dewar was given an ultimatum to conclude the revels by accepting one of them as her husband, or risk being disinherited."

I made a face. "A cruel demand on a bright young woman."

"And a dangerous situation for greedy young men," Holmes said. "The competition for her hand must be fierce, considering the lady's financial status, as well as her personal qualities. It could be enough to cause a murder amid the rivals."

"And that is precisely what we fear has happened," Lestrade said. "One of the suitors disappeared during the night on Christmas Eve. They searched all morning for him, and as he is the son of a viscount, I was called in by luncheon. Flaxen Hill stands rather isolated in a large estate. With the bitterness of the weather, it would be quite impossible for the young man to have departed by foot. No horses or vehicles were missing, no tracks were found, and none of the youth's effects were taken. Only the man himself has vanished – into thin air."

"Did you check the chimneys?" Holmes asked. "That method seems to suit Saint Nicholas."

"Am I wasting my time here?" Lestrade growled. Holmes waved a hand airily.

"My apologies. Do continue."

"I interviewed the family and all of the assembled suitors. One thing became very clear to me: The missing man was seen as the leading contender for the honor of becoming Miss Dewar's spouse. He was thoroughly loathed for this. Perhaps when I show you these files, you will understand." He pulled an envelope from his jacket. "This dossier was compiled by the maiden's father. He was determined that only 'proper' young men would be welcome at his holiday party, and as you can see, the old gent was thorough."

Holmes carried the envelope to his table. I stood over him as he sorted through the pages.

Dewar had indeed been careful in his research. There was a page on each competitor, with a photograph attached. The man's family, social status, education, career, and estimated wealth was included, as well as a number of personal notes, some flattering (*"an excellent sportsman"*) and others not (*"said to drink, gambles too freely"*). Even rumors of insanity in a family line were explored. Half the men possessed noble blood to some degree, one had a direct claim to Plantagenet ancestors, and two were sons of industrial magnates. There was a captain in the Coldstream guards and a surgeon who had once removed a blemish from the neck of Princess Beatrice. Their ages ranged from twenty-five to thirty-eight. The eldest was a widower, but the remainder had never been wed. As I flipped through the photographs, I was struck by the fact that all of the men would be considered handsome chaps, possessing broad shoulders, strong chins, a variety of whiskers, lots of hair, and steely gazes.

"Which one has disappeared?" I asked.

Lestrade grinned. "This one. I've held him back to make a point."

Holmes took the last page, which the inspector now produced.

Of all the men in the dossier, this fellow stood out for all the wrong reasons. He was thin and frail in appearance, nearly bald, and sported a sizeable pair of spectacles. He was the Right Honorable Maxwell Drayton, third son of Viscount Drayton. He was twenty-eight years of age, a graduate of Cambridge, and a noted herpetologist.

"Loves newts, it seems. Not happy unless he's crawling around on his belly in the mire, trying to find them."

"He would hardly have gone out hunting for them in a snowstorm," Holmes said.

"Why on earth would she be attracted to him?" I asked.

Lestrade shrugged. Holmes held out the picture.

"The ways of women are confounding to men – their motives are always obscured – but I will risk a theory. He is different. There may be a kindness to him, a humor that the others lack. He sees his rivals and assumes the game is lost before it begins. Therefore, he has nothing to lose, and acts in whatever manner is natural to him. The lady, weary of the posturing and preening of the other males, is therefore attracted."

Lestrade had wandered over to our cabinet and located a bottle of whisky. He added a dollop to his coffee. "You may be on to something there."

I read the rest of the page. "Dewar notes that Drayton is sickly. That could also explain the attraction. Many women possess a natural affinity for nursing, and nurses often fall in love with their patients."

Holmes pointed to me. "I think I am surpassed as an investigator – at least in the mystery of women's hearts."

"So," Lestrade muttered, before bolting down his drink, "will you two brilliant consulting detectives come back to Flaxen Hall with me or not?"

Within an hour, we were on the train. Never have I felt the cold so keenly in my bones. My wound throbbed. Holmes, as usual, seemed to take the frigid temperatures in stride.

"I do like your theory of the case, Watson," my friend said as we waited for Lestrade to join us in our compartment. "I read Miss Maggie Dewar's entry in the Index as you were dressing. She has an excellent education at an American women's college and produced a thesis on developments in germ theory. She is known for her charitable work, especially in fundraising for hospitals. She is a promoter of medical education for women, as well as measures for public health. Drayton is also a scientist, and therefore a man with whom she might readily converse. This would add an especial appeal."

"Drayton's prospects are good, but not excellent," I said, recalling that detail from the file.

"The common fate of third sons. But the lady knows she does not need to marry wealth, since she will inherit it."

"So which of the rivals caused him to disappear?" I asked.

Lestrade entered the compartment and took his seat. Holmes offered him a cigarette from his silver case and asked him to tell us more about the Christmas party at Flaxen Hall. Lestrade consulted his notebook.

"The guests arrived four days before Christmas. The house is massive, and each fellow could have his own room, even without Dewar opening the old north wing. There were meals and games and larks about outside until Christmas Eve, when the great snowfall began, and the temperatures plummeted. Miss Dewar told me she had organized everything around an Elizabethan theme – there was a troupe of minstrels who performed during the Christmas Eve feast, but they departed before everyone retired around ten."

"That seems an early hour for ending a revelry," Holmes said.

"It was on the order of the old man. He was sleepy."

We both chuckled. "And when was the alarm raised?" Holmes asked.

"At seven on Christmas morning. Drayton's valet went to wake his young master and found his bed rumpled but unoccupied. The other men were unconcerned at first, but over breakfast the lady was most insistent that he be found before any of the presents could be opened. They all went running whither and yon, paired off in hunting parties, all across the house and grounds, but found nothing."

"No tracks?"

"None. But if he had departed shortly after everyone retired, the snowfall would have covered them."

"And a frantic search would have obliterated any others," I said.

Lestrade nodded. "There is a lake, and some of the men were insistent that Drayton threw himself into it, as there was a hole in the ice. I'm afraid it's frozen back over now, and it will take some time to get men out to drag it."

"Where were Drayton's glasses?" my friend asked.

Lestrade started. "His glasses?"

Holmes waved the photograph of the missing youth. "His spectacles, Lestrade. He is obviously blind without them. If they were found in his room, he most certainly didn't walk outside, nor cast himself into a lake."

"They were on his bedside table. Folded."

Holmes dropped the picture. "Then the man is dead, not missing. Someone in the house has done away with him. The challenge will be to find his body."

Flaxen Hill was one of the greatest estates in England. It perched upon a high hillock, with excellent views of a thousand-acre hunting park. The house itself was a classical symphony in marble and glass, surrounded by pleasure gardens that the snow had transformed into twinkling fairylands. Wreaths were hung in a hundred windows, and candles alight even in midday added to the magical appeal. We were greeted by a butler in an ornate and heavy livery who immediately ushered us into a trophy-lined chamber.

"Mr. Sherlock Holmes, Dr. John Watson, and Inspector Lestrade," the butler intoned. A dozen men were littered about the room, taking their leisure. Four straightened from a game of billiards. One turned away from admiring a globe. The oldest of the party, bald but heavily bearded, and clearly the master of the house, rose from a chair by the fire.

"Mr. Holmes, I am glad that the Inspector was able to acquire you. We have all hopes that our missing lamb will be found safely. Maggie is quite distraught – It has entirely ruined Christmas."

"Rather selfish of Drayton, if you ask me!" one of the billiards players proclaimed. "Quite like him, though."

"I say he was careless," the tallest man, whom I recognized from his picture as the Captain of the Coldstream Guards, announced. "Probably ran off after one of his little slimy creatures and got lost."

"Newts aren't about at this time of year." This statement came from the Royal Surgeon. "He would know that!"

"Well, I say the Red Nun took him away!"

Holmes held up a hand. "It seems that every man here has a pet theory. I will hear them in turn, if Mr. Dewar will be good enough to make introductions."

Lestrade sank wearily onto a sofa, and I settled in beside him. It made for a tedious, but occasionally entertaining, afternoon, as each man presented his ideas about what had happened to Drayton. Our host dozed off in his chair, clearly worn out by the affair.

"Tell me about the Red Nun," Holmes said, after listening to presentations about Drayton's obvious carelessness, his clumsiness, and his lack of common sense. There were two suitors – Jack Keller and Carlton Mott – who were cousins, and they were shoved forward by their peers.

"It's a legend of the house," Keller said. "Flaxen Hill stands where a monastery did, back in the olden days. The monastery was torn down in Henry VIII's great dissolution. When Cromwell's men came to force the monks to leave, they found that the abbot had a mistress, who dressed herself as a nun."

Mott took up the tale. "Needless to say, Cromwell's commissioners didn't approve. The abbot was put in prison, the monks sent away, and the entire structure burned to the ground, with the nun chained up inside it. Ever since that time, she walks the grounds, and she glows red like the fires of hell."

"And have you seen her?" Holmes asked.

The party chuckled, all except for Mott and Keller.

"I . . . I have," Mott said softly. "On Christmas Eve. I was standing at my window, taking off my tie, when I saw her moving across the grounds. It was true – she appeared as a woman completely consumed and yet unhurt by fire. And I thought I saw someone following her, but I was terrified."

"My room is next door," Keller said. "I heard him cry out. He threw open the connecting passage and called to me to look, but by that time she was gone."

"We sat up for almost an hour," Mott said, "waiting to see if she would return, but the snow began coming down so heavily we couldn't see the lawn, and so we went to bed."

"It must have been a truly frightful vision," I said.

There was a general nodding of heads, though one man – Sir Frederick Lyon – raised a hand.

"I have also seen something that glowed red upon the snow, but I suspect it was an optical distortion of the lights from the Christmas tree in the great hall. Allow me to explain the nature of how light travels."

There was a communal groan. A number of the men returned to their activities and games as Sir Frederick droned on and on. I understood instantly why Maggie Dewar had eliminated him as a prospective husband.

Halfway through his monotonous exposition on Newtonian optics, the door of the chamber opened and the lady of the house appeared. She was without doubt one of the loveliest women it had ever been my pleasure to behold. She was tall and stately, regal in her bearing, with her head raised proudly and her perfectly formed chin thrust forward. Her hair was a magnificent, lustrous chestnut shade, piled into an artfully imperfect halo on her head. She wore a simple white day gown, and though she clearly needed no adornment, a string of pearls worth a king's ransom dangled from her swan-like neck. Instantly, every gentleman in the room turned from his distraction and struck some sort of pose. I realized that even I had leapt to my feet and offered her a bow.

"I see Father is asleep again," she said, in a musical voice. "I will beg all of you not to tattle if I have a private conversation with Mr. Holmes and his friend."

I sensed that her announcement wasn't pleasing to the assembly, but none dared object as she beckoned us from the room and led us into a smaller suite that was clearly a lady's conservatory, complete with a piano, harp, and a vast collection of lovely paintings.

"Thank you for coming to us," she said, boldly taking my friend's hand. "I realize how disgraceful this affair must appear. It was Father's idea, and all I could do was make the best of it."

"It is certainly a large house party."

"With no other ladies present besides the servants. You have no idea how exhausting it is to have to pretend to be interested in everything these horrible men have to say – to laugh at their jokes and flatter their vanity. But dear Max was different. He expected nothing, he hung back from the crowd. Yet he alone shared my interests in science, and in doing some good for poor sick people – he understood because he was so often ill. His heart was weak. Indeed . . . oh Mr. Holmes . . . I fear I have killed him!"

She seemed poised to weep, but quickly mastered herself. Her strength of character and resolve was clear in her lovely yet sorrowful face.

"You must understand that I planned to stand up to Father – he is such a bully at times, but I am his daughter, and I can bully back to him. I wasn't going to announce a selection at the conclusion of the party. Quite frankly, I have no intention to marry, ever. I want to commit my life to helping others, and I can hardly do that with a husband and a pack of children at my heels. But I was quite taken with Max, I favored him above the rest, and I saw that it made the others angry. I enjoyed making them angry, they who were so prideful of their appearance and their wealth! And then, on Christmas Eve – I was indiscreet. And I fear that indiscretion has led to Max's vanishing, and perhaps even his murder.

"I had been careful never to allow anyone a close dance, or more than a kiss of my hand. I fled from any man who tried to whisper in my ear. But on Christmas Eve, just as we were leaving the dining room, I chose Max for my escort. Father had tottered on ahead, and in the doorway, there was a spray of mistletoe. I halted Max and, quite boldly, I turned and kissed him, in front of all the others! He turned as red as the holly in our wreaths. There was quite a bit of muttering from the rear, for they all surely saw the kiss, but none dared speak out. I dropped Max's arm and went to walk upstairs with Father. That was the last I saw of my sweet little scientist."

"Rest assured, Miss Dewar, that no one blames you for anything," I said. Holmes was about to speak when the door to the conservatory flew open. I was poised for angry suitors, but instead it was a pair of little children, a boy and a girl.

"Aunt Maggie! Aunt Maggie!" they cried. "We want to meet Sherlock Holmes!"

My friend has always had a great heart for children, and a natural aptitude for dealing with them. He is never patronizing and treats their concerns with great seriousness. His Irregulars worship him, and every London newsboy and chimney sweep tips his cap at Holmes's approach. Before any word could be spoken, the two youngsters were at my friend's knees.

"Susan, Michael, where are your manners?" Miss Dewar scolded. "These are my niece and nephew – my late brother's children."

"I had deduced as much," Holmes said, solemnly shaking hands with each child.

"Will you solve our mystery?" Master Michael asked.

"Yes, please – we want to know if it is true or not!" little Miss Susan added.

"And what mystery is that?" Holmes asked.

"Are you talking about the Queen's Christmas Eve dance?" Miss Dewar asked. "Goodness! I am certain Mr. Holmes is much too busy to be bothered with that tale."

"On the contrary, I would like to hear of it. Young person's mysteries are the purest, the most filled with magic."

The children giggled. Miss Dewar blew back a loose strand of hair.

"As you have perhaps heard, Flaxen Hill is a virtual cornucopia of ghost stories. There is the Devil Cat and the Red Nun and even a skeleton that supposedly appears stomping around the grounds on All Hallows Eve. Supposedly, some year in the 1500's – I was never good at history, so you must not ask me the exact date – Good Queen Bess came here for the Yuletide and gave the manor her special blessing. Ever after, at the stroke of midnight on Christmas Eve, the old Tudor Hall comes to life, the suits of armor parade around, and the Virgin Queen herself steps down from her portrait to dance." The lady leaned forward with a conspiratorial tone. "The Tudor Hall is in the north wing of the house, which has no heat and is in great need of repair. Father keeps it locked up – I have only seen it a few times myself! And no one has ever heard the mystic celebration."

"We did!" the little girl insisted. "We heard it."

"We were supposed to be asleep in the nursery," the boy said. "All the grown-ups had gone to bed. But we snuck out and went to the Tudor Hall. It was ever so cold in the middle of the night. And when we got to the door, we heard a clanging! It must have been one of the knights, bowing to the Queen. Sissy got scared."

"I did not! You were scared!"

"We ran back to our room. But tell me, sir, is it true? We heard it! Both of us!"

"Well, my young friends, I have heard a philosopher claim that only those things the heart believes are true," Holmes said. "Do you believe it here?" he asked, gently placing his finger in the middle of the lad's chest.

"Oh, yes!"

"Then you have indeed experienced a Christmas Eve miracle."

The children clapped their hands. A gong rang, signaling tea was being served. Our hostess shooed the young ones away, then turned to Holmes.

"You will stay and continue to investigate?"

"Of course. Perhaps I can converse with your erstwhile suitors over dinner and afterward."

"Oh, sir – better you than I!"

The evening was a painfully long one. True to his word, Holmes spoke with all of the gentleman guests. I attempted to make myself useful – and I confess I was curious to engage the Royal Surgeon as a fellow medical man – but the eleven remaining bachelors clearly found my humble presence beneath their notice. Mr. Dewar dozed off between every course, and Miss Dewar opted to take her meal in the nursery with her niece and nephew. I found myself longing for the company of Inspector Lestrade, who had whisked himself back to London to try and mollify his irate spouse. Just after dessert, Holmes towed me below the stairs to speak with the servants. They were far more concerned with Drayton's disappearance than his peers had been. A few brief conversations communicated that young Drayton was a kind soul, who had, through his valet, distributed small but thoughtful gifts to the entire staff before his vanishing. Drayton's valet, a distinguished fellow named Brighton, was especially remorseful.

"I don't understand it," he said to Holmes. "My master would never have left this house without me. He was a dear fellow who would rescue wounded animals and always thought of those less fortunate than himself, but he also was rather lacking in common sense. Why, he would have worn tweeds to dinner that night if I hadn't stopped him! He couldn't even select his own socks, much less make himself disappear like a magic trick."

"I presume you helped him to prepare for bed on Christmas Eve."

"Yes, sir. I had laid out his pajamas and dressing gown and fixed a hot water bottle for him."

"How would you describe his mood?"

"Ebullient, sir. He practically danced into the room. His face was red and flushed. I immediately assumed that Miss Dewar had shown him some favor, for he was very much in love with her."

When at last we retired to our rooms, I found myself even more puzzled than I had been before. All of the servants, as well as several of the guests, had conducted yet another search of the house and grounds, with no clue being found. Holmes himself had inspected Drayton's chamber, which remained as it had been found on Christmas morning. The young man's possessions likewise made no impression, told no tale. There was something rather sad and pathetic about the folded spectacles on the nightstand. Beside them was a small gift wrapped in bright foil, with Miss Dewar's name attached. Brighton informed us that it had been his master's gift for the lady and was an original copy of *On the Origin of Species*.

I drew back the curtains and stared out onto the lawn, recalling the stories of the spectres that supposedly haunted the property. The snow had stopped falling and the moon shown brightly, a perfect stage for a supernatural debut, but there was nothing more engaging than a rabbit doing some belabored hopping through the snowdrifts.

"The Red Nun will not walk tonight," Holmes said, nearly causing me to jump out of my skin, as I hadn't heard his knock upon the door. "Nor will the Devil Cat appear . . . much to the hare's relief, I am sure."

"Holmes, do you have a theory?"

"One, but I must wait to test it. Good night, old friend. Sleep well."

And with that he departed to the room next door. I amused myself with a historical novel for another hour. Shortly after the clock struck midnight, I went to bed.

I drifted in slumber for some time, but then I heard a sound in the hallway. I listened intently, certain that it was footsteps. Cautiously, I rose from my bed and lit a candle. I opened the door, leaning out into the passage. It was black and cold. Indeed, the entire house was uncomfortably chilled, as aged mansions often are. I squinted into the darkness. Something was moving at the far end of the passage, something tall and dark, like a figure wearing a cloak and cowl. It turned at the end of the hall, and for the briefest of instants I thought I saw a wane light, and a skeleton-like face.

I slammed the door, blew out my own candle, and dove beneath the covers. I felt foolish and resolved to say nothing of the matter until we returned to Baker Street. Perhaps I was as easily frightened as the children, but I was also certain that whatever I had witnessed, walking toward the end of the passage, wasn't of this earth.

The next morning, the entire assembly was at the breakfast table. Having knocked on Holmes's door and received no answer, I had assumed he was already mingling with the house party over coffee and kippers. But everyone was well tucked into their food before my friend suddenly appeared in the doorway. With a quick strike to the ornate gong, he gained the party's attention.

"Good morning. Dr. Watson and I will need to return to London upon the noon train, but before we depart, I will require the assistance of the gentlemen in this room for one final investigation – one which I hope will bring us to the truth as to the disappearance of the Right Honorable Maxwell Drayton. If the men will all rise and accompany me?"

"I will go too!" Miss Dewar asserted. "I want to find Max!"

"This is a man's business," her father answered. "You stay right here, young lady."

Everyone except the furious Miss Dewar stirred from the table, following Holmes. I wondered what he was up to as he gestured to several lanterns and asked that they be borne by the companions.

"There is very little light where we are going," he said, setting a brisk pace through the many public areas of the house, refusing to answer the questions that were flung in his direction. At last, he turned along a passageway that was darker than the rest.

"This is the North Wing," Mr. Dewar said. "We do not use it."

"It's cold!" another gentleman complained.

Holmes never broke his brisk stride as we passed into the unused quarter of the ancient home. "This part of the house is said to date to Tudor times, though my knowledge of architecture tells me otherwise. Am I correct, Mr. Dewar?"

The old man sputtered. "Well, I think . . . yes, blast your sharp eyes, it is just a replica of a Tudor Great Hall. This wing of the house was constructed in the early eighteenth century for a gentleman who had an obsession with Queen Elizabeth's court. My wife wished to have it renovated but died before any work could begin. After she passed, I had no heart to keep it open. This hall hasn't been used in well over a hundred years."

"Which is an ideal amount of time for a legend to grow and spread, especially among the servants and the young people in residence. Surely you informed your guests about the Christmas Eve fete, where Good Queen Bess herself dances?"

"Yes, but that is a story for children!" Dewar snorted. "The great hall is unsafe, so we keep it locked. I secured it myself, several days ago, after I showed it to the gentlemen."

Holmes had halted in front of a massive doorway. "Yet someone has broken in."

He placed his lamp near the lock. The metal was clearly scraped and scratched, a fresh and shiny wound.

"A rather unprofessional job," Holmes said. "Made in a great hurry, and most likely by flickering candlelight. Ah, look at the floor!"

The carpet runner and the wooden floor was splattered with red wax. A murmur rose amid the crowd.

"We never looked here."

"It isn't as if Drayton, blind as a bat, could have burgled his way inside it!"

"Why would he want to go in there?"

"Well, let us see what the room itself can tell us," Holmes said, holding out his hand for a key, which Dewar reluctantly provided. Holmes pushed the door open and held his lantern high, signaling for the rest to bring in their lights as well.

It was a strange sight, a room dressed as if for some Elizabethan drama, with moth-eaten bearskins on the floor, unlit torch scones upon the walls, and great faded tapestries of hunting scenes hanging between the narrow windows. It was barren of furnishings, except for a single chair set under a canopy of state. Behind the chair hung a portrait of Queen Elizabeth, clearly a copy of some earlier work, that showed the queen bedecked with pearls and diamonds, her right hand upon her hip and her left resting on a great ceremonial sword. A wry smile played upon her lips, as if she was enjoying a secret. Along the walls, a host of antique suits of armor were displayed, mounted on heavy iron supports that held them upright. It was immediately obvious how an imaginative soul might craft the myth of kneeling servants of chivalry and a dancing queen.

"I'm freezing!" the Royal Surgeon snapped.

"There is nothing here!" another voice called.

"What is the point of this?" Dewar asked.

"The point is that someone murdered a good and kind young man and had every hope of getting away with it." Holmes walked toward the nearest suit of armor. "But justice will be done."

He lifted the visor of the nearest knight. The old man gave a strangled cry. Instantly, a dozen shouts of horror, revulsion, and terror went up.

The gray, frozen face of poor Maxwell Drayton was revealed. His body was stuffed into the suit, which served as a grim metal casket for him.

Mott and Keller, who stood to the back of the gathering, whirled and fled.

"Stop them!" Holmes shouted.

They had almost reached the door when a figure stepped through. It was Miss Dewar, holding a Scottish broadsword at the ready. The men skittered to a stop. The young woman's eyes blazed.

"I have beaten both of you villains in tennis," she hissed. "Do you wish to try me now?"

They threw up their hands. The other suitors rushed to subdue them.

"Oh Maxwell!" the lady cried, dropping her weapon to the floor with a clatter. Holmes had quickly lowered the visor, to spare her the terrible view, but Miss Dewar had seen the evidence of the tragedy. Her father gathered her into his arms and firmly led her away.

There was an hour before Lestrade arrived at the house. In that time, it was all that Holmes and I could do to keep the other gentlemen from murdering Mott and Keller. At last, Holmes convinced them to allow us a private interview with the pair, who had been tied to chairs in the library.

They made a sad spectacle, their shirts torn and their hair awry. Keller sported a split lip, and Mott's left eye was swollen.

"We didn't kill him!" Mott proclaimed. "Please, Mr. Holmes, you must believe us. We are innocent!"

"We were in the wrong," Keller moaned. "That I will confess. But we did not kill him."

Holmes sat down, crossed his legs, and lit a cigarette. He considered the young men with a cool and appraising gaze. "So what did you do? I warn you to be careful in your recitation, for I will know if you are lying."

The young men shared a woeful look. Mott nodded for Keller to speak.

"This is the truth sir – we swear it upon our parents' graves. We hated Maxwell from the start, and even more when Maggie started mooning over him. Christmas Eve night, we were right there, not five steps behind, when she kissed him. She'd been so cool to us, but so warm for him – ugly, sick, near-sighted Maxwell! We couldn't stand for it. We sat drinking and talking in our rooms until almost midnight. Then, when everyone was asleep, we snuck over to Maxwell's chamber. He hadn't bothered to lock the door, so we went right in."

"And murdered him!" I said.

"No – no, that isn't what happened," Mott sobbed. "We woke him up and shook our fists in his face. We threatened to take him out and dump him in the lake or bury him in the snow. I admit we were cruel, but he was such a weasel, all he could do was curl up and whimper. And then – oh God! – he had a fit! He clutched his heart, and gasped, and then he was dead!"

"He had a weak heart, Mr. Holmes," Keller said. "Ask his valet, Mr. Dewar. Even Maggie. Everyone knew it. But I swear we only meant to scare him, not to kill him. We never actually laid a hand on him."

"If so, why did you hide his body?"

Mott moaned. "We were in our cups. We'd brought up a bottle of Dewar's finest whisky, and had been passing it back and forth, drowning our sorrows over Maggie and getting our courage up to have sharp words with Maxwell. I can only say that in our drunken state we imagined all sorts of things – that we had been heard or seen, that we would be arrested, that we would be hanged. We reasoned that if Maxwell disappeared, no one could blame us. We thought of the Great Hall, and how cold and isolated it was. Dewar showed it to us on the tour of the house, the day we arrived. Someone – I don't recall who – made the joke that there might be frozen knights inside those suits. I guess that inspired us. Maxwell was so small he would fit right inside the armor. Of course, we hadn't thought about the door being locked. We found a metal pin to get it open, all while Maxwell's corpse was leaning against the wall in his pajamas. When at last we got inside, it was even harder to force open that armor. It fell over with a crash. We were lucky no one heard us."

"Please, sir," Keller pleaded, "we are miserable creatures, but we don't deserve to hang."

Holmes rose from his chair. "You are fortunate that the intense cold of the room has preserved the corpse so that the coroner will be able to fix a cause of death. And you are indeed miserable creatures, to have so bullied a young man to a fatal seizure and then been disrespectful to his corpse. You have also deprived a fine lady of a great happiness in her life. Ah, I see our inspector is here. I will leave you in his competent hands."

My readers will no doubt recall the conclusion of this case. Inspector Lestrade received all credit for having "unmasked two vicious murderers". The coroner concluded that Maxwell Drayton had indeed suffered a fatal case of apoplexy, but couldn't state decisively that it had been provoked by the actions of the rival suitors. The young defendants were acquitted, and shortly afterward departed for South Africa, to begin life anew, away from the great scandal. True to her vow, Miss Dewar never married, but instead moved to the Continent, attended medical school, and became a noted expert on cardiac diseases. Following her father's death, she assumed the wardship of her niece and nephew, raising them to be pure-hearted young persons who were worthy of their vast inheritance.

I was adding the final touches to my notes after our return to Baker Street when it occurred to me that I should mention the phantom I had seen in the hallway. Perhaps there was some remaining mystery. I described it to Holmes, only to have my friend laugh loudly.

"The answer is a simple one, Watson. I had brooded upon the youngsters' tale of magical festivities all evening, but felt its veracity would be best investigated when all the other guests were abed. Footsteps and moans might be imagined, but a loud crash is less easily dreamed up. The children's testimony turned my thoughts into the direction of the armor being used for some nefarious purpose. I knew it would be painfully cold in the unused wing of the house. I opened the wardrobe in my chamber and discovered a long cloak and cowl within, which I threw over my garments to keep myself warm. I was the ghost of Flaxen Hall – and it is well that you are so stout-hearted Watson, and not frightened to death, for I would be lost without my Boswell."

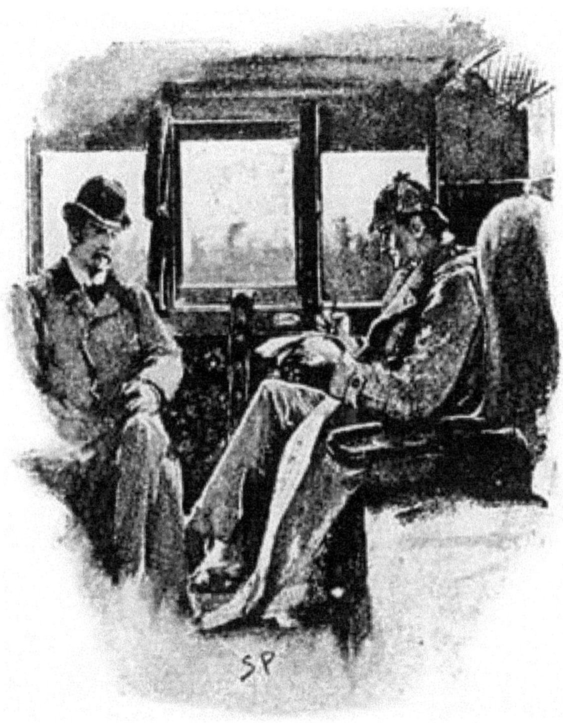
SP

About the Contributors

The following contributors appear in this volume:
**The MX Book of New Sherlock Holmes Stories
Part XXIX – More Christmas Adventures (1889-1896)**

Ian Ableson is an ecologist by training and a writer by choice. When not reading or writing, he can reliably be found scowling at a clipboard while ankle-deep in a marsh somewhere in Michigan. His love for the stories of Arthur Conan Doyle started when his grandfather gave him a copy of *The Original Illustrated Sherlock Holmes* when he was in high school, and he's proud to have been able to contribute to the continuation of the tales of Sherlock Holmes and Dr. Watson.

Wayne Anderson was born and raised in the beautiful Pacific Northwest, growing up in Alaska and Washington State. He discovered Sherlock Holmes around age ten and promptly devoured the Canon. When it was all gone, he tried to sate the addiction by writing his own Sherlock Holmes stories, which are mercifully lost forever. Sadly, he moved to California in his twenties and has lived there since. He has two grown sons who are both writers as well. He spends his time writing or working on the TV pilots and patents which will someday make him fabulously wealthy. When he's not doing these things, he is either reading to his young daughter from The Canon or trying to find space in his house for more bookshelves.

Brian Belanger is a publisher, editor, illustrator, author, and graphic designer. In 2015, he co-founded Belanger Books along with his brother, author Derrick Belanger. He designs the covers for every Belanger Books release, and his illustrations have appeared in the MacDougall Twins with Sherlock Holmes series, as well as *Dragonella, Scones and Bones on Baker Street*, and *Sherlock Holmes: A Three-Pipe Problem*. Brian has published a number of Sherlock Holmes anthologies, as well as new editions of August Derleth's classic Solar Pons mysteries. Since 2016, Brian has written and designed letters for the *Dear Holmes* series, and illustrated a comic book for indie band The Moonlight Initiative. In 2019, Brian received his investiture in the PSI as "Sir Ronald Duveen". Find him online at *www.belangerbooks.com*, *www.zhahadun.wixsite.com/221b*, and *www.redbubble.com/people/zhahadun*

Derrick Belanger, PSI is an author and educator most noted for his books and lectures on Sherlock Holmes and Sir Arthur Conan Doyle, as well as his writing for the blogs *I Hear of Sherlock Everywhere* and *Belanger Books Sherlock Holmes and Other Readings Blog*. Both volumes of his two-volume anthology, *A Study in Terror: Sir Arthur Conan Doyle's Revolutionary Stories of Fear and the Supernatural* were #1 best sellers on the Amazon.com U.K. Sherlock Holmes book list, and his *MacDougall Twins with Sherlock Holmes* chapter book, *Attack of the Violet Vampire!* was also a #1 bestselling new release in the U.K. Through his press, Belanger Books, he has released a number of Sherlock Holmes anthologies as well as new editions of August Derleth's original Solar Pons series. In 2019, Mr. Belanger received his investiture in the PSI as "Albert, the Dove". In January 2020, Mr. Belanger was awarded the Susan Z. Diamond Award in recognition of outstanding efforts to introduce young people to Sherlock Holmes. Mr. Belanger dedicates "The Man of Miracles" to teacher extraordinaire Kimberly Kubsch, for introducing him to the wonderful world of Magical Realism.

Barry Clay is a graduate of Shippensburg University with a BA in English. He's dug ditches, stocked grocery shelves, tutored for room and board, cleaned restrooms, mopped floors, taught cartooning, worked in a bank, asked if you'd like fries with that (and cooked the fries to boot), ordered carpet for cars, and worked commission sales at Sears. Currently, he is a thirty-two year veteran of the Federal employee workforce. He has been writing all his life in different genres, and he has written thirteen books ranging from Christian theology, anthologies, speculative fiction, horror, science fiction, and humor. His Sherlockian volumes include *The Darkened Village* and *The Leveson-Gower Theft*. He volunteers as conductor of a local student orchestra and has been commissioned to write music. His first two musicals were locally produced. He is the husband of one wife, father of four children, and "Opa" to one granddaughter. He is honored to have been asked to contribute to this collection.

Craig Stephen Copland confesses that he discovered Sherlock Holmes when, sometime in the muddled early 1960's, he pinched his older brother's copy of the immortal stories and was forever afterward thoroughly hooked. He is very grateful to his high school English teachers in Toronto who inculcated in him a love of literature and writing, and even inspired him to be an English major at the University of Toronto. There he was blessed to sit at the feet of both Northrup Frye and Marshall McLuhan, and other great literary professors, who led him to believe that he was called to be a high school English teacher. It was his good fortune to come to his pecuniary senses, abandon that goal, and pursue a varied professional career that took him to over one-hundred countries and endless adventures. He considers himself to have been and to continue to be one of the luckiest men on God's good earth. A few years back he took a step in the direction of Sherlockian studies and joined the *Sherlock Holmes Society of Canada* – also known as *The Toronto Bootmakers*. In May of 2014, this esteemed group of scholars announced a contest for the writing of a new Sherlock Holmes mystery. Although he had never tried his hand at fiction before, Craig entered and was pleasantly surprised to be selected as one of the winners. Having enjoyed the experience, he decided to write more of the same, and is now on a mission to write a new Sherlock Holmes mystery that is related to and inspired by each of the sixty stories in the original Canon. He currently lives and writes in Toronto and Dubai, and looks forward to finally settling down when he turns ninety.

Harry DeMaio is a *nom de plume* of Harry B. DeMaio, successful author of several books on Information Security and Business Networks, as well as the seventeen-volume *Casebooks of Octavius Bear*. He is also a published author of Solar Pons stories and stories included in the MX Sherlock Holmes series edited by David Marcum. His latest offering for Belanger Books is a seven-story collection: *The Adventures of Sherlock Holmes and the Glamorous Ghost*. A retired business executive, former consultant, information security specialist, elected official, private pilot, disk jockey and graduate school adjunct professor, he whiles away his time traveling and writing preposterous books, articles, and stories. He has appeared on many radio and TV shows and is an accomplished, frequent public speaker. Former New York City natives, he and his extremely patient and helpful wife, Virginia, live in Cincinnati (and several other parallel universes.) They have two sons, living in Scottsdale, Arizona and Cortlandt Manor, New York, both of whom are quite successful and quite normal, thus putting the lie to the theory that insanity is hereditary. His books are available on Amazon, Barnes and Noble, directly from Belanger Books and MX Publishing, and at other fine bookstores. His e-mail is *hdemaio@zoomtown.com* You can also find him on Facebook. His website is *www.octaviusbearslair.com*

Sir Arthur Conan Doyle (1859-1930) *Holmes Chronicler Emeritus.* If not for him, this anthology would not exist. Author, physician, patriot, sportsman, spiritualist, husband and father, and advocate for the oppressed. He is remembered and honored for the purposes of this collection by being the man who introduced Sherlock Holmes to the world. Through fifty-six Holmes short stories, four novels, and additional Apocryphal entries, Doyle revolutionized mystery stories and also greatly influenced and improved police forensic methods and techniques for the betterment of all. *Steel True Blade Straight.*

Steve Emecz's main field is technology, in which he has been working for about twenty-five years. Steve is a regular speaker at trade shows and his tech career has taken him to more than fifty countries – so he's no stranger to planes and airports. In 2008, MX published its first Sherlock Holmes book, and MX has gone on to become the largest specialist Holmes publisher in the world with over 500 books. MX is a social enterprise and supports three main causes. The first is Happy Life, a children's rescue project in Nairobi, Kenya, where he and his wife, Sharon, spend every Christmas at the rescue centre in Kasarani. They have written two editions of a short book about the project, *The Happy Life Story.* The second is Undershaw, Sir Arthur Conan Doyle's former home, which is a school for children with learning disabilities for which Steve is a patron. Steve has been a mentor for the World Food Programme for several years, and was part of the Nobel Peace Prize winning team in 2020.

Mark A. Gagen BSI is co-founder of Wessex Press, sponsor of the popular *From Gillette to Brett* conferences, and publisher of *The Sherlock Holmes Reference Library* and many other fine Sherlockian titles. A life-long Holmes enthusiast, he is a member of *The Baker Street Irregulars* and *The Illustrious Clients of Indianapolis*. A graphic artist by profession, his work is often seen on the covers of *The Baker Street Journal* and various BSI books.

Paul D. Gilbert was born in 1954 and has lived in and around London all of his life. His wife Jackie is a Holmes expert who keeps him on the straight and narrow! He has two sons, one of whom now lives in Spain. His interests include literature, ancient history, all religions, most sports, and movies. He is currently employed full-time as a funeral director. His books so far include *The Lost Files of Sherlock Holmes* (2007), *The Chronicles of Sherlock Holmes* (2008), *Sherlock Holmes and the Giant Rat of Sumatra* (2010), *The Annals of Sherlock Holmes* (2012), *Sherlock Holmes and the Unholy Trinity* (2015), *Sherlock Holmes: The Four Handed Game* (2017), *The Illumination of Sherlock Holmes* (2019), and *The Treasure of the Poison King* (2021).

John Atkinson Grimshaw (1836-1893) was born in Leeds, England. His amazing paintings, usually featuring twilight or night scenes illuminated by gas-lamps or moonlight, are easily recognizable, and are often used on the covers of books about The Great Detective to set the mood, as shadowy figures move in the distance through misty mysterious settings and over rain-slicked streets.

Arthur Hall was born in Aston, Birmingham, UK, in 1944. He discovered his interest in writing during his schooldays, along with a love of fictional adventure and suspense. His first novel, *Sole Contact*, was an espionage story about an ultra-secret government department known as "Sector Three", and was followed, to date, by three sequels. Other works include six Sherlock Holmes novels, *The Demon of the Dusk, The One Hundred Percent Society, The Secret Assassin, The Phantom Killer, In Pursuit of the Dead*, and *The Justice Master*, as well as two collections of Holmes *Further Little-Known Cases of Sherlock* Holmes, and *Tales from the Annals of Sherlock Holmes*. He has also written other short stories and a modern detective novel. He lives in the West Midlands, United Kingdom.

Nancy Holder, BSI, is a *New York Times* bestselling author who lives in Washington state. She has received 6 Bram Stoker Awards from the Horror Writers Association and the 2019 Grand Master "Faust" Award from the International Association of Media Tie-in Writers. She has written numerous Sherlockian pastiches and articles and is a member of several Sherlockian societies including *The Sound of the Baskervilles* and *The Sherlock Holmes Society of London*. She also writes and edits comic books and pulp fiction. Forthcoming works include two new comic book and graphic novel series with her writing partner, Alan Philipson.

Christopher James was born in 1975 in Paisley, Scotland. Educated at Newcastle and UEA, he was a winner of the UK's National Poetry Competition in 2008. He has written three full length Sherlock Holmes novels, *The Adventure of the Ruby Elephant*, *The Jeweller of Florence*, and *The Adventure of the Beer Barons*, all published by MX.

Roger Johnson BSI, ASH is a retired librarian, now working as a volunteer assistant at the Essex Police Museum. In his spare time, he is commissioning editor of *The Sherlock Holmes Journal*, an occasional lecturer, and a frequent contributor to *The Writings about the Writings*. His sole work of Holmesian pastiche was published in 1997 in Mike Ashley's anthology *The Mammoth Book of New Sherlock Holmes Adventures*, and he has the greatest respect for the many authors who have contributed new tales to the present mighty trilogy. Like his wife, Jean Upton, he is a member of both *The Baker Street Irregulars* and *The Adventuresses of Sherlock Holmes*.

Gordon Linzner is founder and former editor of *Space and Time Magazine*, and author of three published novels and dozens of short stories in *F&SF*, *Twilight Zone*, *Sherlock Holmes Mystery Magazine*, and numerous other magazines and anthologies, including *Baker Street Irregulars II*, *Across the Universe*, and *Strange Lands*. He is a member of *HWA* and a lifetime member of *SFWA*.

David Marcum plays *The Game* with deadly seriousness. He first discovered Sherlock Holmes in 1975 at the age of ten, and since that time, he has collected, read, and chronologicized literally thousands of traditional Holmes pastiches in the form of novels, short stories, radio and television episodes, movies and scripts, comics, fan-fiction, and unpublished manuscripts. He is the author of nearly ninety Sherlockian pastiches, some published in anthologies and magazines such as *The Strand*, and others collected in his own books, *The Papers of Sherlock Holmes*, *Sherlock Holmes and A Quantity of Debt*, *Sherlock Holmes – Tangled Skeins*, *Sherlock Holmes and The Eye of Heka*, and *The Complete Papers of Sherlock Holmes*. He has edited over sixty books, including several dozen traditional Sherlockian anthologies, such as the ongoing series *The MX Book of New Sherlock Holmes Stories*, which he created in 2015. This collection is now up to 30 volumes, with more in preparation. He was responsible for bringing back August Derleth's Solar Pons for a new generation, first with his collection of authorized Pons stories, *The Papers of Solar Pons*, and then by editing the reissued authorized versions of the original Pons books, and then volumes of new Pons adventures. He has done the same for the adventures of Dr. Thorndyke, and has plans for similar projects in the future. He has contributed numerous essays to various publications, and is a member of a number of Sherlockian groups and Scions. His irregular Sherlockian blog, *A Seventeen Step Program*, addresses various topics related to his favorite book friends (as his son used to call them when he was small), and can be found at *http://17stepprogram.blogspot.com/* He is a licensed Civil Engineer, living in Tennessee with his wife and son. Since the age of nineteen, he has worn a deerstalker as his regular-and-only hat. In 2013, he and his deerstalker were finally able make his first trip-of-a-lifetime Holmes Pilgrimage to England, with return Pilgrimages in 2015 and 2016, where you may have spotted him. If you ever run into him and his deerstalker out and about, feel free to say hello!

Sidney Paget (1860-1908), a few of whose illustrations are used within this anthology, was born in London, and like his two older brothers, became a famed illustrator and painter. He completed over three-hundred-and-fifty drawings for the Sherlock Holmes stories that were first published in *The Strand* magazine, defining Holmes's image forever after in the public mind.

Tracy J. Revels, a Sherlockian from the age of eleven, is a professor of history at Wofford College in Spartanburg, South Carolina. She is a member of *The Survivors of the Gloria Scott* and *The Studious Scarlets Society*, and is a past recipient of the Beacon Society Award. Almost every semester, she teaches a class that covers The Canon, either to college students or to senior citizens. She is also the author of three supernatural Sherlockian pastiches with MX (*Shadowfall, Shadowblood*, and *Shadowwraith*), and a regular contributor to her scion's newsletter. She also has some notoriety as an author of very silly skits: For proof, see "The Adventure of the Adversarial Adventuress" and "Occupy Baker Street" on YouTube. When not studying Sherlock, she can be found researching the history of her native state, and has written books on Florida in the Civil War and on the development of Florida's tourism industry.

Dan Rowley is a retired lawyer who practiced for over forty years in private practice and in house for a large international corporation. He lives in Erie, Pennsylvania, with his wife Judy. His father introduced him to the love of mysteries a long time ago. He inherited his creativity and writing ability from his children, Jim and Katy, now enhanced by Sherry and Prince.

Frank Schildiner is a martial arts instructor at Amorosi's Mixed Martial Arts in New Jersey. He is the writer of the novels, *The Quest of Frankenstein, The Triumph of Frankenstein, Napoleon's Vampire Hunters, The Devil Plague of Naples, The Klaus Protocol*, and *Irma Vep and The Great Brain of Mars*. Frank is a regular contributor to the fictional series *Tales of the Shadowmen* and has been published in *From Bayou to Abyss: Examining John Constantine, Hellblazer, The Joy of Joe, The New Adventures of Thunder Jim Wade, Secret Agent X* Volumes 3, 4, 5, and 6, *The Lone Ranger and Tonto: Frontier Justice*, and *The Avenger: The Justice Files*. He resides in New Jersey with his wife Gail, who is his top supporter, and two cats who are indifferent on the subject.

Margaret Walsh was born Auckland, New Zealand and now lives in Melbourne, Australia. She is the author of *Sherlock Holmes and the Molly-Boy Murders, Sherlock Holmes and the Case of the Perplexed Politician*, and *Sherlock Holmes and the Case of the London Dock Deaths*, all published by MX Publishing. Margaret has been a devotee of Sherlock Holmes since childhood and has had several Holmesian related essays printed in anthologies, and is a member of the online society *Doyle's Rotary Coffin*. She has an ongoing love affair with the city of London. When she's not working or planning trips to London. Margaret can be found frequenting the many and varied bookshops of Melbourne.

I.A. Watson was shattered when he failed in his life's ambition to become a Christmas Elf, and turned for solace to writing stories of Sherlock Holmes (which are known to be Santa's favourites). In hopes of being allowed at least a turn as a reindeer, he has produced the books *Holmes and Houdini* and *The Incunabulum of Sherlock Holmes*, and over thirty short stories about the Great Detective, along with eight other novels and many novellas and short stories on less-Sherlockian subjects (most recently *The Death of Persephone*). Having to generate so many "About the Author" paragraphs requires additional eccentric author blurb – but heck, it's Christmas! An up-to-date list of I.A. Watson's work is online at: *http://www.chillwater.org.uk/writing/iawatsonhome.htm*

Emma West is the Acting Headteacher at Undershaw (formerly Stepping Stones), a school for special needs students located at Undershaw, one of Sir Arthur Conan Doyle's former homes in Hindhead, England.

Matthew White is an up-and-coming author from Richmond, Virginia in the USA. A lifelong devotee of Sherlock Holmes, he maintains a Sherlockian blog, Baker Street Forever, at *https://bakerstreetforever.wordpress.com*. He can be reached at *matthewwhite.writer@gmail.com*.

Marcia Wilson is a freelance researcher and illustrator who likes to work in a style compatible for the color blind and visually impaired. She is Canon-centric, and her first MX offering, *You Buy Bones*, uses the point-of-view of Scotland Yard to show the unique talents of Dr. Watson. This continued with the publication of *Test of the Professionals: The Adventure of the Flying Blue Pidgeon* and *The Peaceful Night Poisonings*. She can be contacted at: *gravelgirty.deviantart.com*

The following contributors appear in the companion volumes:
The MX Book of New Sherlock Holmes Stories
Part XXVIII – More Christmas Adventures (1869-1888)
Part XXX – More Christmas Adventures (1897-1928)

Deanna Baran lives in a remote part of Texas where cowboys may still be seen in their natural habitat. A librarian and former museum curator, she writes in between cups of tea, playing *Go*, and trading postcards with people around the world.

Andrew Bryant was born in Bridgend, Wales, and now lives in Burlington, Ontario. His previous publications include *Poetry Toronto, Prism International, Existere, On Spec, The Dalhousie Review*, and *The Toronto Star*. His first Holmes story was published in *The MX Book of New Sherlock Holmes Stories - Part XIII*, with the second in *Part XVI*. The two stories in this collection are the third and fourth. Andrew's interest in Holmes stems from watching the Basil Rathbone and Nigel Bruce films as a child, followed by collecting The Canon, and a fascinating visit to 221B Baker Street.

Thomas A. Burns Jr. writes *The Natalie McMasters Mysteries* from the small town of Wendell, North Carolina, where he lives with his wife and son, four cats, and a Cardigan Welsh Corgi. He was born and grew up in New Jersey, attended Xavier High School in Manhattan, earned B.S degrees in Zoology and Microbiology at Michigan State University, and a M.S. in Microbiology at North Carolina State University. As a kid, Tom started reading mysteries with The Hardy Boys, Ken Holt, and Rick Brant, then graduated to the classic stories by authors such as A. Conan Doyle, Dorothy Sayers, John Dickson Carr, Erle Stanley Gardner, and Rex Stout, to name a few. Tom has written fiction as a hobby all of his life, starting with *The Man from U.N.C.L.E.* stories in marble-backed copybooks in grade school. He built a career as technical, science, and medical writer and editor for nearly thirty years in industry and government. Now that he's a full-time novelist, he's excited to publish his own mystery series, as well as to write stories about his second most favorite detective, Sherlock Holmes. His Holmes story, "The Camberwell Poisoner", recently appeared in the March-June issue of *The Strand Magazine*. Tom has also written a Lovecraftian horror novel, *The Legacy of the Unborn*, under the pen name of Silas K. Henderson – a sequel to H.P. Lovecraft's masterpiece *At the Mountains of Madness*.

Chris Chan is a writer, educator, and historian. He works as a researcher and "International Goodwill Ambassador" for Agatha Christie Ltd. His true crime articles, reviews, and short fiction have appeared (or will soon appear) in *The Strand, The Wisconsin Magazine of History, Mystery Weekly, Gilbert!, Nerd HQ*, Akashic Books' *Mondays are Murder* web series, *The Baker Street Journal*, and *Sherlock Holmes Mystery Magazine*. His latest book is *Sherlock and Irene: The Secret Truth Behind "A Scandal in Bohemia"*. He is also the author of *Murder Most Grotesque: The Comedic Crime Fiction of Joyce Porter*, published by Level Best Books. His first novel, *Sherlock's Secretary*, is published by MX Publishing.

Martin Daley was born in Carlisle, Cumbria in 1964. He cites Doyle's Holmes and Watson as his favourite literary characters, who continue to inspire his own detective writing. His fiction and non-fiction books include a Holmes pastiche set predominantly in his home city in 1903. In the adventure, he introduced his own detective, Inspector Cornelius Armstrong, who has subsequently had some of his own cases published by MX Publishing. For more information visit *www.martindaley.co.uk*

Tim Gambrell lives in Exeter, Devon, with his wife, two young sons, three cats and nine chickens. He has previously contributed to Parts XIII, XVI, XIX, XXIII, & XXVII of *The MX Book of New Sherlock Holmes Stories* from MX Publishing, as well as *Sherlock Holmes and Dr Watson: The Early Adventures*, *Sherlock Holmes and the Occult Detectives*, and *Sherlock Holmes: After the East Wind Blows*, all from Belanger Books. Outside of the world of Holmes, Tim has written extensively for *Doctor Who* spin-off ranges. He is the range editor of Candy Jar Books' *UNIT* series, and has written several novels and short stories for their *Lethbridge-Stewart* and *Lucy Wilson Mysteries* ranges. He has also written a novel, *The Way of The Bry'hunee*, for the *Erimem* range from Thebes Publishing. Tim has written audiobooks for Big Finish Productions, including *Blake's 7: The Palluma Project* (2021), *Signifiers of the Verphidiae* in *Bernice Summerfield: The Christmas Collection* (2020) and *Stockholm from Home* in *Bernice Summerfield: True Stories* (2017).

Jayantika Ganguly BSI is the General Secretary and Editor of the *Sherlock Holmes Society of India*, a member of the *Sherlock Holmes Society of London*, and the *Czech Sherlock Holmes Society*. She is the author of *The Holmes Sutra* (MX 2014). She is a corporate lawyer working with one of the Big Six law firms.

Dick Gillman is an English writer and acrylic artist living in Brittany, France with his wife Alex, Truffle, their Black Labrador, and Jean-Claude, their Breton cat. During his retirement from teaching, he has written over twenty Sherlock Holmes short stories which are published as both e-books and paperbacks. His initial contribution to the superb MX Sherlock Holmes collection, published in October 2015, was entitled "The Man on Westminster Bridge" and had the privilege of being chosen as the anchor story in *The MX Book of New Sherlock Holmes Stories – Part II (1890-1895)*.

Arthur Hall *also has stories in Part XXX*

Paula Hammond has written over sixty fiction and non-fiction books, as well as short stories, comics, poetry, and scripts for educational DVD's. When not glued to the keyboard, she can usually be found prowling round second-hand books shops or hunkered down in a hide, soaking up the joys of the natural world.

Liz Hedgecock grew up in London, England (a train and a tube ride away from Baker Street), did an English degree, and then took forever to start writing. Now Liz travels between the nineteenth and twenty-first centuries, murdering people. To be fair, she does usually clean up after herself. Liz's reimaginings of Sherlock Holmes, the Caster & Fleet, and Maisie Frobisher Victorian mystery series, and the Magical Bookshop and Pippa Parker contemporary mystery series are available in eBook and paperback. Liz lives in Cheshire with her husband and two sons, and when she's not writing you can usually find her reading, going for walks, or cooing over stuff in museums and art galleries. That's her story, anyway, and she's sticking to it.

Stephen Herczeg is an IT Geek, writer, actor, and film-maker based in Canberra Australia. He has been writing for over twenty years and has completed a couple of dodgy novels, sixteen feature-length screenplays, and numerous short stories and scripts. Stephen was very successful in 2017's International Horror Hotel screenplay competition, with his scripts *TITAN* winning the Sci-Fi category and *Dark are the Woods* placing second in the horror category. His three-volume short story collection, *The Curious Cases of Sherlock Holmes*, will be published in 2021. His work has featured in *Sproutlings – A Compendium* *of Little Fictions* from Hunter Anthologies, the *Hells Bells* Christmas horror anthology published by the Australasian Horror Writers Association, and the *Below the Stairs, Trickster's Treats, Shades of Santa, Behind the Mask,* and *Beyond the Infinite* anthologies from *OzHorror.Con, The Body Horror Book, Anemone Enemy,* and *Petrified Punks* from Oscillate Wildly Press, and *Sherlock Holmes In the Realms of H.G. Wells* and *Sherlock Holmes: Adventures Beyond the Canon* from Belanger Books.

Paul Hiscock is an author of crime, fantasy, horror, and science fiction tales. His short stories have appeared in a variety of anthologies, and include a seventeenth century whodunnit, a science fiction western, a clockpunk fairytale, and numerous Sherlock Holmes pastiches. He lives with his family in Kent (England) and spends his days taking care of his two children. He mainly does his writing in coffee shops with members of the local NaNoWriMo group or in the middle of the night when his family has gone to sleep. Consequently, his stories tend to be fuelled by large amounts of black coffee. You can find out more about Paul's writing at *www.detectivesanddragons.uk.*

Mike Hogan writes mostly historical novels and short stories, many set in Victorian London and featuring Sherlock Holmes and Doctor Watson. He read the Conan Doyle stories at school with great enjoyment, but hadn't thought much about Sherlock Holmes until, having missed the Granada/Jeremy Brett TV series when it was originally shown in the eighties, he came across a box set of videos in a street market and was hooked on Holmes again. He started writing Sherlock Holmes pastiches several years ago, having great fun re-imagining situations for the Conan Doyle characters to act in. The relationship between Holmes and Watson fascinates him as one of the great literary friendships. (He's also a huge admirer of Patrick O'Brian's Aubrey-Maturin novels). Like Captain Aubrey and Doctor Maturin, Holmes and Watson are an odd couple, differing in almost every facet of their characters, but sharing a common sense of decency and a common humanity. Living with Sherlock Holmes can't have been easy, and Mike enjoys adding a stronger vein of "pawky humour" into the Conan Doyle mix, even letting Watson have the second-to-last word on occasions. His books include *Sherlock Holmes and the Scottish Question, The Gory Season – Sherlock Holmes, Jack the Ripper and the Thames Torso Murders,* and the *Sherlock Holmes & Young Winston 1887 Trilogy* (*The Deadwood Stage, The Jubilee Plot,* and *The Giant Moles*), He has also written the following short story collections: *Sherlock Holmes: Murder at the Savoy and Other Stories, Sherlock Holmes: The Skull of Kohada Koheiji and Other Stories,* and *Sherlock Holmes: Murder on the Brighton Line and Other Stories,* among others. *www.mikehoganbooks.com*

Christopher James *also has a poem in Part XXX*

Naching T. Kassa is a wife, mother, and writer. She's created short stories, novellas, poems, and co-created three children. She lives in Eastern Washington State with her husband, Dan Kassa. Naching is a member of the *Horror Writers Association,* Head of Publishing and Interviewer for *HorrorAddicts.net,* and an assistant and staff writer for Still Water Bay at Crystal Lake Publishing. She has been a Sherlockian since the age of ten and is a member of *The Sound of the Baskervilles.* You can find her work on Amazon. *https://www.amazon.com/Naching-T-Kassa/e/B005ZGHTI0*

Susan Knight's newest novel from MX publishing, *Mrs. Hudson Goes to Ireland,* is a follow-up to her well-received collection of stories, *Mrs. Hudson Investigates* of 2019. She is the author of two other non-Sherlockian story collections, as well as three novels, a book of non-fiction, and several plays, and has won several prizes for her writing. She lives in

Dublin where she teaches Creative Writing. Her next Mrs. Hudson novel is already a gleam in her eye.

John Lawrence served for thirty-eight years as a staff member in the U.S. House of Representatives, the last eight as Chief of Staff to Speaker Nancy Pelosi (2005-2013). He has been a Visiting Professor at the University of California's Washington Center since 2013. He is the author of *The Class of '74: Congress After Watergate and the Roots of Partisanship* (2018), and has a Ph.D. in history from the University of California (Berkeley).

Jeffrey Lockwood spent youthful afternoons darkly enchanted by feeding grasshoppers to black widows in his New Mexican backyard, which accounts for his scientific and literary affinities. He earned a doctorate in entomology and worked as an ecologist at the University of Wyoming before metamorphosing into a Professor of Natural Sciences & Humanities in the departments of philosophy and creative writing. He considers Sherlock Holmes a model of scientific prowess, integrating exquisite observational skills with incisive abductive (not deductive) reasoning.

Michael Mallory is the Derringer-winning author of the "Amelia Watson" (The Second Mrs. Watson) series and "Dave Beauchamp" mystery series, and more than one-hundred-twenty-five short stories. An entertainment journalist by day, he has written eight nonfiction books on pop culture and more than six-hundred newspaper and magazine articles. Based in Los Angeles, Mike is also an occasional actor on television.

David Marcum *also has stories in Parts XXVIII and XXX*

J. Lawrence Matthews has contributed fiction to the *New York Times* and *NPR's All Things Considered,* and is the author of three non-fiction books as Jeff Matthews. *One Must Tell the Bees: Abraham Lincoln and the Final Education of Sherlock Holmes*, his first novel, combines his passion for the original Sherlock Holmes stories of Sir Arthur Conan Doyle with his interest in American history as told on the battlefields of the Civil War. Matthews is now researching the sequel, which follows Sherlock Holmes a bit further afield – to Florence, Mecca and Tibet – but readers may contact him at *jlawrencematthews@gmail.com*. Those interested in the history behind *One Must Tell the Bees* will find it at *jlawrencematthews.com*.

Julie McKuras ASH, BSI discovered Sherlock Holmes at the age of eleven through the late night magic of the Basil Rathbone and Nigel Bruce films. It was a bonus to learn there were actually books written by Sir Arthur Conan Doyle. She served as the President of *The Norwegian Explorers of Minnesota* for nine years, and has been on the board of *The Friends of the Sherlock Holmes Collections* since 1997, editing their quarterly newsletter since 1999. Julie was the first editor of *The BSI Trust* newsletter as well. She is a frequent contributor to the *Friends* newsletter, and has had articles published in the *Baker Street Journal*, London's *Sherlock Holmes Journal*, *Through the Magic Door*, and *The Serpentine Muse*. Her essays have been included in *The Norwegian Explorers Christmas Annuals*, *Sir Arthur Conan Doyle and Sherlock Holmes: Essays and Art on The Doctor and The Detective*, "A Note on the Sherlock Holmes Collections" published in *The Horror of the Heights*, *Violets and Vitriol*, and *Sherlock Holmes in the Heartland: The Illustrious Clients Fifth Casebook*. She is a co-editor of *The Missing Misadventures of Sherlock Holmes*, and with Susan Vizoskie, she co-edited *Sherlockian Heresies*. Julie has been a speaker at a number of conferences and events, such as *The Sherlock Holmes Society of*

London's Statue Festival, Holmes Under the Arch, the Newberry Library, From Gillette to Brett, and the 2014 Reichenbach Irregulars Conference in Davos. She lives in Apple Valley, Minnesota with her husband, Mike, and with her children, their spouses, and her three grandchildren nearby.

Mark Mower is a crime writer and historian whose passion for tales about Sherlock Holmes and Dr. Watson began at the age of twelve, when he watched an early black-and-white film featuring the unrivalled screen pairing of Basil Rathbone and Nigel Bruce. Hastily seeking out the original stories of Sir Arthur Conan Doyle, and continually searching for further film and television adaptations, his has been a lifelong obsession. Now a member of the Crime Writers' Association, The Sherlock Holmes Society of London, and The Solar Pons Society of London, he has written numerous crime books. Mark has contributed to over 20 Holmes anthologies, including 13 parts of *The MX Book of New Sherlock Holmes Stories*, *The Book of Extraordinary New Sherlock Holmes Stories* (Mango Publishing) and *Sherlock Holmes – Before Baker Street* (Belanger Books). His own books include *A Farewell to Baker Street, Sherlock Holmes: The Baker Street Case-Files*, and *Sherlock Holmes: The Baker Street Legacy*, and *Sherlock Holmes: The Baker Street Epilogue* (all with MX Publishing).

Will Murray has been writing about popular culture since 1973, principally on the subjects of comic books, pulp magazine heroes, and film. As a fiction writer, he's the author of over 70 novels featuring characters as diverse as Nick Fury and Remo Williams. With the late Steve Ditko, he created the Unbeatable Squirrel Girl for Marvel Comics. Murray has written numerous short stories, many on Lovecraftian themes. Currently, he writes The Wild Adventures of Doc Savage for Altus Press. His acclaimed Doc Savage novel, *Skull Island*, pits the pioneer superhero against the legendary King Kong. This was followed by *King Kong vs. Tarzan* and two Doc Savage novels guest-starring The Shadow, and *Tarzan, Conqueror of Mars*, a crossover with John Carter of Mars. He is the author of the short story collecdtion *The Wild Adventures of Sherlock Holmes. www.adventuresinbronze.com* is his website.

Roger Riccard's family history has Scottish roots, which trace his lineage back to Highland, Scotland. This British Isles ancestry encouraged his interest in the writings of Sir Arthur Conan Doyle at an early age. He has authored the novels *Sherlock Holmes & The Case of the Poisoned Lilly*, and *Sherlock Holmes & The Case of the Twain Papers*. In addition, he has produced several short stories in *Sherlock Holmes Adventures for the Twelve Days of Christmas*, and in November 2021 his fifth and final volume of *A Sherlock Holmes Alphabet of Cases* will be released. All of his books have been published by Baker Street Studios. Having earned Bachelor of Arts Degrees in both Journalism and History from California State University, Northridge, his career has progressed from teaching into business, where he has used his writing skills in various aspects of employee communications. He has also contributed to newspapers and magazines and has earned some awards for his efforts. He currently lives in a suburb of Los Angeles, California with his wife/editor/inspiration, Rosilyn.

J.S. Rowlinson grew up on the Staffordshire/Derbyshire border, in the heart of England, near the market town of Uttoxeter where his story is set. He is now an art teacher in Plymouth, with the Mayflower steps to the south and Dartmoor to the north. Conan Doyle, for a short time, had a medical practice in the city, on Durnford Street. When not teaching or writing, he is a freelance illustrator, a singer of traditional English folk songs and ballads, and can often be found walking the desolate beauty of the moor with his dog, Jessie.

Jane Rubino is the author of *A Jersey Shore* mystery series, featuring a Jane Austen-loving amateur sleuth and a Sherlock Holmes-quoting detective, *Knight Errant*, *Lady Vernon and Her Daughter*, (a novel-length adaptation of Jane Austen's novella *Lady Susan*, co-authored with her daughter Caitlen Rubino-Bradway, *What Would Austen Do?*, also co-authored with her daughter, a short story in the anthology *Jane Austen Made Me Do It*, *The Rucastles' Pawn, The Copper Beeches from Violet Turner's POV*, and, of course, there's the Sherlockian novel in the drawer – who doesn't have one? Jane lives on a barrier island at the New Jersey shore.

Geri Schear is a novelist and short story writer. Her work has been published in literary journals in the U.S. and Ireland. Her first novel, *A Biased Judgement: The Diaries of Sherlock Holmes 1897* was released to critical acclaim in 2014. The sequel, *Sherlock Holmes and the Other Woman* was published in 2015, and *Return to Reichenbach* in 2016. She lives in Kells, Ireland.

Brenda Seabrooke's stories have been published in a number of reviews, journals, and anthologies. She has received grants from the National Endowment for the Arts and Emerson College's Robbie Macauley Award. She is the author of twenty-three books for young readers including *Scones and Bones on Baker Street: Sherlock's (maybe!) Dog and the Dirt Dilemma*, and *The Rascal in the Castle: Sherlock's (possible!) Dog and the Queen's Revenge*. Brenda states: *"It was fun to write from Dr. Watson's point of view and not have to worry about fleas, smelly pits, ralphing, or scratching at inopportune times."*

Shane Simmons is the author of the occult detective novels *Necropolis* and *Epitaph*, and the crime collection *Raw and Other Stories*. An award-winning screenwriter and graphic novelist, his work has appeared in international film festivals, museums, and lectures about design and structure. He was born in Lachine, a suburb of Montreal best known for being massacred in 1689 and having a joke name. Visit Shane's homepage at *eyestrainproductions.com* for more.

Joseph W. Svec III is retired from Oceanography, Satellite Test Engineering, and college teaching. He has lived on a forty-foot cruising sailboat, on a ranch in the Sierra Nevada Foothills, in a country rose-garden cottage, and currently lives in the shadow of a castle with his childhood sweetheart and several long coated German shepherds. He enjoys writing, gardening, creating dioramas, world travel, and enjoying time with his sweetheart.

Amy Thomas is a member of the *Baker Street Babes* Podcast, and the author of *The Detective and The Woman* mystery novels featuring Sherlock Holmes and Irene Adler. She blogs at *girlmeetssherlock.wordpress.com*, and she writes and edits professionally from her home in Fort Myers, Florida.

Kevin Thornton is the author of more than a dozen Holmes short stories, as well as other crimonous fare. He has been short-listed quite a few times for awards. He has never won. He has written for *The New York Times* and has been in a top-selling anthology, but he is not an *NYT* best -selling writer. His singular achievement so far has been the locked room mystery he wrote where the door was not, in fact, locked. But that is not in this collection. He lives in Northern Canada. When asked, he will agree that it is quite cold.

Thomas A. (Tom) Turley has been "hooked on Holmes" since finishing *The Hound of the Baskervilles* at about the age of twelve. However, his interest in Sherlockian pastiches didn't take off until he wrote one. *Sherlock Holmes and the Adventure of the Tainted Canister* (2014) is available as an e-book and an audiobook from MX Publishing. It also appeared in *The Art of Sherlock Holmes – USA Edition 1*. In 2017, two of Tom's stories, "A Scandal in Serbia" and "A Ghost from Christmas Past" were published in Parts VI and VII of this anthology. "Ghost" was also included in *The Art of Sherlock Holmes – West Palm Beach Edition*. Meanwhile, Tom is finishing a collection of historical pastiches entitled *Sherlock Holmes and the Crowned Heads of Europe*, to be published in 2021 The first story, "Sherlock Holmes and the Case of the Dying Emperor" (2018) is available from MX Publishing as a separate e-book. Set in the brief reign of Emperor Frederick III (1888), it inaugurates Sherlock Holmes's espionage campaign against the German Empire, which ended only in August 1914 with "His Last Bow". When completed, *Sherlock Holmes and the Crowned Heads of Europe* will also include "A Scandal in Serbia" and two additional historical tales. Although he has a Ph.D. in British history, Tom spent most of his professional career as an archivist with the State of Alabama. He and his wife Paula (an aspiring science fiction novelist) live in Montgomery, Alabama. Interested readers may contact Tom through MX Publishing or his Goodreads author's page.

DJ Tyrer is the person behind Atlantean Publishing, and has had fiction featuring Sherlock Holmes published in volumes from MX Publishing and Belanger Books, and an issue of *Awesome Tales*, and has a forthcoming story in *Sherlock Holmes Mystery Magazine*, as well as non-Sherlockian mysteries in anthologies such as *Mardi Gras Mysteries* (Mystery and Horror LLC) and *The Trench Coat Chronicles* (Celestial Echo Press).
DJ Tyrer's website is at *https://djtyrer.blogspot.co.uk/*
His Facebook page is at *https://www.facebook.com/DJTyrerwriter/*
The Atlantean Publishing website is at *https://atlanteanpublishing.wordpress.com/*

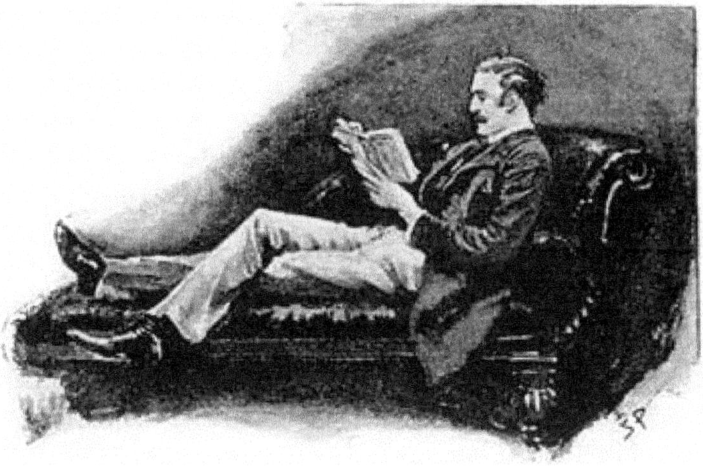

The MX Book of New Sherlock Holmes Stories
Edited by David Marcum
(MX Publishing, 2015-)

"This is the finest volume of Sherlockian fiction I have ever read, and I have read, literally, thousands." – Philip K. Jones

"Beyond Impressive . . . This is a splendid venture for a great cause!
– Roger Johnson, Editor, *The Sherlock Holmes Journal,*
The Sherlock Holmes Society of London

Part I: 1881-1889
Part II: 1890-1895
Part III: 1896-1929
Part IV: 2016 Annual
Part V: Christmas Adventures
Part VI: 2017 Annual
Part VII: Eliminate the Impossible (1880-1891)
Part VIII – Eliminate the Impossible (1892-1905)
Part IX – 2018 Annual (1879-1895)
Part X – 2018 Annual (1896-1916)
Part XI – Some Untold Cases (1880-1891)
Part XII – Some Untold Cases (1894-1902)
Part XIII – 2019 Annual (1881-1890)
Part XIV – 2019 Annual (1891-1897)
Part XV – 2019 Annual (1898-1917)
Part XVI – Whatever Remains . . . Must be the Truth (1881-1890)
Part XVII – Whatever Remains . . . Must be the Truth (1891-1898)
Part XVIII – Whatever Remains . . . Must be the Truth (1898-1925)
Part XIX – 2020 Annual (1882-1890)
Part XX – 2020 Annual (1891-1897)
Part XXI – 2020 Annual (1898-1923)
Part XXII – Some More Untold Cases (1877-1887)
Part XXIII – Some More Untold Cases (1888-1894)
Part XXIV – Some More Untold Cases (1895-1903)
Part XXV – 2021 Annual (1881-1888)
Part XXVI – 2021 Annual (1889-1897)
Part XXVII – 2021 Annual (1898-1928)
Part XXVIII – More Christmas Adventures (1869-1888)
Part XXIX – More Christmas Adventures (1889-1896)
Part XXX – More Christmas Adventures (1897-1928)

In Preparation
Part XXXI (and XXXII and XXXIII???) – 2022 Annual

. . . *and more to come!*

The MX Book of New Sherlock Holmes Stories
Edited by David Marcum
(MX Publishing, 2015-)

<u>Publishers Weekly says:</u>

Part VI: *The traditional pastiche is alive and well....*

Part VII: *Sherlockians eager for faithful-to-the-canon plots and characters will be delighted.*

Part VIII: *The imagination of the contributors in coming up with variations on the volume's theme is matched by their ingenious resolutions.*

Part IX: *The 18 stories ... will satisfy fans of Conan Doyle's originals. Sherlockians will rejoice that more volumes are on the way.*

Part X: *... new Sherlock Holmes adventures of consistently high quality.*

Part XI: *... an essential volume for Sherlock Holmes fans.*

Part XII: *... continues to amaze with the number of high-quality pastiches.*

Part XIII: *... Amazingly, Marcum has found 22 superb pastiches ... This is more catnip for fans of stories faithful to Conan Doyle's original*

Part XIV: *... this standout anthology of 21 short stories written in the spirit of Conan Doyle's originals.*

Part XV: *Stories pitting Sherlock Holmes against seemingly supernatural phenomena highlight Marcum's 15th anthology of superior short pastiches.*

Part XVI: *Marcum has once again done fans of Conan Doyle's originals a service.*

Part XVII: *This is yet another impressive array of new but traditional Holmes stories.*

Part XVIII: *Sherlockians will again be grateful to Marcum and MX for high-quality new Holmes tales.*

Part XIX: *Inventive plots and intriguing explorations of aspects of Dr. Watson's life and beliefs lift the 24 pastiches in Marcum's impressive 19th Sherlock Holmes anthology*

Part XX: *Marcum's reserve of high-quality new Holmes exploits seems endless.*

Part XXI: *This is another must-have for Sherlockians.*

Part XXII: *Marcum's superlative 22nd Sherlock Holmes pastiche anthology features 21 short stories that successfully emulate the spirit of Conan Doyle's originals while expanding on the canon's tantalizing references to mysteries Dr. Watson never got around to chronicling.*

Part XXIII: *Marcum's well of talented authors able to mimic the feel of The Canon seems bottomless.*

Part XXIV: *Marcum's expertise at selecting high-quality pastiches remains impressive.*

The MX Book of New Sherlock Holmes Stories
Edited by David Marcum
(MX Publishing, 2015-)

MX Publishing

MX Publishing is the world's largest specialist Sherlock Holmes publisher, with over five-hundred titles and over two-hundred authors creating the latest in Sherlock Holmes fiction and non-fiction

The catalogue includes several award winning books, and over two-hundred-and-fifty have been converted into audio.

MX Publishing also has one of the largest communities of Holmes fans on Facebook, with regular contributions from dozens of authors.

www.mxpublishing.com

@mxpublishing on Facebook, Twitter and Instagram

Lightning Source UK Ltd.
Milton Keynes UK
UKHW012051271121
394631UK00001B/5

9 781787 059313